T0385418

A SONG OF
LEGENDS
LOST

M. H. AYINDE

A SONG OF LEGENDS LOST

Book One of the Invoker Trilogy

orbit-books.co.uk

ORBIT

First published in Great Britain in 2025 by Orbit

1 3 5 7 9 10 8 6 4 2

Map by Jon Hodgson, Handiwork Games

A CIP catalogue record for this book is available from the British Library.

HB ISBN 978-0-356-52530-3
C format 978-0-356-52531-0

Typeset in Minion Pro by Palimpsest Book Production Ltd, Falkirk, Stirlingshire
Printed and bound in Great Britain by Clays Ltd, Elcograf S.p.A.

Papers used by Orbit are from well-managed forests and other responsible sources.

MIX
Paper | Supporting
responsible forestry
FSC
www.fsc.org
FSC® C104740

Orbit
An imprint of
Little, Brown Book Group
Carmelite House
50 Victoria Embankment
London EC4Y 0DZ

The authorised representative
in the EEA is
Hachette Ireland
8 Castlecourt Centre
Dublin 15, D15 XTP3, Ireland
(email: info@hbgi.ie)

An Hachette UK Company
www.hachette.co.uk

orbit-books.co.uk

For my parents
Alarape and Pat Ayinde
who gave me roots and wings
and always believed in my dreams

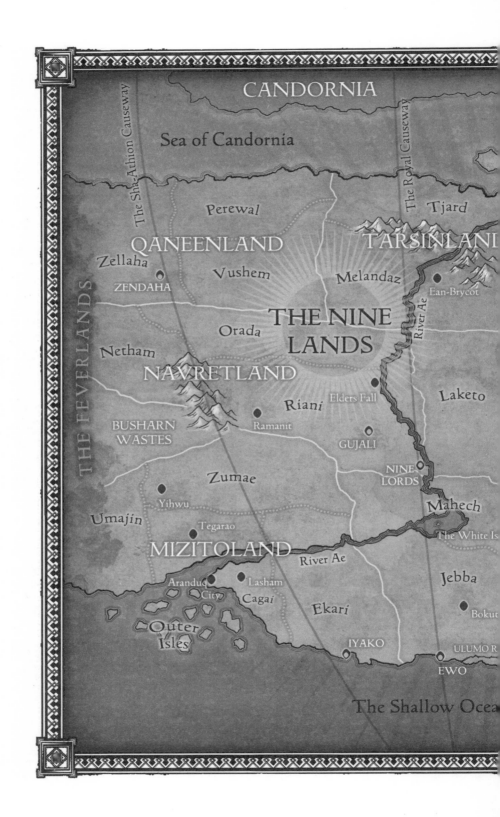

CANDORNIA

Sea of Candornia

The Sha-Athion Causeway

The Royal Causeway

Perewal

Tjard

QANEENLAND

TARSINLAND

Zellaha

Vushem

Melandaz

ZENDAHA

Ean-Brycot

THE NINE
LANDS

Orada

River Ae

Netham

NAVRETLAND

THE FEVERLANDS

Riani

Elders Fall

Laketo

BUSHARN
WASTES

Ramanit

GUJALI

NINE
LORDS

Zumae

Yihwu

Mahech

Umajin

Tegarao

The White Is

MIZITOLAND

River Ae

Jebba

Aranduq
City

Lasham

Cagai

Bokut

Ekari

Outer
Isles

IYAKO

ULUMO R

EWO

The Shallow Ocea

Meli

ENMUTH

FEBAR

QUENON

The Sunken Causeway

FEB

Bal-Mathan

Yenlund

Scattered
Isles

MENIT
WILDERNESS

Kezotl

HARRIA

TAHUALAND

The Ring Ocean

Intiqq

Qenqar

N

Dimadu

Ntuk

W   E

DATALILAND

S

Maadu

Ninshasi

ULAMARA

THE LEOPARD KINGDOM

Souls of Significance, both Highblood and Low

The Royal Clan, Ahiki

Ancestral Markings: Sun
Ancestral Colours: Gold
Leader: His Most Blessed and Golden Grace, Jakhenaten II Ahiki, King of the Nine Lands, High Warlord of the Invoker Clans, Holy Unifier of the People

Princen Tamun, *known as Tamun First Light of Dawn* – A youth who enjoys hunts
Princen Jukanju – A calculating general
Princen Hetemam – Arbiter of the King's Justice
Father Emata, Keeper of Truths – A monk in service to the royal clan

Clan Mizito

Provinces: Cagai, Ekari, Umajin, Zumae
Capital city: Iyako
Weapon: Staff 'Stillness'
Sacred Animal: Eagle
Ancestral markings: Bonetree and Eagle
Ancestral Colours: Silver and Black

Ancestral Incarnations: 90
Leader: Warlord Sohimi, First General in Ekari Province, slayer of the
Farseeker and the Three Dancers, known as Sohimi the Red, Sohimi
Iron Will

Lord Invoker Sulin, *known as Sulin the Bold, Guardian of the Ae* – First
General of Cagai Province
    Captain Bataan – Her spouse
    Lord Invoker Jethar, *known as Jethar River's Son, Jethar Farsight* –
Her eldest child, lost at sea
    Lord Invoker Jemusi, *known as Jemusi Eagle's Shadow* – Her second
child
        Phan – Captain of her quartet
    Jinao – Her third child; a soulbarren sot
    Lord Invoker Julon, *known as Julon Eagle's Heart* – Her fourth child
        Sellay – His spouse; captain of his quartet
    Sister Jassia – A senior nun in the palace of Thousand Domes
        Sister Zalani – A junior nun in the palace of Thousand Domes
    Lakari Tob – An adviser
    Wateng – A nephew
Lord Invoker Wendoa – Lord of the city of Lasham
Lord Invoker Tenutan – First General of Umajin Province

Clan Adatali

Provinces: Dimadu, Jebba, Mahech, Ntuk
Capital city: Ewo
Weapon: Ida 'The Eight Blades'
Sacred Animal: Jackal
Ancestral Markings: The Eight Blades
Ancestral Colours: Green and White
Ancestral Incarnations: 99

Leader: Warlord Daloya, First General in Jebba Province, Slayer of the Blight, the Brethren, the Risen, the Unfolded, the Laughing Twins, the Sand Dancer and the Origin, known as Daloya Scourge of the Feverlands, Daloya Jackal's Claw, Daloya Blade of the South

Lord Invoker Ulacari, *known as Ulacari Daughter of the Flame* – Daloya's fourth child

Lord Invoker Morayo, *known as Morayo Two Blades* – Daloya's fifth child

Imuna – Daloya's spouse (deceased); mother to Daloya's children

Omadella – Daloya's spouse; captain of his quartet

Father Boleo, *known as Boleo the Wise* – A monk, Grand High Curator of Adataliland

Father Ngbali, *known as Ngbali the Just* – A monk, Arch Curator of Ninshasi

Brother Mabasu – A junior Ninshasi monk

Brother Danadu – A junior Ninshasi monk

Sister Ulla – A nun who likes luxuries

Zadenu – An assassin and whispermaster

Remami – A novitiate monk

Father Galumu – A senior monk. Boleo's mentor (deceased)

Grand High Curator Busim – Boleo's predecessor (deceased)

Captain Nchali Betswe Ijunti – A member of the elite Batide warriors

Lieutenant Jamakii Nafula Eliuba Ajwang – A member of the elite Batide warriors

Uchuno Rewali Ilohu Jonneth – A member of the elite Batide warriors

Lande Remmi Tunde – A member of the elite Batide warriors

Shenana Sinethemba Sibusisiwe – A member of the elite Batide warriors

Clan Itahua

Provinces: Intiqq, Kezotl, Laketo
Capital city: Harria
Weapon: Macuahuitl 'Midnight'
Sacred Animal: Jaguar
Ancestral Markings: Mountain and Blade
Ancestral Colours: Blue and Black
Ancestral Incarnations: 88
Leader: Warlord Xinten, First General in Kezotl Province, Slayer of the Mountain Mist, the Sun Singers and the Unfathom, known as Xinten Stone Bringer, Xinten Mountain's Heart

Lord Invoker Manax, *known as Manax the Obsidian Storm* – First General in Intiqq Province

    Dennia – His spouse

    Panali – His spouse (deceased); mother to Manax's children

    Lord Invoker Chinnaro (deceased), known as Chinnaro the Swift – His sibling; Murdered in the Busharn Massacre

        Ashu, *known as the Butcher of Busharn* – A soldier loyal to Chinnaro

    Lord Invoker Cantec, *known as Cantec Mountain's Son* – His eldest child, lost at sea

        Elari, *known as the Black Fury, Sister Death* – Cantec's spouse; captain of his quartet

            Lyela – Her wine buyer; a woman of uncertain background

        Ishaan – A lieutenant in his quartet; former thief

        Osellia – A lieutenant in his quartet; former street performer

        Chellahua – A lieutenant in his quartet; former pillowhouse worker

    Lord Invoker Kartuuk, *known as Kartuuk Son of the Dance* – His second child

        Atanchu – His spouse; Elari's brother

Commander Tanua – A warrior loyal to Kartuuk

Lord Invoker Atoc, *known as Atoc Mountain's Wrath, Atoc the Feared, Atoc Death Dancer* – His third child

Lord Invoker Rozichu – His fourth child

Bayamo – His coincounter

First Envoy Injum – His aide

Incholu – His Captain of the Guard

Clan Navret

Provinces: Natham, Orada, Riani
Capital city: Gujali
Weapon: Chakrams 'The Twins'
Sacred Animal: Tiger
Ancestral Markings: Tiger and Wheel
Ancestral Colours: Red and Yellow
Ancestral Incarnations: 96
Leader: Warlord Uresh, First General in Riani Province, Slayer of the Unborn and the Gatherer, Known as Uresh the Smiling, Uresh the Tenfold Strike

Lord Invoker Darsana, *known as Darsana the Heretic Lord* – Lord of Ramanit

Sister Amira – Her aide

Clan Tarsin

Provinces: Aeli, Melandaz, Tjard, Yenlund
Capital city: Denmuth
Weapon: Bow 'Promise'
Sacred Animal: Bear
Ancestral Markings: Bow and Arrow
Ancestral Colours: Red and Blue

Ancestral Incarnations: 81
Leader: Warlord Lennette, First General in Tjard Province, Slayer of the
Stormrider and the Stone Walker, Known as Lennette Call of the North,
Lennette the Stone Breaker

Lord Invoker Riona, *known as Riona the Daughter of the Bow* –
First General in Yenlund Province

Clan Qaneen

Provinces: Perewal, Vushem, Zellaha
Capital city: Zendaha
Weapon: Shamshir 'Moonrise'
Sacred Animal: Oryx
Ancestral Markings: Horn and River
Ancestral Colours: Red and Green
Ancestral Incarnations: 81
Leader: Warlord Allid, First General in Zellaha Province, Slayer of the Frost
Son and the Clicker, known as Allid the Blade Father, Allid Fever's Bane

Lord Invoker Mavood Qaneen, *known as Mavood the Deathless* – A
friend to First General Sulin
Lord Invoker Rahaam, *known as Rahaam the Blade's Edge* – Lord of
Dakia; Currently in exile
    Lord Invoker Masheem, *known as Masheem the Usurper Lord* – His
cousin

In Lordsgrave, South of the River

Old Baba – Grandfather and Elder to the bakers of Arrant Hill
    Eyin – His spouse (deceased)
        Umadi – Her brother

Deola – *Her sister (deceased)*

Moloko – A nephew

Leke – *A great-nephew (deceased)*

Raluwa – *A great-nephew (deceased)*

Abeni – *A great-niece (deceased)*

Sede – *A great-nibling (deceased)*

Yeshe – His first child

Selek – Her spouse

Nataan – His second child, lost in the war with the greybloods

Kerlyn – His spouse; child of Mama Elleth

Temi – Their first child

Meliti – Her friend

Tunji – Their second child

Amaan – His third child

Mtobi – A child of Amaan

Larmi – A child of Amaan

Maiwo – A child of Amaan

Mama Elleth – Grandmother and Elder to the bakers of Arrant Hill

Mardin – *Her spouse (deceased)*

Braydin – Her second child, Kerlyn's brother

Kierin – His child

Darmin – Her nephew

Jonneth – Her nephew

Gilli – Her niece

Tommo – Her brother

Sutesh – A healer

Sister Poju – A nun

Remmy – An innkeeper's son

Old Javesh – A neighbour

In Lordsgrave, North of the River

Gamani – A member of the Chedu Family

Ba Casten – A member of the Chedu Family

    Krayl – His child

    Harvell – His lieutenant; a woman who buys and sells

    Lakoz – His lieutenant

    Tarn – His lieutenant

    Old Feyin – His aide

    Runt – A pot-girl

      Zee – Her sibling; a sickly child

Pellana – A healer of questionable skill

PROLOGUE

Ngbali

Father Ngbali the Just, Arch Curator of the Sacred Order of the Twofold Path, Holy Guardian of the port town of Ninshasi, and staunch opponent of interruptions, was just biting into his plantain when the knock came.

'What is it?' he snapped.

'Please, Father,' his apprentice said from beyond the bamboo wall. 'You're needed on the beach.'

Ngbali closed his eyes. Needed on the beach. Usually, when he was needed on the beach, it was to identify a supposedly ancient artefact that transpired to be scrap metal washed over from the docks. Sometimes, it was to purify the waters of the borehole. Occasionally, it was to break up drunken arguments between younger monks. Rarely was it anything that necessitated interrupting a meal.

'Mabasu, I would like you to deal with this, as a vital part of your training,' Ngbali said. 'You are an extremely capable soul, and I have every faith that the ancestors will guide you in your endeavour.'

He opened his mouth, the oil of the plantain glistening tantalisingly on his fingers, and was preparing to resume his breakfast when Mabasu's tremulous voice struck up once more.

'Holy Father, a shipwreck has washed ashore.'

1

'Shipwreck?'

'Yes, Your Holiness! Containing a techwork relic.'

Ngbali sighed. 'Then bring the relic back to the monastery for Cleansing.'

'Honoured Father, the relic is too large to carry. I could attempt the ritual of levitation, but the last time I tried that alone, if you recall, the damage to the nearby buildings—'

'Very well!' Ngbali said, slamming his hand on the table and standing. 'I'm coming.'

He shoved the plantain into his mouth and crossed the room to retrieve his sacred staff from its spot by the bookshelf.

Outside, under the shade of the palms, Mabasu fell in beside him.

'Thank you, Holy Father,' he said. 'I've never seen anything like it. The ship lies in near ruin, yet it contains a Scathed artefact of immense proportions!'

Mabasu was a spare, fawning sort of man, always wringing his hands and saying *please* and *Your Holiness*, but Ngbali had been dealing with souls like him since the day the monks scraped him off the streets of Nine Lords, a beggar-boy of six; he knew well the eager light in their eyes. These were souls who would not hesitate to climb over those they claimed to serve if they thought it might bring them to the attention of the royal monks or the king.

Ngbali harboured no such pretensions. He simply wished to live out the remainder of his days in this quiet backwater of the far south-east, eating plantain and cassava, reading the forgotten texts, and absolutely not identifying wondrous relics.

'Tell me what you know,' Ngbali said, licking his fingers.

'Well, Your Holiness, some lowblood children were playing on the beach at dawn—'

'Ah. It always starts with lowblood children playing. We must remember to outlaw that.'

'Yes, Your Holiness. Well . . . they spotted the shipwreck, within which stood a magnificent relic of the purest blackglass. Upon its sides

2

gleamed the ancient glyphs of the lost Scathed People, and the entire find exuded a terrifying energy, like something from beyond the pyre.'

'And have you experienced this terrifying energy for yourself, Brother Mabasu?'

'No, Your Holiness. I was too afraid to go near. Brothers Danadu and Ntalo are there now, fending off the townsfolk.'

Father Ngbali had assumed Mabasu was exaggerating when he claimed the relic was large, but as he descended the grassy hill onto the beach, Ngbali saw that he was not. Beyond the line of palms, where white sand met azure sea, lay a wrecked ship. It was a wonder the thing had made it ashore – the wood of the vessel was rotten and warped, and its cargo immense. And Mabasu had been right: against the ship's portside gunwale lay a large wedge-shaped relic, its glossy contours shimmering like liquid midnight. Blackglass: that unfathomable material the Scathed had used to craft so much of their civilisation. The near end stood perhaps as tall as Ngbali himself, but the front tapered to a narrow point made for speed. It had no wheels, no windows, nor any doors, but Ngbali knew the meaning of the glyphs on its sleek side, glyphs that still glowed a brilliant blue, even after a hundred millennia.

'It is a Scathed travelling carriage,' Ngbali said. He had never seen one so well preserved. It would take years, perhaps decades, to Cleanse the entire thing. As he stalked nearer, pulling his feathered mask down over his face and waving his staff to clear a path through the knot of townsfolk that had gathered, he saw that the wall of the carriage had been shattered on one side. Its silvery innards glinted in the morning sun. Techwork: the cursed remnants of a civilisation best forgotten.

Brothers Danadu and Ntalo stood either side of the shipwreck, staffs gripped in their dark brown hands, feathered turaco masks hiding their faces. Their bead-skirts snapped in the morning breeze, and from the tense set of their tataued shoulders, Ngbali could see they were nervous.

'Father Ngbali, there was a man here!' Danadu said, his voice quavering.

'What do you mean, a man?'

'A man in the ship! He took something and ran off towards the docks.'

'You mean there was a survivor? Well, get after him! Bring him back!'

'Your Holiness, he will be long gone by—'

'Then you had better run fast, hadn't you?'

Ngbali turned back to the ruined ship as the youth sprinted off. The ornately painted name was so faded he could scarcely read it, but something tugged at his memory as he stared. He had seen this vessel before, on his travels, perhaps, in his younger days, when he had visited each of the invoker clans in their homelands and spent time in their palaces and castles . . .

Ngbali peered up at the break in the carriage wall. The blackglass there bowed outwards, as though something had forced its way free. Yet a shimmering light played across it – Forbidden energies, meant to repel. And within . . . within, he glimpsed travelling chests and two white objects perhaps six spans in length.

Bodies.

'There are two shrouded bodies in there!' Ngbali cried, recoiling.

'Yes, Your Holiness!' Ntalo replied. 'We saw but dared not touch!'

'You would not have been able to. Do you see the glowing light? This carriage is sealed by Forbidden means.'

'Father, shall I send the townsfolk away?' Mabasu said.

'No,' Ngbali said. 'No, it is good to remind them that Scathed relics are not to be touched by untrained hands, and that only we who have dedicated our lives to Cleansing may have dealings with them. Let the people watch.'

Ngbali was still contemplating how he was going to get such a beast back up the hill, when it came to him. Where he had seen the ship before. And when. He had a flash of memory. Of crowds, lining the riverbank in the capital, Nine Lords, a thousand leagues from where he now stood. Of the reclusive king himself, come out to watch invokers

4

from each of his warrior clans sailing off to the sort of pomp and fanfare that had not been seen in a generation. Of the hopes of every province in the Nine Lands resting on the invokers' noble shoulders. That they would return with answers. Return with the greatest weapon ever created. Return with a way to end two millennia of war.

That had been five rains ago. And they hadn't returned at all.

'Mabasu, get back to the monastery. Contact Three Towers Palace. Tell them we have located the remnants of Invoker Jethar Mizito's lost voyage.'

'The – the palace, Holy Father?' As if that were the most remarkable part of what Ngbali had just told him.

'Yes, the palace! We need guidance from Grand High Curator Boleo. I know this ship. And he is not going to believe it.'

Ngbali regarded the blackglass carriage one final time. It resembled some great disembowelled sea creature, techwork veins hanging from its broken wall like entrails. Then he set to work. Lifting his staff, he began the sacred dance. As a youth, dancing had been his greatest skill; the fluidity as he leapt, the sharpness of his movements. His body wasn't quite as obedient now as it had been then, but he could still put on a great show.

He began to chant, softly at first, in the Forbidden Tongue. His sacred staff grew warm in response. The crowd murmured in wonder, as they always did when they saw a monk in rapture. Many of them touched their foreheads to call for ancestral protection. Ngbali smiled beneath the calabash of his mask. He danced before the shipwreck, tapping his staff here and there, not letting them see the tiny, silver discs he slipped out of his robe and flicked up towards the deck. When enough of the discs had attached themselves to the carriage, he lifted his staff high, and as he did so, the carriage lifted too, rising from the deck like a bird taking flight.

Behind him, he heard gasps and cries of wonder. He chuckled to himself. Then he turned back towards the hill, and the carriage followed obediently.

'Stand back!' Ngbali declared. 'You see before you a cursed relic of the most potent variety. The merest touch could summon a greyblood attack!'

'Your Holiness!' Danadu cried, appearing at his side. The young man's chest heaved with exertion, sweat pooling between the muscles of his chest. 'I'm sorry, Your Holiness. I couldn't catch him.'

'Catch who?'

'The man! The one who ran from the ship! Perhaps he was just a thief? Or – or a vagrant, asleep in the wrong place?'

Ngbali sighed. Likely the man was lost to the grasslands now. But if he truly had been aboard the ship, letting him go would mean admitting that Ngbali the Just, Arch Curator of Ninshasi, had allowed possibly the most important soul in the realm to slip through his fingers. And that was a thing he could not abide.

'No,' Ngbali said. 'No, that man was no vagrant. Send to the other monasteries. Put out a description – discreetly. We are going to find him. And we are going to recover what he took. Now somebody get me more plantain!'

PART ONE

Temi, Jinao

ONE

Temi

By the time Temi arrived, not even bones remained to send to the ancestors. She stood at the edge of the abandoned wharf, looking out across the small, muddy beach at what remained of her uncle's boat. The hull was charred and blackened, as were the oars, and nothing moved within. No sign of her uncle and cousins. No sign of their cargo. And yet she had heard the screams as she ran down the dirt road. Had seen the strange green flames from the top of the hill.

Temi slipped down onto the riverbank, her bare feet sinking into cool mud. Beyond the boat, the River Ae crawled by, ruddy and sluggish as always. Great galleys slid through its waters, but nobody noticed this tiny, abandoned harbour in a ruined corner of the City of Nine Lords. Beyond the river wall on the far bank stood the shacks and huts of the district of Lordsgrave, and beyond those, like knives thrusting towards the sky, loomed the jagged crystal towers of the vanished Scathed.

Temi dropped to her knees. The curiously sweet tang of the fire caught in her throat as she blinked back tears. Four of her family were dead. An entire shipment of their cargo was lost. Six moons' earnings had been taken by the flames. And the worst part was the driving rain would turn whatever ashes remained to sludge. She'd have nothing left of her cousins to burn on the pyre. Nothing to send on to the ancestral realm.

'This was no accident,' said a voice behind her.

Temi turned to see an old woman squatting in the mud. The many layers of her linen robes were plastered to her portly frame. At first glance, she resembled a nun – the bald head, the tataued feet – but the rings on her fingers and the crystal at her throat told a different tale.

'Do I know you, Old Auntie?' Temi said. Few souls came to the abandoned harbour. Surely this woman had heard the screams too, had smelt the strange, sweet smoke? And yet the smile she offered Temi was calm.

'No,' the crone said. 'But I simply couldn't walk by such terrible grief. Who were they, these poor souls?'

Temi drew in a shaking breath and unclenched her fists. 'Relatives,' she said. 'Cousins, from Jebba Province. Weren't close family, but they're family still. What's it to you, anyway?'

'No ordinary fire could do this,' the crone said, nodding towards the ruined boat. 'What natural flame turns bone to ash but leaves the wood beneath merely charred? And in these rains! No, someone powerful has done this, child. Someone who wanted them gone.'

'They never hurt nobody,' Temi muttered. 'They're just traders.'

'Traders, eh? Docking out here, so far from the market?' The crone settled down in the mud, the rain sliding off her bald head in sheets. 'You know, when I was a girl, this part of the river was used by smugglers. The Ae is the lifeblood of our great City of Nine Lords, and the spine of the Nine Lands. All sorts of things travel up its poisoned waters. Mind telling me what it was your family traded in?'

Temi looked away. 'That ain't your concern, Old Auntie.' Likely the old woman was simply a curious traveller – there were enough of those in Lordsgrave. But the ancestors turned from souls who were loose with their tongues.

The crone stared thoughtfully at the wreckage. 'Such a tragedy,' she muttered. Then she pushed to her feet and set to opening the pack that stood beside her. 'You'll never get a spirit wood fire going in this. By the time the rains stop, everything will be washed away. I heard a story once, about a man who drowned. Swept out on the Ae during a storm. He was never seen again. His family had no body to burn, and so he did not return to the ancestors. When his wife died, though their children burned her body, her spirit lingered, searching for him still. Do you wish to remain forever roaming the city, seeking the bodies of your lost kin?' She jerked her chin towards the river. 'Spirit wood won't burn in this, but I have something better.'

Temi couldn't muster up the energy to question, and so she knelt silently as the crone set to work, her wrapper clinging to her legs, her braids heavy with the rain. The crone hitched up her skirts and darted about the blackened boat, sprinkling something from a pouch in her hand. It looked like sawdust to Temi, and much of it blew away in the wind, but some fell upon the mud and shallows, sparkling like tiny jewels.

Soon, the old woman stood rubbing her gnarled hands and removing her outer robe. The body beneath, in its closeclothes, was wholesomely round and soft bellied. As rain slid out of the grey sky, the crone danced, hands lifting and dropping as she chanted in the Forbidden Tongue. Temi watched her, feeling numb, until she heard a shuffling at her back.

She turned, expecting to see a lizard or a rat, but it was a cat; a scrawny thing hiding in the old woman's pack. Temi held out her hand instinctively, but the creature hissed at her and flinched away.

'Well fuck you too,' Temi muttered, and turned back.

The old woman had worked herself up into a frenzy. Her eyes rolled, and her arms and legs jerked as she danced. Temi was just wondering whether she should say something to stop the crone before she gave herself a seizure, when the dancing ceased, and the crone dropped her hands, and as she did so, a perfect circle of green fire rushed to life around the ruined boat.

11

Temi scrambled backwards in surprise as the keen green flames flared and then softened. Now, a merry ring surrounded Uncle Leke's boat. Neither the wind nor the driving rain seemed to touch it. Even the ruddy waters of the Ae could not wash it away. It was as irrepressible as the City of Nine Lords itself.

'Oh, ancestors!' the crone intoned, lifting her hands to the skies. 'Oh, ancestors, please guide your children . . . *What were their names?*'

'Leke,' Temi said, her voice catching. Who else had been planning to come with him this time? 'Raluwa. Abeni. Sede.'

'Please guide your sweet children, Leke, Raluwa, Abeni and Sede, safely back to you, oh, ancestors. Guide their spirits beyond the pyre and into your realm, that they might be reunited with you for all eternity. Let the tears of those they leave behind serve as an offering, and proof of their worth.'

Temi heard the cat shuffling behind her again as the crone hobbled over, eyes fever bright. 'It is done,' she said, squatting down. 'They have crossed. They will return to those they loved.' She squeezed Temi's shoulder.

'What about the spirit wood?' Temi said.

The crone smiled. 'You see before you an ancestral circle formed from the shavings of a very rare kind of techwork. It is called Dust of Ancestral Light.' She eyed Temi. 'Does that trouble you? I assure you, it has been Cleansed.'

'Techwork, is it?' Temi said.

'Just so.'

'But you've made it safe for me. How kind.'

'Think nothing of it, my child.'

'Just one thing, though.' Temi grabbed the woman's wrist. Held her fast. 'There's no such thing as Dust of Ancestral Light. And you're a fucking liar.'

The crone's face hardened. 'Traders, were they?'

'Yes, traders. And we know a thing or two about Scathed relics. You can't use techwork to send souls to the ancestral realm.'

'Such ingratitude,' the crone muttered, trying to extract her arm.

'Why would you want to trick me?' Temi said, voice rising with her temper. 'I'm sitting here looking at the ashes of my family, and you come serving up this shit. What do—' She heard the shuffling again and turned around to see the cat creeping towards the crone's pack. In its mouth was a coin. *Her* coin. Part of the payment that had been in her satchel.

Temi dived for the crone's pack; tore it open. There lay three more golden suns. There lay little Maiwo's beaded necklace, a gift for Uncle Leke.

'You thief!' Temi cried, grabbing the woman's arm again.

The crone snorted. 'You ungrateful brat. It was a small price to pay for the peace that I was about to give you.'

'A peace built on lies!'

'Let go of me or you shall regret we ever met.'

'I already do!' Temi shouted. She glanced at the pack. 'Where's the rest of my money?'

'What money?'

Temi tightened her grip. 'Give it back, or ancestors help me, I'll take it from you.'

'Oh no you won't,' the crone said, touching Temi's free arm with a sickening smile. Something sharp bit into Temi's skin.

'Ow!' Temi cried, releasing the crone. A perfect circle of blood welled in the brown flesh of her left arm, next to her family tatau. 'You cut me!'

'Yes, and that's not all,' the crone snarled. She lifted her hands. One of her many rings began to glow. 'I place a curse upon you!'

'Oh, *please*—'

'I place a curse upon you, Temi of the City of Nine Lords; Temi of the Arrant Hill bakers—'

'How do you know my name?'

'I curse you! Now, and forevermore!'

The crone began to shake, her eyes rolling up, her lips quivering

13

with unspoken words. The ring – blackglass set with a red gem – glowed more brightly, pulsing ever faster.

'I grew up in Lordsgrave, witch,' Temi said. 'You can't scare the likes of me.'

But then the light from the ring flared, and a great force knocked Temi backwards, and all was darkness and silence.

Temi woke chilled to her core and with a dull throbbing in the back of her head. For a moment, she wondered why her brother had left the window open. Then she remembered. The river. The boat. The ashes.

Temi sat up, rubbing her head. The sky beyond the line of buildings was a rich blue, the remaining clouds tinged with the familiar golden glow that emanated from the king's palace at the heart of the city. Mercifully, the rains had stopped. Traffic crawled by on the river beyond.

Temi groaned and rolled onto all fours, trying to piece together what had happened. Then her hand touched something soft, and she remembered the crone. No; the spirit witch – for that was surely what she was. A nun cast out by her peers for dabbling in techwork. To her surprise, the old woman lay on her back in the mud, eyes open, mouth open, arms spread wide.

'Don't play dead,' Temi muttered, reaching for her satchel. The witch's pack lay a few paces away. Temi could still see the curve of Maiwo's necklace in the half-light. She crawled over and took it back, and her coins too. Then she turned to the witch.

The woman lay unchanged. Tentatively, Temi reached out and poked the woman's hand. Then touched her again, more forcefully this time.

The witch sat up, drawing in a great raking breath. Her eyes had rolled back, but she turned towards Temi and croaked, '*The ancestors have spoken! The king must fall by your hand!*'

Then a terrible choking gripped her, and she clawed at her throat before collapsing back where she had lain only moments before.

'Shit,' Temi muttered.

She watched, wondering for a moment if the witch was playing another trick: trying to escape through feigned death. But as she stared at the crone's chest, looking for movement, counting her own breaths, it became clear. The old woman would never stand again. How she could simply have dropped down dead, Temi could not imagine, and wasn't particularly inclined to. Perhaps, in her rapture, the woman's heart had given up. Or perhaps Leke and her cousins truly had crossed the pyre and had sent the witch her death as punishment for her misuse of their names. It didn't matter. What mattered was that someone had murdered four of her kin, and the last thing Temi needed was to be found at a well-known smuggling cove with a cooling corpse beside her.

She checked the boat one last time, just to be sure. Perhaps she'd been wrong. Perhaps they had swum to safety. But no; there among the blackened sludge was Leke's single gold tooth. She scooped it up, along with the sludgy ashes that remained, and deposited the lot in her satchel. Maybe there would be enough there to burn; whatever the witch had claimed, she could still try.

Something nudged against her leg. Temi looked down to see the witch's strange cat. It mewled piteously at her.

'You two-faced little shit,' Temi muttered. But still, she held out her hand and let it lick her with a hot, rough tongue. Perhaps it saw in her a kindred spirit. They were both grieving now. But when she looked more closely, she saw it was no normal cat. Beneath its matted grey fur, she glimpsed blinking lights . . . A twist of metal where the outer skin had peeled away. This was no cat, not truly. This was something else.

Temi lifted her foot. It would be a simple thing, just to bring her heel down. To grind the creature's glowing eyes into the mud. It was a grey-blood. A tool of the enemy. A destroyer of civilisations. It was her duty to rid the Nine Lands of it.

Temi sighed. 'Follow me if you like,' she said, pulling her satchel full of ancestors over her head. 'I won't stop you.' And she set off home.

*

15

At sunset, Sister Relina the Humble, High Shadedaughter of the Eighth Circle of Enlightenment, sat up in the muddy darkness. She drew in a painful breath and blinked the moisture back into her eyes. Her pack still lay where she'd left it – the foolish girl hadn't thought to take it with her. But the techwork abomination was gone. That was something, at least.

Sister Relina lifted her hands, closed her eyes, and muttered under her breath. She touched the sacred jewel embedded in her skull and called softly to the ancestors to send her words to the Holy Mother.

And presently, the ancestors answered.

[Speak,] the ancestors said. [The Holy Mother is listening.]

'Your Holiness,' Relina said. 'It is done. I have prepared the one who will bring down the king.'

Good, came the reply. *Now let us hope that we have acted in time.*

TWO

Jinao

'Here, let me help you,' the soldier beside him said, as the ox-drawn wagon jolted and rumbled.

She was a slight thing, with quick wary eyes and a serious slant to her mouth. No more than twenty, Jinao guessed, which made her near a decade younger than he, and yet she tightened his grass-pipe cuirass deftly, weaving the straps in and out. He could feel the other warriors watching behind their black and silver warpaint, some not bothering to hide their amusement. To them, this was just another battle in Aranduq bay, another day spent driving the greyblood hordes back into the sea. It had been a year now since the latest attacks began, and these warriors had seen it all.

'Your first time, is it?' she said to him.

'Uh – yes,' Jinao said.

The wagon rocked and the man sitting on Jinao's left slammed into him. He shoved at Jinao irritably before righting himself. At the back, some of the older soldiers had started up a war song. The words were meant to rouse, meant to stir warriors to do great deeds, yet all they did was tighten the knot in Jinao's stomach. Through the narrow window, Jinao watched Aranduq City slide by, a rain-drenched blur of bowing palms and bamboo huts. There could be no running back to the palace of Thousand Domes now, high on its hill at the city's heart. In mere moments, they would reach the mouth of the River Ae – the Gateway to the Nine Lands.

'I'm Leling,' the girl said. 'And you . . .?'

'Er . . . Janzen,' Jinao said.

'Well, Janzen; no need to worry. The invokers are already on the riverbank. You probably won't even need to fight! Since the other clans arrived, we've been able to repel them every time.' She frowned. 'You know, you don't need your mask down yet.' Her own war-mask rested in her lap, its garish eagle-face snarling up at him. 'You'll roast under there.' She reached towards his face, and Jinao jerked his head away. The last thing he needed just then was for someone to recognise him.

'OK, OK!' she said, holding up hands hard with callouses. 'Just trying to help. Want some advice? When they open them doors, just run, you hear me? You start running. Try a bit of roaring, too. Never goes amiss. You run and you roar, and you always aim for the eye. Most greybloods got spines like stone . . . the Scathed made 'em that way deliberately, to do all their heavy work. So you got no chance taking the head. But the eyes – those what still have eyes – is usually crystal, and if you can just shatter one and work through to what passes for brains, only they ain't soft like human brains, you see—'

'I do see,' Jinao said swiftly, swallowing down the sour burn that climbed up his throat.

'Good. Now the other thing is, if you can hook their techwork veins with the end of your . . . what is that, an axe? Who gave you an axe? Captain, this one here's got an axe!'

The captain, a squat man with a blunt wedge of a face, whom Jinao knew he should be able to name, knew his brother and sister would know on sight, looked around from his perch by the door. Jinao felt his pulse quicken.

'You,' the captain called across to him. 'Name?'

'J-Janzen, sir!' Jinao said, disliking the tremor in his voice. 'Uh . . . they told me to bring an axe . . . They said—'

18

'Don't have a clue who the fuck you are. Why's your mask down already? Show me your face.' The captain leaned forward, grass skirt falling about his painted legs – legs that were as thick as Jinao's waist, and all of it muscle.

Jinao fumbled at the feathers, mind racing. 'I, um . . . the catch is stuck. Just trying to lift it, sir, hold on.'

The captain pushed aside the woman next to him. 'Where's your sword? Are you even from this battalion? Show me your—'

And then the world flipped. Jinao was flying; falling. Something smashed into his shoulder. He was aware of shouting, of the captain trying to raise his voice above the chaos. Beyond the walls of the wagon, he heard screaming, pleading, the clang of metal.

And greybloods. The growls, the inhuman screams, the shouts in the greyblood tongue. Jinao landed on his back – on top of someone, he realised. He rolled off and found the wagon lay on its side. The captain had forced open the door and it now gaped up at the dull grey sky.

'Out, you lazy fuckers!' the captain screamed. 'Out out out! You want to see humanity go the way of the Scathed? You are all that stands between your province, your king, and annihilation! Out!'

And out they poured, clambering one over the next, heaving themselves through the opening with weapons drawn. Kampilans. They carried kampilans; he should have known.

'Let's kill some greybloods!' Leling screamed at him, before leaping for the sky and disappearing.

It took Jinao three attempts to reach the opening. Two soldiers remained in the wagon, both injured. One was conscious, and despite the painful angle of his knee, Jinao was sure the man was laughing at him.

Then Jinao was out, and chaos swirled around him.

It was no battle. It was a storm. Bodies piled upon each other. Captains screaming as their soldiers desperately tried to form ranks. Horses rearing, unable to move, their eyes flashing, their crystal bodies bright with exertion. Aranduq estuary spread out before him – their bamboo wagon had flipped over in a great crater in the mud-road that led down to the sea. One of its massive iron wheels still spun. To Jinao's left stood the tumbledown shacks of lowbloods, all abandoned now. To his right, the grey sweep of the River Ae stretched into the distance.

Three large greybloods strode within the tumult. The nearest looked unsettlingly human; only its blunt, triangular head and grey skin marked it as something else. It tore and slashed as it stalked through the mass of soldiers, its ragged clothing billowing around it. Yellow eyes met Jinao's and the creature smiled, revealing a mouth of blinking techwork. Behind it came smaller greybloods, six-legged beasts with heads that were all jaw. They leapt like rabid dogs, biting off faces, slicing souls from navel to neck, ripping limbs from bodies . . .

Where were the invokers? For nearly ten moons now, Jinao's mother had been hosting them up at Thousand Domes: warriors from every invoker clan, come to defend the Gateway to the Nine Lands. Why weren't they here, lifting their hands to call their ancestors back from beyond the pyre?

Jinao blundered towards the riverbank. There was nothing noble about the chaos that whirled around him, nothing grand. It was bodies writhing in the dirt; it was desperate souls using teeth and nails and feet, shrieking and crying and begging. It was blood and piss and dirt and limbs; so many limbs, tossed like offerings to the ancestors. Now and then, a lieutenant would streak past, screaming an order, or slicing down with a sword. But where were the battle lines? Where were the shield-bearers forming up? Where were the spear-wielders, driving the enemy back? He saw none of that here, only—

Something slammed into Jinao as he stepped out of the line of palms and onto the sand, and for long seconds the world was a swirl and a ringing in his ears and a searing pain between his eyes. Then the ground struck, and the breath was knocked from him, and when Jinao opened his eyes again, it was to see a body collapsing towards him. He was fast enough to roll to the side, but it landed so close that his face was splashed with blood and viscera and ancestors knew what else . . . some silver fluid, surely something from the techwork bowels of a greyblood.

Jinao turned his head to one side and vomited.

He'd been a fool to come. An utter fool. Go to battle, he'd told himself. Prove yourself in battle. Show that you are worthy of the blood that runs in your veins. Then, perhaps, the ancestors will finally choose you for the Bond . . .

Jinao's stomach heaved again. He sat up. All around him lay corpses, some crusted with blood, others twitching and sparking – fallen grey-bloods. The metallic tang of blood combined with the familiar ripeness of the river made his head spin. Craning back, he saw the wagon on its side, not more than ten paces away, and emblazoned with the white bonetree of the invoker Clan Mizito. His family insignia. His ancestors' crest. If he crawled . . . If he dragged himself over the sludge and the bodies, he could reach it. He could hide there until their foe had been vanquished. He could creep back to the palace by the rear entrance . . .

'Lotus Company! Form up!'

Lotus Company . . . He knew that name; part of his sister's battalion. And suddenly there she was: Jemusi, standing in the stirrups of her horse, one painted arm raised as she shouted commands, and Jinao's heart soared. How many times, as a boy, had he dreamed of riding out with her? How many times, as they sat together in the palm gardens and counted stars, had he dreamed of them standing side by side, invoking the spirit of Mizito, smashing a thousand greybloods with a single blow?

'Quartet! To me!' Jemusi screamed, and Jinao stared, transfixed, as four masked warriors appeared, encircling his sister, protecting her. Her grass skirt flared around her painted legs as she leapt from her horse onto the sands. Jemusi raised both arms, her tataus already glowing with the light of invocation, and began the sacred dance. She whirled and leapt, her arms a blur. Then she threw back her head, her long black braid snapping behind her in the wind, her eyes closed, her expression beatific.

'Mizito, spirit of my fathers, hear me!' she cried, and Jinao felt tears spring to his eyes, felt his chest tighten. 'Mizito, spirit of my mothers, hear me!' And now it wasn't just Jemusi's skin that glowed. The air around her brightened, and there came a keening from the sky, a quickening that set the hairs on the back of Jinao's neck to rising, made his palms tingle. 'Mizito, Lord of the Eagle, Master of the Bonetree . . . hear me now, and come!'

And so he did. Jemusi's body convulsed as light bled from her every pore and coalesced in the air before her, taking on form and shape: a man, near twice the size of a mortal, clad head to toe in black and silver scale armour. His eyes, just visible behind his eagle mask, glowed an impossible blue. Black glyphs played along the pale length of his staff, *Stillness*, and where it struck, greybloods fell screaming, their techwork innards jolting as they perished. Jemusi knelt on the sand, her eyes still closed, and Jinao imagined he could see the sweat beading on her painted forehead; hear the rasping of her breath as she strained to keep the link with the ancestral realm, strained to keep her forefather here to defend them.

Then a great cry sounded from somewhere to his left, and Jinao turned. A hulking greyblood stood within a circle of corpses, a pale creature that Jinao recognised instantly from a hundred paintings and songs; a towering figure with grey skin, and the swollen body of a man, its hands gripping jagged blades. Its bald head looked tiny atop its muscular shoulders, but nothing could mask the leer of its smile, the shine of its pointed white teeth.

The Bairneater.

A score of warriors surrounded the Bairneater; souls in the armour of every province in the Nine Lands. As Jinao stared, he realised the Bairneater held something, or rather something was caught on its left blade . . .

Impaled there.

It was a body; limp, its blood tracing a red river down the Bairneater's powerful arm. Long black hair fell from the victim's head. Its shining warpaint glinted in the morning sun.

'Sulin!' came a man's cry. 'First General Sulin has fallen!'

22

And even there, Jinao heard his brother Julon shout, 'Mother!' From somewhere off by the shoreline, Julon's nimble blue horse appeared, and Julon rode high, his arms flung wide. 'Mizito, spirit of my fathers, hear me!' he screamed, his voice strained with emotion. He leapt from the horse, rolling as he landed, before he began the sacred dance, his movements rushed and imprecise. Behind him, his quartet scrambled to form up, to surround him. 'Mizito, spirit of my mothers, hear me! Mizito, Lord of the Eagle, Master of the Bonetree, hear me now, and come!'

Jinao stood there, frozen, unable to comprehend what was happening. Fallen. His mother, First General Sulin Mizito, the woman they called the Guardian of the Ae, ruler of the province of Cagai, she who had slain the Farseeker and the Three Dancers, had fallen.

The Bairneater, meanwhile, turned to flee with its prize, and it was only now that Jinao realised he stood in its path. A second incarnation of Mizito appeared, invoked by Jinao's brother. It bore down upon the Bairneater, but the greyblood was fast, and emotion seemed to have weakened Julon's link with the ancestral realm, for Mizito stumbled twice, and twice more seemed to lose cohesion for a heartbeat.

Fallen. Jinao's mother had fallen. As the Bairneater thundered towards Jinao, he saw the creature still held her body. The Bairneater loved trophies – every soul in the Nine Lands knew that – but its trophies were the skulls and trinkets of the young: a lock of hair; a wooden toy; a tiny, severed hand. Sulin Mizito was a woman past sixty.

Jinao's only thought, as the Bairneater thundered towards him, was that if this greyblood took his mother, they would not be able to send her spirit beyond the pyre. There would be no dances around the fire, no wine drunk in her honour, no songs and laughter.

And Jinao would not be able to curse her name as he watched her burn.

So he hefted his axe, and he closed his eyes, and as the Bairneater leapt, he swung.

Then the world came crashing down upon him, and all was darkness.

*

'There's another here, look.'

'Is she alive?'

'Hold on . . . no. *Sisters, another dead one!*'

Jinao blinked against a fine, warm rain. Palms swayed lazily above him. The sun was a yellow smudge behind hazy grey clouds. For a moment, he could not think why he was outside, what had happened, but then it all came back in a terrible flood. The battle. The Bairneater. His mother.

Jinao sat up.

Around him lay a sea of bodies. The riverbank was littered with people picking over the destruction: nuns, soldiers, scavenging lowbloods. Beyond the line of palms, beyond the bamboo rooftops of the city, stood the palace of Thousand Domes, high on its hill: a nest of bulbous blackglass buildings and smaller, bamboo greathouses spread among white bonetree orchards. What a fool he'd been to leave it.

To his left lay the corpse of a greyblood, its fingers still twitching. Flesh covered those fingers, flesh much like Jinao's, but beneath the torn fingernails gleamed metal instead of blood. Had it slipped into the skin of a victim, like a trouper slipping into costume? Or had it grown the skin somehow, in the foul depths of its Feverlands home? This creature, now as dead as the dozens of warriors around it, was ancient beyond measure. It had been old long before humanity had dragged itself up out of the mud. Jinao knew he should hate it, for what it had done to the Scathed, for what it would do to humanity, given the chance. And yet its face – so curiously humanlike – looked sad in its death throes.

Jinao could hear Sister Jassia's voice in his mind, droning on at one of her sermons by the palace shrine. *Do not pity them. Some may resemble people, but people they are not. They fashion themselves after us, but this is only to play on our sympathies. They wiped out their Scathed creators, and they yearn to wipe out humanity, too. So harden your heart against them, because they will not stop until all mortal souls are dead.*

24

Jinao had never quite understood why greybloods were so bent on destroying the Nine Lands. Sister Jassia claimed that it was the techwork that lay buried under human cities and towns – it not only lured them, it nourished them; they needed it to survive. Jinao had heard others whisper that the truth was greybloods sought to stamp out all remaining traces of the Scathed. That included the human cities that were built amid their ruins.

Two pages in the black and white grass skirts of Clan Mizito wove a path among the bodies, scanning for survivors. When one – a gangly girl with a mop of ragged hair – caught sight of Jinao, she rushed towards him.

'Where are you hurt?' she asked. '*Sisters! Sisters, this one is alive!*'

Mercifully, his mask was still in place, but there was no sign of his mother's body, nor of his brother Julon. Jinao's throat felt painfully raw, but he swallowed against it and said, 'The First General?'

The gangly page lowered her head. 'First General Sulin Mizito has fallen. Slain by the Bairneater, may the ancestors preserve her soul.'

Something within Jinao soared. He pushed it down, hating himself. A woman had died. A cruel, vain, monstrous woman, but a woman nonetheless, and beloved of thousands.

'Her body?' Jinao managed.

'Don't worry,' the other page said, touching his hand. He was a squat youth with tightly curled hair and a heavy brow. 'Julon recovered her body. He chopped off the Bairneater's arm! The monks took the arm for Cleansing. If we're lucky, the beast will die of its wounds.'

'*Invoker* Julon,' the girl hissed. She lifted her gourd to Jinao's lips, and he drank gratefully, the water as sweet and smooth as wine. 'Besides, the monks didn't take it. Invoker Jemusi smashed the arm to pieces, right after she fought off the Woodsmaiden.'

Julon? Julon had severed the arm? Jinao was sure he could remember the bite of his own axe hitting skin, the snarl of the techwork beneath, the hot spray of greyblood ichor. But perhaps he'd been dreaming.

'The Woodsmaiden wasn't here!' the boy said.

25

'She was! She came with all her children, and they carried off six palace servants and Lord Jinao Mizito.'

The boy frowned. 'Who?'

'You know . . . the soulbarren one. The middle brother. You remember. Tall, scrawny. He is nowhere to be found, but one of the archers says she saw the Woodsmaiden carrying him off to her lair, to breed with him and add to her infernal brood.'

Tall, scrawny, soulbarren. Jinao was so used to those words that they scarcely registered. His thoughts were of the palace, of all those within it . . .

He struggled to rise. 'There are greybloods in Thousand Domes?'

'Oh no, they're long gone! Invoker Kartuuk of Clan Itahua drove them out.' She pressed the gourd to his lips again. 'I cannot wait for the day of the funeral! It will be the grandest celebration of the year! Maybe even the king will come!'

'Don't be stupid,' the boy said. 'Clan Ahiki never leaves the City of Nine Lords.'

'Maybe they'll come for the Day of Choosing, then!' the girl said. 'I hope the new invoker is Wateng. No one is faster with a staff than he . . .'

And so they prattled on, but all Jinao could think about was that now he had another chance. Now, another from his family would present themselves at the great shrine, and Mizito would answer their call. Now, finally, it might be his turn.

'. . . and anyway,' the squat page said, 'they need another strategist, with Invoker Jethar still missing. It'll be someone like Tiani. Soldier? Soldier, where are you going?'

Jinao swayed, his head a throbbing weight, his pulse a war drum in his ears. But he was upright. Bruised, yes, but otherwise whole. So he gritted his teeth and set off across the sands.

THREE

Temi

Lordsgrave. Easternmost of the nine mighty districts. Cesspit of Nine Lords, the greatest city that had ever stood. The slums, to most, but it was and would always be Temi's world; the most beautiful place in the land. Before her stretched a vista of decaying shacks and bamboo roofs. The streets were narrow and dirty, and the people were barefoot. Ah, the people! So many. Crowds everywhere, arguing and shouting and laughing, a dozen languages rolling over each other. Beggars chortled drunkenly under the shade of palms. Naked children clattered over the rooftops. The ceaseless stench that rose from the docks was as familiar and comforting as a childhood song, and the breeze that kissed Temi's bare shoulders merely spread it around, could never hope to banish it.

Temi stood still, hands still shaking, while the world swirled around her. Dead. Leke and Raluwa and Abeni and Sede, all dead. At twenty-two, Temi was just five rains younger than Leke, and yet she had always known him as uncle. She had only met him once before in her life, when he'd last made the long journey north from Jebba. Every dry season, Uncle Moloko sent a new set of cousins up the River Ae to the capital, their hull filled with techwork they had gathered from the wetwoods or the desert. Temi or her brother Tunji would meet them at the abandoned wharf, coin would change hands, and the techwork would be quietly taken home to their compound. They'd host the southerners for a moon or so, a rite of passage to them now. Tunji would take them to the heart of the city, to the very edge of the Garden, from where they could glimpse the golden ziggurats of the king.

Temi would take them drinking.

But not this time. Temi stood at the bottom of Arrant Hill, the implications only now running through her mind. Someone had killed them – that much the spirit witch had been truthful about. Not the king's monks – they'd simply cart them off to the White Isle, or the gallows if they wanted to make an example to others who might dare to touch Forbidden relics. Not local thieves – they would never have the resources, nor the inclination, since half the thugs Temi knew still came to her family's bakery for their bread.

And there it stood, at the top of Arrant Hill. Her home. Though it was the only brick building in the neighbourhood, it did not look like much. Indeed, aside from the swinging wooden sign painted with a loaf of Yennish blackbread, the building seemed a ruin. Creeping ivy and violets grew across its walls and through the gaps in its tired slate roof. Lizards sunned themselves on the crumbling bricks.

As a child, Temi had thought nothing of her light-skinned relatives sailing down every dry season, their holds filled with techwork. She had thought nothing of her dark-skinned kin sailing up from Jebba during the rains, their boats carrying much the same. Only later did she realise that none but monks should touch techwork, and that no one at all should be so reckless as to attempt to use it. Only later did she learn that techwork was what lured greybloods to attack.

And only later did she hear the whispers that, if you knew the monks' secret ways, well . . . the cursed relics of the Scathed People could prove very useful indeed.

It had been a neat arrangement, their profits split three ways: every morning, customers would line up outside the bakery for gozleme or roti or sweetbread, and when they slipped in a little extra coin, Aunt

Yeshe would reach under the counter and pull out a piece of techwork: a water votive. And that night, if their customers placed this small tangle of silver in their water buckets . . . Why, then they'd find the dirt and disease all gone and their morning drink sweet as a mountain spring.

Temi quickened her pace as she approached, anticipating the smell of cinnamon and cloves. Any moment, she'd hear Yeshe's gravelly voice, bellowing orders or cackling at some bawdy joke. As Temi drew near, she realised people were watching her. Serati, the old seamstress, outside her hut. The elders at the ogogoro tavern. The children scrubbing washing outside their mudbrick homes. She knew the names of them all, but none of them greeted her.

There was no line outside the bakery. Temi could see only one customer within. Old Baba, her grandfather, sat in his usual spot outside the door, dozing in his rocking chair, blanket over his scrawny legs.

Temi strode up to the door, preparing herself, and then the customer within turned.

She was a highblood, or at least someone wealthy, from her flowing silk dress. A woman of perhaps thirty rains. Small wonder no one on the street had greeted her: the woman's muscular brown arms were criss-crossed with intricate blue and green tataus. Everyone in the district knew who wore that pattern of eyes within waves – the Chedu Family, who ran much of northern Lordsgrave.

'I told you, I never heard of no Tunji,' Aunt Yeshe was saying as Temi slipped through the door. Temi's aunt was a hard woman, all angles and sneer, her dark skin smooth despite over sixty rains of life. White peppered her close-cropped, tightly curled hair. She shot Temi a warning glance, then turned back to her customer.

'Are you sure?' the woman said. 'You are the Arrant Hill bakers, are you not?'

'Oh, *Tunji*,' Yeshe said. 'Your pronunciation was all wrong. He lives here sometimes. He's away at the moment.' She turned to the rows of shelves behind her, laden with bread and pastries. 'I take a message?'

29

'It's best if I speak with him myself. When will he be back?'

Yeshe puffed out her cheeks and folded her arms. 'Now there's a question. Could be anything from a day to a moon. He's gone to Jebba Province. Left ages ago.'

The woman's dazzling smile didn't quite reach her eyes. 'Well, he owes me money. I'm here to collect.'

Temi strode up to the polished wooden counter behind which her aunt stood. 'Hello, Auntie,' she said. 'Everything all right?'

'Money?' Yeshe said, ignoring Temi. 'Don't know nothing about that.'

'He stole from me,' the stranger said.

Yeshe leaned on the counter. 'Now you listen here, girl. My nephew ain't no thief, so—'

The woman moved so fast Temi had no time to react. In a heartbeat, she had a knife to Yeshe's neck – where she'd been hiding it only the ancestors knew. She pulled the old woman down onto the counter with her free hand and leaned close, her voice still honey and silk.

'You let her go!' Temi cried.

'Stay back,' the stranger said, 'or I'll slice your aunt's neck open. Understand me?'

Temi said nothing, but rage simmered within her as she stood frozen. 'Now I know Tunji is here somewhere. So you're going to deliver a message to him. The next time he crosses the river and sells techwork on one of our streets, it won't be me coming here with a warning. It'll be Ba Casten, and he isn't as forgiving as I am.' Her grip tightened and Aunt Yeshe squeezed her eyes tight. 'Tunji sold votives up by Northlands. Those are our streets. By selling there, he's stolen from my family. You let him know that Harvell of the Chedu Family will be back here in six days to collect the ten suns he owes.'

'Ten suns!' Yeshe croaked. 'We can't possibly—'

The woman jerked her hand and Yeshe let out a groan as her face pressed into the counter. 'Ten suns. Six days. I'll be back to collect.'

Then the woman, Harvell, pushed Yeshe away and strode past Temi, catching her eye as she walked.

'We'll have your money,' Temi said, watching her go. In the street outside, people curved out of Harvell's path and cast anxious looks after her as she strode away. Temi waited until the woman had gone from sight and then hurried over to her aunt.

'Ancestors, you all right?' Temi said. 'Let's see your neck.'

'Stop being stupid,' Yeshe snapped, batting her hands away. 'I'm fine. Where's Leke? He got the goods?'

Temi drew in a slow breath. 'Auntie, they . . . they was killed. All burned up, not even bones left.'

'Killed?' Yeshe took a step back.

'Yes, Auntie. And not in no normal fire.'

'Shit.' Yeshe drew in a long breath, her scowl deepening. 'Shit. You sure none of 'em got out? Swam or nothing?'

'I'm sure.'

Yeshe strode across the chipped tiles of the bakery floor and turned the sign to closed. 'That explains that Harvell woman. Your brother's done some stupid shit in his short life, but this really takes the prize. What was he thinking, selling techwork north of the river—' Yeshe recoiled. 'Ancestors, what is that thing?'

Temi looked down to find the spirit witch's ugly cat sitting at her heels, its golden stare fixed on Yeshe. She had assumed the creature would lose itself to the bustle and smells of their journey, but no, somehow it had slipped into the shop behind her. Only now did Temi recall the crone's words: *The ancestors have spoken.* Had she foreseen something? Was this all part of her curse? And what was it she'd said about the king?

'It's a cat,' Temi said.

'Don't look like no cat to me. What is it, diseased? Don't be bringing no diseased animals in here, Tem. Last thing we need. *Maiwo!*'

A moment later, a scrawny child of eight rains came scampering out of the kitchen: Maiwo, one of the many nephews and nieces Yeshe minded while their elders worked.

'Go get everyone,' Yeshe said. 'Family meeting at highsun.'

31

'Everyone?' Maiwo said, frowning.

'Yes, everyone. Go on, get going!'

And by highsun, when Temi had had several cups of ogogoro and paid her respects to Leke and the others at the family shrine, they were gathered. The bakers of Arrant Hill. Near thirty souls in total: her aunts, uncles, cousins, all crowded around the old bamboo table. Their home had one main room: the vast family room that opened out onto their yard. Out there, under the shade of the wall, Old Baba sat teaching the children their numbers. The only person absent was Tunji . . . and their mother, though there was nothing unusual about that.

'When your grandparents started this business,' Yeshe said, 'we had only one rule.'

She stood at the head of the table, her wife Selek to her left, and Old Mama Elleth, Temi's Yennish grandmother, to her right. This was the stalwart triumvirate that had long run their business; this was the three-headed beast that kept their family together. Selek, painted and powdered despite her advanced years, stood like a highblood lord who had fallen on hard times. Few swept down the dirt-roads of Lordsgrave with as much poise as she. Mama Elleth was a different creature altogether: plump and pale and soft. But her ready smiles and easy laugh hid a sly wit.

'Any of you dozy lot care to remind me what that rule is?' Yeshe said, leaning her gnarled brown hands on the table.

'No selling beyond the Hill!' Kierin said, smiling broadly. Temi's cousin's pale shoulders were thick with muscle from his days spent hauling at the docks.

'Well done. Now, thanks to Tunji, who's yet to grace us with his presence, we have a problem. I am sorry to have to tell you that Uncle Leke and the others was murdered this morning.'

Temi lowered her head as cries of disbelief rose around her.

'Temi-girl saw it all. Didn't you, Tem? It weren't no accident, neither. Then, next thing, we get a visit from a lovely lady called Harvell. Harvell of the *Chedu* Family.'

32

'What do the Families want with us?' Uncle Amaan said. He sat at the corner of the table, his youngest child sleeping on one shoulder, his long hairlocs swept over the other.

'Turns out our Tunji's been taking water votives across the river and selling right under the Chedus' noses. Now, all your Mama Elleth ever wanted . . .' Yeshe said, and here she jabbed a finger at her softly smiling neighbour. 'All she ever wanted was to bring clean water to these parts. All your Old Baba out there ever wanted was to use his mind to help others. Not to make no profit. Not to muscle in on whatever it is the Families do. Now they're demanding ten suns' recompense, and if we don't get it to 'em, you can bet they'll be dishing out more of what Leke got. So, first thing I'm gonna say is this: you watch your backs in the coming days. Don't be going out at highsun. Don't be talking to no strangers.'

'Where is Tunji, anyway?' Mtobi said, rapping their painted nails on the table. They had their father, Amaan's, slender build, but wore their tightly curled hair in neatly patterned braids. 'Shouldn't he be here?' They shot Temi a knowing look. Temi shrugged.

'Next thing we need to figure out is how we're going to get ten suns to them in six days,' Yeshe continued. 'Now, I'm asking each of you to empty your pockets. Check your secret chests. Call in those favours. We really don't need no trouble from Ba Casten and the Chedus.'

There came a rattling from the kitchen.

'Tem, you go,' Yeshe said.

'Yes, Auntie.'

Temi padded across the room and through the cramped kitchen, where Mama Elleth's brick oven stood cooling. She crossed the empty shop and strode up to the door, where a scrawny beggar-woman was trying to break in.

Temi's mother.

Temi yanked open the door. 'What d'you want?'

'Temi!' Kerlyn said, falling into the room. She stank of wine and sweat and unwashed clothes. How many days had it been since they'd last seen her? Six? Eight? Her mother usually only came home when she ran out of drinking money. Her yellow hair was a matted tangle, her freckled arms burned from so long out in the sun. 'Tun . . . Tunj . . . your brother's up on that hill again.'

'Is he?' Temi said wearily.

'Tem, you got any coin? I just need—'

'Goodbye, Ma,' Temi said, sidestepping her mother and slipping out into the street.

The crowds on Arrant Hill were thinning as highsun drew near. The heat hit Temi like a physical force as she dodged round the side of the building and scampered up the small hill that stood above their yard.

Up there, behind their house, stood Bakery Mount. In truth, it was little more than a small hillock that loomed over the rooftops of Arrant Hill on one side and the River Ae, far below, on the other. But as a child, Temi had thought it the summit of the world itself. A single jagged wall of blackglass thrust through the grass of Bakery Mount; all that remained of the mighty Scathed tower that must have stood there millennia ago. She and Tunji had made up such stories about that wall when they were children. Temi crossed to it now and sat, feeling her skin prickle in response to the energy that still crackled through it. Then she sighed loudly and turned to face her brother.

Tunji sat amid a circle of techwork – veins and discs and tiny flecks of blackglass – utterly absorbed in his work. In his smooth brown hands he gripped a water votive; it was little more than a bundle of battered metal and a knot of flowers. But as he sat, his dark lips moved and he chanted under his breath, chanted in a language he should not know, a language it was forbidden to use . . . And the words worked: at the sound of those five syllables uttered in an aeons-dead tongue, the techwork flared, glyphs appearing then dimming. The votive was complete. And now, any soul who used it could change the nature of water itself.

'Go on then,' Temi said. 'Tell me what you did.'

'Temi!' Tunji said with a start, his large eyes growing wider still. 'What you doing here?'

'Wondering why you decided to sell votives north of the river.'

'Me? Don't know what you're talking about,' Tunji said, turning away.

'Don't give me that shit. You know someone killed Uncle Leke?'

Tunji laughed lightly; he was a man who smiled easily and often, but when she didn't smile back, he sobered. 'You're serious?'

'Course I'm serious. And some woman called Harvell came and threatened Auntie Yeshe with a knife. Said she was a Chedu.'

'Ah, fuck,' Tunji muttered, passing a hand over his face. 'Shit.'

Temi crossed the grass and dropped down beside him, then lifted his chin with a finger. She looked into his dark eyes. Thick as thieves, that's what the family had called them as children. Always scheming together. Getting into scrapes together. They had no secrets from each other – never had. When their father had been sent to war and their mother descended into drunken despair, they had been each other's strength.

'Tunji . . .' Temi said.

'It was just this one time—'

'Ancestors, Tunji!'

'No, listen! It was one time . . . *one time!* There's all these people come over from Vushem, right, after that city out there got sacked by the greybloods. So I saw some of the kids drinking out of the Ae . . . Maybe they don't know the water's no good, or maybe they was just desperate. But anyway, I got talking to this one lady—'

'A lady, was it?'

'And I told her I could get her something to make the water clean. She was scared when she saw it was techwork, but I told her it was safe, told her it's a just an ancient tool, not cursed like the monks call it . . . Tem, you should've seen 'em, little kids, little babies, all skinny and thirsty and—'

'You should have told your lady to walk over to the bakery to collect!' Temi cried, throwing up her hands. 'Not gone across the river to sell her bloody votives! Lords!'

'But nobody saw me, Tem, nobody, I swear, I was so careful, and I didn't charge her or nothing so technically I wasn't selling.'

'You idiot!'

'I didn't know all this would happen, Tem – how could I? Ancestors forgive me, I . . . I didn't know!'

Temi sat in silence for a time, listening to the shouts from the river below, the sun a searing weight on her back. She knew she should be angry with him. She knew she should drag him downstairs to the others. But instead, her gaze drifted to the votive at Tunji's feet.

'You done something different,' Temi said.

They usually used the flowers that grew on the walls of the house to call for the blessings of the ancestors. A thin coil of techwork bound them together. Tunji alone knew the correct way to do that. Something about the knots and folds, the way the pieces of blackglass were woven within it, changed what the techwork could do. Old Baba had taught them both, but Tunji was the one with the gift. He took hold of the votive now and turned it over with a smile. He had an artist's fingers, long and fine, and Temi knew making the votives was an art to him. While she saw it more like Mama Elleth's bread recipes – follow the instructions, same result each time – to Tunji, crafting techwork was a matter of heart and soul.

'It's these discs, see,' he said, pointing to a circle of silver bound up with the veins. 'They was in the shipment that come over from Jebba last time. Uncle Moloko said they're just decorative, but these glyphs here mean something special. You remember when I told you the reason boiling the water don't work is because it ain't infection in the water, it's something else? Well, see these discs . . . they attract the bad stuff in the water. And when I done the chant, they made everything last longer . . . these ones can clean twice as much.' He took hold of her shoulder. 'I reckon it's some kind of techwork in the river. I reckon it's so tiny we can't see it, but it does something to us when we drink it. If I could just get hold of one of them monk's seeing lenses, the ones what make things bigger, then—'

36

'Tunji!'

'What? Temi, we could do so much more than water votives.' He sighed heavily. 'Old Baba knows more than just this one water chant. More'n all the monks in this city, I reckon. We sit here in the ruins of Scathed cities, surrounded by Scathed tools we're told we can't never touch! But if one simple piece of techwork can clean water, what can the rest of it do?'

'Summon greybloods,' Temi said. 'That's what.'

'You really believe if all the techwork buried under the Nine Lands just disappeared, that the greybloods would stop coming? You think they'd just vanish and the war would be over?' Tunji blinked at her. 'Techwork ain't cursed, Tem. The monks should be sharing it with the people, not hiding it away for themselves. We've only scratched the surface of what it can do. Don't you want to try making something more?'

'Nope,' Temi said, pushing to her feet and touching her forehead in the sign for ancestral protection. 'And you shouldn't neither.'

She sensed movement behind her and turned to see No-Cat padding up the hill. Temi strode over and held out a hand, and the creature sniffed at her with a surprisingly wet nose.

'You know that's a greyblood, right?' Tunji said.

'This cat?' Temi ruffled its head. The skin beneath its fur was searingly hot, but it watched her with round, trusting eyes. 'Course it ain't. If it was, it would've ripped my throat out by now, wouldn't it?' But she shot him a wistful look as she spoke.

[Temi.]

'What?' Temi said, straightening.

'Me? I didn't say nothing,' Tunji said.

[Temi. I know you can hear me.]

The voice was a whisper at the edge of her consciousness. Barely audible. But there. She whipped around, but there was no one behind her. No one near the wall, or on the rooftops. Besides, the voice had sounded too close. She looked down at No-Cat, suspicion rising within her.

37

[I am nothing to do with that ridiculous creature.]

Temi thought again of the spirit witch's words. *I place a curse upon you, Temi of the Arrant Hill bakers.*

'Fuck this,' Temi muttered, and crossed to where her brother worked. Evidently, she'd drunk too much ogogoro.

[Temi, you cannot ignore me.]

'We should go to the others,' Temi said, dropping down beside Tunji again. 'This needs sorting out. They'll forgive you.'

'I know,' Tunji muttered, looking away.

[We can help each other.]

'Listen,' Temi said, 'before we go . . . you ever hear of spirit witches . . . cursing people?'

'Cursing? Only in stories. Why?'

'Just . . . just wondering. Could they actually do it, though?'

'What, make the ancestors turn from you or something? Course not. No one can.'

Temi gripped her brother's shoulder. 'Good. Come on.'

FOUR

Jinao

'Welcome, all!' Sister Jassia said, lifting her scrawny arms high as she strode before the shrine of Mizito. At the sound of her voice, the crowd fell silent. 'Welcome to the Day of Choosing!'

In the days since his mother's death, Jinao had thought of little else but this moment. He knew it was foolish to hope. He might be of the right blood, but as his mother had reminded him so often, he would never be of the right heart. Yet perhaps, this time, with Sulin Mizito gone. Perhaps . . .

'Today,' Sister Jassia intoned, striding across the cracked marble of the shrine's floor, 'one of Mizito's descendants will honour the sacred vow and Bond with his spirit.'

Jinao had allowed himself only one glass of wine when he broke his fast that morning, and yet the tataus on the old nun's bald head seemed to shift and writhe. The palace shrine had always been a place of dread to Jinao, a place of failure and disappointment. How many days had he spent within these black walls, kneeling and beseeching while his mother paced and scowled? How many times had the sun shone down through that broken roof, merciless in its indifference?

Jinao averted his eyes from the circle of spectators – warriors from Clan Adatali and Clan Itahua and the rest. Come to witness his enduring

39

worthlessness. Well, perhaps today they would be surprised. Instead, he kept his gaze on the statue of Mizito. It stood against the far wall, a looming bronze monstrosity bedecked in beads and jewels. A sea of sparkling offerings surrounded the spirit wood at its feet. More food and wine than Jinao had ever seen there covered the bronze platter.

'Descendants of Mizito!' Sister Jassia continued. 'In your blood, you carry the most sacred power of them all. The power to invoke your clan's founder.'

Jinao loomed head and shoulders above his fellow hopefuls. Most of those in the line were Jinao's adolescent cousins – eager-eyed and excited. Many had already selected their quartets from among Aranduq City's petty nobles. All ignored him, as though being soulbarren were contagious, as though his many failures might infect them. They thought they knew exactly what outcome awaited him today. Every one of the hundred or more souls standing there thought they did.

'Ninety souls of the blood has he chosen,' Sister Jassia continued. 'Ninety will he always maintain. Today, Mizito will choose his clan's newest invoker. Let the first of his progeny present themselves. Tegana, child of Rocanan!'

Tegana was a girl of not more than thirteen, some second cousin from the Outer Isles. She set down the gift she had brought – an exquisite necklace of diamonds and rubies – and then began the sacred dance. Her every movement was achingly precise. Heads turned as she spun before the statue. When she had finished, she threw herself to the ground, forehead planted on the spirit wood slab as she awaited her ancestor's response.

Silence rippled across the crowd. Jinao heard the northerners muttering as they watched. One hopeful, ahead of Jinao in the line, yawned ostentatiously, and those around her stifled giggles. The nuns taught that, during those moments, all Clan Mizito's ancestors peered into the mortal realm to weigh the hopeful's worth. If they deemed their descendant worthy, Mizito would send a sliver of his soul back into the mortal realm to Bond with them, creating a new invoker. Jinao

40

saw no flash of ancestral light from the spirit wood, however . . . that sacred doorway to the ancestral realm. All he could see was the girl's anxious breath, misting the bronze offering cup.

'The ancestors thank you for your offerings,' Sister Jassia said, voice dripping with compassion. 'Perhaps the spirit of Mizito will answer your call another day. Let the next hopeful present themselves. Wateng, child of Lilani.'

Here came a youth to fill the ancestors with pride: upright, confident and strong. Wateng was not yet sixteen, but his muscles stood out like cords. His warpaint was flawless, accentuating the contours of his back and thighs. Behind him came the four women he had selected for his quartet, all little older than he, all groomed since birth. No doubt Wateng would choose one as spouse, or milkmother should someone with seed catch his eye. Each was exquisite, their black hair oiled and jewelled, their staffs strapped to their backs.

Wateng dropped down before the statue and bent to press his forehead to the spirit wood. Jinao could feel the audience watching, rapt, as Wateng set down a bowl of rice and a single perfect emerald. His painted lips moved in silent supplication as he drew a short dagger from his belt. Several of the onlookers gasped at this. And to Jinao's horror, Wateng pressed his palm to the slab of spirit wood, fingers splayed.

'Mizito!' Wateng cried. 'Spirit of my fathers! Hear me!'

And he jerked the blade, severing the last two fingers of his left hand.

Jinao was not the only one to turn away. Wateng stood, leaving his bloody offerings there beside the rice. He held up his mutilated left hand, triumphant. 'Mizito!' he cried, making a slow circuit for all to see. 'Spirit of my mothers! Hear me!'

Wateng's drummers started up then, filling the shrine with their music, and immediately, Wateng dropped into the first stages of the sacred dance. His moves too were flawless, and yet unlike the first girl, he had added flourishes to each. His expression remained serene, even

41

as his blood continued to drip. Sister Jassia watched on, her eyes sparkling, and Jinao knew what she saw: a man worthy of his blood, worthy of wielding the spirit of his ancestor. A warrior who would earn himself a dozen names before he was thirty. Jinao scratched the stubble at his chin and pushed away unkind thoughts.

'Hear me now, and come!' Wateng finished, dropping to the ground again.

Silence followed. Jinao swallowed a burp. It had been only one glass he'd taken . . . hadn't it? Wateng's shoulders heaved as he lay prostrate. The blood from his wounded hand traced a meandering path towards the spectators. Even from where he stood, Jinao could see insects had landed on the rice. Then, almost reluctantly, Sister Jassia stepped forward, her grey robe sighing on the ground as she walked.

'The ancestors thank you for your offerings,' she said. 'Perhaps the spirit of Mizito will answer your call another day.'

Perhaps he will answer your call another day . . . How many times had Jinao heard those words? Wateng stood, and though his expression was stony, his eyes were not. They shone with emotion. Shame? Anger? Jinao couldn't tell. Wateng strode silently back up the steps, and Jinao resisted the urge to offer him a sarcastic bow as he passed.

'He's going to run out of fingers,' muttered a tall girl ahead of Jinao, and a ripple of laughter ran down the line.

'Jinao, child of Sulin!' the nun called, and Jinao felt a stirring around him. Plainly, many of them had not known who he was. He felt like a giant, striding past them all. He closed his ears to the whispers at his back, feeling all his resolve melt away like morning mist. It had been foolish to hope. Foolish to think that today might be different. Best now to get things over with and return to the solitude of his bathhouse. Jinao crossed to the statue and knelt unceremoniously before it.

He set the remains of his breakfast down beside Wateng's severed fingers, along with a decorative stone he had found on the path.

'Do you not wish to perform the sacred dance?' Sister Jassia said sharply.

'Forgive me, Mother, but the ancestors have seen me dance a time or two before,' Jinao said. Then he closed his eyes and turned back to the statue of his ancestor. 'Mizito, spirit of my fathers, hear me,' he muttered. 'Mizito, spirit of my mothers, hear me. Mizito, Lord of the Eagle, Master of the Bonetree, hear me now, and come.'

He closed his eyes, counted to five, and then stood.

'You may wait,' Sister Jassia said, a line of disapproval creasing her brow. 'The ancestors will answer in their own time.'

Jinao was fairly sure the ancestors had given him their answer long ago, but he turned mechanically, dropped back to his knees, and closed his eyes. He could hear his mother's voice in his head, hear the endless sermons she'd given him as he knelt in this spot. *Invocation*, she would say, *is the act of calling upon the founding warlord of your clan. You are the bridge . . . the physical bridge between the realm of the ancestors and our mortal realm. When Mizito accepts you, he is Bonding a copy of his soul permanently to yours. The more closely you are aligned to him in thought and nature, the stronger the Bond will be. Blood alone is not enough, though being of the blood is essential to the Bond. When you invoke, you are the channel his soul will travel down to become physical for a time. Those tataus upon your arms are the gateway through which he will step. Your body lends him the physical strength to become truly present. That is why invocation taxes both muscle and mind. And that is why you must train.*

Once, Jinao had made the mistake of repeating his sister's mocking addition: that an invoker was the anus through which a warrior shits his family. That had earned him a vigorous beating and no dinner that night.

Time passed. Jinao's mind wandered, and he found himself thinking again of his mother's body, dangling from the Bairneater's arm. How could a woman of such stature fall in her prime? And why could Jinao find no grain of sadness within him with which to mourn her?

'The ancestors thank you for your offerings,' Sister Jassia said at last. 'Perhaps the spirit of Mizito will answer your call another day.'

43

Jinao heard muffled laughter at that, but he bowed to the shrine and strode away. He told himself he felt nothing as he climbed the shrine steps. Nothing but relief that the ritual was at an end. It was past highsun now, the air damp and heavy. He needed wine, and his bath-house and, if the ancestors were kind, to sleep through his mother's funeral. He slipped back through the crowd and out into the chrysan-themum garden.

Up on the hill beyond his sister's greathouse, General Sulin's funeral pyre was nearly complete. He saw the torches they had set around it. A lone figure, all in white, knelt before it, and Jinao didn't need to squint to recognise his brother Julon. He remembered then the words of the page: *He chopped off the Bairneater's arm.* Had his brother spread the lie or was it simply a rumour? Either way, it didn't matter: nobody would believe Jinao had been there.

Beyond, across the city, the grey gleam of the River Ae snaked off into the distance. Jinao could just make out the dark smudge of the statue of Sumalong, the local folk hero, standing astride the river. He knew what people were thinking, out there in the city. With Sulin gone, Aranduq would fall. And then all the Nine Lands, even the City of Nine Lords itself, would be vulnerable.

'My Lord Jinao,' a resonant voice said, and Jinao looked round to see a man in purple robes emerge from among the chrysanthemums: Lakari, one of his mother's advisers. Silver and black jewels hung in great chains about his neck.

'Hello,' Jinao said.

'I am so very sorry for your loss,' Lakari said. 'She was a brilliant woman, your mother. We will all miss her. I must leave Thousand Domes this evening, but I wanted to see you before I left . . . to let you know that, despite what your mother may have said, she loved you very much.'

Jinao mustered a thin smile. 'You are kind to say so.'

'I wonder if we might say a few words for the ancestors together? It would make an old man very happy.'

Behind them, a brilliant flash lit the morning, and a distant cheer rose up. So. Someone had been accepted for the Bond. He wondered who it was. Then reminded himself he didn't care.

Lakari took Jinao's hands and closed his eyes. Touching him was like touching the spirit wood of the shrine; Lakari radiated heat and power. 'Ancestors,' Lakari said, 'we ask you to guide and protect the spirit of our sister Sulin. May she know peace in your embrace.' Then he uttered a stream of words Jinao could not follow.

'Pardon me?' Jinao said, squinting. It sounded like the Forbidden Tongue, but Lakari was no monk.

'They are words of thanks, in my home dialect,' Lakari said brightly. He released Jinao's hands and rubbed his own together. 'Good. Good! And do me a kindness, will you? Place a token or two on Mizito's shrine, for your mother. I know you may harbour her some resentment, but the ancestors smile upon the forgiving, and she did so much good for so many. So remember her in your thanks.'

The rasp of a distant horn cut across their conversation, and Jinao's stomach twisted. But no, this was no herald of greyblood attack. This fanfare was nothing like the long, deep notes he had become so accustomed to over the last two rains. The call was taken up all around the city, and Jinao felt a thrill pass through him.

'Ancestors be praised!' Lakari said, rubbing his hands together, his narrow eyes crinkling. 'Clan Ahiki is here! Come. We must prepare!'

Jinao surrendered himself to the tide of excitement and anxiety that washed over the palace that afternoon. While the grounds filled with soldiers mustering to cross the city and provide escort to the royal convoy, Jinao's bamboo greathouse swarmed with servants come to powder and paint him. He was bathed and oiled and wrapped in a traditional skirt then adorned with warpaint that accentuated his ancestral tataus. Palani, his page, brought him cups of wine whenever Jinao beckoned. After the third cup the boy bowed hesitantly and muttered, 'Sire . . . perhaps it is too early for . . . more?'

'It's never too early for more,' Jinao told him heartily. The day was shaping up to be not so bad! Yes, his ancestor had publicly snubbed his call for the twentieth time – or was it the thirtieth? Jinao couldn't recall. But his mother was dead! Tonight she would burn! And for the first time in his life, he might meet the king!

As Jinao followed the crowds through the gardens late that afternoon, he spotted two household monks, deep in conversation. Ordinarily, the announcement of a royal visit would have come through them, as the king's eyes and ears among his invoker clans. But not this visit, it seemed. Jinao wondered if it was because his sibling Jemusi had not yet been anointed First General. In the distance, coming down an adjacent path, he spotted Marali – some cousin of his from the Outer Isles, and Mizito's newest invoker. There was no point in resenting her. Whatever happened was the will of the ancestors.

Their allies from all across the Nine Lands lined the avenue leading from the Great Northern Gate, every aide, soldier and guest. Jinao stood between his siblings, sweat tracing a line down his bare back, as the heavy iron gates juddered open to admit their most esteemed visitors.

The horses came first: two dozen golden steeds with shining amber eyes and sleek crystal bodies. Their riders wore the familiar golden masks of the king's guard. Their muscular skin, too, was painted gold. So much brightness was hard to look upon. Which, Jinao supposed, was the point.

Then came the Clan Ahiki litter itself, borne upon the shoulders of a dozen gold-painted servants in loincloths. Its curtains hung closed against the city heat. As it drew level with Jemusi and the rest of the palace household, it came to a halt. The entire convoy stopped, and then two more loinclothed servants scurried forward to pull back the curtains and reveal the personage who languished within.

A youth of perhaps sixteen dozed upon the cushions. He wore a headdress of golden spikes, shaped like the sun. His robe, too, was of spun gold. But both headdress and the robe lay askew as the royal youth snored. His slender arms bore intricate golden tataus: the blazing

46

sun of Ahiki, King of Them All. His brown skin and braided hair could have seen him pass as a native of almost any province in the Nine Lands. Jinao cleared his throat. He'd heard that, despite centuries of ancestor-blessed life, the king was young to look upon. But not this young.

'His Royal Highness,' a plump herald sang, their voice carrying across the crowd, 'Princen Tamun Ahiki, the First Light of Dawn, Thirty-Sixth in line to the Blessed Throne of the Nine Lands.'

The drummers struck up then, pounding out a deafening rhythm that startled the youth from his nap. He seized one of the cushions in alarm, his headdress falling over one eye. Then he sat up, straightening his robes and leaning towards the litter opening.

This. This was a descendant of the great leader who had founded the Nine Lands. This soul was Bonded to the spirit of the most powerful warrior to have ever lived. This scrawny youth's forefather held back the greyblood hordes. This bleary-eyed whelp was the one to whom the invoker clans and their progeny must bow.

'Have we arrived?' Princen Tamun said, and then he opened his eyes.

Jinao winced and looked away. He felt all those around him react too, some shielding their faces, others taking an involuntary step back. It was as though someone had opened the sun itself and poured it into Jinao's head. His temples pulsed. His eyes stung. His hearing faded, then surged back again, ringing.

'Do not try to meet his gaze!' Jemusi hissed, her head lowered. 'That pain you feel is the displeasure of our ancestors.'

Jinao had never been to the capital city, Nine Lords, but he had heard it said that the closer a soul got to the king's palace, the Garden, the harder the place was to look upon, until the throbbing in one's ears and the burning in one's eyes became too much to bear. Garden servants, it was said, underwent a special procedure to be able to withstand Clan Ahiki's brilliance. If this was just a taste, then it was a place Jinao hoped he would never have the misfortune to visit.

'Which one of you was it?' Tamun said in his uneven adolescent voice. 'Which one took the Bairneater's arm? We would speak with them.'

On Jinao's right, Julon stirred, then shuffled forwards. 'It was I, Your Highness,' Julon said. He lowered himself to the ground, kneeling and pressing his head to the stone road, his long black hair spreading out in a silky half-circle. 'I took the beast's arm, if it pleases my Royal—'

'You are to be commended,' Princen Tamun said. 'That creature has been quite the blight on our lands for some centuries.'

Jemusi stepped forward and bowed. 'Princen Tamun, on behalf of Clan Mizito and our hallowed ancestors, I bid you welcome to the palace of Thousand Domes. We have prepared the royal dome for you, and all funeral arrangements have been made.'

'Funeral?' Tamun said.

'Yes, Your Highness. For our mother, ancestors preserve her.'

Tamun stared, his searing golden eyes empty of expression, but the corners of his mouth curved in gentle amusement. 'Ah. Yes. We are not here for the funeral, though we would be happy to preside over the ceremonies. We are here with a declaration from my uncle, His Grace King Jakhenaten II Ahiki.'

Tamun gestured, and the plump herald stepped forward again, this time unfurling a coiled papyrus.

'His Most Blessed and Golden Grace Jakhenaten Ahiki,' the herald sung, 'King of the Nine Lands, High Warlord of the Invoker Clans, Holy Unifier of the People, bids every household in his domain provide the kingdom with two souls of fighting age to join in his reclamation of the Feverlands. Furthermore, His Most Benevolent Majesty commands his ancestors' loyal servants, the invoker clans, to each provide an army of ten thousand warriors to join him in reclaiming our lost lands to the west.' The herald let the scroll snap shut, the only sound in the resonant silence that followed.

A joke. It had to be a joke. Some ruse of this young Clan Ahiki upstart, meant to remind Thousand Domes of his power over them

48

all. The invoker clans existed to protect the Nine Lands from what escaped the Feverlands, not go charging in after it. Besides, the Feverlands had been named for how inhospitable they were to humans. Poison, they said. Poison in the air itself. Nothing natural could hope to survive.

Jinao began to smile, then noticed that his sister, still bowing from the waist, had gone rigid. 'Your Highness,' Jemusi said, straightening, 'forgive me . . . perhaps I misunderstood. His Grace the king is intending to . . . invade greyblood territory?'

'It is hardly an invasion when those lands were once ours,' Tamun said, examining his nails.

'Your Highness . . . We are scarcely able to hold the river here in Aranduq. With those numbers, this city and the entire length of the Ae would be vulnerable to—'

'We grow weary after our journey. We will retire to our apartments and refresh ourselves before the funeral rites.' Tamun signalled with one slender hand, and the servants let the curtains fall closed. Before they could meet, however, Jemusi sprang forward, arm extended, holding the curtain open. Within a heartbeat, a gold-painted soldier had a spear to her throat, and two more stood behind her.

'Let her speak,' Tamun sighed.

'Why now?' Jemus said. 'With our mother gone—'

'My uncle the king has become aware of . . . new information about a largescale attack that is being planned. He seeks to forestall that.'

Then Jemusi was driven back into the line of spectators, and the royal procession rumbled on.

49

FIVE

Temi

'Read it again, Tem!' Aunt Yeshe said, from the head of the table. Temi leaned over the sheet of papyrus that had been nailed to their front door. She'd seen the swarm of golden-robed monks that swept up Arrant Hill just after dawn, nailing identical missives to every building they passed. They didn't care that most in the district could not read the Royal Tongue script. They had delivered their directive, and that was all that mattered. Temi had assumed, as she sat counting through the meagre amount of coin they had gathered so far for the Chedu Family, that it was about some wanted criminal. But no. It was something far worse.

'*By order of His Most Blessed and Golden Grace Jakhenaten II Ahiki,*' Temi read, '*King of the Nine Lands, High Warlord of the Invoker Clans, Holy Unifer of the People, every household in the realm must send two souls of fighting age to join in the reclamation of the Feverlands. Members of the Holy Orders will arrive to collect volunteers for transportation and assignment in due course. Refusal is punishable by death.*'

Outside, Temi heard the shriek of children riding a broken cart down the hill. She could not meet Yeshe's eyes. None of them could. Her aunt had been a conscript as a young woman, and though she never spoke of what she'd endured, Temi heard her thrashing and muttering while she slept, trapped in nightmares of that time. Temi's father had been conscripted too, years later, and he had never returned. But never in the history of the Nine Lands had so many been summoned, or for such an ill-fated purpose.

'*Due course*,' Uncle Amaan said. 'So it could be any day.'

'I'll go,' Temi's cousin Kierin said. 'We all know I'm the best fighter. What will it be, a year? I can survive a year.'

'We're drawing lots,' Yeshe said, looking up at them all. 'When the time comes, we're drawing lots. And that includes me—'

'Auntie, no!' Kierin said.

'We leave it all in the hands of the ancestors. They'll know what to do.'

'It makes no sense,' Amaan said. He set his youngest child down on the floor and watched as she toddled out into the yard. 'They should be sending warriors south to Aranduq. There's been sightings of the Bairneater out there.'

'That's just stupid stories,' Yeshe muttered.

'No, I heard it too,' Kierin said. 'A whole galley come up the river from Mizitoland, and they was all talking about it.'

Temi vaguely recalled something about Aranduq. The Gateway to the Nine Lands . . . that was what they called it. Greybloods hauled themselves out of the sea there, and into the River Ae.

'What is this thing, anyway?' Mtobi said, tapping the tiny silver pin with a lacquered nail. 'Looks like techwork.' They lifted one slender dark-brown arm and made the sign for ancestral protection. 'It's techwork that counts who's in a household, right? So can't we just . . . throw it in the river?'

'No,' Yeshe said grimly. 'It's probably done its counting already. Don't matter where we put it, them monks'll know who's here.'

'*Reclamation* of the Feverlands?' said Uncle Amaan. 'That means invade. That means whoever goes isn't coming back, because no human can survive out there.'

[Temi. You cannot continue to ignore me.]

Temi backed away from the table as her family debated. She wiped

51

her damp palms on her wrapper. Every time the voice spoke, it seemed to have gained strength. It had been two days since she'd first heard it, and now its presence felt like a physical weight. It was a tightness behind her eyes and a pressure on her skin, as though she were a prison it sought to escape.

Temi knelt before the family shrine and crumpled the last of her morning bean cake onto the wooden platter. What a cruelty it was that only the nine founding warlords could be drawn back into the mortal realm. How much easier would the war be if every family in the Nine Lands could call upon their fallen kin. Temi closed her eyes and muttered another silent plea to the ancestors to preserve her cousins' spirits. If the voice had been sent to punish her, well – perhaps if she spent enough time at the shrine, she could atone.

[I am not a punishment. And you have no idea what the ancestral realm is.]

'Tem, where you going?' Yeshe called as Temi stood.

'Meliti said she'd lend us coin,' Temi replied. 'Won't be long.'

Temi strode through the kitchen, where little Maiwo was serving at the counter, and on out into the heat of the street. The Feverlands. The Royal Clan was dragging them all to the Feverlands. Even in Aunt Yeshe's darkest tales from the days when the invoker clans had been fighting the Blight, there had never been a conscription this large.

[Temi, look up.]

She reacted without thinking, in time to see Tunji slipping out from between the buildings. He had a large sack strapped to his back and wore a patterned agbada – one of his best, the one usually reserved for weddings.

'Oi!' Temi said, striding after him and grabbing his shoulder before he could slip away.

'Temi!' Tunji said, all nervous laughter. How could he be so calm considering everything they faced? 'I'm just heading to the docks for work, and—'

[The sack.]

Temi jerked at the sack and looked inside. Votives. Dozens upon dozens of them. He must have taken all their stores from the bakery and their personal stock, too.

'What are you doing?' Temi said.

'Everything's gonna be fine,' Tunji replied, lifting a hand. 'I sell this lot, we're laughing. I told you, I added something new; can sell them for twice as much.'

'Twice as much? Where you going?'

Tunji inhaled. 'Not into Chedu territory, promise. Just . . . just west into Lordsheart. But look, I'll be careful, and I'll—'

'Tunji, no! You can't go selling techwork in the highblood districts!'

'You'd be surprised, Tem, what them highbloods do when no one's looking. And they need clean water as much as the next soul.'

'What if the monks catch you? Or some other Family? You can't just—'

'Relax! This is the only way! We got four days, Tem. Four days for all them suns. Or do you have a better plan?'

Temi glanced up at the late-afternoon sky. She knew she couldn't stop him. Even if she ran back to Yeshe, he'd only sneak out while they slept.

'Please, Tem,' Tunji said. 'I need to make up for what I done.'

Temi let out a slow breath. 'Just watch your back, you hear?'

'Promise,' Tunji said, backing away. 'And I promise it'll all be OK!'

'You don't fuck with the Families,' Meliti said as she slipped Temi the pouch. They stood on Market Road, outside the South Lordsgrave Convent, the afternoon crowds swirling past them. Temi could feel the unease in the snatches of whispered conversation, in the drawn faces, in the exchanged glances. Hundreds of these people would soon be heading to a war from which there was little chance of return.

What had changed? For as long as the Nine Lands had existed, greybloods had been trying to invade it. And yes, at times the losses were big – a city here, a town there. But aside from the annihilation of Clan Kzani, things rarely got significantly worse. The invoker clans held the greybloods back. The greybloods took all the metal they could, then retreated. That was the way things were.

'Seriously, Tem, you listening? I said you don't fuck with the Families.' Meliti's baby was strapped to her back, dozing with his head lolling to one side. He alone seemed peaceful in the simmering heat. Meliti herself wore a green kameez damp with her sweat. She watched Temi count out the coins – six moons and twenty crescents: nearly ten days' wages for Meliti, far more than Temi had hoped for.

'It's too much,' Temi said.

'Maxood advanced my pay,' Meliti said, shrugging and looking away. 'My ma and auntie gave some. You know, one time Maxood's cousin borrowed money off of one of them Families, then lost it gambling with some Intiqqi sailor. You know what they did when he didn't pay up? They chopped off his hands.'

Temi laughed and looked away. 'Come on, Meli—'

'This is serious,' her friend said, punching her shoulder. 'You said this Harvell mentioned Ba Casten? He's a complete lunatic, from what I heard. I asked the regulars – I heard them mention him before. They say his speciality is taking the tongues and feet of those what disobey. Once, they found a dozen bodies in the canal, all with their throats slit and the Chedu family sign carved in their foreheads, them two staring eyes. Their households didn't even go to the bluehawks. Knew better'n to speak out. The Chedus run half the pillowhouses and gambling dens north of the river.' Meliti shuddered. 'So you get them their money and you stay the fuck away.'

'I plan to.'

'Look, I got to get back to work. Tell your stupid brother to keep his head down. I'll see if I can get any coin from my sister's wife – her family's got their own cloth business; might be they can help.'

Temi watched her friend melt back into the heaving afternoon crowd.

[We can help each other. If we work together, we can help each other.]

54

'Not interested,' Temi muttered, crossing the street. She stepped over the low blackglass wall and into the convent gardens, where the orphans who lived in the catacombs were pulling up weeds. The children watched her as she passed. To many of them, she was a familiar face: she'd been bringing Sister Poju bottles of Jebbanese red for many years now. The old nun had first befriended her when Temi was an angry girl of twelve, mourning a lost father and a mother who had given herself to drink.

[These nuns cannot help you.]

'Yes, they can. You're the curse that thieving witch placed on me. I'm going to find out how to undo her work.'

[There is no such thing as a curse.]

'All right, so how do I get rid of you?'

[You cannot.]

Something hissed behind her, and Temi turned to see No-Cat sprinting away towards the road. She hadn't even been aware it was following her.

[That creature knows it is not welcome here.]

'That creature is *welcome* to go away whenever it bloody wants,' Temi muttered. 'It don't need to keep following me.'

Sister Poju stood outside the convent's marble entrance, polishing a statue of Warlord Navret holding her chakrams. The convent was dome shaped, and from its summit stretched a ruined Scathed tower.

'Temi Baker,' Sister Poju said. 'It's been a while. How may I help you today?' Temi did not miss the way the old woman's eyes flicked to the bottle she carried in one hand.

'I seek the wisdom of the ancestors,' Temi said.

'Then follow me, child.' Sister Poju led her into the echoing coolness of the remembrance hall, her bare feet slapping on the stone. She was a spare, wiry woman, the tataus on her bald head faded with age. They crossed the circular hall, the nine statues of the founding invoker warlords looming above them. Just the smell of incense and damp and the distant chanting of the nuns calmed Temi. It was going to be all right. Everything was going to be all right. She'd ask the ancestors to get rid of the voice. Ask them to grant her the means to appease the Chedus. And then, with their blessing, somehow evade the king's draft.

'The ancestors smile upon those who seek counsel,' Temi muttered, unclenching her fists.

She felt a wave of dark amusement bubbling up in response to that.

A noviciate girl of no more than six or seven knelt at the feet of First King Ahiki, lighting nine candles in his honour. Ahiki's marble eyes stared disinterestedly out from beneath the hood of his cloak. In one outstretched hand, he carried a glowing sun.

'Here, miss!' a second noviciate said, crossing to her eagerly and pressing a candle into her hand. Temi took it and followed Sister Poju into the tunnel leading down into the catacombs.

Many of the chambers they passed were occupied by dozing orphans or vagabonds, but after a time they came to an empty chamber, dug like them all from the earth itself. One candle burned low before a modest shrine, illuminating the sketches laid out before it. Elders with kind eyes. A smiling child. Two cats and even a pet lizard.

'Kneel, child,' Sister Poju said, 'and perhaps the ancestors will hear you.'

Temi closed her eyes, the musk of the catacombs filling her nostrils. 'Ancestors,' she said, 'your daughter Temi Adaduna Irine Omolele Yawo Baker seeks your wisdom and counsel so – so that she might find the path you would not turn from.'

Temi swallowed. Her father had given her that first name, after one of his aunts. Mama Elleth had chosen Irine, the name of her long-dead sister, though there was no naming tradition in Yenlund, not as there was in Jebba. Temi might not be an invoker, but calling on the names of those who had gone before, those she had been named after herself, had to have its own power. That was what Old Baba had always said.

'And what have you brought them?' Sister Poju said.

'A morsel from my own plate.' Temi pulled a crust from the fold of her wrapper.

'The ancestors smile upon the generous hearted. And for a thirsty nun?'

'Jebbanese red.' Temi slid the bottle across the earthen floor.

She stole a glance and saw that though Sister Poju's eyes remained closed, one bony hand crept out, feeling for the bottle.

'Ancestors, lend us your wisdom,' Sister Poju intoned. 'Let the life-times you have lived strengthen your daughter here. Speak, child, and perhaps the ancestors shall answer.'

Temi swallowed. 'Ancestors,' she said. 'I—'

Her thoughts were interrupted by the pop of the bottle, followed by the wet sound of several deep swallows.

'Go on,' Sister Poju said thickly. 'The ancestors smile upon those who unburden themselves before their shrines.'

'I think a spirit witch has cursed me,' Temi said.

The nun stifled a belch. 'Spirit witch, you say?'

'Yup. Feels like something's . . . inside me. A presence. It happened after I met her. I hear it . . . talking to me sometimes. Smiling.'

'Child, one cannot hear a smile.'

'Can't one? Seems to me I can. He's always smiling, or—'

'*He?* This faceless smiler is a *he?*'

'Yes. It feels like he's trapped there and he wants to come out like, well . . .'

'Like an ancestor invoked? Temi, my dear: only the descendants of the nine mighty warlords can Bond their spirits. You know that.'

'I know, but—'

'Are you under any strain at the moment? Anything troubling you? I know this city is reeling from news of conscription.'

'No, nothing's bloody troubling me. Look, can you banish this thing or not?'

Sister Poju was silent for so long that Temi feared the old woman had fallen asleep, as had happened more than once in the past, especially when Temi brought the Jebbanese red. But when she stole another glance, she found the nun was pouring wine into the little glasses set before the shrine.

57

'I fear the ancestors need more than a mere crust in order to guide you, child,' Sister Poju said wearily as she poured. 'We nuns cannot help you with a sickness of the mind, and you are old enough to know that there is no such thing as a spirit witch. This is what happens when those outside the Holy Orders dabble with techwork.'

Temi feigned outrage. 'Techwork? Mother Poju, I have no idea what you mean. I—'

'All techwork is cursed, child. It is not meant for human use. Your sickness is the result of ignoring that fact. I suggest you seek the help of a healer.'

'That woman, whoever she was, did something to me, the day my cousins were killed, and—'

'Ah! Now we get to the heart of it. You have suffered a trauma. Your cousins.'

[This person is a liar. A liar and a sot. And we are wasting time.]

The rhythmic thrumming of the catacombs was like a heartbeat and had always comforted Temi. But just then, she felt only creeping unease. She pushed quietly to her feet.

'Thank you, Holy Mother,' she said.

Sister Poju smiled up at her. 'Trust in the ancestors, Temi, and they will provide the answers you seek.'

At the entranceway, Temi turned and saw Sister Poju still watching her. The empty smile the old woman flashed could not quite mask the frown of unease that had preceded it.

The crowds were thinning out on Market Road when Temi turned back onto it, ahead of the evening lull. Temi knew Yeshe would be wondering where she'd gone, but Sister Poju was right: perhaps a healer was the answer.

By the time she reached Sutesh's apothecary, it was near fully dark. The tumbledown hut stood on the quayside between a pillowhouse and a smithy. Down here, the ripe stench of the River Ae was over-powering, but it had never bothered Temi. She rapped on the wooden door and listened to Sutesh humming within. A light rain had started up, fine as mountain mist. Temi watched it drip from the assorted signs that swung from the lip of the roof. Sutesh had been healing Lordsgrave for Temi's entire life, and they were usually happy for Temi to pay them in bread.

'Come!' Sutesh called in their musical Riani accent.

Temi pulled open the door, releasing a waft of hot, fragrant air, and stepped into the bright interior of Sutesh's hut. Sutesh sat at the cooking pot that hung over their fire, humming and chewing on a stick of sweetweed. They were a small soul, round-bellied and wrinkled with age. Their brown head had been bald for as long as Temi could remember, but their smile was keen, their gaze sharp, and the thin arms that stuck out of the orange tunic they wore were strong with sinewy muscle.

No-Cat crept in behind her, sniffing the air, its tail held high. Sutesh shot a glance at it, then chuckled to themself. 'I'll be a moment,' they said, crumbling something into the pot. Temi watched the smoke curl up through the hole in the roof, where the thin rain floated down like tiny jewels. 'More lovers' tea, is it?'

'Not this time,' Temi said. 'Got a delicate problem.'

The walls and floor of the apothecary were thick with vials and bottles. But it was the rear of the hut to which Temi's gaze was drawn, and the screens that did not quite hide the stacks of techwork piled there. Sutesh might earn their meals selling wart-portion to elders, but their true calling lay there, among the metal and the blackglass.

'I heard about your cousins,' Sutesh said. 'Nasty business. You have my condolences.'

'Thank you, Old Elder.'

'Not many souls could burn a body but not the boat it stands on,' they continued, stirring the pot. 'Hope my Arrant Hill bakers aren't in any trouble?'

'Nothing we can't handle,' Temi said.

'Good. To business, then. Take a seat on the cushions. Tell me what it is.'

Temi sat cross-legged and let out a slow breath. 'Well . . .'

Sutesh smiled knowingly. 'I understand. How many days late is your blood?'

'No! It's not that. Look, I've got this voice. In my head. No one else can hear him. It's, er . . . it's like something is imprisoned within me, wanting to get out. Sister Poju said it was caused by . . . techwork.'

Sutesh's brown eyes narrowed. 'The holy ones will tell you techwork will poison you, mind and body, and that using it will summon greybloods. But that is merely because they want the Scathed's tools all for themselves. Temi, voices are caused by an imbalance of the mind.'

'Could someone curse you with something like that?'

[Ask them about that crystal, there by the waste pot.]

Temi glanced across the room and saw what she had taken to be a large black stone. It was a crystal, she realised, with so many facets it seemed almost round. Its inky darkness shifted as she stared, brightening into a deep and luxurious blue.

'Old Elder, what's that crystal?' Temi said, nodding with her chin.

'That? Oh, nothing. An ornament.'

[Ask them how many other memory domes they have masquerading as decoration.]

'The . . . *thing* inside me says it's a memory dome,' Temi said.

Sutesh froze, one bony hand suspended over the cooking pot. 'What did you say?'

'He says it's a memory dome?'

'How could you know that?' Sutesh said quietly.

'I told you. The thing inside me said it.'

Sutesh heaved a heavy sigh and then pushed to their feet, knees creaking. 'There are not many who would recognise this for what it is.' They crossed to one of their crowded bookcases, their back turned. 'Why did you come to me?'

'Sister Poju said I needed a healer. Have you got something that can . . . send the voice away?'

Sutesh pulled a curious metal tool down from their shelf. They slipped their fingers into it, like a Yennish boxer preparing for a fight. They sat beside her in a waft of sandalwood and sweat, and lifted their hands so that they framed her head. 'Close your eyes, please.'

Temi closed her eyes.

For several long moments, all she could hear was Sutesh's slow breaths and the clamour of the river outside. Then she heard a rumpled thud, followed by a clang, and when she opened her eyes, she saw that Sutesh had collapsed sideways. They lay sprawled on their back, legs still crossed beneath them, the ring tool lying several handspans from their fingers.

'Old Elder?' Temi said. She leaned forward and shook their arm. 'Sutesh?'

Within her, the voice chuckled. [I told you this was folly.]

'What's happened to them?'

Sutesh drew in a great breath and then sat up. When they caught sight of Temi, their eyes grew wide, and they began shuffling backwards. 'Stay away!'

'What?' Temi said. 'What happened? I didn't do anything!'

'Just stay away! Go!'

'Did you find the man?'

'No, I didn't find any men!' Sutesh snapped, jostling her to her feet. 'Now go home.'

'Would—'

'Go!' They made the sign for ancestral protection and then bundled her through the door and out into the night.

'Thank you, Old Elder!' Temi called over her shoulder.

'Go!'

Temi trudged through the drizzly darkness, past homes lit up in pools of light. The scent of evening meals being prepared reached her nostrils, making her stomach grumble.

'Why was Sutesh scared of you?' Temi said.

[Because they do not understand me.]

'Of course,' Temi said. 'Right. Well. Tell me what you need to leave my body, and I'll do it.'

He was silent for several heartbeats. Finally, as Temi turned back onto Market Road, he stirred and said, [There is no one alive today with the skill to set me free.]

'So I'm stuck with you? For the rest of my life?'

[I said there is no one *alive* who may help. I did not say that there is no one in existence.]

Temi straightened. 'The ancestors, then? The ancestors can help you?'

She sensed him hesitate. [If I were stronger, I might be able to free myself. But I am a shadow of what I once was.]

'Well, why didn't you say? So how do we get you stronger?'

[That is . . . complicated.]

At the bottom of Arrant Hill, Temi saw someone had torn down and partially burned a pile of papyrus announcing the conscription. She wondered what would happen if the entire district refused to comply. If they all just turned away. If they attacked the press gang when it came.

[Look. Outside your compound. Quickly.]

Temi squinted as she climbed the hill. Something lay beside the door. A large package, wrapped in cloth. Whoever left it could not have been gone long, and clearly didn't know Lordsgrave – it was a wonder the package hadn't been whisked away the moment it was set down. Locals often left her family gifts – rice, yam, cloth, spices . . . But this was larger, and no local would be fool enough to leave it in such plain sight.

As she drew closer, passing the noise and music of the ogogoro inn, Temi saw that the cloth was Jebbanese: bright purple and green wax-dyed cloth. But a dark stain marred the pattern, black in the feeble light from nearby windows . . .

Temi's heart lurched. She blundered forwards and fell to her knees.

She pulled at the cloth with shaking fingers, a swirling nausea rising within her.

He was almost unrecognisable, so beaten and bloody was his face. But that was his agbada. Those were his beautiful, slender hands.

Tunji.

Temi covered her mouth, a silent scream building in her throat.

SIX

Jinao

As the last light of the setting sun bathed the hillside of Thousand Domes red, Princen Tamun Ahiki lifted the flaming torch and turned to face the crowd.

The pyre loomed above Jinao. If he craned his neck, he could just glimpse the figure within, dressed in the silver and black of Clan Mizito. Its arms lay lovingly wrapped around something that glinted in the waning light. *Valour* – his mother's staff – and that was how Jinao knew she had truly gone. Its arcane metals would remain solid while Sulin's body crisped and burned, just as her father's had before her, and his parent before him. How small Sulin seemed now. How insignificant. How mortal, this woman who had once loomed so large.

'I thought she'd live for ever,' Jemusi said, slipping her hand into Jinao's. His older sister was dressed much as he was: white silks, white armour, white sandals, her long black hair bound with white ribbons, her face painted silver and black. Behind her stretched the grounds of Thousand Domes, the ancient Scathed structures glowing despite their blackness. Though only twelve stood now, Sulin claimed that once, there really had been a thousand. The bonetrees that stood among them looked piercingly white by contrast.

'Invoker Sulin,' Princen Tamun intoned as a hush descended, 'First

64

General of Cagai. Descendant of Warlord Mizito. Guardian of the Ae. Slayer of . . .' The Princen paused, before glancing at the small scrap of papyrus he held in his free hand. '. . . of the Three Dancers. To many, she embodied . . .' He glanced again. 'To many, she embodied the struggle against the greybloods. A woman who loved her people, loved the continent of the Nine Lands, and loved her king.'

Jinao felt a stirring at this but did not look up. The darkness only accentuated the unnatural glow in the young princen's eyes. To his left, he heard Julon sniff loudly.

Princen Tamun glanced at his papyrus again, and then abandoning all pretence at emotion, he read out, 'The spirit of Sulin, loyal servant of the ancestors and His Most Blessed Grace King Jakhenaten, lives on. It lives on in her child Jemusi. It lives on in her child Julon. And it lives on in each of you whom she touched with her light.'

Jinao did not even feel surprise that the princen failed to mention his name: only a dull sense of inevitability. Only a vague resignation. Only the desire that this whole thing be over so he could return to his bathhouse.

Tamun lifted the torch high. 'Lord Sulin, we bid you good journey. In the name of the warlords who defend our Nine Lands even in death, we bid you good journey. May your ancestors welcome you as you cross the pyre.'

But as the whelp turned to throw his torch, the wind gusted up around them and the flame faltered and went out.

Jinao heard stifled gasps at his back, but no one spoke, and a moment later one of the princen's golden-robed monks bustled forward and muttered a soft incantation, and the flame flared to life again. Tamun plunged the torch deep within the pyre, where lay twigs taken from every bonetree in the palace, as well as spirit wood to send Sulin on to the ancestral realm, and many of her most treasured possessions – carvings, paintings, and words for the ancestors written on papyrus and sealed within lengths of bamboo. The flame danced hungrily among it all. More torches were brought forth then, and Jemusi stepped forward to place hers within the pyre, and then their brother Julon, and then one found its way into Jinao's hand, and when it was time for him to step forward, he did so. The heat of the blaze stung his face, fierce as his mother's temper.

'May the ancestors preserve you,' Jinao said flatly, and then tossed his torch among the growing flames.

One of Tamun's round-cheeked heralds started up the Song of Legends Lost, his shrill voice sharp enough to startle half a dozen of those nearest him. Others joined him, voices rising into the night. They surrounded the pyre now, the family closest, then his mother's captains and envoys and the inner household, and beyond them warriors from the other clans who had been steadily pouring into Aranduq City to help defend the Ae. Tapers passed among them all, and heartfelt words were shared as all lamented the loss of such a great woman, such a kind woman, a woman who had given so much to them all.

'If Aranduq falls, the Nine Lands fall!' Julon railed, standing before the roaring fire. 'Why is the king sending us west, when the threat here has never been greater?'

More than one head turned to look for the princen as Jemusi hissed at her sibling to be silent, but Jinao could see Tamun had already lost interest in the proceedings and was stalking up the path towards the Greatdome, trailing a procession of gold-clad monks and servants, a gilded river in the dusk.

'The Ae no longer has a guardian!' Julon said, turning to the crowd.

'Julon!' Jemusi hissed, but Julon shook her off and stalked into the night.

Now that the fire was blazing, the mourning began. Jinao's father, Captain Bataan, led the way, falling to his knees and screaming at the sky, and then Jemusi joined him. A dozen voices took up the call, a hundred, until the hillside shook with it. Jemusi drew her kampilan and slashed her braid in half, then cast it into the flames. Wateng, missing fingers bandaged now, tore at his face with his good hand, scratching until the blood dripped from his cheeks. Jinao had heard of souls offering ears, limbs, of some who would climb into the pyre and turn to ash beside the ones they had lost. Jinao hoped that none would have the poor judgement to do so today.

As he stood watching the flames, he realised that more than one eye had slid round to take him in. Invoker Mavood Qaneen and the other warriors from his clan had begun their ululating death cry, kohl-rimmed eyes fixed disapprovingly on Jinao from behind their veils. Invoker Morayo Adatali shouldered into him as he danced by in the first movements of the Jebbanese Dance for the Lost.

Jinao knew he had to show some emotion. If he stood there, eyes dry, voice silent, they would claim he had not loved her, that he did not mourn her passing, and so was no worthy son.

Jinao dropped to his knees and willed the tears to come. *Most people are failures*, Jinao's mother had told him, time and again. *Their lives are a slow slide into failure, or sometimes a fast one. Most set targets they'll never meet, have dreams they'll never realise. But not us. Not our family.*

Jinao let a thousand memories of his mother come into his mind, memories he'd spent so long trying to banish, to package up and hide deep within. Sulin the Bold, taking her staff to his knees when he could not recite the name of the sixth Warlord of their clan. Sulin the Wise, shutting him outside when the rains came because every other child had bested him on the wrestling mat. Sulin the Guardian, turning away from the shrine time and again when the ancestors ignored her son's call.

The tears came easily now. Jinao stared at the pyre, remembering every cruelty, every humiliation, every harsh word and cold glare. His mother had had such love for others, such a warm heart, but he was the fulcrum of everything else . . . All the darkness she hid, all her rage and despair.

When the last light of the sun was gone, Jinao found that he was as spent as the rest of them. The pyre roared now, and the skin of his arms and face was raw with it. Beside him, Jemusi stood and bowed one final time to her mother. Her hair looked strange, flapping raggedly around her broad face. Now she was First General of Cagai, and Guardian of the River Ae.

'I know she was unkind to you,' Jemusi said softly as they led the way up to the Greatdome. 'But she did love you. Truly.'

Jinao could not bring himself to tell her she was wrong.

In the distance, he saw Julon standing alone on the hillside.

'He blames himself,' Jemusi said. 'He wishes he'd taken more than just the beast's arm.'

'I heard it was . . . another soldier who took the arm,' Jinao said quietly.

'I can't imagine where you heard that,' Jemusi said.

The Greatdome was filled with more tables than Jinao could ever recall having seen. Even then, not everyone could be accommodated. Eating mats lay on the lawns surrounding the dome, with great awnings set above them, should the rains come early. Now that the pyre was lit, and the people's grief and rage spent, they would celebrate. They would drink and dance and laugh and rejoice at how blessed they were to have known Invoker Sulin Mizito.

Jinao had never seen so many descendants of Mizito in one place. He realised now how very different they all were – their skin, their hair, their clothes, their mannerisms, their local tongues. Strange to think that they had all descended from the same warrior.

As Jinao stepped between the ornamental palms and into the hall, his gaze was drawn to the dais, and the long, low table at which the inner family would sit. But reclining there now upon his mother's cushion was Princen Tamun. Already, the youth was eating from a banana leaf platter and joking noisily with a circle of fawning advisers. He did not look up as the mourners entered, instead lifting his cup and shouting loudly for more wine.

Beside Jinao, Jemusi's jaw tightened. 'We can greet the guests here,' she said flatly, and motioned Jinao to her side.

The palace herald, Chiyu, who had been standing beside the drummers, scampered over to them, straightening his white headdress as he ran.

'Warlord Sohimi Mizito, ruler of the four provinces of Mizitoland!' Chiyu sang as the first guests stepped between the palms.

Heads turned as the leader of Jinao's clan entered. Sohimi was a slight woman, and dressed modestly – no flowing cloaks for her, but a simple Ekari battle dress, wide about the sleeves and tied with a broad belt in the Mizito colours. Jinao's mother had claimed Sohimi was proud and vain. When she stopped before them, she made a slight formal bow, but there was no hint of warmth on her pinched face.

Jinao leaned forward, looking down the snaking line that led out into the darkness. He would have to stand there all night, bowing and accepting condolences he had no use for, while on the dais, the young royal got steadily more drunk.

'Invoker Tenutan Mizito, First General of Umajin Province of Mizitoland!'

The Umajin plains-dwellers wore their long hair loose beneath conical, silk-draped hats. Lord Tenutan led them; their long hair was white now, but their unreadable eyes remained ageless.

'Sulin was unparalleled,' Tenutan said as they bowed. Their eyes glittered as they shifted to Jinao, dwelling on his just a moment longer than necessary. Jinao remembered when Tenutan had found him as a child, crying in the gardens after a beating. *Here*, Tenutan had told him. *It is a carving of Mizito fighting the Blight. If you twist it just so, you can see his staff move.* And it was true. When Jinao turned the carving to the light, it seemed as though his forefather struck down with his staff. Jinao had the carving still, somewhere in his greathouse.

Tenutan smiled imperceptibly before turning, and Jinao knew in that moment that there went a soul who had seen his mother for what she truly was.

Jinao bowed and nodded as nobles streamed by, these souls who'd fought beside Sulin. So many of them held a terrible grief in their eyes,

69

and he realised, with a sickening dread, that this was not for the loss of his mother. It was for what they would all lose if the Ae opened its waters to the enemy. Aranduq was doomed. With the king's conscription, the city would fall along with its First General. And then, what would become of the Nine Lands? Jinao thought of that day on the riverbank, of how the dead had carpeted the sands. If they were barely surviving now, how would they stop greybloods entering the Ae once the best of them were sent west? He glanced wistfully at the wine-bearers weaving between the steadily filling tables. He needed a drink. A drink, and his bathhouse.

'They think we're finished,' Jinao muttered.

'Then they too are finished,' Jemusi said, smiling through clenched teeth. 'Ten thousand warriors heading west will leave us with virtually nothing to defend the river. Every province that sits on the banks of the Ae will be vulnerable. While the king hurls us against the Feverlands, his kingdom will be overrun.'

By the time the last of them had paid their respects, Jinao's legs were stiff and his stomach grumbling. He followed his sister and the rest of their family across the floor to a new high table that had been hastily set up before the drummers. A flood of servants swept in from the gardens, bearing platters of steaming breads and rice fried with rare spices. Wines from every corner of the Nine Lands were poured, and behind their table, the drummers began their first song.

Jinao ate, and drank, and drank some more. Nobody spoke to him, and he was glad of it. His sister balled food absently in her hand, while her eyes drifted ever to Julon's empty cushion.

Finally, when the stews and sizzling vegetables of the main meal were brought forth on platters of woven banana leaf, Jemusi stood.

'I'm going to find him,' she said.

A servant passed with a jug of wine, so Jinao waved her over. *Wine and spirits are for weak souls*, Sulin had told him as a child. And so he could think of no more fitting way to celebrate her memory.

Later, when the sweet dishes had come and gone and the teas had

70

been drunk, the drummers began their duelling songs. Jinao knew he was already drunk. He was aware of people coming and going, sharing their stories, filling his cup from their own, weeping and holding his hands. But after a time, they all blurred into one. It reminded him of the parade of suitors his mother had produced for him over the years, souls Jinao might find entertaining for a day, or a moon, but who ultimately looked to him only as a route to the inner clan.

'Boring, isn't it?' came a woman's voice.

Jinao looked up through heavy eyes to see First General Riona Tarsin manoeuvring herself to sit beside him. Northerners were not floor-sitters, and Riona's bulk had grown as she had aged, but still her laughter filled any room. It took some negotiating before she had arranged her heavy dress-armour. Her yellow hair fell down her back in a simple tail. Over by the drummers stood more of her pale-skinned kin, including Riona's supposititious son, whom Jinao had heard was already Bonded to the spirit of Tarsin. A child of twelve and of unsanctioned birth, yet stronger in invocation than Jinao would ever be.

'I'm sorry?' Jinao said.

'I don't think you are,' Riona said with a wistful smile. 'But that can be our secret.'

The stage erupted with the throaty boom of the greatdrum, calling all to a friendly sparring bout in Sulin's honour. Nearby, Riona's young husband tipped his head back, draining his wine cup, his light skin flushed.

'I fear I've angered him again,' Riona said, shaking her head. 'That man . . . he will be the death of me. Lennette told me not to marry one so young, after Ulran died, but I didn't listen, and now where am I? My husband hates me. My children squabble over who will lead when I am gone. And I am stuck with this!' She patted her round stomach with one pale, meaty hand. 'Six children and too much ale will do that to the best of us, I suppose.'

'Mother used to say you were the strongest invoker of any Tarsin she knew,' Jinao said.

71

'Ah, but you won't repeat the other part, will you?' She leaned close as the drums drowned out her voice and cheers rose up around them to greet the first fighters. 'That she thought Tarsin the weakest of the Nine. Or should I say seven? I don't know why we continue to say *nine lords* and *nine lands* when two of the invoker lines are extinct. No need to blush; I know what your mother thought of me.'

'She thought that about everyone,' Jinao said, trying to keep the bitterness from his voice. 'She didn't give compliments easily.'

'She was a sour, prideful fucker with hate in her heart,' Riona said lightly, and when Jinao looked round, she laughed. 'Deny it! I see it in your eyes, Jinao. You bore little love for her. As she did for you, no doubt.'

'She always told me you northerners have no inhibitions when you speak,' Jinao heard himself say.

'She is lucky, your mother.' Riona continued, heedless. 'She leaves only memories of greatness behind her.' She took a long draw from her wine cup. 'If only I had the strength to join her. When I go, they'll say, *Riona fought well once, but she spent twice as many years drinking and fucking and suffocated on her own vomit at the ignoble age of ninety-nine.*'

Jinao didn't know what to say to that, so he sipped his wine and tried to think of a way to politely excuse himself.

'I don't know how they can stand to be near that little princeling,' Riona said, looking across the room to where Lord Tenutan sat before Tamun, chatting amiably. 'Those bloody eyes . . . Have you ever been to the Garden, Lord Jinao? It is fifty times worse there. The whole sky is bathed in gold, and it feels as though the weight of it could melt your wits. They say that it is the greatness of our king and his ancestors that we feel, but I call that goatcrap.' She gulped from her cup again. 'This invasion the king wants is doomed. And if your city falls, we will see our people go the way of the Scathed.'

Jinao scratched his nose and began to organise his limbs to rise. Too much wine, ancestors save him. And now he could scarcely stand. 'Yes,' Jinao said. 'Well, erm, if you'll excuse—'

'I've heard that Mizito has yet to heed your call,' Riona said. 'Do not let them tell you that you are any less worthy just because you are, what – twenty-two?'

'Twenty-eight,' Jinao said.

'Twenty-eight! A mere pup! You must know the tale of Invoker Petann Tarsin, the Sun in the North? Or perhaps you don't. Sulin wasn't the sort to tell her children northerner stories before tucking them in, was she? Petann had no tongue, they say, and could not hear even the loudest of sounds. *How*, his mother fretted, *will he ever Bond? He has no words to call upon his ancestors, nor make obeisance before them. They may have marked him as blessed, but how will he ever serve the Nine Lands and our king?* And sure enough, he reached manhood without Bonding the spirit of Tarsin, though his mother thrice presented him to the shrine. Then, one day, when he was four and forty, he visited the shrine alone. He was gone for eight days and eight nights and his husband and children feared him dead. But on the ninth day he reappeared, smiling, and that night, when the greybloods attacked, he stepped out of Highsee Castle, lifted his arms, and invoked Tarsin for the first time. They say he marched ahead of his army and slew great swathes of the enemy before the first captains had even mustered their warriors.'

'How did he invoke, if he had no words?'

Riona slapped Jinao's thigh, her grin wide. 'Don't ask me that, you monster! That's not the point of the story. The point is, if four and forty is good enough for Petann Tarsin, the man who slew the Grey Terror, then it is good enough for you. If you'd like, I will show you some tricks I know. You may not believe this, but it took me years to master invocation. Yes, I am strong when Tarsin's spirit is with me, but drawing his spirit out? That is the hardest part. You have a practice room, I'm sure. It will be quiet now, yes?'

He caught her eye, and it occurred to him in that moment that the tricks Riona Tarsin planned to show him in a quiet practice room would have little to do with their ancestors.

'I – I must find my sister,' Jinao said, and lurched to his feet.

Behind him, Riona cackled heartily. 'You can't blame a woman for trying!' she called.

Jinao stumbled past tables of laughing, chattering people and out into the cool of the night. The pyre was a thundering column of fire now, high upon the hill. Two figures sat before it: Julon and Jemusi. They looked comfortable there, talking softly together, sharing a grief that he never could. He felt no resentment, watching them now. Only detachment. Perhaps if he volunteered to answer the king's summons, they could remain. Together, perhaps they could hold the Ae long enough for the armies to return.

Jinao meandered through the night, stepping gingerly to remain upright, the sounds of drumming and cheering fading as he descended towards the dark gardens. He was so consumed with not passing out, or – ancestors forgive him – vomiting, that at first, he took the new shouts and the clanging of the gong that followed to be part of the celebrations. But then he realised they were coming from the wrong direction: there, deeper into the darkness at the edge of the grounds. And the words, clearer now, sent a chill running through him.

'Bairneater! The Bairneater is here!'

Jinao turned to see an enormous grey shape bounding towards the pyre. On the opposite side, Julon and Jemusi had begun to rise. But ancestors, the creature moved fast! Within a heartbeat, it had reached the pyre. It seemed to be taking something from within it. For one horrified moment, Jinao thought it sought to reclaim what was left of his mother's body to add to its collection of grisly trophies. But when its hand came away, Jinao saw that whatever it held was too narrow.

Her staff. The Bairneater had taken Sulin Mizito's staff.

Already, the creature was bounding away, and as figures streamed out of the Greatdome – his siblings' quartets, followed by a line of other warriors and invokers – Jinao realised that, once again, he stood in the creature's path. It thundered towards him, eating up the stretch of lawn between them in heartbeats, and Jinao, fool that he was, just stood there mutely, wondering how the same calamity could befall the same man twice.

'No!' Jinao cried, shielding his face like a child. But no blow came. No sting of metal.

'Five days!' the Bairneater boomed, its voice carrying across the gardens.

Jinao lowered his arms. The Bairneater stood before him. Ancestors, but it was massive! Its left hand gripped his mother's staff, still glowing red from the pyre. The skin there had blistered and wept grey fluid that glimmered in the night like molten silver. Its right arm ended in a jagged stump – the stump caused by the swing of Jinao's axe. The creature reeked . . . of heat and metal and something earthy and rotten. Its yellow eyes gleamed at Jinao, and he tried not to ascribe emotion to what he saw there. Hatred? Disgust? But no, this was a greyblood; a mindless creation of the Scathed – it did not feel.

'Five days for the one who took my arm to face me!' the Bairneater continued, sweeping Sulin's staff to encompass all those who approached. 'If they do not, I will take this city. I will await them in the abandoned slum. There, we will fight.'

Jinao's stomach twisted, while in the distance, the sky brightened as though with the rising dawn. Twin warriors stepped into the mortal plane: Jinao's black-clad ancestor. As the light of the ancestral realm dimmed, the two incarnations of Mizito strode forward, solid as mortals now, blue tendrils of ancestral energy limning their bodies. And behind them, golden robes all aflutter, came the king's nephew.

'The beast is wounded!' Jinao heard Princen Tamun shout. 'We have a chance to claim it!'

'Five days!' the Bairneater cried, and then it leapt, passing clear over Jinao and on into the dark.

SEVEN

Temi

T hey burned her brother's body at sunset.
Aunt Yeshe threw open the side door, and all afternoon, guests filed into their yard. Most Temi knew, but such celebrations always drew strangers, and these they welcomed too. The ancestors smiled upon those who shared what they had.

They moved the old bamboo table out into the yard and set it up before Mama Elleth's rows of spinach. Each group that arrived brought a contribution: fried cassava, sugared breads, bean cakes baked with peppers and onions . . . Elleth and Selek had been in the kitchen all morning, making stews and flatbreads and dumplings. Temi's uncle Amaan built the pyre under the shadow of Bakery Mount, his children coming and going with driftwood from the docks. There was no need to seek spirit wood at the convent – Temi's friend Meliti arrived with an armful of it, her baby strapped to her back. Temi and Meliti sat together as Temi's cousin Larmi carefully placed the strange black sticks around the pyre. Within the nest they'd created lay Tunji. Aunt Selek had draped a cloth of Vushemi lace over his mangled face. The children set trinkets on his chest: favoured toys, food they had saved . . . offerings for him to take to the ancestral realm.

By the time Aunt Yeshe lit the pyre, her dark hands trembling as she held the flaming torch, the yard was filled with people. 'Tunji Adareke Omodio Mareth Baker,' Yeshe said, her voice taut with emotion, 'we bid you good journey. In the name of the nine warlords who defend these lands even in death, we bid you good journey. May our ancestors welcome you as you cross beyond the pyre.'

Meliti held Temi's shaking shoulders as the flame leapt from place to place, climbing towards the boy who had been so full of passion and cheer. Hearing all the names his family had given him – names of his forebears, in the Jebbanese tradition – released something within Temi. He truly was gone. He was gone, and as the flames climbed higher, devouring all that he was, Temi let the tears come.

On the far side of the pyre, she glimpsed Old Baba shaking his head as he watched from his rocking chair, as though the force of his denial could undo what had already happened. Selek was the first to start up the Song of Legends Lost, her rich, deep voice filling the yard. Others joined her, but Temi had no will to sing. There was nothing to celebrate here.

[An injustice has been done. An injustice that must not go unanswered.]

Temi watched a stream of people pass Aunt Yeshe, kissing her cheeks, touching the ground in a bow, and slipping coins into her hand. For Tunji's spirit, they said. But they knew full well who it was for and why it was needed. The people of Arrant Hill did not have much, but they shared what they could. And before the flames had reached Tunji's agbada, Yeshe squatted down beside Temi to say that they now had the Chedus' ten suns.

Temi gripped a single length of spirit wood, brittle and black, as she watched the flames take hold. For invokers, it could call spirits back from the dead. But all it did for lowbloods was send loved ones away.

Temi's cousin Kierin arrived after dark with a dozen other youths, each carrying a cask of Yennish ale. No one asked how they had come by them, and soon the yard rang with laughter, and Kierin stood loudly sharing memories, and each of Tunji's friends lined up to pour drink at his hands. Temi's uncle Umadi arrived with his children and grandchildren. They wore white agbadas and geles, and two of the younger men had talking drums. Then Mtobi started the dancing, and soon they were all on their feet, all but Temi and Old Baba.

Her grandfather sat by the pyre, muttering and sucking restively on his gums. Temi stared at the flames as they leapt hungrily from plank to plank in their own wild dance.

'I can't understand it,' Uncle Amaan said, dropping down beside Temi as the heat from the pyre grew. He was a spare, angular man, his face all but hidden by his waist-long hairlocs and braided beard. But his sunken eyes had always had a way of seeing within her. If she fibbed as a child, it was Amaan they took her to. He was the one who would gently hold her shoulder and ask her to speak the truth, and she found she could never lie to his kind, knowing face.

So she kept her gaze low, but after a time he touched her shoulder and said, 'Tem. Why did they do this to him? We've got their money ready for tomorrow.'

Temi realised No-Cat lay curled by the edge of the pyre, its yellow eyes narrow slits as it watched the flames contentedly.

'I don't know,' Temi said.

'You sure?'

Temi closed her eyes and drew in a slow breath. 'He told me he'd made something new out of techwork. He was going to sell it over in Lordsheart, to get more money.'

Amaan was silent for several heartbeats, and when she glanced at him, she saw he was studying the flames. 'And he told you this when?'

'The day they killed him,' she said.

Amaan heaved a great sigh. 'You should have brought this to us, Tem. But the mistake was his. Might be the monks did this, if they caught him.'

'I don't think it was. I think it was *them*. The Chedus.'

Amaan turned to her. 'You keep that thought locked away, you hear?

They're coming here in the morning. We're going to pay them, and that'll be the end of it.'

[They should fear to return here. Fear what you will do to them now.] She felt him lashing within her, a stirring in her blood, a heat on her skin. His fury matched her own, amplified it, until Temi had to clench her fists to keep from screaming.

'So we just give them the money,' Temi said tightly. 'Obediently. Like good little children.'

'That is exactly what we do.'

[Unpunished. While your brother burns, unavenged.]

'You had something else in mind?' Amaan said.

'Course not.'

'Good. Because believe me, the Chedus are not people to get entangled with. Whether they did . . . *this* or not. We give them their money, and then we . . . try to move on.'

But there could be no moving on. Temi knew that as she watched the flames. They'd taken Leke and the others. They'd taken her brother. And tomorrow, they would take their coin. A cold anger lay coiled deep within her, and the Chained Man seemed to feed on its hardness.

[By what right do these people tell you where you and your family may go, or to whom you may sell what you make? By what right do they kill with impunity?]

This is what happens when those outside the Holy Orders dabble with techwork. That was what Sister Poju had said. And one way or another, she had been correct.

'You remember when he used to want to be a monk?' Temi said.

Amaan laughed softly. 'I remember that stupid staff he made out of driftwood. Old Baba was so angry. *Monks don't use techwork; they destroy it! Ah-ah!*'

'You think we're being punished,' Temi said, 'for what we do?'

Amaan gripped her shoulder, his dark eyes shining. 'Helping people get clean water? No. So don't you go thinking that.'

It was fully dark when Temi's mother Kerlyn arrived. A hush fell as she staggered out into the yard. She came to a stop, swaying on the spot and staring at the pyre as though not quite sure what it was. Then she stumbled a few steps in Temi's direction before collapsing to the ground. The flames had climbed so high by then that Temi could see nothing of Tunji within, as though a curtain of light had been thrown up to shield him from mortal eyes.

Temi left them all to their drinking and their memories and stepped over her mother's body to enter the cool of the house.

The family shrine glittered in the far corner of the room. Its velvet base bristled with food scraps and cheap trinkets. The polished back-board bore the sketched likenesses of those who had crossed the pyre. None for her father – because perhaps he was still alive out on the war front, slaughtering greybloods in their dozens. But her grandfather Mardin was there. Several of her uncles. Leke and the others. Tunji would be joining them now.

Temi curled up by the shrine and dozed until dawn, then rose early to prepare the bakery. The yard and house were filled with sleeping bodies, and few locals would call upon them today. But she fired up the oven and used the last of the water to scrub down the counters. By then, the street was stirring, and she could hear Yeshe yelling for someone to collect the day's water. Temi was just wringing out her cloth when there came a tap at the door.

Harvell Chedu.

She stood smiling outside, dressed in a green wrap dress and woven shoes. Across the street stood two strangers, watching silently, and a third soul appeared on the roof of the ogogoro inn. Lookout guards.

Temi crossed to the door, her heart thumping. Heat pooled into the tips of her fingers, a fierce itching that made her clench her fists. Temi wanted nothing more than to scratch Harvell's face off, but she unlatched the lock and pulled open the rickety wood.

'Greetings,' Harvell said. 'I've come for your brother's payment.'

'It's here.' Temi returned to the counter and grabbed the pouch that lay beneath. She held it out until the Chedu woman reached her, then opened her hand, letting it drop at the woman's feet.

[Look at her clothes. Her shoes. She does not need your coin.]

'Well, that was unnecessary,' Harvell said, squatting to collect the pouch. She counted silently, while Temi watched her. How easy it would be to lean across the counter now, seize the woman by her hair, and slam her face into the wood. How long would it take those lookouts to reach her? Ten breaths? Twenty?

[You could do this woman much damage in that time.]

'Is your brother home?' Harvell asked.

'What's that supposed to mean?' Temi said. Had she come to gloat? To wallow in their pain? Temi dug her nails into her palms.

'Well, when he returns . . . from his moons-long journey to Jebba,' Harvell said, 'tell him I need his assistance with something.'

'He crossed the pyre last night,' Temi said. 'Someone smashed his face in and dropped his body at our door. As you well know.'

'He crossed the pyre?' Harvell said flatly. 'How awful. So your brother, whose services I seek, is no longer in Jebba? He's dead this time, is it?'

[Look at her eyes. Her mouth. She is taunting you. Are you going to let her mock you?]

Temi leaned on the counter with both hands, her heartbeat thudding in her ears. 'You calling me a liar?'

'Ancestors, no,' Harvell said, touching her chest with one delicate hand.

'Because I might say the same to you,' Temi said, still holding the older woman's eye. 'You come in here acting like you don't know my brother's dead when it's you people what did the deed.'

Harvell stepped back. 'I have no idea what you're talking about.'

'You threatened us. You told us there'd be consequences for what he done. Then I come home and find his body at my door. Take your bloody money and go,' Temi said.

'My sincere condolences for your loss,' Harvell said. 'But I know nothing at all about Tunji's death.' She tossed the pouch of coins through the air. 'Here. Take it back.'

Temi watched the pouch land on the counter. 'You can't buy my ancestors' forgiveness—'

'Now, I would rather have done this with your brother, but since he's not here, you will have to do,' Harvell said. 'You see, I was lucky enough to get a closer look at those votives he's been making. Quite exquisite work. Truly beautiful. And this gives Ba Casten a problem. A problem your brother created. Many of our customers are asking for the *new* votives. The ones we sell simply will not do. So we are in something of a quandary.'

Temi stared at her, not trusting herself to speak, not trusting any word she heard.

'I would like to purchase more from you,' Harvell said.

'My brother was the one that knew how to make them. And his ashes are cooling out in our yard right now.'

'Oh, I'm sure you're doing yourself a disservice there. Rumour has it that this is very much a family business. We've seen your little boats, sailing in from Jebba and Yenlund. What a tidy little arrangement you had.'

'We ain't interested.'

'Oh,' Harvell said, offering Temi her dazzling smile, 'you misunderstand me. This is not an offer. It's an instruction. Ba Casten would like you to make more votives. Three dozen each Starsday will do. We will be here at highsun, when we will exchange the votives for your payment.'

'Listen, lady, I don't—'

'Your nephew, is he?' Harvell said, turning. Temi glanced through the window and saw little Maiwo talking to one of Harvell's lookouts. Maiwo was Amaan's son, and at eight, no fool. He stood very still, glancing at the bakery, an empty water bucket at his feet.

'Lordsgrave can be such a dangerous place for children,' Harvell continued. 'It breaks my heart. Every day, bodies come floating past on the Ae. Every day, I hear tales of bairns disappearing in the night, or not returning from their chores. It truly is a tragedy.'

She leaned forward and covered Temi's hand with her own. 'I'd hate for that to happen to you,' she said softly. 'Particularly after all you've clearly suffered.'

Temi swung with her free hand. She had no skill with her fists, not like her cousins Larmi and Kierin, but Old Baba always said she had temper enough to make up for what she lacked in brawn. It was a wild swing, and Harvell caught it effortlessly with a lazy overarm block. Then she twisted her hand round, viper quick, and jerked down on Temi's arm until she slammed her into the counter.

'Try that again,' Harvell said sweetly, 'and I'll have one of my guards cut off that hand. Understand me?'

[Now is not the time to confront this woman. She is stronger than you, and better prepared. We must be patient.]

'*Do you understand me?*'

'What's going on out here?' It was Yeshe, standing in the doorway. From the corner of her eye, Temi saw her aunt held her large kitchen knife in steady hands.

'Nothing, Old Auntie,' Harvell said.

'Auntie, just go,' Temi said thickly.

'You got your money,' Yeshe said, not moving. 'Now leave us all in peace.'

'You have a beautiful, loving family,' Harvell whispered, leaning down so that her fragrant breath brushed Temi's ear. 'I'd give a lot to have a family like yours. Cherish them. Protect them. Do you understand?'

Temi nodded, her throat dry.

'Good.' Harvell shoved her away. Temi stumbled backwards, her arm throbbing, her breath coming in bursts. Yeshe caught her, staring hard at Harvell. Temi scanned desperately for Maiwo and saw him smiling as Harvell's guard showed him a spinning toy. But when Maiwo caught her eye, Temi knew that he had seen – and understood.

'Starsday,' Harvell said, striding towards the door. 'Have them ready. No excuses, please.'

Temi watched her go, massaging her arm, her legs weak and wobbly. Even beyond the pyre, Tunji's mistakes haunted them all. Three dozen votives each Starsday. Even with every member of her family helping, it would not be enough.

'They still ain't content,' Yeshe spat. 'Still ain't happy.'

'She gave the money back,' Temi said, massaging her neck.

'We'll muddle through. We'll figure it out, between us.'

'Yeah, but when does it end? They could threaten us for ever.'

'We'll talk about this later,' Yeshe said, stomping back into the kitchen. 'You get the shop open.'

[I will help you,] the voice said, when Yeshe was gone.

'Help me how?' Temi snapped. 'Gonna bring my baby brother back across the pyre? Gonna chant life into him?'

She felt that dark amusement again, rich and knowing. [I will teach you Tunji's technique. Perhaps an even better one.]

'No.'

[Do you want that woman and her cohorts to pick your family off, one by one? Have no doubt that she can do it. You are nothing to her, all of you. I have known a thousand of her ilk and you are but dirt beneath her feet. She would not blink to order you all executed. Now, where do you keep your tools?]

Temi watched Maiwo pick up his bucket and continue on to the borehole.

The pyre had turned to smouldering ash when Temi strode back into the yard. Kierin and a number of others sat awake, smoking sweetweed and talking in low voices. She and Tunji had always made the votives up on their hill, under the sun. Tunji claimed daylight helped his creations function. But Temi harboured none of his superstitions. It was Old Baba's workshop where most of their tools were kept, so it was to the workshop she crossed now. She pulled open the trapdoor in the dirt of the yard to reveal a set of rickety steps.

'Just need a moment alone,' Temi called over to Old Baba, where he stood leaning on his cane and inspecting Elleth's vegetables.

Temi descended the stairs into the darkness, pulling the trapdoor closed behind her. Old Baba's workshop had been a place of wonder

84

and fascination to Temi once. As she descended the worn wooden steps, she remembered how she and Tunji had sat on the floor by Old Baba's sleeping mat, while he told them some tale of the Old Country or tried to show them the correct way to speak to blackglass so that it listened. Because that was what he'd always called it . . . just *speaking*. The Forbidden Tongue was a language of pure will, he said, and techwork simply made that will a reality. And though Temi knew, as a child, that she and Tunji could not share their knowledge of that strange language, it had been a long time before she'd understood why.

She thought of Tunji's wide, white smile as his blackglass flared with life, while whatever piece she'd been given remained cold and dormant. She'd always been clumsy and impatient with techwork, where her brother was an artist. The things Old Baba had had to explain five or six times to her came instinctively to Tunji, so that he was always leaping ahead, making connections, drawing huge grins of pride from their grandfather's round face. Once, she'd been so jealous, she'd knocked the blackglass from her brother's hand, and it had smashed in two on the earthen floor. Old Baba hadn't shouted. He hadn't even been angry. He'd simply shaken his head, muttered *ah-ah*, and turned away from her. But it was the last time Old Baba had tried to teach her the Forbidden Tongue.

[There is very little here,] the voice said, as Temi swept her eyes over the bare shelves.

The workshop was small and lit by a single techwork candle that brightened whenever it sensed mortals nearby. The room was carved from the earth itself, and aside from the shelves, the sleeping mat and Old Baba's rotting work chair, it was barren.

'You say you can help me,' Temi said. 'But what are you?'

[What I am does not matter.]

Temi sighed. Only invokers could bring their ancestors back into the mortal realm. And only the nine founding warlords could return. And yet . . .

'So what do you get out of this?'

85

[As I work, I will grow stronger. Eventually, we may be able to separate. But there is so little here.]

'My family brings artefacts over with them,' she said. 'When my cousins died in that boat, they took six moons' worth of goods with them. So our stores are low.'

[Then we must work with what we have. Temi Baker, I will help you make your three dozen water votives, and they will be the finest this city has ever seen. Take the filaments from that shelf.]

'The what?'

[The . . . *veins*. Take hold of the veins.]

Temi pulled a tangle of techwork veins from the shelf and began untwisting them.

[Stop. There is no need to pull them apart.]

'But Tunji always—'

[Your brother had only a rudimentary understanding of what it was he did. He was a child groping at shapes in the darkness. You are going to work in the light. Hold your hands over the veins.]

'You have to chant when—'

[Hold out your hands!]

Temi sighed and extended her arms. The moment she did, the place where the spirit witch had sliced her forearm began to sting. Temi turned her hand over and saw the skin around the scar brightening, as though the sun itself were rising within. The brightness swelled, creeping down into her palms and the tips of her fingers, then jumping across to her other hand. As she stared, the techwork veins began to glow in sympathy, began to brighten with shifting glyphs – the Forbidden Tongue, moving faster than her eye could follow, as though fed from her skin itself.

'Are you my ancestor?' Temi said, pushing down the swell of excitement that stirred within her. 'How is this possible?'

[I am not your ancestor, but I was alive once.] And he chuckled mirthlessly and filled her skin with his warmth.

EIGHT

Jinao

*F*ive days. Five days for the one who took my arm to face me.
   Under the shade of woven palm fronds, Jinao watched the last few bouts of Princen Tamun Ahiki's games. The princen himself sat on a golden dais opposite, surrounded by his aides and with Julon at his side. As the man who had claimed the Bairneater's arm, and the one the beast had challenged, Julon was to be the second judge in the games to select warriors for the hunting party.

Jinao watched his brother, wondering. Perhaps Julon truly had taken the Bairneater's arm. Perhaps Jinao had witnessed his brother's act of prowess, and in his battle-crazed hysteria, had projected the event onto himself. That day on the riverbank had been the most terrifying, most confounding of his life. Perhaps he had been fooling himself.

'Who will face Lord Velita?' yelled someone seated behind Jinao: Atoc – one of the Clan Itahua invokers, and a man Jinao had rarely seen sober. Atoc gripped a wine cup in one hand, as did many of the lords on the spectator stand. How had the threats of an infamous greyblood become cause for drunken celebration? Only one among them looked sober: Captain Elari, a renowned Itahua warrior of middling years. She sat motionless, as though the entire event were a personal affront, her feathered headdress stirring in the breeze.

'There are warriors here I have never seen before,' muttered Jemusi, on his left. She nodded at the line of warriors who had already been selected. Many came from the Outer Isles, tall souls whose family tataus covered their bare torsos and who wore circlets of woven flowers to denote their highblood lineage.

Jemusi had been in a foul mood since the funeral, and Jinao knew their mother's passing was the least of it. On the city outskirts, two thousand Cagai warriors were preparing to head west to war. Jemusi had charged newest invoker Marali with leading them, the ever-eager Wateng Three-Fingers at her side.

Invoker Velita Navret, a scarred and towering woman, strode around the sparring circle, hands raised as she awaited a challenger. Behind her cheered a dozen of her captains, hardened warriors in conical helms and orange warpaint. Everyone on the hillside had seen how much wine Velita had consumed. When she belched and lost her footing, the crowd roared with laughter.

'Come on!' Atoc cried. He leaned forward, his alcohol-laced breath sour. 'The woman is clearly drunk! Now is your chance to best a legend. What about you, Lord Morayo?'

He nudged the man seated next to Jemusi, a round-eyed youth in the green and white warpaint of Clan Adatali. His tightly curled hair was twisted into gleaming coils. Beside him sat a wizened monk wearing a beaded skirt.

'But she can scarcely stand,' Morayo said. 'It hardly seems fair.'

'It will teach her to be cocky,' Atoc said.

Morayo glanced at his monk, who spread his hands noncommittally. 'Well, I suppose I could give her a try.'

'One thousand suns on Lord Velita!' Atoc shouted as Morayo shrugged out of his cape of coloured grass.

Morayo looked wounded. 'You believe a drunk can best me?'

Jinao wasn't sure when the wagers had begun, or exactly who was running them – he suspected it might be Atoc himself – but half the palace had come out to see the games, and the coin and glory to be won were considerable.

A cheer rose up from every bright-robed Adatali warrior as Morayo climbed down from the dais and stepped out into the sun. Morayo strolled around the perimeter of the circle, smiling shyly.

'I wanted to speak with you, My Lord,' Morayo's elderly monk said, shifting closer to Jemusi. 'About a delicate matter.'

On the lawn below, the towering Velita sprang. Jinao could see she was good – she teetered as she landed, and though her aim was off, presumably from the drink, she slapped the back of Morayo's legs with her practice chakram, and the hillside rang with laughter.

Morayo whirled around in surprise, but Velita was gone again, dancing at the edge of the circle, both chakrams in her hands now. She swayed there, then seized a drink from one of her captains, to the raucous cheers of all who looked on, before twisting to land a blow on Morayo's rump.

'Who are you?' Jemusi asked the monk, as more laughter rang around them.

'I am Father Boleo, Grand High Curator to Warlord Daloya Adatali. Daloya, who was your mother's greatest friend.'

Jinao saw the way Jemusi's jaw tightened as she strove to appear disinterested. Her eyes remained on Morayo, whose fine brow had creased with the beginnings of irritation.

This monk, with his wary, watchful eyes, did not look like the most senior of the king's holy ones in Adataliland. But when Jinao stole another glance, he realised that beneath the man's beaded necklace, his dark brown skin was patterned with a complex tatau in the Forbidden Tongue.

'My mother spoke fondly of Warlord Daloya,' Jemusi said. 'How is his health? I hear that he rarely leaves Three Towers now.'

Velita landed another mocking blow on Morayo's rear. Behind them, Atoc cackled.

'My Lord's health is as good as can be expected,' the monk said. 'But we received a message from him, not two days past. A message of some import. I wondered if I might arrange a meeting with you and your siblings to discuss it.'

'Father Boleo, I have many constraints on my time. Tell me what it is you want.'

The monk cleared his throat and glanced behind him, then lowered his voice. 'Two moons ago, a ship washed ashore in Ntuk Province. A ship that was . . .' He sipped from his wine cup, dark eyes glistening. '. . . very familiar.'

On the sparring lawn below, Morayo fell flat on his back. Velita raised her fists, earning cheers from every side.

'What does this have to do with us?' Jemusi said.

'We believe it belonged to Invoker Jethar, your missing brother.'

Jemusi turned to fully face the monk, while on the lawn below, Morayo groaned in pain.

'Impossible,' Jemusi said. 'Jethar and the others set off on their voyage five years ago. They perished either at sea or in whatever new land they found as they headed north. *North*, Father Boleo. Not south. How is it this wreckage was found in the south?'

Velita leapt to drop down on Morayo's chest in a final blow. Jinao winced, feeling a stab of pity for the Adatali youth.

Morayo rolled. He was up in a heartbeat, and now Velita's chakram was in his hand. The spectators cheered, and over on the royal dais, Princen Tamun howled with laughter.

'I do not have the answers to those questions,' the monk said. 'But I was hoping you might help me. You see, we found something on the ship. Techwork; locked, in a manner of speaking. We cannot get to its contents. My holy brothers have studied the arcane energies suffusing it and have surmised that someone of Mizito blood is needed to open it. I ask that you come back to Three Towers with me to assist.'

Below, Velita rolled and came to her feet. She grinned as Morayo circled her.

'A bargain,' Velita cried, for all to hear. 'I'll stop being a drunk, if you stop being an untried upstart. Agreed?'

Morayo frowned. 'But, My Lord – I am untried!'

Morayo threw himself sideways, legs spinning as he went, and Velita's second chakram whirled into the crowd. A child caught it, and leapt in the air, white veil fluttering as he joined the laughter and held it out of Velita's reach.

Velita laughed too, but Jinao saw the irritation beneath it. She had been tricked, and in front of a member of the royal clan.

'I cannot leave Aranduq,' Jemusi said. 'Not when the river is so vulnerable.'

'There is techwork within the locked carriage,' the monk said. 'That much we know. But we also discovered two shrouded bodies. By rights, I should have sent this on to my holy superiors at the Garden, but due to my warlord's . . . special relationship with your mother, I wanted to give your clan the opportunity to see it first. If the body is your brother Jethar, we will grant you the chance to send him beyond the pyre. A chance he will not have if he is taken by my superiors.'

Jinao made the sign for ancestral protection and took a swallow of wine. It had been five rains since Jethar and his friend Cantec Itahua had left on their voyage north. Jinao had paid little attention to the details – something about a map and a place where spirits gathered. At the time of Jethar's departure, many had speculated about what this could mean: a doorway to the ancestral realm, a place to receive ancestral blessings, perhaps even the location of a powerful weapon. They hoped the fleet would return within a year, perhaps two, with a way to destroy all greybloods.

But of course, not a soul among them had come back, surely meaning they had all perished at sea.

The hillside rang with laughter as Morayo danced on the balls of his feet in mockery of the Riani style of combat. Velita breathed hard now, barely dodging Morayo's strikes, and her anger was plain to see. Her captains snorted and jeered, but their voices were drowned out by those chanting Adatali's name. As Morayo came up out of a roll, he caught Father Boleo's eye, and the old monk nodded.

A distraction, Jinao realised. All this had been a distraction so that the old monk could speak to them unobserved.

'Please think about it,' Boleo said. 'We leave tomorrow, and I would like very much for a member of your inner family to accompany us. Someone you trust, of course.' Then the monk stood and descended the dais to meet a grinning Invoker Morayo.

'This concludes our games!' Princen Tamun cried, standing at the front of his dais. 'Come dawn, when the beast is at its weakest, we will ride out to face it!'

All around Jinao, people were striding out into the sun to congratulate the chosen. Jemusi remained seated, staring off into the distance.

'He must be mistaken,' Jinao said. 'Or lying.'

'I'm not sure that he is,' Jemusi said. 'Did you notice the jewel on his staff brightening as we spoke? He was doing something, perhaps hiding our words from unwanted ears. Besides, what reason could a holy one have to lie?'

'Perhaps we can send one of the Outer Islanders. Or . . . or one of the Mother's squires?'

'No,' Jemusi said, standing, her white robe of mourning falling about her muscular legs. 'It has to be one of us. There are . . . things you do not know about Mother's friendship with Clan Adatali. Things few people know.'

Jinao watched her stride down onto the lawn to join the others. Jinao followed at a distance, his thoughts churning. Should he go with them? Nobody had thought to ask him, just as nobody had asked him to go west to war. He was as redundant here as a third wheel, and yet he could not shake the cloying dread that had settled in the pit of his stomach.

Five days. Five days for the one who took my arm to face me. If they do not, I will take this city.

It was an empty threat, of course. The Bairneater was powerful, but still it was only one greyblood. Fearsome, feared, fabled, yes, but still only one. How could a single entity destroy an entire city? It was laughable.

'My Lord Jinao,' a voice called, and Jinao turned to see Sister Jassia bustling towards him wearing one of her condescending little smiles. 'My Lord Jinao, there you are. Your brother and sister and all the great warriors in this palace have a job. As do you.'

Jinao bit back the urge to ask her if his role was invisible spectator. 'Yes, Holy Mother,' he said, standing.

'At times like these,' Sister Jassia continued, 'we are wise to seek the blessings of the ancestors.' She tapped his arm, and then wandered off in the direction of the Sun Gate.

Jinao wandered the grounds for a time, resisting Sister Jassia's suggestion that his job was pleading with the ancestors to lend strength to the hunting party. He could join them, he supposed. No one would turn him away. Or he could go in disguise again, and then reveal himself to the Bairneater. But what would that achieve? He possessed little fighting skill and even less combat experience. Besides, the hunting party numbered fifty now. The Bairneater was one creature against them all. It was doomed.

Somehow, his feet had taken him to the palace shrine after all. As Jinao descended the black steps, he saw only a single nun in attendance, cleaning one of the many small carvings that stood beside the main Mizito bronze. Several of the offerings remained from the Day of Choosing, although Jinao noticed that someone had cleared away poor Wateng's severed fingers. Jinao had no offering to give, he realised, but Sister Jassia had taught them that sincerity and passion were what the ancestors valued most.

Jinao nodded a greeting to the nun, then knelt before the spirit wood of the altar and allowed his eyes to drift closed. 'Ancestors,' he said. 'Mizito. All of you. Please . . . please protect Julon and Jemusi. Please give them the strength to defeat the Bairneater. I didn't know my actions that day would lead to all this. Please . . . just please forgive my cowardice.'

Jinao bent forward to kiss the spirit wood, as he had a thousand times before, as he did every time he came to offer respect to the fallen.

But this time, the dark surface responded, seizing him, and dragging him headlong into its depths.

Down and down he tumbled, into blackness, into a cloying warmth that pressed upon him and into him. When he opened his mouth, the blackness poured in until it seemed it would choke him. When he turned, he saw only more blackness.

The palm wine. What a fool he'd been, drinking so much of Invoker Morayo's palm wine. And now, drink and fear had consumed him, and his mind had come untethered. He lifted a hand, but there was no light for him to see by. He tried to speak, but the silence swallowed every sound.

His thoughts began to drift then, slowly at first, then faster and faster. Unbidden, he saw himself before the shrine as a boy: whispering, kneeling, pleading. His mother was there sometimes, watching or shaking her head. Twenty-two. That was how many times he'd presented himself to Mizito. Twenty-two, though how he suddenly knew this number, he could not say. Sujil Two Blades had given up at thirteen. One-Eyed Ujimu, exactly ten. None had come close to Jinao's number. And none in the history of his clan had spent as many days beseeching.

His thoughts travelled faster then, crowding together like a fever dream. He stood in the gardens, watching the Bairneater grinning down. He knelt at his mother's pyre, cursing her name. He rode to battle in secret, sick with terror and excitement. And other memories came to him, ones he could not place. He flew above a landscape of mountains and trees. He marched beneath a star-filled sky, a daughter he did not have riding at his side. He wandered a city of pastel-hued towers and opulent gardens, a city that covered everything . . .

Faster the thoughts came, until it seemed his mind would explode with them, that his sanity would melt away before them, and he heard voices, so many voices, all of them whispering his name . . .

And then he was on the ground.

'He moved!' a woman cried. 'Sisters, he moved!'

Hands touched him. Someone dripped water into his mouth. He swallowed. His throat was raw and his lips painfully cracked. When he opened his eyes, candlelight assaulted them, merciless in its brilliance.

A face floated before him: Sister Jassia, her eyes radiant.

'I think I fainted,' Jinao muttered. 'The wine . . .'

'Your mind wandered the ancestral realm for some time,' Jassia said. 'But we knew your forebears were watching over you.'

Jinao tried to rise but found his muscles would not obey. His arms burned, as though he'd dipped them into boiling water. 'My arms . . .'

'It is your tataus,' Sister Jassia said.

Jinao lifted his arms. His clan tataus glowed brightly, lines of silver running along his skin like blood in his veins. There was the eagle. There the bonetree. He felt an energy in them that hadn't been there before. A coiled power.

'Yes!' Sister Jassia intoned. 'You have Bonded the ninety-first incarnation of Mizito. The first ever to do so. Lord Jinao Mizito, you are now an invoker.'

NINE

Temi

Temi stood before the bakery counter, the crate of water votives at her feet, when little Maiwo came running in from the street.

'Fighters!' he cried, leaning on the counter to catch his breath. 'The Chedu woman's here and she's brought fighters!'

Temi squinted through the bakery window and saw people turning to look down the hill. Yeshe had already closed the shop, so Temi shooed Maiwo through to join the others out back, then smoothed down her wrapper.

Thirty-six water votives. That was what she had spent the last four days crafting. Thirty-six votives, and never in her life had she felt more exhausted. Her family had cycled in and out, helping her when they could, not questioning why she was using Old Baba's workshop, not noticing the glow that spread from her hands to the techwork. She used no Forbidden chants, which meant the work went quicker: the Chained Man claimed these were not needed with him at her side. All that was needed was the correct twist of the veins, and a little of the Chained Man's light. Temi was reduced to a mere pair of hands, guided by a voice from another realm. She wondered what Tunji would have made of his beloved art being reduced to such cold function.

Harvell pushed open the door of the bakery, then held it aside for

the half-dozen fighters who came behind. And they were all fighters . . .
anyone could see that from their coiled muscles and fluid movements.
Most were young, with the look of many lands about them. Temi did
not need to see their swirling blue and green tataus. The way the street
had cleared before them told her everything she needed to know.

'Hello, Temi Baker,' Harvell said, striding up to join her at the counter.
'I see you have our supplies.'

'Yes,' Temi said, lifting the crate. Why did her voice shake like that?
She told herself she wasn't afraid of these people, that it was anger, not
terror, that quickened her pulse. But she thought again of Meliti's words.
His speciality is taking the tongues and feet of those what disobey, and
she realised her throat was dry.

Harvell gestured, and one of the young men with her stepped up to
take the crate, his gaze passing dismissively over Temi.

'Lonu,' Harvell said, 'have a look at this place, would you?'

A fidgety, angular young man with pale skin squeezed into the
bakery and held up a small disc of techwork. Temi swallowed as he
made a slow circuit of the bakery, holding the relic before him like a
talisman.

'T-twenty behind the counter,' the young man, Lonu, stammered.
'Two more up on the high shelf there, b-behind the buckets.'

Another man stepped forward and seized Temi's arm, bending it up
behind her back.

'What are you doing?' Temi cried as Harvell's fighters swarmed past,
some bending to look under the counter, others sliding their hands
over the shelves, knocking down the fresh baked loaves, the fried
breads, the sweetcakes.

'You stop!' Temi cried, but the one who held her – he smelt of
peppermint, of all the things – twisted her arm up so that her shoulder
burned. Temi was tired . . . so tired she could cry. So tired she could
scarcely think. She lifted her leg, ready to slam her heel down on her
captor's foot.

[No. Not yet. Patience.]

'Here, Harvell!' cried a black-haired youth. He produced the box of votives intended for their usual customers. Temi had needed to thin that out in order to meet the Chedus' quota, but now it appeared the locals would be left with nothing at all, because the boy carried these off towards the door, along with the spares they kept for emergencies.

'Well, this is unfortunate,' Harvell said, smiling sweetly.

Temi bit down on the inside of her cheek. She would not let Harvell see her tremble. She would not look away.

'When I instructed you to make votives for us,' Harvell said, 'I meant *us*. Only us. Is that understood?'

'You never said—'

'Perhaps I'm not speaking clearly. We are now the only ones who will be selling the bakers' votives. That means no more of this . . . under-the-counter nonsense. Is that understood?'

Temi inhaled slowly. 'The people round here need—'

'The people *round here*, as you put it, are no concern of mine. Ba Casten has taken a special interest in your work. If I find out you, or any of your family out there . . .' She lifted her voice and looked in the direction of the kitchen. 'Yes, lovely family! This includes all of you! If I find out you're selling votives . . . *giving away* votives, to anyone other than us, there will be consequences. Your dear sweet cousin first, the yellow-haired one at the docks. Then perhaps the uncle with all the offspring. If you really test us, we'll move on. The old man. Your sour aunt . . .' She took hold of Temi's braids and leaned forward until Temi could smell the cinnamon on her breath. 'You we'll come to last. When all the others have gone. Now: do I have your full cooperation?'

Temi stared at the tiny scar on Harvell's cheekbone. It looked old and was paler than the rest of her skin. She could spit in the woman's eye from here. Smash her forehead into Harvell's pretty little nose . . . Oh, no doubt they'd beat her bloody afterwards, but perhaps it would be worth it to see her recoil. She could—

[Not yet, Temi. I have told you . . . we are not ready yet.]

98

'Yes,' Temi said. She wet her lips. 'Yes, you have our cooperation.'

'Good!' Harvell said brightly, stepping back. 'I knew you were sensible.' She nodded to her crowd of fighters, who fell in step behind her as she swept back towards the door. The man holding Temi released her and shoved her at the counter. Temi made no move to straighten as she landed against it.

When they were gone, Temi sank down onto the chipped floor, every muscle in her body shaking. She felt suddenly heavy, as if all the sleepless nights of the past days had descended on her at once. She longed to glimpse Tunji's broad smile, even just once; she'd never felt its absence as keenly as she did in that moment. His jokes and enthusiasm could lighten any load, but Harvell had taken all that from her.

'Tem!' Yeshe cried, rushing out, touching her cheek, her shoulder. 'Oh, Tem. You OK, girl?'

'I miss him, Auntie,' Temi said. 'I miss him so much.' Yeshe's narrow face was lined with such sadness that Temi felt the tears she'd been holding back spring to her eyes. 'What we gonna do? If we can't sell to the locals, can't even give 'em away—'

'We'll figure out something.'

'But what? How's everyone gonna clean their water?'

'We'll leave it to the ancestors.' Yeshe sat beside her and took her hand. 'Most lowbloods in this city don't have votives to clean their water. Most take their chances. That's what we'll have to do, all of us.'

'Yeah, but it ain't fair! Ain't right!'

'The world ain't fair, Temi,' Yeshe said, stroking her cheek. 'But we still have to live within its rules. Now let me get you some tea.'

When Yeshe stood, Temi leaned back and closed her eyes. There was no way out. She would be working for the Chedus her entire life. They could demand any price they wanted, any number of votives they desired, and there could be no escape. If she fled – or worse, sought refuge beyond the pyre – she'd be leaving her family behind, and she had no doubt they'd be punished for her absence. Besides, the ancestors turned from those who did not face their responsibilities.

[If you truly wish to be rid of them, I can help you.]

'No,' Temi said. 'If we cross them, they'll hurt someone I love. Again.'

[Not if we are careful.]

'How? You know how many of them there are? Because I don't. You think we can run in and slit their throats while they sleep? Is that it?'

[There are other ways.]

'No!' Temi rubbed her hands over her face.

When Yeshe returned with the tea, she said, 'Don't mention any of this to Old Baba. He don't need to hear it. You know, after me, he had three more kids before your baba and Amaan was born? All three died of the river sickness. Old Baba swore he weren't gonna let that happen to no other family, not when he had the gifts to stop it. Hearing this . . .' Yeshe shook her head. 'Well, let's just say it'll break his heart.'

Starsday became a day of tension on Arrant Hill. A day the entire neighbourhood came to dread. Every local knew that just before highsun, it was best to be elsewhere. Because every Starsday, just before highsun, the Chedus came to collect. Sometimes Harvell came with two guards. Sometimes a group of her young fighters came swaggering up the hill. These last were the most difficult . . . they often spent all highsun at the ogogoro inn, drinking without ever offering payment, picking fights with any who crossed their path. When they came striding into the bakery, they helped themselves to whatever lay on the shelves. Even when Yeshe took to hiding all but a few of the driest loaves until the Chedu youths had gone, they bellowed and threatened until fresh goods were brought out.

'You're a rebellious little thing, ain't you?' one youth said, looking Temi over as she stood holding the Chedus' third delivery.

She knew he could feel the simmering rage behind her eyes. Not just her hatred, but whatever arcane power the voice within her exuded. A nameless force shone through her like sunlight, and it was getting harder to disguise. It didn't matter that only she could feel the burning in her skin, hear the dark muttering in her ears. Others sensed it. She wanted to hold the young man's gaze; but she forced herself to look away until he had taken the crate and gone.

[You could bow before them and they would still name you insolent. Power such as ours cannot be hidden.]

A few days after the Chedus' second visit, the price of grain rose at the docks. First wheat, then oats, then maize. The King's Quota, they said. The provinces were emptying of farmers as the Nine Lands began answering the conscription. Yeshe took to turning the loaves sideways, so that the bareness of the shelves was less noticeable.

Temi found herself spending many sleepless nights kneeling before the family shrine. Reciting her own names, reciting the names of the lost, was the only thing that brought her solace. She felt as though her entire family were being drawn inexorably towards their doom.

'Please, Uncle Leke,' she whispered, 'lend us your strength. Tunji, lend us your strength.'

Within thirty days of the start of their arrangement with the Chedus, they were no longer able to afford grain at all. All they could manage, with their diminishing funds and the spiralling costs, was enough to keep their family fed, and soon barely that. Within a moon, Yeshe placed a board outside the bakery, informing the neighbourhood they were closed until further notice. Only two members of their household had work outside the bakery – Kierin, hauling at the docks, and Amaan, who took coin for teaching local children their words and numbers. The rest began asking around.

At mealtimes, they let the children eat first, then ushered them out into the garden while the rest of the family ate what remained. Despite everything, Yeshe made them all sit down together and bid thanks to the ancestors. No matter how hungry they were, they each dropped a crumb on the family shrine. Sometimes, Amaan took payment for his lessons in rice or yam, and once, Kierin came home with an entire crate of cassava he claimed someone had been giving away. Temi took to carrying crusts in the fold of her wrapper, to nibble on through the

101

day. It was easier than letting her stomach grow empty, especially as she needed energy to make the votives.

One mealtime not long after their fourth visit from the Chedus, Kierin slammed his fist on the table, cutting short their muted conversation. 'We all just gonna sit here and pretend?' Kierin said. 'There ain't enough food for us all!'

'Quiet,' Yeshe snapped.

Kierin shoved his chair back and stomped off. Mtobi rose to follow, but Yeshe lifted a hand. 'Let him be. Just needs to cool off; you know what he's like.'

But that evening, as Temi was taking the night air and a cup of ogogoro that Remmy, the son of the inn's owner, had brought over for her, Kierin came up the hill, supported between two of his friends. His hands and knuckles were bloody enough to tell her he'd got in some hits of his own before he went down, but his pale skin was blue and bleeding, and one eye was swollen shut. As he came closer, she saw at once that his arm had been broken.

'You bloody fool,' Yeshe muttered, rushing out into the street. 'How you supposed to work in this state?'

It took them all night to dress his wounds and splint his arm. Mtobi agreed to take over Kierin's work at the docks, though Temi's powdered and poised cousin was not made for hauling. A knot of despair formed in Temi's stomach; one she knew wouldn't loosen soon. The Chedus could hurt people she loved whenever they wanted. They had proved that with Tunji. The lives of her family meant nothing to the Chedus, and she would spend for ever dancing to their tune.

[If you want to be free of these people, I can help you.]

'It's too dangerous,' Temi said, just as she did every time he slid into her thoughts. 'All it will do is bring more trouble. We keep our heads down. We keep going. Just like Auntie said.'

At night, when the golden haze of the Royal Garden lit up the sky to the west, Temi muttered, 'How can we live in the richest city in the Nine Lands and not have enough to eat?'

Finally, they ran out of materials for the votives. With Leke's delivery burned up along with him, and Darmin not due down from Yenlund until after the northern frost, they had precious little techwork in their store. When Temi told Harvell this, the Chedu woman sent a dozen of her men into the compound to comb every cupboard and shelf and corner. Once she was satisfied, she turned to Temi and said, 'We'll supply you with materials from now on.'

From then on, every Sunday at dusk, a different set of lowbloods would appear at their door with crates or sacks or barrels filled with techwork scraps. *Tribute*, they called it, as they watched Temi carry it into the bakery. At first, Temi didn't understand the fear and deference in their eyes.

[They think you are Chedu too. They think you are part of the organisation.]

Temi burned to tell the tribute-bringers that she wasn't of the Families. That she too was a victim. That she also longed for escape. But what was the point? They couldn't help her – no one could.

[I can help you. I've told you before, there are ways.]

'We can't!' Temi cried, as she knelt at the shrine. 'You saw what they did to my brother! We can't fight them. We can't run from them.'

But when Temi closed her eyes at night, she saw Harvell's smug smile. She saw Harvell's smile as she washed and as she helped Old Baba dress. As the days went by, as the sun rose and set, the hate and the rage within her hardened until it was like stone lodged in her throat. Until she felt it would choke her . . . or consume her. Until it felt like more than she could continue to endure.

'You killed my brother,' Temi whispered to Harvell's back, as the woman turned out onto the street with her most recent collection. 'One day, the ancestors will punish you. One day, you will know pain.'

[Let me help you. Let us work on a way. We were brought together for a reason. Perhaps this is it.]

'No. No! The ancestors turn from those with vengeance in their hearts. The ancestors turn from those who would do violence. The ancestors—'

[This is not about the ancestors, Temi. This is about the survival of your *living* family. Because believe me, if this continues, your family will not survive. The Chedus will squeeze and squeeze and squeeze until only you remain, working for ever on their little votives while around you, all else crumbles.]

Temi's pulse thudded in her ears. Every muscle in her body felt taut as a bow. He was right; she knew he was right. But what choice did she have?

[What if I show you something? If, after you have seen it, you do not want my help, then I will never offer it again. But first, permit me to show you something. Please.]

Temi missed her brother. Ancestors, but she missed him! She missed his laugh and his smile and his wide-eyed wit and, ancestors help her, she even missed nagging him.

'This is his fault,' she muttered. 'Why'd he have to be so bloody brilliant? Why couldn't he just make the votives the way Old Baba showed us?'

[Will you do it?]

She didn't trust him. She didn't trust his smooth words and silken promises. She didn't trust the way his emotions twined with hers, like gripweed round a tree, until she didn't know where her thoughts ended and his began. But he had only offered to show her. No promises were made. Besides, the ancestors turned from those who spurned the gifts they offered.

'If it means you'll leave me alone,' Temi said, staring out into the street, 'then yes, I'll bloody do it. What is it you want to show me?'

[Something that will change your mind.]

TEN

Jinao

Jinao woke the next morning to find a group of nuns swarming into his sleeping chamber. He had spent a fitful night sweating and thrashing through dreams of unfamiliar faces and unfamiliar cities, and the waking world was no less disorienting. He lay blinking on his sleeping mat while his servants folded away the bamboo screens, flooding the room with sunlight. The nuns bustled around him with their holy instruments while at the screen door, a messenger signalled to him.

'I won't be a moment,' Jinao called, pushing up on his elbows.

One of the young nuns kneeling at his side pressed something cold to his neck. Jinao flinched, then held still while the nun's eyes fluttered as he listened to whispers from the ancestral realm. So Jethar truly was dead. Jinao supposed he had always clung to the hope that his older brother might return alive from his voyage; even when the monks said it was impossible, even when his mother began placing offerings for him on the shrine. But if Jinao had made the Bond, it meant another incarnation of Mizito had been released. And it meant the body in Adataliland really was Jethar.

'The ancestors see nothing strange here at all,' the young nun said, his eyes sparkling with excitement. 'They see only the spirit of Warlord Mizito!'

Sister Jassia gripped Jinao's bare forearm with a papery hand. 'Only once before has Mizito's spirit Bonded more than ninety times: in the days of Rejanitzu Twin-Blades, and even then, there were still only ninety invokers.'

'There still are only ninety invokers,' Jinao said. 'My brother is dead.'

'Yes, Lord Jethar is dead, ancestors preserve him, but while his body remains lost, his incarnation of Mizito will not have been released. My Lord, you must not question what we had seen, nor should you question the will of the ancestors. They truly have blessed you, to have granted you this sacred gift!' When Jinao said nothing, she patted his arm reassuringly and added, 'Do not fear, Invoker Jinao. We are in the process of selecting a fine nun to guide you in matters of the ancestral realm. You will not be left to flounder.'

Jinao opened his mouth to tell her had no intention of floundering, and would she mind taking her fluttering sisters away, when the messenger signalled to him again: one of his sister's runners, he realised, a long-legged youth with the strong calf muscles of one used to travelling the city.

'I look forward to meeting them,' Jinao said. 'If you don't mind . . . I'd like to dress and break my fast before my training begins.'

'Of course, My Lord,' Sister Jassia said, pushing to her feet and signalling for her flock of nuns to follow. Was it Jinao's imagination, or was there a newfound respect glittering in the woman's eyes? She seemed to hold his gaze a little longer, smile a little more broadly than before. Jinao bit back a sour laugh. As a youth, he had craved her approval. Its presence now felt like an insult.

The skin of his forearms still itched, as though his sacred clan tataus had been freshly cut and weren't years old. So this was what the spirit of his forefather felt like: a skin malady. Jinao found himself wondering why, after all his years of practising the words and the dances and the correct way to bow, after all the gifts he had placed on the shrine, after all the longing, Mizito had decide to Bond with him now, when he hadn't even been trying to call upon him at all.

106

'Come,' Jinao said, signalling to the messenger. Through the open screens, he spotted two of his servants weaving a path through the ornamental trees, bearing the platters of fruit that would form his morning meal. And wine, he saw: they had got used to his requests for that. Perhaps today he would send them away.

'Sire,' the messenger said, squatting down before him, his grass skirt fanning out around his legs. 'Sire, your sister left this message for you.'

The papyrus scroll was fixed with his sister's seal, and as Jinao eyed it, wondering why she had gone to the formality of writing the message down, he registered what the boy had said.

'What do you mean, *left*?' Jinao asked him.

The messenger blinked anxiously. 'I was told to give this directly to you.'

Jinao broke the seal and read.

Dearest brother. I have gone east to Adataliland with Invoker Morayo and his party, as well as most of Clan Itahua. If Jethar's body lies in the carriage the Adatalis found, we must bring it home for burning. I hope you understand. Please apologise to Julon for me; I told him I would meet him at the northern slums so that we could face the Bairneater together. When I return, I will head north to Nine Lords, where I will plead with the king for more warriors to hold the river. Until then, Julon must cope alone.

Jinao cursed under his breath, then read the message again before closing his eyes and leaning back against the bamboo wall.

'My Lord,' the messenger said, pressing his forehead to the ground in a bow, and then slipping away.

Jinao watched as his servants set up his breakfast on an eating mat. Gone. Jemusi had gone, leaving Aranduq at its time of greatest need. He knew that sending Jethar across the pyre would bring them all peace, but it had been five years. Five years to come to terms with their loss. Jinao found himself thinking again of Jemusi's words as they had watched Princen Tamun's games: *There are things you do not know about Mother's friendship with Clan Adatali. Things few people know.* Of course there were. And of course, not a soul would share those things with him. Jinao picked at a bowl of mango salad. He was finally Bonded to Mizito. He had expected to feel elation, excitement, but all he knew was disquiet.

One of his servants was padding across the room with his clothing for the day. 'Rujong, isn't it?' Jinao said. 'Rujong, please can you ask my brother's steward if I could dine with him? We to need to talk.'

'Oh, have you not heard, sire? Invoker Julon has yet to return from the princen's hunt. They say the Bairneater has surrounded itself with lowbloods and refuses to fight! Every bell, it tears the head from one captive and throws it at the hunting party. It is quite terrible!'

But Rujong did not look as though she found it quite terrible. Her mouth curved upward and her eyes gleamed. Yet all Jinao could think about was the heads of lowbloods, and that each one of them had died because of him.

Jinao pushed away the breakfast mat, his appetite entirely gone. What a fool he'd been. What a selfish fool. He hadn't told a soul about the implications of the Bairneater's words at the funeral because he hadn't believed them . . . At least, that was what he'd told himself. But he felt the ugly truth of it now like a stone in the pit of his gut. He hadn't told them because he'd been afraid. Just as he'd been paralysed by fear that day on the beach. If he had acted decisively then . . . if he'd buried his axe in the Bairneater's head instead of closing his eyes and swinging blindly, his brother would be heading to Nine Lords now and ancestors knew how many lowbloods would still be alive. But instead, as always, he'd let fear and apathy control him. Now, more people would die, and it would be entirely his fault.

Five days for one who took my arm to face me. If they do not, I will take this city.

*

108

It had been years since Jinao had visited the stables. His horse stood like a lump of stone under the bamboo shelter, her blue, crystal skin dull with dirt, her eyes flat stones. In the field beyond, grooms oiled and exercised a dozen of the palace's colourful mounts, joyful beasts with iridescent eyes and shining, jagged skin. But not his Liet. She sat unloved, the grass long around her hooves.

'Lord Jinao?' a stooped senior groom said, rubbing her hands on a rag and approaching with a bemused smile. 'Can I, er . . . help you?'

'How long will it take for my horse to be rideable?'

The groom sucked in a slow breath. 'Liet? Well, sire, that's hard to say. She'll need several days o' sun, if she's even capable o' life at all.'

'If?'

The woman shrugged apologetically. 'Well, sire, see when a horse ain't ridden for many years, sometimes its soul returns to the ancestors. Liet's the only one what's been left here so long. Even the master never heard o' such a thing!'

Jinao felt a stab of shame. His mother had given him Liet on his ninth birthday. She'd belonged to an aunt, and three generations before that, a First General of Cagai. Sulin had claimed the creature was one of the oldest in the palace, three centuries at the least. Jinao had ridden her only a handful of times. And now her soul might have returned to the ancestors due to his neglect.

'Just do the best you can within the morning,' Jinao said, and stalked away.

'Might I ask where you're taking her, sire?' the groom called after him. 'She won't be up to a long journey!'

'It won't be a long journey.'

Jinao knew he had come to the right place when he turned a corner to find the dirt road eerily empty, and the bamboo houses of the lowbloods deserted. The palace guards had been reluctant to let him ride out alone but knew they couldn't stop him. So, eight of them had followed him through the city at a respectful distance, shouting for the crowds to clear the way if they drew too close. Jinao would have felt less troubled by their presence had Liet not frozen several times on their journey, her dusty eyes dimming, the soft hum of her muscles winding down to silence. On the third such occasion, Jinao had been midway across Winterblossom Square and under the shadow of the towering statue of Sumalong, bestride the river beyond. The crowds outside the teahouses and smoking dens had stopped to watch him as he sat by the fountain statue of Mizito, gently stroking Liet's angular head and pleading for her to *please, please wake*, even as the guards steadfastly averted their eyes from the spectacle. When she had finally lurched into motion, it had been so sudden that Jinao was nearly thrown from the saddle. Liet had a jaunty, faltering gait, and Jinao wasn't certain whether this was due to her disuse, or a feature of who she was. Either way, he tried to smile and wave when the people of Aranduq came out onto their balconies to see him.

As he had headed out of the highblood districts the roads became uneven, and after a time there were no roads at all. Here, the buildings were conglomerations of mudbrick, scraps and bamboo. Here, naked children watched him solemnly from beyond the open sewers. Here, elders seated outside their homes turned their faces away. At one point, a rotten papaya exploded in Liet's path. Jinao did not see who threw it, but one of the guards at his back galloped towards the line of grim hovels, kampilan raised, yelling for the culprit to show themself or see the whole street arrested.

'It doesn't matter,' Jinao called, keeping his gaze on the shadow of the city wall. The lowbloods were right to hate him. He had brought this on them.

Now, as he trotted through the empty street, he felt the first stirrings of fear. Would the creature be angry with him for arriving so late? Jinao knew he stood no chance against the beast. He could only hope that, with its focus on him, the rest of the hunting party would be able to take it down.

110

A woman ran out from between two dilapidated buildings: a scout, he realised, dressed in the grass-pipe armour of a palace guard.

'Who are you?' she said, drawing her sword, before registering his tataus and taking a step back. 'F – forgive me, Lord Jinao. I did not recognise you.' She stepped aside, allowing him to pass. He could smell it then. The unmistakable reek of the Bairneater. Hot metal, like the smell from the palace smithy, but with the sickly-sweet undertone of rotting flesh. For a moment, memories of the battle on the banks of the Ae consumed him, and he gripped Liet's pommel, fighting down a surge of nausea. He was an invoker now. Mizito would come out. Mizito would protect him.

In a clearing up ahead, he spotted the vast crowd of the hunting party. Somebody was shouting in the distance, too faint for Jinao to recognise their voice. He tapped Liet in the signal for *stay* and then slipped down awkwardly from her back. His legs were already sore. He was going to suffer tomorrow.

'Lord Jinao,' said one of the warriors at the edge of the crowd: one of Riona's pale-haired northerners, Jinao realised, sweating beneath their heavy metal armour. 'It is . . . an unpleasant sight.'

Jinao pushed through the crowd of fighters, guards and locals, as well as grizzled warriors in mismatched armour whom Jinao supposed were mercenaries of some sort. As he neared the front of the crowd, he recognised the shouting voice: Princen Tamun. His gold-painted warriors stood at the front of the line, spears tipped forward to the centre of the clearing.

It was not a clearing. It was the wreckage of several dozen huts, the outlines of their original shapes the only discernible remnants of what had once been lowblood homes. At the centre of this stood a monstrous, bristling structure. A colossal den, formed from the hastily assembled wreckage of the surrounding homes. And chained to it, surrounding it like offerings to the fallen . . .

'Oh ancestors,' Jinao muttered, the strength going from his legs.

Lowbloods covered the structure. Children. Elders. They were packed in, chained together like a macabre net. Some wept. Some beseeched the ancestors. Some looked scarcely alive, their heads lolling, their eyes rolled back. Many had clearly soiled themselves. Their expressions were flat; resigned; the hopeless stares of people who believed themselves already dead. Jinao covered his mouth with his arm as he stepped out of the circle. Only a tiny opening was visible in the structure, and from within came more weeping.

Princen Tamun paced before the nightmarish edifice. At his feet lay what Jinao had taken to be more wreckage but realised now were heads. Human heads. And as he approached, a chorus of screams issued from within the Bairneater's lair, and a new head came sailing through the air, trailing a spray of blood before landing beside the princen.

'That's it!' Tamun said, shaking a knobbly fist at his hidden quarry. 'Do not say that you weren't warned.'

A crescendo of pleading and wailing rose up from the captives chained to the structure as Tamun turned his back. From off to the left, Julon appeared. He had a bruise to one cheek, Jinao saw. His eagle mask was pulled back on his head and his warpaint was faded.

'I told you we should wait!' Julon said, approaching Tamun. 'There are over fifty lowbloods on the structure, and ancestors know how many within.'

'They are dead either way,' Tamun said, shaking his head with a baffled smile. 'You know that as well as I. And address me as *Your Highness* next time, unless you wish my bodyguard to furnish you with another of those.' He nodded towards Julon's bruised cheek.

'Jin,' Julon said, rounding on him. 'What are you doing here? Go back to the palace.'

'I . . . I have something to tell you,' Jinao said, swallowing.

'Prepare the battering rams!' Princen Tamun cried, his face alight.

'Go home,' Julon hissed at Jinao, before turning back towards the Bairneater's hovel. 'Creature! I am here, as you requested! Release the innocents and meet me in honourable combat, as you promised you would!'

The wind stirred in the tall palms beyond the city wall. The distant chittering of monkeys and whooping of birds could not mask the soft cries of the lowbloods.

'Bairneater!' Julon shouted, a note of desperation in his voice as, on the far side of the circle of spectators, Princen Tamun's warriors prepared for a charge. 'You slew my mother! Come, so that I might finish the job I began that day!'

A low, echoing chuckle issued from within the hovel. It seemed to pulse in the very ground. All around Jinao, warriors tensed, pointing spears, lifting bows and blow-darts.

'Finish the job?' came a rumbling voice. '*Finish the job?* You did not even begin it. But the one I sought is here now, at last.'

Jinao's stomach tightened. It was true. It was all true. He realised then that part of him had hoped he was still mistaken. Julon pulled his eagle mask down over his face. 'It was I who took your arm. *I.* Who else do you think it was?'

'Why, I do believe it was *him,*' the Bairneater said, and Sulin's staff, *Valour,* emerged from the darkness of the hole, pointing clean across the clearing. Pointing at Jinao.

Jinao took a step backwards as every face turned to take him in anew.

'That is my soulbarren brother,' Julon said. 'He wasn't even present that day.'

'Wasn't he?' the Bairneater said, its rumbling voice dripping amusement. 'You thought to take the credit from a lowblood grunt, but it was your own *brother* who stood before me. I am glad to see he is here now, and ready. Let him face me, and every one of these people may go free.'

Incredulous muttering rose at Jinao's back, and some muted laughter. Julon looked from Jinao to the Bairneater's hovel. He made no denials now.

'Jinao . . . is no warrior,' Julon said.

'He will be.'

Shouts of alarm rose from within and a moment later, a shape stirred in the mouth of darkness. The Bairneater's hand came out first, its remaining hand, clutching a shining metal disc. Its massive shoulders followed, and then it uncurled in the sunlight, towering above them all. Its shadow fell across the clearing. Its stench filled Jinao's mind.

'Stop!' came a thin voice from the far side of the clearing. 'Please, nobody move! Your Highness, do not move.'

A monk emerged from the line of royal warriors opposite, one of Princen Tamun's golden-robed monks. His narrow face was lined with fear as he scurried over to where Princen Tamun stood.

'The beast carries the . . . the Judgement of the Scathed!' the monk cried, and behind him, the Bairneater's mouth split in a wide grin, displaying too many teeth. The greyblood's yellow eyes gleamed within its massive head as it watched them. It wore only a dirty loincloth and a battered, northern-style chest plate, but its grey skin looked more hardened than any armour. Its long toes curled in the dirt, claws gouging deep into the mud.

'The Judgement of the Scathed will summon cursed energies that can level the entire city!' the monk said, his voice quavering. All around the clearing, warriors touched their foreheads for ancestral protection. Jinao copied them, but not Julon, he saw. Julon was slipping quietly backwards.

'Creature,' the monk said, 'is that a dead man's latch?'

The Bairneater tilted its head. 'Why, yes, holy man. How astute.'

'Please!' the monk cried, waving his hands and turning to address the crowd. 'He will kill us all if his thumb does not remain pressed to that cursed artefact!'

'As I said,' the Bairneater replied. 'If the one who took my arm does not face me, I will take this city.'

Jinao did not mean to move, but he realised, as the Bairneater turned its massive head towards him, that he had taken a step towards it. Every muscle in his body trembled. He could not remember ever feeling more exposed, more alone. Out of the corner of his eye, he saw Julon look up in confusion.

'It's all right!' Jinao cried, his voice strangely steady. 'I'm – I'm going!'

And, ancestors help him, he walked forwards.

ELEVEN

Temi

Temi backed into the shadows of a banana plant and squinted across the street.

The Scathed ruin stood back from the dirt road; a pale thrust of crystal within which nestled a brick inn several storeys high, incongruous in the sea of wooden shacks of Little Dimadu's eastern shanty. Beyond, the land fell away to the ruins of the collapsed portion of the Lordswall and the scrubland beyond.

[She is in there. She and others.]

'The Cascade,' Temi muttered, reading the swinging wooden sign. 'So Harvell lives at this inn?' Yeshe had always forbidden them from venturing so far to the north in Lordsgrave. Temi had thought it was due to the rumour that rogue greybloods sometimes came wandering out of the wastes, buried relics of some long-ago battle. This had certainly felt like the edge of the world itself when she'd been a child. But Temi realised now how wrong she'd been. This was Chedu territory. Temi had seen it in the packs of well-dressed youths that strutted around these streets; in the wagons that sometimes trundled past, and in the furtiveness of the locals. This was Chedu territory, and Yeshe had known to keep her family well away.

[Yes, this is Harvell's home.]

'And this is what you planned to show me to make me agree to your scheme?'

[Keep watching. She is with customers.]

'What d'you mean, customers?' Temi said, but at that moment the doors at the top of the steps opened, and a number of people in the high collars and silks of Zumae spilled out.

[Conceal yourself.]

Temi pressed deeper into the shadows and watched as two men in Dimadi kanzu tunics carried a crate between them. *Her* crate, she realised, filled with the votives she had crafted. Harvell came last of all, wearing a white, flowing dress, her hair unbound, her face painted.

[They are her customers. And guess what she sells them?]

The party stopped at the gates, and Harvell exchanged words with a stately looking elder woman. Temi found herself smiling sourly; of course Harvell sold on what she took. Why else would she need so many votives so quickly? But clearly these were not bound for locals who needed clean water.

As Temi watched, three rickshaws came rattling up the hill.

'A true talent,' the stately woman was saying, gripping both Harvell's arms. 'It is a true talent you have, Harvell Chedu.'

Harvell placed a demure hand to her chest and made a show of looking abashed.

'You mean they think *she* makes them?' Temi said. She shook her head, unable to hold back the laughter. 'Ancestors!'

Bows and smiles were exchanged, and then the visitors climbed into their carriages, taking Temi's water votives with them.

'Who are they?' Temi said as she watched the customers go, the few people they passed darting out of their path.

[The Sengs. Another Family. Very ancient. Very powerful. I wonder how much they paid for Harvell's wondrous votives?]

Harvell gestured impatiently to one of her guards, then turned back towards the inn.

'That's my bloody techwork,' Temi muttered, and started off in pursuit.

Her trailing of the Seng Family led her south, to a fortified compound where Temi watched her votives change hands with a group of people in Ntuki dress. From there, they were taken up into the slums of Lordsbasin District, the lawless northern district of Nine Lords, and a sprawling bamboo estate. She watched the gates of that building all afternoon, until a smartly dressed man arrived alone, and bought a single water votive for the lordly sum of twenty suns.

'Twenty suns,' Temi muttered. 'Twenty fucking suns for one votive.'

[Follow him.]

Temi trailed the smartly dressed man into the wide avenues of Thousandlords. She could hear Yeshe's admonishments in her mind, telling her no barefoot lowblood should be venturing into the inner districts, telling her the bluehawks would lock her up just for setting foot on the wrong street. Here, looming buildings of sandstone or brick looked down on paved avenues noisy with carriages and carts. Servants followed their well-dressed masters, shopping balanced on their heads. The only beggars and vagrants she saw kept well to the shadows. Shops and stalls seemed to line every street, selling anything imaginable, and everywhere she heard music, and smelt flowers, and not a soul looked short of a meal.

The estate the stranger led Temi to stood on the hills of Lordsheart. By the time Temi got there, it was near sunset, and she was hot and thirsty and in a temper so foul only one thought remained in her head. Her techwork. The Chedus were only buying it to pass off as their own before selling it on to another Family, who in turn delivered it to . . . whoever these fine highbloods were. And all for a price that could feed her own family for moons.

'Twenty suns,' Temi muttered again. 'Twenty fucking suns for one votive.' She shifted her grip on the acacia tree she had scaled to look within the walls of the estate.

The building loomed over a garden on three sides, its balconies dripping with flowers. Down in the garden itself, among the ornate bushes, uniformed servants just like the one she had followed busied themselves setting up tables and chairs.

'They're having a party?' Temi said.

[Yes. The owner of this mansion is named Falani. She is the spouse of a highblood general. While he is away at war, this is how she entertains herself.]

A woman with much the same mid-brown skin as Temi drifted out into the crowded garden. She floated between the guests as they arrived, giggling with one group, exchanging raucous gossip with another. Most of those who drew up to the estate in their horse-drawn carriages seemed connected with the invoker clans, but Temi spotted monks among the chattering crowds, as well as merchants and highblood storytellers. A band of drummers played on small stage, and a painter – highly renowned, from the deferential way people approached them – sat sketching exaggerated portraits for a series of guests, all for more coin than Temi's family would make in moons.

'Highbloods are fucking sick,' Temi muttered as she watched their increasingly rowdy celebrations.

If she craned her neck, she could see the golden haze of the king's palace, the Garden. There, at the heart of the city, dwelt the Ahiki Royal Clan. Beneath that cloud of gold, the man who could command all the invoker clans of the Nine Lands reclined on a silken bed. While his people drank poisoned waters, or marched to a war they could not win, he hid safe within his palace.

After the endless rounds of tiny snacks, the children were herded away into the house, where Temi spotted an arokin preparing to entertain them. Falani emerged again, now wearing an elaborate gele that twinkled with jewels. A hush spread over the garden as she crossed it with all the sombreness of a nun on the Day of Choosing. Upon the cushion she carried nestled Temi's water votive.

'What the fuck do they think it is, Adatali's sun blade?' Temi muttered.

[Quiet. Watch.]

Falani set the cushion on the ground while one of the monks strode solemnly forward. He began a flamboyant dance to the frenzied drumming of Falani's musicians. Temi watched him leap and dive around the votive as he chanted in the Forbidden Tongue.

'What the bloody—'

[Watch!]

And to Temi's astonishment, something began to emerge from the votive. It was smoke-like at first, but as it expanded, it began to take on form. Its colours shifted as it moved in undulating synchronicity with the monk, turning now blue now yellow now green. Within its flowing lengths, Temi glimpsed shifting images: waves, leaping fish, swirling vortices and boats. Higher and higher it crept as the monk sweated and whirled. The highbloods *ooh*ed and *aah*ed and touched their bejewelled heads in rapturous wonder.

'What is that thing?' Temi said. 'Did it come out of the votive?'

[Yes. I believe it is the spirit of the Ae.]

'The spirit? The River Ae has a spirit?'

[All things have a . . . a *spirit* that determines their nature. Though I do not believe any of the people below are aware of this. To them, what emerges from the votive is a Forbidden spectacle. An evening's illicit entertainment. And word of it has already begun to spread.]

'So how did my votives do it? Can techwork . . . attract spirits? Like it attracts greybloods?'

[You said your brother Tunji was trying something new before he was killed? We merely replicated what he did. Did he tell you where his new idea originated?]

'Actually . . . no.'

[Interesting.]

'It's beautiful,' Temi muttered, unable to look away.

[Yes.] The voice was a satisfied purr deep within her. [As I've said, word will spread. This is not something we can contain, unless we stop making the votives. These monks already know, but are content to keep it to themselves, for a few extra coins. But eventually, others will find out. Then, less *corrupt* holy ones, perhaps even the invoker clans, will come seeking answers. And the trail will lead them to your door.]

The monk dropped to the floor in a deep bow, his tataued shoulders glistening as they rose and fell with his laboured breaths. The Ae continued its graceful undulations until it stretched over the garden like a vast, flowing tree. It curved down in viscous drips, and the guests lifted eager hands, not quite close enough to touch.

Temi heard a shuffling beneath her. Her heart skipped, but when she looked down, it was into a pair of familiar yellow eyes.

'What?' Temi hissed at No-Cat.

The creature tipped its head to one side and stared up at her.

When Temi turned back to the garden, the Ae had begun retreating, flowing back down towards the votive, its colours dimming. Her eyes drifted to a well in a far corner of the garden. Flowers surrounded its walls and base, and its smooth techwork sides shone with Forbidden glyphs.

[Yes . . . These people do not need your votives to clean their water. They have Cleansed techwork built into the very pipes and boreholes of their homes, and monks in their pay to perform the necessary chants. Their water always flows clean; meanwhile, would you like to see what happens on Arrant Hill?]

Temi looked west again, to where the golden haze of the Garden filled the sky. Though it was fully dark, the clouds glowed with their own irrepressible light.

[Do you know why the water poisons?]

'Tunji reckoned there's techwork in it,' Temi said. 'He told me—'

[It is the Garden. Do you know what the golden light is?]

'The blessings of the ancestors,' Temi said. 'It's how they show their love for the Royal Clan.'

His dark chuckle swelled within her. [Do you truly believe that?]

Temi sighed. 'What does it matter? It's got nothing to do with the water.'

[It has everything to do with the water. Corruption flows out of the

Garden and into the Ae, and spreads all over the Nine Lands. An intricate network of pipes lies below the earth, connecting a thousand rivers and streams and lakes across this supercontinent. Oh, it is strongest here, most dangerous here, because this is its source, but it is everywhere.]

In the garden below, the dancing had resumed, and yet more food was being brought out. A card table appeared, and an erotic dancer climbed onto the stage to begin their routine.

'Look,' Temi said, 'I don't care about no pipes, and I have no idea what a supercontinent is. I need to think. Can we go?'

Returning to Lordsgrave was like cool air after the ravages of highsun. As its sea of bamboo roofs swung into view, so dull after the well-lit streets of Lordsheart, Temi felt a wave of relief. This was where she belonged, and her votives too. As she walked, the voice directed her down this alley or that street, having her pause outside mudbrick huts or compounds as he told her what occurred within.

[That crying you hear is a mother, weeping over the loss of her newborn.]

[He is vomiting because of the poison. It won't kill him yet, but his life will be the shorter for it.]

[You knew her as a child. Now she is forced to do this, to be able to afford clean water for her own child.]

When they stopped outside the compound of Samun, an elder who used to bring meals to the beggars, Temi heard drumming and singing within, and the acrid scent of a funeral pyre filled her nostrils. Temi closed her eyes. She was so hungry and hot and tired. She leaned on the outer wall of Samun's home.

'What do you want from me?' Temi whispered, her eyes stinging.

[I want you to free us both. Temi, if we continue to do as the Chedus say, many people in your neighbourhood will suffer and die. The monks will find out, and your family will be punished. Whatever happens, unless you act, your household, your family, are doomed. *I* have a way out. It will require time, and work, but I have it.]

121

Temi slid down the wall and rested her head back. She was so very tired. She wanted to hear Tunji's laugh, to play with Maiwo in the yard, to listen to Old Baba tell stories of his homeland while she dozed beside the shrine.

[Nothing will change unless you act.]

The teahouse opposite was still busy – gambling, she guessed, from the shouts that drifted into the street. In the shadows outside, the old beggar, Chaakin, lifted his cup in greeting. Temi waved back in response and pushed to her feet.

By the time she arrived home, the ogogoro inn was emptying of its regulars. A lone figure sat outside the bakery, in his usual chair. Old Baba. He stared down the street as though he'd been expecting her.

'Want me to help you into bed?' Temi said, flopping down beside him. Inside, she could hear Mtobi and Kierin arguing; about coin, most likely.

'Oh no,' Old Baba said, sucking on his gums and staring out at the night. 'Think I'll sit up tonight.' He glanced down at her. 'You know, there's a saying, out in Jebba. First saying I learned when I came to these lands from the Old Country. *The ancestors turn from those who refuse the gifts they offer.*'

Temi snorted. 'I know that saying.'

'Oh really? Seemed like you forgot.'

'What if the gifts on offer ain't of the ancestors?'

'All gifts are of the ancestors, Temi-girl.'

Temi felt a shifting beneath her skin. 'What if the gifts are dangerous?' she said quietly.

'Hah!' Old Baba chuckled and slapped his bony knees. 'All gifts are dangerous in the wrong hands!' He took his cane from its spot against the wall and pushed shakily to his feet. 'I'm going to lie down.'

Temi jumped up. 'I'll help y—'

'No, no, you stay out here,' he said, tapping her arm with a warm, dry hand. 'You stay. Look like you need a moment . . . *alone.*'

Temi held the bakery door open and watched her grandfather hobble inside.

[He is a wise and noble elder.]

'Course he bloody is. What, did you creep into his mind too and tell him to say all that?'

[No. But the ones we love often have a way of knowing what we need to hear.]

'Fine,' Temi said. She wet her lips. Across the street, Remmy waved goodnight. 'Fine. So if . . . *if* I was gonna do what you want. What would I have to do?'

[Invoke.]

'Oh, is that all!'

[Yes; it is.]

'I'm no invoker, in case you ain't noticed.'

[An invoker is merely one who invokes.]

'An invoker is a highblood,' Temi said. 'You need noble blood to have a strong enough a connection with your ancestors. Only the nine founding warlords of the clans can be brought back. You need the words and the dances and—'

[I am not your ancestor. And there is no such thing as noble blood. But I will show you the way.]

Temi closed her eyes. Of course he wasn't her ancestor. How could he be? More likely, he was something conjured by her own mind. But if she brought him into the light, if there truly was a way, then perhaps he was a gift from the ancestors, and she would be spurning them if she turned away.

'And if I do it . . . if I do it, you can free us?'

[Yes.]

Across the rooftops to the west, at the heart of the city, the sky shimmered with the golden haze of the Garden. *When the Greyblood Kings rise again, so too will the ancient Warlords Nine.* That was the Song of Legends Lost. But every soul alive had ancestors who had come before them. What could be wrong in seeking their protection?

'All right,' Temi said. 'All right. Tell me what I do.'

*

The following morning, after dressing Old Baba and taking a single spoonful of gari to break her fast, Temi descended into her grandfather's workshop to invoke.

'I'm ready,' she said, leaning on the table with both hands. 'You said I don't need to dance or chant or nothing.'

[That is correct. Prepare yourself. The initial sensation may not be pleasant.]

Temi opened her mouth to ask what he meant, but without warning she found that she was falling; falling backwards through the floor and then out of the workshop itself, out of the very world. She fell through darkness, then through a swirl of colour and images – forests, oceans, stars, cities – faster than her eye could track. She flailed, panic flaring within her, as a terrible vertigo seized her. She knifed through the streaking confusion, moving faster and faster.

After a time, she realised she could see faces in the tumult. Some looked kind and some harsh. Some cringed from her while others swept her way. Many seemed human, but others bore horns or feathers or gills, and still more defied comprehension altogether. She saw flickering bands of light, with the mere suggestion of a body at their core. She saw expanding clouds that radiated amusement or wrath, but had no face.

Then, abruptly, she found herself standing. Her heart pounded as she turned, taking in her new surroundings.

She stood upon a small, grassy island; a modest swell of land in a vast, still, silvery sea. Other islands dotted the sea, she saw; hundreds of them, punctuating the tranquillity in every direction. But none, so far as she could tell, was inhabited, and each seemed as barren as her own.

There was something curious about the light here, and when Temi tipped back her head, her breath caught. The sky was a spectrum of colour and shape. A dozen spheres populated the deep blue. The sun hung there to her left, either rising or setting – she couldn't tell which. It shared the sky with stars and moons and a large red sphere encircled by a ring of the palest blue.

It felt like a dream, and yet it also felt too real: the colours too sharp, the brightness too dazzling.

'It's beautiful,' Temi muttered.

'Yes,' a voice said. And there he stood, beside her, a man several handspans taller than she, swathed from head to foot in a dark, threadbare cloak. All but his hands were hidden from view, and these were skeletal; white bone and the pink glisten of muscle, as though someone had flayed all the flesh from his body. Manacles bound his wrists, their loose blue chains glowing almost as brilliantly as the stars above her. They did not seem to constrict him, and yet Temi felt a throbbing power from them, a keening that intensified when he moved.

Temi's heart thudded as she reached out to grasp his hood. She had to see his face. Had to look into his eyes.

'Not yet,' the Chained Man said, stepping away.

'It's you,' Temi said. 'It's really you.'

'Yes, it is me,' he said, his voice emanating from within the darkness of his hood.

'Where are we?'

'The Throxx.'

'The what? Sounds like something you catch in a brothel.' Temi turned around. 'This place . . . this is the ancestral realm, ain't it?'

'It is the Throxx. Endless. Everlasting. All of everything is contained here. But yes, your people refer to parts of it as the ancestral realm.'

'And this island is your . . . prison? It's better than the oubliettes of the White Isle, let me tell you. Least you got a view.'

Temi sensed movement above her, and when she looked up, she saw a streak of light and laughter go cavorting by. It was gone in a heart-beat, but then she spotted another, this larger and slower than the last. It was scarcely more than an explosion of colour, yet it made Temi think of the flowers that bloomed over the walls of her house, and she found herself reaching towards it.

'No,' he said, placing a skeletal hand on her wrist, the keening in his chains increasing in pitch. A great heat rose off him, so strong that Temi snatched back her arm in shock.

'Are they ancestors? Can you show me my ancestors? Is Tunji here somewhere? Can I speak to him, or—'

'We must focus on the task before us. In order to build what we require, I will need to join you in your realm. For that, I need strength. Strength that you can give me. We are lucky. My brethren have already sensed you. You must be ready. If we are fortunate, it will be a strong one.'

'What do you mean?'

'Prepare yourself!' he cried, and then he seized her, whipping her around to face the sun.

A surge of light raced purposefully towards them, gaining speed as it plummeted, and though it was beautiful, Temi found herself cringing away. The Chained Man's hands dug into the flesh of her arms as he held her in place. The swell of light grew larger and larger. There were faces within the cloud, she realised; dozens of them. The eagerness she sensed there, the desperation, made her pulse quicken.

'All will want to claim you,' the Chained Man said. 'But we need only one to begin.'

'One what?'

Then the cloud fell upon them, and Temi found herself buffeted from all sides. She felt herself being pulled in a dozen directions as hands and teeth and wings and claws grasped for her. Some held her for a time, and shining eyes regarded her with hungry relish before another would snatch her away and she would be pulled in a different direction.

'Stop!' Temi shouted, groping blindly for the Chained Man, but if he heard her pleas, he gave no sign. 'Where are you? Do something!'

Then she spotted him, standing at the edge of the island, his chained arms folded, his hood obscuring all but the jutting white bone of his chin. A circle of emptiness surrounded him, as though the swirling faces feared to go near. Temi strained towards him, but he made no move, simply watching her without comment. A desperate thought overtook her then: that he had brought her here to trap her. That she would never leave this place.

Then a creature with a feminine form of blue and green light with wide, shimmering wings seized Temi's shoulders and lifted her from the ground. Her touch permeated Temi's body, her being, like blood in a bowl of water. Its darkness spread over her, consuming, constricting, cloying—

'Let me go!' Temi screamed, twisting left and right, realising the world was fading and her movements slowing.

'No!' the woman snarled. 'You are mine!'

She jerked her head towards Temi's face, and before Temi had time even to cry out, the winged creature passed through her, *into* her. Cold suffused her, crept up her throat and into her bowels. She felt a tumble of emotions that were not her own – elation and triumph and relief and terrible fatigue and aching loneliness – and Temi felt herself diminishing, felt the world around her fading, felt—

Something seized her shoulder, warm, powerful. It lifted her away, gaining speed, moving so fast that all was a blur around—

Temi gasped, coming back to herself, still clutching the edge of Old Baba's table. She stood in the workshop, her sweat-drenched tunic clinging to her legs and breasts. She drew in long, grateful breaths of musty air, then turned.

A feminine scream pierced the air. The Chained Man stood behind her, cloaked and hooded as before, the azure light of his chains pulsating tremulously. One skeletal hand encircled the blue-green woman's neck. It was she who had screamed. Half her body was gone, somehow buried inside the Chained Man, and though she thrashed and fought, he drew her ever closer. As her luminous body was absorbed into his, networks of light played across his cloak, flaring with Forbidden glyphs.

'What are you doing to her?' Temi cried, and at the sound of Temi's voice, the woman reached for her. Her legs and half her torso were gone now, but on instinct, Temi took her hand. Blistering heat seared Temi's skin, and she snatched her hand back.

'Help me!' the woman cried, before the Chained Man gave one final pull, like a lover drawing his beloved into an embrace.

The woman's face twisted, contorting as the last of her light melted into the Chained Man's cloaked body. He arched his back, a crackling energy playing across the white bone of his hands as he hissed in pleasure.

Temi stepped back, revulsion seizing her.

The Chained Man seemed to fill the whole workshop as he turned towards Temi. She felt behind her for the stairs. If she was fast, she could still escape.

'Temi—'

'Ancestors preserve us! Did you just . . . just *eat* her? With your whole body?'

'I did not *eat* her,' the Chained Man said, his amused voice resonating across the room, sounding so strange outside the confines of her head.

Temi inched onto the first step. 'You killed her, though.'

'That aberration is not dead.' He turned towards the shelves, and Temi felt a pulling on the skin of her arms and hands. She looked down to find that a blue glow now suffused her brown skin.

'What did you do to me?' Temi cried, brushing at her skin. But the light clung to her like cobwebs.

'We now share the same energy.'

'Then you're Bonded to me? Like a clan ancestor?'

'I now have the ability to exist physically within your realm for a time.'

Temi's foot was on the bottom stair. She could run. Call for help. A dozen of those who loved her most in all the world lay just beyond that door. Would he try to stop her? Would he devour her, the way he had devoured the blue-green woman?

'Temi,' he said, lowering his arm, 'if I had not brought you back, she would have destroyed you.'

128

'You killed her.'

'I told you, she is not dead.'

Temi felt her way up the next step. Kierin would be home soon. She could call to him, and he would come running. Even with one arm broken, he was strong.

'This is what we came to do,' he said, advancing. 'Do you want to save your family or not?'

The ancestors turn from those who refuse the gifts they offer.

'I would never hurt you,' he said. 'I swear it. We were brought together to help each other.' He did not touch her, not quite, but she felt the energy of his hand as it hovered above her own; the energy that connected them now.

'What do I have to do?' Her voice sounded small in her own ears. She could not bring herself to lift her eyes.

'Now, we repeat the process.'

TWELVE

Jinao

Jinao tipped his head back to take in the Bairneater's face, dark against the bright afternoon sky. Now that he stood before it, the heat of it blazed like a funeral pyre. Jinao forced himself not to look at the crowd, who stood around him in stunned silence, nor at his brother, still turned incredulously his way. Even the Bairneater's hideous tangle of victims, chained to the hovel it had built, watched him through blood-shot eyes. The only person who spoke was Princen Tamun, arguing with his monk at the edge of the clearing. But Tamun's voice faded to insignificance next to the ceaseless whir of the Bairneater's body.

Jinao wondered how much of the beast was flesh and how much aeons-old techwork. This close, he realised he could see shifting glyphs in the Judgement of the Scathed the beast held. Tamun's monk claimed that tiny relic could level the city. Wordlessly, Jinao lifted his hand, making the sign for ancestral protection.

The Bairneater chuckled. 'Techwork is not a contagion and your ancestors cannot *protect* you from it.'

'I – I am sorry I took your arm,' Jinao said. 'I didn't mean to . . . and honestly, I wasn't even sure that it was me. But you held my mother's body and, well . . . I just wanted to make sure she really was dead.'

The Bairneater blinked down at him for several heartbeats before

130

erupting with thunderous laughter. The creature arched backwards, its great mouth splitting wide as its howls echoed around them all.

'Jinao,' the creature said finally, looking down at him again. 'Yes . . . Jinao Mizito. Well, now you are an invoker, I see. So invoke.'

'I, um . . . I mean—'

'Invoke. Call upon Mizito. Do it now.'

'Jinao is soulbarren!' Julon's call came from somewhere off to the left.

The Bairneater grinned. 'Not any longer.'

Jinao willed himself not to look round at his brother, but he did not miss the exchanged glances in the crowd, the mutters of disbelief. So, they hadn't heard, then. None of them had. None save the Bairneater. Somehow, the creature knew.

Jinao closed his eyes, summoning the words he had longed to speak in battle but never believed that he would. 'Mizito,' he said, his voice scarcely a whisper, 'spirit of my fathers, hear me.'

'Louder,' the Bairneater said.

'Mizito,' Jinao continued, holding out his hands the way he had seen Jemusi do, 'spirit of my mothers, hear me.'

'That's it. Call upon him. Bring him here to face me.'

'Mizito, Lord of the Eagle, Master of the Bonetree, hear me now, and come.'

He threw out his hands, as he had seen his siblings do so often. He knew he needed to dance, to make the sacred movements, but it had been so long he could not remember how. He squeezed his eyes, willing himself to feel the heat in his skin, to feel a rush of something coursing through his body and out through his tataus. But instead, he felt nothing.

'Again,' the Bairneater said, pacing, the Judgement of the Scathed glinting in its hand. 'How many times have I told you that Mizito abhors hesitation? Doubt repels him. Be sure of yourself and he will come to you.'

And unbidden, a memory flashed in Jinao's mind: he stood in his mother's sparring room, his shins burning where she had struck him with her staff. *Stop crying*, she snapped at him. *How many times have I told you that Mizito abhors hesitation?*

'W-why did you say that?' Jinao asked softly, ice stealing over his skin.

'Invoke! Or pick which of these lowbloods you'd like me to eviscerate first.'

'Mizito,' Jinao said, more loudly this time, 'spirit of my mothers, hear me.' The dance began with the move they called *sunrise*, that much he could remember. He stooped down and swept his arm out.

'No,' the Bairneater snapped, head jerking round. 'You are not pleading with your wetnurse for one last sugar-fruit. You are calling upon the spirit of the greatest warrior who ever lived! Where is the respect? Mizito has promised to protect you for all time. Show him the honour he deserves!'

Even the creature's voice was different, Jinao realised as he turned. The timbre. The intonation. *Where is the respect?* his mother used to ask him, time and again. *You sound like a child, asking for just one more sugar-fruit.*

'Mizito, spirit of my fathers, hear me!'

'Good. He wants to join you. He exists only for battle. Feel him straining to join you. It is what he was made to do.'

And, ancestors turn from him, but Jinao *could* feel Mizito. Something in the Bairneater's words crystallised the sensation in his mind. That tingling was indeed a pulling, flowing in one direction as though he were a conduit, as though if he just threw his arms out hard enough—

'Hear me now, and come!'

Jinao staggered forwards as a great force surged into the tips of his fingers and out into the air beyond. The morning shifted around him and the crowd rippled with astonishment as Mizito materialised, first a mere outline, then more solid, until he stood silent and looming, a towering man in silver and black scale armour. Blue-white light shimmered on his armoured shoulders. His hair hung down his back

132

in a long black tail, and behind the feathers of his eagle mask, his eyes shone. The energy of him, as he stood gripping his staff, *Stillness*, pulled on the hairs of Jinao's arms and tugged on the skin of Jinao's face and chest.

'Now strike me,' the Bairneater said.

Jinao could scarcely move, let alone strike anyone. His muscles felt leaden and his mind untethered, as if he were about to collapse drunk. Mizito was a throbbing potentiality in his muscles, in his lungs, in the tips of his fingers. His ancestor's presence spread over him like sunlight at dawn, warming his skin, lifting his heart, as welcoming as an embrace. But it was so very heavy; so heavy it pulled on every pore of his skin, as though it might rip Jinao's spirit from his body.

'Are you deaf? Strike me! Now!'

Jinao ground his teeth against the weight of his ancestor's presence. How could a greyblood know anything about invocation? Jinao had to move to will Mizito to move – that was what he'd been taught. But as he trained his gaze on his left hand and dragged it up through the air, that glorious heat begin to fade. He couldn't lose him! Not yet! Jinao grunted and curled his fingers into a fist. He needed this moment to last a little longer, because he had done it – ancestors be praised, he had done it!

'Focus! Then *strike!*'

Jinao jerked one heavy arm and Mizito's arm jerked too. It was like dancing underwater; like dancing underwater in full Yennish armour, after an entire bottle of Jebbanese red.

'Mizito is not your absurd lizard puppet,' the Bairneater shouted, as the captives on its edifice cringed and moaned. 'He is not a doll, to be pulled around. You are merely the channel, the river flowing into the sea. Let him out!'

And Jinao roared, a sensation that started deep in his belly, a knot of fear and anger and desperation that swelled within him until it burst out, and as it did, Mizito leapt forward, *Stillness* spinning, and the Bairneater – laughing, triumphant – hopped back out of reach.

Jinao had no control over the fight, he realised. He provided only the energy, only the will to do harm. He kept his eyes on the Bairneater, channelling all his fury, and Mizito drew it into himself like water into a dying plant. Jinao felt a tugging on his arm, and so he extended it. It was as though Mizito only sought permission from Jinao, sought to pull on the parts of Jinao's body that he wanted to use to attack, and Jinao had only to let him do so.

Ancestors, but it was exhausting. Every breath he drew was harder to take. Every second that passed made it more difficult to stay upright. Jinao could hear his own pulse in his ears, pounding as his vision misted. He had to blink, to grit his teeth to keep from passing out. Each movement Mizito made pulled on Jinao's heart and hands, draining a little more of him. This: *this* was what invocation was. Why had nobody told him before? His mother, his siblings . . . all his family; they taught that the invoker wielded the Bonded ancestor, but that seemed a lie now. There was no true skill to it. It had nothing to do with martial prowess or control. It was the utter surrendering of one's life force to another, and it came easily to him now.

'Good,' the Bairneater said. 'That is all for today.' Then the creature reached out with its stump and clubbed Mizito across the face in a monstrous blow. Jinao staggered, feeling the sting on his own skin, and all at once, Mizito winked from existence.

Jinao caught himself before hitting the ground. In the distance, he saw Julon take a step towards him before his wife, Captain Sellay, placed a staying hand on his arm.

'You will meet me in Ramanit, Riani Province, in thirty days,' the Bairneater said, holding up the Judgement of the Scathed. 'There, you will face me again, alone.'

'Pardon?' Jinao said. 'I don't—'

'Ramanit,' the Bairneater said. 'Thirty days. Face me alone, or more innocents will die. These people are now free to go. Let us see if you can save the next.'

'Wait. I cannot leave Aranduq. We—'

134

'You can . . . unless you want more lives to be lost in your name.'

'But why? I don't understand why you—'

'Attack!' came a shrill cry, and Jinao looked round to see Princen Tamun bouncing on the balls of his feet, face lit up with exhilaration as a swarm of gold-painted warriors thundered past him, spears extended. 'Attack! Do not damage the head! The head is for my collection!'

The Bairneater whirled around as the warriors reached it. In one smooth motion, it tossed the silver Judgement of the Scathed at the crowd and drew Sulin's staff. On the far side of the clearing, Jinao saw the princen's monk – bleeding from the nose and head, Jinao noted with surprise – leap towards the techwork device as it went twinkling through the air. Jinao's heart twisted as the monk dived, arms outstretched, and the Judgement of the Scathed passed clean over the old man's head to land in the mud behind.

'Fools!' the Bairneater roared, sweeping the staff around again, catching the first wave of spear-wielders like a scythe through maize.

'Mizito!' Julon cried from the far side of the clearing. 'Spirit of my fathers! Hear me!'

Jinao backed away as chaos consumed the clearing. Many of the warriors were preparing to join the charge, but others surveyed the scene uncertainly, and one group had set about trying to free the lowbloods. The monk sat in a sobbing heap on the ground, tapping desperately at the Judgement of the Scathed. But nothing had happened. There had been no—

The ground shifted. An earthquake, perhaps . . . they were not unknown in Cagai. Jinao spread his arms, keeping himself upright. Shouts of alarm rang out behind him and when Jinao looked around, he saw a plume of thick black smoke rising into the air above the city perhaps a league away. There came another jolt then, this one closer, and a second plume rose. Jinao swung his gaze over to the sobbing monk, terror climbing up his throat as the ground shook again, then again, and the people around him began to cry out and make the sign for ancestral protection.

135

'Ancestors preserve us . . .' Jinao breathed.

The Bairneater growled and Jinao looked back to see the creature covered in warriors; hacking, slashing, jabbing, so many of them that the greyblood itself was buried beneath. But as the creature's growl intensified, there came a rush of wind, and Jinao was driven backwards, along with twenty or more warriors, who were sent sailing in all directions. The Bairneater stood at the eye of the storm, its skin suffused by an arcane blue glow. Those warriors who remained near swung at the beast, but their attacks rebounded off the creature's skin. The Bairneater strode forwards, heedless of those who leapt and slashed at it, advancing irrevocably towards where Princen Tamun stood shouting in excitement.

'*You*,' the Bairneater said. 'Ahiki.'

Another jolt rocked the ground. In the distance, the convent bell clanged: *fire*. Multiple fires. Somehow, the Judgement of the Scathed had kindled fires all across Aranduq, fires that had shaken the very ground with their force. What kind of power could do such a thing? Jinao felt a ripple of energy to his left, and there was Mizito, invoked by Julon and striding towards the Bairneater, staff raised.

Jinao should join him. He was an invoker now: that was his duty. But his hands felt as lifeless as the ground beneath him.

'Get away from me, beast!' Princen Tamun shrieked. The Bairneater was mere strides from the young man now, and the princen's warriors had formed a protective circle around him. '*I said desist!*'

A hail of arrows hit the Bairneater, and its skin rippled and shook them free like so many mosquitos.

'You are a small, useless thing,' the Bairneater said. 'Send my regards to your forefather.'

Then the Bairneater leaned forwards, its massive body curling over the protective line of warriors, its mouth hinging wide. Horror replaced the amusement on Tamun's face, and though his arms began to glow, it was too late. The Bairneater jerked forward, mouth descending over the princen's head. For a moment, the Ahiki youth's cries were muffled. Then the Bairneater clamped shut its jaws and stood upright.

Jinao stared, transfixed, as Princen Tamun Ahiki, nephew of the king of the Nine Lands himself, dangled from the Bairneater's wide mouth. Then his headless body fell to the ground, to be surrounded by his screaming warriors.

'Ramanit,' the Bairneater said, chewing, turning. 'Thirty days. Then, we shall continue.'

The Bairneater leapt, gaining the lip of the crumbling city wall. Archers loosed at a cry from their captain, their arrows arcing upwards. Mizito, invoked by Julon, leapt also. But the Bairneater was so incredibly fast despite its bulk, and its skin tough as mountains. It hauled itself up with its good arm and leapt down into the wetwoods beyond.

'Here,' Julon said, dropping down beside Jinao. 'Drink.'

Thin afternoon light shone across the ruins of Aranduq City. The convent bells had ceased their ringing, though the fires still burned. Jinao took the gourd in trembling hands and swallowed, scarcely tasting the liquid. He had done this. All of this was because he had failed. And now the entire Nine Lands would suffer.

Across the clearing, the last of the lowbloods were being helped down from the Bairneater's structure. Most of them stood about crying, looking out over a city now shrouded in smoke. The thunder of collapsing buildings filled the afternoon. The last messenger to arrive from Thousand Domes had reported that most of the palace wall had been destroyed. The western docks and the canal district had been flooded. Fires still raged near Winterblossom Square. Hundreds had been buried alive.

'This was all my fault,' Jinao muttered.

'Your fault? The only one to blame here is Tamun. The creature was preparing to leave when he attacked.'

'Sire!' One of Jemusi's commanders appeared, a heavyset woman with thinning grey hair. She glanced uncertainly at Jinao, then swung her gaze round to Julon. Her face was streaked with soot. 'Sire, we have completed the evacuation of the palace. The remaining warriors are setting up camp at the mouth of the Ae, ready for First General Jemusi's return.'

First General Jemusi. Jinao had done this to her, too. She would return from Adataliland to rule a home in ruins.

'Send messengers ahead to Lasham City,' Julon said. 'Let my uncle know we will need horses and wagons to transport the wounded. Have Captain Talung lead the convoy there.'

'Yes, sire. But surely you yourself—'

'I am not going with the convoy. That is all.'

The messenger bobbed her head in a bow, her eyes filled with a terrible dread. Jinao looked across the burning rooftops as the commander jogged away. If he had been stronger, if he had been a better invoker, perhaps he could have defeated the Bairneater and saved the city. The ancestors had given him a chance to prove himself, and he had failed.

Across the clearing, a circle of monks stood around Princen Tamun's body, chanting softly in the Forbidden Tongue. Many of them wept openly. Did they truly mourn the princen, or did they merely fear reprisal? Perhaps they should all fear reprisal. A member of the royal family had died while staying as a guest of their clan.

'Look, I didn't know it was you,' Julon said. 'Who took the Bairneater's arm, I mean. I . . . I thought it was just a lowblood.'

'Does that make a difference?'

'Yes, it makes a difference! Jin, these people look to us for hope. They need to believe that we are powerful. That we can save them. I was told the man who took the Bairneater's arm was dead, so I did not believe I was . . . stealing anyone's glory.'

In the distance, there came another rumble . . . another building collapsing.

'What's going to happen to Aranduq?' Jinao said.

'Have you seen the devastation that monster caused? Hundreds killed. Thousands without homes. When I climbed the wall earlier, I saw fallen buildings in the Musicians' Quarter and among the

138

greathouses near the monastery. The statue of Sumalong has collapsed into the river. Do you remember the songs? When Sumalong falls, so does this city.' Julon looked away. 'We are finished here now. And ancestors only know what this means for the realm. It is just a mercy that Mother didn't live to see it. How proud she would be.' Julon chuckled miserably. 'Not even a moon since she crossed the pyre, and already her city is burning!'

'She always did say we should surpass her in all things.' Jinao looked down. 'Did you hear what it said?'

'About what?'

'About me. It sounded just like her.'

'A coincidence.'

'Do you truly think so? It knew about that stupid lizard puppet I had as a child. How could it possibly know?'

'I don't know, Jin.'

'What if it has Mother's memories somehow? What if part of her spirit lives in it? Maybe that's why it wanted *Valour*. Maybe that's why it wants me.'

Julon sighed and brought one hand to his head. His tataus rippled with the light of invocation, coursing up and down his arm as though Mizito sought to break free.

'*If* a greyblood somehow does have our mother's memories,' Julon said, 'then that is all the more reason for us to focus now on ridding the Nine Lands of it.'

'You should go to Lasham,' Jinao said. 'I can find passage to Ramanit alone.' Though the thought of leaving Cagai, of leaving Mizitoland and striking out on his own, filled him with despair.

'Don't be absurd,' Julon said. 'You can't cross the Nine Lands on your own. And I'm not letting you face that creature unprotected. You don't even have a quartet. No, we go on together. Until the monster is destroyed.'

Jinao took another sip from the gourd.

Ramanit. Thirty days. Face me alone, or more innocents will die.

139

Ramanit . . . That city was somewhere in Riani Province, to the north in Navretland. It had to be three hundred leagues at the least, perhaps more. That did not give them much time. But he had seen what happened when people doubted the Bairneater's threats. Aranduq, Gateway to the Nine Lands, was on fire. Already, word would be spreading. Now the king would see, Jinao hoped, what his mother had long been saying. Now he would see why holding the mouth of the Ae had been so crucial. When the greybloods poured in – and they would; nothing could prevent that now – all the Nine Lands would see.

There could be no running back to the palace for Jinao now. No hiding and waiting for everything to go away. His siblings, his mother, would not arrive to take care of it all. His home was gone. And he was an invoker. There could be no return to the time before.

Julon gripped his shoulder. 'You did it, Jin. You were accepted for the Bond. And a new iteration of the spirit, too! This is a sign from the ancestors. They have strengthened our hand.'

There came a shout, and a group of weary-looking warriors appeared, among them Captain Sellay, Julon's wife and the leader of his quartet. She dropped down beside them, her grass skirt fanning out around her. Her brown skin was scratched in a dozen places – wetwoods plants, Jinao supposed.

'It's gone,' Sellay said. 'After your last invoking, we tracked it for a while but . . . the scouts think it is up among the trees. I sent Remal and Uchin on into the wetwoods, but rain is due. I doubt we'll catch it.'

'That's all right,' Julon said. 'We know where it's going. *Rendau!*'

A youth who had been helping to bandage an old woman's leg lifted his head, and then sprinted across the clearing.

'Rendau, return to the palace,' Julon said. 'See if any of the stores survived . . . We need provisions, weapons, camp equipment. We'll be taking the northern road.'

'Yes, sire,' Rendau said, bowing. Just a flicker of uncertainty creased his smooth brow. 'Might I ask where—'

'After the Bairneater. That creature killed my mother and a member of the royal family. And it destroyed the City of Aranduq. I am going to hunt it down and present its head to the king myself.'

'Yes, My Lord,' Rendau said, before scampering off.

'Is this wise?' Sellay said. 'If we regroup at Lasham and gather enough warriors from Uncle Wendoa, we can return here and—'

'Jemusi is First General of Cagai.' Julon pushed to his feet. 'Let her deal with this, when she decides to return from her little trip. Mizito roils within me, Sellay. You . . . you wouldn't understand. He *hungers* for vengeance. And vengeance he shall have.' Julon extended a hand towards Jinao, his eyes blazing. 'The creature wants you. So that is what we shall give it. All the might of Aranduq. All our strength. Channelled through you.'

Jinao had as much desire to channel the might of Aranduq as he did to walk across a field of burning coals. He looked out over the clearing to where his horse, Liet, stood still as stone. Dormant again. Or perhaps just sleeping. Perhaps she too hoped that if she turned her face from the world, the world would forget she existed. Jinao was no warrior, and he was certainly no invoker. But the Bairneater had asked for him. And he had seen what it could do when it was refused.

Ramanit. Thirty days. Face me alone, or more innocents will die.

'At your side,' Jinao said, and took his brother's hand.

THIRTEEN

Temi

Temi sat cross-legged on Bakery Mount, the morning sun hot on her shoulders. Opposite her stood a man in a threadbare cloak, his brown hands bound with glowing blue chains. His face was still not visible within the shadow of his hood, but gone were the bone and sinew of previous days. He had flesh now. Substance now. And as the wind stirred the hem of his cloak, Temi could almost hear him smile.

'We are going to destroy everything Harvell Chedu has built,' the Chained Man said. 'We are going to ensure she can never trouble your family, or any other, again.'

Eight times they had returned to the ancestral realm over the past days, and eight times he had drawn creatures of light into him. Not killing them, he still claimed; merely letting them exist within him, and gratefully so. With each, he grew more solid, and his Bond with Temi stronger. Now, if she focused, the Chained Man could remain in the mortal realm for a half a day before Temi tired.

'Destroy how?' Temi said.

The Chained Man stared out over the river, his ragged cloak snapping. Here, in the mortal realm, the rich blue of his chains was paler. She watched the line of his jaw as he spoke.

'Harvell Chedu has been passing your techwork off as her own creation. I want you to imagine what will happen if, suddenly, her wondrous creation were found to . . . fail.'

'Harvell will come for my family,' Temi said. 'That's what.'

'No. Imagine this: that highblood woman, Falani, at another of her parties. Her guests are gathered round. She presents her votive. But this time, no strange spirit comes dancing out. She has been tricked. Robbed, in effect. And she will be angry. She will direct her anger at the Seng family who, in turn, will shine their anger on Harvell. They will want to make an example of her, since someone like Falani will ensure word of the Sengs' failure gets out – to all her highblood friends or, if she is especially angry, the senior monks. The Sengs will come down upon Harvell with the full force of their fury. And then, in one elegant manoeuvre, you and your family will be free.'

Temi watched a lizard scampering towards the old Scathed wall. 'You mean they'll kill her.'

'Yes. None but she and a few of her cronies know that you make the votives. The Sengs are unforgiving, and once she is dead, you will be free.'

'No,' Temi said. 'No. It won't work. What if Harvell tests them first and finds they're broken? What if the Sengs ain't as angry as you say, or what if they believe her when she says it's really us? And anyway, Harvell will know it's me, and she'll come after me.'

'We shall craft them to fail only once they have arrived with their final purchaser.'

'We can do that?'

'I can, yes.'

Temi closed her eyes. 'It'll come back on us. Somehow, it'll come back on us. And I can't be responsible for someone's death, even Harvell.'

'Can't you?' The Chained Man drifted towards her and lifted her chin. She could almost see his face, deep in the shadows of his hood. The heat of his fingers on her skin was at once alarming and enthralling.

'What if they don't kill her?' Temi whispered. 'What if they let her live, and then she comes for us?'

143

'If you do not act,' the Chained Man said, lowering his hand, 'there will be no one left for you to save. Your family will break apart or starve. Your brother's killer will roam free. The people of Arrant Hill will sicken and die. And, eventually, the monks will hunt you down. Is that what you prefer?'

'Ho-ho! Now I see!' came Old Baba's voice.

Temi spun around, and the Chained Man melted to nothing, but not quickly enough.

Temi's grandfather hobbled up the hill, his walking cane piercing the ground.

'Old Baba,' Temi said, making a quick bow. 'I – I didn't see you there.'

'Who is your floating friend?'

Temi looked over her shoulder. 'Floating friend?' She forced out a small laugh. 'It's just me here, Baba.'

Old Baba cackled and shook his head. 'My hands don't work so well no more, but my eyes is good. Which ancestor did you call upon?'

'I can't call upon ancestors, Baba. I'm lowblood. Only the clans invoke. Only the nine warlords return.'

'That one is not of this realm,' Old Baba said, waving his stick. 'So tell me: what is their name?'

Temi sagged. 'I don't know his name. I call him the Chained Man.'

'So,' Old Baba grinned, 'what does he want?'

'He helps me with the votives. Here.' She took one out of the pocket of her tunic and handed it to him. 'Not as good as Tunji's, but—'

To her surprise, Old Baba straightened, confusion crossing his face. He turned her votive over and over, studying the glyphs, shaking his head in wonder. 'How did you do this?' he said.

'I don't know. I just follow the Chained Man's instructions. It's based on what Tunji made.'

Old Baba lifted his rheumy eyes. 'This is why that woman, that Harvell . . . this is why she comes.' He stared at her – that frank, open stare she had found so disarming as a child. 'Do you know why I left the Old Country?'

144

'Baba told me it was bandits in your town,' Temi said.

Old Baba puffed out an irritated breath and waved his cane dismiss-ively. 'Bandits? Ah-ah! It was the *Amfi . . .* The Twelve Houses, we call them then. Powerful. Untouchable. They came to our town; told all the people we must pay them to stay safe. My ma grew tired of it, yes? Tried to make a stand.' Old Baba sucked on his lips and looked away. 'They would not let me see what they did to her. But I saw the anger in my own baba's eyes. The day after, we left. I am the only one to make it here alive to the Land of the Nine.'

'I'm so sorry, Old Baba.'

'When I came here, I told myself, never again. Never again would I run because of the Twelve Houses, or anyone. You start running, you don't stop your whole life.' He glanced over his shoulder. 'Door! Door, come here!'

To Temi's surprise, No-Cat came trotting obediently up the hill. Old Baba held out a hand and the creature sniffed his fingers. 'This thing here, now. This is very interesting. I came to show you. Where you said you find it?'

'At the wharf,' Temi said, as her grandfather worked gnarled fingers under No-Cat's fur. He pulled free a single techwork vein, which he then looped around a jagged shard of blackglass.

A series of glyphs streamed across the blackglass as Old Baba grinned. 'Come, come!' he said.

Temi shuffled forwards.

'You see those four lines?' Old Baba said, pointing one trembling finger. 'This cat is a doorway to those four lines.'

'Doorway?'

'Yes, a doorway!' Old Baba disentangled the blackglass then pushed to his feet. 'You keep it close. Might be there's something useful on the other side.'

He turned away and began hobbling back to the edge of the hill.

'Old Baba, I—'

There came a shout from the street below, followed by several screams.

'Stay here,' Temi said, lurching to her feet and heading for the hillside.

She scrambled down the dry grass. Harvell couldn't have come again. She wasn't due for several days. And Temi had done everything the woman asked, everything . . .

She stumbled out into the street to find a group of locals clustered around the jerking form of a beggar. No, not a beggar. A greyblood. Its rags were half rotten and clogged with riverweeds, and its metal head studded with lichen. Its face was a sparking mass of techwork veins where Remmy, son of the ogogoro innkeeper, had smashed it in with the chair leg he still brandished. Shock marred the faces of all those who looked on as she approached.

Temi hadn't seen a greyblood since she was a child, and even then, it had been from her father's arms. Yeshe and Selek had hacked the thing apart, and to her young eyes it had seemed feeble, pitiful.

'I'll've seen seventy-six rains this dry season,' Old Javesh said, leaning on his cane, 'but I ain't never seen a greyblood climb all the way up here.'

'It came from the river!' cried a small boy, pointing. 'There's three more.'

'Three more!' Javesh said, making the sign for ancestral protection. 'These is dark days indeed.'

'There'll be more,' Remmy said, tucking his chair leg under one arm. 'Now that Aranduq has fallen.'

'What do you mean?' Temi said.

'Aranduq City was destroyed,' Remmy said. 'It was the Bairneater what done it.'

Several voices scoffed at this, and Remmy's smooth brow creased in irritation. 'You don't believe me? Go ask at the docks and you hear the stories what's coming in.'

'And I guess the Woodsmaiden was with it, eh?' someone said, but the laughter was muted as Javesh began shaking his head.

'I heard it too,' Javesh said. 'You think this is bad? There'll be more coming out of the river now, you watch!'

As Javesh and the others chattered on, about an invoker who was chasing the Bairneater, about the war, about the end of all things, Temi backed away. 'If we do this,' she said, 'if we take on Harvell . . . you have to promise it won't come back on my family.'

[I promise you I will do everything in my power to ensure that it does not. But if our plan does not work as expected, I promise there are other ways I can keep you all from harm.]

'Good,' Temi said. 'Then let's get on with it. But ancestors save you if anything goes wrong.'

While the children cleared away their meagre dinner of rice soaked in vinegar, all talk at the table about the Bairneater, about greybloods in the river, Temi slipped out into the yard and pulled open the trapdoor to Old Baba's workshop. Down in the darkness, they got to work quickly, the Chained Man swirling out with scarcely a thought from her. He stood at the workbench, his long fingers darting over the veins and discs, weaving and interlocking, telling her again and again to watch closely.

'There,' the Chained Man said finally, holding out a tangle of techwork. 'It is ready.'

'And this is it?' Temi turned it over in her hand. It looked identical to every other votive they had made. But Tunji always said the real power of techwork lay in what couldn't be seen. 'And it's going to work? It's going to free us from Harvell?'

'It's going to free us all,' he said. 'And they will be powerless to stop what is coming.'

Harvell Chedu smiled when Temi stepped out onto the street and handed her the crate.

'Thank you,' Harvell said.

'I hope you enjoy them,' Temi replied, with as much deference as she could muster. She offered Harvell a tiny bow, ignoring the flicker of confusion that crossed the older woman's face.

When the last of the Chedu fighters had descended the hill, Temi released a breath. 'Now what?'

[Now, we wait. It will not happen immediately. It may be a moon or more. And in the meantime, we continue as usual.]

'How will we know the plan's worked?' Temi said.

The Chained Man chuckled. [Oh, believe me. We will know.]

PART TWO

Boleo, Jinao, Elari

FOURTEEN

Boleo

'Welcome, friends!' Father Boleo said as they crested the final hill. He steered his horse around to face the ragged convoy that had accompanied him all the way from Aranduq. 'Welcome to Ewo City!'

Invoker Jemusi Mizito broke away from the line of mounted warriors, her horse trotting up to join him. 'Where is my brother's shipwreck, Father Boleo?' she said. 'I need to return home. I need—'

'My Lord Invoker,' Boleo said, inclining his head politely, 'we all mourn the destruction of Aranduq. But at this moment, you are serving your clan and your ancestors by being here.'

That was always the best way to placate invokers: remind them of their duty to their ancestors. Jemusi was a serious, calculating woman, and he knew she had grown impatient over the long days of their journey through the wetwoods. She'd brought only the four warriors of her quartet with her – which was well. Boleo had impressed upon them all the need for discretion, a thing their Clan Itahua counterparts seemed incapable of comprehending. Boleo looked past her, to where two dozen members of Clan Itahua waited on their colourful horses. Ancestor-cursed fools! Their definition of discretion seemed to include ten servants, half a dozen warriors, and a wagon full of clothing and

151

wine. Boleo had explained to them that he had to keep the techwork carriage hidden. He'd told them of the need to inform no one why they journeyed east. And yet they had travelled with almost their entire party, in full warpaint and feathers. If there had been a way to do this without them, Boleo would have leapt at it. Unfortunately, the findings could not be denied . . .

As though reading his thoughts, Jemusi said, 'Can't you just leave them here while we go straight to my brother's shipwreck?'

Boleo smiled patiently. 'Lord Invoker, if we want to identify the bodies in the techwork carriage, we will need to open it. As I have explained, the ancestors spoke to my holy brothers and me in a vision. Members of *both* your bloodlines, Itahua and Mizito, are required to open the carriage. If you attempt it alone, you will be repelled by its arcane energies.'

Over by the treeline, Atoc Itahua, a man who had spent most of their twenty-day journey in a drunken stupor, stood urinating against a tree.

'I cannot imagine why the ancestors saw the need to bring us together with them,' Jemusi muttered.

'The ancestors turn from those who question their will,' Boleo said.

That silenced her, but Boleo felt a pang of sympathy. Her home city, a city over which she had only just become First General, had been destroyed in her absence. One of Boleo's messengers had brought them the news. When Jemusi returned home, she would be guardian of a city of smoking rubble.

'Your brother Jethar and Cantec Itahua led the voyage together,' Boleo said. 'Perhaps that is why—'

Boleo's holy staff flared to life, a stream of glyphs in the Forbidden Tongue sliding across its crystal heart.

'Ancestors preserve us,' Jemusi said, making the sign for protection.

Boleo pushed down the unease that prickled within him and slipped from his horse. He had given his noviciates express instructions not to risk contacting him.

152

'I must offer thanks to the ancestors for our safe journey!' Boleo called down the line. Then he turned back towards the city and lifted his staff.

Ewo spread out before him, a glittering valley of palms, a vast warren of winding streets, a teeming port on the southern tip of the Nine Lands. Four-sided Scathed towers, tiered and dripping with gardens, stood among the white-washed human-built houses. And there, looming over it all, stood the shattered Scathed ruin that was the palace of Three Towers. Its famous twin shards – Moon and Star – rose to narrow summits of the palest blue crystal. Its gardens spread out below like the skirts of a bride. Boleo smiled. He was home. With the help of these people, he would open Jethar's carriage. And then, whatever treasures Jethar Mizito had found on the voyage would be his.

'*Repeat Message!*' Boleo cried theatrically in the Forbidden Tongue. He heard movement at his back. Perhaps they craned to watch a monk communing with techwork. Perhaps they touched their foreheads for ancestral protection, to ward against the corrupting language of the Scathed. Boleo made a show of dancing in a slow circle, his beaded skirt fanning out, his old knees creaking, until the message rippled across his staff again.

Do not bring them to palace. Royal monks everywhere.

'Wonderful,' Boleo muttered, straightening.

'Problem?' a voice said behind him.

Boleo started. Invoker Morayo Adatali, Warlord Daloya's youngest son, came sauntering past. He wore his travel agbada, blue lined with yellow embroidery, along with his customary easy grin.

'Please don't sneak up on me like that!' Boleo snapped.

'I thought it best not to interrupt until you had finished . . . *chanting*,' Morayo said in a mock whisper, leaning towards him. 'Do we need to be worried?'

'Perhaps,' Boleo said. 'There are royal monks in the palace.'

'Royal monks? They must have come about the king's draft.'

'I don't think so.' Boleo glanced back at the convoy. 'Take our guests

153

to the hillside summerhouse. Have them remain there until I send word. We'll need to bring them into the palace via one of the tunnels.'

'They aren't going to be pleased,' Morayo said, then shrugged and stalked back towards the waiting line. 'Friends!' he cried. 'I have an exciting announcement!'

Boleo did not wait to hear what the exciting announcement was. Morayo was almost as skilled with his words as he was with the ida blade: much like his father had been, before the Battle of Maadu. With his open smile and easy laugh, Morayo could charm even the most jaded of hearts. He would soon have their guests not only eager to head to the summerhouse, but believing the idea was theirs. Boleo secured his staff against his black and red horse and pulled himself back up.

Children ran to the roadside as Boleo galloped past yam farms and humble roundhouses. Many made the sign for ancestral protection, while their elders in the fields shielded their eyes against the sun. Royal monks. Dread uncurled within Boleo as he pulled down his turaco mask. They were so close now. So close to opening the most pristine Scathed relic he had ever seen. But the arrival of these monks could mean the ruin of it all.

The crowds parted as Boleo thundered towards the main city gate, his skirts flying out behind him in a staccato of beads. People peeled away, many bowing, others stopping to stare. City guards, high on the blackglass battlements, shouted for travellers to make way, make way for Father Boleo the Wise, Grand High Curator of all Adataliland, most senior monk in the south.

Boleo willed himself to stay calm as he wound his way through the city. Perhaps the royal monks were on a pilgrimage. Perhaps they were just travelling through. The noviciates he had spying for him were mostly street children and petty criminals – perhaps they had made a mistake.

But no, as he rounded the corner onto the Lords Road, the walls of Three Towers rising in the distance, he began to spot them: royal monks in their distinctive, looping golden robes. They wandered down the alleyways in twos and threes. They stood conversing with market-goers and street vendors. A fierce protectiveness rose up within Boleo. He had worked so hard for Warlord Daloya, so loyally, to ensure that here, at least, his holy superiors' influence could be kept at bay. Yet now, the royal monks had their crooked fingers in everything.

'Open the gates!' Boleo yelled as he galloped towards the palace walls. 'Open the gates!'

Two men leapt down from their stations to work the rope and pulley mechanism as Boleo charged onwards. The gardens of Three Towers unfurled before him, winding paths and bushes of towering violets clustered beneath bowing palms. Palace servants, in tunics of green, looked up as he flew past. Many were in his employ, but just as many were ignorant of the . . . extra duties he performed for his warlord. How obscene that this place, a haven of such peace to him ordinarily, now crawled with those he had come to consider foes.

Boleo slid to the ground before his horse had come to a stop, stag-gering to stay upright and ignoring the groom who came scurrying over from the stables. His greatest concern was to check on Jethar's carriage and the protections he had placed around it. Then, he would need to secure his personal vaults. Much of his techwork lay hidden in the city slums, but not all . . .

'Holy brother,' came a voice from off to the left, 'we have been awaiting your arrival.'

Boleo came to a halt. His chest still heaved and sweat dripped from under his mask onto his bare shoulders. He turned to see a dozen warriors in the golden warpaint and loincloths of the royal clan. Walking ahead of them came a large monk in equally golden robes. From the tataus that snaked around her fleshy arms, she was senior indeed.

Boleo dropped into a Jebbanese-style bow, head low, arms wide, the feathers of his turaco mask brushing the lawn.

'Welcome to Ewo, Your Holiness,' Boleo said. 'Had I known to anticipate your arrival, I would have arranged for—'

155

'I am Father Emata,' the woman said, 'Keeper of Truths. I am here to check Three Towers' artefact records. It seems it has been eight rains since a curator of the Garden last successfully logged a report from this province. I am here to remedy that. You may rise.'

Boleo straightened. Keeper of Truths. Boleo kept his breath steady as he removed his mask, but fear rose within him like bile. If the Garden had sent their Keeper of Truths then it meant they were more than suspicious about activities in Clan Adatali. It meant they believed they had proof of unholiness.

'Please join me, Father,' Emata said, turning back the way she had come . . . Not towards the twin towers of the palace or the dining gardens, but up the hill, towards the small, stone building that housed the Adatali shrine.

'Father Boleo, I have heard a troubling whisper,' Emata said as they walked. 'A whisper that a large artefact washed ashore in the Adataliland town of Ninshasi. I have heard that this artefact was something highly unusual. But curiously, when I contacted the Ninshasi monastery, Arch Curator Ngbali told me I was mistaken, that it was only a rotten boat containing no artefacts at all. Do you know anything about the matter?'

'Nothing whatsoever,' Boleo said, meeting her gaze. 'Ninshasi is in the far east of Ntuk Province. We rarely hear anything from there . . . unless it is about the price of goats.'

His smile died on his lips as she studied him, her pale gaze boring so deep. 'Father Boleo, with the demise of Aranduq City, the Nine Lands are vulnerable. Now more than ever, we servants of the king must work to protect the realm. Do you deny knowledge of a wreckage on the shores of Ninshasi?'

Oh, but she was going to have to try much, much harder than that. 'Yes,' he said. 'I deny knowledge – as I have already told you, Your Holiness. If something had washed ashore, I would have heard of it, and reported it, as is required of my holy station.'

'It is curious,' Emata said, turning onto the path leading up to the shrine. 'My predecessor fell to bandits on the road home from your lands.

Bandits that stole all his records. The holy brother who came before him succumbed to a snake bite while staying as your guest. And Father Yeshini, who came before him, apparently renounced her holy calling and took up residence across the seas. We hear of her occasionally. It seems she has come into substantial riches since abandoning the holy ways.'

'That is most unfortunate,' Boleo said. Sweat slid down between the contours of his chest. But as Emata had so helpfully pointed out, he had dealt with her predecessors: he would deal with her, too.

'Is it?' Emata said. 'Father Boleo, our role as monks is to keep the Forbidden knowledge. Knowledge is dangerous, my child. Look what it did to the Scathed! Our role is to find the cursed relics that wiped out that species, to Cleanse them, and then never to speak of them again. We are given only such tools as are necessary to do that job. But some monks gorge themselves on the corrupting knowledge to which they are privy. Like drunks on a city dock, they want more, always more, and their desire can never be sated.' She turned to study him as they reached the shrine doors. 'Eventually, Father Boleo, it kills them.'

Boleo inclined his head. 'I have served Clan Adatali tirelessly for nearly fifty rains,' he said. 'I am Warlord Daloya's most trusted aide. There have been no incidents involving Scathed artefacts in decades. There is little smuggling to speak of, and any misuse of techwork is dealt with swiftly and decisively, which is why our provinces are deemed the safest in all the Nine Lands.'

'Oh, I am sure you have served your *clan* very well,' she said.

He followed her into the shrine, unease crawling over his skin. Instead of the usual young, unquestioning nuns who served Sister Ulla, a woman long in his employ, the hall swarmed with golden-robed monks. The statues of Adatali that lined the walls had been stripped of their jewels and offerings. The contents of the silver platter that stood before the main statue had been tipped into a gourd. Two monks worked to remove the spirit wood altar where every Jebbanese invoker for the last five thousand years had knelt to receive the blessings of the ancestors.

'What is the meaning of this?' Boleo said, turning to Emata. 'This is a sacred place.'

'Indeed,' she said. 'Which is why it is such a shame that it has been sullied.'

She gestured, and the two monks working the spirit wood slipped behind the largest statue of Adatali.

'I had always heard that Three Towers' shrine was unique,' Emata said. 'Away from the main palace. In a modest building. Smaller than all the others. How strange, I thought. How strange that a people who love their ancestors so deeply should show them such scant respect.'

Boleo realised his tongue had gone dry. Because yes: they had begun to slide the great bronze statue aside. He worked saliva into his mouth, then said, 'Stop at once! This is sacrilege!'

'Adataliland has always possessed more techwork than anywhere else,' Emata said as the two monks lifted the trapdoor – the trapdoor Boleo had spent half a lifetime trying to protect. 'It is why our best minds have often come from your lands. Your mentor was Father Galumu, was he not? He is something of a legend in the Garden. His knowledge was unparalleled. It is such a shame that he was taken from us in his prime.'

Boleo could still remember Galumu's smile when Boleo had arrived back first during the Trials. Boleo had bested all the other youths. Tasked with finding, identifying and neutralising the artefact of greatest worth, most were still splashing through the trial caves when Boleo was bowing on his mentor's floor, presenting him with what he had found: a talking drum, its cords spun from the finest woven blackglass, its skin stained in a language Boleo had never seen before. It had lain buried under the caves – perhaps even the monks hadn't known it was there. And yet when Boleo had presented it, beaming, the look of horror that had crossed Galumu's face had been terrible to behold. Galumu had snatched the drum from Boleo and bid him never speak of it again. Then he had beaten Boleo bloody.

As Boleo had limped back to his sleeping mat that night, bearing the wounds whose scars he still possessed, he had understood the grim truth of it. A monk's duty was not to seek knowledge. It was to destroy it. That was what Cleansing was: the destruction of techwork. The removal of everything the so-called cursed relics could do. And yet, over the years, Boleo had found so many wonders created by the Scathed. Techwork that could heal. Techwork that could count. Techwork that remembered all you whispered to it.

Yes: a monk's sacred duty was to destroy techwork, the world's most valuable tools. And Boleo wanted no part in it.

'Follow me, please,' Emata said.

Boleo followed her to the trapdoor, painting bewilderment onto his face. 'This is astonishing!' Boleo said. 'In all my decades here, to think there was a secret room all this time! By the ancestors, how did you find it?'

Emata, holding her robes in one hand as she descended the worn steps, made a sniffing sound which Boleo chose not to interpret. He felt the eyes of the royal monks on him, just as he had felt the eyes of the other noviciates on him the night he returned from presenting Father Galumu with that drum. But now, just as then, he kept his head held high.

Boleo followed the Keeper of Turths down the narrow, earthy tunnel to the room at the end. The room he knew so well. The room he had discovered quite by accident during his earliest days at Three Towers.

At the end of the tunnel stood a small cavern lit by glowing techwork lamps. Twenty statues stood in a broad semicircle: crumbling, ancient, chipped. Twenty statues depicting souls in clothing from across all the provinces of Adataliland, and more besides. One held a talking drum: she wore clothing resembling garments from across the sea. One wore long, overlapping lengths of patterned fabric and something like a gele headwrap. One carried a strange, curved spear. At the feet of all stood spirit wood platters for offerings. Offerings to Clan Adatali's true ancestors.

'Goodness, what is this place?' Boleo said, looking around.

'No more games, Father Boleo,' Emata said, turning to him. She smiled, but her eyes were steel. 'We both know I am here because Clan Adatali has been withholding techwork from us for decades. This clan, aided by you, has been hoarding and misleading for as long as you have been its most senior curator. I believe I have only scratched the surface here. I believe that the techwork that washed up in Ninshasi is hidden somewhere in this palace. I believe you knew about this room, this room that goes against all that we are. I am going to prove all this, and then I am going to bring you before His Golden Majesty for judgement.'

Boleo turned, studying the statues that he had knelt before almost every day of his life in this palace. The day he had found it, Daloya had come upon him silently. Back then, Daloya had struck a powerful figure – tall and broad and muscular. His hairlocs, oiled and set with green jewels, had hung almost to the backs of his knees. He had been a man who commanded any room he entered, a man possessed of a presence that swelled beyond himself to encompass all those around him. Boleo remembered the smell of him as he knelt and dropped a few crumbs at the feet of each figure. Boleo had known in those moments that he would do anything for this man, anything to defend and protect him. Daloya had not sent Boleo away or chastised him for what he had discovered. Indeed, he had seemed pleased.

You must never speak of this room again, Daloya had said.

Who are they? Boleo had asked him.

Warlords, Daloya had told him. *All of them, warlords. Adatali's companions. Our ancestors.*

Boleo rounded on Emata as royal monks began to flood the room. 'I have no idea what you are talking about,' he said, fixing her with his gaze. 'This is the first time I have set foot within this room. Your predecessors' ill luck is nothing to do with me. And I know nothing about a techwork carriage. But by all means, have the run of the palace,

160

the city, the province . . . of all Adataliland. You will find nothing. See nothing. That I promise you.' He smiled. 'Your Holiness.'

Her lip curled in a mocking smile of her own, and then she turned to her monks. 'Break it all,' she said. 'Ensure no part of it remains. Then bury the accursed rubble at sea.'

Boleo stood unmoving as hammers and chisels were brought out, as the monks hacked at faces that had stood here for centuries, safely hidden. He did not flinch as features he had come to know so well were chipped away, as stone limbs thudded to the earthen floor. Emata watched him as she destroyed Clan Adatali's hidden legacy, but he had spent decades bringing down souls like her. She wouldn't see a flicker of emotion on his face.

That day, when Daloya had found him in the hidden shrine, the warlord had said, *I am told that you requested specifically to be sent here. You were gifted enough to receive a summons to the Garden itself, but you turned it down in favour of Three Towers. Why?*

Boleo's reply had been simple. *Because I am Jebbanese. This land is my home. My blood.*

Daloya had placed a hand on Boleo's shoulder as he stood. The warlord's palm had felt warm and strong. *Do you truly wish to serve me? Even if I ask you to do something that runs . . . counter to all you were taught?*

Boleo's reply had been immediate. *Unreservedly, My Lord.*

Then I believe this is the start of a great friendship. Though I must warn you, your superior, Arch Curator Busim, has no love for those who question the diktats of the Royal Clan. He is quite the thorn in my side.

That night, Busim had fallen from the top of the Moon Tower, plummeting to his death. And the next morning, Boleo had woken to find a gift waiting outside the door of his room: a tiny talking drum, carved from ebony.

It had indeed been the start of a very great friendship.

'Will that be all, Your Holiness?' Boleo said, turning to Emata as destruction reigned around them.

161

'I want all your records,' Emata said as the final statue crumbled. 'All your ledgers. Everything.'

All that remained of those nameless warlords was rubble now. But Boleo inclined his head. 'Of course, Your Holiness. I live only to serve.'

FIFTEEN

Jinao

Sixty souls headed north from Aranduq City on the hunt for the Bairneater. Jinao had never journeyed so far on horseback before. Every trip he'd taken around the provinces of Mizitoland had involved sumptuous carriages and nights hosted in the greathouses of minor nobles. But as they passed through the wetwoods and towns of northern Cagai, there were no leisurely stops at roadside inns. Instead, they drove the horses hard, pausing only to eat or to sleep under rough canvas tents, and after three days, Jinao was sore and tired and miserable.

It wasn't just the physical pain. The warriors he travelled with, many from his brother Julon's company, shunned him, as if the fall of Aranduq were his personal doing. And perhaps it was: Jinao still couldn't shake the feeling that if had known how to fight, the creature could have been defeated. It was a shame he would carry with him until the day he crossed the pyre.

Lowbloods came out to watch as they passed through towns or rice paddies, but not a soul among them deigned to cheer the convoy on. An impenetrable miasma of hopelessness seemed to hang over them all. Hopelessness, or perhaps disapproval.

'They think we've abandoned our station,' Jinao said to Julon. They rode side by side, behind Julon's quartet and two dozen of his most trusted warriors. At the rear, the rest of their party followed in mournful silence.

Julon snorted. 'Their despair has nothing to do with us. It's the war draft. Every one of these households will be sending loved ones to die.'

Jinao supposed he was right. As they entered the highlands of northern Cagai, their convoy passed a procession of terrified-looking lowbloods flanked by monks in travelling garb: conscripts answering the king's draft. They carried farming tools for weapons, and death already haunted their eyes.

They were deep into the bamboo forests of Zumae Province when Father Tuvo received word that the Garden had ordered them home. They stopped by the roadside while Tuvo performed a dance that let him receive the message via his holy staff. Tuvo was a fussy, officious monk whom Sulin had always considered workshy. One look at the triumph in his eyes when he relayed the order told Jinao exactly how devastated the man was at the news.

'What do they intend to do about the Bairneater's threats?' Julon said.

'The threats of one greyblood are not our concern,' Tuvo said briskly. 'Our job is to prepare for war.'

'Our job is to protect the people of the Nine Lands,' Julon said. 'No one is safe until that creature is brought down.'

Tuvo straightened. 'I am afraid that I cannot in good conscience continue to journey with you!' he declared. But the way he stamped his staff into the road made Jinao think of a small child refusing to go to bed.

'Then you and your conscience may return south,' Julon said. He murmured softly to his horse and continued on.

'This is unconscionable!' Tuvo called after them as the convoy followed their invoker. 'My holy brothers will not stand for it!'

The last thing Jinao saw as he rounded the bend was Tuvo standing alone amid the swaying bamboo.

They crossed the border into Navretland after twenty days of journeying steadily north. Riani Province was in monsoon season, and it was nothing like the gentle rains in Cagai. Sheets of water pounded out of the grey sky, stinging Jinao's eyes and turning the wetwoods to a swamp. The heat hung like a heavy cloak over everything. And the insects! Biters were commonplace in Aranduq City, but the monstrosities Jinao had seen out here made toys of the pests back home. Twice on their journey, he had needed the nuns to heal the swollen results of their attentions, and they lost three warriors to fevers from the stings.

They were passing through Ilurat, a sweltering, low-lying river town at Riani's heart, when a group of monks came riding out of the rain up ahead. They wore local garb, as monks so often did – orange lungis, their chests bare save for looping necklaces of sandalwood.

'Great,' Julon muttered. 'Another command to return home.'

But instead, the lead monk, a tall man with a thick beard, called out, 'Party of Clan Mizito! We have a message from Warlord Uresh!'

Julon lifted a hand for the convoy to stop, then trotted his horse forwards. 'Go on,' he said, eyes sceptical beneath his rain-drenched hair.

'Warlord Uresh has heard of your plight,' the monk said, his eyes twinkling as he looked from one face to the next. 'He will not permit the Bairneater to terrorise his people. My holy brothers in the palace have sent word that Uresh has dispatched two hundred of his finest warriors to join you. They will meet you outside the gates of Ramanit, and together, you will destroy the beast. Once the creature has been dispatched, Warlord Uresh insists you join him in his summer mahal, as honoured guests of Clan Navret.'

Warlord Uresh's mahal. That meant real beds. Hot baths. Meals consisting of more than one course. But as Julon nodded, and the convoy trundled on, Jinao saw the unease in the monks' eyes.

They arrived on the outskirts of Ramanit on the twenty-eighth day of their journey, when the Mizito convoy reached the broad highway leading down into the valley. The dense green wall of the wetwoods, to their left and right, rose like the ranks of soldiers that would be awaiting them at the city. Beneath Jinao, Liet thrummed unhappily.

'Riders!' came a cry from up ahead.

Jinao lifted his head. Rain angled down out of a slate-grey sky.

'Uresh,' Julon said. 'We have little time now to prepare a plan.'

A ripple passed along the line, and then a warrior in a conical helm, riding a red and yellow horse, streaked past at full gallop.

'Perhaps they forgot the wine?' Jinao muttered.

'The ancestors turn from those who succumb to base pleasures,' said Sister Zalani. She rode to Jinao's right, her sodden grey robes clinging to her slight body, giving her the look of a drowned rat. She was one of a great many new attendants Jinao now boasted as an invoker, including a fight master, an armourer and a haughty page of no more than twelve, who made it clear how displeased he was to be assigned to Jinao. As Julon reminded him almost every day, he would also need to select his quartet, a task for which he could muster very little enthusiasm. It was plain from the way their warriors continued to shun him that no one in the convoy would willingly endure that particular honour.

Sister Zalani was harmless enough – earnest and enthusiastic. But her tasks for him were either tedious or impossible: study the ripples of water in her contemplation bowl; memorise the exact shape of a leaf. She had him pull Mizito into the tips of his fingers and hold him there without release. Everything he did, she claimed, would bring Jinao closer to his ancestors, but all it truly achieved was to remind him of how much he had failed to learn as a child.

'Wine clouds the mind, and thus our connection to the ancestors,' Sister Zalani continued. 'Your Bond with Mizito will be stronger if you call to him with a clear head.'

When a second Riani warrior went galloping past, Julon straightened. 'This is not good. Why aren't they stopping?'

A moment later, Captain Sellay appeared out of the rain, her grass skirt plastered to her muscular thighs, her mouth a grim line.

'Our scouts say they're leaving!' she said.

Julon peered at her. 'What do you mean?'

'Warlord Uresh's warriors are here, but they're leaving. Two hundred of them were just spotted heading west.'

166

'They claimed the Bairneater was in the woods to the east!'

'I know! But I don't think this is anything to do with the Bairneater.'

Up ahead, their line had come to a stop, and Jinao could hear shouts from their lead riders. 'This is absurd!' Julon growled, then barked a command at his horse and charged on along the line.

Why would Clan Navret leave, when they had been so keen to help? Jinao had met Clan Navret's warlord only once, as a child: he recalled a smiling, jovial man. Sulin always said Uresh was proud and protective. Jinao followed Julon at a trot, past ranks of soldiers and aides who sat hunched and grim in their saddles.

Julon stood on the edge of a hill overlooking a sprawling city of domed mansions and floating slums. Off to the left, the snaking line of a great army was indeed marching west, baring banners in the red and yellow of Clan Navret. But Jinao's eye was drawn to the figure riding up to meet them, a man in golden robes seated upon a golden horse. Three other riders in the royal colours came behind him, travelling at a distance. Royal monks.

'Lord Julon of Clan Mizito?' the lead monk called.

'We're here to meet Warlord Uresh,' Julon said. 'This doesn't concern the king.'

'All matters in the realm concern the king,' the messenger replied, his narrow, pinched face tightening with disapproval. 'His Most Blessed Grace commands you and your brother Jinao Mizito to present yourselves at the Garden to explain the death of his Most Blessed Highness's nephew, Princen Tamun.'

'There's nothing to explain,' Julon said. 'The Bairneater bit off the princen's head. I'm sure the advisers who scurried back to the Garden were able to tell His Blessed Majesty that.'

The monk smiled humourlessly. 'Perhaps you do not understand me. His Highness Jakhenaten II command you and your brother, his loyal subjects and servants of the Blessed Clan, to return to the Garden. This is not a request. It is an instruction.'

'Why are Warlord Uresh's warriors leaving?'

'His Most Golden Majesty's noble invoker clans have been commanded to provide your party with neither succour nor military personnel until the investigation in to Princen Tamun's death head been concluded.'

'You . . . fucking—' Julon lunged forward, tumbling off his horse and breaking into a sprint. Jinao slipped from Liet and followed, the rain lashing his skin. Julon had almost reached the royal messenger when Jinao seized him around the waist. They slammed into the mud together, Julon thrashing, his tataus flaring erratically. Jinao clamped his legs around his brother, as his fight master had taught him, and held fast. Julon was broader than him, and stronger, but the rage seemed to melt out of him as quickly as it had come on. Julon went slack, watching with hard eyes as the royal monk wheeled his horse away.

'The directive has been delivered!' the monk cried, somewhat shrilly, and then he tapped his horse and swung back towards his companions waiting by the trees.

'Why would they do this?' Julon groaned as Sellay came trudging towards them. 'Why would they try to stop us?'

'I don't know,' Jinao said.

Sellay flopped down beside them in the rain-soaked damp. 'We don't need Clan Navret,' she said, gripping Julon's shoulder. 'We can do this ourselves, kill the Bairneater ourselves, and then go home and rebuild.'

'There's nothing to rebuild,' Julon replied, staring off into the lashing rain. 'You know how many greybloods come out of the sea. Aranduq will be crawling with them by now.'

'But we'll manage,' Sellay said.

'What, with half our force already sent west?'

The sound of galloping hooves cut across Jinao's thoughts. Another local rider appeared out of the rain, wearing a conical helm and red scale armour, a scimitar set with red and yellow gems strapped to their waist.

'Stop them!' Julon said, reaching forward.

'Seize the rider!' Sellay cried, pushing to her feet and setting off at a run.

'Help me stand,' Julon said.

'What's wrong?' Jinao asked.

'Nothing. An insect bite perhaps. Help me up.'

As Jinao helped his brother to stand, several riders peeled away from the line at their back, heading off the mounted warrior. The warrior's horse reared as they drew their scimitar. Julon winced and began hobbling forwards. Jinao darted after him, offering an arm in support, but Julon shoved him away.

'Who are you?' Julon called. 'And why aren't you leaving with the rest of Clan Navret?'

The man snorted. 'I am nothing to do with those cravens. I am Ramaniti. I am here to ask you to leave our city. You've caused enough trouble.'

'So you're planning to just let the Bairneater prey on your people?'

'No. We are planning to kill it.'

'If you attack the Bairneater without my brother Jinao, the beast will be angry. You heard what it did to Aranduq. If Jinao does not face it, the same will happen here.'

The warrior eyed them all, his dark eyes gleaming as he weighed Julon's words. Finally, he slid his scimitar back into the wide sash at his waist. 'You three, follow me,' he said, nodding towards them. 'The rest of your party must wait.'

'We should not go alone with this man!' Sellay hissed.

But Julon ignored her. 'Follow you where?'

'To Invoker Darsana's war camp. She is Lord of this city.'

The warrior steered his horse about and galloped towards the line Sellay had hastily assembled. Julon signalled to them to allow the stranger through.

'Who is Invoker Darsana?' Jinao said.

'I've never heard of her,' Julon said, his face still tight with pain. 'But if she wants to save her city, she'll have to listen to what we have to say.'

*

Shortly after highsun, the Ramaniti warrior led Jinao, Julon and Sellay out of the wetwoods and towards a great camp. It lay in a rain-drenched valley, and had Jinao not known differently, he would have taken it for an encampment of outlaws. No Clan Navret banners flew from the tents. No drummers heralded their arrival. And the wagons and pavilions they passed were a motley of fabrics and designs from across the Nine Lands.

Hard-eyed warriors watched them silently from their cook-fires, souls with filthy armour and many scars. Beside Jinao, on Julon's horse, Sellay hissed under her breath, 'If they decide to turn on us, take your brother and run. Do not wait for me.'

Julon sat slumped against Captain Sellay, one arm coiled loosely around her waist, seeming scarcely aware of their surroundings now. Whatever was wrong with him, he had deteriorated rapidly, and Jinao tried not to think of the three warriors they had burned following fevers just like this.

'Guests for Her Lordship,' their escort said when they reached the faded walls of a command pavilion. The warriors on guard there stood aside, one raising her eyebrows. Their escort muttered something to her in a local tongue and she laughed throatily.

The command tent was blissfully cool and dry after the ceaseless onslaught of the rains. Jinao felt a stab of guilt as he strode across the rich carpets, his muddy boots leaving dark prints in his wake. A group of musicians sat in a circle off to the left: three drummers and a shehnai player, all staring at their party as though they had risen from the dead. At the low table up ahead sat a dozen souls eating a light dinner, among them the woman Jinao supposed was Invoker Darsana. There was something strange about the group, though Jinao couldn't put his finger on what.

Darsana, a woman of perhaps thirty, wore silks and jewels enough to shame any Ahiki princen. As Jinao and his brother stopped before her table, dripping a tattoo upon the carpet, Darsana tipped her head to one side, her elaborate earrings jangling.

170

'Yes?' she said.

'You're planning to hunt the Bairneater,' Julon said, still leaning on Sellay. 'You won't be able to defeat it without us.'

Darsana spluttered with laughter, then glanced at a warrior with a jewelled beard. 'Are they a comedy troupe? Or have the rains washed away their wits?'

'The Bairneater destroyed Aranduq City,' Julon growled. 'If my brother Jinao does not face the beast, it will destroy your city, too.' He straightened. 'If we pool our resources, our knowledge, perhaps we can finally defeat the thing.'

'Do you know how difficult it is to kill a named greyblood? When the attentions of such a beast turn your way, all humanity should quake.'

'My brother severed its arm,' Julon said, and Jinao tried not to turn towards him. How strange it sounded, finally hearing those words on his brother's lips.

Darsana's eyes flicked to Jinao. 'And this is him, is it?'

'I am he,' Jinao said flatly. 'Him.'

Darsana turned to Sellay, a light frown creasing her brow. 'What is wrong with your invoker, Captain?'

'He's fine,' Sellay said. 'Just tired.'

Darsana passed her wine glass to a servant and rose. She crossed the room, her dark gaze sliding over Julon. 'Your brother has a fever.'

'He'll be fine,' Sellay said.

'Is that what your clever little nuns told you?' Darsana smiled, and though her face was level with Jinao's chest, he still felt the smaller under her stare.

'Forgive me,' Darsana said, 'but I do not understand why the creature is so interested in you.'

Jinao cleared his throat and said, 'Um . . . back in Aranduq, the Bairneater spoke using . . . using my mother's words. It said things only she could know.'

'Curious,' Darsana said, a faint smile tugging at the corners of her painted mouth.

171

'My nun, Sister Zalani, says that it could be my mother's staff. The Bairneater took it from her pyre, and Sister Zalani says that over time a warrior's weapons become imbibed with their essence.'

Darsana's lip curled with amusement. 'What do you make of it, Amira?' she said, glancing over her shoulder.

In the shadows sat a shrunken old woman who on first glance resembled a street beggar. Her clothes were rags and her eyes bloodshot and grim. But a collection of Forbidden crystals glinted at her neck. It was then that Jinao realised why the tent had seemed curiously empty. There were no nuns present. Nor monks; nor any signs of a quartet.

'They say the Forest King used to eat the slain,' the ragged beggar-woman said in her sing-song Riani accent. 'Each soul he ate made his mind larger, until eventually, his head exploded.' She offered them a menacing little smile and Jinao saw that the woman's teeth were all crystal too and gleamed more brightly than the candles in their sconces. 'But that is only a story. Greybloods cannot capture human souls.'

'Might I ask who you are?' Jinao said.

'Amira is my adviser,' Darsana said. 'And a very learned woman. If she says there are no records of greybloods acquiring the memories of the fallen, then such records do not exist.'

'That doesn't mean it hasn't happened,' Jinao said.

'Perhaps, but it makes no difference to us,' Darsana said, taking her wine glass back and sitting again. 'Very well. I will permit you to join us. I'm told the rest of your convoy waits in the hills. Bring them down into our camp so that they might rest and eat. Amira will see to your brother's fever.'

'I have to be the one to face it,' Jinao said. 'That's part of the arrange-ment.'

'Your attempts to kill the Bairneater will fail if you meet it in open combat, even if you have ten thousand warriors at your back,' Darsana said. 'Its skin can repel blades. That is why it has survived for centuries. In order to defeat the beast, you need to create a trap that can penetrate the arcane energies of its skin. I will not let it continue to prey on the people of my city while my clan and king sit idly by. Face it, if you wish, but know that you will fail unless you have a plan.'

Jinao watched Darsana lift her wine glass to her lips. He did not trust this woman and the strange company she kept. But if she knew a way to defeat the Bairneater, that was all that mattered.

'Then let us plan,' Jinao said, removing his cloak.

SIXTEEN

Boleo

As the hidden door in the garden wall creaked open, Father Boleo paid silent thanks to the ancestors. He might not have been able to prevent the destruction of the hidden shrine, but he had successfully kept Father Emata from finding this place. Boleo had provided the royal monk with enough ledgers and accounts to drown her for a decade. He had a whole roster of coincounters in his employ whose sole task was to provide false records for the techwork that passed through Ewo City. And now, ancestors be praised, his guests had safely arrived to open the techwork carriage.

'Greetings to you all,' Boleo said, bowing as the party stepped out into the daylight.

Jemusi Mizito came first, stumbling through the tangle of vines that kept the door hidden. She took in the squat trees and manicured lawn with naked suspicion. Behind her came Invoker Kartuuk Itahua, a man Boleo still hadn't puzzled out. The brother of missing Cantec Itahua was too composed, too cautious, for Boleo's comfort. He strode into the brilliant sunlight, the feathers of his headdress fanning out behind him as he muttered to one of his warriors.

'I promise you,' Morayo said, hurrying out behind them. 'Travelling through Ewo underground is much the best way!' He gestured to the servants waiting nearby with platters of frosted fruit and jugs of wine, the sleeves of his purple agbada sliding down his arm. A dozen or so palace guards in green tunics stood under the shade of the wall, but they kept well back.

Invoker Atoc Itahua strode towards the wine at once. The rest of the Itahua party drifted forwards in reverential silence.

'And this is it?' Kartuuk said. 'This . . . lump of blackglass?'

Boleo turned. Up ahead, rising from the lawn like an ominous boulder, stood the techwork carriage. Blue glyphs gleamed along its sleek, black length. The gaping hole in one side did not diminish how well preserved the relic was. Only the faintest sheen of silver in the air betrayed the existence of Boleo's warding protections . . . protections he sincerely hoped Father Emata did not possess the skill to detect. Because in all his years, in all his studies, Boleo had never dreamed he would encounter a wonder such as this.

'Yes,' Boleo said. 'The Scathed needed no wheels to navigate. Millennia ago, Forbidden energies would have held this carriage aloft. A specimen as pristine as this is a rarity indeed.'

'Was nothing else found in my brother's shipwreck?' Jemusi said, her dark eyes gleaming.

'Nothing,' Boleo replied as he led the way through the trees. 'Perhaps now you understand the need for discretion. My holy brothers in the Garden, whose will I respect unflinchingly, would take this carriage and never reveal the identity of the two bodies that lie shrouded within. Their diligence would prevent the spirits of the deceased from finally crossing the pyre. That I cannot, in good conscience, abide. Which is why I brought you here.'

'So it's got nothing to do with all that techwork you can't get at?' called Atoc Itahua, from where he slouched against a tree. He held an entire jug of wine in one casual hand, as though completely indifferent to the proceedings. Lieutenant Ishaan, another Itahua warrior, shot him a look. He pushed his long black hair out of his eyes and added,

'I mean, that's what this is really about, isn't it? You need us to open the carriage so you can have the treasure within.'

'Whatever Forbidden relics lie within belong to my holy brothers in the Garden,' Boleo said. 'As all Scathed artefacts do. I have done my best, but these will need further Cleansing, lest they summon grey-bloods or ill fortune.'

How easy it had become, over the years, to say such words. Easy, because it was what most souls expected to hear. The lie had been hammered into him as a noviciate – even as his eyes and mind told him something very different – and it was so very easy to repeat.

Jemusi stood before the carriage as she might before her clan's greatest ancestral shrine. She leaned forwards, studying the gaping hole in its side. 'Something broke through here.' She extended a tentative hand, then snatched it back as the arcane energies flared. 'What was that?'

'The same power that prevents me from opening the carriage door,' Boleo said. Some of Father Ngbali's noviciates claimed to have seen a person sprinting away from the shipwreck. In all likelihood, it was merely a local thief who had been repelled by the carriage's energies. But something about the broken wall – and the man – unsettled Boleo.

'What do we do?' asked Kartuuk, striding forward to join Jemusi.

'Approach the Forbidden lock,' Boleo said, 'so that its arcane energies might know your blood. I assure you, you are quite safe while I stand at your side.'

The lock took the form of a square of blackglass, protruding from the carriage's side. It had no features to speak of, but Boleo had spent days studying its many intricacies. His staff revealed that the device was designed to locate particular patterns in blood. Two patterns, unique to two bloodlines.

Jemusi made the sign for ancestral protection. 'Ancestors preserve us,' she muttered, and then extended her hand.

Boleo gripped his staff as the techwork lock brightened. A blue light slid down its length, as though something within was casting its gaze over Jemusi's hand. Each time Boleo had attempted to open it, the light had flared red and then the thing had fallen still. But this time, it flared a brilliant green.

'Did it accept me?' Jemusi asked, looking round.

'We won't know yet,' Boleo replied. 'Please, My Lords . . . could one of you from Clan Itahua present yourself?'

Kartuuk rolled back the wide sleeve of his beaded tunic and then pressed his palm to the lock just as Jemusi had. At once, the blue light appeared. And this time, when it flashed green, Boleo heard a crackle of energy.

'Stand back!' Boleo cried, marching forward with his staff raised. 'All of you, stand back! Allow me to determine if it is safe.'

Kartuuk stood aside as Boleo approached the doors at the end of the carriage. Instead of repelling his touch with a burst of warm energies, the carriage permitted him to close his hand around the blackglass handle. Boleo sucked in a breath, and then twisted.

A gust of cool air greeted him. He could see little within, but when he lifted his staff and muttered in the Forbidden Tongue for it to light the way, the harsh yellow light glinted on a hundred metal surfaces.

Techwork. There stood a dozen silver discs, all intact. There stood a slab of Forbidden glass with only a single scratch to mar it. Boleo climbed in. He had to hunch against the low ceiling as his eyes darted from place to place, unable to settle on any single thing. On the shelves lay artefacts he could not name: a basket filled with white gems; three plates, curiously ridged with tiny stones . . . Boleo ran his hand over these and found they gave way at a press, and that each bore a different glyph.

'Let me see the bodies,' Jemusi said from behind.

Boleo shuffled hastily aside and let Jemusi pass. The two shrouded corpses occupied much of the floor at the carriage's front. The sunlight from the gaping hole cast them in an ethereal glow. Boleo had not noticed it before, but Forbidden glyphs streamed faintly across their shrouded torsos. And he realised, with interest, that a third tangle of the same white material had been stuffed under one of the far shelves. Curious.

'Which one is he?' Jemusi said thickly.

'Over fifty souls journeyed north on Jethar's voyage,' Boleo told her. 'This might not be him.'

'The ancestors meant this carriage for us,' she said, wiping her eyes. 'You said it yourself, Father. For us, so that we can ensure Jethar returns to them.'

'The bodies are likely to be very decayed,' Boleo said as Jemusi shuffled forward. 'They may be difficult to look upon.'

Jemusi pulled at the bindings on one body, heedless, as the others gathered in the doorway behind them.

'Ancestors . . .' Jemusi muttered, sitting back.

'What is it?' Boleo leaned forward.

Beneath the shroud lay the peaceful face of a man in middle years. Not Jethar – Boleo could see that at once – this man had the broad cheekbones of the eastern mountains. How his corpse had been so well preserved, Boleo couldn't imagine.

Jemusi had already shuffled round to the second body, and after pulling the shroud away, she stifled a cry.

'It's him!' she said, her voice catching. 'Ancestors preserve us, it is him.' She leaned down, her tears darkening the white fabric of the shroud. 'Oh, Jethar . . .'

She pressed her lips to his cheek, then straightened abruptly. 'He's breathing!' Her eyes sought out Boleo. 'Father, he's breathing!'

'It is your imagination, child. Sometimes the body—' But his words died as he saw Jethar's eyes move beneath their lids.

'*Call the nuns!*' Jemusi cried. 'Send for help! My brother is alive!'

Alive. The bodies in the carriage were still alive. As Boleo's aides swarmed the mango orchard, several Itahua warriors set about carrying the bodies out into the sunlight.

Boleo strode over to the two bodies, now laid out under the shade of a large mango tree. Several young nuns darted about them, unwrapping the shrouds, tapping the holy jewels in their heads. He sincerely hoped he would not have to summon Sister Ulla out of her drunken stupor to advise them, because palace nuns were selected solely for their slow wit and preference for riches over righteousness; if they bungled aiding Jethar, Boleo would not be able to keep the matter secret.

But his fears proved unnecessary . . . by the time Boleo reached his side, Jethar had already coughed twice, and the second man was attempting to lift a hand. These men, who had lain shrouded for moons, were rising of their own will.

'Cantec?' came a woman's cry: Captain Elari, an Itahua warrior of some renown, and Cantec's wife, if Boleo recalled correctly. She knelt at his side, her feathered skirt fanning out around her. Though her long black braid was shot with white, she looked supple as a woman half her age. She reached for Cantec gingerly, as though fearing her touch might shatter him.

Cantec's mouth worked. He lifted a hand, pointing towards the carriage. 'It's—' His voice cracked, ragged with disuse. His dark gaze swung round. 'Elari . . . it's—'

Invoker Jemusi's cry cut across whatever Cantec strove to say. Jethar Mizito was standing and pulling off the remains of his death shroud. His long black hair and beard were matted and caked with dirt. The brown skin of his arms bristled with hideous scars, where once his clan tataus had been. He took in the orchard, eyes wild and desperate, while Jemusi stood blinking at him in disbelief. Boleo could see at once that the man was disoriented. Disoriented, and not quite sane.

'They are coming!' Jethar rasped. 'They will destroy you all!'

'Jeth, it's me! Jemusi!' She turned desperately to the nuns. 'Help him – he's delirious!'

As Jemusi spoke, Cantec Itahua lifted shakily to his feet. He pushed past his wife Elari, turned towards Jethar, and leapt.

Jemusi fell back as the two skeletal men crashed to the ground. Boleo stared in disbelief at these warriors who should have been dead. Cantec fought to seize Jethar by the neck while Jethar babbled incoherently.

179

Captain Elari lurched forward, reaching for her husband before being knocked sideways as the two men rolled into her.

'Brother, stop this!' Kartuuk Itahua said, dancing out of Cantec's path, bewilderment creasing his smooth brow.

'Can't you do something?' Jemusi wailed at the two nuns, who stood staring in shock.

Boleo strode forward, staff extended. These men who had once been friends fought like street beggars, like animals – clawing, biting, scratching. These warriors who had once commanded armies, who were masters with sword and fist, were reduced to scrapping and snarling under the hot sun.

Boleo had nearly reached them when Jethar twisted round and seized the knife hanging at Jemusi's belt. She cried out, but her brother was already moving, lifting his hand as he threw himself at Cantec.

'*Stop!*' Jemusi screamed, grabbing Jethar's free arm, but the blade came arcing down. Metal slid into the side of Cantec's neck and he reeled backwards, blood spurting. Jethar stood back, watching dispassionately as Cantec Itahua clutched at his neck, trying to stem the flow. But there was too much blood. Boleo could only watch, powerless, as Cantec toppled forward into Elari's arms. She cried out, falling with him to the ground, pressing desperately at his neck as the blood spread over them both. Cantec's eyes sought Elari's, lips moving – speaking, Boleo realised. Passing on some final message as the light in his eyes began to fade.

Jethar Mizito backed away from them all, a terrible, triumphant grin spread across his sunken face. He twisted the blade still gripped in his hand and in one devastating motion, buried the weapon in his own chest.

Jemusi screamed and leapt towards her brother, but the moment her hand touched his body, Boleo saw a crackle of energy and she collapsed to the ground.

'Nobody touch him!' Boleo cried, holding his staff high, pushing down the swell of panic rising within him. He'd had everything under control! Everything had been perfectly ordered! The Itahuas and the Mizitos were to take whoever they found within for burning. Boleo was to study the techwork. And nobody was to speak of the matter again. Yet now, as Captain Elari began to scream, everything was falling apart. A small voice within him, a voice he was certain he'd silenced long ago, whispered that this was what happened to those who betrayed the Holy Orders.

Kartuuk Itahua drew his weapon – a macuahuitl, the dozens of obsidian edges on the imposing club catching the morning light.

'Stand aside,' he said coolly.

In response, Jemusi's quartet fanned out around her and the fallen body of Jethar. More Itahuas joined Kartuuk, among them his quartet and three warriors in matching blue tunics. They outnumbered the Mizitos by two to one.

'Stop this!' Boleo cried, striding between them. Beyond, Morayo was signalling to his own warriors to spread out.

'Is he dead?' Kartuuk said, only the slightest hint of strain in his soft voice. He pointed with his macuahuitl. 'Is Jethar Mizito dead?'

'Do not touch him!' Boleo cried as one of the nuns motioned to check. 'You saw what happened to Invoker Jemusi. Sister Ogonu, is she alive?'

The nun crawled over to where Jemusi lay and tentatively touched her neck. 'Invoker Jemusi appears to be unconscious, Father.'

Boleo turned back to the two parties. 'I suggest everyone return to their lodgings—'

'We're not leaving them!' cried the captain of Jemusi's quartet, a stocky, blunt-faced man named Phan.

'I would like you all to calm down,' Boleo said. 'Put away your—'

'Is Jethar alive?' Captain Elari growled, looking up from her husband's corpse. Fury etched every line of her face. Blood coated her tunic and arms, obliterating the warpaint and the family tataus. She turned to Morayo, who stood silently with his line of warriors. 'Invoker Morayo, if Jethar Mizito lives, your people will hand him over for justice—'

'Only a nun may dispense justice,' Boleo cut in. Ancestors, but he was going to have to summon Sister Ulla after all.

'Is Jethar alive?' Elari repeated, standing. Blood dripped from the feathers of her skirt. Behind her, Cantec stared glassily at the tops of the mango trees, the grass all around him dark with his blood. The wound at his neck flapped obscenely. Boleo felt a stab of pity. To come all this way . . . to survive and bring back such marvels as Boleo had glimpsed within the carriage, only to be struck down by his friend at the moment of his return; it was a tragedy indeed.

An Itahua lieutenant placed a hand on Captain Elari's shoulder, but she shook them off angrily and strode towards Jethar. Jemusi's blunt-faced Captain Phan moved to block her, but Boleo said, 'Let her through.'

The captain glared at Boleo but made no move to stop Elari as she strode past, then squatted beside her husband's killer and friend. She extended a hand towards the knife still buried in Jethar's chest. Ancestors – such a wound should have killed him instantly, but Boleo glimpsed movement beneath the man's lids.

Elari had scarcely made contact with the hilt before Boleo saw the spark of energy again, and then she too crumpled to the lawn beside Jethar.

'Does anyone else wish to try?' Boleo cried, lifting his voice and turning in a slow circle. 'Shall we continue until I am the only person left awake in this orchard?'

Someone snorted with laughter. Atoc Itahua sat slumped under a tree, two of Morayo's wine jugs at his side. The man observed the scene through bloodshot eyes, as though it were a play he watched, and not the death of his eldest brother.

Boleo wet his lips. 'My Lord Morayo, would you be so kind as to escort our guests and their . . . sleeping kin back to their lodgings?'

He turned his back on the Itahuas and strode past Jemusi's quartet. How could Jethar still be alive? He looked down at the man's body while, behind him, he heard Morayo speaking to their guests, offering careful measures of sympathy and reassurance. If anyone could calm restive hearts, it was Morayo Adatali.

No blood lay around the knife in Jethar's chest, and only the faintest tinge of pink marked the surrounding skin. And was it Boleo's imagination, or was the blade less deeply settled than it had been? He had been sure the thing was buried to the hilt, but now he noticed a glint of clean blade as thick as two fingers. Tentatively, he reached out with his staff and poked Jethar's leg.

'What are you doing?' Captain Phan said.

'Quiet,' Boleo snapped. He lifted his staff higher, then brought it down with more force. This time, Boleo felt the cushioning energies that were surely protecting Jethar's body, much as there had been strange energies protecting his carriage not long before. So, some force was guarding him. Curious indeed.

Boleo held his staff over Jethar. '*Observe*,' he commanded in the Forbidden Tongue.

The familiar yellow light of observation bled out of his staff and ran along Jethar's body in a slow sweep. Behind him, someone muttered soft words to the ancestors.

His staff was just completing its work when a strange coil of silvery light surged out of Jethar's chest. Boleo did not have time to react before it seized his staff and tried to tug it from his grip. Boleo looked down.

A hand.

Boleo pulled back, clamping both hands around his staff. Behind the hand came a slender arm, then a second hand, as though an entire being was preparing to climb from beneath Jethar's skin. Could it be Mizito? No . . . how could a Bonded ancestor ever climb from an invoker's unconscious body? But if it wasn't Jethar's ancestor . . .

Boleo gave one final jerk then wrenched his staff free. At once the arms collapsed back into Jethar, leaving Boleo breathing heavily on the grass where he had fallen.

SEVENTEEN

Elari

Captain Elari dressed for war on the morning she would kill her husband's friend.

While the rest of the Clan Itahua company slept, Elari descended the steps into the courtyard of the townhouse the Adatalis had set aside for them. It was a fine estate on the very outskirts of Ewo City, high in the hills overlooking the lagoon. Four storeys of pale sandstone rose around her, the balconies dripping with blue and black flowers. But no matter how prettily Invoker Morayo Adatali spoke, nor how many luxuries his people lavished upon them, he could not make up for what they had taken. Her husband Cantec was dead. His murderer slept on, under their protection. Elari had no choice but to deliver justice herself. And yet now she prepared to do the deed, she felt the first creeping tendrils of doubt.

It had been a full day since whatever foul power Jethar possessed had put her to sleep in the Adatali orchard. A full day since Cantec's last whispered words. And what words they were. No declarations of love. No promises to see her again in the ancestral realm. No, instead, he had given her his last ever command.

It's in the carriage. Find it.

Elari paused beside the statue of Invoker Belu Adatali, looming over a small fountain that glimmered in the pale dawn light. The household shrine stood at its feet, and so Elari knelt before it, the feathers of her battle skirt folding beneath her knees. It seemed an eternity since she had last presented herself to the ancestors – the day the monks had told her Cantec would likely never return. But she knelt before them now, removing a single feather from her headdress, followed by the jade ring Cantec had given her on the day of their betrothal. All her life, Elari had done what was expected of her. Every command she had ever been given, she had followed unquestioningly. But the ancestors had shown how they rewarded those who followed the paths they laid out.

Elari rose and crossed to the casket on its stand at the centre of the courtyard. A sea of flowers surrounded it in a protective ring . . . As though their beauty could ward off the ugliness of what had happened.

Cantec had aged greatly in the five rains he'd been missing. The thin dawn light could not disguise the new scars that spoiled his face. Ancestors, what had he suffered out there beyond the Nine Lands? And what could have happened to Jethar to cause him to turn on his friend? Jethar and Cantec had been like brothers since their days fighting on the Feverlands border, the only two invokers on a long campaign. They had been future First Generals who shared a fascination with history and a determination to end the greyblood war. But they had returned to her as empty shells.

A cry from outside cut across her thoughts: guards shouting, followed by the clang of the household gong. Elari turned in time to see the main gate swing open. A trio of household guards burst inside, their faces tight with alarm. And small wonder: behind them came a monk with a dozen noviciates in tow.

'Search the premises,' the monk said, pointing her staff at the balconies. 'Every room, if you please.'

Elari saw at once that this was no ordinary clan monk: she wore the looping golden robes of the Garden. Her noviciates, too, wore gold tunics as they swarmed over the building, heading through doors and into quarters while the servants looked on impotently.

Finally, the monk's eyes came to rest on Elari and the casket she stood beside.

'I am Father Emata,' the monk said as she advanced. 'Keeper of Truths and Holy Servant of the Royal Clan and His Golden Majesty. Who are you, child?'

'Elari,' she said. 'Captain of Cantec Itahua's quartet.'

Father Emata came to a stop beside Cantec, her gaze sliding down his body, taking in his clan tataus. 'Well, this is quite the surprise,' she said, eyes gleaming. 'Invoker Cantec Itahua, supposedly lost at sea.'

Why had Elari's throat grown so tight? She had nothing to fear. It was not her clan that had been withholding Forbidden relics. That old monk, Father Boleo, had warned them questions might be asked. She'd never dreamed the questions might come from his own holy brothers.

'His body washed ashore near here,' Elari said, keeping her voice steady. 'We came to bring it home, so that he might return to the ancestors.'

The monk smiled as she studied the corpse in a way that made Elari's skin prickle with discomfort. Emata was a tall, broad woman, with a shock of short white hair in a fleshy light brown face. The yellow jewel in the heart of her holy staff hummed, studying Cantec too. Elari's chest tightened at that. The last time she had stood so close to a royal monk had been out in the Feverlands, during the—

Who will you sacrifice, Captain?

The hot spray of blood.

The screams of the dying.

Elari closed her eyes against the memory.

'Washed ashore,' Father Emata said, 'and yet so beautifully preserved! Why, that wound in his neck looks fresh! It is almost as though he left us yesterday!'

Elari heard footsteps on the stair behind her and looked around to see her three doves – her lieutenants, really, but she had always called them her doves. They wore identical white sleeping tunics: Lieutenant Chellahua, fair of skin and hair, in the way of the north; Lieutenant Osellia, willowy and dark, her braided hair falling to her waist; and

Ishaan, their raven hair cut short, their small frame belying their fury on the battlefield.

'We wondered where you'd gone?' Ishaan said, giving Elari a pointed look.

'Ah, you must be the rest of Invoker Cantec's quartet,' Emata said. 'Although in truth, you are a quartet without an invoker, are you not?'

Elari watched a vein pulsing in the monk's neck. A sharp blow, just there, and she would crumple like a felled tree. Anyone could see the woman was no fighter. Elari could hit her before any of her aides heard. She could squeeze the life from—

'So tell me, Captain Elari, how did your husband's body come to be found here in the south, and as fresh as newly fallen snow?'

'He was . . . preserved—'

'In a shroud,' Ishaan cut in. 'The shroud preserved him.'

Emata's pale gaze swung round to Ishaan. 'A shroud. It must have been a unique shroud indeed to have achieved . . . this. There is no bloating from the waters. No wounds from curious fish. It is almost as though the method of preservation were . . . unnatural.' She inhaled slowly. 'It is a perversion, you know, to withhold techwork from the Holy Orders. Techwork is corrupting. Dangerous. And by law, it must be surrendered to us.'

It's in the carriage. Find it.

'There is no techwork here,' Elari said.

'Why did the Adatalis not simply send you this . . . perfectly preserved corpse? After all, have you not been commanded back home to prepare for the assault on the Feverlands?'

The hot spray of blood.

The screams of the dying.

Elari closed her eyes against the familiar swell of disorientation. But though she tightened her jaw and began to recite the Song of Legends Lost in her head, the courtyard receded, the voices receded, as the need to run, to flee, swept over her. The crash of weapons filled her mind, the mud, the darkness, the swirling chaos.

187

The Bairneater, its grey skin gleaming in the moonlight as it told her to choose.

Who will you sacrifice, Captain?

The eyes of the captives upon her, pleading, imploring.

Cantec in the distance, unconscious, beyond her reach.

Who will you sacrifice, Captain? Choose who lives and who dies.

'Captain!'

Elari jerked, crashing back into herself as Ishaan squeezed her hand. She swung her gaze around the courtyard – in chaos now, as her people rose from their sleeping mats and monks flung open every door. She was here, in Adataliland, far from the Feverlands border. And the Bairneater was in the west, being hunted by Jethar's brothers.

Emata peered at her, her small mouth pulled up in a tiny derisory smile.

'What else did the Adatalis show you?' Father Emata said. 'What else washed ashore with Cantec?'

'Nothing,' Elari said. 'We came because—'

'You mean to tell me Invoker Cantec Itahua's body washed ashore after five rains, perfectly preserved in this miraculous shroud, and that you travelled all this way to see it.'

'Yes.' Elari turned to Ishaan, gripping them with both hands now. 'I need to sit down.'

'Not yet. How did Cantec receive that neck wound?'

'I do not know!'

'The wound is fresh!'

'Cantec died at sea!'

'Who killed him, Captain Elari? Who killed Cantec? Was it Father Boleo?'

'No!'

'Where is the techwork carriage, Captain Elari? Where are the Adatalis hiding it? It is a perversion to lie to a holy one, a sin against your clan, your ancestors, against the memory of your husband! You would betray—'

Elari wrenched herself free of Ishaan and sprang, knocking Emata back, landing astride her. She could hear her doves shouting, could feel their hands trying to pull her loose, but just then her head throbbed, as though too much blood filled her body, and Emata's neck, so soft, called to her, called to her . . .

Choose who lives and who dies.

'Do you know what happens,' Emata whispered, making no effort to free herself, 'when a royal monk comes to harm?' Elari saw no fear at all in the other woman's eyes. Only utter calm, utter certainty. 'A warrior monk visits,' Emata continued. 'If I do not make regular reports, a warrior monk will visit. Do you know what gifts a warrior monk has? They can peer into your mind, Captain Elari. They can peel back the layers of deceit to see who you truly are. I wonder what they will find when they peer within you?'

Who will you sacrifice, Captain? Choose who lives and who dies.

And for a moment, Elari did not see a large monk of middling years. Instead, she saw a monstrous greyblood, tall as two men, its wide mouth grinning as it pointed at the captives and then at Cantec and told her to choose, choose. She heard their screams. She felt the hot spray of blood as her macuahuitl fell and fell and fell.

Elari collapsed backwards, her skin ablaze with that familiar fear, that familiar loathing.

'Captain,' Ishaan murmured, pulling Elari to her feet.

Father Emata was on her feet again too. She rubbed at her shoulder as she watched Elari warily. 'We will be taking Invoker Cantec Itahua's body with us for Cleansing,' she said. 'He has been preserved by unholy means. It is not safe for you to be around this corpse.' She signalled to two of her noviciates just emerging from the kitchens. 'Some cloth for the corpse, please! Any cloth will do!'

A slow, simmering rage rose within Elari. What had she done in her life to deserve such cruelty? The ancestors must truly hate her to have visited so much upon her. To deliver Cantec back to her, alive, and then rip him away again. And now, to deny her the chance to send him beyond the pyre. She gripped Ishaan's hand, not trusting herself with any other movement, not when her body yearned to crush the life from this woman.

'Please,' Elari said. 'He . . . he must be allowed to return to the ancestors. If we cannot light the pyre—'

'You may petition the Garden for the release of this cadaver,' Emata said. 'I believe they respond to most cases within a mere eight moons – seven, if you are lucky. You may also petition the Garden for leniency following your attack on a monk of the Holy Orders.'

Emata's eyes shifted to the others who had entered the courtyard – Cantec's reserved brother Kartuuk, still in his sleeping tunic; his drunken middle brother Atoc, blinking in confusion, his long black hair obscuring half his face; his youngest sibling Rozichu, her eyes watery and wide. 'We seek to understand the mystery of Cantec's survival!' Emata said, addressing the entire courtyard now. 'Of course, if there was something *else* to study that might explain how he came to you like this – a techwork carriage, perhaps – then we would have no need of this . . . corpse.'

It's in the carriage. Find it.

It would be so easy just to say it. Just to tell the monk that the carriage lay in the palace mango orchard. Imagine the wrath of the Garden then, once they discovered all that the Adatalis had been withholding? She hated the way Father Boleo had used them. She hated what Jethar had done, and she hated all those who sought to protect him. But Cantec had died to bring the contents of the carriage back to the Nine Lands. She would not betray that. She could find a way to retrieve his body later.

'There is no carriage,' Elari said stiffly. 'Now please let me—'

'The techwork carriage is in the palace orchard,' Atoc called across from where he leaned against a pillar.

'No!' Elari cried, whirling. They were all looking at Atoc now, even implacable Kartuuk, his jaw flexing.

'We were all sworn to secrecy,' Atoc continued nonchalantly. 'The bloody thing wouldn't open without our assistance, so that's why—'

'Atoc, stop!' Elari cried.

'We were tricked into coming here by that sinister old monk. My brother's preserved body lay beside Jethar Mizito. They both woke up, then Jethar slit my brother's throat in a manic rage.' He looked across at them and shrugged. 'What? She was going to find out, and I for one do not wish to be punished for something in which we had no say.'

Rage bubbled up within Elari. Atoc lifted his wine glass, but Elari saw a tension behind his eyes. Could it be he feared for his brother's spirit? No. No, it was just another example of Atoc's selfishness, and she had had her fill with that . . .

'Captain, don't,' Ishaan whispered softly, their hand closing on Elari's wrist.

'Thank you, Invoker Atoc,' Father Emata said, inclining her head. She scarcely smiled, but her eyes blazed with triumph. 'Thank you for continuing to protect the realm. I would recommend that your clan not be found in Ewo City when I make my . . . troubling discovery.'

'Cantec wanted me to protect it,' Elari whispered, reaching for Ishaan.

'Not like this,' Ishaan said. 'Not if it meant keeping him from his ancestors.'

Elari watched, utterly powerless, as Father Emata strode towards the outer gate, signalling for her novitiates to follow. Elari's pulse sounded in her ears again, pounding, pounding. The Bairneater seemed to grin at her from every shadow. It had got worse since the day of Sulin Mizito's fall. Worse than it had been in many moons. But Chellahua's hand brushed her right arm and Ishaan steered her towards the stairs, and so she let them lead her away while behind her Atoc and Kartuuk began to argue.

Back in their sleeping chamber, dawn crawling grey over the pale walls, Ishaan took both Elari's hands in theirs.

'Cantec was not himself,' they said. 'When he spoke to you—'

'There is something in that carriage,' Elari said. 'S-something important. He didn't ask me to tell his father, or the holy ones. He asked me to find it. Me.'

'He wouldn't want you to lie to a monk,' Chellahua said, dropping down onto the wide sleeping mat they all shared. 'I know Cantec was interested in techwork, but—'

'He brought something back. Maybe – maybe their quest didn't fail! Maybe they found a weapon! Cantec told me that the symbol on the map they followed, the word *vunaji*, means a gathering of spirits. Imagine that! Perhaps they received ancestral blessings that could—'

A noise from beyond their bathing-chamber door stopped her short. In a heartbeat, Ishaan had crossed the room and flung the door wide, allowing Chellahua to leap inside. Elari's pale-haired dove was on the stranger in a heartbeat, dragging her out, obsidian dagger pressed to her neck.

Elari peered at the stranger. Most of the household servants had the dark brown skin and tightly curled hair common in Adataliland, but this one could have come from a dozen places across the Nine Lands. She was of middling years, with a round, homely face and kind eyes that shone a striking tawny yellow in the mid brown of her skin. Her dark, gently curling hair was clipped short. But most striking of all was the smoothness of her arms; Elari saw no tataus of family or identity at all. The stranger was as unmarked as a child.

'My doves are a bloodthirsty three,' Elari told her, 'and it is a long time since their blades have claimed a human life. Tell me why I shouldn't I indulge them?'

'Forgive me, Captain Elari,' the servant said, in the flat accent of Nine Lords. 'I . . . I was not spying, and I swear I heard nothing! Nothing at all! I just wanted to speak with you!'

Osellia stepped forward. 'By hiding behind doors? Let me take an ear, Captain. That will teach her not to listen.'

'I – I want to help you!'

'Help me to do what?' Elari said.

'Help you with Lord Cantec's carriage.' The servant wet her lips and looked between them all. 'I know how to help.'

192

Elari sighed and looked across at Ishaan. 'Lieutenant, who should get the honour of this kill? Osellia or Chellahua? I simply can't choose.'

'Wait!' the servant cried, awkwardly lifting one hand. 'I mean it. I can get you the contents of the carriage! I can get them all for you tonight, before the monk takes them. I can make it so that she doesn't even know.'

Chellahua snorted back a laugh. 'You?'

Elari held up a hand. 'What do you mean?'

'I can use . . . arcane distractions. Techniques to make her think the techwork is still there.'

Elari studied the woman. Despite the green tunic, she was no servant, that much was plain. She looked as unremarkable as a lowblood, which was exactly the sort of forgettable person who made the perfect tech-doctor. What she spoke of – taking techwork from a royal monk, using arcane distractions – that was dangerous talk indeed.

Who will you sacrifice, Captain?

As the shouts of the battlefield closed in around her, Elari focused on the vein pulsing in the woman's temple. 'And will you protect me from the corrupting energies of the techwork? From the greybloods it will summon?'

'I – I know a way to make it safe. Your husband was a scholar, Captain Elari, I know he was. I know neither of you feared the Forbidden ways.'

Elari's hand curled into a fist as she remembered how many hours Cantec had spent poring over rare books and scrolls. She remembered the first time she had come upon him studying a piece of techwork. The thing had been splayed open, its veins and plates naked to the world as he picked at its innards like a crow over a corpse.

Elari, he had said. *I . . . I am sorry.*

He had covered the techwork and stood abruptly, all awkward embarrassment. But Elari had found that she had no desire to turn away, or to run to the palace monks, or even to make the sign for ancestral protection. Instead, she'd felt only a delicious, burning curiosity.

What does it do? Elari had asked, joining him.

The childlike joy that spread across Cantec's face at her words was as glorious as the sunrise. *I think it makes music, Elari! Music from a lost age!*

'Who are you working for?' Elari asked the stranger, bringing herself back into the present. 'Speak quickly.'

'I'm working for no one!'

Chellahua snarled and pressed her obsidian blade harder against the woman's throat. A single trickle of blood snaked down her fleshy neck.

'Truly!' the servant said. 'I . . . I was a monk, once. I was expelled and . . . and now I collect and study techwork.'

'You are a techdoctor.'

'If you wish to call me that. I am a scholar, like you, like Cantec! Please . . . release me, and I'll get the techwork for you.'

'And what is it you expect in return?'

'Nothing . . . except . . . passage with you. I have enemies here too. I wish only to begin a new life. Please, Captain! I could have taken all the techwork for myself, but—'

'You will not touch Cantec's things,' Elari said, stepping forward. 'Do you hear me?'

'Of course, of course! I wouldn't dream of it! I have no use for techwork now : . . . it has brought me much heartache. But I wanted to help you because . . . because I owe you and Cantec my life.'

'Your life,' Osellia said flatly.

Elari touched her dove's arm. 'What do you mean?'

'You are Captain Elari, the Black Fury. Y-you and Cantec once fought the Frost Maid out in the mountains of Tjard. I . . . I was among the people you freed that day.'

Tjard. She had almost forgotten. She supposed she had done some good, in among so many, many mistakes. 'And do you plan to just walk in and out of the palace of Three Towers, carrying armfuls of Scathed artefacts? Father Emata is already on her way there, and the palace is heavily guarded.'

'It will take Emata time to break through Father Boleo's protections. I can . . . get to the carriage first, using the hidden passages.'

Elari studied the stranger, taking in the roundness of her arms, the curve of her belly. She did not look to be made for stealth. But Elari saw the position of the woman's leg – she was ready to throw Chellahua, should she need to. She saw the way her eyes darted from one face to the next, gauging distances. This was a soul who knew how to fight.

'Very well,' Elari said. 'I'll release you. Bring us the techwork and I will grant you passage to Intiqq. I suspect we will be leaving rather soon after all that has happened. But if you betray me, or if you attempt to take even a single artefact for yourself, my doves here will find you, and your death will not be swift.'

'Captain, no!' Chellahua cried, still holding the stranger.

'Let her go,' Elari said. 'This may be my only way to fulfil Cantec's last instruction.'

Chellahua sighed and shoved the woman roughly away. Elari did not miss how her balance never wavered.

'May I have your name?' Elari said. 'Since you know ours.'

'Lyela,' the woman said. 'I am Lyela of . . . of Lordsheart.'

'Lyela of Lordsheart,' Elari said. 'We shall speak again.'

They watched the woman cross to the door and slip out.

Osellia said, 'How can an old homemaker like that break into Three Towers and through the protections of a senior monk?'

'I do not know,' Elari said. 'But the ancestors turn from those who scorn the gifts they offer.'

'If she betrays us,' Chellahua said, fingering her blade, 'I will flay the skin from her face.'

'Delightful as always, Chell,' Ishaan said.

Chellahua curtseyed daintily and flicked her knife into its hiding place.

EIGHTEEN

Boleo

Warlord Daloya Adatali, Scourge of the Feverlands, Slayer of the Brethren and the Sand Dancer, the greatest warlord of his age, lifted the spoon with a shaking hand as drool slipped from the corner of his mouth. His lips puckered to meet the implement . . . though not on the left. That side of him had not moved since the Battle of Maadu, when he had taken a grievous blow to the head, dealt by the Blight itself. It was a wonder that he'd lived at all. But he had always been blessed by the ancestors.

Boleo knelt on the stone floor of the Three Towers circleroom, before the gently flickering fire of the Circle. Around him sat the innermost members of the Warlord Daloya's household: his siblings, their children, his senior advisers. They watched him hungrily, drinking in every word he spoke, their bright geles and agbadas belying the fire behind their eyes. These were souls who had not forgotten the slaughter at Maadu. These were souls who had dedicated their lives to Daloya and his great work.

Daloya's wife, Captain Omadella, sat at the warlord's side. She leaned over to dab at his chin with a cloth. She was a painted, ornamental thing. Her green gele gleamed with emeralds. Her slenderness lent her frame a delicate air, but Boleo knew better than to underestimate the leader of Warlord Daloya's quartet, and the mouthpiece of all his plans.

'He wishes you to continue,' Omadella said, without looking round.

'I saw no weapons at all,' Boleo told them. 'But I am now certain that the rows of squares were used by the Scathed to communicate. Many of the other techwork artefacts were likely used for entertainment; blackglass that shows pictures, devices that can recreate music . . .'

Beyond the high pillars of the circleroom, the rain pounded down ceaselessly. No walls divided them from the colourful bushes of the palace gardens, but it was treason for the uninvited to approach while the Circle was in progress.

'Then there is no great weapon,' Omadella said. 'Nor any gateway to the ancestral realm. Despite all their work and all they clearly suffered, Lord Jethar's voyage yielded nothing. And all we have to end the war with is . . . music and colourful pictures.'

Daloya gave no sign that he understood any of their words, and for a moment, the only sound in the room was the loud slurp he made as he sipped his chilli and okra stew. How like an infant he looked, propped up by a nest of cushions, his dark eyes roving here and there. How far from the towering, vibrant warrior Boleo had spent a lifetime serving.

'What of Jethar?' Omadella said, dabbing at her husband's chin again with one slender hand.

'He remains in the mango gardens. Sister Ulla tells me he is stable. The knife that was buried in his chest was ejected, and after examination, appears to be nothing extraordinary. A simple steel blade. The wound itself has left no scar. But we cannot touch him or move him. I even had the gardeners try to dig below his sleeping body to see if we can lift the ground he rests upon, but it appears the energies that protect him extend in a column from the sky to beneath the earth. And he remains asleep.'

Omadella stirred. 'My husband would like to know what you have determined about the hand you glimpsed within Jethar. You are still certain it was not Mizito?'

'I have read reports of warriors prone to talk during sleep accidentally invoking their ancestors,' Boleo told them all. 'But they are few in number, and never while in the deep sleep of unconsciousness. The hand I saw . . . was not Mizito's hand. I am not certain what it was. And I have gleaned little from my . . . investigations into that. There is a stillness within him; a spiritual silence. I cannot penetrate it.'

It was a pretty way to say his staff could not read anything from Jethar. But then, Omadella did so like pretty things. She lowered the napkin and looked across at Boleo for the first time. 'Any day, the king will begin his invasion of the Feverlands. Tens of thousands will die. Every soul in the Nine Lands knows that this plan is doomed. The greybloods cannot be defeated by our people hurling ourselves against them, and we cannot fight on ground that is poisonous to life. Meanwhile, the mouth of the Ae lies unprotected, leaving every province in the realm in danger. My husband believes protecting the river is the most important use of our resources.'

'Captain, we do not have the numbers to rebuild Aranduq. Not with so many of our warriors being sent west.'

Omadella gave an enigmatic little smile that made Boleo's palms itch. 'Father, what do you know of the Busharn Massacre?'

Boleo looked at the faces that surrounded him in the Circle. How many of them knew Daloya's full plans? How many of them had been brought entirely into Daloya's trust? After all his decades of service, after all that they had achieved together, Boleo had never truly been shown it all. He knew it was because of what he was – a monk and, ultimately, a tool of the king. Kneeling there now, Boleo felt the great weight of the knowledge they possessed and he lacked, and it twisted at his gut.

'I don't remember all the details,' Boleo said. 'Something about a solider who killed her entire company over a map? It is the map Jethar and Cantec followed. Perhaps that is why their voyage failed. The history of that map is cursed.'

Omadella sighed wearily. 'Seven rains ago, Chinnaro Itahua led an expedition into the Busharn wastes, searching for ruins among the lands of the fallen Clan Kzani. Moons later, a single survivor stepped out of those wastes, dragging the severed heads of the rest of the party behind her, as well as a map for Chinnaro's brother, Cantec. It is a sad tale. The soldier admitted to massacring her entire party in a fit of madness. But she found it within her to honour her invoker's dying wish and hand over the map they found.'

Omadella gestured, and one of Daloya's nephews strode forward holding a scroll, which he placed at Boleo's side with a bow.

It was Chinnaro Itahua's map. Certainly not the original, but the thing had been copied many times prior to Cantec and Jethar's departure. Boleo recognised it instantly from how unfathomable it was. No units of measure, no placenames, no landmarks of any kind save for one. Simply a series of broad strokes that resembled the Nine Lands, with an ancient symbol over what appeared to be an island far to the north. *Vunaji*, a word translated from an old Kzaniland language as *gathering of spirits*. It was what Jethar and Cantec had wagered their lives on. Wagered, and lost. How sad for the Itahuas that first the aunt and then the nephew should die because of its existence.

'The land of Vunaji does not exist,' Boleo said. 'Either that, or Jethar and Cantec failed to find it.'

'Vunaji most certainly does exist,' Omadella said. 'It is simply that Jethar and Cantec were not equipped to find it. We would have you return to the ruins to investigate.' She leaned forwards. 'A gathering of spirits, Father. Do you know why Chinnaro, why Cantec, dedicated their lives to this? They believed this pointed to a way to strengthen the ancestral Bond. Now, more than ever, we need strength, Father. We need strength if we are to help our friends in Aranduq reclaim their city. We need strength if we are to survive this accursed war.'

They were sending him away again. Now, when the Garden was breathing down their necks and they had an unknown entity residing within their walls. Perhaps the map was cursed. Perhaps all those associated with it were doomed to die. Perhaps that was why Omadella wanted him to have it.

'You are planning a second expedition to find the gathering of spirits?' Boleo shook his head. 'It will take many moons to explore the Busharn wastes thoroughly, then many more to organise a second voyage. If these Clan Kzani ruins—'

'We must have faith that the ancestors will provide.'

Boleo swallowed the curse that made its way onto his lips. He watched her face as she balled pounded yam between her fingers and offered it to her husband.

'What are you omitting?' Boleo asked softly.

'As my husband has told you many times over the years, the less you know, the better.'

'Surely I have proven already that you can trust me? The more I know, the more *effective* I can be. My hands are tied when you do not provide me with all the information.'

'It is not a matter of trust, Father Boleo. It is a matter of safety. It would not be safe for you to know everything. It would not be safe for any of us.' She offered him another simpering smile. 'Find Chinnaro's ruins. Learn how Jethar and Cantec went wrong.'

Ah, and here was the truth of it! He was indeed being banished. Disposed of, via an impossible task that would keep him busy for moons. Clan Adatali could then distance itself from him. After all he had given them. After all the lies he had told, the rules he had broken, the lives he had taken. He knew Omadella, a woman half his age, resented the history he and Daloya had together. With Father Emata in the palace, scrutiny would be placed on Clan Adatali such as they had not endured in decades. Omadella meant to rid herself of Boleo and, in his absence, blame him for anything the Keeper of Truths found.

'You will not sweep me aside like dust from a crumbling book,' Boleo said softly.

Omadella had the insolence to actually laugh at that. 'Father, you are not being swept aside! Far from it. You are being entrusted with our most important task, brought forward because of circumstances.'

Omadella sighed. 'Besides, we both know Father Emata will take you back to the Garden when she leaves. She will bring you before the Holy Circle or perhaps even the king. If you stay, you are doomed. If you go, you will be helping us with the greatest task we have undertaken yet, one that could avert thousands of deaths.'

Warlord Daloya caught his wife's wrist by one of her jade bangles, his eyes boring into hers. Omadella looked round at Boleo and said, 'My husband asks you to have faith. He says . . . he loves you, as he always has, and that he knows he can rely on you in all things. He says that his work is so very, very near to fruition, and that this is the final, vital stage.'

Boleo lifted his gaze and saw that Daloya still had hold of his wife. But now, his dark, rheumy eyes studied Boleo. The slant of his mouth gave the impression of distaste, though Boleo knew this was only because he had so little control of that side of his body. Boleo's jaw tightened. Omadella was right about one thing: Father Emata would not leave until she had found proof of Boleo's misdeeds. Therefore, what did it matter if the task Boleo had been given was simply a diversion? His days at Three Towers were numbered either way.

'I will need to study the reports of the massacre,' Boleo said, sighing, 'if I am to stand any hope of finding this place.'

'That won't be necessary. We have arranged for a guide. Someone who has been there before.'

'A guide? Captain, the only person alive who has been there before is—'

'The Butcher of Busharn herself. Yes, Father. She is to be your guide.'

Boleo snorted. From what he knew of the butcher, the woman was a lunatic. A senior soldier who had turned on her entire company and her invoker, and slaughtered them all in a fit of bloodlust. Last he had heard, she was rotting in the oubliettes of the White Isle. The only reason she hadn't been executed was because the clans had called for her to suffer.

Boleo heard a stirring at the Circle and caught sight of an unfamiliar face: a man, with the look of Cagai about him, wearing a collection of techwork crystals about his neck. He and Omadella exchanged glances.

'Everything has been prepared,' Omadella said. 'The Butcher is being brought here as we speak. We have arranged for her . . . *death* so that no suspicion arises. You will leave at first light, with a party of my husband's own Batide warriors.'

'I shall accompany him!' Morayo announced, standing in his spot to Omadella's left.

'No!' Boleo said. Too fast. He cursed inwardly. He should have known Morayo would jump at the chance of going on such a mission: he courted controversy and danger, had been Boleo's shadow since his childhood. Boleo gritted his teeth. 'Invoker, your presence is surely needed here, particularly given the king's draft.'

'My husband thinks this is an excellent idea,' Omadella said. 'Morayo will accompany you.'

Of course Omadella would want Morayo gone. She leapt at any opportunity to have him out from beneath her bejewelled sandals. Of all the family, Morayo was the only one who challenged her, who questioned her when she spoke for Daloya. Likely she would send nightblade assassins after them and be rid of her husband's youngest child for good. Perhaps *this* was what it was all about . . . Omadella was ridding herself of sceptics so that she could continue to enjoy all the luxuries and power of being a warlord's wife. All this talk of protecting the Ae and evading Father Emata were mere excuses. Boleo bit down on another curse and painted on a beatific smile. If Omadella wanted whatever lay in those ruins, then he would give it to her. He would give it to her, and when he returned, he would deal with both her and Father Emata.

'Then I accept, Captain Omadella,' Boleo said, bowing to the floor. 'I live only to serve Clan Adatali and its ancestors.'

When Boleo returned to his chamber to pack, he opened his door to find a man blocking his path.

'All right, Father?' the man said, grinning.

'Zadenu,' Boleo said. 'How did you get into my chambers?'

'I have me methods,' Zadenu said. He was a small man, lean as a whip, with a shark-like jut to his forehead. Gold studded his broad grin. Boleo had never worked out Zadenu's age – past fifty, certainly. Though he was a lowblood, he was Daloya's favourite assassin and whispermaster, and despite his appearance, the man's work was flawless. Zadenu lifted a bottle of Jebbanese red to his lips – a bottle Boleo realised was from his own store.

'What do you think you're doing?' Boleo snapped, and snatched the bottle from Zadenu's grasp. He pushed past him into his room to find a figure huddled on the floor. 'Already? And Omadella told you to bring her *here*?'

'Yes, well,' Zadenu said, 'it were this, or leave her where that royal monk might find her. I can take her back, if you like. Think she prefers them oubliettes to freedom anyway.'

When Zadenu kicked her, the woman didn't flinch. She wasn't even bound, Boleo saw to his horror. She was not a large woman, and with her knees drawn up and her face buried, she seemed smaller still. Yet there was something undeniably coiled and powerful about her and the muscular curve of her brown shoulder.

'I had to dunk her in the Ae,' Zadenu said. 'Stench was unbearable.'

Dark eyes watched Boleo from beneath a tangle of matted hair. Ragged fingernails fluttered as she rapped her fingers on her knees. 'And you're sure this is her?' Boleo said. 'The Butcher of Busharn?'

Zadenu's eyes hardened. 'How many rains you been dealing with me, holy man? You doubting me now?'

'If I find you've made an error—'

'Yes, yes, I know, and right scared I am too. If all's in order, I'll be off. Pleasure as always. Oh, and there's about fifty guards from the White Isle coming up the causeway, looking for an escapee so, er . . . best be off sooner rather than later, if you catch my meaning.'

'They said you'd make it seem she'd been killed!'

Zadenu shrugged. 'Them prison guards is a wily sort, ain't they? Had to improvise a bit. Plus she weren't so keen to leave the darkness, for some reason. You ask me, her wits is gone. All rotted right out of her head.'

And with that, Zadenu took his leave, slipping through the high window and out into the rains.

Boleo closed his trunk and studied the creature on the floor of his room. She was approaching middle years. Her lips – just visible behind that mass of hair – were cracked and dry, but as he watched, they curved upwards into a smile.

'Something amusing?' Boleo said.

For a moment, he thought she wasn't going to reply or – terrifyingly – that Zadenu was right, and she was now beyond language altogether. It was said few could endure more than a rain or two in the oubliettes of the White Isle, and this monster had been down there for nearly seven. But then, finally, she uttered something.

'I didn't catch that,' Boleo said, turning towards her.

A strange choking sound seized the woman. Laughter. The Butcher of Busharn was laughing.

'What's so funny?' Boleo said.

Her voice was hoarse and cracked and strangely slow, as though she found each word a labour, and only reluctantly gave the syllables their freedom. 'You,' she said. 'I am. Laughing. At you.'

Boleo took a step towards her. 'You shall find, to your sorrow, that I am not a man to cross. You may be a monster, but I too am capable of horrors. You will do as I command, or things will not go well for you. You may believe you have already endured more than a human can endure, that I have nothing to throw at you, but you are wrong. You have one task. Lead us to Chinnaro's ruins. Fail us, and—'

There came a sharp rap at the door. Boleo froze. None of the palace servants would dare seek him out uninvited, and neither would the hapless youths he chose to serve him as noviciates. Perhaps Omadella had sent him a messenger, but if so, she was courting danger.

'Leave the message by the door,' Boleo snapped. 'I am in holy contemplation.'

But the voice that replied spoke with the flat accent of Nine Lords. 'My child, it is Father Emata. I have need of you.'

Boleo closed his eyes. Curse the woman! Had she been following him? He thought he'd lost her when he'd taken a convoluted route to the circleroom. He'd led her past a room filled with techwork he'd been certain would keep her occupied all day. But apparently not.

Boleo turned back to the Butcher. 'Draw attention to yourself, and you will die,' he said, knowing as he spoke that such threats would do little to sway such a broken creature. Then, being careful to keep his room hidden, he seized his staff and slipped out through the door.

Father Emata stood on the balcony. The courtyard below was hazy with the pounding rain. Behind her stood two of her underlings – the tallest, Boleo noted.

'Father Boleo, I wonder if you might accompany me. I have found something curious and would welcome your counsel.'

'I'm afraid I'm rather busy at—'

'The ancestors thank you for your service,' she said, and turned to lead the way.

Gritting his teeth, Boleo swept after her, staff stomping on the sandstone floor.

'Father Boleo, I'm afraid I have some disturbing news to impart. I believe your coincounters have been making . . . errors.'

'Errors?' Boleo said. They came to the stairway that led down the side of the Moon Tower and into the gardens below. It was nearing sunset now, and Ewo City was shrouded in cloud. He could just make out the palace wall in the distance, and beyond it the nearest mansions of the city's highbloods.

'Yes,' Emata said. 'They've been cataloguing artefacts as sent to the Garden that never actually arrived. Counting others twice. And then there are all the rooms of items waiting to be processed.'

'We are rather behind. Much washes up on the shores of Ewo City and I have but a small number of holy brothers to aid me here.'

'Indeed. Which is why am surprised, given all that you find, how little there is of any value. There are mountains of energy veins. Oceans of Panels of Sol. But no Thought Plates. Not a single shard of unbroken blackglass. Why, it is almost as though someone has already studied it all and hidden everything of real worth.'

'Alas,' Boleo said, 'we do tend to get . . . a lot of detritus here in Jebba.'

'Indeed,' Emata said, before turning towards the path leading to the mango orchard.

Boleo slowed. 'Where are we going?' he asked. Already, the rain had soaked through his beaded skirt.

'I found something in the mango orchard,' Emata said. 'I would welcome your thoughts on it.'

So, it had happened. Despite all the protections he had placed around Jethar's carriage, the woman had found it. He'd hoped the wards would be complex enough to keep Father Emata occupied for a moon at least, but apparently he had underestimated her.

They entered the clearing where Jethar and his carriage lay. And yes, as they approached, Boleo could see them both clearly. . . the haze of protective obfuscation was gone. There stood the awning shielding Jethar from rain and sun. A dozen monks squatted around him, only two of whom Boleo recognised. And there stood the tech-work carriage.

'By the ancestors!' Boleo made himself say, striding forwards. 'What is this?' He lifted his staff and whispered for the light of observation to come out, as though seeing the thing for the first time.

'Let's not play games, shall we?' Emata said. 'You sought to hide this from me. But you have been found out. You may have skilfully hidden all your other crimes, but this . . . *this* is undeniable. Oh, don't look coy; I have already sent for more of our holy brothers, and believe me, they are going to tear this place apart. They are going to uncover the full extent of your corruption, and then you will explain yourself to the king.'

'A techwork carriage!' Boleo said. 'Remarkable! One of my noviciates must have found it this morning. And who is that man there? Why, he looks like—'

'Stop the pretence. I have seen what lies in the carriage. Perhaps you'd like to look, too?'

Boleo tried not to hang his head as he walked forward. He'd thought the shrouds he'd placed on the shelves would last longer. But clearly, Emata had removed them easily, just as she'd removed the protections around the mango orchard itself. Boleo placed his hand on the door handle. 'I was intending to show you,' he said. 'I only wanted first to give the families concerned a chance to—'

'Open the door,' Emata said, triumph glittering in her eyes. She had caught him. She now had her proof. Reluctantly, Boleo pulled opened the door.

Empty.

It wasn't just the techwork that was gone. The shelves were gone. The storage chests. The carriage was as bare as if someone had stripped every physical thing from it save the walls themselves.

'What have you done?' Emata cried, shoving him aside and climbing in. 'Where did you put it all?'

Boleo was as stumped as she was, so it was no effort to look at her in confusion. 'I don't know what you're talking about.'

'Brother Lalu!' Emata cried, blundering out of the carriage. 'Brother, has anyone been in here since I left? Anyone at all?'

'No, Father!' one of her young monks cried. 'No one at all. We've been watching it the whole time, just as you said.'

Father Emata seized Boleo by the necklace of shells that hung around his neck. 'You—'

'Please!' Boleo said, pouring as much terror into his voice as he could, hoping they were all watching. 'I don't know what's going on! I don't know what you're talking about!'

207

'Father Emata!' one of the monks called from the far side of the garden. 'Father, Clan Itahua? The ones you had me watching? The glyphs tell me they're leaving Ewo City! And they have some . . . some significant *siganaals* emanating from their convoy.'

Emata shoved Boleo away from her. 'I will deal with you when I return,' she said, then turned towards the monk who had spoken.

'We will have to be quick, Father,' the young monk said as Emata joined her. 'Someone is masking their passage.'

Boleo smiled. He had an unwitting ally, it seemed. But that mystery would have to wait. Emata would take him into custody when she returned, he had no doubt. Quietly, Boleo backed out of the garden. His departure would have to take place that night.

NINETEEN

Elari

Captain Elari sat upon a barrel of Jebbanese red as the Itahua convoy trundled steadily north. If she looked ridiculous in full battle paint and feathers while the rain drummed down around the rickety cart, nobody said it; just as nobody questioned her bringing so much of the sweet wine with her. She knew what they whispered . . . That she planned to drown her grief, just like Cantec's brother Atoc. And if sometimes, they heard a metallic rattle coming from one of the barrels, well, Lieutenants Ishaan and Osellia were there to silence them with a look.

It's in the carriage. Find it.

Elari's three doves sat opposite, each perched upon barrels of their own. Only when they were completely alone did they risk talking freely. Then, Elari surrendered herself to every fear that clutched at her heart. What if the object Cantec wanted her to find wasn't there? What if it was, but she couldn't identify it? What if he truly had been delirious and his words meant nothing at all?

And above all, what if Father Emata came upon them in a blaze of golden-robed fury? Mercifully, Invoker Kartuuk had kept their travelling party to the minor roads that wound through wetwoods far from Adataliland's towns and cities. But by now, Emata must have discovered

209

the techwork was missing, which meant she would doubtless be upending the palace trying to locate it. Lyela claimed that, as a tech-doctor, she could use Forbidden energies to hide them. But she was one woman against the might of a royal monk and all her aides. The crime could not remain secret for long.

They were ten days into their journey when their party set up camp in a clearing near a jagged blackglass ruin. The rains had stopped, for now, so their servants set about putting up conical tents while Elari and her doves unfurled their eating mat beside the cart. Around them, the looming, slender trees sang with life. Every branch held a scampering lizard or chittering monkey. Elari closed her eyes, willing herself to calm. She had Cantec's body and his techwork. She knew she should feel relief. But once she returned home, they would all be preparing for war. War, and the Feverlands.

The spray of hot blood.

The crunch of the macuahuitl hitting bone.

Who will you sacrifice, Captain?

'Captain!' Chellahua said, taking hold of her shoulders. Elari hadn't realised she'd been crying until she felt the wetness on her cheeks. She looked up to find that the camp had been made, and the sun was close to setting. Cantec's siblings sat by the fire, eating and laughing as though their brother hadn't recently been murdered in front of them. Servants were bringing round a simple supper of squashes roasted with hot peppers. Elari's doves took portions for her as well as themselves, and Chellahua fed her while Elari watched the flames and tried to stop trembling.

'We don't have to go back,' Ishaan said. 'We no longer have an invoker to protect.'

'Everyone knows we have been fighting in Aranduq,' Elari said. 'They will expect me to go to war. First General Manax will expect me to go to war.'

Seeing the Bairneater again, back in Aranduq City, had undone something deep within her. She'd thought she'd been getting better, the last few moons. Her thoughts spiralled less often. Sometimes, she even slept the night through. But when the creature had thundered past with Sulin Mizito impaled on its blade, it had seemed as though she was back on the border again. And that feeling had remained. Perhaps, if the Mizito brothers managed to kill it, she would be able to sleep again. She only knew that, however many greybloods she slew, she would never have the strength to face the beast again herself.

Once the feasting was over, the Obsidian Dance began. Invoker Kartuuk led the way. He held the macuahuitl before his masked face, the light from the fire shimmering in each of the weapon's dozen bladed edges. Behind him, the Itahua siblings and their quartets fanned out.

Still as a midnight lake, Elari heard Cantec saying in his rich, melodious voice. *Poised as a serpent preparing to strike.* Elari had been practising the Obsidian Dance since she was old enough to stand. She knew its hundred and eight moves better than she knew the contours of her own body. Once, she and Cantec had practised the dance together. She had never felt more content, more at peace, than in those moments. It was as though their thoughts, their movements, resonated as one, just as they did when they fought. She realised she had been holding on to the hope that, somehow, he would return. No one had successfully Bonded the eighty-eighth incarnation of Itahua, not in the five rains since Cantec's voyage began. She had clung to that as proof that Cantec still lived. But now, all hope had ended, because his body lay there, in Kartuuk's travelling coach.

Elari looked up to find the camp in darkness and the fire burned low. Chellahua dozed at her feet in a pool of pale hair. Lyela slept out under the stars, along with the other servants. Only the three lookouts remained outside the tents. They, and the drunken figure that sauntered towards her now.

Atoc. Elari had managed to avoid him for most of their journey. Just looking at him now made her muscles stiffen. She could not forget Father Emata's triumphant little smile as Cantec's brother had told her everything. Neither could she forgive.

'Go away,' Elari said.

'Still angry with me, Captain?' Atoc leaned against the cart, a flagon of palm wine in one hand. He was taller than his siblings, his eyes an unusual green. Elari had once thought him among the most handsome men in the clan, but all she saw now was a wasted shell whose brilliant eyes had become pits of sunken emptiness. His existence was a warning to her, she supposed: how easily she could have chosen his path of self-destruction. They had both endured the horrors of the Feverlands, but he had chosen the coward's way out.

'I have nothing to say to you,' Elari said.

'That monk would have found the carriage. We both know that. We came to Adataliland for those bodies . . . for the chance that it would be him. Now, we can take him home and see him safely across the pyre. Isn't that what you want?'

'You don't care about what I want,' Elari said. 'You ceased caring about anyone but yourself long ago.'

Atoc shrugged and sipped from the lip of the flagon. 'Who's that woman you've got scurrying about all the time? She's not a local, and she wasn't with our party when we left. There's something suspicious about her – I can smell it.'

'I can smell *you*,' Osellia muttered drowsily.

'She's my new wine buyer,' Elari said flatly.

Atoc barked out a laugh, sending palm wine spraying into the night. 'Since when has Captain Elari, the – what was it they used to call you? Ah yes, the *Black Fury*. Since when has the Black Fury needed someone to choose her wines?'

'Go away, Atoc,' Ishaan said.

'Captain Elari, Flame of the East! Captain Elari, *Sister Death!* Ancestors, such *names!* Don't believe the names they give you, Captain. They make you feel you have to live up to those names every time you step out to fight. They make you think that's who you are.' He took another sip. 'Do you know how many warrior names Jethar Mizito had? Twelve. Twelve names! Nobody needs twelve names.'

There came a shout, and a disturbance on the far side of the camp. Elari and her doves stood as the familiar clap of weapons reached their ears. Up ahead, among the trees, Elari saw a flash of movement. A moment later, the lookout toppled backwards, an arrow lodged in their chest.

'Greyblood!' Ishaan cried.

'Not just one,' Atoc said.

It was true. A stampede of ragged figures flooded the clearing, makeshift weapons drawn as they loped towards the tents. Their yellow eyes studded the darkness as they leapt down from the trees. Elari came to her feet, heart thudding. So many, and out here in the wilderness while the camp slept. Ancestors preserve them all.

'Attack!' Osellia screamed. Chellahua snapped awake, and Ishaan jerked their knife from beneath their skirt. 'Wake up! Attack!'

Ululating cries filled the air as the camp came alive, but Elari strode forwards, the familiar heat of battle flooding her with calm. It swept away all thought, all fear, bringing to her the soothing nothingness of the fight.

Choose who lives and who dies.

Elari met the onrushing greyblood in an explosion of rage. Her macuahuitl was tucked away back in the cart, so she fought with only the short dagger she kept strapped to her leg. But it was all she needed. Because she was the *Black Fury*. She was *Sister Death*. As a man-shaped greyblood with goat-like legs charged towards her, Elari dropped low, sweeping smoothly under the swing of its club to thrust her dagger up under its chin. She kept tight hold as sparks flew around the hilt, jolting her hand, but the pain was good; this was why she fought. Because with that pain she did not remember. With a savage grunt, she twisted, and a great gout of silver fluid bubbled out of the creature's neck. Elari kicked it away, wiping her hands on her bare shoulders, bathing herself in silver. Let them see. Let them all see.

Something leapt at her from behind. Fool! Did they think her a green novice? She dodged to the side, not bothering to turn, so that the leaping creature crashed to the ground ahead of her. This one was dog-like, with four legs ending in long claws. But when it turned, the eyes she saw in its canine face looked almost human, and bright with intelligence.

The dog-thing growled at her, and so she roared back before jumping, knife raised. It was still turning when she landed astride it. Claws raked her thigh, but what did she care? She brought the knife down, sliding the blade clean into the creature's eye. It jerked once, then fell still.

Elari looked up to see the camp in chaos as warriors stumbled groggily from their tents. Osellia and Ishaan fought somewhere off to her right, the two of them taking swipes at a towering greyblood with the head of a boar. Ishaan, ancestors smile upon them, stood in the cart holding Elari's macuahuitl.

'Captain!' they called, before hurling the massive weapon through the air.

Elari caught the obsidian-edged club in her left hand. Its familiar weight was sweeter than the sweetest fruit, sweeter than the sweetest wine. Another human-shaped greyblood was loping towards her, this with an injured arm.

But it was the Bairneater whose face she saw as she grunted, swinging, hitting the thing clean in the neck. The head snapped back, not quite severed but yawning open to reveal blinking techwork innards. Elari spun to see a greyblood in jagged black armour limping away, dragging a wounded leg. But when it turned to regard her, she saw no visor, no helm. She saw only the Bairneater.

Choose who lives and who dies.

Elari charged, running the macuahuitl into its back, the weapon's many obsidian blades sharp enough to rip through the feeble armour. It babbled something in the greyblood tongue, but Elari heard only the Bairneater's voice, asking her *who lives and who dies*.

'You die!' Elari screamed. 'You!' She looked round for another to kill. Kartuuk had come out of his tent, hands bright with the first light from the ancestral realm, but there was confusion as his quartet scrambled to position themselves. Meanwhile, greybloods swarmed everywhere, slaughtering servants as they woke, setting tents ablaze. The stench of burning filled the air as people came running from their tents, clothing in flames.

This was her fault, she realised. All her fault. The barrels of techwork had lured them. It was more than she had ever seen in one place in her life, and now the ancestors were punishing her, as they always did, for all she had done.

A scream cut the air, and Elari spotted Cantec's youngest sister, Rozichu, standing near the treeline, her night tunic snapping in the wind. The captain of her quartet, a woman named Xulia, had taken a blade to the thigh. Two of her lieutenants lay on the grass – dead? Elari couldn't tell. She couldn't see the fourth, and though Rozichu was close to invoking, nobody was there, nobody was there.

Elari broke into a sprint, macuahuitl held over one shoulder, eating up the distance between them. But then a pair of yellow eyes appeared in the shadows, and a huge greyblood with rock-like skin emerged, mere paces from where Rozichu knelt, arms held aloft.

'*No!*' Elari screamed.

A shape leapt in from Rozichu's left, a grey bundle. They sprang at the greyblood, the force of their attack knocking it back. Rozichu's saviour wore the rough-spun robes of a servant but fought like one born to war. In a heartbeat, they had buried the knife in the greyblood's shoulder; in a place, Elari realised, where there was a gap in the stony skin. The creature wailed, staggering backwards, giving the servant time to remove the knife and slide it into the creature's open maw. Then the servant did something, some twisting motion with the knife, three quick but precise movements. At once, the looming greyblood fell still before collapsing gracefully backwards.

Elari had reached them now, but she knew at once that she wasn't needed. The servant jumped away from the body as it crashed, then came to stand before Rozichu.

Lyela. Her face and ample chest were splattered with silvery ichor, but her tawny eyes looked alight. Elari knew that light well. Here was a fellow warrior. Here was a woman with battle in her heart.

'Itahua! Rejoin us!' Rozichu cried, her voice so high, so small. 'Rejoin those you have sworn to protect!'

Elari twisted as a two-headed greyblood charged in from the left, but before she could lift her weapon, the creature crashed sideways as Lyela barrelled into it. Elari watched, enthralled, as the other woman leapt onto its back, then kicked the weapon from the hands of a second greyblood . . . Ancestors, but she could fight!

'Lord of the Mountain, rejoin us!'

Itahua stepped into the clearing, xir feathered jaguar mask gleaming red in the light of the fire. Xir heavy skirt spun as xe pulled xir macuahuitl into existence, the weapon the same size as Elari herself and shimmering with all the power of the ancestral realm.

A greyblood swung at Elari, so she leapt back and slammed down with her macuahuitl, hitting it in the shoulder. She spotted Atoc, off near the fire. There was no light of invocation for him: Elari could not remember when he had last called upon Itahua. But he fought like a rabid dog – snarling, biting, seizing a greyblood that stumbled past him and twisting its neck . . .

Behind her, Captain Xulia lay dead, eyes staring glassily. Her invoker trembled, tataus agleam, but as Elari looked, she no longer saw a green girl of seventeen rains.

'Don't worry, Cantec,' Elari said. 'They won't get near you.' Then she positioned herself before her invoker and fought.

Elari did not know when her doves joined her, their faces splattered with silver fluid. She did not know what happened to Lyela, only that the woman tore across the battlefield like a vortex of death. Every greyblood that leapt at Elari wore the Bairneater's face, just as they did on the beaches of Aranduq, just as they did wherever she fought. And no matter how many she killed, no matter how much of their blood she bathed in, it was never enough to banish the memory of that creature's smile.

'Captain Elari?' Someone touched her hand. Elari whipped round.

Lyela stood before her, concern creasing her face. She had a bruise on one cheek, and a gash in the meaty muscle of her arm, but otherwise looked unharmed. Beyond, the camp was a wasteland of burned tents and greyblood corpses. But the enemy was slain, all of them.

'Cantec!' Elari said, whirling, triumphant.

The blissful calm of battle melted away, and reality came crashing back. It was Rozichu who knelt on the ground behind her, weeping uncontrollably beside the bodies of her dead quartet. The Bairneater did not lie broken at Elari's feet – only a circle of twitching greybloods with no names.

Elari collapsed to one knee, her chest tight. They had won, but more than half their people had died. Behind her, Ishaan and Chellahua were helping Rozichu to her feet. The young invoker was pale, and still splattered with the blood of her fallen quartet. That was Elari's fault, too. This girl would now be sent to war without a quartet because of the choices Elari had made.

Choose who lives and who dies.

Elari stumbled as the forest around her blurred. When had the heavy darkness been replaced with the ethereal glow of the Feverlands? And there, over by the trees? Could nobody see it? The Bairneater. Smiling, smiling, always smiling.

Elari growled and charged forwards, hefting her macuahuitl.

'Captain, stop!'

Elari slammed into the ground, knocked sideways by an attack she had somehow failed to anticipate. She sat up to find Lyela kneeling before her.

'Captain—'

'You said we'd be safe!' Elari cried.

'This isn't our doing. This was a coordinated attack. Didn't you see their formations, the way their archers hung back?'

'They were lured by the techwork! By your protections!'

'No! All that is . . . is not as the monks claim. And this won't happen again, now I know what we face.'

'That girl has lost her entire quartet!' Elari trailed off as she saw Kartuuk striding towards them, long black hair unbound, eyes bright.

'You saved my sister's life,' he said, looking at Lyela with an intensity Elari had rarely seen on his stoic face. 'You have my eternal thanks.'

'It was nothing,' Lyela said, unable to meet his eyes.

'That was not nothing. Where did a wine buyer learn to fight like that?'

'My . . . mother,' Lyela said. 'She taught me the Jebbanese fighting art emii. It is a tradition in our family.'

Kartuuk inclined his head in a bow. 'Then she has my thanks, too. Please, come – let my healer see to your wounds. It's the least I can do.'

Elari watched as Lyela pushed uncertainly to her feet, then followed Kartuuk back across the broken camp. Beyond him, in the shadows, the Bairneater grinned.

TWENTY

Jinao

Rain ran down the unpaved road in snaking rivulets. Invoker Darsana Navret rode her scarlet horse between Jinao and his brother. She wore a wide farmers' hat and churidars; unadorned, her clan tataus covered by a loose cloak, she looked like any local lowblood. Jinao squinted out through the rain at the circular huts of the Ramanit slums, all the windows and doors boarded, the vegetable gardens untended, and felt a twist of sadness.

'Those few who remained here after the king's draft fled once the Bairneater arrived,' Darsana said, following his gaze. 'Lord Jinao, you look pensive. You must not fear. We have an excellent plan, and a hundred of my finest warriors at our backs.'

Oh, Jinao knew all about their excellent plan. They had spent the last day discussing what to do with him as if he were a piece on a forces board, to be moved around on a whim. He wasn't a powerful piece; that much was clear. He was a pawn, who by ill luck had found himself the last piece on the board. With the improvement in his brother's health, thanks to the aid of Darsana's strange little healer, Amira, Jinao had been relegated to his usual position of spectator in his own life.

'The Bairneater said I should come alone,' Jinao said.

'And alone you shall be, brother,' Julon replied, his long hair plastered to his face. 'Just with one hundred of us waiting in the shadows. Exactly as we agreed.'

As they neared the top of the hill beyond which lay the valley they sought, Darsana lifted a hand, and a stream of youths dressed as beggars peeled away from the line, each carrying a heavy slab of techwork. Or perhaps they were beggars – from what Jinao had seen of Darsana, she acquired all sorts of people. None of them appeared to be troubled by touching Forbidden relics. But then, as Jinao had learned in recent days, Darsana and her followers did not bow to convention.

Jinao watched them disappear among the trees. He had seen Amira chanting over the techwork that morning, dancing and touching the smooth surface. Jinao had counted nine slabs in all – an auspicious number, he supposed, though how the things could stop the Bairneater when they were to be placed many hundreds of paces apart, he couldn't say. They were part of some kind of trap, that much Jinao had come to understand. Darsana's techwork would trap the Bairneater, then Julon and his warriors would sweep in and Jinao, well . . . Jinao was to be the bait.

On Jinao's left, Sister Zalani made the sign for ancestral protection.

'Our techwork will not infect you, Holy Mother,' Darsana said, leaning forwards to address Jinao's nun. 'It is quite harmless to those who know how to use it.'

Sister Zalani straightened. 'Only those trained in the holy ways from childhood know how to withstand techwork corruption,' she declared, somewhat shrilly. 'I see no holy ones here!'

Darsana laughed. 'Ah, but what you *do* see are many learned souls. Watch, and you might learn something too.'

As their party descended the hill into the wetwoods, Jinao felt the first stirrings of fear. He was about to face the Bairneater again. One of the most dangerous named greybloods in the history of the Nine Lands. Alone, this time, despite the army that would be waiting among the trees. And worse, he feared what else he might see when he looked into the monster's eyes.

You sound like a child, asking for just one more sugar-fruit.

The path ended abruptly at the edge of a rocky precipice. And there, in the meadow below, a lone boulder stood amid the long grasses. Then the boulder moved, and Jinao's stomach turned over.

'Remember,' Julon whispered, leaning past Darsana, 'keep it talking. Keep its focus on you.'

'Ancestors watch over you,' Darsana said, smiling, and Jinao tapped Liet and let her carry him forward.

It seemed to take an age to descend the rocky path and enter the long grasses at the centre of the clearing. Jinao slipped down from Liet, trying not to watch the surrounding wetwoods, trying not to imagine the ring of techwork being laid out there, ancestors forgive him, nor the soldiers moving into position. As Jinao approached, he saw the Bairneater sat tending an unnatural green fire that flickered keenly despite the lashing rain. Though Jinao had thought the creature to be drowsing, he quickly realised that it was not. It was merely hunched as though with fatigue.

'I hope you have been practising,' the Bairneater rumbled as Jinao drew closer.

Jinao stopped, trying to still the thumping in his chest. He had forgotten how massive the greyblood was. Even seated, it was taller than him, and Jinao was taller than most. Sulin's staff looked like a toy in its free hand . . .

In its free hand. Jinao swallowed against the dryness in his throat. Yes: the arm he had taken had regrown, like a new branch from a tree. The skin looked a paler shade of grey, Jinao noticed, and the new arm seemed smaller, too. But the veins beneath the new skin pulsed near bright as the Bairneater's eyes. This was what the Scathed had made: monsters that could regrow their own limbs. Creatures that lived on aeons after annihilating their own creators. Abominations that had given themselves names and taught themselves human words. And yet nothing that moved was more unlike humanity. Jinao forced his gaze up to the Bairneater's face. It was like looking into stone.

221

'I did what you said,' Jinao said. 'I'm here.'

'Good.' The Bairneater pushed to its feet. Its shadow loomed over Jinao, the now-familiar metal-and-rot stench of it filling his nostrils.

Remember: keep it talking. Keep its focus on you.

Every instinct within Jinao told him to back away, to run. But instead, he said, 'Those things you said, in Aranduq. They were things my mother used to say to me.'

'What things?'

'Things about me. The way I am. Do you know something about her? Can you . . . *hear* her spirit? Something like that?'

The Bairneater snorted. 'Our kind do not listen to your *ancestors*.'

'But do you hear them sometimes?'

'Enough. I did not come here to talk about your family. I came to see if you have improved. Come. Bring Mizito out into the world. It is time for you to reach your potential.'

Jinao fell at once into the first moves of the sacred dance, but the Bairneater held up one grey hand and said, 'No. I told you we would be doing this alone.'

'We are alone.'

'Are we?' The Bairneater closed its eyes as though listening to distant music. 'I sense one hundred and forty-three heartbeats in the woods around us. I hear their breaths. I smell the fear in their sweat.'

'But they're not here,' Jinao said, pushing away the surge of panic that rose within him. The creature hadn't mentioned Darsana's techwork slabs, and that was all that mattered. 'They won't interrupt us, I swear it. They're merely waiting for me.'

'No,' the Bairneater said, and then lifted its hands. As it did so, the long grasses all around Jinao came to life. Metal gleamed between the damp green blades. Jinao backed away as a techwork arm appeared before him, followed by a human-shaped torso and legs. Glowing eyes regarded him. Jinao looked up to see a dozen, two dozen, more than he could count, sloughing off mud and coming to awareness in the clearing.

'You said we'd fight alone!' Jinao cried as inhuman chattering filled the air. 'I'm facing you *alone*.'

The Bairneater spread its arms. 'You have an army waiting in the wings. So do I. Now we will not be disturbed.'

Jinao had to warn them. Had to tell them to stop, to wait—

'Something wrong?' the Bairneater said.

Then came the signal: three sharp blasts of Darsana's horn. A line of blue fire arced up into the rain-darkened sky . . . then another, and another, nine in all, meeting high above the clearing. The Bairneater tipped its massive head back as the blue fire leapt from line to line, forming a dome.

'What have you done?' the creature growled, rounding on him.

The dome flared, and all the hairs on Jinao's body stood erect as a wave of pressure hit him from above. The Bairneater roared, clutching its head and doubling over, its army of greybloods jerking spasmodically.

Now. Now was Jinao's chance. He allowed one hand to close on the staff strapped to his back.

'No!' the Bairneater screamed, arching its back, and as it straightened, the wave of pressure surged back up towards the sky.

A series of distant claps echoed from somewhere among the trees, loud as sudden summer thunder. Then, one by one, the lines of blue that formed Darsana's dome began to disappear.

Jinao froze. Many of the greybloods lay crackling in the mud, and the stench of burning metal filled the damp air.

'Close,' the Bairneater said, turning, 'but foolish. And now you will all pay.' As the Bairneater descended on Jinao, it lifted one hand, and the surviving greybloods charged out into the wetwoods.

Jinao took a step back. 'Mizito, spirit of my fathers, hear me.'

'Why did you defy me?' the Bairneater roared, swinging *Valour*, knocking Jinao off his feet.

He slammed down into the mud, the breath driven from him, his legs stinging just as they had when he had displeased his mother.

'I told you to come alone!' The staff came slicing down through the air and Jinao rolled aside. He felt the impact of it hitting the mud as he scrambled to right himself.

Why had Jinao ever believed that, even with an army at their back and the arts of a techdoctor to guide them, they could hope to best this monster? Darsana had been so sure that her plan would work. But Sister Zalani was right: the ancestors were punishing them for their hubris and their use of the Forbidden ways.

'Stand!' the Bairneater thundered, its chest rising and falling. It had been hurt by Darsana's device, Jinao saw: a dozen dark burns marred its bare grey chest.

Jinao pushed shakily to his feet. He could hear Darsana's commanders calling for a charge, followed by the bellows of warriors running.

'Mizito,' Jinao said, 'spirit of my mothers, hear me.'

'You grasp for it too tightly. Yearn for it too deeply. You cannot control it. You are merely a channel for its release.'

'Hear me now, and come!'

Something tugged at every part of Jinao's body, and with a jerk, leapt out of him. Mizito – rolling across the grass as he materialised, coming up clutching *Stillness* in both hands.

'Good,' the Bairneater said, smiling.

Jinao dropped to his knees. Why was it so hard to remain upright when he invoked? The pull of Mizito on his muscles, on his mind, was overpowering. It was as though the very sky pressed upon him, shortening his breath, tightening his muscles and heart.

'Now *fight!*' The Bairneater swung *Valour* at Jinao's ancestor as he charged, catching Mizito's overhead blow and twisting it aside.

'*Come on!*' the Bairneater roared, circling. 'Don't you want to know where I've hidden the captives this time? Don't you want to save your new friends?'

'I stood before you *alone!*' Jinao said, and Mizito leapt, swinging his staff down, kissing the air where the Bairneater's shoulder had been, rising again to sweep the creature's legs.

The Bairneater danced backwards. 'Oh, Jin. You have too much of your father in you. You are too literal. Too linear in your thoughts.'

'*Stop speaking my mother's words!*'

'These are not your mother's words. Your mother is dead. These are my words.'

A cry rang out behind him and Jinao looked around to see Invoker Darsana Navret sprinting out of the wetwoods, her tataus glowing. Before her came a towering woman in a tiger mask: Navret herself. Darsana's ancestor wore no armour, only silks of red and yellow. She carried a chakram in each hand, and her black, jewelled hair flew out behind her in tendrils as a dozen greybloods swept in to intercept her. Ancestors, but Darsana was strong! She had no quartet, and even while her soul was tethered to the ancestral realm, she could run like a soldier.

Amira appeared at the treeline. As Darsana dropped to her knees, hands raised, Amira came to her and began to dance. The old woman chanted and spun in a wide circle around Darsana, the crystals at her neck glowing in time with her Forbidden words. Then she dropped to the ground, pressing her palms into the mud, her eyes rolling back in her head. The ground beneath Jinao's feet shifted as deep fissure appeared before Amira, splitting wider as it angled towards the Bairneater.

Jinao watched, transfixed, as Amira drove more fissures into the earth. He had never seen power like it. Was there techwork beneath the ground, techwork Amira somehow communed with? The stories Jinao had been told about techdoctors featured power-hungry lunatics who sowed chaos in their wakes, but this woman—

The air burst from Jinao as the Bairneater knocked Mizito off his feet. Jinao stumbled and felt his hold on Mizito waver . . .

No. Jinao closed his eyes. No. Mizito was his. He would not let him go.

'Focus,' the Bairneater said. '*Focus!* You must be stronger than this!'

Jinao roared. Every pore in his body was full of the strain of holding

Mizito present. He knew that if he breathed too deeply, if he looked away again, Mizito would disappear.

The Bairneater slid under Mizito's swing and came upwards, sending *Stillness* flying end over end before it winked from existence, returning to the ancestral realm.

The Bairneater straightened, rumbling with low laughter. 'What will you do now?' it said. With one hand, it seized Mizito by the neck: squeezing, as Jinao's own throat constricted and his vision began to mist. 'Your ancestor has no weapon. He is in my power. Why do you still fight?'

Why do you still fight? Sulin asked him, time and again.

Jinao closed his eyes. It was easier that way. With his eyes closed he could see the Bairneater as his ancestor did. The creature seemed smaller now, as Jinao looked through eyes that were not his own. Jinao knew that he knelt in the tall grasses of a Riani wetwoods, but just then he was also a well of potential, a living weapon poised to strike. And he knew exactly what to do.

The nuns claimed that an ancestor's form was fixed. But that had never made sense to Jinao. He remembered asking, in the days before he had learned better than to voice his opinion, why Mizito appeared the same way to everyone. In the ancestral realm, thought became form. No ancestor bowed to the laws of the living. Surely, if his forefather wished to, if his invoker desired it, he could appear in any guise.

'Why do you think I brought you here?' the Bairneater said. 'Do you think your ancestor is only what they told him to be?'

Mizito spread his arms and two kali fighting sticks fell into his open hands. Jinao felt their weight as they came into existence: Cagai fighting sticks, more ornamental than the sort soldiers wielded – smoothly polished, with delicate bonetrees etched into the darker wood at the ends.

The Bairneater snarled as Mizito struck its neck, dropping him as it stumbled back. It swung *Valour* round in a sweeping arc, but Mizito danced away and lifted his left stick to meet the blow with a clack that reverberated up his arm, up Jinao's arm. Jinao felt the pull on his

226

muscles, and let Mizito charge forward, right stick crossing left and back again as he struck out. The Bairneater was driven backwards, laughing triumphantly, on the defensive now, ducking and blocking as Mizito bore down upon him.

Navret sprinted in from the left, free of the greybloods who had descended on her. One of her chakrams sailed through the air, catching the Bairneater in the shoulder, knocking the creature to its knees. It rolled sideways, then came up as Navret leapt towards it in a storm of silk, hands extended. In one swift motion, the Bairneater brought *Valour* up, catching the Darsana's ancestor in the head and slamming her down.

The Bairneater staggered as the ground beneath it fissured and shifted. It looked over to where Amira knelt, trembling, her skinny arms still planted on the earth. Wordlessly, it hefted a rock and sent it sailing across the clearing towards the old woman.

Jinao didn't have time to see if it struck her. '*Again!*' the Bairneater roared at him, shoulders heaving as it swung its gaze back. '*Again!*'

Mizito charged forward, and Jinao realised he had given the action scarcely any thought. The need to move had simply passed from Jinao to his ancestor as naturally as a river flowed into the sea. Jinao's only task was to clearly know his own intent. That was what invocation was. Why had he ever sought to force it? Jinao let his muscles relax. It was easier that way. Mizito was here to protect his descendants. Their needs, the needs of family, would always be one.

'*Again!*' the Bairneater cried, whirling. From somewhere distant, Jinao heard voices. Familiar voices, all whispering his name.

Navret rose, her chakrams in her hands, preparing another charge, but then several greybloods dropped down from above, wielding battered swords. Navret spun, chakrams flying, slicing heads from shoulders. Beyond, Amira trembled, the rock the Bairneater had thrown lying in pieces all around her.

'Enough!' the Bairneater said. 'I told you to come alone. You diso-beyed.'

For one dizzying moment, Jinao saw himself through Mizito's eyes: a gangly Cagai man, trembling with effort, eagle mask askew, long hair heavy with sweat. Then the Bairneater fell upon him, and the heat of invocation, that exquisite, excruciating heat, fell away, and darkness replaced it.

Jinao blinked. His head throbbed. In the distance, someone wept softly. He felt as though days had passed, but when he sat up, he saw it could only have been heartbeats. He pushed onto his knees, scanning desperately for the Bairneater, but instead a sea of bodies greeted him. They lay everywhere in the long grass, many unmoving, others in their death throes.

Darsana lay unconscious near the trees. Amira stood over her, a scimitar in each hand, still protecting her lord. Blood streaked the old woman's face, perhaps where fragments of the Bairneater's rock had struck her.

Jinao heard a familiar cry and turned to see Julon at the edge of trees. And there was the Bairneater, raining down blow after blow on Julon's incarnation of Mizito. Where was Julon's quartet? He spotted Lieutenant Jexaan, unmoving in the grass nearby. And Captain Sellay fought some paces away, desperately hacking at a wolf-like greyblood.

'Stop!' Jinao croaked, pushing to his feet, stumbling, righting himself again. He felt utterly spent, every muscle in his body throbbing. 'Please . . . Stop.'

'Do not disobey me again,' the Bairneater said, and then it slid under Mizito's next swing and rose up before Julon, who knelt trembling and alone.

'*No!*' Jinao shouted, stumbling forwards as soldiers rushed in from left and right. Sellay screamed in rage and shouldered past the greyblood she fought. But they were too far away, all of them; too far away.

For a moment, the Bairneater seemed to hesitate, its shoulders trembling as though it fought a silent battle within. Then, with a great roar, it brought *Valour* down on Julon's head.

Jinao felt the crack in his gut, in his soul. His legs folded beneath him as his brother crumpled like a felled tree. Julon's incarnation of Mizito flicked instantly to nothing. Captain Sellay, in a blaze of fury, swung wildly at the Bairneater, uttering an animal cry of pure grief and rage. But the Bairneater was already on the move. It stepped back, watching impassively as Sellay tumbled into empty space, then it knocked her aside.

'You should have come alone, Jin,' the Bairneater said, stalking towards him. 'But you always were a disobedient child.' Jinao couldn't take his eyes from the tip of *Valour*, dark with blood: his brother's blood.

Jinao wet his lips. 'Mizito, spirit of my fathers, hear me . . .'

'That is enough for today. I will see you in Herinabad in forty days. Bring others with you and they will die. The forty innocent locals I trapped in a cave here will now also die. Slowly. Of starvation. Their deaths are on your conscience.'

Then it turned towards the trees and strode away.

Jinao crawled after the Bairneater, dragging himself forwards with fistfuls of long grass, too spent to stand. Darsana's warriors leapt at the creature as it passed, but it batted them aside like flies and was soon lost to the murk of the wetwoods.

The outriders would kill it. Darsana had posted guards in the forest all around, hardened mercenaries all. Yet as Jinao pulled himself closer and closer to the place where Sellay knelt howling over Julon, the truth crept over him like morning mist. Darsana's army was broken. Half her warriors had been slain. She herself had taken a grievous wound.

'Someone get the nuns!' Sellay screamed. '*Get the nuns!*'

Sellay propped Julon up against one of the twisting banyans. Julon's brow was dark with blood. His eyes were closed as though he were resting. Jinao pulled himself up beside Sellay as his brother's lips began to move.

'Jin,' Julon said. The voice that had always been so full of vigour was broken and scarcely audible now. 'Kill it. For our family, Jin. Kill—'

229

'Stop talking!' Sellay said. 'Save your energy. *Where are the nuns?*'

'Swear it, Jin. Swear it.'

'I swear,' Jinao said. 'But Julon, you—'

'Swear on our ancestors. Swear you will finish it.'

Sister Zalani appeared, trailing Julon's tall household nun. They set to work, brushing Sellay gently aside, bringing out their little boxes . . .

'I swear,' Jinao said, taking his brother's hand. 'I swear on our ancestors I'll kill the Bairneater.'

'Please sit back, Lord Jinao,' Sister Zalani said.

Jinao could not take his eyes from his brother's face as the nuns swarmed around him. Behind, Jinao heard Darsana, conscious now, barking out commands. Send riders to Invoker Mahesh; his soldiers could patrol the east. Send scouts to track the Bairneater. Prepare horses; she would lead a team in pursuit. The words drifted in and out of Jinao's mind like leaves on a breeze. Julon still wasn't moving. Though the nuns chanted softly, he still wasn't moving and his head lolled to one side.

You should have come alone.

'Ancestors,' Jinao muttered, closing his eyes, 'please help Julon. Please lend him your strength.'

Jinao opened his eyes to see Sister Zalani and her companion standing and exchanging looks. It was over. Julon's spirit had left the world. Sellay howled, a terrible, raw cry, and threw herself upon the ground. Something awakened within Jinao then. An anger cold as Mizito's eyes. He reached out and touched Julon's cheek. Still warm. Still so full of life.

'He will rejoin the ancestors,' Sister Zalani said heavily, placing a hand on Jinao's shoulder. 'It was their will.'

'Fuck their will,' Jinao muttered, shaking her off.

Swear on our ancestors. Swear you will finish it.

Jinao looked round. Most of the soldiers he saw were wounded – he supposed any who were strong enough had joined the pursuit. Darsana stood by her horse while Amira bound her wounded head. Sellay had crawled back to Julon, and now her head rested on his lap as she wept silently.

Jinao didn't remember standing. Sister Zalani said something to him, something about getting the ancestors to check his wound, but Jinao let the words wash over him like his mother's insults.

I will see you in Herinabad in forty days. Bring others with you and they will die.

Jinao turned towards the trees. He was not as weak as he'd thought. The rain had slackened to a soft, warm mist. He cast a final look back at his brother's corpse, and then slipped into the wetwoods, alone.

TWENTY-ONE

Boleo

At the top of the ridge, Father Boleo called their company to a halt. The Great Busharn Desert spread before them, a ragged red landscape stretching from horizon to horizon. No signs of human civilisation remained, but the ancient blackglass ruins of the Scathed dotted the landscape, jagged shards many hundreds of paces high, thrusting towards the turquoise sky. Once, this had been a great Scathed city, and its remnants had long outlived the humans who had come and gone since.

'They say the lands of Clan Kzani were quite beautiful,' Invoker Morayo said, reining up beside Boleo. He wore a Mahechi-style turban, its veil wrapped about the lower part of his face. He had eschewed his usual warpaint in favour of a loose agbada, but the cloth that had started out as white was now a dirty brown, after so many days of sand and mud. Still, Morayo was a man who could appear regal in rags. His scarlet horse, Relentless, pawed the ground with its crystal hooves.

'Pass me the long-glass,' Boleo said to his noviciate, Remami, a dull-witted boy of fifteen. The child rummaged in the saddlebags of Boleo's nameless red and black mount until he located the long-glass. Boleo pressed the device to his eye and scanned the horizon.

Hyenas often roamed the wastes, and occasionally the desert lions that had been sacred to Clan Kzani. But the deeper in they went, the fewer wild beasts they would have to contend with.

Once they crossed the border into Busharn, Boleo had stopped looking back. If Father Emata had seen through his diversions in time to send underlings in pursuit, they had lost them somewhere back in Adataliland. Boleo suspected he had the thief to thank for that. Whoever had stolen the contents of the techwork carriage must have Father Emata's full attention, ancestors be praised.

'If you look west,' Morayo said, leaning towards Remami, 'you can see the ruins of a palace of Clan Kzani. They were all found dead in their beds, you know; every soul of Kzani blood, murdered on the same night. With the ruling clan gone, the lands withered. Where once lush gardens and plentiful farms stood, now only rock and sand remain. They say any human who dares set foot upon these lands will find the same curse laid upon them.'

Remami stared with round eyes. 'Is it true?'

'Of course not,' Boleo snapped. 'Invoker Morayo enjoys the sound of his own voice far too much.'

'Everyone enjoys the sound of my own voice,' Morayo said.

'There is no great mystery here,' Boleo told Remami. 'There was a drought, and when Clan Kzani was obliterated in a targeted attack by the greybloods, the people left for surrounding provinces. It is as simple as that.' Boleo handed the long-glass back to Remami. 'Bring the prisoner.'

Morayo nodded to Captain Nchali, commander of the forty Batide warriors they had brought with them from Ewo. These were no ordinary clan soldiers. The Batide were Daloya's personal guard, souls he had hand-trained himself, warriors descended from families who had dedicated their lives to defending the clan. Boleo did not like taking them so far from his warlord's side, but Omadella claimed Daloya was insistent. Nchali, a willowy man wearing the black crane helm and swirling white warpaint of the Batide, nodded to a second warrior, and together they crossed to the cage that held their guide.

The Butcher of Busharn lay curled upon the wooden floor of her horse-drawn prison. She ate and drank when they brought her provisions, and the rest of the time she dozed. But Boleo had been told she spent her nights pacing the cage and testing its chains and edges for weakness. And while the camp slept, the Butcher suspended herself from the upper bars, strengthening her muscles until her clothes were heavy with sweat.

Preparing.

Captain Nchali rapped on the cage with his spear and then signalled for his companion to open the locks.

At once, the Butcher sprang out. This time, they were ready. The soldier she was aiming for ducked, and Nchali lashed out with his spear, catching the woman by her legs and sending her sprawling.

Nchali hauled her up and dragged her by her clothes to the edge of the ridge, where Boleo stood watching dispassionately.

'Which way to the ruins?' Boleo said.

The Butcher straightened. Since they'd hacked off her matted hair, she seemed younger and smaller, but her shoulders were still powerful, and her eyes filled with cold rage. She wiped a trickle of blood from her mouth.

'Well?' Boleo said. 'We know it is somewhere in this region of Busharn. Now it is time for you to talk.'

'Send me back,' the Butcher said, in her slow, deliberate way.

'Back to the oubliettes of the White Isle? Do you truly wish to return?'

'I will not help you.'

'You will. Eventually.' He motioned to Nchali, who bundled the Butcher back towards her cage. 'Leave me, all of you. I wish to contemplate.'

Once he stood at the edge of the ridge, Boleo lifted his staff. '*Observe*,' he commanded in the Forbidden Tongue.

The yellow light of observation spread out of his staff, dimming as it sliced through the bright morning. Boleo's staff was one of the better ones. The structure itself, carved from painted bonetree, had the usual patterned diamond shape at its tip, along with a sharpened point for combat. But it was the jewel at the centre of that ornate twist of wood

234

that was the key. The only thing he had done as his mentor Galumu had lain bleeding out on the floor that day – before yelling for help because thieves had come, thieves in the monastery and oh, ancestors preserve us, they had *killed* Father Galumu – was switch the jewels in their staffs. He had hoped that the thinking jewel at the heart of a senior monk's staff could do more than simply read techwork and provide illumination, but he'd been wrong. Aside from its greater range, the thinking jewel in Galumu's staff had been identical to Boleo's.

That range was useful to him now, though. It couldn't quite stretch to a hundred leagues, but it wasn't far off. Within minutes, the glyphs on the length of his staff flashed with the symbol for *complete*.

Boleo lay the staff before him so that the images its jewel displayed would be hidden from those behind. 'Show me an overview,' he commanded in the Forbidden Tongue. '*All structures larger than six paces by six paces. Distances. Bearings.*'

His staff flashed up another glyph: *working*.

'So, it's a torch,' Morayo said, sauntering up. 'And a map. And what else?'

He leaned down to take hold of the staff, but Boleo batted his hand away. 'Never touch a monk's staff,' he snapped.

Morayo grinned at him. 'Oh, Father, don't knock it until you try it.'

'Leave me to my contemplations,' Boleo said.

'I just want to understand. I thought you monks could . . . summon fire and ice and twist nature. The tales our wetnurse used to tell us about your powers! But after all these rains watching you, Father, all I can see is a torch and a . . . kind of very, very clever eye.'

'Oh, it is much more complicated than that,' Boleo said, but in truth, it wasn't. In truth, the only tool a monk really possessed, apart from their understanding of the Forbidden Tongue, was a thinking jewel that could speak to other techwork. It was down to the individual monk to glean the tales that techwork had to tell.

'This is a map, yes?' Morayo continued. 'And those blue points . . .'

'They are all Clan Kzani ruins.'

'So many,' Morayo said, leaning down. 'We can't possibly search them all.'

'We don't need to. We can cross-reference this with the ruins we already know about from our maps, most of which are old Clan Kzani cities and towns. The only ones we are interested in are those that do not appear on the maps . . . Ah, such as this one, not three leagues from here.'

'And do you know what we're looking for when we get there?'

'Your father believes something else was hidden in the ruins Chinnaro found. Something in addition to the map, that might help explain where Jethar and Cantec went wrong.'

'*Something else.* Is that it? No details on what this thing might be?'

'Your father believes it can help us defend the river.'

'And you believe my father knows. How does he know? We are talking about a man who hasn't spoken in rains. And even if we find that something, what then? Set off on another voyage north for this mythical land where spirits gather? This is a rains-long undertaking! Not the quick solution to war that Omadella wanted.'

'I am well aware of that.'

Morayo sighed. 'I heard what you said – about how he should give you more information. You trust him, even without it?'

'Yes, I trust him.'

'Then you are a better man than I.'

Boleo looked across at Morayo, uncertain if the younger man was teasing him again, or perhaps testing his loyalties. But Morayo turned and trudged back towards his horse, shouting, 'Make haste – a storm is in the air!'

Morayo had not been wrong: by highsun, the wind had picked up, and as their shadows grew long, Boleo's staff told him a sandstorm of significant power would be upon them by dusk.

Boleo found himself thinking about Morayo's words as their convoy headed steadily west, veils pulled down against the wind. He had always thought Morayo's brashness was mockery; it had not occurred to him that the young man might feel just as ignorant of his father's work as Boleo himself did, or that he might yearn just as strongly for Daloya's approval. Morayo sped ahead of the main convoy, his agbada billowing behind him like a banner. He was restless, Boleo knew. He had not brought his quartet with him, and though he claimed it was because he wanted them to rest before joining the king's draft, Boleo wondered if this was entirely true.

It was near dark by the time they reached the rocky outcrop that his staff told him was the location of some ruins. By now the wind was so strong that it howled like a lost soul, and most of their warriors had dismounted to lead their horses by hand.

'How do we get in?' Morayo shouted at him above the swirling drone. 'I see no structure, no doors . . .'

Boleo squatted down. '*Search for openings,*' he murmured.

The glyph for *working* flashed up on his staff.

After a moment, he had it: an entrance not five paces from where he stood. And to his surprise, it appeared as though it was sealed by techwork. Boleo strode forward until he stood over it. 'Remami, come and help me!'

His moon-faced noviciate scampered forward and together they swept at the sand, beneath which Boleo could see the faint blue glow of forbidden glyphs. Their group huddled against the shelter of the rocks as they waited, while beside them, the Butcher's cage swayed dangerously.

'Did she really kill all those people?' Remami asked.

'The Butcher? Yes,' Boleo said. 'And the woman does not deserve a shred of your sympathy.'

Soon they had uncovered a blackglass panel, which Boleo was able to unlock with a simple command to *open*. The thing sighed upwards, revealing a metal ladder leading down into darkness. The soldiers behind them exclaimed in wonder, and even the foolish boy Remami made the sign for ancestral protection.

'This ladder will not bite,' Boleo snapped. 'Have the horses fall dormant under the rocks and let us all get out of this accursed wind!'

Once the horses had been secured against the rocks, their party descended the ladder. They had no choice but to remove the Butcher from her cage, but Nchali had her bound like a sack of grain and lowered to the bottom, where two Batide warriors held her at spear point. Boleo was the last to descend, by which time the wind was strong enough to lift him from his feet and the swirling sand sharp enough to cut skin. Boleo descended hastily, commanding for the door to seal shut above him.

At the bottom, their party stood about in an uneasy circle. To Boleo's surprise, there was light here: blue techwork torches illuminating the walls at regular intervals. The warriors eyed the techwork warily, as though at any moment it might spring to life.

'This is a cursed place!' Nchali said. 'Are you certain we will be safe in it?'

Boleo was tempted to snap at him, but instead he lifted his staff and chanted in the Forbidden Tongue, a meaningless babble of commands that made his staff flash dramatically but did little else. 'There,' he announced. 'This room has now been Cleansed.'

Appeased, the warriors fanned out, talking in low voices. Whatever this place was, it was not like any Scathed ruin Boleo had seen before. The walls nearest him were of smooth metal, and Boleo did not need his staff to know that more techwork lay behind them. But the floor up ahead fell away to reveal a drop about twice Boleo's height, down into what appeared to be an abandoned excavation site. Morayo was already making his way towards it, while his warriors set about assembling a meal of dried okra and cassava.

'What is this place?' Morayo said when Boleo joined him, his voice echoing down from the walls. 'It looks like a Scathed ruin, but that statue . . .' Morayo jumped down into the gloom, his agbada billowing out as he landed. And though Boleo was hungry, and tired, he followed. Because Morayo was right . . . the excavation site before him was like nothing he had ever seen before. Someone had been working on it – the Scathed, presumably . . . and yet it seemed too recent for that. They had been partway through uncovering a sandstone monument before they had abandoned their work. As Boleo's eyes adjusted, he saw that two pillars lay either side of the site. Towards the back, and almost consumed by shadows, stood a statue: a creature with a head much like the Jebbanese jackal for which Clan Adatali was known, but with four arms and the body of a human. One arm held a sword, the other what looked to Boleo remarkably like a Scathed trinalgram.

'Is that a Scathed?' Morayo said. 'Are we looking at a statue of a Scathed? It has no wings, but . . . clearly, it isn't human.'

Boleo had reached the statue's feet, where a techwork panel shaped like a book lay open.

'*Activate*,' Boleo commanded in the Forbidden Tongue.

'Careful,' Morayo muttered. 'You'll have them climbing back up that ladder again.'

'Quiet! *Activate panel.*'

The slab of techwork remained dormant. Boleo ran his fingers over it, removing the thick layer of dust. Beneath, he saw it was decorated with a curious script: something foreign to him, and certainly not in the Forbidden Tongue. In all his years, in all his journeys, he had never come across techwork marked with any language other than the language of the Scathed. But perhaps these markings had been added afterwards, for decoration.

Boleo brought his staff around. '*Is this device functional?*' he said.

'Ooh!' Morayo gave a mock shiver, then touched his forehead for ancestral protection. 'Ooh, it gives me chills to hear you chant Forbidden words!'

'Be quiet!'

The jewel on his staff set to work, the light of observation sweeping out and sliding up and down the ancient techwork.

'Are you certain this place was built by the Scathed?' Morayo said, turning in a slow circle. 'I've never seen such pristine ruins.'

'Nor have I. But this is techwork – all of it. So the Scathed must have built it.'

His staff flashed with the glyph for *complete* then flashed a second series of glyphs: *Memory device functional.*

'Well, why won't it listen to my commands, then?' Boleo muttered. He sighed and touched his staff to the book. '*Manual activation.*'

His staff flared and sent a line of energy down into the strange panel. The script brightened a searing blue, and then a booming, masculine voice filled the room.

'Ancestors!' Morayo cried, dancing back. Behind them, Boleo heard the other warriors shouting in alarm.

'Remain calm!' Boleo called above the clamour, as the voice droned on in a language he could not name. '*Deactivate!*' he commanded, then removed his staff from the contraption.

'What in Adatali's name was *that*?' Morayo said, looking at Boleo.

'Go and join the others,' Boleo said. 'I will be with you soon.'

'But I want—'

'Please leave me!'

Boleo stood before the statue, his thoughts aswirl, his heart hammering.

'*Identify language of recording,*' Boleo said, placing his staff back on the panel.

Glyphs streamed across his staff. *Working . . . Closest match: Early Leopard Tongue, Ulamara continent.*

The Leopard Tongue. Here, in the Nine Lands, on a piece of Scathed techwork. It was a language they spoke in the same continent the techwork talking drum had come from, the one Boleo had found all those years ago during the trails.

'*Translate,*' Boleo said.

Complete.

It took Boleo several repetitions of the glyphs before his mind would accept the full meaning. *Senjorr, the Wayward Brother, as he was once worshipped. This replica uses the exact techniques the First Dwellers*

240

would have used, when such a statue would have taken decades to complete. Tap the 'more information' button on your panel to see an animated diagram of the process.

Button . . . Panel . . . Animated . . . Words pertaining to techwork. But how could that be? The Leopard Kingdom – indeed, humanity itself – did not exist during the days of . . . whatever this four-armed jackal thing was.

Drumming cut across his thoughts as one of the soldiers brought out a talking drum. The Batide began to sing . . . Some Jebbanese folk song in a local tongue. Several warriors had set about making a tiny shrine and were reciting their many Jebbanese names. Boleo had never known a group of soldiers to be so obsessed with provincial traditions as the Batide.

After a supper, Boleo sat cross-legged, sipping ogogoro from his hip flask and watching the Butcher across the leaping flames. Despite the gloom, Boleo could see the tightness of her jaw as she stared into the darkness. He stood and closed the space between them. She did not move until his shadow fell across her.

'Are these the Chinnaro's ruins?' Boleo said.

The woman turned to him. Her lips were cracked and the skin of her cheeks sunburned. They had left her bound at ankle and wrist, and propped her against one of the metal walls. She stared at him for a time, then turned her head to the side and spat.

Nchali, standing nearby, was beside them in three strides. He lifted his spear then slammed the haft into the Butcher's head, knocking her sideways. When he raised it to strike again, Boleo lifted a hand.

'No more,' he said.

'Let me take a finger,' Nchali said. 'She will soon be singing a different song.'

'No fingers, thank you,' Boleo said. The Butcher stared at Nchali, a faint smile playing at her lips, almost a challenge. 'Why won't you help us?'

The Butcher sucked on her cheek and turned her gaze back to the gloom.

'He asked you a question, dog!' Nchali snarled, lifting his spear again. Boleo knew how much the Batide despised this woman. He'd heard them asking her how it felt to kill her own, and whether she looked forward to the ancestors turning from her when she crossed the pyre. Batide warriors were always close – training together from childhood, selected from the same Jebbanese family lines . . . the idea that one among them could ever kill another was unthinkable. That first night, Lieutenant Jamakii had thrown the Butcher's breakfast bowl at her, and watched her eat garri off the floor of her cage. Yes, they despised her, and Boleo could not blame them.

'Go ahead,' the Butcher said, looking up at him. 'Hit me again. Maybe I'll feel something this time.'

Nchali growled and swung his spear round, but Boleo caught it. Even now, he could still surprise them with his strength. 'Leave us,' Boleo said.

'But Father—'

'I'll be fine. I'll call to you if I need help.'

Once Nchali was out of earshot, Boleo squatted in front of the Butcher. 'There are dozens of unmarked ruins in the Busharn wastes,' Boleo said. 'I'll search them all if I have to. But it would be quicker and easier if you helped. Why do you refuse? Our success may enable us to save many lives.'

The Butcher laughed. 'How? You think a map can end a war?'

'I believe it may lead us somewhere that will strengthen our hand. If further clues lie in Chinnaro's ruins, then we must find them.'

The Butcher snorted. 'Do not look for the ruins. They are not what you think.' Then she settled her head on the cracked ground and closed her eyes.

Boleo stood and made his way back towards the cook-fire, something gnawing at the back of his mind.

'*Find me all reports that were brought to us on the Busharn Massacre,*' Boleo commanded his staff in the Forbidden Tongue. 'There's something I'm missing here.'

TWENTY-TWO

Elari

Little Rozichu Itahua spent the entire journey north weeping for her lost quartet. As the Clan Itahua convoy trundled out of Jebba and through the eastern scrublands of Mahech, Rozichu found no solace in the company of her brothers. Instead, she took to riding in the wine cart with Elari and her doves, lying curled between the barrels as the days came and went.

Elari sat swathed in heavy blankets as they entered the Intiqqi mountains. She had scarcely spoken to Lyela since the greyblood attack. She blamed Lyela, yes, but she also blamed herself. But Lyela had been true to her word: since that night, they had not seen a single greyblood. If the techwork had lured them, then whatever Lyela did afterwards had driven them away again.

As they came out of the mountains, and the vast, rolling wetwoods of Itahualand spread before them, a change came over Rozichu. She took to leaning on the edge of the cart, staring at the dirt road and the villages that swept by. Eventually, she began to talk.

'I see it in my head,' Rozichu said. 'Over and over. I can see them dying. Even when I close my eyes.'

For a moment, Elari couldn't speak. Then she knelt down beside the girl and put an arm around her. 'I know it is small comfort, but a quartet exists to protect their invoker.'

The hot spray of blood.

The screams of the dying.

Choose who lives and who dies.

'I . . .' Elari swallowed. 'I know what it is to be unable to get past a single moment in time. But you will find ways to cope. Sometimes I . . . recite the Song of Legends Lost. My brother used to sing it to me after my father beat me for making errors in my forms. And it has always brought me comfort. Knowing that the nine warlords are always there, always ready to return, has always given me strength.'

Lyela, riding at the head of the cart with the horses, made a strange grunt low in her throat.

'I don't want to go to the Feverlands,' Rozichu whispered, taking Elari's hand. 'Atoc told me what it's like. He said greybloods crawl out of the ground, out of the trees. That some are as big as houses. He said the trees themselves are poison, like a weight pressing on your chest. He said war turns even good souls into the sorts of monsters they loathe. He said—'

'Atoc enjoys tormenting people.'

Rozichu looked up at her, her dark eyes rimmed red. 'I will have so little time to find a new quartet, to train with them, for them to learn each other's ways. If I could find a quartet with experience . . . warriors who already know each other, and who already know war . . .' She gave a sheepish smile and Elari looked away.

'Atoc says Father will insist you go,' Rozichu said softly, 'because you are the best captain in Intiqq and your presence on the battlefield will inspire the troops.'

'I am past forty rains of age. There are younger warriors just as skilled as I.'

Elari felt a small hand touch hers tentatively. 'Please, Captain Elari. Please. Will you and your lieutenants be my quartet?'

Elari could not meet her eyes. It was an honour to be asked to serve an invoker of the blood. An honour that one could not politely refuse. But Rozichu was young – she needed a young quartet who could serve her for life. Elari tapped the girl's hand. 'I am too old for you,' she said, and shuffled away.

Finally, over a moon after their hasty departure from Ewo City, they came out of the hills to see Qenqar gleaming before them in the afternoon sun. Elari leaned forward, drinking in the sweeping valley of whitewashed estates and bright piazzas that lay beneath the stepped pyramids for which the city was famed. In the distance, beyond the hills, lay the glittering sea.

Naked lowblood children ran beside the convoy, pointing at the horses or calling out Itahua's name. Chellahua smiled and tossed them crescents from her little purse and waved when they told her the ancestors smiled upon her. Elari closed her eyes. She was home. Now Cantec would be sent safely beyond the pyre and his techwork could be placed in the palace vaults for her to search at her leisure.

As their convoy descended the switchback road that led down into the city, sending lowblood pedestrians scattering, Elari studied Lyela. She supposed techdoctors might also learn to fight, but Elari had spent her entire life studying the combat arts and she had never encountered that curious move the woman had used against the greybloods. Those three sharp strikes had scarcely seemed to touch her opponent at all, and yet she had used them to fell a greyblood thrice her size.

They passed through a wide, busy square. People stood on the pavement or leaned from their balconies to watch them pass. From their shutters and balconies hung long swathes of white cloth. White for mourning. Which meant First General Manax had finally passed, ancestors be praised.

'Father . . .' Rozichu muttered, leaning on the edge of the cart.

'I am sorry, My Lord,' Elari said, though in her heart she knew it was a mercy. Manax had always been a stern man, but since Cantec's disappearance, his sternness had turned to cruelty. It was good for them all that he would never learn of the awful things Cantec had

245

endured. Cantec had always been his favourite, and they would all have been made to suffer for failing to protect him.

Clusters of lowbloods gathered before the palace walls, placing offerings by the twin statues of Itahua that flanked the main gates. But Elari noted that no shrouds of mourning bedecked the crystal of that entrance.

'That is Livinghall?' Lyela said, as they passed the guardhouse and into the gardens. Up ahead spread a low stone building.

'What you see is only the very top,' Chellahua replied, amused. 'Most of the palace lies in the cliff-face itself.'

At the end of the main road through the gardens stood a group of warriors in the blue and black feathers of the palace guard. None wore robes of mourning. Osellia, leaning out of the front of the cart near Lyela, straightened. 'Look!' she cried. 'Look, it's him! Out front!'

'Who?' Elari asked, climbing past the barrels to join her.

Then she saw. Standing between the guards was an older man in a warrior's paint and headdress. His long raven braid was streaked with white, and though he was thin, and his eyes sunken, he seemed upright and strong. His arms bore the distinctive blue and black Itahua tataus. There could be no mistaking him: it was First General Manax. The man had been half a corpse when Elari had last seen him, a skeletal shadow of the looming tyrant she had once feared. Three times the convent chirurgeons had cut the sickness from him, and three times it had grown back, taking more of him with each return. Before Elari had left to join the fighting in Aranduq, Sister Anatuan had declared he would not live more than a few moons.

The convoy came to a halt as shouts of astonishment rose all around. Elari climbed over the lip of the cart and joined the crowd of travellers hurrying to greet their first general, Kartuuk leading the way.

'Father,' Kartuuk said, stopping short before him. 'Shouldn't you be resting?'

'No. I've rested enough in recent months,' First General Manax said stiffly. He looked past Kartuuk at the rest of the convoy. 'Where are the others?'

'We were attacked by greybloods on the road,' Kartuuk said. 'And there is more I need to tell you, in private, concerning Cantec.'

Rozichu ran to join them, a sob of delight escaping her. She extended her hands, then lowered them. Manax had never been one to embrace his children: even less so now, it seemed.

'How is this possible?' Rozichu said.

'The palace nuns were trying to poison me,' Manax said. 'Their mistakes nearly cost me my life.'

'We found some new healers!' said Dennia, Manax's vacuous young spouse. The girl hovered at Manax's side, the blue beads threaded through her hair snapping in the wind. 'They gave him a special medicine, and now look!' She took Manax's hand. 'We must have a feast tonight, to celebrate everyone's return!'

Kartuuk cleared his throat. 'Father, I really need to speak to you about . . .' He trailed off, his gaze drifting towards the obsidian statue of Itahua that stood before the palace entrance. Wedged on top of Itahua's macuahuitl was a misshapen lump.

A head.

'Father?' Kartuuk said, nodding in the direction they all now stared. 'What's happened here? Isn't that—'

'The king sent a messenger to inform me that I must send the people of Intiqq to their deaths,' Manax said. 'I refused. That person attempted to insist. I made my response.'

Atoc, already halfway to the palace entrance, barked out a laugh. 'By all the ancestors who fuck, you killed an Ahiki!'

'They came to our province last. They think nothing of our people. Yet they would have us throw away our lives for their whims.'

Beside Elari, Lyela went still. And yes, Elari could see it now . . . the golden tataus across both the woman's cheeks. The slight golden tint to her sightless eyes. Not just a messenger: an actual descendant of the Nine Lands' founder.

'Father . . .' Kartuuk said, his voice faint.

'We should all stop pretending we owe anything to the Royal Clan,' Manax said. 'We obey the Ahikis because we fear them. But no more.'

With that, he turned, striding back towards the palace, his long headdress sighing on the stone path in his wake. Elari glanced at Ishaan, whose eyes were still on the severed head. Never, in all her years, in all her studies, had Elari heard of an invoker attacking an Ahiki. Manax had always complained about the demands of the Royal Clan, yes, but she'd never imagined him capable of anything like this.

'See that the barrels make it to our apartments,' Elari muttered softly to Ishaan. 'I do not want to chance the vaults.'

The feast went on all afternoon and well into the night.

The doors to the Fountain Hall were thrown open, and its tiered balconies rang with music and laughter. It was no hall, really, standing open to the sky, descending the cliffside towards the azure sea. Fountains surrounded each circular level, where pipers sat playing and servants drifted among the guests with platters of food.

Elari strode through the crowds, ignoring the voices that called to her. It seemed every soul she passed wanted to talk to the fabled Captain Elari. Had she seen the fall of Aranduq? What was the fighting like out there? Would she like to meet their child, a promising warrior?

Elari sweated beneath the constricting blue fabric of her feathered robe. It was a long time since she had worn anything but battle dress. She grabbed a glass from a passing servant and drained the contents in one long swallow. The crowds seemed to press upon her, so many bodies, so much noise, so much heat. Their chatter merged into one, until it sounded much like the cacophony of the battlefield. Elari closed her eyes.

'Captain,' Ishaan said, touching her arm.

'What is it?'

'I can't find a single nun in the palace,' Ishaan said. They and Elari's other doves wore identical robes of lavender silk. 'I've seen no monks, either.'

Elari stared off to where First General Manax sat apart from his guests, at a circular table that occupied the lowest tier of the Fountain Hall. His senior envoys and commanders sat around him, as well as his children and their spouses. Elari could not help but think that they looked like so many preening birds, all jostling for attention.

'No one seems to know about the Ahiki envoy,' Osellia added. 'At least, no one from outside the palace. None of the servants will talk to us.'

'Who are they, down with Manax?' Lyela said from Elari's side. Elari's seamstresses had thrown together a hasty celebratory gown for the portly woman – close about the hips, leaving the shoulders bare. Though Elari did not think the garment suited Lyela's frame, she wore it with ease, as though she were used to fine clothes.

Down beside Manax's high table, a little show was being performed. Two curious people in unfamiliar dress were bowing to Manax. Kartuuk, seated on the cushions nearby, wore a dark expression.

'I do not know,' Elari said. She squeezed her doves' hands in farewell and then descended towards the high table. Manax's guards eyed Lyela, but they made no comment as she and Elari passed.

'Sister!' Atanchu cried, leaping from the cushions where he sat beside Kartuuk. 'I've been trying to find you all afternoon!'

'I missed you,' Elari said softly, embracing her brother and inhaling his familiar scent. Atanchu wore his favourite jewelled jaguar mask, and matching jewels glinted on his fine fingers. His deep blue robe left one of his muscular arms free. He had never had Elari's aptitude for combat, and so their father had groomed him for betrothal. Not long after Elari and Cantec married, he caught Invoker Kartuuk's stoic eye, but Kartuuk would never bring his sweet, cheerful husband with him on campaigns.

'Look at them!' Atanchu said, taking her hand and gesturing to the two strangers. 'Can you believe it? It is they who healed Manax! I know they don't look like much, but they are skilled healers.'

'What is going on here?' Elari muttered under her breath. 'All the nuns gone, an Ahiki *dead*—'

'What do you mean?' Atanchu said. 'There was an Ahiki emissary here, but she left days ago on a barge! And the holy ones were all called away on urgent business.'

'There was a head at the front of the palace.'

Atanchu regarded her, his smile wavering, as if uncertain whether she was joking.

'Never mind,' Elari said, and steered her attention to the little show that was being put on. The two men in foreign dress stood before a travelling chest filled with bottles and jars. Both men were stout, but this was the only way in which they resembled each other. One was dark skinned, the other light; the light one was bald, and the dark one had his long hair braided elaborately down his back. There was an odd synergy to their movements, to their ready smiles. They wore identical robes of curious yellow silk, voluminous about the wrists and legs, and covering their arms.

'Where are they from?' Elari asked.

'Ertla!' Atanchu said. 'Across the sea and beyond the land of Quenon.'

'There's no such place,' Lyela said, and Atanchu turned to her. She did not flush, but lowered her head and said more softly, 'I have never heard of such a place, and I have travelled much . . . My Lord.'

'Who is this?' Atanchu said with grin. 'A new friend of yours?'

'My wine buyer,' Elari said. She hated lying to her brother, but Atanchu had never been discreet, and explaining all that had happened would be too much, at least for now.

'Well, *wine buyer*, the place must exist, because these two men are from it! Oh look, they've got new things to show us!'

Elari heard titters as the two men set about unpacking their wares. Up on the tier above, she saw a wider audience watching, and glimpsed Osellia's dark, doll-like face within the crowd.

'Gentlesouls of this grand land,' the light-skinned foreigner intoned. 'Please to let us present these finest rarities of our wonderful home.' The man wrung his hands as he spoke and glanced about anxiously at the gathered faces. His accent was sing-song and like nothing Elari had heard before. But in all her life, she had only ever met one other person from beyond the Nine Lands.

'Here is an herb of the greatest value and worth,' the foreigner continued, lifting a jar of pink flowers. 'In all the many great cities and lands we have passed through, *this* people please to ask for again and more times. Smell the scent of this bloom, and your warriors will need no rest, will know no fear, will follow any command. Eat of the petals, and they will have the strength of ten persons.'

'This . . .' the dark one said, lifting a bunch of what looked to be grass. 'This herb grows in the highlands of our fair country. Please to know that its uses are many. If you have pain in your muscles, a poultice will ease them. Wrap it on festering wounds, and infection will flee. A strong tea brewed of its leaves will see anyone with a member satisfy their lover.'

Elari heard more laughter at this, but Manax watched sombrely, almost fervently, his dark eyes glittering.

Kartuuk, seated down upon the cushions, straightened. 'Tell me, my friends,' he called out, 'I am unfamiliar with your homeland. Who rules it? Is it part of Quenon? Candornia?'

The men whispered to each other and then the dark one said, 'Oh, no one. No one rules.'

Laughter rang around them, but Kartuuk's expression did not falter. 'No one? Perhaps you misunderstand the question. From whom do you take orders?'

They conversed again, and the dark one replied, 'Our master. We take orders from our master.'

'And who is that soul's master?' Kartuuk asked. 'From whom does *your* master take commands?'

'Why, from the master of our master!'

Atanchu laughed brightly and said, 'And what of your invokers?'

The light-skinned one frowned. 'Invokers? Please to explain this word.'

Gasps of astonishment and more laughter peppered the air.

251

'The ones who fight the greybloods,' Atanchu said. 'The ones who Bond the spirits of their ancestors.'

'Ah. Invokers. No, no. We do not have the taint of mindwraiths in our home. No.'

'You have no invokers in your lands?' Kartuuk said. 'None at all?'

'Yes, it is true, none at all, no.'

'But how can that be?' Atanchu cried. 'Every land has its invokers, even the barbarian lands. Who defends your homes when the greybloods come?'

'*Pai?*' the man said. 'Ah, you mean the broken ones. Yes, these we see from time to time but they do not trouble us. We send them away.'

The crowd gasped, and Atachu laughed, shaking his head as though he'd been entertaining the fancies of a small child. But Elari did not like the way the healer smiled as he spoke, nor did she like the way his eyes darted eagerly from face to face, weighing the impact of the words.

Before he could speak again, loud drums announced the first of the banquet's courses.

'Come,' Atanchu said, taking both her hands. 'Sit! Tell me about Aranduq. Tell me about your journey home! Kartuuk won't explain yet, but he said something important happened?'

It's in the carriage. Find it.

'I am tired,' Elari said. 'I came to greet Manax and then leave, but—' Her voice cut off as she saw one of the traders studying her with a strange little smile.

'Sister,' Atanchu said, touching her cheek, 'go and sleep. We can talk tomorrow. I'll tell Invoker Manax where you have gone.' He peered at her. His damaged right eye, white within white where the fire had burned it, was just as piercing as the brown. 'What's happened? What's wrong?'

'I—' Elari swallowed. 'I can't talk now.'

She turned away as her eyes began to sting, then headed for the stairs. She could hear Lyela behind her, but didn't dare look round. She felt as though all the air had gone from the night and she could

252

no longer breathe. She passed Osellia and gave her a nod, enough to signal that she wished her to remain. She passed Atoc, too, sprawled out drunk beside a fountain. She was nearly at the entrance to the main palace hallway when someone crashed into her from the left.

'Captain Elari!' Rozichu gripped her arm. Her face was wild, her eye paint smudged, and her feathered headdress askew. She gulped in long breaths then said, 'Captain I – I feel trapped! This place!'

Elari took her hand. 'Tell them you are ill. Then go to the training gardens and practise the Obsidian Dance. Or . . . or just run laps of the grounds. Something to exhaust your body and divert your mind.'

'Exhaust my body?'

The spray of blood.

The screams of the villagers.

Choose who lives and who dies.

'When I was . . . out there,' Elari said, 'I brought the fear back with me. That fear has been chasing me ever since. Sometimes, it comes close to catching me. You must outrun the fear, Invoker. You must learn to ignore its lies. It tricks you, but you can trick it back.'

Rozichu nodded, her wide mouth hanging open as though Elari had spoken a profound truth.

'That is why you still fight,' Rozichu said, 'isn't it? It brings you peace.'

'It—' Elari stopped. She had been about to deny it, but what was the point? Every greyblood she cut down brought her closer to banishing the spectre of the Bairneater. One day, she would dispatch enough to be rid of its shadow entirely.

'Th-thank you, Captain!' Rozichu said, bowing. Elari watched the girl dart along the promenade towards the steps leading up the cliffside. In that moment, she felt a swirling despair. Only seventeen rains of age, and yet the girl was already set upon the same path as she. It was not a path Elari wished on anyone.

'You would make her a good captain,' Lyela said softly.

Elari glared at her. 'You know nothing about what it is to serve one who invokes.'

The halls were quiet, with much of the staff still engaged in the banquet, but as they approached the walkway leading out into the darkness of the wanaban grove, Elari heard voices up ahead. There, beside the door, two figures stood before a towering statue of Itahua: Manax's first envoy and his coincounter. Elari could tell from their postures that they had been arguing.

'Let's go,' Elari muttered, turning back the other way, but Lyela pressed herself against the wall, listening. Elari had no desire to get pulled into a conversation with more of Manax's fawning sycophants, but Lyela was staring round the corner with an intensity that gave her pause.

'My mentor tried to overrule his First General once,' said the coincounter, a wiry, sour-faced man whose name Elari couldn't recall. 'Now he balances books for the mountain garrisons. There is only one month of thaw up there, did you know that?'

'We simply cannot stand by while he refuses a direct order from the king,' hissed the first envoy. 'Warlord Xinten must be made aware of . . .'

She trailed off as movement came from the darkness of the gardens beyond. The two outland healers appeared, speaking softly to each other. They paused when they saw Manax's aides.

'How did you get in here?' the first envoy, a shrunken sparrow of a woman, said sharply. 'This wing of the palace is only for members of the inner household.'

'Oh, please to know we are lost,' the dark one said, ringing his hands and smiling ingratiatingly. He looked at his companion. 'You are having war here, no? We have many things to sell for war. Many wondrous things.'

'We don't need your wondrous things,' the first envoy said scornfully. 'Now leave, please, before I have the guards throw you out.'

But there were no guards. And the two little traders did not move. Indeed, the light one cocked his head and said, 'Oh, I'm afraid you do need what we have to offer, my friend.'

His accent had changed. Gone was the sing-song lilting. Now, he spoke like any lowblood born in the Nine Lords slums.

'Bayamo, kindly escort these people out,' the first envoy said, just a hint of unease in her voice.

But the healers did not leave. Instead, they held out their hands, and blue smoke rose from their bodies like heat from a fire. No, not smoke; Elari saw now that the blueness had form. Laughing eyes. Groping hands. Long, smooth limbs.

The first envoy stood, gaping, but her coincounter companion Bayamo had the good sense to try to flee. He did not get far; in a heartbeat, one of the blue things was on him, melting into his body then streaking out through the top of his head in a spray of blood and bone and brain. As the coincounter collapsed, the blue creature smiled, its teeth white and pointed, and swept towards the first envoy.

Elari seized Lyela's arm, pulling her back the way they had come. And as the first envoy screamed, Lyela stopped resisting, and together they ran.

TWENTY-THREE

Jinao

Rain dripped from Jinao's nose. Rain squelched in his boots, in his closeclothes, in his hair. The bush was dense, and Jinao had no machete, and so his journey slowed to a crawl.

How foolish he'd been to set off with nothing. No food. No horse. Not even his water gourd. An afternoon into his abandonment of his dead brother's army, Jinao found himself stumbling blindly through the Riani wetwoods with nothing to live on and no idea where he was going.

You should have come alone, the Bairneater had said. Jinao did not intend to hear those words again. How many people had died because of him? How many more would die if Jinao did not heed his brother's final words? *Swear on the ancestors. Swear you will finish it.*

When he closed his eyes, Jinao could still hear the dull crack of his mother's staff landing on Julon's head. He could still hear Sellay's terrible scream as her husband crumpled to the ground. It didn't seem real. Julon was so full of vigour and strength and heart. He couldn't simply be gone, and by a single blow. If Jinao had been stronger, if he had been a better warrior, Julon would still be walking the mortal realm.

A sharp pain cut through Jinao's thoughts, something slicing into the meat of his calf. It was so sudden that he thought he'd cut himself on one of the sharp roots that sometimes jutted out of the ground like traps, but when he stooped down, he could find nothing.

It was nearly dark when Jinao heard distant shouts. They were searching for him, he realised with a stab of guilt. He felt guilty, too, for Sister Zalani, who would surely blame herself, and for poor Liet, riderless now. All who came with him came to meet their deaths, and so it was better for him to carry on alone.

If the Bairneater had his mother's memories, Jinao had to reach it before it could convey them to its fellow greybloods. All of Sulin's battle strategies; all of their people's vulnerabilities; ancestors help them, all the plans Jemusi claimed Sulin had been working on with Warlord Daloya . . . If the greybloods had them, what further damage could they do?

Jinao scratched at his calf – an insect bite, then, and a large one from the feel of the lump that had formed beneath the skin. Jinao knew Herinabad lay to the north. Somewhere along the way he would have to find a town, find transport. Fortunately, he did have a small pouch of coins under his battle skirt, which would serve to get him transport on a cart or perhaps a ride with a trading caravan. If Invoker Darsana Navret was still streaking through the wetwoods, he hoped that the Bairneater would know that she acted alone.

The forty innocent locals I trapped in a cave will now also die. The first thing Jinao needed to do when he reached a town was find help for the captives. If the cave the Bairneater had spoken of could be found, they might still be saved. There couldn't be that many places to hide forty people in such a damp, forested—

Something snared Jinao's ankle and then he was down, twisting awkwardly to one side. He reached his hands out to catch himself and slammed hand-first into a moss-covered boulder.

Jinao's left wrist snapped back painfully. He cried out, and twisted to the side, then plummeted to the forest floor.

Rain pelted down on him as he lay amid the sodden, muddy leaves. He would not weep. His mother always told him the ancestors had no use for his tears, that he dishonoured them when he shed them. His wrist was on fire and the insect bite on his calf was beginning to throb. Perhaps he should just stay there and never move again. The Bairneater couldn't challenge him if he were dead, and he was of no use to anyone alive – he never had been. He had killed Julon. Ancestors! He had killed Julon, as surely as if he had wielded the staff himself. He did not deserve to live while better people died all around him.

'Need a hand, sire?'

The voice was so close by that Jinao started, then winced. A knife of pain angled up his arm from his wrist, and when he lifted his hand, he saw an ominous red swelling at the base of his thumb. His feet had become entangled in a vine, he realised. He craned his neck, looking for the speaker.

'Go away,' Jinao mumbled at the darkness. 'Just turn around and pretend you didn't see me.'

'Erm . . . can't do that, sire. Been sent to fetch you.'

'Tell the others I'm not coming back. It's not safe for them.'

'Well, see, the thing is, sire . . . I'm not from the others.'

Jinao slid his good hand down to his belt, where he carried a single small knife. Bandits. What a fool he'd been! He knew these wetwoods could be riddled with bandits, even in monsoon season, and he had been blundering through them like a drunken elephant. Likely there were dozens poised in the trees above, watching him. Well, if they wanted his pouch of coins, they would have to take his life first.

Jinao jumped up, jabbing at the air, whipping around, then round again.

'Easy, sire! I'm a friend!'

He spotted the man then, leaning on a nearby tree. His accent suggested the City of Nine Lords, but the man looked like a local. He stood wearing loose pantaloons with no shirt or shoes, common as any lowblood. But the stranger watched Jinao with a half-smile that was cockier than any lowblood had a right to be. Jinao's eyes drifted to the tataus snaking round the man's sinewy brown arms. Simple, but larger than most lowblood family tataus. A traveller, perhaps; though what he was doing out in such a place was beyond Jinao.

'I don't need any friends,' Jinao said, turning and limping away. His ankle was sore, he realised, though mercifully not broken.

'Looks to me like you do,' the man said, scampering after Jinao. 'I'm Amit.' Brightness flared to Jinao's left, and he looked round to see the lowblood had lit a small techwork candle. Its red glow threw the surrounding wetwoods into eerie shadow. Night was coming, Jinao realised. The way would grow even more treacherous then.

'Don't worry about those *others*,' Amit said. 'They set off south ages ago, and they wasn't looking back. I've got a message for you, sire. From me masters, the Bhuten Wives.'

'I don't know any Bhuten Wives.'

Amit laughed as though Jinao had made a grand joke. 'Course not. Well, see, the wives, they take responsibility for these parts, and the Bairneater's been terrorising locals left, right and centre.'

'Responsibility . . .' Jinao paused. 'Have they found the cave? The Bairneater took forty lowbloods there and has left them to starve. If these wives you mention are part of the local guard, have them send out—'

'Don't you worry, sire. Don't you worry about none of that. It's all in hand. But the Bhuten Wives would like to meet you, if you'd be so kind. They want to offer you their help.'

'Tell them I don't need help,' Jinao said, kicking at a tangle of bush ahead of him. 'I hunt the beast alone.'

Amit slid a machete off his shoulder and sliced through the bush in one smooth, alarmingly violent motion.

'Course you don't. But they'd like to speak to you all the same.'

Jinao stepped through the opening. 'No. Thank them, but no.'

'No? So what is your plan? You heading off to fight one of the most feared named greybloods unarmed, with no map, no food, no water and no shelter?' He touched Jinao's arm. 'The wives' home is less than a day's walk from here. They have supplies. Weapons. You don't need to stay long – just listen to what they have to tell you.'

Jinao trudged onwards, shoulders hunched against the rain.

'That way leads to the south road, sire!' Amit called after him. 'And that snake bite on your leg . . . Might want to get that looked at.'

Jinao had thought the man was exaggerating, but before long, the pain in his leg had spread until it reached his hip, and he was beginning to feel dizzy. He staggered forwards from tree to tree, shaking off the vines that snagged at him, heedless of the direction now. He just needed to keep going. If he could just keep going . . .

'Easy, sire,' Amit said, catching him. Jinao hadn't seen the lowblood appear again but knew he had been following. The wetwoods swayed dangerously as though he was on a boat. 'Easy. I'll have them bring a cart to the Kalepur Highway. I reckon we can make it that far.'

Then he was moving, Amit half dragging him as he supported Jinao with his shoulders. Faces leered at Jinao from the shadows as he passed. His mother. The Bairneater. Julon. Sumalong, the folk hero's statue a ruin now in a ruined city.

'They're all dead,' Jinao heard himself say, his voice repeating around his head.

He was aware of a thinning in the trees up ahead, of figures running in from left and right. Then he felt nothing, heard nothing except the Bairneater's cruel laughter.

'Welcome back, Lord Jinao.'

Jinao opened his eyes.

He sat in the shade of a sweeping portico, looking out over the garden courtyard of a decaying mahal. Aged, moss-covered walls looked down on a busy, functional garden. Jinao saw rows of vegetables and herbs, and on the far side of the garden, a pen with goats, chickens and a single cow. The building that rose around it had once been grand, but its windows were now dirt-stained and its walls cracked by creeping plants. It was lived-in: Jinao could feel that without seeing the many dozens of souls he was sure dwelt within.

'Get him a drink, would you, Amit dear?'

'Yes, Nani.'

Jinao straightened. Two women sat in chairs to his left, sharing a bowl of lychees. The first was fleshy and jewelled and so heavily painted Jinao found it hard to tell her age. The tataus that swirled out from under her pink sari were intricate and detailed, all red and blue. He saw flowers, a dozen scarab beetles, and a long, lance-like weapon.

The woman caught him studying her and grinned. 'Pleased to meet you, Lord Jinao. Our wise-elder has given you something for the snake bite, although I fear that leg will take several days to heal.'

Jinao looked down and found that his calf had been bandaged and from the pungent scent, treated with some ointment. Out in the garden, a gaggle of ragged children ran past waving, and the plump woman waved back.

Amit appeared, holding a glass of water, which Jinao accepted gratefully. As he gulped down the blessed sweetness, he realised that Amit's tataus matched the woman's. He wondered how lowbloods could afford such exquisite work. But then, what lowbloods lived in a vast, decaying mahal?

'Show us his tataus,' the second woman said, and Amit lifted Jinao's hand – the thumb was in a splint, he saw – and pulled back the sleeve of a tunic Jinao hadn't known he was now wearing.

'It seems to be him,' the fleshy woman said. Her voice was disarmingly girlish, but her gaze was intent.

'How long have I been here?' Jinao said.

'Eight days.'

'Eight *days?*' Jinao started to rise, but Amit pushed him gently back down.

'Do you know who we are?' the second woman asked. She was a sinewy, stern-looking soul of fifty rains or more, and wore a plain grey kameez with a masculine cut. She regarded Jinao with naked hostility, and Jinao found himself flushing under her stare.

'You are . . . the Bhuten Wives, I presume,' Jinao said. 'But I have not heard of your noble household.'

'Oh, we are not *noble*,' the fleshy woman said with a giggle. She turned her luxurious feline eyes to her companion. 'Could it be he doesn't know?' Then she looked back at Jinao and said, 'I am Neena of the Kalepur rice farmers. Neena Farmer, if you will. And this is my wife, Nisha. You'll forgive her her face, My Lord of Cagai. I assure you it is nothing personal.'

The thin woman, Nisha, said nothing, still studying Jinao sceptically.

'And now, to business,' Neena said. 'We would like to lend our assistance in defeating the Bairneater. It has been rampaging through our province for nearly a moon, leaving a trail of death in its wake. Our family found forty of its most recent victims starving in a forest cave. We will not allow what happened in Aranduq to happen here.'

Jinao felt a swell of relief. 'They're OK? The forty lowbloods?'

'The *people* whom the creature imprisoned have been rescued, yes,' Neena said. 'But in this very town alone, ten souls have fallen to the Bairneater. Our friends further afield report graver losses. And everyone has heard about the destruction of Aranduq. But sadly, the invoker clans are rarely sympathetic to the plights of those they deem beneath them, and so the duty falls to us.'

Jinao swallowed more water. 'Invoker Darsana Navret is hunting the Bairneater,' Jinao said. 'But it is me it wants.'

'Oh, yes, we heard about Darsana,' Neena said, with a sparkle in her eye. 'Perhaps you do not know, but Warlord Uresh disowned her over six rains ago. He struck her from the family and seized her holdings. They call her the Heretic General in some parts, or the Wandering Lord. From what I hear, she squanders what wealth remains her on an army of outland mercenaries.'

Her eyes glittered merrily again, and Jinao had the feeling that his reaction was being weighed. He kept his expression as neutral as he could and said, 'If you're not part of Clan Navret, then . . . Forgive me, but then you do not have the resources with which to fight the beast.'

Neena glanced at Nisha and giggled, and the thinner woman rolled her eyes and leaned forward. 'Let me speak plainly,' Nisha said. 'We didn't need to involve you at all. My wife here thought it a courtesy that we—'

'I wanted to meet him myself!' Neena said, clapping her hands excitedly.

'A *courtesy* that we inform you of our intentions.'

'Yes, but also,' Neena said, 'if a creature as powerful as the Bairneater has a particular interest in him, it would serve us to know why before we go charging into the fight. I have never heard of a greyblood behaving in quite this manner before.'

'I was in favour of your capture and surrender to the greyblood as bait,' Nisha said coolly, 'so that we might finish the work you seem incapable of finishing yourself.'

'It doesn't want to kill me,' Jinao said. 'But I am the one who has to kill it.'

'You see!' Neena said, gesturing again. 'Here is information that is useful to us. What did you mean by that, Lord Jinao? Why doesn't it want to kill you?'

'The beast seems to want to . . . teach me. When we fight, it wants to bring out my skill in invocation. And it doesn't like it when others are with me.'

'Absurd,' Nisha muttered.

'Before we continue,' Neena said, 'we have something of yours.' She stood and clapped her hands, and a moment later a young girl appeared from behind a bed of tall beans, leading a familiar, rust-coloured horse.

'Liet?' Jinao said, lowering his glass.

'She arrived the day after you,' Neena said. 'She refused to leave our gardens. She simply shut down and nobody could move her! My niece recognised her genus as being popular in Mizitoland. She is yours, I take it?'

'Yes . . .' Jinao shook his head. 'How could she know I would come here?'

'Horses are ancient creatures, Lord Jinao,' Neena said. 'They know many things.' She took a sip from her glass. 'Now, My Lord of Cagai . . .

In your pursuit of the Bairneater, you believe yourself to be its hunter. But this is not the case. Do you know what you have become?'

'I told you; it's not a hunt. It tells me where to go and I . . . follow.'

'Lord Jinao, you are this creature's *carrier*. That is what you have become. It is a disease and you are the one spreading it. Wherever you go, death follows. You are, quite simply, a source of infection. This leaves us with two options: use you as bait to lure the creature here—'

'The option I favour,' Nisha said.

'Or lend you our resources and expertise.'

'Forgive me,' Jinao said, 'but I don't see how you could help. Even with an army, Lord Darsana and my . . . my brother Julon, ancestors preserve him, were not able to defeat it.'

'Your brother is dead?' Nisha said.

'Yes. It killed him. The Bairneater.' Jinao's throat tightened, so he took another swallow of water.

Neena clasped her jewelled hands together and sat forward. 'Do you know the Song of Legends Lost, Lord Jinao?'

'Of course I do.'

'Tell us.'

Jinao sighed. He certainly wasn't going to sing for them, but he recited the words flatly. '*When the Greyblood Kings rise again, so too will the ancient Warlords nine. Mizito, Lord of the Staff. Navret, Lord of the Chakram. Tarsin, Lord of the Bow. Qaneen, Lord of the Shamshir. Adatali, Lord of the Ida. Itahua, Lord of the Macuahuitl. Kzani, Lord of the Spear. Menit, Lord of the Axe. And Ahiki, Lord of Them All.*'

'Such pretty words!' Neena said, clapping her hands. 'But allow me to correct one minor point.' She cleared her throat and began to sing in a surprisingly rich, melodious voice. '*When the Greyblood Kings rise again, so too will the ancient Warlords ninety-nine. Eight bowed their heads to the Traitor King. Eight fled across the seas, new fortunes to bring. All the rest crossed beyond the pyre or faded back into the mire.*'

'What does that mean?' Jinao said.

Nisha snorted. 'It means, Invoker Jinao, that there were never just eight warlords under the king. Our best guess is it was closer to eighty. Our beloved Ahiki kings insisted that all warlords bowed to their rule. Many did not wish to. There was a war. The Royal Clan won. The defeated warlords either fled across the seas or took their own lives, or they agreed to fade into obscurity – fallen soldiers, if you will, and their descendants would be fallen families, although we prefer the term *Families*.'

A young girl with wide, dancing eyes appeared, carrying wine and paratha stuffed with lentils. Neena set upon the food immediately and gestured for the girl to pour. When she offered Jinao a glass, he took it, and after a moment's hesitation, tipped the contents back in one swallow.

'Just what are you saying?' he said thickly.

'We're saying this . . .' Nisha drew to her feet. Her body was as lean and hard as a soldier. When she threw up her hands, the sleeves of her kameez fell back, revealing the tataus that glowed all along her sinewy arms. When she closed her eyes, the intricate patterns came to life. Light spilled out of her hands and ran across the lawn. She spoke no words. Performed no dance. But the light cascaded out.

A woman took form, plump and fleshy. Not just plump, Jinao realised – plump and with child. She stood eight, perhaps nine feet in height, her painted face arch and knowing, the jewels at her forehead swinging in an unseen breeze. She held a gold-tipped lance in one chubby hand, its sharpened tip shimmering with light.

'Lord Jinao,' Neena said, extending her arm, 'meet Bhuten, Lord of the Barcha. Our ancestor. Leader of our Family. And now, if you'll excuse us.'

She clapped her hands, and two men appeared, carrying chains and manacles.

Jinao braced his hands on his seat, preparing to rise. The heat of invocation crept down his arms, setting his skin ablaze.

'I wouldn't if I were you,' Neena said. 'Bhuten here will slice off those beautiful arms of yours before you even have a chance to speak your forefather's name.'

'I thought you were going to help me!' Jinao said.

'Yes,' Neena said, with a slight pout. 'I did favour that option. But I'm afraid my wife here always gets her way.'

TWENTY-FOUR

Elari

'Captain, please, sit down!' Ishaan cried, as Elari strode to check the main door for the third time. Still locked. As was the door to her dressing chamber, where Cantec's barrels of techwork remained hidden. Once, she'd loved the high limestone ceilings and sweeping windows of her apartments, but that had been before the Feverlands, before the Bairneater, before she had to *choose, choose*. Now, her bedchamber, with its wide sunken bed and stone floor, seemed too open, too vulnerable to attack. Her main windows looked out on the gardens, one storey below, and the city of Qenqar in the valley beyond. It seemed a thousand eyes could see within. Elari had found ways to cope, over time. But the events of the evening had brought all the old fears crashing back down.

'Blue monsters,' Chellahua said flatly, regarding Lyela. 'Blue monsters with claws and teeth. And the healers no longer had foreign accents but spoke like Nine Lords lowbloods.'

'I know it sounds absurd,' Lyela said, 'but I saw it with my own eyes.' She stood by the small ebony table where Elari's pitcher of night wine stood. Lyela was on her third glass, and that fact alone was enough to trouble Elari, because in the short time she had known the woman, she had never seen her look afraid, not even when she faced the grey-bloods. But she looked afraid now.

267

'Atanchu knew nothing of the Ahiki head,' Elari said, stopping. 'He said the nuns—'

A burst of drunken laughter sounded from the gardens below, and Elari jumped, her heart hammering.

'Captain,' Ishaan said, 'let's rest. By morning, the crime will have been discovered and we can tell Invoker Kartuuk what we saw.'

'What if they're coming here?' Elari said. 'Wh-what if they try to silence us, like they silenced . . .'

She trailed off as she caught movement in the corner of her eye. A figure, rising among the shadows. Grey limbs. Low laughter.

An invoker, the Bairneater said, *or all these people? Who will you sacrifice, Captain?*

'Leave me alone!' Elari screamed at the corner that was now empty. Then Chellahua was standing before her, her blue eyes filled with tears as she pulled Elari into her arms.

'What happened out there on the border?' Lyela said.

'That's not your concern,' Osellia replied. She led Elari over to the daybed and helped her to sit, then poured her a glass of wine. But all Elari could hear was the Bairneater's laughter and the cries of the dying.

'There's something monstrous in the palace,' Elari whispered. 'S-something invoked like an ancestor but definitely not of them.'

In the end, Elari tipped her daybed onto one side and positioned it against the wall. It was an old trick, but there had been moons, when she'd first returned from the Feverlands border, when it was the only way she could sleep. She brought her macuahuitl into the nook she'd created, and curled up around it, closing her mind to the clamour in her head. Not long after she lay down, she felt Ishaan slip in beside her, followed by Osellia. The familiar press of their bodies felt like the sweetest wine, as Ishaan reached up to stroke her hair and Osellia took her hand. It was times like this when Elari ached for Cantec, when his absence felt like a great void between the four of them. She realised that she hadn't spared even a thought for how they too might be grieving. She had been with him longest, true, but that did not mean she was the only one who had lost the man she loved.

Elari woke before dawn and padded naked across the cool stone to fetch more wine. Sleep had dulled the churning fear to a gnawing in the pit of her stomach.

'So all four of you are dedicated to each other?' Lyela said from where she sat by the wall. 'All five of you?' Her face looked drawn; Elari guessed the other woman hadn't slept at all.

'The bond between an invoker and their quartet is the most intimate bond there is,' Elari said, pouring herself a glass of wine. 'Every night we slept together like that, Cantec between us. Every day, when he invoked, when he let the spirit of another enter his body, he entrusted himself completely to our care.'

'I can't imagine sharing the one I love with four others.'

Elari smiled. 'I can't imagine choosing only one love from among the four I have.'

'And who is that?' Lyela said, nodding towards the etched portrait of a woman which hung above the door.

'That? That is Chinnaro Itahua, First General Manax's sister. She died in the Busharn Massacre, but it was her map that Cantec followed on his voyage.'

Lyela smiled sadly. 'So two members of this family were lost chasing the same legend?'

'Cantec took up her work, yes. They were very close.'

The door-gong sounded, crisp and clean. Chellahua, sleeping alone in the sunken bed, snapped upright in a tumble of pale hair.

'Yes?' she called loudly.

'F-forgive me, Lieutenants, Captain!' came the tremulous voice of a messenger. 'You brother Atanchu and Invoker Kartuuk have sent for you! It is most urgent!'

Elari and Chellahua exchanged looks.

'What do you mean?' Chellahua called.

'It is Invoker Cantec! They are burning his body!'

Twenty pyres burned upon the stony beach when Elari flew down the final staircase. Twenty, for the twenty dead they had brought back with them from Jebba. Elari had put on the first white robe she could find: a simple sleeping tunic. It was a poor way to honour Cantec – a poor way to honour anyone – but she'd had no time to don her feathers or paint her skin. Ancestors curse Manax! Why would he seek to exclude her from the moment Cantec finally crossed the pyre? She had never spared Manax much love, that was true: she saw too much of her own father in him. But she had obeyed every one of his commands, and she had given her life to serving his clan.

They all turned as Elari's feet crunched upon the shingle, and immediately she knew something was amiss. Kartuuk's face was even more unreadable than usual, and Atanchu, at his side, gripped his hand as though his husband might drown if he let go. Elari's brother wore one of his simpler masks over the scarred half of his face – smooth jade set with a single onyx – but his good eye was red from weeping. Atoc stood off at the water's edge, skipping stones across the surf, his back turned to dead and living alike. First General Manax himself stood some distance from them all, arms folded, his long hair snapping in the breeze. From what Elari could see, he still wore his sleeping tunic.

But it was the sight of little Rozichu, kneeling alone by a roaring pyre, her hands red with blisters, that told Elari all she needed to know.

'Captain!' Ishaan cried, seizing her arm, but Elari lurched forward.

'Where is the spirit wood!' Elari shouted. She slipped past Kartuuk and stared wildly from pyre to pyre. Which was him? It was impossible to tell one shrunken, blackened corpse from the next. They burned hungrily deep within the piles of driftwood and kapok, the sickly-sweet aroma of their burning filling the morning. But Elari had stood at more pyres than she could count . . . every warrior of the clans had.

Spirit wood burned slowly, and with a distinctive blue flame. She saw none of that here. None. Neither did she see any weapons, any etchings, anything personal to send the slain on their way.

'General Manax!' Elari cried. 'Please . . . where is the spirit wood?'

'There is no spirit wood in the palace,' Manax replied without turning.

'He needs spirit wood! How else will he rejoin the ancestors?'

'There's no such thing as rejoining the ancestors,' Manax said. 'The dead are gone, and their will has no bearing on the living.'

'No!' Elari turned to Ishaan. 'Find spirit wood! In the city – there must be some.'

'Captain . . .' Ishaan looked past her, their small face lined with pain.

'*Please!*' Elari cried.

'I'll go,' Osellia muttered.

'We need buckets! Atanchu, someone get the servants! We need water! If we can put out the flames—'

'Captain,' Ishaan muttered, enfolding her in their arms.

'We can still send them on! If we put out the fires now, there will be something left to send. Kartuuk!'

Kartuuk turned, but it was Manax who spoke, crunching across the smooth stones to face Elari. 'You will not touch the pyres,' he said. 'I will order you removed if you try to intervene.'

'*How could you!*'

'Aranduq City has fallen,' Manax said, addressing them all. 'Yet the king would send our warriors west to die in his doomed invasion. Jakhenaten Ahiki may be ruler of the Nine Lands, but I am the Guardian of Intiqq. I refuse to send my people to a needless death. I know you all returned to join the king's war. But instead, we will be pressing south into Mizitoland. If First General Sulin's children would abandon the river, then I will take their place. We will reclaim Aranduq and secure the southern border.'

'Please! We must put out the flames . . .' Elari began, then trailed off as she caught movement on the steps: the two little healers, standing in the palace entrance, wearing identical robes of white linen. Why were they still in Livinghall? Why hadn't they fled?

Elari pointed as the two men descended the steps. 'They—' She swallowed. 'First General, those two men are a danger to us all. I saw them yesterday, with Coincounter Bayamo and Envoy Injum. They . . . they attacked . . .'

Elari faltered as more people emerged from the palace, all dressed in funeral whites: Manax's aides and advisers; several senior members of the household . . . and there, adjusting his white headdress, Coincounter Bayamo, with fussy little Envoy Injum at his side.

Ishaan caught Elari as her legs weakened. 'I saw them,' Elari murmured. 'I – I saw them die.'

'Father,' Kartuuk said, staring across at Manax while the pyres crackled behind him, 'we cannot fight in the lands of another clan without their invitation.'

'An invoker's duty is to protect the Nine Lands, yes?' Manax said. 'That is what I intend to do by retaking Aranduq.'

'Aranduq is not ours to retake,' Kartuuk said. 'When our warriors fail to arrive on the war front, there will be consequences. When the death of that Ahiki is discovered, there will be consequences. The ancestors turn from—'

'The ancestors have nothing to do with this!' Manax shouted. 'The ancestors should be left to rest, and not dragged into the affairs of the living. Too much of our lives is driven by what others tell us our ancestors want.'

'Bayamo,' Elari called as the coincounter passed her. 'Bayamo, are you well?'

Bayamo looked around in confusion, then made a hasty bow. 'Captain Elari. My sincere condolences to you on this day when we remember Cantec.'

'Last night,' Elari said. 'Last night, I . . . near the wanaban grove, I saw . . .'

What? What was she going to say? She saw the top of the man's head burst open? She saw blue apparitions climb into his body? She saw two outlanders murder their own hosts? She could feel the eyes of those around her watching. It was no secret that the horrors of the Feverlands plagued her still. Servants talked, soldiers talked, but Elari had always thought she inspired them by fighting on. Yet now, as Kartuuk looked away and her sweet brother Atanchu's good eye filled with tears of sympathy, she felt hollow.

'Please accept my deepest condolences for your loss.' Bayamo shuffled off, and as Elari watched him go, she could hear the Bairneater's laughter in her mind.

'You wish to see more of our wares?' the light-skinned healer said, picking his way over to her as the other new arrivals fanned out. 'We have much and many herbs for pains of the mind.'

His hand came to rest on her arm. His palms were rough and calloused – lowblood hands, or the hands of a soldier. His eyes glittered with mirth as he peered up into her face.

'I'm not interested in your wares,' Elari said stiffly, as Ishaan took a step towards the man.

'You sure, Captain?' the healer said, dropping his sing-song accent, switching to the flat tones of the City of Nine Lords. 'I think you're very interested. But looking too deeply ain't good for your health, if you catch my meaning.'

Ishaan leaned forward. 'If you mean to threaten—'

'We got no quarrel with you, love. But get in our way and that'll change.'

Then he made a small, mocking bow and drifted further down the beach.

His words leeched something from her. Elari dropped to the ground, feeling suddenly weak and old and tired. Ishaan held her while she wept. Nobody spoke to her except Atanchu. And after a time, they all began to drift back into the palace in ones and twos. Elari was scarcely aware of them. Because all her work had been for nought. After everything Cantec had suffered, after everything that took place in Ewo City, he had still been kept from passing into the ancestral realm. Instead, Cantec had been burned to ash like kindling under a cook-fire. They had spoken no words. They had sung no songs. Not a single holy one was in attendance. It was as if his life, his death, had meant nothing.

'I've heard the Hill People say that nothing can keep a soul from rejoining their ancestors,' Ishaan said softly as they stroked Elari's hair. 'I met many of them in my days on the streets, and they don't use spirit wood at all. They believe the bond between us and those who came before is more powerful than anything holy ones can bestow upon us. That power is carried in our blood. Nothing can erase that. I'm sure that, wherever Cantec is now, he is loved and he is not alone.'

Elari stared at the flames. The last time she had sat before so many funeral pyres had been the day after the Bairneater had forced her to *choose, choose*. The greyblood watched her now, from the corner of her eyes, smiling, laughing, mocking.

Elari squeezed her dove's hand. 'Cantec used to tell me he could feel a power greater than himself when he practised the Obsidian Dance. He believed the hands of those who wielded his macuahuitl before him joined their skill to his. I suppose that weapon is somewhere out across the ocean now.'

'Wherever it is, one day it will find its way back to him, I am certain.'

The sun was past its zenith by the time Osellia returned, her dark brown skin glistening with sweat. Under her arm she carried a bundle of spirit wood bound with twine. Elari tugged at the bindings as soon as her dove set the bundle down. No one else remained on the beach now save Kartuuk and Atanchu. When they saw what she was doing, they moved silently to help.

Three of the pyres had burned themselves out, leaving behind blackened circles of shingle and ash. The remainder smoked wanly, their contents all but lost to the wind. Still, Elari set a length of spirit wood upon each and with Osellia's help, lit the flames anew.

'Cantec, we bid you good journey,' she whispered as she stood over the nearest pyre. 'In the name of the nine warlords who defend these

274

lands even in death, we bid you good journey.' It occurred to her then that none of the others had family present to send them on with kind words. She didn't know who was who, but surely the ancestors would recognise them still. She ran through the names of all those who had been killed, then added, 'We bid you good journey.'

She was staring at the final pyre, the tide now lapping at the blackened mess, when Ishaan appeared at her side, dark eyes dancing with alarm.

'Captain,' they said, 'apologies, but I think you should come. We found a thief in your apartments.'

Elari blinked at them. 'A thief?'

'It is best if you come.'

The towering doors to Elari's apartments stood ajar as they approached. Elari swept forwards and stepped into the brightness of her receiving room.

Lyela lay face down on the cool stone floor, Chellahua astride her, obsidian knife pressed to the side of the older woman's neck.

'I caught her,' Chellahua said, baring her teeth, 'in your dressing chamber, going through Cantec's techwork. She is a liar and a thief. Let me slit her throat!'

Lyela tried to lift her head. 'If you'd just let me explain!'

'Silence!' Chellahua snarled. 'You were told never to touch those barrels. But I knew from the first that you sought to abuse my captain's kind heart.'

'This is why she came with us,' Osellia said. 'It's what she wanted all along.'

Elari crossed the room and sat on the broad window seat, the night sky at her back. She turned to Lyela, a dull anger rising within her. What a fool she'd been to trust the woman. 'Talk,' she said. 'And quickly, before I give my doves what they want. And I warn you, they are not gentle.'

Lyela's hazel eyes swung round. 'I – I saw an assassin. A nightblade! I saw them in your chambers, Captain, and—'

275

'Goat-spit,' Osellia said, squatting to point her knife in the older woman's face. 'There was no nightblade. The truth now. All of it, or would you prefer to lose an ear?'

'Who are you working for?' Chellahua said, pressing down with her knee.

'Nobody! As I said, I—'

Chellahua struck her hard with the back of one hand, her jewelled ring catching Lyela across the cheekbone. As a single trickle of blood traced a line down the woman's brown skin and onto the stone floor, she began to weep softly . . .

No; not weep, Elari realised. She was laughing.

'Keep going,' Lyela said between laughs. 'Far worse has been done to me a thousand times over.'

Elari stood. 'I took you into my trust. I brought you into my household. And this is how you thank me?' She looked across at her doves. 'I have no further use of her. Just be sure to dispose of the body beyond the palace grounds.'

Ishaan strode forward, elbowing Osellia aside and pulling Lyela's head up by her hair, exposing her neck.

'Wait, wait!' Lyela cried as Elari strode towards the door. 'All right, I admit it. I was looking through the techwork. I – I am sorry. I should have asked you, but I . . . I just couldn't take the chance that you would say no!'

'She admits it!' Chellahua said.

'I found something! In one of the barrels! It's . . . it's in my tunic, if you'd just untie—'

'Oh no!' Chellahua said, laughing. 'Do you think us complete fools?'

'Where in your tunic?' Ishaan said.

'The left pocket!' Lyela said. 'I was going to bring it to you once I realised what it was!'

Ishaan fumbled roughly at Lyela's side for a moment, then straightened, holding a crumpled square of strange, thin papyrus.

Elari took the papyrus and unfolded it to reveal several columns of neat, looping symbols.

'The ink looks relatively fresh,' Lyela said.

'Silence!' Chellahua snapped.

'It's in Old Tiku,' Elari said, eyes swimming. 'I – I know because my father forced me to learn ancient poetry in the language, as a child. Cantec was the only other person I've met who had studied it.'

'Can you read it?' Lyela asked.

Elari frowned. Old Tiku was a slippery language, many of its words possessing multiple meanings, much of its phraseology figurative. 'If I use Cantec's books, then yes.' She felt a swell of hope. This had to be it. The object Cantec had wanted her to find: a message in a language only she was likely to recognise, and which only she possessed the tools to translate.

It's in the carriage. Find it.

'I need to think,' Elari said. 'Get her away from me.'

Ishaan sheathed their blade. 'I'll have the guards take her to the dungeon.'

'Yes. Wait, no. No; we keep her here, for now. I do not want the wider household involved, not with everything that is happening. Put her in Cantec's old study.'

'I still think we should cut her,' Chellahua said as she hauled Lyela to her feet.

TWENTY-FIVE

Jinao

Jinao paced the darkness of his cell. Each time he reached the bars, he threw out his hands. Each time, ancestral light surged within him, momentarily dazzling, and then . . . *Nothing*. The urge simply fled. The energy faded. It was as though, without the Bairneater near, he couldn't muster the passion to do anything.

There were no windows in the Bhuten Wives' dungeons, but going by the number of bowls of okra soup his silent guard had brought him, Jinao guessed he'd been their captive for three or four days. Did his siblings know the truth about the Fallen Families? Likely they did. Likely he was the only one who had lived in ignorance. Of course more than nine families were strong enough to Bond the spirits of their ancestors. And why would the ancient king Ahiki, saviour of humanity, have had only eight warlords at his side? He had brought an entire civilisation east to settle the empty lands that, aeons before, had belonged to the Scathed.

Jinao knew why his mother had never told him: she was too proud. She hated lowbloods. She'd always been convinced of her family's superiority over everyone. She would have been loath to ever admit lowblood invokers might exist.

A noise sounded from the end of the corridor. Jinao pressed his face against the bars. A light approached, accompanied by voices.

'Open the cell,' came Neena Bhuten's girlish voice. Light assaulted Jinao, and he threw an arm across his eyes. Keys rattled, followed by the groan of a creaking hinge.

'My Lord Jinao, I hope you can forgive our lack of hospitality,' Neena said. 'We simply couldn't risk you gallivanting off around the country-side, sowing destruction in your wake.'

'If this is how you people treat guests,' Jinao said, 'it's no wonder they call you Fallen Families.'

'Please,' Neena said. 'Just Families. We are the Families. Tonight, there is to be a celebration, ahead of our departure to hunt your nemesis. We would like you to join us, as guest of honour.'

Jinao stole a look at her, an ample silhouette against the light. 'What if I say *fuck you*?' he asked.

'Then I must, regretfully, insist. Bring him, if you please.'

Jinao was bundled out of his cell and into the corridor, then up stone steps and out into the blinding sunlight of an overgrown court-yard. He considered making his body slack, or catching his feet to trip them up, but what would be the point?

The gardeners and children he passed scarcely looked up as he was manhandled onwards. Perhaps ragged highbloods in chains were everyday sights to them. Who knew what these Fallen Families were capable of?

They marched him to a dilapidated bathhouse, and for the remainder of the afternoon, Jinao was scrubbed and trimmed and powdered. Then two women dressed him in an Ekari-style shirt and slippers – because, of course, one province of Mizitoland was indis-tinguishable from another. He noticed tents in the gardens he passed, with lowblood families sitting outside at small cook-fires. When he asked, the guard sneered at him and said, 'Your bloody king's war quota is driving thousands from their homes. The wives offer them somewhere safe to hide.'

It was nearing dark when they led him out into the misty rain and onto a hillside that climbed away from the decaying mahal. Children in red and orange swept past, carrying platters of steaming food up to a pavilion that was bright with music and laughter.

Noise and colour greeted Jinao as he passed through the entryway and into the heaving interior. The raucousness was nothing like the stately affairs his mother had presided over. People. So many people. Lowbloods that smelt of sweat and fields. Children. Elders. All jostled cheek by jowl, loading their plates, shouting and arguing in a dozen different tongues. If anything could confirm these people's birth, it was the rowdy way they celebrated.

Many of the faces that turned to regard him had a local look about them, but he saw people from across the Nine Lands. Performers entertained circles of cheering drunks. Acrobats twisted their bodies into knots, or swallowed blades or flames. One man in barbarian dress stood talking loudly, while at his side sat a great bearded cat of Ulamara, and not a soul present stared. What such people were doing here in a Riani backwater, Jinao couldn't imagine. He only hoped they didn't intend to join the wives' accursed hunt.

'Ah, there you are,' Neena said brightly, patting a cushion at her side. She and her wife sat on a dais with a dozen others, and Jinao was marched up and seated with them at a low table heaving with food. 'Thank you for joining us, Lord Jinao. You're just in time for the play.'

Jinao said nothing, letting his gaze sweep the room, wondering how many people present knew he was a captive. He had to get out. He had to get out, and soon, to have a hope of reaching Herinabad on time.

'It is *The Death of the Second Singer*,' Neena said, as six outland troupers stepped into the space that had been cleared before them. 'A classic Febari tale. Perhaps you know it?'

'You need to let me go,' Jinao said.

Most of the troupers performed naked; only their musicians wore clothes – grey damasks and heavy skirts. Jinao found their music to be a meandering, discordant mess. They had no drums at all, and the main instrument seemed to be a circular, stringed monstrosity with a

280

sound like a Yennish piano. They babbled away in their strange outland tongue, emoting and regaling while the party continued on noisily around them.

A parade of people came to the dais while the play trundled on, ostensibly to speak to Neena and Nisha, though Jinao saw the way their eyes slid round to him. He wondered what they would do if he sprang up and bolted for the exit. One scruffy-looking woman attended by a waif-like child insisted on shaking Jinao's hand, in the northern style, and told him she was a great admirer of his mother. Jinao plastered on a thin smile in response and let her pump away until she had finished speaking.

Jinao sampled every morsel that was brought before him. After the stringy okra soup, everything that passed his lips tasted exquisite. He had just swallowed some pistachio barfi when Neena beckoned over a man in a sweeping robe of brown and gold. The stranger was bald save for a circle of pale yellow hair on the crown of his head, which had been braided with silk threads in a dozen colours. His hands were long and bejewelled, and his smiling mouth had a leering quality to it that Jinao did not like at all.

'Lord Jinao, this is Princen Hothin ab an Tak,' Neena said.

The outlander made a sweeping bow, his gaze wandering unashamedly over Neena's ample bosom.

'Princen Hothin, Lord Jinao here has a particular interest in the invokers of other lands. He was telling me just the other day that the shadow he invokes is mightier than all the others.'

Shadow. Jinao supposed the outlander meant a Bonded ancestor. And yet he could not help but feel that the word sounded somehow insulting.

The princen smiled, revealing a single gold tooth. 'Across the sea, we have shadows to make even your Ahiki quail,' he said, in his curious, flat accent. 'The Death Singer, who can melt minds and raise the bodies of the dead. The Thousand, an entire army Bonded to a single mortal. The Six Sacred Beasts. And more besides. I even know a man who has travelled beyond the Feverlands.'

'Surely not!' Neena cried, her hand going to her chest.

'You do not believe me?' Hothin said. 'Have you heard of the palanquin riders of Quenon? Some claim they are from noble families, and many are, but when I was a boy begging on the streets, one such rider took pity on me and stopped. They dropped three golden queens at my feet, and though I was half starved, I did not take the coins, for the hand that reached beyond those velvet curtains was not human.'

'So, in the barbarian lands,' Neena said, 'greybloods ride palanquins, and beggars may become princens, is that it?'

'No, no!' the outlander said, all mock outrage. 'It was no *sottotharn* monster that rode within. It was a mortal, but not human.'

Neena slid her eyes round to Jinao, so he tipped his head back and drained his glass. His fifth now? He couldn't quite recall. Hothin caught his eye. 'This one, this lord, does not believe me, I think,' he said.

Jinao leaned forward. 'You're saying the outland ancestors are animals and monsters?' he said. The drink was making him bold, he realised. Unwise, if he was going to find a way to escape.

'Who said anything about ancestors?' Princen Hothin replied with a chuckle, and then he turned and drifted away.

Neena watched Jinao closely, and he knew then that the entire exchange had been for his benefit. 'You're trying to show me the world is filled with invokers summoning all sorts of . . . people out of the ancestral realm,' Jinao said. 'Is that it?'

'Me?' Neena said. 'Why, I merely wish you to have a pleasant evening before we begin our expedition.'

'If you go anywhere with me, you'll all be killed. Everyone here; all these foreign warriors. Killed. You said so yourself: where I go, death follows. I need to face the Bairneater alone.'

'These souls you see before you are among the most experienced in the world at hunting greybloods. If all goes well, you will live to tell this fine tale. But look now: the murder of the Second Singer is about to take place.'

A young boy stepped out onto makeshift stage, naked but for a wreath of flowers about his neck. Perhaps it was because this was his first performance, but to Jinao he looked genuinely fearful as the man playing the First Singer seized his hand and spoke his grand, incomprehensible lines.

Then a blade came out and two women stepped forward and slit the child's throat.

Jinao cried out. He was on his feet before he could stop himself, his hands aflame with the heat of invocation. Many heads turned his way, faces creased with amusement. Jinao stared, aghast, as blood pulsed down the boy's chest. The troupers let him crumple to the floor, while the First Singer uttered more meaningful, incomprehensible words, his hands still red with the dead child's blood.

'That's real blood!' Jinao cried.

'Yes,' Neena said, smiling. 'In his country, it is a great honour for that boy and his family to perform this scene. Only those of the noblest birth and the highest blood are able to play the part of the Second Singer. That boy is now destined a position of great standing in his troupe.'

'He's destined for the pyre!' Jinao cried, but as he stared, the women sat the child up, and another trouper waved a shard of techwork before his neck. The child gasped, and coughed, and then his fellow actors pulled him to his feet. They stood before the audience, basking in the applause and cheering, and the boy's eyes shone with pride. Jinao squinted at the child's neck and saw a thin scar there; nothing more.

'These people value the sanctity of childhood above all else,' Neena said. 'They do not send their young to war. They do not train them to be killers. Neither do they force their ancestors, the ones who should be most hallowed to us all, into endless centuries of battle. In their culture, only the most reviled, the most condemned, are chosen for a martial Bond. *Possession*, they name it. The very concept of an entire clan of warrior invokers is abhorrent to them.' She lifted her glass. 'Has it never occurred to you that perhaps invocation is no different from the king's draft? The unwilling forced into pointless war?'

Jinao looked round and saw that, for once, she wasn't smiling. Her gaze was hard as she watched the troupers clear away their props.

'You hate the clans,' Jinao said.

'Yes. I do. But I also pity you. The killing of the Second Singer, who is always played by a child, symbolises the loss of innocence that forced invocation results in. I thought that you, coming so late to invocation, might understand.'

'Why do you care if I understand?'

'Because, if you survive our encounter with the Bairneater, I want you to take what you have learned back to your clan. I want you to think about how different things could be if a handful of families did not spend their lives and the lives of their children in combat while others exist who could help them end their war. I want you to refuse the king's draft. And I want you to think about who your true enemy is.'

'What do you mean?'

'You call yourself invoker, Jinao Mizito, yet what do you truly know of communing with your ancestors? Have you ever felt the joy of generations of learning pressing upon your mind? Have you harnessed the love, the resolve, of your forebears, and felt them lift you when you fall? Have you ever performed the Dance of Broken Blades and channelled the will of your people into one? Have you ever fought with the fists of fifty warriors as you moved through the poses of emii? Have you ever peered beyond the pyre to see the truth of those who came before, and vowed never to forget? Well, My Lord Jinao? Have you?'

'You people are insane.'

Neena stood and clapped her hands, and two guards appeared.

'Invoker Jinao is tired,' she said. 'Show him to his rooms, so that he may rest before we begin our journey.'

'*Let me go!*' Jinao cried as they bundled him away. 'Let me go, or all these people are going to die!' But Neena had turned to whisper

284

coquettishly in her wife's ear, and soon the guards were marching him through a side door.

He had expected them to return him to his cell, but instead they marched him to a room high in the southern wing of the mahal. It was small, but well furnished, with a large, Riani-style bed, and rugs upon the floor. A narrow window was set into the far wall, too small to climb through, but wide enough to admit a pleasant breeze.

'Sweet dreams, My Lord,' one of the guards said mockingly, and then the heavy door shut, and Jinao heard the rattle of keys.

A bottle of Jebbanese red stood on a small table. Jinao pulled out the cork and helped himself. In the morning, he would start working on a way out. When he had downed half the contents and the room was spinning nicely, he lay back on the bed and closed his eyes.

It seemed only an instant later that he jerked awake. The bed was wet where he'd let the bottle fall. The candle had burned low, and the room stood in semi-darkness. He had a moment to wonder what had roused him when it came again – a hurried knocking at his door.

Jinao crossed the room, which lurched dizzyingly as he walked.

'Whoever you are,' Jinao slurred, 'I don't have a key, so I can't open the door.'

There followed a silence long enough for Jinao to wonder if his visitor had gone, before the rattling started up again. It seemed to go on for a long while before the door swung open, forcing Jinao to dart back.

A ragged child of perhaps ten or eleven stood there, staring at him with wide dark eyes. She gripped a length of techwork in her little hand. After a moment, Jinao placed her from the banquet: she had been standing in attendance on the scruffy-looking elder who had gripped his hand so firmly. Her tightly curled hair made a halo around her dark brown face.

'I suspect you have the wrong room,' Jinao said wearily, turning away.

'Oh no, begging your pardon, Your Lordship. I definitely got the right room.' The girl glanced uncertainly over her shoulder and then stepped inside.

'What do you want?' Jinao said.

'We can help you,' the girl said. 'With the Bairneater. We can help you get it, alone. Save the lives of all them people. Make sure it don't come for no one ever again.'

'You?' Jinao said. The girl looked scarcely able to help herself, let alone others.

'My family,' the girl said. 'We heard about you. We want to help. And might be, my grandba says, that you can help us too.'

Jinao's mind felt as thick and sluggish as the mud-road out of the wetwoods. He rubbed his eyes. 'You want to help?'

'Oh yes, Your Lordship,' she said, nodding earnestly. She lowered her voice and then said, 'My grandba says there's a certain technique to killing a named greyblood. My family know all about it.'

'Your family?'

'Clan Kzani,' the girl said, all wide-eyed sincerity. 'I'm Adimu Kzani, daughter of Warlord Mukisa Kzani.'

'Of course you are,' Jinao said with a sigh, passing a hand over his face. 'Clan Kzani, wiped out over two hundred rains ago. Close the door on the way out, please.'

'Oh no, milord,' the girl said. She rolled back her sleeve, revealing a simple tatau, meant to grow with her as she did: a black and yellow lion that lit up her face when it flared to life. 'We wasn't wiped out. Been hiding, is all. Hiding from our enemies.'

Jinao studied the girl: her deferential demeanour, her eager eyes, which flitted about the room as though she rarely beheld such riches. Chances were, the Bhuten Wives had sent her to him as some manner of joke. Chances were the crone she travelled with was a fantasist, and the grandfather she mentioned a product of her imagination. And yet . . .

'You're serious,' he said.

'Course I am. My grandba wants to help you. But we can't talk here.' She turned towards the door. 'Come on. It ain't far.'

Lowblood invokers. Barbarian invokers. And now, dead invokers. Either the ancestors were playing the cruellest of tricks or the mortal

286

realm was not what he'd believed it to be. He studied the girl. She looked Jebbanese or Ntuki. He'd heard it said that those in the east of Kzaniland had had similarly dark skin.

'You realise I'm a prisoner here?' Jinao said.

'Course, sire. But that won't be a problem now you got me.'

TWENTY-SIX

Elari

The limestone walls of Cantec's library were etched with thousands of tiny carvings: warriors, all said to be descendants of Itahua, fighting leering, masked greybloods. Ebony bookcases stood beneath them, reaching for the centre of the room like rays of sunlight. Every shelf was crammed with ancient books, scrolls, tablets and maps. Elari sat at the heart of it all, before a bloodwood table laden with Old Tiku texts. Cantec's letter lay pinned before her, its neat columns of script all that stood between Elari and fulfilling her husband's final command.

This was what she had needed. Absorbing herself in the detail brought on a calm she had not felt in moons. As the night stretched on, and Elari's doves hovered anxiously by the door, Elari lost herself to her work.

Occasionally, the spectre of the Bairneater visited her, from within the dark corners or the tops of the bookcases, reminding her that she had to *choose, choose*. The message was clear. The ancestors had turned from her. That was why everything had happened. She had chosen, and now she was paying the price. Cantec's burning, the outland healers, perhaps even the Feverlands invasion . . . all of it was to punish her for what she had done. She had never been able to recall the faces of the villagers — not a single one. But the Bairneater's smile was burned into her mind, as eternal as the sun. It was because they were the same, she supposed. Killers. Unnatural creatures. After all, what sort of person slaughtered ten innocent souls to save one man?

Come nightfall, Ishaan brought her a light supper of amaranth cakes steeped in honey. 'Go to bed,' Elari said, after she had finished picking half-heartedly at the food.

'You need sleep, Captain.'

'I'm not tired. Go on, all of you.'

She spent all night teasing out the few symbols she knew. Apart from her name and his, Cantec had also spelled out *Jethar* and *Nine Lands*, using the Old Tiku form of phonetic writing. But it was such slow, painful work translating the other words.

What was it Jethar had shouted before he slit Cantec's throat? *They are coming! They will destroy you all!* She had assumed he had meant the greybloods, but now she was beginning to wonder.

'Captain,' Osellia said, standing sleepily in the library doorway, the grey light of dawn at her back. 'You haven't moved. You look terrible.'

Elari knew the thin tunic she wore was plastered to her body with sweat. She'd been twining her hair around her fingers and pulling out the knots – a habit she'd developed in childhood, and one of the few her father had failed to beat out of her. She looked down to discover with embarrassment that black and white strands now carpeted the stone floor.

'I'm getting you breakfast,' Osellia said. 'Then you're coming outside with me for a walk.'

When they brought her a platter of fruit, Elari found she was ravenous.

If you are reading this, then I have died. That was what the first column said. She read it again and again, her eyes swimming. Cantec had known he was in danger. He'd known he was in danger, and he'd sought her help.

Elari looked up, surprised to find the sun was setting again. Had she slept? Perhaps a little, head on her arms. She'd been aware of her doves fluttering around her – collecting her chamber pot, refilling her water – but she hadn't even acknowledged their presence.

If you are reading this, then I have died before I can reach you. There is much to say, and I have little time . . .

Elari chewed her quill. It was all falling into place now. The more words she identified, the easier it was to decode the rest. *Should something happen to me, you must put an end to this.*

The next morning, Elari realised she was being shaken awake. The candles in the library had burned low. A single sheet of papyrus lay beside her, filled with neat columns of words in the Royal Tongue. She had done it. She had translated Cantec's letter.

'Captain,' Chellahua said.

'What is it?' Elari said.

'It's Lyela,' Chellahua said. 'She is asking for you. She says she has an offer to make.'

Elari realised she hadn't given Lyela a thought since her doves had locked the woman away in Cantec's study. Had solitude broken the woman already? She'd thought her far stronger than that. 'Tell her I'm busy,' Elari said.

'With pleasure,' Chellahua replied, smiling broadly.

When she was gone, Osellia and Ishaan crept into the room. With shaking hands, Elari stood and began to read.

'My dearest Elari. If you are reading this, then I have died before I can reach you. There is much to say, and I have little time, so I shall keep to the essentials. A thief deceived his way onto our ship; a member of the Fallen Families. He stole a treasure during our travels, a thing of great value. That treasure was guarded by an entity of terrible power, and it pursued us. The entity will do anything to retrieve its charge, including destroying the Nine Lands, and I have no doubt that it can. This entity resides within Jethar now, controlling him. He does not know that I have discovered this. Should something happen to me, you must stop

290

him. No invoker will ever see him as the enemy. But enemy he is. Elari, I am sorry: the only solution is to kill him. I know you will find a way.'

Elari looked up, her eyes swimming. That was it. No words of love. No tales of what had befallen him those last five rains. Just the directive that she must kill his greatest friend. She had expected so much, but not this, and not the anger it conjured within her.

Elari cast aside the papyrus and sat, a single tear streaking down her face. At once, her two doves were at her side, kissing away the tears, holding her hands.

'We all saw the hands that reached out of him and seized the monk's staff,' Osellia murmured. 'That must be the creature Cantec speaks of. I assumed it was Mizito, but . . . in truth, it didn't look like him.'

'If it is not an ancestor,' Elari said, 'then what is it? Where did it come from? Who is this lowblood thief, and where are they now? He gave us so little!'

'You need rest,' Osellia said. 'Come to bed. Let us talk about it tomorrow.'

'If he, an invoker, could not stop this creature,' Ishaan said, 'then what chance do we have? We should show Kartuuk what we know and ask for his aid.'

Elari gripped Ishaan's arm, then stood. 'Get me a clean robe. And tell Chellahua I'll speak to Lyela after all.'

Elari was soon sweeping through her apartments, her doves at her side, wearing a clean robe, her thick hair freshly braided.

She pulled open the door to Cantec's study to find Lyela seated in the window, her gaze fixed on the glittering sea.

'I have been imprisoned before, you know,' Lyela said without turning. 'More times than I care to count. But never anywhere quite as beautiful as this. Nobody knows I'm here, do they?'

'What is it you want?' Elari said. 'They told me you wish to make me an offer.'

'I do.'

'Why now? What has changed?'

Lyela sighed and lifted her chained arms. 'Search beneath the cabinet. Over there.'

Osellia shot Elari a look, and Elari nodded. Her dove crossed the room to search under the polished wooden cabinet. After a moment, Osellia straightened, her expression incredulous. She held an ornate wooden box between her fingers.

Elari felt a stab of recognition. 'That is Cantec's!'

Lyela sighed. 'I found it in the barrels of techwork,' she said. 'I told you I remained your captive voluntarily. I can free myself whenever I wish.'

Chellahua was on her in a heartbeat, her blade drawn and pressed to Lyela's neck, her face etched with fury.

'Let me take an eye,' Chellahua began but Elari held up a hand, understanding creeping over her.

'You're still searching his things, aren't you?' Elari said. 'All these days of supposed captivity, you have been escaping and going through Cantec's techwork.'

'Nights, actually,' Lyela said. 'And now I have found what I sought.' She slid her eyes round to the box Osellia held. 'It is an irony, really. After all my work and planning. To find what I seek yet be unable to reach it.'

Elari smiled. 'It is a Perewali puzzle-box. Cantec learned to make them himself. People spend decades studying them, trying to determine their secrets. They were a speciality of his. He never found one he could not solve.'

Lyela smiled thinly. 'I have spent three nights with the bloody thing and still cannot open it.'

'You're telling me you wormed your way into my trust, into this palace, all so you could steal a puzzle-box the likes of which you could find in any Perewali souk the Nine Lands over?'

Lyela rolled her eyes. 'I seek what lies within.'

'And how would you know what lies within?'

'You would not understand if I told you.'

'Try.'

Lyela wet her lips. 'My eyes are . . . stronger than yours. I am able to see things you cannot.'

'Let me take one from you, then,' Chellahua said, bringing her blade to the woman's cheekbone. 'Let us see how strong your ancestor-cursed eyes truly are.'

'Techwork!' Lyela said tightly, trying to raise a chained hand. 'I have a kind of techwork in my eyes! It enables me to see . . . other techwork. I went to Three Towers to look for techwork among the relics in the carriage, and now I have found what I seek, hidden in a place I cannot reach.'

'There is techwork in your eyes?' Elari said, folding her arms. 'How? Why can we not see it?'

'It is too small for you to see.'

Chellahua made an impatient sound and pressed her blade closer to the white of Lyela's eye.

'I am no different from you,' Lyela said. 'I too seek justice for one I have lost. It is why I need this.'

'What do you mean?'

'My father took . . . my child from me,' Lyela said. 'When she was just a baby. He told me she would never know my name, nor my face.' Lyela closed her eyes. 'He cast me out. He left me with nothing.'

'Why?' Elari said.

'I tried to leave him,' Lyela said, her voice a whisper now. 'I tried to leave our family. I tried to take my child and run. My father, my family . . . they are not good people. They are proud. Cruel. And powerful. I did not want my child to become like them, to become what I had been forced to be. My father would seek to shape her as he shaped me, with cruelty and malice and no regard for her wishes or for what she might become. Our home was a prison. I was held there all my life. You asked me where I learned to fight? My father

293

taught me. I was trained in hand and spear and blade. Honed, like steel. Every soul in our family is a living weapon, and my father wielded us all.' Lyela swallowed, and Elari knew in that moment that here, at last, was the truth. She could tell at a glance that the woman had not meant to say so much; could see from the way her eyes swam and her nails dug into her palms that here were words from the heart.

'My father is a man who sees enemies everywhere,' Lyela said. 'When he cast me out, I was broken. But no longer. I will work my way back to him. And I will take everything from him, as he took everything from me. I will make him watch as it all comes crashing down. Then I will spit on his corpse and leave it to the crows; unburned, unmourned.'

Elari shifted. 'Who are they, your family?'

Lyela looked away, a single tear escaping her eye to land on Chellahua's blade. 'I cannot say.'

'You're from the Families,' Ishaan said. 'Aren't you? Which is it? The Sengs? The Bhutens?'

Elari studied Lyela, and Lyela held her gaze, unflinching, unmoving. 'Take my eye, if you wish. It won't stop me. If I desire, I can walk from this room, from this palace, and I will leave only destruction in my wake.' She flicked her eyes around at Chellahua. 'Go on. Try. I will give you the fight of your life, I promise.' She smiled thinly. 'Or, we could help each other.'

'How can you possibly help me?' Elari said.

Lyela's gaze drifted down to the puzzle-box. 'Show me how it opens, and I will show it all to you. Everything in the carriage – how it works, what it does. What it *means*. I can show you.'

Elari turned away. 'Let's go, lieutenants—'

'Wait!' Lyela said. 'Wait! I can give you more. More techwork. And money, too, if that is your wish. A way out of here? We both know this place is doomed. I'll help you leave Intiqq before Clan Ahiki arrives to crush Lord Manax.'

'No water for her,' Elari said to Ishaan. 'And no visits either. Leave her to rot.'

'Please!' Lyela cried. 'Please, Captain. Name your price. Whatever it is, I will pay it.'

Elari paused, hand hovering above the door handle. 'Jethar,' she said, turning. 'Kill Jethar Mizito. If you can do that, I will show you how to open the box.'

There. She had said it. And yet they felt like words of such treachery. She was fulfilling Cantec's wishes, and yet she felt only shame.

Choose who lives and who dies.

Lyela sagged. 'That would be . . . complicated—'

'Let's go,' Elari said, nodding to Chellahua, who stood.

'No, wait! Fine. Fine, I will kill Jethar. But it will not be easy.'

'Nothing in life ever is,' Elari said. She strode towards Lyela. 'I want Jethar dead. I know you can do it. You can fight. You can break through the monks' protections. You are the only one alive who can kill him. And believe me, he must die. *This* is why the ancestors brought us together. Bring me Jethar's head and I will open this box.'

At Elari's side, Osellia and Ishaan hissed in anger. 'We cannot trust her!' Chellahua snarled, reaching for her knife. 'The moment you let her leave Livinghall, she will flee and never return.'

Elari lifted a hand and then knelt. She reached for the puzzle-box, being careful to keep the side with the catch facing her. Three quick motions, in just the right places, then three more with both hands together, were all it took. 'I only know how to solve these,' Elari said, 'because I memorised so many ways. There are patterns, once you know to look for them.' The box sprang open, its nine segments falling apart like the petals of a flower. On the velvet cushion within sat a small blackglass orb.

'Don't touch it!' Lyela cried as Elari reached forward.

Elari set the box down. 'Why not?'

'It is very dangerous. Why do you think I didn't just smash the box? If mishandled, that could—'

'What is it?' Elari said.

'A weapon,' Lyela said. 'A very powerful, very specific weapon.'

'It must be the weapon they sought!' Osellia said. 'They found it after all, in the place where spirits gather!'

But Lyela was shaking her head. 'Jethar and Cantec were chasing a myth. A place where spirits gather? No such land exists.'

'Cantec surely would have told us in his letter if their voyage had been a success,' Ishaan said.

'And why do you want this weapon?' Elari said.

Lyela closed her eyes. 'To use against my father.'

Elari began the motions that would seal the box again. 'I know what it is to have a father who moulds you with cruelty,' she said. 'If I let you have this, you must bring Jethar's head to me. No one can see you. No one can know.'

'Captain, we cannot let her go!' Osellia cried.

'I must not be followed,' Lyela said. 'And I must not be contacted.'

'Captain, please!' Chellahua said.

'Captain, if she is traced back to us, you will be executed,' Ishaan said. 'If she is traced back to us, it could start a clan war.'

'Oh, she won't be traced,' Lyela said, smiling. 'She promises.'

Elari studied her. She looked more like a farmer than an assassin, yet there was nothing but confidence in her gaze. Besides, how would Elari ever get close to Jethar again? Even if she could leave Livinghall, even if she could manipulate her way back into the palace of Three Towers, an unknown entity of great power resided within him, and she was an ageing warrior with no ancestor at her side.

'If you betray us,' Elari said, 'we will hunt you across the Nine Lands and beyond.'

'Naturally,' Lyela said, with a smile.

Elari clicked her fingers and her doves joined her, their faces lined with unease. 'You have three moons to bring me Jethar's head,' she said, and turned towards the door.

PART THREE

Runt, Elari, Boleo, Jinao

TWENTY-SEVEN

Runt

It was nearing dark when the healer flicked aside her curtain and let them in.

Runt manoeuvred her younger brother's limp body over the threshold and stepped into the hut. It was small, almost as small as the shack Runt and her brother shared at the top of the hill. Techwork swung from the low wooden ceiling – glinting silver shards and blackglass. Runt didn't much believe in the ancestors, and she was pretty sure if Scathed artefacts really were cursed, half of Lordsgrave would have passed beyond the pyre. But she made the sign for ancestral protection anyway; no sense in taking chances.

The healer herself sat at the back of the hut, stirring a large pot of stew and humming. She was an ancient thing, with dirt in the folded wrinkles of her face and nails long as claws. Runt and her brother stumbled over the filthy rugs, and then she set him down by the woman's fire.

'My brother's got the river sickness,' Runt said. 'Can you help him?'

The healer looked up and heaved a great sigh. Her watery grey eyes slid over Zee's body. Runt knew what she saw: a boy of seven, scarcely a bag of bones now, his brown skin tinged yellow, his breath shallow and fast. The evening was hot, but the film of sweat that covered Zee's body had nothing to do with the weather. Besides, he was shivering, and in those rare moments when he was lucid, he kept repeating that he was cold, so cold.

'Tricky,' the healer said, shuffling over. Pellana, that was her name – Runt remembered it now. *Don't you never go to old Pellana,* Ma used to say. *She dabbles in the Forbidden ways, and is as likely to kill you as to heal you.* But Runt had no choice. She'd tried Veiled Aya, over by the docks, but she'd claimed greybloods from the river had destroyed her supplies. Sutesh near Arrant Hill had sucked their teeth and shaken their head. Baba Eshun had actually shed a tear when Runt had arrived on the doorstep of his townhouse. He'd sent Runt away with a bundle of herbs to brew up, *so your brother can return to the ancestors in comfort.*

That was when Runt had still had coin, which she'd planned to take over into Lordsheart. She could find a real healer there, not these charlatans of the slums. But then she'd run into Ramanan's Curs, who'd beaten her and taken everything she had. She supposed she'd been asking for it, using the short cut through their territory, but by that point Zee was shivering and Runt didn't think he had long.

'Very tricky,' Pellana said, touching Zee lightly with the back of one filthy hand. She lifted her eyes to Runt. 'I got the goods to heal him,' she said. 'But it ain't gonna be cheap.'

Runt chewed at her lip. 'Can I owe you? My word's my honour, I swear.'

The old woman chuckled. 'Word's your honour, is it? How old are you, girl? Twelve? Thirteen?'

Runt tried not to let her irritation show. 'I'm eighteen,' she said. People always took her for younger than she was, on account of her small frame.

'Ain't you Yunonu's girl? Up by the Lordswall?'

Runt's stomach tightened at the sound of her mother's name. 'Yep.'

'What happened to her? Ain't seen her in moons.'

Don't touch me, she could still hear Ma crying. *Don't you dare touch me.*

'She's dead,' Runt said, watching Pellana's face. 'Just me and him now.'

'Two suns,' Pellana said. 'You'll need to get it to me tonight.'

Runt closed her eyes, willing away the panic. 'I got half a moon,' she said. 'That's all my money in the world. Please, can I just owe you?'

Pellana eyed her before sighing and saying, 'Tell you what. You leave him here. I'll make sure he don't get no worse. You go and sort the money. Two suns. Tonight. That's the best I can do.'

A rush of anger stole over Runt then, and she had to clench her fists to stop herself from flying at the woman. Deep within her, she felt a stir, as she so often did since Baba had given her the pendant. *You're its guardian*, he'd told her. *Its keeper. See that nothing happens to it, you hear?*

'I'll get you your money,' Runt said, pushing to her feet. She was almost at the strip of material that marked Pellana's door when she stopped and added, 'But I'm telling you, if he dies, I'll burn this place down, with you inside. I work for the Chedu Family, you know.'

Pellana's chuckles followed her out into the night.

It was fully dark when Runt stepped out onto the dirt road everyone called Low Hill. The stirring within her grew more insistent, and before long, they were bubbling up inside her, filling her mind with their overlapping chatter.

[You are special.]

[Chosen.]

[Ours.]

[We could do much together.]

[So very much.]

Runt clenched her fist and cursed her father's name for the hundredth time that day. Why? Why had her father returned, after so many rains, just to give her a piece of jewellery she couldn't even sell and then disappear back into the night? The pendant's weight bumped between her breasts beneath the thin linen of her tunic. Outwardly, it looked like a cheap trinket from the market, an ugly thing of conjoined faces all leering out. But Baba said it was special, said *she* was special as its keeper. *Can't trust no one but me own daughter in this, you hear? The ancestors chose you for this job.*

He'd placed it on a chain of blackglass beads – and *these*, Runt knew, were priceless. But why would the man who hadn't seen her since Zee was in their ma's belly give her something of such value? At the time, she'd decided Baba was soothing his own conscience; that he'd given her this gift to make up for his long absence. Even when he'd brought two of his friends to her, and bid her show them the pendant, she hadn't thought it was anything more than trying to placate the child who'd missed him.

That had been moons ago now; before the pendant had started talking.

Runt rounded the corner and there stood the Cascade, a beacon of light in the darkness, looming above the shacks of the Lordsgrave shanty. It dwarfed the tents of Lordsgrave's newest residents – families fleeing Aranduq City. Lordsgrave had always been a place in flux, as changeable as the wind, as fluid as the Ae. Runt couldn't imagine a city any other way, and loved her home all the more for it. But lately, as stories crept in of greyblood attacks all along the Ae, Lordsgrave had begun to transform in ways she didn't wholly like. The district seemed taut as a drum; like an intake of breath before a shout; like a pot close to boiling.

'You're late, you lazy fuck,' Asham said as soon as she descended the narrow steps into the pot room. 'You're lucky I ain't gave your job to someone else.'

'My brother's sick,' Runt said, crossing the uneven tiled floor to take her place at the largest wash bucket.

'Course he fucking is,' Asham said, before throwing a dishcloth at her head and turning back to chopping yam.

Runt wondered what Asham would have done if she simply hadn't shown up. Because really, why did she bother? She and Zee lived alone, which meant when the monks finally came, she would be heading to war for their household of two. The pay the Chedus gave her was scarcely enough to keep her and Zee in bread, but once Zee was better, he could take over her job, and at least she'd die knowing he had enough to eat.

Asham was a moody, temperamental sort, with close-set eyes and messy black hair. The youths who worked in the kitchens spent their lives tiptoeing around his fickle ways. As Runt set to work on the stew pots that lay submerged in the grimy water, she watched Asham out of the corner of her eye, waiting for her moment.

It came after Asham had had his break and was laughing at something Cessa, the girl who worked the ovens, had said.

'I need a favour,' Runt said, putting on her most winning smile as Asham swept back to his mountain of vegetables. 'I know I ain't due pay till Sunday, but I wondered—'

'You asking for an advance on your pay? Cause you ain't gonna get it.'

[You should not beg.]

[The chosen never beg.]

'My brother's sick,' she said. 'River sickness.'

'You deaf? I said no. Now get to work.'

Runt turned back to her bucket, face hot with anger. What did they know, any of them who worked in the kitchens? Most lived in Ba Casten's worker quarters, or else over in Northlands where the roads were wider and the air sweeter. They had food, and they had a table to put it on. She'd even heard they had a way to avoid the king's draft. None of them had a mother so useless she'd lived in terror of a man who had been missing for rains.

The Cascade was in full swing above, the sound of singing and drums reverberating through the ceiling. The laughter and shrieks of merriment grew louder as the evening wore on, and Runt's mood grew darker. Her brother could be dead already, while she stood here scrubbing plates.

Finally, near midnight, opportunity arrived in the shape of a man named Tarn.

'You got my usual, Asham?' Tarn said, lumbering down the stairs. Tarn was a heavy man dressed in embroidered silks. Runt hadn't worked out exactly what he did for the Chedus, but it was something to do with trading a type of techwork people called water votives.

'Of course, my friend,' Asham said, reaching for one of the shelves.

[You are chosen.]

[You should not beg.]

So when Runt set down her cloth and crossed the room, she made sure to keep her shoulders square and her gaze steady, and the voices liked that. Tarn had taken a package from Asham and was already turning back to the stairs. This was her moment. Her last chance for Zee.

'Excuse me, Tarn,' Runt said. 'I wanted to show you something.'

Tarn froze part way up the stairs, as though someone had struck him.

'And just who are you to use my name?' he said, turning.

'She's the pot-girl,' Asham said. 'Don't pay her no mind. What are you doing, Runt? Get back to work!'

Six rains. That was how long Runt had been working there. Six rains, and she saw Tarn almost daily.

'I got something special to sell you. You trade in techwork, right? Look at this.' Runt unclipped the chain of blackglass beads – there were twenty at least: worth quite a sum. She was still fumbling to remove the ugly pendant and slip it into her pocket when Asham reached her and began manhandling her back to her pots.

'They're blackglass!' Runt called over Asham's shoulder. She held up the beads and the pendant slipped out of her hand and onto the floor.

'I'm sorry, Tarn,' Asham said. 'Don't know what's got into this idiot, but it won't be forgotten.' He shot Runt a look.

[You are chosen.]

[Destined for greatness.]

[Why do you listen to these fools?]

[Why do you obey them?]

'Wait a minute,' Tarn said, holding up a jewelled hand. 'Come here, girl.'

Asham narrowed his eyes at Runt, but let his hands drop. Runt slipped past him and returned to the foot of the stairs, scooping up her pendant as she went. 'Here,' she said, letting the blackglass chain dangle from one finger. 'Worth three suns at least.'

'Not those,' Tarn said. 'The other thing. In your hand.'

Runt's throat closed up. *You're its guardian, girl. Its keeper.* 'That . . . ain't for sale.'

Tarn leaned forward. 'Take the pendant out of your fucking pocket. Now.'

Wordlessly, Runt fumbled and removed her father's gift. She'd meant to pass it to Zee when she went to war, but what use was it to him if he was dead? Tarn peered at it through his tiny, stupid eyes, and Runt tried not to wrinkle her nose. The man smelt like powder and perfume, but beneath it all was stale sweat. The stale sweat of a weak man.

'I'll give you a moon for the carving,' Tarn said with a shrug, though she could see from the way his jaw tightened that the shrug masked a deep interest.

'I can't,' Runt said. 'The pendant ain't for sale.' But she thought of Zee, back in Pellana's tent, his tiny body plastered with cold sweat. 'For – for less than three suns.'

'Three suns!' Tarn laughed. 'I told you. A moon.'

You're its guardian, girl. Its keeper. Baba had trusted her. But surely he would understand? Surely, if he had seen Zee shivering on the floor of Pellana's hut, he would have agreed. Besides, if she took it to war with her, it would be lost for ever. Runt gritted her teeth. 'It's rare,' she said. 'My baba got it from across the sea. It's worth ten suns at least. You can have it for three, but I can't go no lower.'

'*Can't go no lower!*' Tarn laughed, glancing over at Asham, who laughed too. 'Listen, you little shit. You're lucky to get a moon for it. I've met a hundred souls like you, pretty little brats who think the world owes them something. Well, the world don't owe you nothing. You take what you're served. One moon.'

'My baba said—'

'*My baba said* . . . Listen to it!' Tarn said. 'I don't care about your filthy beggar of a father. If I say it's worth a moon, it's worth a moon. Just who do you think you are?'

'My baba ain't no beggar,' Runt told him, the heat rising in her again.

[He should not speak to you like that.]

[Should not look at you like that.]

Without warning, Tarn jerked his hand forward, snatching the pendant from her grip. Then he kicked out with one meaty leg, sending Runt staggering back into a pile of plates. Crockery clattered all around her as she hit the ground hard.

'Here you go, you ungrateful whelp,' Tarn said. 'One moon.' The coin spun through the air, glinting, before landing at Runt's feet. Runt was still trying to right herself when Tarn went stomping up the stairs with her father's gift.

Runt lay on the floor of the pot-room, unwilling to open her eyes to the world. She'd lost the only gift her father had ever given her, something he'd trusted her to look after, and she still didn't have enough for her brother's medicine. Baba was right – she hadn't earned herself a proper name yet. Her ma had tried to name her once, but Runt had let her fist show what she thought of that. No one but Baba had the right to name her, and until he did, she would remain Runt.

'Them broken plates is all coming out of your wages,' Asham said, standing over her. 'You're lucky I don't kick you out.'

Runt spent the rest of her shift in a haze of fury that only worsened as the night continued. But within her, she could still hear the voices of the pendant, and they roiled and churned and whispered.

[He took what's yours.]

[Stole from you.]

[Cheated you.]

306

[That should not go unpunished.]

By the time Asham closed up the kitchen for the night, Runt could scarcely breathe for the rage. She climbed the narrow staircase out onto the street and looked up at the main door of the inn. The Cascade loomed above her, each of its windows an oasis of gold in the dark brick. Above the drinking rooms and the kitchens, above the pillow-house and the bathing suites, there, at the summit, lived Ba Casten. She'd seen him once, from afar. A great bear of a man who dominated any room he stepped into. Runt's father had told her that he knew him, but that seemed unlikely. Casten was a Chedu, one of the oldest and most powerful Families in Lordsgrave. Runt and her kin were nothing.

How she'd dreamed of joining their ranks, earning a place among them, earning respect. She'd imagined that after a few moons in the kitchens, she'd be one of their messengers, perhaps even a street-watcher. But instead, nothing. Six rains of washing pots. Six rains, and not even a low-ranking rat like Tarn remembered her face.

[He's in there.]

[With your money.]

[With your father's property.]

Before she could stop herself, Runt climbed the steps up to the main doors. If she brought Pellana nothing tonight, then her brother would die. Besides, what did she have to lose? Any day now, the monks would sweep through Lordsgrave and drag her to war. Who'd be looking out for Zee then? Not a single soul.

Runt pulled open the doors and was greeted with a flood of heat and noise and sweetweed smoke. The main taproom still heaved with people: people drinking around tiny tables, people arguing, people playing cards or dice.

And there he was: Tarn, seated at a table near the back, beside a striking woman with dark hair and wide-set eyes. As Runt stood there, trying to still the thumping of her heart, running through what she was going to say, she realised how many of them were looking at her. Even the boy behind the bar, a wolfish youth, had stopped cutting sweetweed to eye her with amusement. She was aware of how out of place she must look: a short, scrawny thing, her wrapper stained from cleaning pots, her face flushed with emotion.

Tarn was one of the last to look up, and though the musicians on the mezzanine above continued, a certain stillness fell over the room.

'You owe me three suns!' Runt shouted.

She ignored the stifled laughter and dancing gazes of those who watched. Instead, she kept her eyes on Tarn, leaning back in his chair.

'Don't you have pots to wash?' Tarn said, folding his arms.

[He insults you.]

[Mocks you.]

[You should show him you are chosen.]

'You took my pendant from me,' Runt said, her voice shaking. 'The price was three suns. You gave me a moon, and the end of your boot. That money was for my sick brother. I'm here to collect what I'm owed.'

She felt a deep satisfaction at the silence that followed. It spread around the room in a wave, causing heads to turn and conversation to falter. Runt clenched her teeth against the flush creeping up her neck. But the voices in the pendant swelled beneath her skin, adding their fury to her own.

'Well,' Tarn said at last. 'I've your money right here. Come and get it.'

Runt ignored the mutters and laughter that rose up around her and shook her head. The voices chuckled deep within her, and she let their laughter spill out until she heard it on her own lips.

'No,' Runt said with a grin. 'You come here.'

And so the man did.

He moved quickly for someone of such a solid frame, and though Runt backed away, Tarn caught her by one arm. Before she could duck, Tarn jerked his head back and slammed it into her nose.

Runt reeled, her head ringing, her eyes streaming. From somewhere distant, she heard jeers and clapping. She stumbled into someone, who shoved her away, sending her staggering straight into Tarn's fist. Runt fell back, and then the man was on her, fists coming down. Runt lifted her arms, tried to protect her face, but the blows kept coming. Everything seemed to slow then, and the ringing in Runt's head threatened to obliterate all else.

'That's enough,' came a distant voice.

Instantly, the blows ceased. Runt pushed herself into a seated position. Tarn stood off to one side, his chest heaving, his fists bloody. Runt sucked in breath. Her cheek felt tight, but none of her teeth were loose and, thank the ancestors, her bloated nose felt intact.

It was the dark-haired woman who had spoken. Her voice was soft, but somehow her words carried. She sat opposite a man who could have been her twin, so alike did they look. Tarn's eyes still blazed with anger, but he made no move to attack.

'He owes me money,' Runt slurred, pointing with one bloodied, shaking hand. 'Three suns. My brother's dying, and I need that coin tonight, to save his life.'

'That piece of junk is not worth three suns,' Tarn said.

'It is and you know it.'

The woman watched them closely. 'Tarn, give this young person what she's owed, and three more suns for her trouble.'

Tarn hesitated for a heartbeat before emptying his pockets. 'I only have two here, Harvell.'

'Then you'll have to owe me,' the woman, Harvell, said. She gestured, and a girl of nine or ten, sitting somewhere in the shadows, scampered forward holding a small bag. As she approached, Runt tried not to react to the sum she saw glittering within the bag. The child counted the coins out then tipped them into Runt's bloody hand.

Runt closed her fingers, scarcely daring to breathe. Six suns. She would be leaving the Cascade tonight with six whole suns.

'This pendant is techwork, you know, and very rare,' Harvell said. She reached under the table, and there it was: Baba's gift. How strange it looked in the hands of another. 'Why would you part with it?'

'For my brother,' Runt said. She pushed shakily to her feet.

'Well, your brother is very lucky to have you.' Harvell smiled. 'Come here, sweet. You need a drink.'

Runt wanted to turn away, to leave with the money she had, but just then she couldn't trust her legs to carry her, and she was indeed thirsty, and Harvell's smile was as dazzling as the sunrise.

They cleared a path for her as she limped across the room. Her chest burned with every breath. By the time she reached the table, her entire left side felt aflame. Someone passed her a chair, and someone else gave her a drink. Runt gulped it eagerly, hands still shaking as sweet liquid fire slid slide down her throat. Her fingers left smears of blood on the glass, but under the gaze of Harvell and her companion, Runt felt strangely calm.

'I'm Harvell,' Harvell said, inclining her head in formal a bow. 'I buy and sell techwork for Ba Casten, and I must say, I have never seen anything quite like this. Where did you get it?'

She let the pendant spin beneath fine, soft fingers.

'My baba gave it to me,' Runt said. 'He got it from across the ocean.'

'He travels, does he, your father?'

[She seeks power over you.]

[Tell her nothing.]

'Sometimes,' Runt said. She was close enough that her elbow touched Harvell's companion. He smelt exquisite – like cinnamon and sandalwood and sunlight. Harvell watched her, lip curled in amusement, and Runt felt a deep flush building in her cheeks.

'You knew this was techwork,' Harvell said, 'didn't you? Tell me: what does it do?'

[She seeks power over you.]

[Tell her nothing.]

'It talks,' Runt said. Behind her, she heard the door swing open. She needed to get back to Zee. All this would be for nothing if she arrived too late.

'Goodness, it talks, does it?' Harvell said. Then she clapped her hands brightly and nodded to the cards. 'Do you play?'

'Yes,' Runt said, before she thought to stop herself. 'Though I should—'

'Excellent. One hand, then. As thanks to me, for saving your brother's life.'

Runt watched as Harvell's companion began to deal, his long fingers quick and deft. 'I have to pay the healer,' she said.

'One hand,' Harvell said. 'I insist.' She smiled softly, but there was steel behind her eyes.

Runt lowered her gaze. The trembling in her fingers had returned. 'Of course,' she said. 'I'd love to.'

TWENTY-EIGHT

Elari

'I do not understand why my presence is required at the Circle,' Elari said as she followed the guard along the portico. 'I am a widow in mourning, and not of the family blood.'

Elari's doves followed silently at her back, each in matching tunics of white. She too wore mourning white, and for the first time since returning to the palace had strapped her obsidian knife to her thigh. She was surprised at how comfortable the weapon felt, though its weight did little to combat the fear that swirled within her. Only four days had passed since Lyela's departure, and yet the woman was all Elari could think about. And now, with the sun scarcely up, a guard she did not recognise had roused them all from bed.

'All senior clan members are to present themselves at the Circle,' the guard said, not meeting her gaze. 'First General Manax has an important announcement to make.'

'What has happened to my usual messenger?'

'Lord Manax found traitors among his household staff. They have been dealt with accordingly.'

As they passed the courtyard containing the palace shrine, Elari slowed. The flowers had all died, she saw, and the statue of Itahua that resided at the courtyard's heart had been sealed away behind a looming wooden barrier. Tall weeds choked the pathway, and the spirit wood of the shrine itself appeared to have been broken into splinters.

'This is an affront to the ancestors,' Elari said.

'The ancestors must be left to rest,' the guard replied. 'It is an affront to drag them back to the realm of the living.'

Chellahua reached for the man's belt. 'You know, you wear your weapon too high. If you'd like, I can—'

He seized Chellahua's wrist. There was nothing human in his feral smile. Blue smoke rose from his skin as he snarled, 'Do not test us.'

Wordlessly, her expression tight, Chellahua snatched her arm back and marched on.

Livinghall's circleroom stood high above the ocean, at the end of a narrow crystal bridge that marched out over the waves far below. From those heights, the entire cliffside palace was visible in descending tiers, all its terraces and balconies bright in the dawn sun. Elari looked out over the edge, down to where the surf crashed against the rocks. Why had she never noticed how impenetrable the circleroom was, with only one way in or out?

The circleroom itself lay open to the sky on all sides, its high ceiling held aloft by limestone statues of Itahua performing the Obsidian Dance. The fire pit was out – ordinarily an ill omen, but Elari was unsurprised: there hadn't been nuns to tend to it in moons. Rarely had Elari seen so many at the Circle. Every member of the inner household seemed to be present, from the youngest child to the most senior clan aide. People crowded the Circle's periphery: noted warriors, pages, squires, even several people in the beaded skirts of story singers. But despite the numbers present, a terrible hush lay over the crowd. Those who spoke did so only in whispers, and every face looked drawn with concern.

Elari was not the only one to have been disturbed by the early call. Rozichu appeared on the bridge behind her, looking red-eyed and tousled. A gaggle of envoys hurried ahead of her, some still straightening their headdresses, their voices hushed.

Elari took her place behind the spot reserved for Cantec. As ever, she left his cushion empty, no matter that now he would never return. Her brother Atanchu caught her eye as she straightened her skirts. He sat on the far side of the Circle, wearing a plain mask of ebony over his burn scars and seated behind a weary-looking Kartuuk. Kartuuk wore a simple tunic and travelling boots, his macuahuitl strapped to his back.

Heads began to turn, and there came Manax, striding along the bridge, the two traders trailing behind. The crowd fell silent as he stepped into the Circle. Elari watched him as he walked, his feathered jaguar headdress framing his face. She tried not to look at the traders for fear of what she might see behind their eyes. When Manax reached his spot beneath the statue of Itahua in the sixth pose of the Obsidian Dance, he did not sit, as was customary. A murmur of astonishment rippled across the crowd, and when Elari saw why, her breath caught.

Manax's tataus were gone. His arms looked as unmarked as a newborn, as did his shoulders, beneath their patterned mantle. How it had been done, Elari could not imagine. She had heard of souls burning their skin to remove the mark of their family and ancestry, but Manax's slender brown arms were utterly free of scars. Manax held his hands high, turning them this way and that, allowing everyone a good look.

'Clan Ahiki has long controlled us,' Manax said. 'They send us to fight while they remain secreted within the Garden. Even now, I am told, they have sent one of their legions here, to punish us for not answering their call to war. But how many centuries has it been since Clan Ahiki joined us in battle? Why should they among the nine warlords command us when our people believe all in a circle should have equal voice? I ask you all: when did you last hear of a scion of Clan Ahiki invoking the spirit of their ancestor? Not for decades. Some say this is because they have forgotten how. I tell you it is not. I tell you that they have had them *removed*.'

Elari felt dread uncoil deep in her gut. Something was very wrong here. What mortal power could remove an ancestral Bond? She felt

Ishaan, at her back, place a hand on her crossed legs, so she reached down to clasp their fingers.

'These are not mere symbols!' Manax continued, lowering his arms. 'The deed has been done. I have freed myself of my ancestor, and xem of me. Now, ahead of our departure for Aranduq, it is time for each invoker among you to do the same. Beginning with my own children.' He turned his head to his left, towards Invoker Kartuuk and Atanchu. 'Come, my son. You must be the first. Step forward and embrace freedom.'

All around the Circle, the inner household of Livinghall stared. Kartuuk remained motionless.

There came a commotion from the edge of the Circle and Elari looked round to see three huge guards dragging a ragged man between them. The man cursed and thrashed, and only when they brought him to the centre of the Circle did Elari recognise Atoc. His hair was a matted mess and his beard bedraggled. One look at his face was enough to reveal how drunk he was. Indeed, when he threw back his head, she saw that he was laughing.

'Forgive me, Your Grace,' one of the guards said. 'He was trying to scale the walls.'

Atoc thrust out one tataued hand and stared intently at it. The skin brightened then dimmed, then brightened again. Atoc cackled at this, then threw off one of the guards before launching himself at another.

'Enough,' Manax said. 'Atoc, once you are freed of the burden of the ancestor that possesses you, you will find peace in your heart. Bring him.'

Atoc struggled, but the guards dragged him forwards. As Manax's healers approached him, carrying a strange box between them, Atoc's eyes went wide.

'Stop!' Atoc shouted, bracing his feet on the floor. 'Please! Father, stop this!'

'Father, I think we should discuss this,' Kartuuk said.

'No,' Manax said. He turned to his healers. 'Please begin.'

The traders set the box before Atoc, then placed their hands on his shoulders. Atoc tried to shake them free, but the guards held him firm as the traders started to chant.

'What language is that?' Ishaan whispered, leaning forward. 'It is nothing I have ever heard.'

'That is because they are making it up,' Chellahua said.

'I'm sure nothing will happen,' Osellia whispered, gripping Elari's shoulder. 'Nothing can undo an invoker's ancestral Bond.'

'Captain,' said a soft voice said at her back, and Elari looked round to see a messenger of eight or nine kneeling behind her. 'Your brother says come to the west side of the Circle now.'

'Tell him I will find him later,' Elari said. Atoc had stopped fighting, and now he stared wide-eyed, teeth gritted, growling deep in his throat.

'It will be over soon, my son,' Manax said as he watched. 'The pain does not last, and then you will be free.'

'Please, Captain!' the messenger said, tugging on Elari's elbow. 'Your brother says to *come now*.'

Elari looked round and realised what the child meant.

'We should go!' Osellia said. 'If Atanchu has a way out—'

'No. We have to wait for Lyela.' She turned to the messenger and took hold of her shoulder. 'Tell my brother I love him. And that I will follow. Tell him not to wait.'

As Elari stared, the skin of Atoc's face began to ripple and warp, as though it were being pulled free of his body. No, not *his* face, she realised. Another face, being drawn from within Atoc's. As Atoc shook and strained, another body was dragged out of his own, a body made of shifting light. For a moment, Atoc's scream of pain took on two tones as a second soul was pulled from within the first. Elari had an instant to glimpse the form of Itahua, xir jaguar mask down, xir feathers shifting with glyphs, before Atoc's ancestor disbanded in an explosion of light and wind that pushed them all back as it sped past.

Atoc collapsed onto the marble floor, his body convulsing.

'*Attackers!*' someone screamed, and Elari looked up in alarm to see a flood of warriors in full feathers and warpaint streaming over the sides of the bridge. They had used ropes and claws, she realised, climbing from the rocks below. Atanchu and Kartuuk stood at the edge of the Circle with Rozichu trembling at their side, and as they backed away, the warriors closed around them, encircling.

'What is the meaning of this?' Manax said, stepping over the twitching form of his youngest son. He scanned the faces of the warriors assembling before him – souls Elari realised she knew. Kartuuk's soldiers. Those who had fought beside him, camped with him, dined with him.

'Commander Tanua, will you turn your blade towards your First General?' Manax said. 'And you, Ujimin. What is the meaning of this?'

'My company and I are leaving!' Kartuuk cried from across the Circle. 'I'd urge all others to do the same!'

'Stop them!' Manax cried.

The palace guards started forwards uneasily, some looking to their captain, but Kartuuk's warriors charged towards them, heads lowered and macuahuitls raised high. Only the four warriors of Kartuuk's quartet fled with him, Rozichu and Elari's brother, and she caught one final glimpse of them sprinting back into the palace before they were gone.

'Manax cannot attack his own people,' Elari said, her chest tight. 'He cannot.'

Chaos descended on the circleroom. Manax bellowed at his guards but was caught up in the press of people surging to flee across the bridge.

'Get after my son!' Manax shouted.

'Let him go,' said Kartuuk's Commander, Tanua. He was a lean, compact man, and softly spoken, but fire now burned in the eyes behind his jaguar mask. He did not expect to leave alive, Elari realised. None of Kartuuk's warriors did.

'Kill them,' Manax said. When the captain of the guard, a tall bull of a woman named Icholu, looked around at Manax uncertainly, a ripple of rage crossed the First General's features. 'Did you not hear me? *Kill the traitors! Now!*'

'We should leave, Captain!' Osellia said, pulling Elari's arm. 'Lyela will find us!'

Elari's stomach tightened as her people set upon each other, Manax's guards drawing their scimitars and Commander Tanua shouting Itahua's name one final time.

'Captain!' Chellahua cried, as one of Manax's guards fell backwards, almost knocking into them. Then her doves were on their feet, obsidian daggers drawn, pulling Elari into the press of people trying to escape the madness.

Nobody noticed the healers' spirit-stealing box. Elari shook off Osellia's hand and crossed the Circle, gripping her own obsidian blade until she stood before it. She placed a finger on the smooth surface – from a distance, it had looked like spirit wood, but up close, she could see that it was not. It was acacia, she realised; acacia painted to look like the sacred material. She rapped on it and heard a hollow echo.

Empty. Nothing but an empty wooden box.

Someone charged into Elari, knocking her to the floor: one of Kartuuk's young warriors, her weapon raised defensively as she backed away. And Elari could see why. As the light-skinned trader bore down upon her, a blue cloud burst out of him, seizing the warrior about the neck. The cloud rose into the air, chuckling merrily, taking the warrior with it. Then it plummeted down, smashing the poor woman's head on the stone floor in an explosion of blood and bone.

'Did you see?' Elari cried, turning to her doves as they joined her. 'Tell me you saw!'

'We saw,' Osellia said.

Others had seen too, many crying out, several pointing in disbelief.

'Look,' Chellahua muttered, and Elari looked up to see Commander Tanua making a final stand. Bodies surrounded him as his macuahuitl swung. Then one of Manax's guards blew a dart across the room and caught him in the throat.

The circleroom seemed to still as Tanua fell, dead before his head struck the ground. Elari heard weeping behind her. Manax's hulking captain, Icholu, threw her scimitar to the floor and screamed in rage. Behind her, two of her lieutenants lifted their voices in an ululating death cry.

'Captain Icholu,' Manax said, 'I told you to get after my son.'

'I did not dedicate my life to the obsidian blade for *this*,' Icholu said.

'Go!' Manax roared, sweeping an arm towards the bridge. 'All of you. Back to your chambers. Nobody is to leave or enter the palace.'

At his words, Elari found herself caught up in the current that swept across the bridge. She grabbed Ishaan's hand, then Chellahua's, and let herself be carried by the human flow. But looking back over her shoulder, she saw Icholu, captain of the palace guard, standing before Manax with her head bowed.

'Don't look,' Osellia hissed.

'What is he going to do to her?' Elari said.

'Captain, don't look.'

Out on the bridge, the river of people sped up. Elari passed souls crying, others with weapons drawn, still more shouting to their friends or scooping up howling children. Sometimes she glimpsed the Bairneater, grinning in the distance.

Elari's heart hammered, but she also felt a strange relief. Everyone had seen now. Finally, they all knew.

'We can use the hidden passage,' Ishaan said. 'I'll get food and water gourds from the kitchen. Chellahua, you assemble our travelling packs.'

'I shall oil the horses,' Osellia said, 'and meet you all by the underground gate.'

Back at her apartments, Elari packed with shaking hands. An ancestral Bond had been broken. She had seen Itahua dragged from Atoc's body. How was such a thing even possible? Manax was systematically removing his ancestor from his line. What claims could the healers have made to make him think this a good thing? And what foul craft had they used to undo the ancestral Bond?

319

'It was nothing but a wooden box,' Elari said as Chellahua fastened her travelling cloak. 'It was all a charade.'

'But that was Itahua we saw,' Chellahua said.

'I know.' Elari stood. 'W-what if Lyela cannot find us?'

Chellahua gripped her arm. 'If she succeeds in killing Jethar, we will hear of it. The Mizitos will ensure word reaches every corner of the Nine Lands. We do not need his head for proof. All that mattered to Cantec was that he is gone.'

Elari knew she was right. If Lyela could break into Three Towers Palace and kill Jethar, she could track Elari and her doves to wherever they hid. But she still felt a twist of sadness as she looked around her apartments for the last time. She would have to leave all Cantec's techwork; she guessed the ancestors had never meant them to have it after all.

The door banged open and Ishaan entered, their face bloody, two large guards holding their arms. 'Everyone must remain in their apartments,' one of the guards said, throwing Ishaan to the floor.

'How dare you lay hands on a lieutenant of a clan quartet?' Elari said, rounding on them.

'The city is under siege. Everyone must remain in their rooms for their own safety.'

'What do you mean, siege?'

The guards began to pull closed the doors. As Chellahua ran to Ishaan, helping them up, touching their face, Elari heard the rattle of the key.

'They're locking us in!' Chellahua cried.

Elari threw herself against the door, banging on the heavy wood. 'Unlock this door! I am a captain of the clan! I command you to open!'

'He said siege,' Chellahua said, steadying herself against the wall. 'Do you think—'

'We need to find a way out.' Elari strode across to her nearest daybed. 'Help me lift this. We can use it on the door.'

Between them, they lifted the daybed, then charged as one into the door. Wood clapped against wood, but the door did not move.

'Again!' Elari said.

Chellahua dropped her corner to the ground. 'Captain, this will not work.'

'*I said again!*'

They indulged her until all three of them ran with sweat and the end of the daybed was a splintered ruin.

Chellahua flopped to the floor. 'Maybe Osellia will escape,' she said. 'She can go for help.'

Elari crossed to the window and gazed outside.

Her apartments were among the few in the palace that looked west-ward over the city. Down in the valley, and beyond the palace garden, Intiqq was bathed in afternoon calm. The tiered earth-mounds of highblood estates stood like islands among the smaller, whitewashed buildings. But as she looked beyond the stepped pyramids of the Noble Quarter, she realised she could hear distant horns. In the far hills, up in the wetwoods, an army was approaching.

It was nearly dark when Osellia climbed in through the window. Mud and grime caked her dark brown skin, and a bruise gleamed on one shoulder, but she was otherwise unharmed.

'I couldn't get to the horses,' she said. 'Every gate is guarded, even the hidden ones. I've seen six of those blue monstrosities now. I think every guard in the palace must have them.'

'We've been locked in our rooms,' Chellahua said.

Osellia shook her head. 'It doesn't matter. We won't be leaving this city. There is an army descending the hills.'

'Whose army?' Elari said.

'Clan Ahiki,' Osellia said. 'The king's response has come.'

TWENTY-NINE

Runt

For ten glorious days, Runt's luck seemed to have finally turned a corner. Zee's health improved. They had coin enough for hot meals every day. And Asham was polite to her, even deferential. Something about her visit with Harvell in the taproom had changed the cook's view of her, for the moment at least.

Runt often found herself thinking of the pendant. She missed its weight around her neck. She missed the voices, too: the further she strayed from the Cascade, the weaker they became, and without them, she felt less herself. Would her baba be angry that she'd sold it? *You're its guardian*, he had said. *Its keeper.* But Baba wasn't there. And once she left for war, she'd never see him again. So she put it out of her mind, and focused on enjoying her last days of freedom.

Then one morning, she woke to find her brother lying on his side in a pool of blood-streaked vomit. His brown skin was grey and clammy and his tight golden curls damp with sweat.

'Zee,' Runt said, shaking him awake. Outside, Little Dimadu was just waking for the day. Children shrieked and elders banged pots ready for the day's cooking. 'Zee, wake up.'

Zee opened his eyes. Blue, like Runt's, and like Runt's they were striking in the dark of his skin. 'I feel . . . so cold, Run,' he muttered.

Runt folded away the soiled bedclothes and wrapped her little brother in the remainder of the rags they slept on. *Run*. That's what Zee always called her. Runt never corrected him. *Run* spoke of flight and speed and power. She'd always hoped that when Baba finally named her, he'd pick something similar. But now, with the call to war, it seemed *Run* was as close as she'd ever come to a true name.

'I'm getting you more medicine,' Runt said. 'You wait here and don't go out.'

'I want you to stay!'

'Just wait for me, you hear?'

Runt fixed a Jebbanese wrapper under her arms and then stumbled out into the morning.

The sun was bright on High Hill – or Last Lane, as some called it. Beyond the row of wooden shacks standing opposite their hut lay nothing. The land fell away in a tumble of stone and crystal until it met the barren scrubland beyond. It was the very edge of the great City of Nine Lords and here not even the Lordswall stood to protect them. The stretch of collapsed wall ran the entire length of Lordsgrave. Some battle against the greybloods had been fought there, long ago, and now the land was littered with the discarded husks of their bodies. A cursed place.

At the bottom of High Hill, the mud road joined Low Hill and there, on the corner, stood Pellana's hut. The folds of fabric that marked her door were all down, but Runt didn't let that stop her. She flung them aside, heedless of the two youths who stopped to watch her with their empty water buckets on their heads.

Inside, the shack was musty and dark. She spotted Pellana's bulk on a sleeping mat off to the left. Runt poked at her with one bare foot until the woman started and blinked awake.

'My brother's sick again,' Runt said. 'You told me you'd heal him.'

Pellana peered at her for a few moments, clearly trying to place her. She was drunk, Runt realised – she smelt it in the air now. Drunk and useless, just as Ma had been.

'I did heal him,' the old woman croaked. 'He got better, didn't he?'

'For a while, but now he's bad again.'

'I never said I'd heal him permanently.'

'You *what*?' Runt said. She grabbed the central pole of the hut, steadying herself against the wave of rage that swept over her.

'I told you that weren't no normal river sickness,' Pellana said. She sighed. 'What are his symptoms now?'

'I don't know. He's cold. Sweaty again. He brought up everything we ate last night, and there was blood in it.'

'Blood?' Pellana closed her eyes and rolled onto her back. 'Can't help you.'

Something within Runt hardened. 'What do you mean, can't help?'

'Just that. Nothing I can do. If the blood's back, he's beyond healing. Best you can do is make him comfortable. For a price, I can—'

'No,' Runt said. 'I got you two fucking suns just so you could stretch out his death? No.'

'I don't have nothing that would work.'

'Nothing that would work? So what is all this shit then, eh?' Runt jabbed a hand at the techwork dangling from the ceiling. 'This just here for decoration?'

'I think you need to leave.'

'So what's this?' Runt yanked down a metal box, badly battered, and threw it at Pellana's head. 'Can't this do nothing?'

'Now listen—'

'What about this?' Runt seized a shard of crystal and lobbed it at the cowering woman. 'Can't this help?'

'I—'

'How about this?' And suddenly, Runt found she couldn't stop. All those useless artefacts, put there just for show, all so Pellana could take money from souls who had so little and use it to drink herself into a stupor. Runt strode around the hut, pulling it all down, throwing every Scathed relic at the mat while the useless woman jabbered and covered her head. The monks taught that techwork was not to be touched by

324

untrained hands, and this was why – they didn't know what to do with it. Perhaps there was something here that could heal. But a woman like Pellana would never know it.

Runt realised after she'd thrown the last box that the healer wasn't moving. A dark pool spread out beneath the sleeping mat.

Blood.

Runt stood staring at the healer, her chest rising and falling, not sure how she felt. Angry, yes. Sickened. But also relieved. Exhilarated. She took a cautious step forward, shaking, though not with fear, and felt for Pellana's pulse as she had done that day she'd lost her temper with Ma.

Nothing. No breath, either. Runt closed her eyes.

She hadn't meant to kill the woman – of course she hadn't. But Pellana had pushed her over the edge. Tricked her, lied to her, stolen from her. Really, Pellana was the murderer, because now Zee was going to die. Really, this was justice. Really, it was Pellana's own doing.

Runt realised she felt strong. It was as though taking another life had fed directly into hers, enriching her, heightening all her senses. It was a sign from the ancestors, she knew. A sign that she had done the right thing.

Pellana didn't deserve to join the ancestors. Runt's instinct was to burn her right where she lay and see that nothing remained. But any fire she started here would quickly spread through the entire neighbourhood, with so many living crammed together in their tiny wooden shacks. She'd seen it happen more than once: whole locales destroyed by one errant candle. Whole communities rebuilt from the ground up the morning after.

Pellana was too heavy to carry, so Runt left her where she lay. Found her bottle of Jebbanese red and emptied it over her corpse. Then she worked loose a couple of boards at the rear of her hut and slipped out through the back.

Two elders sat between the homes up ahead, peeling yam and chatting in Urobi, but Runt didn't care if they saw her. What did it matter?

Soon, she'd be heading to war. She strode by them, heedless of the blood on the hem of her wrapper, and turned out onto Low Hill for home.

She found Zee sleeping peacefully, but his face was crusted with dried vomit. Runt wiped at it absently, knowing she had to start her shift at the Cascade, but not quite able to stand.

'Pot-girl?' came a voice from without, and Runt's heart leapt. They'd found Pellana. Traced her death to Runt. Now they were going to hand her to the bluehawks. 'Pot-girl? I'm sorry, I still don't know your name. It's me – Harvell. I have a favour to ask.'

Runt scrambled to her feet and removed the piece of wood that covered the doorway. There she stood, Harvell, barefoot in the dirt of the road, wearing a simple tunic, her hair tied back.

'I'm Runt,' Runt said. 'I was just coming. But my brother's sick again.'

'Runt?' Harvell said. 'Well, er, *Runt*, I have a favour to ask of you.'

'Of course. Anything.'

'Well, you see, we've been looking at that pendant we bought from you for days now, and we can't seem to fathom it out. We've had our keenest minds on it, turning it over, poking and prodding it. They assure me it is techwork, but we can't get anything from it. You said it talks?'

'It does! There's these voices, and—'

'I'd hate to think you were misleading me. You see, I showed it to Ba Casten, and he's very curious about what it can do. But he is not a forgiving man when he thinks he's been tricked.'

'Ba Casten?' Runt said, her mouth dry. 'It – it ain't a trick. It really is rare techwork; my own baba told me.'

'I know,' Harvell said, touching her shoulder. 'Which is why you're going to come with me and show him.'

She didn't wait for Runt to answer. Nor did her gaze flick once to Zee, despite the stench of sickness in the air.

'I'll be back, Zee,' Runt said, though she knew in her heart her brother couldn't hear her. Then she fixed the door-wood back in place and hurried after Harvell.

This was it. Her biggest chance to earn the Chedus' respect. And coin for more medicine; perhaps even a place among them for Zee, once she'd gone. Harvell strode ahead of her, hands in the pockets of her tunic. Heads turned as they passed. Runt saw caution in every pair of eyes that flicked away; and adoration in those that nodded quick bows. Everyone they passed knew Harvell, knew the Chedus. They were a Family who inspired respect.

As soon as Runt stepped within the shadows of the Cascade's taproom, the pendant voices crowded her mind like a pack of eager dogs.

[We have missed you.]

[Missed you very much.]

[Longed for you.]

[Worried about you.]

[Do not leave us alone again.]

[Abandoned again.]

Harvell led her up the spiral staircase of the mezzanine and then beyond, down a narrow hallway lined with a rich Perewali rug and towards another set of stairs. These were the pillow rooms, Runt knew. But the pillow-workers of the Cascade did not have to ply their trade from windows and street corners. Elanna the Quenoni and Gifted Mikim and all the rest had long waiting lists and all the jewels they could want.

Runt had always assumed Casten's apartments lay at the top of the Cascade, but she'd been wrong. At the end of a short hallway stood a pair of doors carved with a woodland scene. A series of eyes floated within the curving path of a river. They matched the swirling tataus that wound up Harvell's left arm.

The doors opened as they approached, and Runt found herself stepping out onto a balcony crowded with people. Beyond stretched a glorious view of sky. They were so high up that the encampment of people fleeing Aranduq, which lay below, was invisible, as was the fallen Lordswall itself. It was as though the Cascade stood at the very edge of civilisation, as though it floated in the sky.

The Family sat in a loose circle: Casten's sons and lieutenants, among

327

them a sour-faced Tarn. This was their circleroom, Runt realised, their most sacred gathering of elders. The fire in the middle was almost out, but a man knelt before it, eyes closed in contemplation. Even kneeling, Casten was an imposing figure; tall and heavily muscled, with wide, strong features. His black hair was shorn short, but his beard was long and twisted with beads.

'That her, Vell?' Casten said.

'This is the pot-girl,' Harvell said.

'Come closer,' Casten said.

Runt stepped within the circle, aware of all the gazes that fell upon her as she knelt down by the smouldering pit.

An offering lay on the floor beside the small fire – food and a number of jewels. There, to the left, lay Runt's pendant. Her heart lurched at the sight of it. It was hers. It had been given to her, and it took all her willpower not to reach out and snatch it back.

'Now, I'm a patient man,' Casten said, holding Runt in his gaze, 'and I know what my strengths are and what they ain't. Vell here's the one that sniffs out the techwork, and Feyin's the one with the eye for its workings.' He nodded his head at a skinny, grinning old man with wild white hair. 'But my patience don't last for ever. Feyin's been turning this pendant here over and over these last few days, prodding and poking it, twisting it up with all them little veins.' He lifted the pendant as he spoke, and Runt felt a burst of annoyance as he did. It swung from his rough hands, too close to the fire. Runt realised she was following it with her eyes. She couldn't look away.

'And you know what Feyin said? He said this thing weren't made to talk. He's pretty sure about what it *was* made to do, though all them Forbidden words he knows couldn't get nothing out of it. But he did notice that every time you was down in the pot-wash, the thing would start to give off . . . techwork heat—'

'A *siganaal*,' said Feyin, the wild-looking elder. So it was true: some Chedus knew the Forbidden Tongue. 'It starts to give off what we call a *siganaal*.'

'Now Harvell here, she assures me you're a good girl, and that you wouldn't try no tricks, and she also tells me how hard you fought for this. Harvell ain't wrong about tech, or people. So what I'm trying to work out is this: are you a liar or just bloody stupid?'

Runt swallowed, heat rising within her. Out of the corner of her eye, she caught Tarn's wild grin. They thought she was a fraud, she realised. All of them. That was why they were all here: not to witness a miracle, but to enjoy an execution. Harvell's face was a mask; so her reputation was at stake too.

'It does talk,' Runt said. 'On my life, on my ancestors, it talks. Whenever I'm near it, I hear them . . . whispering to me. So it don't matter what you say. I know what's true.'

Silence fell over the room. Runt kept her eye on the pendant, there by the fire. The only movement came from Feyin, rocking back and forth where he sat. Then he chuckled and said, 'Son, I think she really doesn't know.'

Ba Casten glanced at the old man, then tossed the pendant through the air. Runt caught it smoothly, its weight a familiar comfort in her hands. She wanted to close her eyes and press it to her face, but she forced herself to keep her gaze on Casten.

'It heals,' Casten said, tipping his head. 'Feyin says all them glyphs tell him that it heals. What we can't work out is how. Which is where you come in. Show us. Make it heal. Or I'm going to need my money back. With interest.'

Runt closed her hand around the pendant, her mind aswirl. That day Baba had visited her with his two friends, he'd made her hold the pendant. She'd watched as he jerked his knife across his friends' hands, calm as you please. Runt hadn't flinched – her baba didn't like flinchers – and afterwards he'd whispered, *Go on, tell the pendant to heal them.* She'd thought it was some kind of game, some joke, especially as Baba had bound the men's hands immediately. But she hadn't seen what happened after she passed out, and woke up later that night, utterly alone.

'I—'

[We heal.]

[We fix.]

[We make things better.]

Runt drew in a slow breath. 'I can try. But I'll need a wound.'

Casten lifted a hand and beckoned. 'Krayl, come here.'

A hawk-faced youth with the look of Ntuk about him peeled away from the line of Casten's sons, each as different as their various mothers had been. He was a handsome, smiling man, and stared openly at Runt, lips curled with scorn as he sat at his father's side.

[He mocks you.]

[Looks down upon you.]

[You should teach him.]

[Show him.]

'Now Krayl here, he likes a fight,' Casten said. 'Just this morning, he had himself a grand old time, taking care of a thief that stole from me. Gets carried away sometimes, though, and this thief had the temerity to actually try to fight back. Show him, son.'

The youth, Krayl, held out one hand. It was a mangled, flopping ruin. How he'd been able to sit there so calmly with that smile on his face, Runt couldn't imagine. Two fingers stood out at an odd angle. A third was torn to the bone. Krayl had to support the damaged hand with the good. He grinned at Runt's expression and let out a soft laugh.

'Off you go, then,' Casten said with a shooing motion. 'Fix him.'

Runt looked up. 'Fix him?'

'You deaf? I said fix him.'

Runt closed her eyes. Baba's men – if the pendant really had healed them, if *she* had healed them – had only flesh wounds. Here were broken bones and severed muscle.

[We can fix him.]

[Heal him.]

[Make him better.]

Runt shuffled forward and held her hands out above Krayl's wounded one. 'Please,' she whispered, 'heal him.'

330

She heard movement behind her, a stifled giggle, but ignored it all and let the voices rise up. Something streaked past her, the air kissing her cheek, and Runt opened her eyes to see a swirling blue form manifesting. It was little more than a streak of light, but within its churning cloud shone feline eyes, an arch smile, the suggestion of long, smooth limbs. A second joined it, and then a third, and soon they formed a swirling, living mass.

Runt glanced at Casten, but he stared straight through the churning cloud. Everyone did. Even when the blue creatures swept towards Krayl, not a soul reacted, not even Krayl himself. They couldn't see, Runt realised. Only she could, just as only she could hear their voices.

'This is stupid,' Krayl said.

'Wait!' Feyin cried. He sat frowning at the shard of blackglass in his palm. Green glyphs streamed across the relic's ancient surface as a slow smile crept onto the elder's face.

Round and round the blue creatures streaked, forming a vortex high above Krayl's head. Then they began to descend until they encircled Krayl's kneeling form, faster and faster in a thin blue cloud.

At once, Krayl's arm began to shake. The youth looked up uncertainly, then clasped more tightly with his good hand.

One of Krayl's fingers jerked, then snapped back into position, and Krayl let out a grunt of pain. Others had noticed now, kneeling forwards and whispering to each other, and even Casten himself began to nod.

The second finger snapped back, and then the flesh began to re-knit itself, growing across the finger that had been cut to the bone. Krayl let out a cry, and the blue creatures burst from existence in a cloud of echoing laughter.

Runt opened her hand. She'd been gripping the pendant so tightly her fingers were numb. She looked up and allowed herself a small smile.

'Astounding!' Feyin cried, staring at his blackglass. 'I've never seen anything like it!'

'And only the pot-girl can do it?' Casten said.

331

'I suspect only she can do it. It . . . responds to her somehow.'

'Then you got yourself a new job,' Casten said, turning back to Runt. 'From now on, you're our healer. You'll report to Feyin so he can learn how to replicate this thing. Krayl?'

'You have my thanks,' the youth said, head bobbing in a bow.

They were all watching her. Some grinned excitedly. Others regarded her with hard suspicion. Harvell smiled broadly. Lakoz, the man who looked so like her, had taken hold of her hand.

'Please,' Runt said, turning back to Casten. 'My brother is sick. If – if this could help him—'

'Go on,' Casten said, gesturing. 'Go on and heal your brother. Seems the ancestors gave that to you for a reason, so you'd best use it. Just see that you bring it back. You run off with that thing and you'll regret it.'

Runt summoned up a smile and climbed to her feet.

THIRTY

Boleo

Tap the 'more information' button on your panel to see an animated diagram of the process.

Those words had become a mantra in Father Boleo's mind over their days searching the Busharn wastes. They were words that should not be. Words out of time and place. Words written in a language from across the ocean, on an artefact made by the Scathed. The Forbidden Tongue was the only language that could control techwork. Every monk knew that. Yet he had heard a Scathed artefact speak words in the Leopard Tongue.

As they combed the desert, travelling from ruin to ruin in the shadow of broken Scathed towers, those words were all Boleo could think about. Yes, he knew his task here was to find the ruins, and whatever clues lay within. But Boleo had the sense that something of greater import loomed just beyond sight, and that only he could reach it. It was the end of the path the ancestors had set him upon at the age of sixteen, when he had found that techwork talking drum during the monastery trials.

The Butcher of Busharn remained resolute in her refusal to aid them. From what Boleo could glean about her from the old reports, she'd been an exemplary officer. In receipt of many tataus of honour. Not a blemish

333

on her record. In service to Chinnaro for over five rains before she took the woman's life. It made no sense that she would slaughter so many, not only because he did not believe the claim that she had temporarily lost her grip on sanity, but because there had been thirty souls in her party, hardened warriors all. How had she, a single soldier – talented, yes, but not even an invoker – managed to singlehandedly slaughter them all?

By the second moon of their journey, things began to deteriorate. Their food supplies had dwindled, and one of the Batide warriors took a bad insect bite and died. The mood among them grew increasingly sour, with many whispering that they should be heading home, not wandering the wastes in pursuit of a myth. Even Morayo grumbled about wanting to rethink things. Boleo didn't dare tell them that they were out here because of him, because he had been banished. They were not meant to solve this riddle, only to stay out of the way until the Garden had turned its gaze from Clan Adatali. He supposed he could have sent them all back and carried on alone, but he knew Morayo would not permit that. The boy stuck to him like a barnacle, just as he had as a child.

One evening well into their second moon of travel, they made camp at a small oasis. A single wall of blackglass stood amid the palms. It was the first water they had come upon in days, and Boleo felt the mood lift at once. While he examined the slab of blackglass, the Batide fanned out, filling their gourds, some stripping naked to bathe. Remami found some edible grasses growing near the water, and a scrawny, aged Batide named Uchuno set about making a stew with dried fungus and powdered peppers.

Morayo came to Boleo as he stood oiling his horse under the shadow of a palm. The boy had stripped to his loincloth to practise his fighting forms, and sweat glistened on his dark, muscled skin. The green and white tataus of his clan glimmered on his forearms. He had grown his hair and beard into stubby twists.

'We only have six ruins left,' Morayo said.

'I'm aware of that.'

'What are we going to do if none of them yield anything of value? Do you think perhaps we've missed something?'

'No,' Boleo said. 'I am certain of it.'

'I wish I shared your faith,' Morayo said, before dropping to the sand. Boleo watched the boy assemble a makeshift shrine using a collection of decorative stones and a cassava cake. 'Oh ancestors,' Morayo intoned loudly. 'Please lend Father Boleo your wisdom, so that he might know when to give up. Please lend him—'

'You are welcome to return to Jebba whenever you wish,' Boleo snapped.

'—lend him your strength, so that pride no longer guides him. So say I, Morayo Adabowale Adalele Ibiko Adatali.'

Boleo had never heard Morayo list all his names before . . . he supposed because beseeching the ancestors was usually a private affair – a fact Morayo would have done well to remember. Boleo had always associated that particular Jebbanese tradition with lowbloods. Curious that Daloya would observe it within his own family, just as he did with his Batide guard.

'You have ancestral family names?' Boleo said.

'Of course – how could I call myself Jebbanese if I didn't have twenty names given to me by aunties I've never met? Father always said that the clans have it backwards giving us names for the enemies we defeat in battle. It is the names of our forebears that have the most power, names given to us with love.' Morayo eyed him. 'Do you not have any family names, Father Boleo?'

'Monks do not have family.'

'Not even your holy brothers?'

'Most especially our holy brothers.'

'Well, Father always said that when I am most in need, I must recite the names of the ancestors I am named after at a shrine. I believe we are most definitely in need of ancestral guidance, Father Boleo.' Only the slightest twitch at the corner of Morayo's mouth betrayed his amusement.

Boleo ground his teeth. 'Then I will leave all twenty of you to your contemplations.'

While the rest of their group sat around the cook-fire as the sun set, singing Urobi folk songs again, Boleo leaned against the slab of blackglass and had his staff flash up those words in Leopard Tongue, words that should not be.

Tap the 'more information' button on your panel to see an animated diagram of the process.

He recalled the day he had asked Warlord Daloya why their palace was called Three Towers when only two towers stood on the grounds. *Sometimes words blind*, Daloya had said. *Sometimes words seek to obscure, not illuminate. To ensnare. If there is one thing you should know as a monk, Father Boleo, it is the reductive nature of words.*

'What is that thing you keep looking at, anyway?' Morayo said, stepping out from behind the blackglass.

'I do wish you'd stop sneaking up on me!' Boleo snapped, tapping his staff to take the words away. 'It is not an appropriate way to behave around a member of the Holy Orders.'

'Oh, spare me, Father,' Morayo said, flopping down beside him. 'Haven't you and I come too far for all this? What are those symbols you keep looking at?'

'It is an ancient language from the Leopard Kingdom – the most powerful nation on the continent on Ulamara. It was inscribed on a piece of techwork, but I do not understand how it could be, given that the Scathed died out long before the Leopard Kingdom existed.'

'Is that the language the invisible voice was speaking?' Morayo said.

'Yes. But it makes no sense. Only the Forbidden Tongue can command techwork. And humans did not exist in the days of the Scathed.'

'Many things about the Scathed make no sense,' Morayo said. 'If they were such a peaceful species, why did they create the greybloods? And how could their own creations annihilate them when they were said to wield such power?'

'I was taught not to ask such questions,' Boleo said.

'Could your staff be wrong? Maybe it's not the Leopard Tongue . . . maybe the Scathed had more than one language.'

'It doesn't matter what language it was,' Boleo said, 'Only the Forbidden Tongue can command techwork . . . and that language wasn't the Forbidden Tongue.'

Boleo looked up to see the Butcher watching them from the shadows of her cage. She turned away, but not fast enough to disguise her interest.

Boleo stood and crossed to where the Butcher's carriage stood facing the dark mass of the desert night. 'Open the cage!'

'What are you doing?' Morayo asked, springing after him.

'I've had enough of playing games,' Boleo told him. 'Lieutenant, open the cage!'

Lieutenant Jamakii called to the two Batide nearest her, who fell into position while she unlocked the door. Boleo leaned his staff against the carriage wall and climbed in.

The Butcher sat in the far corner, knees drawn up to her chin, watching him warily.

'Seal the door, please,' Boleo said to Jamakii. 'Then leave us. You too, Invoker, if you'd be so kind.'

'Father?' Jamakii said, her smooth brow creasing. 'I do not think this wise.'

'I will speak to the Butcher alone. Please seal the door – I do not want her running off.'

'As you command, Father,' Jamakii said, and she swung the cage door shut and secured it with bolt and lock. Though she moved away, she did not go far, and stood watching with spear in hand.

'Let me quote something to you,' Boleo said. 'Something from the many reports I found on the Busharn Massacre. I think you will find it quite interesting.' Boleo cleared his throat. '*Her only request was that she be permitted to attend Lord Chinnaro's funeral. She was kept well away from the family and wept bitterly the entire time.*'

The Butcher stared at him mutely, radiating hatred.

'Does this sound like the actions of the insane?' Boleo said.

'Are you still quoting now, holy man?'

'No. I am asking you. Did you lose your mind and murder your entire party singlehandedly? Then drag their severed heads across the desert and surrender yourself to the nuns?'

'Yes,' the Butcher said, showing him her teeth.

'I don't believe you.'

Silence stretched between them. Boleo stared out at the night, determined not to be the one to break it. After a time, he glanced at her and, to his surprise, saw tears standing in the woman's dark eyes. When one spilled down her cheek, she made no move to wipe it away.

'Who really killed them?' Boleo said. The Butcher turned away, but Boleo leaned forward, insistent. 'Who? And why did you take the blame?'

She looked round slowly, her eyes still swimming.

'We could bring them to justice, you know,' Boleo said softly. '*I* could bring them to justice.'

A faint, scornful smile curved her lips.

'Do you not yearn to show the Nine Lands the truth?'

For a long time, the Butcher watched him quietly, her expression unreadable as she weighed his words. Finally, she lowered her gaze and said, 'I heard what you and the invoker were saying about names. We should not name greybloods. People, yes. Weapons, yes. But not greybloods. Naming them gives them power. Father, I may not have killed them, but I am responsible for their demise.'

'But those people did not die by your hand.'

'You have no idea of the horrors I took part in that day.'

'You were innocent,' Boleo said softly. He reached forward and took hold of her arm. So many tataus of honour, intertwined with the scars.

She looked at him and for the first time her guard seemed to slip. 'Do not walk this road, holy man. It will bring you only death.'

Boleo smiled faintly. 'As we speak, tens of thousands of warriors just like those who died in the massacre are marching to the Feverlands. Meanwhile, Aranduq has fallen and the River Ae lies unprotected. The king cannot win against the greybloods. His invasion is doomed. Warlord Daloya is the greatest invoker of his age. He can protect our people. Show me the way to Chinnaro's ruins. Help us stop more innocent souls from crossing the pyre.' Boleo leaned forward. 'Ashu,' he said softly. 'That is your name, the report says. Ashu: you must show me the way. You cannot bring back those who have already been slaughtered, but you can save countless others from a slaughter yet to come.'

She straightened like a viper preparing to strike, and for a moment Boleo thought she meant to leap at him. Jamakii noticed it too, for through the darkness Boleo saw her grip tighten on the spear.

But Ashu, the Butcher of Busharn, merely turned her head.

'We must head west,' she said finally. 'We can be there within a few days.'

The next morning dawned bright and clear, and they set off early, heading west again. By nightfall, the landscape began to change, the deep gullies and looming outcrops giving way to an arid scrubland. Then, four days after agreeing to help them, Ashu, the Butcher of Busharn, led them out of the desert and onto a wide, grassy savannah dotted with majestic acacias.

By Boleo's reckoning, they were approaching the western borders of what had once been Kzaniland, and he was all too aware of how close they were coming to the warfront and the Feverlands beyond.

'Not long now,' Ashu called back from her place at the head of the main column.

Boleo slept poorly that night, and the next day rain swept in from the west and did not leave them until nightfall. By then they were cold, and miserable, and the grasslands had given way to the beginnings of wetwoods. From the top of the plateau on which they stood, the sun setting off to their left, they could see for many leagues across the wetwoods, to the hazy green glow on the horizon.

'She has been wasting our time!' Morayo shouted, steering Relentless up to where Ashu stood. He removed his ida from his belt and pointed it in her face. 'That glow is the Feverlands. You have brought us to the very edge of the realm. Where are Chinnaro's ruins? Tell us now, or ancestors help me, I will run you through.'

Ashu smiled slowly. 'You already have everything you need.'

Boleo slipped from his horse and strode towards her, the rain streaming through his beard. 'There's nothing here,' he said. 'No ruins. Nothing. You swore to lead us to—'

'The ruins don't matter! Don't you understand? There's nothing more there!'

'Then tell me how we're ever supposed to find the place where spirits—'

'Place!' Ashu said. 'Whoever told you Vunaji was a place? Look again at the map. Look carefully. Everything you need is there.'

Morayo swung. In response, Ashu lifted her hand and slapped away his blade.

Morayo grunted in surprise. Then he swept the leaf-shaped blade back round in a savage arc. But Ashu was ready. She jerked backwards, ducking under his blow, and then threw herself forward, knocking Morayo to the ground.

They had given her no weapons, but she didn't need them. Though Nchali leapt from his horse and sprinted across the ground and Jamakii fumbled for her bow, Ashu was on Morayo in a heartbeat. Ancestors, but she was fast! She knelt on his hand and jerked the blade from his grip. In all Boleo's years watching Morayo train, watching him dance around the central courtyard of Three Towers with a smile upon his face, Boleo had only ever seen Morayo disarmed once. By the time Nchali was within striking distance, Ashu had the blade pressed to Morayo's neck.

'Let me go,' she said, looking round at Nchali. Morayo's forearms were bright with the light of invocation, but Boleo knew he would not be able to invoke before she slit his throat. He cursed inwardly. How

340

had he let it come to this? Why hadn't he been keeping closer watch? 'It is for your own good.'

'Why did you lead us in circles?' Morayo said.

'Because I hoped that you would change your minds!' Ashu said. 'You want to know why Cantec and Jethar failed? You want to know why my entire company died? Then I'll—' Ashu fell still, her face slackening. 'No. It can't be . . .'

Singing. Distant singing. A feminine voice, high and serene.

'You have to run!' Ashu said. 'She's found us!'

'Look out!' Nchali cried.

The bush parted and a woman appeared. No; not a woman. Something bearing the semblance of a woman, but wrong in every way. Her body was too thin, too angular, and her grey skin shone with its own light. Her eyes were yellow within black and it was not hair that fell from her head, but a tangle of leaves and flowers. Boleo could not deny that there was something alluring about her. She wore a dress, but it was transparent as moonlight, revealing the breasts and woman-hood beneath. She offered them all a wide and wicked smile, revealing dozens of tiny, sharp teeth. She was even more beautiful than the paintings. Even more revolting.

'Ashu,' the Woodsmaiden said, no longer singing, her voice soft and musical. 'What an unexpected joy!'

'Please,' Ashu said, releasing Morayo and standing. 'Please, not again.'

'And what delightful treats you've brought me,' the Woodsmaiden said, clasping her hands together. Her metallic claws clicked as she rapped her fingers against each other, and for a moment, Boleo saw a flash of Forbidden glyphs slide across the grey skin.

Then her children appeared, a dozen, two dozen. Some were small and some large. Some looked almost human, while others were jittering conglomerations of metal and techwork, and still more seemed ghastly, slavering beasts. One of them, a female in rotting feathered armour, looked almost familiar as she turned towards Ashu.

'Ashu, just go,' the feathered greyblood said. 'Please.'

'I won't let her take any more people, My Lord,' Ashu replied, striding towards them.

The Woodsmaiden grinned, sliding a proprietary arm around the familiar-looking greyblood. *My Lord.* Ashu had referred to the greyblood as *My Lord.* And as Boleo looked more closely, he realised why the creature had seemed so familiar. She had the same compact, warrior's frame. She had the same narrow jaw. He could not see her clan tataus, true, but then her skin was caked with dirt and twisted with techwork veins.

'I don't understand,' Boleo said. 'Is that—'

'Oh, so you know Invoker Chinnaro Itahua!' the Woodsmaiden said, smiling malevolently. 'Granted, she might have changed somewhat over the last seven rains, but I do believe she's never been in finer form!'

Boleo stood. The greyblood before him had once been a woman. She had once been Chinnaro Itahua, warrior and scholar, but now all that remained was a decaying, emaciated ruin held together by Forbidden arts. Her head was made entirely of metal, as were the heads of dozens of others Boleo saw. And now he understood why the Butcher had returned with only the severed heads of her company. The bodies had been taken elsewhere.

'What did you do to them?' Boleo said, revulsion crawling over his skin.

'Ashu begged me to save them,' the Woodsmaiden said, pouting. 'And so I did.'

'You preserved their bodies with techwork?' Boleo said. And though he knew he should feel nothing but disgust, a deeper part of him swelled with wonder as he began to understand. Of course techwork could safeguard life – it could heal, couldn't it? Of course the creatures the Scathed had crafted from it would seek ways to adapt their forms. And this explained why so many greybloods took on a human aspect. Despite what his holy brothers claimed, it had nothing to do with mockery or emulation.

342

'Were you all human once?' Boleo said. 'Or do you just take our body parts?'

The Woodsmaiden placed a silver hand to her narrow chest. 'You wound me! Take body parts? I do no such thing! I save people! Don't I, dearest?'

She gave Chinnaro – if the techwork abomination truly was Chinnaro – a little shove, and Chinnaro's silver head flicked Boleo's way. 'Sh-she saved us all!' Chinnaro said emphatically. But her voice cracked as she spoke, and Boleo saw the way her shoulders stiffened in what was such a human response. It was a response that spoke of fear and obedience and so many things. It was a response that left no room for doubt in Boleo's mind.

He tightened his grip on his staff. 'By what right do you mutilate us?'

'By what right?' the Woodsmaiden cried. 'Why, if I had not saved these people when Vunaji attacked, they would all have perished. Instead, I have given them eternal life.'

'She tricked me,' Ashu said. 'She promised to bring them back, but instead . . . she did this. You ask if I killed them, holy man? I did. Because it was I who caused *this*.'

Nchali and several other Batide warriors had begun spreading out. But Boleo's attention remained fixed on the Woodsmaiden. 'What do you mean, when Vunaji attacked?' he said. 'Vunaji is an island.'

'When the creature attacked!' the Woodsmaiden sang. 'And now, Chinnaro here has come to save you from a similar fate.'

'How could you?' Morayo growled at the Butcher. 'You have led us to our deaths!'

'I didn't know that she would come again!' Ashu cried, her voice stricken. She faced the Woodsmaiden. 'Please, just let them go. Let them go, and they will promise not to call upon Vunaji.'

'What do you mean, call upon Vunaji?' Boleo said. 'Vunaji is a *place*.'

'Oh, I'm afraid I can't let them go,' the Woodsmaiden said. 'These lands are mine, and I have a duty to protect them.'

343

'What is she talking about?' Morayo said, turning to Boleo. 'Father, what does she mean?'

But the Woodsmaiden lifted her hands, and her children swept forward with wide, feral smiles.

THIRTY-ONE

Elari

The palace of Livinghall was under siege, and Elari was a prisoner in her own apartments.

It took less than a day for the Clan Ahiki to seize the city of Qenqar. Elari and her doves watched from their sleep-chamber window, silently holding hands. From what Elari could see from the hillside of Livinghall, the people of the city had offered no resistance. She saw warriors out on the battlements of the palace wall, but to her surprise, no Clan Itahua companies marched to meet the advancing ranks of the Garden. By mid-afternoon on that first day, the golden horde of Clan Ahiki's soldiers filled the boulevard beyond the palace. The city was the king's now, and Clan Itahua had done nothing to prevent it.

'Why don't they storm the palace?' Osellia whispered as the sun began to set. 'There must be two thousand royal soldiers down there.'

'I don't know,' Elari said. 'I don't understand it.'

Ishaan, the stealthiest among them after so many years as a street thief, was able to explore the palace every few days and report back on what they saw. What they described did nothing to allay the knot of terror that tightened in Elari's gut.

'I've not seen Atoc at all,' Ishaan said as they all ate the simple supper of seed crackers their gaolers had given them. 'I've searched his entire apartments now. From what I overheard in the kitchens, there are enough stores of food to last the palace three more moons at most. Several servants have been caught trying to surrender – they were brought before Manax's traders and are compliant now.'

'It is only a matter of time before we too are brought before the traders,' Osellia said. 'If what you say is true and they are slowly transforming the whole palace, our time will come.'

'Why isn't the Royal Clan attacking?' Elari said.

'They have taken over the administrative and holy districts and dismissed all clan officials, from what I could gather. Princen Jukanju leads them. He is a calculating man, I am told – shrewd and patient. He has both the skill and the numbers to seize Livinghall, yet they whisper that fear holds him back.'

'Ahikis do not know fear,' Chellahua muttered.

'Perhaps they know what has taken hold here,' Osellia said softly. 'Perhaps they have heard about those . . . those blue things.'

Sometimes they saw warriors training out on the lawns, but none seemed to be practising the Obsidian Dance. Elari guessed that this too had been deemed of the ancestors and was therefore unsanctioned now. Part of her longed for the Ahikis to storm the palace and destroy the traders and their creatures. Surely no one could stand against the Royal Clan? But the days rolled on and a moon came and went and the Ahikis did not advance.

Each time the lock sounded, Elari's stomach tightened with the certainty that it was the two little traders, but nobody came except the ever-changing cycle of guards.

'Iqdaa,' Elari said, on the morning she finally saw a warrior she recognised. 'Please! Can you tell us no news? Can we at least be permitted to go out and exercise?'

'Iqdaa is busy,' he replied, turning yellow-tinged eyes on her and offering a mirthless smile.

'What did they do to you?' Elari whispered, backing away.

'They healed me,' Iqdaa told her as he set down their food. 'Made me better.'

Then one night, some time before dawn, Elari woke to a scrabble of movement outside the window.

'Go,' she mouthed to her doves, before reaching beneath the cushions for her dagger.

Chellahua slipped from the sunken bed and crossed to the window, blade in hand.

A boy stumbled into the room, a youth of perhaps fifteen. He wore travelling garb and his eyes were wide with fear. At once, Chellahua was on him, blade pressed to his throat.

'Please!' the youth said shrilly, holding up both hands. 'I'm unarmed! C-Captain Elari, your brother Atanchu sent me, and Invokers Rozichu and Kartuuk. I am to bring you to safety. I am to rescue you!'

Osellia raised her eyebrows, and Elari gestured for Chellahua to let the boy go.

The youth sagged as Chellahua stepped away from him.

'How do we know you are not an assassin?' Ishaan said, sliding from the bed.

'Your brother sent this,' the boy said, and reached into the pouch at his belt to produce a bright red ring. It was a garnet Elari had given her brother on the day of his betrothal. Her throat tightened, and for a moment she couldn't speak.

'He could not risk a written message,' the youth said.

'That is his,' Elari said tightly. 'Osellia, find this young man some water – he must be thirsty.'

'Would you like me to draw you a bath?' Chellahua said, looking him over. 'I can scrub your back.'

The youth looked horrified. 'No, I – I . . . A drink would be welcome, if you please, Lieutenant.'

Chellahua turned away, laughing, and Osellia gave her a playful kick. Elari let them chatter as she approached the boy, taking both his hands in hers. They were calloused – from the Obsidian Dance, she guessed. So perhaps he was a squire.

'You did a brave thing, coming here,' she said. 'It must have been dangerous.'

'I had to kill a guard,' the boy said, staring past her. She led him to her broken daybed and sat him down. 'Something came out of him. Some kind of . . . blue smoke. After I slit his throat, I said sorry. Imagine that!' He made a sound that was half laugh, half sob, then covered his eyes. 'I was trained to kill greybloods, not people.'

'You see! The blue things can be killed,' Osellia hissed at Ishaan.

'Then why does the Royal Can hold back?' Ishaan replied.

'I am sorry that happened,' Elari told the boy. 'Now tell me: do you believe we can escape the same way you came in?'

'Yes. Captain, Livinghall Palace will fall. Lord Kartuuk says the Ahikis will burn it to the ground. You must escape before they do. You will be safe with Invoker Kartuuk. They have a camp on the borders of the Menit Wilderness. And they are planning a rebellion against Manax!'

Chellahua arrived holding a cup of water, which she pressed into the boy's hand. The youth tipped his head back and swallowed deeply.

'Truly, Captain,' the boy said, wiping his mouth on his bare arm and turning to her, 'you should come with me. I would n-not presume to command a captain of a quartet, of course, but—'

Ishaan had been quiet for some moments, but now they stepped forward and said, 'You killed one guard? Only one?'

'Yes, thank the ancestors.'

'Which passageway was it you used? The Moon or the Serpent?'

Elari ensured her smile didn't falter, but her skin grew cold. There was no Moon passage, and the Serpent passage was on the eastern side of the palace. Ishaan stood lightly, hands behind their back, but Elari knew when they were preparing to spring. Out of the corner of her eye, she saw Chellahua nudge Osellia.

'I – I am not familiar with the names, Lieutenant,' the boy said. 'I—'

Elari threw herself backwards over the daybed as Ishaan sprang. She was up in a heartbeat, her knife in her hand, but Ishaan had the young boy by the throat. They planted themself behind the daybed, their arm around the boy's neck, the blade pressed to the youth's side with their free hand.

'Please!' the boy said. 'It really would be better if you just came with me. They said it would be better! Don't you want to escape?'

'My brother didn't send you,' Elari said, feeling an icy rage grip her.

'Yes, he did!' the boy said. His face shifted then, as though trying on several emotions for size. His eyes grew calm, and his mouth curved with just a hint of mockery. The voice he spoke with then was smooth and sweet as honey. 'Oh, your brother did send him,' the youth purred. 'He just . . . met with more resistance in the passageways than he was expecting.' His back arched, and Ishaan strained to keep hold of him as something melted out of his body; it was human shaped, but with a long, tapering head, glowing yellow eyes, and skin a smoky blue.

Elari leapt, slashing downwards with the knife, catching the blue creature in its shoulder as it twisted towards her. To her astonishment, her arm passed through air as the creature's shoulder parted like fog, before reforming as it whipped around. To her left, Ishaan grunted as they struggled with the boy.

Osellia joined Elari. The edges of her macuahuitl caught the candle-light. She slashed downwards in a devastating swing, but the heavy weapon sliced through the creature's body as it parted like smoke again.

'It can't be harmed!' Osellia cried, whirling around.

'The boy!' Chellahua said. 'It is tethered to the boy!'

Choose who lives and who dies.

'He's just a child!' Elari cried, the Bairneater's laughter echoing in her mind. But Chellahua leapt onto the daybed, straddling the youth, and in one quick motion, plunged her blade into his eye. His body convulsed as dark liquid ran down his face.

The creature whirled around, its wide mouth curving in a smile. 'We're everywhere now,' it said. 'You have no choice but to join the hunt.' Then its body streaked upwards, fading and twisting. By the time it reached the high limestone ceiling, all that remained was its echoing laughter.

'Fuck,' Chellahua muttered, rolling off the boy's corpse. 'Ancestors!'

Elari clutched at her chest, unable to look at the youth, unable to take in his face.

'It couldn't be helped,' Osellia said, slipping an arm around Elari's waist.

Elari gripped her hand. 'That *was* my brother's jewel. It could only have come from him. Do – do you think the creatures are—'

'No,' Ishaan said sharply, standing. 'This boy must have been sent by Kartuuk and Atanchu originally, but been attacked in the passageways here, just as that thing said. There's no possibility that he only encountered one guard – I've seen dozens down there. They must have caught him and infected him as they have infected so many in Livinghall.'

Elari steadied herself on the back of the daybed, closing her eyes against the wave of nausea that swept over her. 'And if we'd followed him,' she said, 'we would have carried that infection to my brother's camp.'

'Thank the ancestors we did not,' Osellia said, making the sign for ancestral protection. She took Elari's hand and traced a finger across her tatau of union, the tatau all five of them received the day they pledged themselves to each other. 'Kartuuk is one of the greatest warriors in the east. Your brother will be safe.'

Elari drew in a shaking breath. 'We can trust no one,' she said. 'Only each other.' She closed her eyes and pressed her face to Osellia's shoulder.

They did not sleep that night, and the following day, they took turns to guard the door.

Elari snapped awake. She sat up in the darkness, listening to the tap-tapping coming from the main door.

Osellia, who had been on guard duty, was already on her feet, a blade in each hand. Chellahua had been curled at Elari's side, but silently she uncoiled herself and slipped across the room, her thin night robe billowing out behind her.

'Breakfast for the captain!' came a feminine voice.

Elari frowned, then motioned for Chellahua to answer. 'It is not yet dawn!' Chellahua said, removing her own knife. 'And we are not hungry!'

'Oh, I think you'll want this meal.' It was only then that Elari registered the voice. At once she dashed across the room, heart racing, and pushed past Chellahua.

The door opened before she reached it, and there stood Lyela, dressed in the uniform of a palace guard, a radiant smile on her round face. The portico beyond was all in shadow, but Elari could just make out the dark shapes of two bodies slumped on the stone floor.

'I'll need a hand with those,' Lyela said. 'It might be best not to leave them out there.'

Elari's doves set to work at once, dragging the corpses into the room and behind the door.

'I see much has been happening in my absence,' Lyela said brightly. Elari noticed that there was not a mark on her skin, nor on the guards, whose eyes stared sightlessly.

Ishaan had noticed too, for in a heartbeat, their knife was at Lyela's neck. 'Are you one of them?' they hissed. 'Tell us now if you are one of them.'

'One of what?'

'The blue things!'

Lyela sighed. 'If I was, would I say so with a knife to my neck? You'll have to take a gamble.'

'Did you do it?' Elari said. 'Did you kill Jethar?'

'My mission was a success,' Lyela said. 'But as you can imagine, I couldn't bring the proof here. You'll need to come with me.' She slid her eyes round towards Ishaan. 'I trust you'd prefer to leave the palace, rather than remain until the Royal Clan destroys it? I'm your best chance at escape.'

'If you lie—' Ishaan began darkly.

'Yes, yes, I know,' Lyela said. 'You will cut out both my eyes and make me eat them with broken teeth.' She smiled brilliantly. 'You know, I have missed you four.'

Elari's doves packed quickly while she opened the door to her dressing-room one last time. Cantec's barrels of techwork stood neatly stacked against the far wall. The monks would burn it all once they stormed the palace, and no one would ever know what Forbidden wonders lay within.

She swept on down the short hallway and into Cantec's library. It made her heart hurt to leave all his books and scrolls behind. The monks would likely burn everything in this room, too. But they could not burn her memories. And that would have to be enough.

'Captain, we must hurry,' Ishaan said from behind her. They wore a travelling wrap and a loose shirt, their short black hair unadorned, their face unpainted. It was curious, seeing her doves so plainly dressed, but they would need to pass inconspicuously. Elari herself had dressed in a light linen dress and belt and had gathered her long hair into a modest bun. She stuffed the scroll into her satchel, along with Lyela's puzzle-box, then pulled on a travelling cloak that covered her tataus of honour. Lastly, she reached for her macuahuitl. It had gathered dust, there upon the wall, but when she strapped it to her back, she realised how much she was comforted by its weight.

They slipped quietly out onto the portico. Far below, the descending tiers of the palace marched like steps towards the black expanse of the ocean. Elari glimpsed guards patrolling, and silently begged the ancestors to ensure that none chanced to look up.

Halfway along the portico, Lyela paused and placed her hand to the stone.

'What are you doing?' Ishaan hissed. 'The hidden passage is two floors down!'

Lyela's entire hand shone a brilliant yellow colour, and the wall flared with blue light. Forbidden glyphs flashed brightly in sequence, and then a glowing line traced a door-shaped rectangle across the stone. As Elari stared, the stone sighed inwards, revealing a dark recess and a ladder leading down.

'Did you know this was here?' Ishaan said, turning to Elari.

'I did not,' Elari said. She placed a hand on Lyela's shoulder. 'How did you find this? I know every hidden passage in the palace.'

'I have ways,' Lyela said. 'The other passages are filled with guards, even your hidden ones. This old thing is the safest option.' Without waiting, she strode in and began to climb down into the stale darkness.

Osellia still stared warily at the glyphs. 'Captain—'

'We'll be safe. Techwork cannot harm us.'

Elari ensured she was last to descend. She cast one final look back at the palace before swinging round onto the ladder. It was made of a strange, light metal that was warm to the touch. As the brightness of the palace began to recede, Elari hissed, 'How do we shut the door?'

As though commanded by her words, she heard a rumble of stone and slowly the last of the light was obliterated as the entrance sealed itself.

When she reached the bottom, wan orange light flared as Lyela held up a shard of glowing crystal. It illuminated the smooth, pale walls of a passageway that headed steadily downwards. Elari traced her hands along the glossy material and found it too was warm. Osellia made the sign for ancestral protection.

'Where are we going?' Chellahua said as they walked in single file.

'To the edge of the city,' Lyela said. 'The streets are swarming with Ahiki soliders. This was the best I could do. But I would suggest we hurry.'

They broke into a run, following the passage as it descended, moving in silence. The light threw dancing shadows up on the walls. They had covered perhaps half a league when Elari glimpsed a shape up ahead. The others came to a halt and Chellahua strode forward, knife drawn.

The shape resolved into a man, sauntering towards them. He appeared to be in no hurry. By the time he stepped into the orange glow of Lyela's techwork candle, Elari knew who she would see.

'You lot are in the wrong place,' the light-skinned trader said in his flat Nine Lords accent.

'Don't come any closer,' Chellahua snarled, extending her weapon.

The trader stopped. 'Just go back to the palace, there's a good lieutenant.'

'Who are you?' Elari said, her voice echoing down the tunnel.

The trader shrugged and smiled again. 'Oh, I'm nobody. Nobody at all.'

'We're not going anywhere,' Osellia said, pulling her macuahuitl from her back.

'Have it your way,' the trader replied with a sigh. He lifted his hands, letting the blue smoke bleed out of him and coalesce into grinning, monstrous life.

THIRTY-TWO

Boleo

The Woodsmaiden's chittering children spread out behind her, some climbing the trees, others loping out onto the grass to form loose ranks. So many. Boleo counted over sixty greybloods before he abandoned keeping track. His people were outnumbered, that much was certain, and with the sheer drop of the ridge behind them, poorly positioned for a battle.

'*Form up!*' Nchali cried as the Batide warriors scrambled into a tight line. '*Protect the invoker!*' The invoker who had left his quartet at home in Ewo City, ancestors curse the boy.

Nchali pointed his spear at the Woodsmaiden. 'You are outnumbered, dog!' he shouted. 'I suggest you retreat, before you are destroyed!'

Boleo had to admire the man's brashness. But the Woodsmaiden's children were already drawing makeshift weapons and preparing to charge. Many still wore the vestiges of humanity – rotting flesh, a human hand – but every member of Chinnaro's party now bore a techwork head with piercing yellow eyes. Could they still think and feel, within their twisted forms? And why did those silvery faces still look so very human?

'Outnumbered?' The Woodsmaiden giggled, the loose fabric of her dress flapping in the breeze. 'I see only forty of you, against me and all my children!'

'There are more than forty of us here.' Nchali looked around. '*Batide! It is time!*'

Jamakii, at the end of the line, leaned forward. 'In front of the monk? Lord Daloya forbade—'

'Unless forced.' Nchali grinned. 'He said only if forced. Besides, he is going to awaken Adatali soon anyway. *Batide! Speak your names!*'

And to Boleo's horror, the Batide warriors all fell to their knees, spears pointed towards the sky.

'*I am Nchali!*' Nchali shouted. '*Named Nchali Betswe Ijunti for the ones who came before!*'

'*I am Lande!*' cried the next warrior in line. '*Named Lande Remmi Tunde for the ones who came before!*'

And as the Woodsmaiden's children charged, claws and teeth glinting, the Batide warriors remained kneeling as they shouted their family-given names. The greybloods were nearly upon them when Nchali roared, '*Batide! Return!*'

The line of Batide warriors rippled and Boleo stared, awestruck, as a host of spectral forms burst through their skin. Warriors: more Batide warriors in black crane helms and white warpaint. As they solidified, they swung their spears round and crashed into the oncoming horde.

'Ancestors be praised,' Boleo breathed. 'Their namesakes have come!'

The Batide remained kneeling while their ancestors fought; two or three for every mortal soul. Morayo, standing beside Boleo, gestured incredulously. 'Do you see this?'

'Yes,' Boleo said. 'But it is impossible.' He groped for the bag that hung at his waist, not once lowering his eyes from the Woodsmaiden, waiting back by the trees. Nine warlords returned to the mortal realm. Only nine. And yet before him fought an entire Batide army from beyond the pyre.

Morayo shook his head in disbelief, then lifted his hands skyward. 'Adatali, I call upon you! I call upon you in the name of the fallen!'

Boleo groped in his bag. So much techwork there, yet so little that might be of use.

'Adatali, I call upon you! I call upon you in the name of those yet to come!'

Beside him, the green and white tataus on Morayo's arms came to life, illuminating eight interlocking blades.

'Adatali; Lord of the Flame; Master of the Eight Blades: I call upon you now!'

The twilight sky blazed bright as highsun as Adatali stepped out of the ancestral realm. His battle skirt blazed like fire, and behind the swinging beads of his jackal helm his eyes gleamed white. Morayo trembled as he knelt on the grass, arms held aloft. Adatali, standing before the Batide invokers, reached into the air and his dark brown hand closed around the hilt of a green sword: the Living Blade. He reached out with his free hand and plucked another sword from the air: the Sun Blade, brilliant and blinding. This was Morayo's speciality. Few souls could master more than one of Adatali's eight idas, and fewer still could wield two together.

Boleo's heart soared. The sight of Adatali, towering above them, the green and white warpaint that covered his bare torso and arms gleaming like liquid metal, never failed to rouse him. When Adatali lifted the Living Blade, Boleo felt the beads of his skirt shift towards it and saw the long grass of the clearing bend that way too. Boleo felt Adatali in the prickling of his skin, in the way the forest shifted, as if it recognised a power from beyond the mortal realm.

Boleo resumed his desperate search through his bag as Adatali swung the Sun Blade. He had almost forgotten about Ashu, the Butcher of Busharn, but spotted her now fighting among the ranks of invoked Batide. She had found a jagged sword, and now darted among the greybloods, slashing and ducking furiously: working her way towards Chinnaro, it seemed. But when any of her silver-faced former soldiers leapt towards her, Ashu sidestepped them entirely.

Finally, Boleo's fingers closed on something useful: a narrow disc of silver that hummed beneath his touch. And just in time – a single greyblood had broken past Adatali and was bearing down on Nchali;

a squat thing with a fleshy body and tiny, lifelike hands. Ancestors, but it looked so much like a human child: the too-large eyes, the chubby limbs. Boleo strode towards it and brought his techwork disc up in his free hand. Had this poor creature been human once too, or had it been sired on one of the Woodsmaiden's victims? Did its second parent still live, trapped in one of the Woodsmaiden's fabled breeding lairs? They said some of those she took gave her a hundred young before insanity finally claimed them.

The child-thing leapt at Boleo, and Boleo thrust the disc at it, chanting low in the Forbidden Tongue. The techwork sprang to life, sending out a burst of blue light, and the child-thing fell out of the air. But still it came on, crawling now, limbs moving quickly as it ate up the ground.

Boleo lifted his staff. For each Batide who was cut down, they would lose three or more invoked spirits. As the child-thing reached for Nchali, Boleo slammed his staff down on its back with a grunt.

There came a squeal, followed by a terrible cracking, squelching sound as Boleo twisted. He gritted his teeth and brought the staff down three times more. The squealing ceased, but Boleo dared not look down to see what lay at his feet. Instead, he strode past Adatali, the techwork disc held aloft, and chanted for it to make blue light again.

Boleo scanned for the Woodsmaiden. She stood beneath the trees, her arms folded as she chewed on her lip and watched. Chinnaro stood at her side, silver face unreadable as Ashu hacked a path towards her. Around Boleo, the Batide warriors fought, spears spinning. Any that fell faded back into the ancestral realm before they hit the ground. It was working, Boleo realised; they were holding the greybloods back. But they could not hope to win, even now. Within the darkness of the trees, a second wave of greybloods waited. Boleo had to do something about that.

'*Behind you, Father!*' shouted a sinewy, older Batide wearing a style of battle skirt not seen in decades. Boleo spun in time to see a wolf-like greyblood with wide jaws and claw-tipped hands leaping in from the left. He ducked, but not fast enough. The thing landed on his head, knocking him backwards, driving the air from his lungs. Claws flashed, tracing a hot, wet line down the side of Boleo's face.

Panic flooded him. He had to get to the Woodsmaiden. He had to complete the work Daloya had set him. His mouth filled with the reek of the greyblood, but Boleo smashed wildly at its back with the techwork disc. His other hand, still clutching his staff, remained pinned by the creature's hind leg. He was going to die here. Unless he could free his other hand, he was going to die.

Then a woman's roar sounded above him, and the greyblood was torn from his face, raking fresh cuts across his neck as it flew away through the air. Boleo scrambled to his feet in time to see Ashu sprinting away. The Butcher of Busharn had saved his life.

Boleo held the techwork disc high and turned back towards the Woodsmaiden. He could not let himself be distracted. If he went down again, he would not rise. Though greybloods leapt in from left and right, Boleo resumed his chant. The blue light returned, angling out of the disc, leaving greybloods jerking and sparking as Boleo passed.

Finally, when he was perhaps ten strides from the Woodsmaiden, she took note of him, her bright eyes flicking round with amusement, her lip curling. For a moment, she looked to be considering him, perhaps deciding if he was worth her time. It was all the opportunity Boleo needed. He lifted the techwork disc, chanted another word, and a blue wave leapt out of the device, sweeping around him in an expanding circle.

The force of this stronger blast knocked Boleo backwards. Every greyblood the wave touched fell twitching. But the Woodsmaiden, inhumanly fast, merely ducked behind a tree, and when the wave had passed, she came dancing out.

'*Call them off*,' Boleo said in the Forbidden Tongue, '*or I will kill every one of your children here, human or otherwise. I may not be able to harm you, but I can harm them.*'

The Woodsmaiden peered at him. '*You speak the Old Tongue well*,' she said.

'*It is a particular interest of mine*,' he replied.

From the corner of his eye, Boleo saw Adatali stalking across the grass, trailing a line of Batide ancestors ... coming for the Woodsmaiden. But beyond, Morayo convulsed, his raised arms wavering. The young man was close to his limit, as were many of the Batide kneeling before him, some of whom had already collapsed. It would not be long before they all needed to rest, and then they would be overrun. Boleo had to keep the Woodsmaiden distracted. He had to give Adatali a chance.

'*How many of you were once human?*' Boleo said, trying to keep her attention. '*It's not just Chinnaro's group, is it? There are others.*'

'*Many*,' she said, smiling wickedly. '*A great many.*'

'*Why? Isn't it enough that you slaughter us and destroy our cities?*'

The Woodsmaiden laughed sweetly. '*I know what those shells around your neck mean. You are a servant of the invader king, sworn to destroy the ancient knowledge. You ask me why – I might ask you the same. Your beloved king stole from you. He took everything you were, everything you made, then hoarded it for himself. And now you do not even know who you are. You consider yourself a creature of honour, holy man, but in truth, it is you who is the monster.*'

'I am no man of honour,' he said, switching to the Royal Tongue. 'I first killed a soul when I was eight – a child my own age, over a single mango. When I was sixteen, I killed my own holy mentor. I have lied and manipulated and slaughtered more times than I can count. Let us go, and in return I will do whatever you ask. I know many of your kind can tell a lie from the truth. Look at me. Read my face. Tell me if you see deceit there now.'

She studied him, and he found himself drawn to her gaze. Deep within her eyes, he saw tiny movements. He could almost hear something, some mechanism, working within. '*You are fearful*,' she murmured. '*Your body betrays that. But I sense no deceit. I believe I could hold you to—*'

Adatali struck, the Sun Blade thrusting out, sliding through the Woodsmaiden's narrow grey chest. She staggered as Adatali withdrew

360

his blade, grey ichor sliding down her naval and into the scant hair between her legs. Boleo leapt away, hoping she would not fall on him, but she did not fall at all. She straightened, her grey lips working as she struggled to speak. Then she lifted a hand, and two of her larger children broke off their attacks to return to her. They caught her, then bore her up and back among the trees.

Boleo released a breath. Though many of the Woodsmaiden's children followed her into the darkness, many more did not.

Finally, Morayo collapsed, and Adatali winked from existence.

'*Protect Lord Morayo!*' Boleo cried. '*Form a circle!*'

Never had Boleo fought so hard as he did during the night that followed. The press of Batide ancestors gathered in a ring around Morayo's unconscious form. Darkness came on quickly, and the battle seemed unending. The greybloods targeted Nchali and those who knelt beside him, and with every warrior they felled, three Batide melted back into the ancestral realm. Boleo was able to use his techwork disc twice more before it fell dormant, starved of the sunlight it drank. Then he took up his staff, set his feet, and bludgeoned anything that leapt. Teeth glinted like jewels. Rusty swords swung at him out of the gloom. Snarling, dog-like creatures with claws like knives sprang in from left and right. But Boleo fought on, blinking against the sweat that stung his eyes, a soaring energy coursing through him. Batide warriors could invoke! They could call upon their namesakes! And what that implied, what that meant, was incredible indeed.

A scrawny, manlike greyblood growled at Boleo as it charged, mace lifted for a killing blow. Boleo growled back, feeling buoyed by the resilience of his people – his glorious, defiant people – and ducked, slamming the tip of his staff into its gut. His arms burned with exhaustion, but Boleo had seen the ancestors tonight, and so he staggered forward, using his weight to pin the beast down. When its claws scraped his back, Boleo scarcely registered the pain. He clamped his hands round the greyblood's thick neck and squeezed.

'For the ones who came before!' Boleo screamed, squeezing harder while the greyblood batted at him feebly until, finally, it fell still.

When he looked up, raking in painful breaths, his shoulders trembling he realised he could see no more foes. A circle of misshapen corpses surrounded him. Greybloods. Boleo fell to his knees. His arms were caked with silvery greyblood ichor, all the way to the elbow.

'*Morayo!*' he called raggedly, scanning the gloom. And there his lord knelt, a beacon of light in the darkness, Adatali looming beside him with the burning Ida of the sun. Adatali, who would soon awaken – that's what Nchali had said, though Boleo had not known his clan's ancestor was ever asleep. Boleo rose and took two steps towards the boy to tell him that it was over, that they had won, when exhaustion claimed him, and his legs gave out, and he collapsed where he stood.

Come sunrise, the full extent of their losses was revealed. Bodies of the slain lay strewn across the ridge, its grass red with blood and silver with the vile fluids of greybloods. Some of the Woodsmaiden's children still crawled towards the trees, but Nchali strode among them, his spear plunging up and down as he picked them off one by one. Boleo pulled himself upright, head throbbing. He arms felt heavy as stone. His left shoulder burned, and when he touched it, his fingers came away sticky and red. He had no memory of taking that wound, nor of the lump that throbbed on the back of his head. But he found himself laughing. He was alive. Ancestors be praised, he was alive! And last night, he had witnessed something wondrous.

Morayo sat slumped against a rock, staring off into space. Remami, Boleo's hapless noviciate, lay near the ridge's edge. His hand still gripped a skyward-pointing knife. Boleo couldn't find a single wound on the boy and had to conclude that he had died of fright. He closed the youth's eyes and made a silent plea to the ancestors to see that he fared better beyond the pyre.

'You are wounded, Father,' Nchali said, stalking towards him.

'It's nothing,' Boleo said. 'I have never felt better. How is what I saw possible?'

'You mean our ancestors living and breathing through us?' Nchali laughed softly. 'What else would they do?'

'But you invoked. All of you. And so many! How did you learn it, and what—'

'We did not learn. Our lineages simply never forgot.' Nchali turned back towards the battleground. 'Batide! Was anyone carried off alive? Anyone she could steal seed from?'

'I can't see Uchuno,' Jamakii called back. 'Or Shenana. Or Lande.'

'Uchuno is here,' Nchali said. 'He's dead.'

'I'm here,' Shenana called, her voice coming from among the trees. 'I think my leg is broken.'

There followed a desperate search for Lande. Finally, Nchali dropped down on the grass, face drawn. 'She took him,' he muttered. 'She'll get children from him. Break him.'

But not long afterwards, Lande came limping out of the undergrowth, one arm hanging slack at his side, his expression haunted.

'Did she harm you?' Jamakii said, taking hold of him. 'Did she try to take your seed?'

Lande shoved her away. 'I'm fine,' he said.

But then he fell where he stood, and though they were at his side in a heartbeat, working to staunch his wounds and rouse him with herbs, he did not rise again.

The Butcher had gone too. Boleo had not seen her flee but couldn't find her among the corpses. He had no doubt that she still lived – she was a woman born to survive. Had she reached Chinnaro? Boleo couldn't recall. Perhaps she intended to free her former company. Or perhaps she sought to finish the job so many before her had started and finally slay the Woodsmaiden.

'We should leave before highsun,' Morayo said, joining Boleo. 'She may return, and we will not survive a second attack.'

'I don't think she'll be back soon. You gave her a grievous wound, Invoker. One she will not heal from quickly.'

'Did you know?' Morayo said. 'About humans becoming greybloods, I mean. You're a holy one . . . you must have known.'

'I can assure you I had no idea.' Boleo glanced at him. 'Did *you* know about the Batide?' Now that he considered it, he supposed the signs had always been there. *Batide*: that meant *father returns* in Urobi, a local language. They always trained in secret, they always observed Jebbanese traditions that Boleo dismissed, that so many dismissed, because they were lowblood traditions.

Morayo laughed softly. 'This is the point at which I should pretend, isn't it? Why yes, my father shares everything with me! What else would he do? Hoi! Commander!'

Nchali looked up from binding a warrior's leg.

'So when your families give you all those lovely names, they're really giving you secret weapons, is that right? And you didn't think the son of the clan warlord needed to know this?'

'It is better this way, My Lord,' Nchali said. 'My family, and the families of all my Batide brethren, have served the clan's warlords for generations. It is a long tradition in our lines.'

'Bloody tradition,' Morayo muttered, then turned back to Boleo. 'What did the Butcher mean about us being doomed? Please tell me this whole journey wasn't in vain.'

'It wasn't,' Boleo said, opening his pack, which had mercifully remained intact. 'And the Butcher kept her promise.'

'But where are the ruins?'

'Make a pyre!' Nchali was shouting. 'We burn the fallen tonight! Lieutenant, find the spirit wood!'

While the survivors worked around them, dragging bodies into a pile, setting perimeter guards, rounding up horses, Boleo opened Chinnaro's map.

Whoever told you Vunaji was a place? Ashu had said. *Look again at the map. Look carefully. Everything you need is there.*

364

No city names. No distance markers. Yes, parts of it resembled the Nine Lands and the edges of the surrounding continents, but only if that is what one sought to see. And Boleo above all others knew the danger in that.

'Tell me what this is,' Boleo said.

'It's a map,' Morayo sighed. 'It shows a place where spirits are said to gather. Chinnaro found it out here in some ruins.'

'Yes, but how do we *know* that? What are the actual *facts*?'

'What do you mean?'

'We know Chinnaro's explorations of the Busharn wastes led her to ruins where she found *this*. Everyone assumed it was a map pointing to a place where spirits gather. What if it wasn't?'

'Father, I tire of your games. Spell it out for me, would you? Are we wasting our time here or not?'

'This isn't a map,' Boleo said. He stood and began flattening out a wide circle on the grass. 'It's a *diagram*.'

Tap the 'more information' button on your panel to see an animated diagram of the process.

'A what?'

'It is a Forbidden word. It means . . . a mathematical drawing. In this case, a mathematical drawing of a shrine. This was never a map to a place where spirits gather. Vunaji was never a land. And the thing Chinnaro overlooked, the thing your father sent me to obtain: it's here, within the shrine that this *diagram* shows us how to build. Didn't you hear what the Woodsmaiden said? About Vunaji *attacking*? Vunaji is a person, and if we build this shrine, we can invoke them.'

Boleo had completed the circle. They would need all their spirit wood supplies. The only problem was they had no nuns with them, no one who could perform the ritual to link a mortal soul with the ancestral realm. But there were ways around that.

'Um . . . what?' Morayo said.

'Shall I tell you what "Vunaji" means, in that old Kzaniland language? I should have seen it sooner. It means *gathering of spirits*, yes, but also *spirit who gathers.* It never was a location; it is a *person*. The ancestor we must Bond: what your father seeks, using this shrine.'

'I don't understand. How can we just build an ancestral shrine?'

'Lowbloods do it all the time, in the corners of their homes! My Lord, a shrine is merely a means to connect one to the ancestral realm. The truth is, we can build one anywhere.'

Morayo grew still. 'You're serious.'

'Yes, I'm serious! Think what we both saw last night! The ancestral realm is vaster and more wondrous than we were ever permitted to believe. I suspect Chinnaro worked all this out the moment she discovered the map. I suspect that wherever she happened to be when she realised, she built the shrine. And in doing so, she unwittingly doomed herself and her company.'

'Wait,' Morayo said, shaking his head. 'Wait just a moment. This ancestor is the treasure my father wants us to use to reclaim Aranduq?'

'I believe so, yes.'

Morayo rubbed at his head. 'I'm too tired for all this. Why didn't he just tell us, if he knew? And this ancestor . . . won't you need their descendant in order to Bond them at all? And if they're not one of the nine founding warlords, how can they be Bonded in the first place?'

Boleo squatted down again. 'We have both seen that the nine founding warlords are not the only ancestors who can form the Bond,' Boleo said softly. 'I had heard rumours about the Fallen Families, but I thought they must just be fanciful thinking. I suspect that, in theory, any ancestor can be Bonded to any living soul . . . provided the ancestor is willing and the living party has been correctly prepared.' He stood. 'I need every able-bodied soul to help me with the walls! Send scouts to look for edible plants in the woods! And spirit wood! All our remaining spirit wood!'

'No,' Morayo said. 'No. We are not doing this. Look at us – we've lost half our party! We should return home and tell Father what we have learned about the greybloods. If this shrine can be built anywhere, then it can be built there.'

366

'Listen to me,' Boleo said, gripping Morayo's arm. 'That royal monk, Father Emata, will be watching for us. If I return, I will be captured and taken to the Garden. Do you honestly think we could build a secret shrine right under her nose?'

'I'm sure you could take care of things,' Morayo said quietly. 'As you always do.'

'The last time I . . . *took care* of things with a royal monk, they sent a warrior monk to investigate. You have never met a warrior monk, My Lord, and count yourself fortunate. I thought that I had left fear back on the streets of my childhood. But it returned eagerly to me the day one of our king's holy warriors walked the gardens of Three Towers—' Boleo broke off. It would not do to speak of such things. But he still remembered the unnatural way the air seemed to still when that gold-tataued monk came near. He still remembered the empty-eyed gaze of the nun chained to the holy man's side. Boleo cleared his throat. 'Believe me, My Lord, we are safest here, at the edge of the Nine Lands.'

Morayo studied Boleo with hard eyes. 'This is madness, all of it. Once we build the shrine, what then? Someone Bonds this ancestor who nearly killed Chinnaro? When we are already weakened?'

'We are not going to fail the way Chinnaro Itahua did. She was missing something, just as your father said, and we are going to determine what. I have faith in him, and in the ancestors, to show us the way. And once they do, we are going to Bond the most powerful ancestor in the Nine Lands.'

THIRTY-THREE

Jinao

For four days, they had been climbing steadily into the mountains. Four days, with the monsoon-drenched wetwoods falling away behind them, to be replaced by a snowy, rugged land of jutting outcrops and towering pines.

Jinao pulled his cloak close and looked out across the endless vista of woodland. When the child, Adimu Kzani, had come into his room, saying that she could set him free and take him to her family's home, he had imagined she meant in another part of the town, or perhaps a nearby village. But that had been four days ago, and each time he asked, the girl claimed they were nearly there. He should have known what to expect from the amount of food her accomplices had left them in the hidden tunnel: dozens upon dozens of neat packages bound with banana leaf. Liet had been waiting there too, along with Adimu's small, scruffy-looking mount.

'How much further?' Jinao said.

'No far, milord. Honest.'

Jinao sneezed. It was years since he'd had a cold, but his throat was raw and his head throbbed dully. 'You should have told me from the start how long this journey would take,' he said, wiping his nose on a rag. 'I need to be in Herinabad in ten days.'

The girl glanced over her shoulder. 'We ain't even left Riani Province, sire. As journeys go, this is a short one.'

Jinao pressed his face to Liet's neck. The warmth of her crystal body seeped into his skin, soothing. The thrum of her innards calmed him as they steadily climbed. Herinabad. He wondered if the Bhuten Wives and their collection of outlanders had pressed on there without him. Perhaps they would meet up with Invoker Darsana and form a great host in his absence.

The forest was a dead thing all around them, unmoving as though frozen in time. Angular trees, stripped of their leaves, loomed above them like statues. Birds of prey circled high above, and twice Jinao spotted animal tracks; but nothing else there seemed alive. At night, they heard wolves, but Adimu assured Jinao they were perfectly safe. Yet the higher they climbed, the closer those unsettling howls grew.

Adimu's horse, Keke, was the strangest creature that Jinao had ever seen. Its crystal hide was a motley of colours and textures, and beneath, Jinao glimpsed channels of pulsing blue light. When he had commented that it looked like techwork, Adimu had peered at him and said, 'Course, sire! All horses is made of techwork.'

The pounding in Jinao's head grew stronger the higher they climbed, and by the time the sun began to descend towards the peaks on the fifth day of their journey, a terrible sweat broke out over his skin.

'Adimu,' Jinao said. 'Adimu, I think I might need to rest. I . . .' He paused to let a roiling wave of nausea pass over him. 'I feel unwell.'

'It's OK, sire, look – we're here!' She turned, pointing, her face lit up. And yes; through the trees, Jinao could just make out a light. The way had been levelling off for some leagues, but now the trees were thinning too. Jagged rocks angled up out of the snow. Not rocks, Jinao realised – blackglass. Up ahead, a circle of blackglass stakes formed the boundaries of a curious palisade. Beyond them stood a small encampment, nestled against the sheer face of the mountain. No snow settled there – indeed, the grass looked lush and green. Off to the left lay paddocks, with vegetable gardens beyond. Though everything about the encampment seemed utilitarian, someone had taken the time to place dozens of ornate carvings around the central clearing: a lion, often with a spear beside it, a crown-like circlet around its brow.

A cluster of curious, rectangular buildings stood on the far side of the camp, but Jinao was distracted from these by the sensation that hit him as they passed beyond the palisade.

Warmth. It spread over him like a blanket, thawing his face, his hands, his feet. Up ahead, Adimu shed her cloak as several ragged people stepped out of their tents to greet them. Many bore dark brown skin similar to Jinao's guide; but he saw several with the pale skin common in Tarsinland, and others who would have looked at home in Cagai. Though all were thin, they seemed hale enough. One boy took Adimu's cloak, and several naked toddlers kept pace with her horse. Jinao untied his own cloak and shed his hat and gloves as sweat trickled down his forehead. The tents gave the camp the look of a city shanty, but Jinao's eye was drawn again to those curious, long buildings, nestled there against the mountain; narrow, metallic dwellings that sat upon a crystal road which bisected the camp.

'I'll take your horse, milord,' a young boy said.

'Milord is sick,' Adimu said, dropping from her saddle and letting a small girl lead Keke away.

The youth helped Jinao from Liet's back, and then Liet allowed herself to be led off. A great fatigue descended upon Jinao the moment his feet touched the ground. Each step demanded a wealth of effort, and the pounding in his ears grew ever louder as Adimu led him on.

Jinao studied the rectangular structures as he stumbled towards them. Each bore a series of tiny square windows along its sides. The buildings stood upon wheels, like carriages, though Jinao had never seen any so monstrously large before. They were great wheeled vehicles upon an ancient crystal road.

'The mighty Sha-Athion Causeway,' came a voice from up ahead. 'No doubt you know it. But few realise how far it truly goes. They speak of it ending in the Netham mountains, but it continues on south, out beneath the ocean. They say the shining capital of the Kingdom of the Leopard Throne lies somewhere upon its path.'

A wizened man descended the steps of one of the wheeled buildings, a bald soul swathed in rags. His painted lips stood out a glossy blue against the dark brown of his skin. Jinao's first thought was that this man was a monk, though he carried no staff.

'Grandba, this is Lord Jinao Mizito, the man who wishes to slay the Bairneater,' Adimu said. 'Jinao, this here is my grandba, Nirere Kzani.'

The old man, Nirere, looked Jinao over, then shrugged and muttered, 'Come. I'll make tea.'

Jinao shuffled after him. Adimu did not follow, and when Jinao looked back she said, 'I ain't allowed up there yet.' She smiled shyly. 'Good luck!' Then she was off, sprinting back towards the centre of the camp.

Inside, the metal building was dark and musty. Techwork filled the long, thin room. Veins and boxes and crystal slabs covered the battered furniture. A large, thrumming crystal stood before a northern-style bed. Rugs carpeted the floor, but they were so aged and dirt-caked that their patterns were impossible to decipher. More ornate lions crowded the corners: wooden carvings, bronze castings, lions wrought in glass . . .

Nirere struck a flint under a small kettle and hummed to himself. Beneath his rags, the man was all angles and sinew. Small and ancient he might be, but Jinao could see Nirere was sturdy.

'I was troubled to hear of the destruction of Aranduq,' Nirere said. 'Your people have guarded the Ae for generations.'

'The Bairneater did it singlehandedly,' Jinao said. He cleared his throat. 'Your granddaughter told me you might know how to slay the beast. I swore to my brother that I would kill it, before he died.'

'Yes. Yes, indeed. Hold this.'

The old man passed Jinao a silver disc. Its searing heat nearly startled him into dropping it.

'She also said you are the descendants of – of Clan Kzani. How can this be?'

'Press the disc to your forehead,' Nirere said. 'It will help with the sickness.'

'This?'

Nirere gestured impatiently. Jinao examined the disc, noting the tiny grooves that ran across it. But the old man was watching him, so Jinao pressed it to his forehead. Immediately, the skin around the disc began to tingle. Jinao winced as the tingling blossomed into a sharp heat that spread across his face.

'Keep it still,' Nirere said, as he poured water from the kettle into two mismatched cups.

Jinao held the disc in place, feeling the burn encircle his whole head. He felt himself slipping towards unconsciousness again and gritted his teeth, willing himself to stay present.

'That will do,' Nirere said.

Jinao opened his eyes to see the small man had one claw-like hand extended expectantly. Jinao handed him the disc, and then took the tea that was offered. It tasted bitter but brought with it a welcome warmth. And his head felt better, he realised, the pain almost gone.

Jinao swallowed more tea. 'Forgive me, but how can you be Clan Kzani? The greybloods destroyed your lands centuries ago.'

'Many of our lands were destroyed,' Nirere said, placing the kettle back on its strange little ring. 'Many more became part of what is now Navretland, or the lands of your clan. But some of us survived. Look out there and tell me what you see?'

He indicated the windows facing the mountainside, so Jinao crossed to them and rubbed the dirt away with his sleeve.

A group of people had gathered before a cave. The entrance shone with flowers and gems. Ornate plates lay upon the ground, covered with vegetables and fruit.

'That's a shrine!' Jinao said. 'I thought all Kzani shrines were destroyed!'

'Mm, they were, but we came here and built a new shrine.'

Like lowbloods, then. They honoured their ancestors symbolically, like lowbloods did, with offerings that could never yield the return of a spirit. 'But surely you can't—'

'*Can't* is a dangerous word, best used sparingly, my friend.'

'But the other clans—'

'Do not know. And we stay hidden.'

Jinao rubbed at his eyes. The things he'd heard these last days; the impossible things . . . He still could not shake the feeling that the world sought to mock him, with these revelations about Fallen Families and dead clans. 'I don't believe this,' Jinao muttered.

'Originally, there were nine clans, yes? Yet only seven remain. We were said to have been annihilated. They claim Menit destroyed itself with infighting. Do you want to know the truth of it?'

'Go on.'

'The Royal Clan obliterated our family and its lands following a failed coup. Together with Clan Adatali, we led an uprising against the Garden. It failed. When it did, we were punished. Clan Adatali surrendered and pledged fealty again, but we refused, and so we were destroyed.'

Eight bowed their heads to the Traitor King, Neena Bhuten had told him. *Eight fled across the seas, new fortunes to bring.*

'Is this some kind of joke?' Jinao said, looking away, his thoughts aswirl. The Royal Clan would never attack their own people. It was was too monstrous to comprehend. And no one, not even Clan Ahiki, was powerful enough to destroy the land itself.

Nirere offered him a gap-toothed smile. 'Is it really so hard to believe?'

'You're telling me your ancestors were traitors.'

Nirere blinked, then laughed softly. 'I'm telling you they sought a better way for us all, and paid a terrible price.'

'And I suppose Clan Menit staged a coup too?'

'That I do not know. Certainly none that we know of. But believe me when I say that if the Royal Clan knew we were here, they would wipe us out. So we move from place to place, and bide our time. Now. Do you want our help? Yes or no?'

373

If Nirere spoke the truth, then this was a camp of outlaws. But then, it wasn't their fault they were descended from enemies of the king. He didn't need to know their history – he just needed the knowledge they possessed. Jinao swallowed the last of his tea. 'If you can tell me how to defeat the Bairneater alone, then yes.'

'Good,' Nirere said, grinning and standing. He crossed to the slab of crystal sitting at the end of the bed. 'Once we begin the lesson, you will have to see it through to the end. Do you understand?'

'Um, lesson?'

'And you must promise me something in return.'

And there it was. Jinao sighed. 'What did you have in mind?'

'When you have defeated the Bairneater, I want you to give me its head. Do not search for us. We move around a great deal, and we will know how to find you when the time comes. But you must promise to give us its head.'

Jinao studied the old man, trying again to decide if he was serious. 'Its head.'

'Yes, its head. A named greyblood – a greyblood that has language, that is self-aware, that is not connected to what we call the Great Horde – is a special thing. A piece of one would be most useful to my family and our cause. That is my price, Jinao Mizito.'

A creeping unease stole over Jinao. 'If you want the creature's head, and you have the means to kill it . . . then why not do it yourself?'

Nirere laughed softly and shot him a wistful look. 'You do not trust me! That is well. I believe there are a great many people who have betrayed you on this strange journey of yours. But to answer your question: we would not be able to get near the creature. I have heard the reports and the rumours. If the beast is happy – eager, even – to face you, then you have an advantage that nobody else has ever had.'

Jinao looked through the window at the cave shrine. He had never thought of his entanglement with the Bairneater as advantageous. But perhaps it could be.

'Very well,' Jinao said. 'I agree.'

Nirere clapped his hands sharply, and two large men entered.

'What's going on?' Jinao said, standing.

'Easy, sire,' the larger of the two men said, pushing him back into his seat. 'We don't want no one getting hurt.'

'What are you doing?' Jinao said, craning round to look at Nirere.

'Helping you,' Nirere replied, standing. He shrugged, and added, 'And helping me. And helping all the Nine Lands. Hold him, please, Toshin.'

'There's no need for this!' Jinao said, as the two men pinned him to his seat. Jinao jerked forwards and felt the hands tighten on his shoulder, clamping him in place. He braced his legs against the crystal, pushing back. He could force his way outside, then make a run for the trees. But the one called Toshin kicked his feet away, then pressed a booted foot on Jinao's knees.

'Ah, but there is,' Nirere said, lifting a large, black crystal from a crate.

Jinao cast about the cluttered room, scanning for anything he could use if he could just break free. There was no sense in calling for help – he was among enemies again. Perhaps Nirere and his cohorts were not Clan Kzani at all. Perhaps they were associates of the Bhuten Wives, or another criminal organisation, or a cult led by a madman. Perhaps he'd travelled leagues out of his way on a fool's errand, and—

'His hands, please,' Nirere said, sitting opposite Jinao, the crystal grasped between his palms. It was the smoothest crystal Jinao had ever seen, and within it shone a bristling network of techwork veins. They throbbed dully, exuding a heat that already reached him where he sat. As the men grabbed his arms and brought his hands forwards, Jinao realised that he very much did not wish to touch the thing.

'That's it,' Nirere said, smiling. 'This will give us what we both want. If you survive the transition.'

'Survive? Now you listen to me—'

'There we are,' Nirere said, as Jinao's palms touched the crystal. A dozen tiny points of life buzzed beneath the tips of his fingers.

At once, a surge of heat passed through Jinao, and he gasped as Mizito flooded down through his arms to coalesce at his side. His ancestor seemed to fill the entire room. But something was wrong. Behind the looming warlord, Jinao glimpsed a strange landscape, and an even stranger sky, as if the way to the ancestral realm hadn't yet closed. Beyond that opening, Jinao could hear voices – people calling to him in his father's tongue. The tataus on his arms throbbed, now silver now black, the heat of them burning like naked flame.

Nirere touched the crystal, and then uttered a string of words. The Forbidden Tongue, its lilting music unmistakable. But Jinao had never heard it spoken by someone outside the Holy Orders. And this stranger was most definitely not a monk.

'How is it you speak the Forbidden Tongue?' Jinao said.

'Oh, it is easy enough to learn,' Nirere said. As he spoke, a strange energy rippled over Jinao's body, driving him to his knees. The heat of it passed through him as waves of surging nausea, while Nirere lifted his voice, repeating his words in the ancient language.

'What are you doing to him?' Jinao cried, as Mizito fell to all fours. But Nirere ignored him, his voice rising to a shout. Jinao tried to keep hold of the words. Tried to memorise the sound of them. *Siprata. Siprata kod, iraz—*

A great rending seized Jinao, as though someone were trying to tear him apart from the inside. He jerked backwards while his captors struggled to hold him in place. Beside him, Mizito began to convulse. Glyphs rippled over his armour in an endless, overlapping stream.

Then something tumbled from Mizito's abdomen. Mizito grabbed at it, like a dying warrior grabbing his entrails, but the light bled between his fingers and spilled upon the floor. Nirere stood to one side, arms folded, chuckling softly as though watching his favourite grandchild at play. The light that had spilled from Mizito rose up, taking on its own form. Two figures, the mirrors of Mizito; indistinct smudges of light and dark. Then the two contracted into beams of luminescence that shot back into the ancestral realm.

'All done!' Nirere said. The doorway to the ancestral realm collapsed, the many voices that called to Jinao cutting off mid-stream. Jinao's captors loosened their grip and he snatched his hands back. At once, Mizito snapped out of existence. Then all was silent, save for the tremulous pulse in Jinao's ears.

'What did you do to me?' Jinao growled, his breath still ragged.

'Helped you sharpen the best weapon in your arsenal,' Nirere replied.

'You said you would give me the tools to defeat the Bairneater!' Jinao said.

'And so I have,' Nirere said. Then he drew back his arm and punched Jinao to the floor.

Jinao woke to darkness and the steady drip-drip of water high above. His body ached and his stomach growled, but he was alive.

'It will take all you are to leave the gorge,' came an echoing voice.

Nirere. Jinao opened his eyes. He could not make out much in the half-light, but somewhere high above, three figures stood silhouetted against a circle of velvety night.

They had tricked him. Offered to help and then attacked him. Harmed his ancestor and then thrown him into some sort of pit, from what Jinao saw materialising around him now, its jagged, overhanging sides just visible in the gloom.

'At the age of twelve,' Nirere shouted down, 'each of our children is placed in pits such as these. Those who climb out have come of age. Those who don't, well . . . they return to the ancestors.'

'Let me out of here!'

'Remember, Jinao: the Bairneater's head. I have given you the tools to invoke what truly lies within you. Now let us see if you have the skill to use it.'

'Fuck the Bairneater's head! I'll never let you have it!'

'It may take days, or moons. But if you survive, you will thank me for this.'

'I'll fucking kill you for this!' Jinao shouted.

'You'll find edible fungus in the shadows. Sometimes tubers, if you are lucky, though neither will sustain you for long. Each highsun, a pack of greybloods come down here searching for metal. Be ready for them.'

'You fucking monster!'

'Good luck, Jinao Mizito! And remember: keep the head!'

Then they were gone, and Jinao lay alone in the darkness with a steady drip-drip echoing all around.

THIRTY-FOUR

Elari

As the blue smoke-creature streaked towards Chellahua, she swung her knife in a wide arc. The creature melted out of the weapon's path, laughing, and thrust forward one slender arm. Chellahua tried to dive out of reach, but the tunnel was narrow. When the smoke-creature's long fingers closed around her wrist, she screamed as if burned by its touch.

Osellia leapt, slicing downwards with her macuahuitl, but the weapon passed through the creature's smoke-like body and sent her staggering forwards under the momentum.

'Oh, this is ridiculous,' Lyela muttered. She placed her right hand to the wall and made a curious gesture in the air with the left, as though plucking the strings of an invisible musical instrument. At once, the skin of her right hand glowed yellow, and there came a rumbling from the ground below. Elari dropped into a fighting stance, casting around for the source of the shaking.

A thrust of blackglass leapt from the ground and sliced into the ceiling, sealing the passage completely, trapping the trader behind. The moment the smoke-creature was separated from its human host, it faded away to nothing. Chellahua collapsed where she stood, a ring of blue encircling her pale wrist where the creature had seized her.

'Stand back,' Lyela said, and Elari obeyed without question, pulling Ishaan and Osellia with her. Lyela fumbled with her stolen guard's uniform and produced a slender tube of gleaming metal, which she pointed at the newly risen wall.

A muffled cracking reached Elari's ears, then the smoke-creature came bursting through the barrier, sending shards of blackglass flying. But Lyela was ready; a line of red light angled out of the metal tube she held. The smoke-creature giggled, its chest splitting apart to allow the light to pass through.

Beyond, the trader stood unprotected, and as the blue creature turned, the light caught the man full in the chest. For a moment he stood in place, disbelief in his eyes, his hands going to the charred circle in the middle of his robe. Then he fell, hitting the floor with a soft crumple. The smoke-creature faded to nothing, its laughter echoing as it rose towards the ceiling.

Elari sagged against Ishaan. Osellia dropped to Chellahua's side, examining her wrist. Lyela wandered forward and tapped the trader's corpse with one foot.

'What are those smoke things?' Elari said, unable to keep the fear from her voice.

'I don't know,' Lyela said. 'I've never seen or heard of anything like them before.'

'Why can't we hurt them?' Elari said. 'Our blows mean nothing.'

'They're connected to people,' Ishaan said. 'I don't think they can exist without them. Maybe they're . . . not really here, somehow.'

They proceeded in silence after that, Elari turning over and over what they had just witnessed. So, Lyela was indeed a techdoctor; how else to explain the appearance of the blackglass barrier? And yet Elari had not heard her utter a word in the Forbidden Tongue. Elari watched the other woman stalking ahead, her heavy shoulders hunched. She could not recall ever seeing Lyela so pensive.

'The trader almost seemed to invoke it,' Elari said, catching up. 'Like . . . like an ancestor.'

'That was no ancestor,' Lyela replied without turning. She still clutched the silver tube in one hand.

'What is that weapon?' Ishaan asked. 'And the wall – how did you make it rise?'

'You would not understand if I told you.'

Ishaan snorted. 'Try.'

Lyela laughed softly but made no reply.

A light glimmered up ahead and soon they found themselves beneath a bright circle of starry sky. Another metal ladder led straight up, and the air beyond smelt fresh and sweet. Elari inhaled, willing calmness into her veins. It was the raw dampness of the wetwoods. They were free.

'I'll go first,' Osellia said. She climbed quickly, hand over hand, and one by one they followed.

Elari pulled herself out onto a hillside that stood at the edge of the wetwoods, overlooking the city of Qenqar far below. How calm it looked, at that height. The great curve of Livinghall's hillside stood black against the starry sky on the far side of the city. The stepped pyramids and townhouse mounds of the highblood districts gleamed bright as jewels. It did not look like a city under siege or infected by rampaging monsters. It looked peaceful.

'Come,' Lyela said, turning towards the forest.

They had travelled perhaps two leagues when the bush began to thin up ahead. By now, Elari's clothes clung to her body with sweat and her skin blazed in a dozen places from insect bites. Her walking boots were already wet through, leaving her feet damp and clammy.

'He is there,' Lyela said, holding aside the foliage.

In the middle of the clearing stood a curious cage, with sides but no discernible bars. A man sat huddled within, a soul as thin and ragged as a vagrant. But Elari knew him at once. Invoker Jethar Mizito. The man who had murdered Cantec. The man she had been ordered to kill, yet still drawing breath.

Choose.

She charged forward, jerking her macuahuitl from her back in a single sweep. What reason did she have to pause? There was nothing to consider. Her only task was to act. This man had killed Cantec and brought a dangerous power back into the Nine Lands. Of course he had to die.

Elari leapt at the open expanse of the cage, but her foot met an invisible barrier, sending her crashing back into the grass.

'You were supposed to kill him!' Elari cried. She extended one hand towards the cage. The air before her looked empty, and yet she could feel the humming warmth of the hidden energies that had repelled her.

'No harm will come to you while he is in there,' Lyela said. 'I will take his head, if that is what you still wish. But first, I thought you might like to hear what he has to say.'

Choose who lives and who dies.

Elari could not see Jethar's face, where it rested on his knees. He was dressed as a commoner, in wide pantaloons and a waistcoat. His long, black hair hung in greasy clumps. He gave no sign that he had noticed them, but she could see he wasn't asleep. Elari's breath caught as she spotted the burn scars that networked his left arm. All his tataus were gone – his clan tataus, his tataus of honour . . .

No. She should not pity this man. Yet she found herself remembering the first time she had met Jethar, the day of her wedding. He had brought her a gift – a small jewelled dagger; priceless – and when she had commented on it, he'd looked at her with tears in his eyes and told her it was the least he could do for making his friend so very happy.

'Invoker Cantec Itahua was the greatest man alive,' Elari said thickly. 'Learned. A gifted warrior. The kindest soul you could meet. And he was your *friend*. Why? Why did you betray him?'

Jethar sat like stone, his face still hidden.

Something curdled within her then. Where was his grief? Where was his loyalty? He sat there placid as a monk in contemplation, utterly indifferent to all the pain he had caused.

'Look at me, ancestors curse you!' she shouted, striking the invisible barrier with her palm.

At first, she thought he would never respond, but then slowly, Jethar lifted his head. His bright, wild eyes shone with a terrible desperation. 'I did it,' he said, 'because she cannot be refused.'

The wind stirred, bringing a chill to Elari's skin despite the humidity of the wetwoods. She leaned forward. 'Who?'

'Aan,' Jethar said.

Elari thought of Cantec's letter. *This entity resides in Jethar now, controlling him.*

She should end the conversation. She should instruct Lyela to do it. Yet when she looked at Jethar, she thought of how she had not bathed and had scarcely eaten for two moons when she returned from the Feverlands border. She thought of how, every night, she had heard the low rumble of the Bairneater's laughter.

'I will read you a letter Cantec left me,' Elari said, reaching beneath her tunic with trembling hands. 'Perhaps you can explain it. And then, you will tell me why we shouldn't kill you where you sit.'

Jethar watched her silently, his sunken eyes unreadable, his body still as a cat marking its prey, while Elari read her translation of Cantec's letter, her voice quavering. When she had finished, she looked up to see Jethar studying her, his eyes swimming, his mouth a grim line.

'What is she,' Elari said, 'this entity?'

Jethar made a disgusted sound. 'A monster.'

'A monster. Yet it was *you* who killed Cantec.'

'I had no choice,' Jethar said. 'If I hadn't killed him, Aan would have slaughtered you all. Razed Three Towers, possibly all of Ewo City. What would you have done in my place? It was an impossible choice.'

Choose who lives and who dies.

Elari staggered backwards as Jethar came shakily to his feet. He was not as emaciated as when she had first seen him all those moons ago, but he still looked hunched and ragged. 'If I disobey her, she causes me pain. If I question her, she causes me pain. If I hesitate, she causes me pain. Day and night. On and on, without end. You cannot even begin to imagine it.' He reached the barrier between them then closed his eyes as he placed his hand upon it. 'She knew that Cantec suspected. I tried to steer her from him – she cannot always hear all my thoughts. But I was not strong enough.'

'She commanded you to kill him because he knew of her existence?'

'Yes.'

'What is she?'

Jethar laughed sharply. 'What is she? It is as Cantec told you. A guard. A keeper of treasures.' And to Elari's horror, he began to weep. These were not the silent tears of a great warrior, but the desperate sobs of a madman, and the sound cut through to Elari's core.

'He was my friend!' Jethar said, his voice thick with misery. 'He was my friend, and I would have died for him. But not at the expense of so many others.'

For a moment, Elari could not speak, because she no longer stood in the wetwoods above Qenqar. Instead, she stood before a burning village, beside ten locals kneeling in the mud. Some wept. Some begged. But Elari had eyes only for Cantec, lying motionless behind the monstrous bulk of the Bairneater.

'Captain.' Ishaan slid their hand gently into Elari's, and Elari came back to herself.

She swallowed. 'Did you find the place where spirits gather? Was there . . . some weapon there, something the thief took?'

Jethar laughed sourly. 'There is no gathering of spirits. Our whole history is a lie. Who we are. What the greybloods are. What our world is. All of it. It is a lie, made to keep us in our place.' He pressed both hands upon the barrier, his eyes seeking hers. 'Please,' he said softly. 'You must let me go. I have to find the thief. What he took is no weapon – it is something . . . infinitely worse. Something that corrupts. And he means to unleash it on the Nine Lands.'

Ishaan tightened their grip on Elari's hand. 'Don't listen to any more of his lies.'

384

'Who is this thief?' Elari asked.

Jethar looked down. 'He is a lowblood from one of the Fallen Families that live in the Nine Lords slums. He is cunning. And resolute. And he manipulated us all. But we are not his target. His target is the king. He believes that if he threatens the Nine Lands with a danger terrible enough, the Ahikis will return to us the power they have denied us for so long.' Jethar's eyes found hers. 'But this man, this lowblood; his plan will fail. The force he means to unleash will overrun us. Set me free. Let me find him now, while the threat is contained. Aan can stop him. Once her work is done, I will surrender myself to you, and you can do with me as you wish. With our ancestors as my witnesses, I swear it.'

She should never have talked to him. Curse Lyela for letting him live! She should have had Lyela strike his head from his body the moment she saw him. Not listened to more of his lies.

Yet when she looked at his ragged fingernails, all she saw was a broken shell. All she saw was a man carrying an impossible weight. All she saw was herself.

'I don't think Cantec ever told you what happened to us during our last moon on the border,' Elari said softly. 'He didn't even know the full story himself. The Bairneater was sighted in a village in western Netham. Cantec was the only invoker nearby. And he and I were hungry for the glory that comes with defeating a named greyblood.'

'You do not have to tell him this,' Ishaan said.

'My lieutenants were cut off from us. So Cantec and I . . . we . . .' Elari swallowed. 'We went alone to face the beast. It was a mistake. I was unable to protect Cantec.' Elari inhaled slowly as she heard the soft crumple of Cantec's body as the Bairneater cut him down. 'The Bairneater said I could take Cantec and leave, but first I would have to sacrifice all ten of the villagers it had captured. Myself. With my – my own weapon.' She lifted her macuahuitl. Part of her body. Part of her shame. 'Or I could save them, and leave Cantec to die.'

Jethar watched silently from behind the greasy curtain of his hair.

'I never told Cantec what his life cost. Neither did my lieutenants. But

I know what it is to be forced into the vilest of actions.' Elari closed her eyes. 'If I release you, how do I know that you will keep your word?'

'Captain, no!' Ishaan said. 'This creature killed Cantec. He is a murderer and a coward.' They drew their knife. 'Let me do it for you.'

'He is manipulating you,' Osellia hissed.

'I shall cut out his lying tongue,' Chellahua said.

Jethar smiled thinly. 'Aan could kill you with a thought.'

'Let her try.'

'Stop,' Elari said, lifting a hand. She turned to Jethar. 'This treasure the lowblood stole. What does it look like? What does it do?'

'It was a game, to begin with,' Jethar said, laughing again. 'Only a game.'

'The man in insane!' Chellahua cried, throwing up her hands.

'Carry on, My Lord,' Elari said, touching Chellahua's arm to silence her.

'Aan calls them the Cloistered, though I do not think that is their true name. They are old; perhaps even older than the Scathed. Once, they were *playthings* – prey in a great game of hunt.' Jethar smiled bleakly. 'When their masters grew bored with the game, they sealed the Cloistered away and placed guards over them, to recapture them should any escape. Aan is one such guard.'

Elari slid her gaze down Jethar's arms. Scarred, perhaps burned, all sign of his clan tataus erased. That word, *hunt*. Where had she heard it recently? 'You still have not explained what it is these Cloistered do.'

'I told you; it is a game of hunt! The aim is not to be caught! If you are caught, you join them until none are left, and then the game is over.'

Elari's stomach tightened as she recalled the smoke-creature's final words. *We're everywhere now. You have no choice but to join the hunt.* 'Join them?' she said. 'Join them how?'

'You physically join them. They will merge their spirit with yours. They are capricious, and wily. They will disguise themselves as anything to get close. As children, or elders, or—'

'Traders?' Osellia said, standing very still.

'Yes! They must . . . touch you, or be near you, to join themselves to you. Each one they have touched can then spread the curse to another, and so it goes on; like a disease.'

'Oh ancestors,' Chellahua muttered, turning away.

'What do they look like?' Elari said, her voice shaking. 'Tell me quickly what they look like!'

'They dwell within us. Much like ancestral spirits. Their true form is human, after a fashion. Yellow eyes—'

'Blue-smoke skin,' Elari said.

Jethar's head snapped up. 'Yes.'

'They are here already. Dozens reside within Livinghall.'

Jethar closed his eyes. 'Then it has begun.' He looked across at her. 'Listen to me. It is still not too late. There is always a – a source. An origin. The first to be touched by them. Kill that soul, and they all fall. It is part of the game, you see? Find their base, and win.'

'I am telling you, they are here in Itahualand.'

'The source is in the Nine Lords slums,' Jethar said. 'That lowblood is too clever to place his most important piece where it will be noticed. If the Cloistered are here, too, that is only because they have somehow spread. Aan can feel the source. She need only get close. She was waiting for me to heal fully first but your . . . your *friend* here accelerated that, in order that I could travel.' Jethar's eyes flicked to Lyela, standing in the shadows. 'Do you even know who this woman is?'

'And this source person,' Elari said. 'If they are killed, the Cloistered are no longer a threat? They all fall? What happens to the people they've already taken?'

Jethar grimaced. 'Aan does not know. The Cloistered were not made to join with . . . minds like ours.'

'You mean they could die.'

'Possibly. Possibly not.'

'Captain, please,' Ishaan said, 'let us talk. Away from . . . whoever this is.'

387

Elari let her doves lead her into the trees, where they took her hands and stood in a circle, much as they did before battle.

'I say he is lying,' Chellahua said. 'He is trying to confound us.'

'But what he described!' Osellia said, shivering. 'It matches what we have seen.'

'Ask him to bring this Aan creature out,' Ishaan said. 'Let us see this all-powerful monster and talk to her ourselves.'

'There is no creature within him!' Chellahua snapped.

The thunder of drums cut the night, followed by distant ululations. Elari's breath caught.

'Soldiers!' Chellahua cried.

They walked back to the clearing together to find Lyela pacing impatiently. 'I'll take that box now, if you please.' There was a curious light in her eyes. Fear? Impatience? Elari could not tell. Wordlessly, she reached into her travelling pack and removed the puzzle-box.

'Here,' Elari said, twisting three times, then three more.

'Captain, she hasn't delivered on her promise!' Chellahua said.

Elari offered the box to Lyela.

Lyela reached forward and used a square of dark silk to take hold of the tiny black ball that rested within. Her mouth twisted in a smile as she dropped it into the pouch of her guard's uniform. 'Despite everything I have seen in this strange world of ours, there are still things to surprise me. What a clever little box! Your Cantec must have been an interesting man.'

'Why didn't this Aan creature kill you the moment you captured him?' Elari said.

Lyela smiled. 'I wouldn't let her.' She glanced back at Jethar, pacing in his cage. 'If you still wish to kill him, I will help you before I leave. You will not be able to do it without me.'

'Captain, we can't let him go!' Chellahua cried as Elari stalked back towards the cage. The drums were growing steadily louder. Ahiki drums or Itahua? Elari could not tell.

'If I release you,' Elari said, 'will Aan retaliate?'

388

Jethar was silent for several long moments before finally he looked up and said, 'She agrees not to harm you so long as no harm befalls me.'

'And you promise me, when your work is done, you will surrender yourself for judgement.'

'I will.'

'And if you do this, if you find this source in Nine Lords, the smoke-beings, those Cloistered, will disappear?'

'Yes.'

Elari turned to Lyela. 'Do it. Let him out.'

'Captain!' Chellahua cried, but Lyela had already extended a hand. The sides of the cage shimmered as Lyela's hand glowed bright yellow.

Jethar crept forward, reaching out with both hands. The drums were close now, and Elari recognised the ululations of the advance. Clan scouts. Manax.

Ishaan scaled a nearby tree and looked out across the canopy. 'They're everywhere!' they called down.

'Coward!' Chellahua cried, and Elari looked round to see Lyela sprinting away towards the trees.

'I'm sorry – truly!' Lyela called back. 'I wish you luck!' Then she was gone, lost to the wetwoods with scarcely a sound.

Elari looked south and saw the tallest trees moving as drumbeats filled the air.

'I did not want to kill him,' Jethar said, reaching towards Elari, then dropping his arm. 'Ancestors know I didn't want to.' He passed a hand over his eyes. 'I do not know what you have seen of the Cloistered, but it can only have been the beginning. The longer they stay, the more they change the one who hosts them.'

Elari closed her eyes. 'Go. Find the source in Nine Lords. Stop this purge of our ancestors before it spreads.'

She saw no relief in Jethar's eyes. She saw very little at all. But as he straightened, he said, 'The things they make us do . . . they do not define who we are.'

She watched him flee into the trees, feeling something lift within her. Cantec should never have died. One day, she would punish this Aan creature for his death. But not now. Not yet.

'Come,' Ishaan said, taking her hand. 'If we head north, we can—'

Pain blossomed in Elari's left side. She looked down, surprised to find an arrow lodged in her thigh. A slow, dark stain began to spread over the pale fabric of her tunic.

'Captain!' Ishaan cried as Elari dropped to one knee.

THIRTY-FIVE

Jinao

Jinao lay in the dark all that night and well into the next day. Hunger and thirst clawed at his aching body, but he did not want to move. Indeed, he found to his surprise that he would be quite happy to never move again. If the stones that hung over his head fell and crushed him, then the world would be a better place. He had failed. Failed his brother. Failed his ancestors. Failed the captives in Herinabad, who were surely dead by now. He had failed them all.

I have given you the tools to invoke what truly lies within you. Now let us see if you have the skill to use it.

Nirere. The man was clearly some kind of techdoctor, some lowblood who had slipped on the identity of Clan Kzani like a trouper's mask.

'I'm sorry, Julon,' Jinao muttered. 'I'm sorry I couldn't keep my promise.'

As highsun blazed down through the distant mouth of the pit, the chittering cries of greybloods carried to Jinao's ears. They came loping over the edge, agile as goats as they descended the jagged rocks. Their eyes were twin points of yellow light. Their long hind legs scampered expertly down from rock to rock. There were perhaps two dozen of them, vaguely canine in appearance, their metal hackles raised. Jinao lay back, willing them to take him. Willing them to tear him apart and end it all.

But they showed no interest in him. They gathered on the far side of the cave, nibbling hungrily at the rocky surface like cats that had scented prey. Their claws were long and deft and clever. How many years had they been coming here, hollowing out the bottom of the cave? They picked among the rocks, examining, casting some aside. A few glanced his way, but none of them advanced, not until they had finished gorging themselves on whatever mineral it was they sought.

When they were sated, most of them scampered back up into the daylight, but a few remained, their massive shoulders hunched like hyenas as they advanced. Despite Jinao's resolve to do nothing, to simply lie there and die, he found himself shuffling backwards. His hands groped in the damp behind him, seeking out anything that might make a weapon.

Jinao hefted the sharpest rock he could find and then backed himself against the wall of the pit. 'Go!' he shouted, his voice echoing from the rocks above.

But the greybloods did not obey.

Jinao lobbed the rock at the nearest greyblood but missed by several handspans. Still they came, their mouths leering, taking their time not out of fear, but out of relish.

'Mizito,' Jinao muttered, closing his eyes, 'spirit of my mothers, hear me.'

The remaining greybloods fanned out in a wide circle, like the children who came to taunt him growing up.

'Mizito, spirit of my fathers, hear me.'

What chance did he have, seated here in despair, as though his forefather's memory was not worth standing for? Not even forming one move of the sacred dance? But he pushed everything from his mind, focused only on the heat that lay coiled within him, and willed his ancestor to heed his call.

'Mizito. Lord of the Eagle, Master of the Bonetree, hear me now, and come.'

When the burning came, Jinao thought one of the greybloods had clawed him. But no, it was the light of invocation, bleeding steadily from his arms. Soon it filled the pit with a dazzling blue glow. There was no heady rush this time. No sense of losing himself. He called, and the light of invocation answered, and for the first time, Jinao felt the stirrings of control.

The greyblood backed away as Mizito began to take shape.

'Where are they?'

Jinao started. The cave was gloomy, but he could see no other figure within. Had one of the greybloods spoken? These did not look like named greybloods; usually such creatures took on a more human aspect, and these could be mistaken for domestic dogs.

'I see. I have been separated from them. Curious.'

'Who's there?' Jinao cried.

Mizito coalesced into existence, and Jinao's heart climbed into his throat.

The founder of his clan looked scarcely larger than Jinao himself now. Instead of glowing black armour, he wore an Ekari iron-scale chest-plate and skirt, with a wide triangular helm that left his face bare. Ah, his face! It was no more remarkable than the face of any east Mizitoland general. He was just a man, his skin a shade lighter than Jinao's, his eyes a rich brown. He had a scar over one cheek. A missing tooth. Crow's feet around his eyes.

'You're . . . small!' Jinao cried.

'Ah, so you can hear me now,' Mizito said with a slight smile.

'Tell me what's going on!' Jinao said. Had Jemusi ever mentioned anything like this? Had his mother? Not that he could recall. Sister Jassia taught that invoked ancestors were silent because mortal ears were too crude to hear the words of the blessed fallen. But this man sounded like anyone's uncle from Ekari Province, so perhaps that had not been entirely true.

Two of the greybloods scampered away as Mizito pulled the staff from his back. The nearest leapt at him. Mizito dropped into a horse-riding stance and slammed the staff over the creature's head, knocking it out of the air and sending it flying across the cave. The others rose up then, attacking as one, but Mizito spun among them, darting in and out, dashing slavering heads to splinters, one after the next, until all lay sizzling at his feet. Only when Mizito returned his staff to his back did Jinao realise he had played no part in it at all. His ancestor's essence pulled on him, yes, but it was nothing like when he faced the Bairneater. His skin did not burn, nor did his head pound as though it might split apart. He felt only a vague tethering, a sense of being stretched. But no danger of his very self being overwhelmed. Like this, Mizito could surely remain with him for as long as he wished.

'How is it I can hear your voice?' Jinao said as Mizito stood before him, chest heaving. And lords, but was that sweat Jinao could see beaded on his ancestor's brow?

'Someone appears to have separated me from the spirits I was trapped with,' Mizito said. 'They have also destroyed the restraints on your tataus.' He rolled one shoulder as though loosening a knot. 'Ah, it feels good to be free! Of course, he'll discover in time. We'll have to be very careful from now on.'

'He . . .' Jinao swallowed against the dryness in his throat. 'He who?'

'Our good friend Ahiki.'

'Ahiki . . . the king's ancestor? Um, you were *hiding* from him?'

'I was not *hiding* from him,' Mizito said, arching his back. 'I was beholden to him. No longer, thanks to whatever your friend did.'

'Nirere? He is not my friend.' Jinao eyed him slowly. 'And Ahiki – Ahiki is not your friend?'

'Hah!' Mizito began to crack the knuckles of his left hand, pulling on each finger in turn. He shot Jinao a wistful look. 'Now where to begin with that question.' He looked up at the looming walls of the cave. 'Might I ask what we're doing down here?'

'I'm . . . stuck,' Jinao said, looking away. 'Um, *Uncle*. Lord. I don't suppose you know how I can get out.'

'Well, I'm not carrying you, if that's what you mean.' Mizito laughed brightly – he had a warm, smiling face, Jinao noticed, so different from the severe warrior in all the statues and songs. But the smile fell away when Mizito took in Jinao's expression. 'Let me speak to the others first. They'll be very interested to hear what's happened.' He pointed a finger at Jinao. 'You need to be careful from now on. Your link to the ancestors is fully open. It will be easier for . . . other things to come through.'

'Things?'

Mizito looked up at the distant circle of bright sky. 'Goodbye, Jinao.' Mizito turned, and a shimmering doorway opened before him. Through it, Jinao glimpsed a shoreline and a star-filled sky. Whispers drifted out of the opening: voices again, calling to him in his father's tongue. Then Mizito stepped through and the doorway closed and Jinao was alone once more.

[Oh, and it might be a good idea to build yourself a shrine,] Mizito said.

Jinao jerked. 'Ancestors! Where are you?'

[I am speaking directly into your mind through our . . . our sacred Bond. You will need to build a shrine in order to enter the ancestral realm. I can act as your link, since you have no spirit wood, but you'll still need blackglass. And filaments, to connect the processors of your tataus with the transmitter.]

'I have no idea what you are saying!'

[Open the carcass of one of those creatures. I shall instruct you.]

Jinao knelt over one of the greyblood corpses, not wanting to touch it.

[Pull off the plates.]

Jinao's mother had forced him to pull apart the corpses of greybloods on many occasions. When he had baulked, she had pressed his hands to them until the heat of their hides burned his skin. But these were almost cool, he found. Their plates came away easily. Beneath, their innards were a tangle of techwork, grey ichor and flesh.

[There will be blackglass at the core. Find it. Lay the fila— the *veins* out to dry. The rest you can set aside.]

Jinao obeyed. It was growing dark by the time he'd finished with all six bodies. He had enough veins to encircle the cave floor three times. The fragments of blackglass were tiny – most scarcely larger than the nail on his thumb.

'This won't harm us, will it?' Jinao said. 'I mean, none of this has been Cleansed . . .'

[No, Jinao. There is no such thing as Cleansing.]

'What do you mean? When a monk—'

[I'll be back in the morning. We'll need more. But this is a start.]

'Wait! How can techwork even reach the ancestral realm? And why did you say Ahiki wasn't your friend? Uncle? Uncle!'

Jinao supposed he could have brought Mizito back, but something about forcing his return by invoking felt impolite now. The nature of their Bond had changed, perhaps for ever.

Jinao rubbed a hand over his sweat-streaked face. He had so many questions. But he was hungry, and so thirsty his lips had begun to crack. He remembered spotting some mushrooms part way up the cave wall, and water pooling beneath one of the larger overhangs. It would not make much of a meal, but just then he felt ravenous enough to eat the rocks themselves.

At highsun the following day, the long-legged greybloods came again, leaping and bounding down into the gloom. Jinao spoke no word to call on Mizito. His ancestor simply bled out of Jinao's hands and charged forward. After a moment's hesitation, Jinao rushed to join him. He lifted a rock and smashed wildly about. By the time they had finished, ten greyblood bodies lay around them, and the survivors were scampering back up to safety.

'You need to learn to fight,' Mizito said, leaning forward, chest heaving.

'So I've been told.'

Jinao stripped the bodies down quickly this time. By the time he had finished, he felt curiously energised. That afternoon, he located the tubers Nirere had mentioned, and by nightfall, he had a fire going, using sunlight reflected in a greyblood's metal hide onto the fleshy matter that lay within their bodies. He boiled the tubers with more mushrooms in the hollow skull of his enemy, and that evening he feasted like a king.

Within a few days, the greybloods stopped coming. By then, Jinao knew he could not subsist on the tubers and fungus for long. He had already lost weight, a thing he could ill afford to do, and stomach cramps kept him awake long into the night. They had a good pile of blackglass gathered behind some rocks, but Mizito claimed it was scarcely half of what they'd need, and Jinao did not think he would survive long enough to gather the rest.

[Word has spread,] Mizito said. [They are not fools. We will have to find some way to coax them down.]

They built something Mizito referred to as an *amitaar*, as high up in the pit as Jinao could climb. Jinao cobbled it together from plates and veins of techwork, using his forefather's guidance. When it was complete, Jinao wrapped the veins around his arms and summoned the power of invocation, and when he did, the *amitaar* lit up, shining bright as a thousand candles.

[It is the waves that will attract them.]

'Waves? So far from the sea?'

It seemed an eternity before a single, rangy-looking greyblood came limping over the lip of the cave. Jinao watched it hop down from stone to stone, almost pitying the poor thing. Much of its exterior plate was gone, exposing the glowing veins and flesh beneath. One of its golden eyes no longer glowed. Mizito burst out of Jinao and came running into the world, but Jinao grabbed his arm.

'Wait a moment – look.'

The greyblood hopped over to the wall of the cave and began scrabbling at the place where Jinao had seen so many of them gathered that first day.

'There's something there,' Jinao said.

Mizito was silent, eyes narrowed. After a moment, he said, 'Why, I do believe you are right!'

They watched as the wretched-looking greyblood scrabbled away before apparently finding something. It leaned down, nibbling, and then turned with a start, seeming to notice them for the first time. Within a heartbeat, it was moving. Jinao's ancestor tensed under his touch – his skin felt as smooth and cool as any mortal man – but he did not give chase. When the creature was gone, Jinao crossed to the place.

'It's a vein,' Jinao said, pulling at a line of silver thread that drooped down between two rocks.

Mizito chuckled. 'Yes, a *vein*,' he said. He stroked his chin – one of the many mannerisms that Jinao was becoming used to, becoming fond of. 'Try attaching it to your tatau . . . pressing it to your skin will suffice. Let us see if we can pull out whatever lies within.'

Jinao squatted down and braced his arm against the cool rock, then took hold of the vein and pressed it against his skin. Instantly, Mizito faded to a beam of light that shot down into Jinao's arm and on into the techwork vein. Jinao felt a brief tingling as the seconds passed. He was just wondering if he should give the thing an experimental tug – see if perhaps some techwork stuck there over the ages might come tumbling out – when the entire cave began to rumble and a line of blue light bisected the rock before him.

Jinao dropped the vein and staggered backwards as the wall began to shake . . . began to *move*, he realised. The cluster of rocks rumbled outwards and then proceeded to slide sideways, smooth as the screen doors between rooms in Thousand Domes. Beyond, Jinao saw a hallway of smooth metal and blue light.

[Interesting,] Mizito said. [It seems you were right to be intrigued.]

Jinao shuffled forward cautiously as the rumbling walls came to a stop. The corridor continued on a few paces and then ended in darkness. All Jinao's instincts told him walking forwards was a bad idea, but he couldn't help himself. He had never seen a corridor quite like it. Every part of it was made of a smooth, metallic material and the glowing blue lights were as arcane as techwork candles. Jinao felt the darkness at the end opening up before him and sensed the vastness of what lay beyond.

The room flared to life the moment Jinao's foot stepped into it: a space as cavernous as the rocky pit behind him, yet infinitely different. Silver walls rose to the left and right. Up ahead, on the far wall, stood a series of geometrically perfect techwork plates, glossy enough for him to see his face in. It was a Scathed ruin – there could be no question of that. Yet Jinao had never encountered one so perfectly preserved. In the centre of the room stood a bronze statue: a woman, with the head of a lion and holding a gold-tipped spear.

'Welcome, dedicant of Warlord Kzani,' a voice boomed down from above. 'And well done on making it this far in your trial.'

'Nirere,' Jinao muttered.

'You have only one step more on your journey before you can claim your place in our clan.'

'Not fucking interested,' Jinao said. 'Can you see this, Uncle? This is a Scathed ruin.'

[I see it.]

'Within this room, you will find a number of artefacts and records that can help you during this important final stage, as well as the possibility of sustenance: I expect by now you are rather hungry!'

'Fuck you, you spineless dog!' Jinao called to the distant ceiling. He knew Nirere was not there. Somehow, this room had captured the man's words and preserved them for later listening. But it felt good to curse the soul he would one day visit vengeance upon.

'To aid you in taking this final step, please open the box in the floor. It contains an artefact from this region, one I think may explain a lot. Good luck, and may the ancestors smile upon you!'

Something was rising from the ground before the lion statue. Jinao stepped forward and saw that it was a picture, surrounded by an ornate wooden frame. But it was a picture unlike any Jinao had seen before.

It looked so lifelike, it was as though the artist had captured a moment in time and frozen it, made it smaller, distilled it upon the canvas – if this glossy material was canvas at all. Jinao lifted the frame from the ground. Its contents made his breath catch.

Kzani. It could only be Kzani, as Jinao had seen her depicted in sculpture: a woman with dark brown skin and tightly curled hair, her arms bright with yellow and black lion tataus. She stood holding her white spear, *Truth*, and smiling. To her left and right appeared more warriors with the look of the south about them. Some wore kufi hats. Some dashikis. Some wore clothing he did not recognise. They stood with arms around each other's shoulders, as though they were equals, friends. And behind them—

'I don't understand,' Jinao muttered.

Behind them rose a vista of looming towers, all crystal and glass. Scathed towers. There could be no mistaking them. They rose towards the clouds, gleaming majestically. And these were no ruins. Gardens brightened their upper levels. Each looked as pristine as the day the Scathed must have constructed them. Behind, in the sky, floated curious objects, sleek as birds but many times larger: airborne traffic on a glorious afternoon.

'I don't understand this,' Jinao said. 'This is an artist's creation, yes? They're imagining what it would have been like if Warlord Kzani was alive in the age of the Scathed.'

[Warlord Kzani was alive in the age of the Scathed.]

The vastness of the room seemed to grow around Jinao, as though suddenly he stood at the edge of a great precipice.

'H-how can that be?' Jinao said softly. 'They say the Scathed were wiped out tens of thousands of years before humans came east with King Ahiki. Before humans even existed.'

[They say. And who are they? Look around you, Jinao. This is a Scathed ruin. You hold a Scathed artefact. A lie repeated a thousand times becomes a truth. Think!] Mizito sighed. [Those warriors she is with are the other Kzaniland warlords. The Ahikis would have you

400

believe Kzaniland is one place, one culture, because that is what they made it, just as they made each of the Nine Lands, including ours, into neat little packages that fit their whims. But it is because they sought to keep the truth from us. They sought to stop us realising what we really are. Why, here in what we now call Riani there were once hundreds of languages, dozens of cultures, each with their own unique ways of living, their own—]

'What do you mean, *what we now call Riani?* This land has always been called Riani, hasn't it? That is what the ancestors named it when we arrived.'

But understanding was blossoming within him. Terrible, impossible understanding, and he could not hold it back.

[Jinao,] Mizito said, [that image is less than five thousand years old. They told you this continent was empty because the greybloods wiped out the Scathed aeons ago. They told you the Scathed created techwork and that it is dangerous to humans and attracts greybloods. They told you the Scathed were extinct and nothing like humanity at all. But they lied. They lied about it all. Do you understand what you are seeing? There were no Scathed. These lands were always ours. And Ahiki . . . Ahiki was not our saviour.]

THIRTY-SIX

Elari

As the approaching warriors stirred the wetwoods all around them and the sound of drums filled the pre-dawn gloom, Elari stared down at the arrow lodged in her thigh, watching the blood slowly seep into her tunic.

Chellahua charged forward just as the archer emerged from the trees: a woman in the tunic and warpaint of the palace guard. As the archer adjusted her aim, tracking Chellahua, Elari's dove threw herself into a roll, then slid inside the other woman's guard and slashed down with her macuahuitl.

The archer had begun to turn, but not quickly enough. The multi-bladed club caught the warrior in her side. Chellahua slapped the bow away then kicked in the woman's knee. It was a simple thing, then, to slice down and into the archer's neck.

'Stop!' Elari tried to call, but it had become difficult to find her breath. Poison. They'd used poisoned arrows. Manax had always abhorred the use of poison. But the man who now ruled Intiqq was not Manax Itahua.

The archer gagged, a terrible, strangled sound that bubbled up from within her as her hands went to her neck. Chellahua scrambled backwards as blood pulsed through the woman's fingers. Then the palace warrior fell still, and her skin rippled, and something blue streaked out of her towards the sky.

'She's another host!' Chellahua cried, looking round.

'Time to go!' Ishaan called. They slid under Elari's arm and tried to haul her to her feet, but the moment Elari put weight on her wounded leg, white-hot pain lanced up her left side. She clung to Ishaan, head swimming, as her leg collapsed beneath her, driving her back onto one knee.

'We have to go!' Ishaan said.

Elari shook her head. She felt no fear. If anything, she felt a kind of peace. She was tired . . . so very tired. And soon, she would rest. 'No – *you* must go,' she said. 'All three of you. Find my brother and Kartuuk—'

'Captain, *no*—'

'Tell them everything that has happened. Pledge yourself to Rozichu, as her quartet.'

'Spread out!' Ishaan cried. 'Defend the captain!'

In the distance, Elari could hear the Bairneater's laughter. Fading now. Another arrow sailed past, and as Ishaan reached for their macuahuitl, Elari lifted a heavy hand.

'No,' she said. 'They . . . they are still our people. We are still . . . Cantec's quartet. We . . . *defend* the people of the Nine Lands.'

'I will cut down anyone who comes near!' Chellahua growled.

'No . . . no more innocents must die,' Elari said. 'No more.'

'Captain Elari!' a voice rang out from among the trees. Manax. 'Why have you left the palace?'

'We cannot abandon you,' Osellia hissed.

Elari jabbed a finger towards her leg. 'I can't run. Just . . . go.'

'*Please*, Captain.'

'I said go. Now! As your captain, I . . . I command you.'

It was Chellahua who acted first, her face hardening with resolve as she backed away. She took Ishaan by the arm, pulling them with her and leaving Elari to balance on one leg, the rest of her weight resting on her macuahuitl.

Osellia gave Elari's cheek one final caress. 'We will come back for you,' she said. 'I cannot believe that they will kill you.'

Elari watched them sprint towards the trees, her three fearsome doves, feeling calmer and freer than she had in a very long time.

When they were gone, Elari let the macuahuitl fall to the ground. She had no use of it now. She lowered herself to the damp grass beside it as the drums grew closer. A cold sweat covered her skin, but her leg felt like fire.

Manax's voice sounded from among the trees again, there, up ahead. 'Several of my guards were found slain near your apartments! What do you have to say?'

'Those were . . . no longer your guards!' Elari called out.

When the first warrior broke through the trees, Elari lifted her hands in surrender. It was Commander Chuhat – one of Manax's closest friends. He advanced slowly, arrow nocked, his long white hair stirring in the breeze. He wore no warpaint, no feathers, and his clan tataus were gone.

'Commander Chuhat,' Elari said. 'W-why are you doing this?'

'Chuhat is not here,' the man replied, grinning. 'He is busy.'

As more of them spilled from the trees – souls Elari had known for half a lifetime – she wondered how they had managed to leave the palace, unhindered by the army that had them under siege.

Manax emerged last from the trees, dressed in full battle regalia and jaguar headdress, his eyes bright but his expression hard.

'You should not have left,' Manax said. 'We are at war.'

Elari laughed softly. 'First General, we are always at war. We have been for centuries.'

'Not the greybloods,' Manax said. 'The real war. Reclaiming Aranduq is only the first step. We must free every clan from the curse of ancestral possession. And I want you at our side.'

'The Ahikis . . . will destroy you.'

'Will they?' Manax said. The trees around him shifted, and more warriors stepped out. Not just warriors: household servants. Farriers. Even lowbloods. And behind them—

404

'Ancestors,' Elari breathed, her hand going to her throat.

The monks' staffs were broken, but they did not seem to care. Blood dirtied their golden robes, but not one of them was injured. Warriors in gold warpaint and loincloths came behind them, some armed, some not. All wore the same mocking smile.

'It is freedom, you know,' Manax said as he ambled towards her. 'It is freedom, to no longer answer to the dead.'

'You mean . . . no longer . . . honour them.'

'What right do they have, the so-called holy ones? We are children when we are marched before the shrine. We are children when we receive our first markings. We have no choice. And from the moment our ancestor claims us, we serve their ambitions, their whims. I did not even know who I was without Itahua. But I am learning.'

Elari found herself laughing softly. 'Is that even you . . . I am speaking to?'

'It is me,' Manax said.

'But it's not. Not truly. You are just a . . . monster with a collection of someone else's memories.'

Manax smiled sadly. 'What are any of us, if not a collection of memories?'

'Where is Lord Manax?'

'I am Lord Manax.'

As she toppled sideways, the feeling gone now from both her legs, she knew she would not rise again. She looked up at the sky, red with the coming dawn. Red, like the fires of the village, where she'd burned all those she had slain.

'I am sorry,' Elari said. 'I am . . . sorry for my choice.'

'She is wounded,' Manax said. 'Where is the healer?'

Elari tried to say no, but she could not seem to find the air to speak. A face appeared above her: the dark-skinned trader, smiling broadly.

'I will make her better,' he said, as he leaned over her.

Elari found herself batting feebly at him, but what was the point? She was wounded. Surrounded. Defeated. Someone held down her hands, and someone else raised her head while the trader pressed his bottle to her lips.

Elari spat the first lot of the tincture back in the trader's face, but then someone pinched her nose, and she was forced to swallow the second.

Water. It was nothing but water. Once she had taken enough gulps to satisfy them, they lowered her head, and Elari let out a small laugh. Even now, they were continuing with their little charade. The trader took her hand while others shouted orders to begin combing the wetwoods.

'You'll never find . . . my doves,' Elari whispered. 'They are too fast.'

'Ssh now, love,' the trader said in his Nine Lords accent. 'Don't fight it.'

'You want the king,' Elari said. 'Don't you? Y-you brought those things . . . to kill the king.'

'You lot know nothing about the king,' the man said. 'You're all part of the problem.'

'Who . . . are you?'

'Name's Artenn,' the man said. 'Artenn of Lordsgrave. And I promise you, you'll be happier this way.'

Elari smiled, because that much, at least, was the truth. He was waiting for her, beyond the pyre. 'I am going . . . to be with Cantec,' she said.

But Artenn of Lordsgrave smiled wanly and said, 'Oh, I'm afraid you ain't.' His face rippled, and then it sped out of him, something feral and laughing. It streaked past her in a haze of blue. Its yellow eyes stared and its mouth leered and it was laughing, always laughing.

Then more swept out, dozens upon dozens of them, encircling her in the vortex they formed.

'*We will heal you,*' they seemed to say. '*Make you better.*' As the vortex descended, a glorious warmth spread over Elari. It was going to be all right. Everything was going to be all right.

The Cloistered took her hands and lifted her to her feet, and when she straightened, she found herself elsewhere.

She stood upon the shore of a great blue ocean that stretched to the horizon. At her back stood a city of soaring crystal towers. There were people there, countless, teeming masses, but she could not focus on them.

Before her stood a dozen or more of the Cloistered, vaguely human but with no genitals, no noses, no hair. Their yellow, feline eyes dominated their narrow faces, and their broad grins revealed pointed teeth. But she no longer feared them. Her arms tingled, and when she straightened them, she realised she had grown wings. Great, glorious, brown wings.

'*We have fixed you.*'

'*Made you better.*'

Elari stepped forward to thank them, but then the one nearest her backed away.

'Oh no,' the creature said. 'You may not come.'

And it reached out, placing a clawed hand on her forehead, and as it did so, she felt herself tumbling, falling, descending. Faces streaked past as she fell, and she thought she saw souls she knew: the villagers she had chosen to die in place of Cantec; her father, her uncle, a dozen more kin who had passed beyond the pyre. And others . . . souls with the look of Intiqq, whom she was sure she knew but couldn't name. Some reached to her sadly, trying to save her, but they could not grab hold. She fell past them all into a place of swirling chaos and endless screams. If she looked, she could still see the beach, through a tiny window high above. She could even see herself, standing on the sands, smiling widely, admiring her wings.

Then one of the Cloistered stepped up to that version of herself; stepped *into* it, and Elari knew then that it was that creature who saw through her eyes, who turned over her hands, who spread her glorious wings.

[No!] she tried to say. [Stop!]

But she had no voice in this place, nor any form, and she was still falling, falling, forever falling.

THIRTY-SEVEN

Jinao

Jinao sat on the cave floor, biting into his third loaf of the morning. Before him sprawled a patchwork carpet of blackglass, stretching from wall to wall. At last, their techwork shrine was complete. It had taken five days to assemble, to ensure each plate touched the next. Mizito had told him the shrine would need to be powerful to pull him into the part of the ancestral realm that they needed. Jinao still didn't understand how such a thing could work without spirit wood, but his ancestor assured him that their Bond was all that was required.

Jinao twisted the veins around forearms that were stronger now. Thanks to the arcane powers of the relics in the hidden room, he had all the food he could want. Ancient the artefact might be – although nowhere near as ancient as Jinao had been told all his life – but it was still capable of transforming whatever rock Jinao placed within it into edible food.

It wasn't just his forearms that had strengthened. Mizito had had him up every day, hefting rocks, practising new fighting forms, running laps of the secret room. Jinao's body had already begun to feel different; he felt a new sense of power, of control, that was all his own. A faint hope began to kindle within him, a hope he didn't dare acknowledge – that perhaps he now stood a chance.

[When you invoke,] Mizito said, [you will feel an *opening* before you. Go into it.]

'An opening?'

[Just as you did the day we Bonded.]

'I see,' Jinao said, tying the last knot. 'I'm ready.'

Mizito chuckled softly. [Jinao, no one is ever ready for this.]

Jinao closed his eyes, letting the heat of invocation surge into him. The energy crackled through, crawling over his body, making the hairs on his arms rise. It lit the floor like liquid fire, filling every space between the blackglass. When he closed his eyes and felt the tugging on his mind, he did not have to focus to fall into it. The force seized hold of him and snatched him out of the mortal realm and down into darkness.

'Jinao.'

Jinao opened his eyes. He stood on a beach, before a motionless ocean. High above him stretched a sky crowded with stars and moons. He felt no breeze from this place, nor any heat from the distant, setting sun. But the grasses around him stirred under a force he could not see.

Behind him, at the centre of the island, stood a mudbrick greathouse: the sort of building Jinao saw out in the wetwoods of Cagai. He sensed movement from the building, sensed eyes watching him, but the harder he stared, the more still the place became.

'Welcome, Jinao. And well done.'

Mizito sat on a rock at the water's edge. His triangular helm lay on a rock beside him, leaving his long black hair to tumble freely down his back.

Jinao stumbled towards him, unable to tear his gaze from the sky. 'Am I dreaming?' he said. He lifted his hands. The same scratches covered his skin, and the dirt of the cave still caked his nails. 'This is the ancestral realm! Is Julon here? Can I speak to him?'

'Patience.'

Jinao felt a stirring all around him as figures coalesced to his left and right. People; shimmering suggestions that were little more than outlines. If Jinao looked directly at them, they flickered and blurred before his eyes. They gathered around him in a loose circle.

'Hello?' Jinao said.

'You came with questions,' Mizito said, from the edge of the circle. 'Your ancestors are here to give answers. And aid.'

'Why can't I see them?' Jinao asked.

'Because you have never known them, not truly.'

Jinao counted more than twenty now; glowing, pearlescent heads all turned his way. If he looked hard enough, he could make out the suggestion of a barong, the sense that one held a walking cane and another a sword. But the images were as fuzzy and indistinct as distant figures glimpsed through fog, and each seemed to slide away from his comprehension the harder he looked.

'Well,' Mizito said, 'go on. If you want the wisdom of those who have gone before, you need to know who they are. You cannot move forward in the present without acknowledging the wounds of the past.'

The shimmering forms crowded round him, arms spread as though offering to embrace him. But he would have to take the first step – he understood that now. And so he stepped towards the figure nearest and closed his eyes, and felt his thoughts drift as they had the day he had Bonded—

—He bounced his daughter on his knee, beneath the shade of a tree, while around him towers stretched like mountains towards the stars—

—He ran along the beach as his father returned home in a metal vessel that descended from the sky—

—He sat on horseback at the top of a hill, Mizito and a dozen other warlords at his side. *Sumalong, my friend*, Mizito said, gripping his forearm, and Jinao gripped back and said, *Welcome to the nation of Aranduq.*

He saw Scathed cities, vibrant and alive, and filled with faces as human as his own. He walked a dozen lands and spoke a hundred tongues and lived a thousand lives in each beat of his heart. The thoughts overlapped and intertwined, as they had the day he Bonded Mizito, but this was so much richer, so much more. So many wants

410

and fears and regrets, piling one upon the next, images and sensations he scarcely knew before they were snatched away.

Finally, a single image came to him, crystal-clear. He knelt upon the steps of a ziggurat, while above him loomed a man in a golden mask and robes. To his left and right, a city crumbled, towers collapsing, pyres of techwork burning, while clouds of gold light bled from the hands of the robed man. When the light reached Jinao, it sunk into him, choking, corrupting, poisoning, *erasing* . . .

Jinao knelt on the grass, breath ragged as the visions faded and he returned to the ancestral realm. The shimmering figures drifted away: all but one, whose spectral hand rested on Jinao's shoulder. Jinao felt a curious connection there, a deep fondness. He looked up to see Mizito sitting cross-legged some distance away, his face lined with sadness. Jinao shook his head: the images, the knowledge still roiled within him in a sickening jumble.

'I saw the Scathed,' Jinao said. 'Except they weren't another species. They were human. They looked like us.'

'Yes,' Mizito said softly.

'We built those cities. We crafted that techwork. And then Ahiki . . . Ahiki destroyed it all.'

'Yes.'

'Aranduq wasn't even a city then . . . it was a *nation*. I saw so many different lands and peoples.' Jinao stared at him. 'Am I even your descendant?'

'No. Not by blood. By blood, you are descended from Warlord Sumalong.'

'Sumalong the folk hero?'

Mizito laughed softly. 'Yes.'

Jinao became aware that a circle of people sat watching him, and that he could see them fully now. Excitement swelled within him; they had accepted him! He had shared their stories, and now he could sit among them. He straightened, looking from face to face as they regarded him with amusement or suspicion or hope. Most had the look of Cagai about them – the same mid-brown skin, the same broad features and high cheekbones. But two looked dark enough to be from Jebba or Ntuk and a third had the pale skin of the north. They wore grasspipe armour, or shimmering white tunics, or a strange close-fitting fabric that clung to their bodies like a second skin. Many seemed past sixty rains of age, and all but one wore fighting sticks at their sides.

One of them addressed Jinao in a staccato, flat language that sounded vaguely like Jinao's father's home dialect. An older version, perhaps. Jinao squinted, trying to pick out the words.

'What are they saying?' he asked.

Mizito smiled. 'What do you think they're saying? They are elders. They are discussing your problems.'

Jinao watched the faces as they talked on. One woman gestured angrily at Jinao before standing and stalking back to the greathouse.

'Are they criticising me?' Jinao said.

Mizito chuckled deeply. 'You are lucky. Most of them are very fond of you. And they admire the promise you made to Julon.'

Finally, a shrunken sparrow of an elder with missing teeth and wispy white hair rose from the circle to come and sit beside him. She lifted a stone from the ground and made a sweeping motion, then babbled to him in her language.

'I don't understand,' Jinao said.

The old woman sucked her teeth then made the sweeping motion again. She patted her chest, then let out a string of words.

'Her name is Rulei,' Mizito said. 'She is a stonemason.'

Rulei lifted the stone, made the sweeping motion again, then gestured impatiently at Jinao. At once, understanding seized him. So simple. So obvious. Jinao drew hastily to his feet.

'Th-thank you!' Jinao said, bowing to circle of elders. 'Thank you, Auntie Rulei!'

'Time to go,' Mizito said, then Jinao felt himself falling, flying out of the ancestral realm, until finally, he opened his eyes to Nirere's cave.

*

Within three days, Jinao's work was complete. He stood looking up at the circle of sky, a bundle of provisions strapped to his back. He glanced back at the shadows, feeling a momentary yearning for the hidden room behind him, for the secrets contained within. He longed to take the strange picture of Warlord Kzani with him and show everyone, to shout it from the hills. *Look! They are the Scathed! We are the Scathed! Our ancestors were the Scathed, and somehow everything was taken from us!*

The elders' idea had been wonderfully simple, but it had taken him time to shape the blackglass shards and then hammer them into place. Some had shattered. Some could not bear his weight. When he had run out, he had used wall panels from the hidden room. He felt Rulei's hand with him as he worked, gently guiding.

[I shall not be able to catch you if you fall,] Mizito said as Jinao looked up at the makeshift stair he had built. It would take some getting used to – knowing that Mizito wasn't truly his ancestor. At least, not by blood.

'I know,' Jinao said. 'I'm ready.'

He climbed. He remembered Julon's instructions – his brother had been an excellent climber when they were children. Keep the body flat. Always have a plan before you move. Every fall he'd experienced while constructing the stair had made the path clearer in his mind. And he was stronger than he once had been. More supple.

Jinao climbed from hold to blackglass hold, keeping his gaze ever ahead. At the edge of his hearing, the whispering resumed, the whispering he'd been hearing since the day Mizito first wielded kali fighting sticks. It was them: his family. His ancestors. Talking in their many tongues. Encouraging him. He wasn't the only one leaving that cave, he realised as he climbed. They were coming with him, every one. That was why he felt both heavy and strangely light. The weight of them, the strength of them, was part of him now.

He reached the last of the metal plates, those he had wedged in before that final slip, which he'd only survived by seizing one of the lower holds. Now he was climbing bare rock. He forced himself not to look down. It was easier up here, where the rocks were dryer. Would Nirere be waiting at the top, ready to cast him back down for cheating? Or perhaps it wasn't cheating – perhaps this was how every hopeful escaped.

And then sunlight touched his face, and his hand closed on a clump of grass, and he pulled himself out, out under the blessed sky and the echo of insect call and the sweet, earthy scent of the forest.

'Well done,' Mizito said, stepping out of the air at his side.

When he had recovered, Jinao sat up and scanned his surroundings. He was high in the mountains; the trees were thinner here, and the ground dusted with a scattering of snow. He set off east. He was certain the cave lay somewhere above Nirere Kzani's camp: if he combed the land heading downwards, at some point he would encounter it. He knew it was foolish to seek out the man who had trapped him, but he needed supplies, provisions. And a map, if he was going to reach Herinabad.

It was nearing sunset when he found the camp – or what remained of it. A spread of flattened grass dotted with patches of scorched earth stretched before him. The stinking remains of a cesspit steamed away to the left, and the shrine cave stood empty of its trinkets and offerings, just a hole in the mountainside now.

And there, under a tree, stood Liet.

Jinao's horse held herself like a statue, so still that Jinao wondered if she had fallen dormant again. But when he started towards her, she lifted her head and whinnied tinnily, and moisture sprung to Jinao's eyes.

'You're late,' a voice said as its looming owner resolved from the shadows among the trees.

The Bairneater wore a threadbare cloak. Sulin's staff, *Valour*, lay strung across its back. The creature lumbered forward slowly, yellow eyes agleam. 'I see you have been honing your skill,' it said. 'Good. You almost look like a man.'

'I won't let you take my mother's memories,' Jinao said, dropping his pack.

The Bairneater threw back its colossal head and laughed, a booming

414

sound that sent birds scattering from the treetops. 'You think I want her in here? She is a monster, your mother. I am sick of her churning thoughts. Her anger. Her righteousness.' He looked Jinao over. 'You people. You make me sick. Living in perpetual denial. Never questioning. Never thinking about anything beyond your tiny, ignorant lives.' It stepped forward. 'Fight me.'

Jinao had no need of words. Mizito sprinted out of his body, staff raised. Liet reared, then streaked away, angling off into the forest. The Bairneater turned, meeting Mizito's blow with *Valour* in a deafening crack.

'Why, old man,' the Bairneater said, 'you appear to have shrunk.'

Jinao charged forward. No longer would he sit back and let an ancestor do the work. He had made a promise to his brother, and to his ancestors, who had helped save his life. Mizito had shown him new forms, new wrestling techniques. While Mizito struck high, Jinao slid in, meaning to take the Bairneater's feet from beneath it.

'It is true,' the Bairneater said, dancing out of Jinao's path, 'you really are the worst of them both, Jin. Your mother's stubborn intractability. Your father's linear mind. What a terrible combination they make in you.'

Mizito turned, staff spinning, but the Bairneater was stronger, and larger, and Jinao felt the beginnings of panic.

'Do you really think you're ready?' the creature said. 'I have slain thousands. I have brought armies to their knees. What are you?'

Mizito charged, meeting the Bairneater's thrust, but the Bairneater twisted its body away. Mizito did not stagger past; he simply winked from the air, appearing a moment later on the Bairneater's right, the staff descending in an arc.

'You are no match for me like this,' the Bairneater said, spinning to block with its forearm.

Jinao watched, his heart thumping, as Mizito struck and spun away. No matter how fast he was, no matter where he struck, the Bairneater was there to meet him. The creature was toying with them, Jinao realised. It was still in control.

'She always thought the lectures and the name-calling, the shaming and the shunning, would make you stronger,' the Bairneater said. 'She thought they would enflame you and strike a fire in your belly. But how wrong she was. There is nothing in your belly. Nothing but worms and fear.'

Something snapped in Jinao then – he couldn't say what. Perhaps it was exhaustion. But an animal roar escaped him, a sound of pure rage. In that moment, the whispering voices became clearer, and a flood of energy surged into his hands. His ancestors dwelt there, in his blood, in his bone – encouraging, advising, strengthening. The weight of them pressed against his skin as they crowded his mind. It was just as Nirere had said. His link with the ancestral realm was stronger now. Who knew what might come through?

'*Sumalong!*' Jinao screamed, and at once a man appeared, with the brown skin and wide cheekbones of Cagai. He wore a skirt in the style of the isles, and in each hand he carried a kali stick. There was no triangular helm for the warlord of Cagai, nor any gleaming scaled armour. An eagle mask was pulled high upon his head, feathered and glaring as any island warrior.

Sumalong charged forward, kali sticks a blur. At the sight of him, Mizito laughed joyously. 'It is good to see you, my brother!'

Sumalong leapt over Mizito as the taller ancestor ducked; it seemed they knew each other's plans, each other's minds. Sumalong landed on the Bairneater with both feet. It was twice his height and girth, but the creature was off balance. For a moment, shock crossed the grey-blood's face. Then it tumbled backwards, crashing to the ground.

Mizito materialised behind the Bairneater, staff raised. The creature's skin rippled with that same dangerous energy Jinao had seen it use back in Cagai. But before it could act, Mizito slammed *Stillness* down with a cry of triumph that seemed to contain a hundred voices, a thousand wills. The staff plunged into the Bairneater's neck, glyphs flashing along its length, the force so great that the head was torn free and spun away. Its techwork veins sparked and danced in the

416

air as it rolled through the grass. The Bairneater's hands still batted feebly at Sumalong, but Jinao's ancestor, his true ancestor, swatted them aside.

Jinao stared at the headless corpse of the monster who had taken so much from him. He stared until the hands stopped moving, then turned his attention to its head, over by the trees. The yellow eyes sparked once, and then grew dim. Jinao advanced, a fierce relief washing over him. The Bairneater was dead! Jinao had done it. He had kept his promise to Julon. And he had called a new ancestor back to the mortal realm.

Sumalong rolled off the Bairneater's corpse and lay still on the grass, chuckling. He was heavier-set than Mizito, and not quite as tall. His long black hair, pulled into a loose braid, looked thicker. Was it Jinao's imagination, or could he see Jemusi in this man, and also something of Jethar?

'Hello . . . Uncle,' Jinao said, as Sumalong sat up. 'I'm Jinao. Your descendant.'

'It's good to meet you properly,' Sumalong said. Lords, but even his accent was of Cagai. Jinao felt a tightness in his throat. 'It has been a long, long time since anyone called me back.'

'Yes, and you are still not wanted,' a feminine voice said from the far side of the clearing.

Cold terror gripped Jinao. That voice. He knew that voice. He knew it better than any other. Once, it had filled him with dread.

He looked up to see a figure striding across the grass, cradling the Bairneater's severed head in the crook of its arm. It was another grey-blood; this one tall and lithe and almost human, with gazelle-like legs and darting eyes. As it approached, Jinao realised something shone out of the Bairneater's lifeless eyes and into the world. It was like a painting made of light; a tiny depiction of a woman he knew well. That face, pinched and proud; that hard lean body; black hair, shot through with streaks of white.

'Hello, my son,' First General Sulin Mizito said, her flickering image turning to Jinao. 'You have done well.' Her eyes darted to Mizito and Sumalong. 'I'm afraid you two are not needed.'

She uttered a stream of words in the Forbidden Tongue, and at once Mizito and Sumalong winked from existence. The long-legged grey-blood, still holding the Bairneater's head, squatted down beside the Bairneater's immobile body.

'How?' Jinao said, staring. 'How are you here?'

'Oh, I am not truly here, my son,' Sulin said. 'This is merely an approximation of me. A copy of my will.'

He didn't realise he'd been backing away until he knocked into something. He turned to see a second greyblood rising from the grass behind him. Jinao leapt forward, but the greyblood seized his arm, then pulled him back into its solid metal embrace. Hot arms pinned Jinao's own arms to his side.

'Mizito?' Jinao muttered. 'Sumalong?' But he felt nothing: no spark, no warmth, no connection.

'Do not be disheartened,' Sulin said. 'You have far exceeded my expectations. We wished only for you to achieve the mental fortitude to Bond more than one spirit once your inhibitors were removed, but you have managed to bring forth a second ancestor all of your own volition!'

The long-legged greyblood had begun to position the Bairneater's head back atop its shoulders. Then, to Jinao's horror, the creature jabbed its fingers between the plates of its own belly. It tore the metal back, then pulled out length after length of veins.

'What have you done?' Jinao asked his mother's flickering likeness.

The greyblood worked deftly, twining its own veins around those dangling from the stump of the Bairneater's neck. Faster it worked, until the Bairneater's fingers twitched, then twitched again. The Bairneater's headless body sat up, and as it did, the long-legged grey-blood collapsed, lifeless, beside it.

'I am very proud of you, Jinao,' Sulin said, and then his mother faded away to nothing.

The Bairneater's body plucked its severed head from the grass. Jinao watched, transfixed, as veins from neck and head sought each other out, intertwining; remerging.

'No . . .' Jinao said, his mouth suddenly dry as before him, the beast he had finally killed slowly returned to life.

'Good,' the Bairneater said, fixing its head in place, its yellow eyes brightening and brightening like a fire. 'Your mother says you are ready.'

'What do you mean, ready?' Jinao said. He flexed his fingers. Perhaps he had simply been distracted. He had the Bond now – that couldn't be taken away again. But even when he closed his eyes and extended his hand, as he had done the very first time, he still felt no heat.

'It – it was her,' Jinao said, something cold uncoiling deep within him, a terrible understanding unfurling in his mind. 'All of this was her, wasn't it? I thought you had captured her spirit somehow, but the truth is, it was the other way around.'

'Bring him,' the Bairneater said.

'I'm not going anywhere with either of you!' Jinao said. He lurched forward, but the greyblood tightened its grip and then rose, and Jinao felt himself being hefted into the air like a sack of grain. He twisted, kicking out, groping for the greyblood's head, but his captor bundled him forward.

The Bairneater chuckled. 'Even now, you do not give up! How right she was. No matter how many times she knocked you down, you rose up stronger. That is why she chose you, you know. Because you were strongest where it mattered most.'

'Chose me for what?'

The Bairneater struck out, smacking the end of *Valour* onto Jinao's head. Pain exploded behind his eyes as Jinao collapsed to his knees. The Bairneater leaned forward as swirling darkness descended. 'For her great rebellion.'

419

PART FOUR

Boleo, Runt, Jinao, Temi

THIRTY-EIGHT

Boleo

In a remote wetwoods on the very western edge of the Nine Lands, Father Boleo the Wise, Grand High Curator of Adataliland, was slowly losing his mind.

Each morning, he rose at dawn to work on the shrine to Vunaji. While the surviving Batide warriors felled trees, foraged for edible plants or patrolled for greybloods, Father Boleo built. The spirit wood was the most important part: Boleo used all their remaining stores to set it out in the neat formation that resembled less and less the Nine Lands map so many had taken it for.

As Boleo stood surveying the finished product, the rain lashing down around him, the Batide huddled under the wooden shelter they had erected with the help of their invoked ancestors.

Next, Boleo constructed the sides of the shrine. After all, a shrine needed to be majestic, to evoke beauty and grandeur, if it was to honour the ancestors enough to entice one of them back to the mortal realm. Boleo helped strip the trunks of bark himself, and ensured the roof was a perfect cone. He then encouraged every remaining warrior to help decorate the insides – carvings of flowers, animals, the faces of loved ones; anything to show how much they honoured and cherished the fallen. He had them gather the most colourful plants from the wetwoods and hang garlands from the ceilings. He selected two warriors to see that the shrine was never unattended, to show the ancestors that their party always kept them in their thoughts.

By the tenth night, the shrine was complete, and after a supper of roasted roots and berries, Boleo waited until the warriors had posted guards or retired to their sleeping shelter, before slipping back into his glorious creation.

Boleo placed his staff down on the pattern of spirit wood he had constructed, his pulse racing with anticipation.

'You'll need an invoker,' Morayo said, sidling up behind him. 'You know, to . . . invoke.' He cracked the muscles in his neck. 'I am ready.'

'You are Bonded to a spirit already.'

'That didn't seem to stop Nchali and his three aunties. One of them has been helping build the fire every night, you know.'

'Yes, but none of them is Bonded to a founding warlord. Someone else will need to be selected.'

Boleo crossed to where his pack lay against the wooden wall. He rummaged within until his hand closed around the cloth wrapping one of his most treasured possessions, something he had never dreamed he would need on this journey. He had only brought them at all because if that accursed Father Emata had found them in his rooms, they would have incriminated him beyond all measure. It had cost him an entire cliffside mansion and the fabled Golden Elephants of Maadu to purchase them from Sister Ulla. He had never dreamed that they would prove essential to their quest.

'We have seen that all that is needed to connect us to the ancestral realm is a nun's tatau needle and ink,' he said, holding up the cloth. 'And it so happens that I have both.'

'I'm going to skip over the part where I ask how you came by those,' Morayo said slowly, 'and instead go straight to the heart of it. You believe that anyone – *anyone* – could Bond an ancestral spirit, if they were tataued by something like this?'

'So long as the ancestor chooses them, yes.'

424

Morayo fingered the ink pot, an incredulous smile on his face. 'So it really is meaningless. All of it. Our bloodlines. Our nobility. Meaningless. Anyone can Bond! Anyone's dead auntie could be out there building a campfire. You don't need training and dances. You just need special ink!'

'If I were to cut a street urchin and offer him to Adatali, I do not believe your forefather would deem him worthy. But I believe there is nothing inherent in the process preventing him from doing so should he wish to; yes. Now if you don't mind, I need to check this shrine can actually reach the ancestral realm. Why don't you go and rest?'

'Can't I watch?' Morayo said. 'I promise to be quiet.'

Boleo opened his mouth to object, then sagged. What was the point? He had always sought to protect the boy from truths that would harm him, endanger him. But they were well beyond that now.

'If you wish,' Boleo said. 'But don't talk. And don't breathe too loudly.'

Boleo sat cross-legged before the spirit wood, his staff placed upon it. He had ensured he'd left his staff out in the sun all day, to give it maximum potency. Now, he could hear the soft hum of its arcane energies as they rippled across the spirit wood, filling it.

'*Establish connection with the ancestral realm,*' Boleo commanded in the Forbidden Tongue. He heard Morayo shift behind him, and wondered if the boy recognised those words, usually chanted by nuns on the Day of Choosing.

A glyph flared up on the crystal of his staff: *connected.*

'*Which minds have passed through this type of shrine? Show me their patterns.*'

'All that chanting,' Morayo said brightly. 'Are you asking the ancestors to hear you?'

'Yes,' Boleo snapped. 'Now be quiet.'

A series of complex patterns flashed up on the crystal. Ancestors, but he had never seen anything like it! On and on it went, a tangle of glyphs and numbers. But these were not multiple minds. These were all part of one interconnected being. They were part of the same network that formed a single ancestor's spirit. He knew enough about the nuns' techwork ink to see at once what Chinnaro's problem had been. A mind this large: the tiny beads of techwork that passed down the tatauing needle and into the blood of an invoker could never hope to hold such a thing. Adatali's spirit contained half, perhaps a third of the information he saw here.

'Oh,' he muttered.

'What?' Morayo said.

'I believe . . . I believe I see Chinnaro's problem.'

'And do you see a solution?'

'I'm not certain. We will have to experiment.'

Nobody objected the next morning when he explained that he would be using a nun's ink and needle on himself. He supposed none of the Batide warriors had a desire to risk displacing their Bonds with their own kin. He knelt before the shrine and dipped the needle into the pot, then made a long cut in the flesh of his left forearm. Then he pressed his palms to the spirit wood and set to work.

'Spirit of Vunaji, attend me,' he said softly. 'I humbly offer myself to you.'

He felt nothing. No stirring of reality. No rush of heat and light. It felt strange, using the Royal Tongue, but then that was the language invokers used to call upon their ancestors. After a time, he tried again in the Forbidden Tongue, then had the watching warriors bring more food offerings.

Nothing.

'We'll try again tomorrow,' Boleo said, standing. 'The ancestors smile on those who persevere.'

But he found no success the following morning, nor the day after. The next day, Jamakii came to volunteer herself. She stared at him with round eyes when he made the cuts beside her family tataus, then knelt patiently while he chanted.

'It is the shrine,' Boleo declared. 'It is not grand enough. More flowers! More carvings! We must show the ancestors that we care!'

Over the days that followed, he cycled slowly through every remaining member of their group. Even Morayo himself tried, first with his existing clan tatau, and then with a new cut Boleo made. That night, Boleo tataued himself three more times, thinking that perhaps piercing a greater number of places would mean he could Bond a spirit as complex as Vunaji. But he was rewarded with only cold silence. He was rewarded with utter indifference.

The next morning, Morayo entered the shrine just as Boleo was placing their remaining food stores on the spirit wood. It was a good plan – after all, what could be more valuable than the last of their food? But Morayo looked incredulous.

'Ancestors! What are you doing?' Morayo cried. 'It took us days to gather all that!'

'We need more! More! This is the most powerful ancestor to ever be Bonded; they won't be content with mere crumbs.'

Morayo stalked away silently, then left the camp unguarded while every warrior and ancestor among them foraged for supplies. Boleo saw the way they slid their eyes round to him when they returned that evening. He heard the way they whispered to Morayo at the cook-fire. They thought Boleo had lost his sanity. They thought he'd led them into the wilderness to their deaths.

But success was close. Boleo was certain of it. His nights became an unbearable stream of churning nightmares, a ceaseless cycle of images from his past and his research. He saw Daloya, standing over him in the hidden shrine. He saw Daloya on the Maadu battlefield, the day the Blight nearly took his life. He saw Morayo, laughing, mocking. He saw Adatali, stepping out of the ancestral realm.

Morayo came upon him one morning rocking before the shrine, muttering over and over. 'Nobody suitable,' Boleo mumbled to himself. The words were soothing to him now. If he said them enough, just repeated them often enough, the answer would come to him. 'There's nobody suitable. Nobody suitable.'

'What do you mean, nobody suitable?' Morayo said.

427

'I – I believe that this spirit can only Bond a particular type of mind,' Boleo said in a rush. 'Given time, I could do it, I know I could do it. I could train myself or even one of you.' He turned and gripped Morayo's arm. Was that fear he saw in the boy's eyes? 'I believe some of us here could possibly be trained to develop the right pattern of thoughts. Yes, it's about the right pattern of thoughts, an aligning pattern. It is always about the pattern. But, ah, but it would take years. Decades, even, to prepare someone suitable. To prepare someone suitable.'

'Father, what are you talking about?'

'Chinnaro. It is where Chinnaro Itahua went wrong. Look at Vunaji! Look at them! Look at the *complexity!* They would have torn apart the mind of anyone who tried to Bond them. Perhaps this is what happened. Perhaps Chinnaro herself, or another, attempted to invoke, and after destroying the host, the ancestor went on to tear apart her army. It might have been an accident. Yes! An accident! It must be benevolent, after all, it is an ancestor and ancestors are benevolent after all, aren't they? Aren't they, Daloya?'

'I'm Morayo,' Morayo said slowly. 'And I've come to tell you it's time to leave. We've failed.'

'Failed? We haven't failed! Morayo, we – we haven't failed, we haven't. We're nearly there! We are supposed to lead the way. It is we, it is Adatali, who will lead us all! We're—'

'I'm sorry, Father. We're going home. It's time to acknowledge this isn't working.'

Morayo left him there, and Boleo turned his attention back to the shrine. 'It's all connected,' he muttered, because it was, and saying it aloud helped remind him it was true. 'It's all connected. The Scathed. The greybloods. The ancestors. Connected. *Tap the "more information" button on your panel to see an animated diagram of the process!* Leopard Tongue words! In a Scathed ruin! In a—'

A series of glyphs rippled across the crystal on the end of his staff. That was curious. More curious still was what those glyphs said: a repeating message in the Forbidden Tongue.

428

Father Boleo, I hope the shrine is ready. Because the recipient is. Remain where you are. We will be with you in three days.

Clarity came crashing down on him. Clarity and understanding. At once, Boleo sprang up. He blundered outside into the sunshine, for the first time in – how long? He wasn't sure. He'd been sleeping and eating in the shrine for days now. Morayo sat wrapping a wound on Nchali's leg. Had they been attacked again? Boleo couldn't recall. They looked up at him, all of them, and Boleo felt a stab of guilt. They had trusted him. He had promised them he would deliver the ancestor to them, that he knew what he was doing, and he had failed. Worse, he had failed Warlord Daloya. He understood their anger.

'The ancestors have sent me a message!' Boleo declared, lifting his staff high. 'In three days, one will be brought to us, one destined to Bond Vunaji!'

They all looked at Morayo. None of them spoke. For a moment, Morayo couldn't meet Boleo's eyes. Then he turned and said, 'Father—'

'Please, My Lord,' Boleo said softly. 'Please. I am begging you. Three days. That's all I ask. Just three more days.'

After what seemed an eternity, Morayo sighed. 'Three days,' he said. 'But after that, we are going home.'

THIRTY-NINE

Runt

'Here,' Runt said. 'I got you a present.'

She placed the votive on the bed between them.

That bed had been the first thing she'd bought with her new wages. It was made from polished Ekari cedar and was wide enough for six. Even so, it did not dominate her new room, up on the third floor of the Cascade. Many things had become possible with her new Chedu Family wages: new clothing, the best she'd ever had; as much fine food as she and Zee could eat; and, most importantly, a proxy who would go to war on her behalf.

This last, she had not even had to arrange herself. Harvell had called her out into the yard one day to present her with a ragged young man with anxious eyes.

'Lisu here is to become a member of our household shortly,' Harvell had said, resting a hand on the young man's shoulder. 'When the bluehawks come to collect, it is he who will step out of those doors on your behalf. We have added him to the ranks of those we've already hired as brave proxies for the rest of us. It is a great honour, to serve the Chedus in this way! And Ba Casten believes the ancestors smile upon those who look into the eyes of one who will fight in our place.'

Runt had looked, and she had seen in the young man the kind of fear she'd once harboured herself. That fear of being always in danger, always one step away from death. He'd tried to smile at her, a smile that cut straight through to Runt's core. Because it also showed another fear she'd once nursed – the fear that she would not live out the year.

'He . . . gets paid?' Runt had said.

'Well, his family do. This fine young man has volunteered to answer for us, and in return his parent, siblings and spouse will receive thirty suns. A small fortune to them!' And Harvell had squeezed the man's shoulder again, so hard the tips of her brown fingers grew pale.

'So he volunteered?'

'Yes, he did,' Harvell had said. 'Didn't you?'

The young man had nodded vigorously, and after Runt had bowed in thanks and told him she'd light a candle for him on the Cascade's family shrine, he'd turned back for the street. But Runt had not missed the way he limped as he walked, nor the fresh bruises on the backs of his arms.

Back in her room, a pleasant breeze stirring the chiffon at her window, Runt smiled up at Gifted Mikim, her companion this last moon. Mikim placed his fine, square hands around the votive. 'But she should be on shrine, no?'

'This is a special kind of votive,' Runt said. 'Watch!'

She crossed to the window, where a techwork candle drove out the dusk of the street beyond. Her window looked directly down on the stairs to the kitchens, and each night, when the new boy arrived, Runt made sure she sat there to watch. The pleasure she got from seeing someone else trudge down to scrub at old Asham's pots was almost as sweet as that to be found when Mikim used his tongue between her legs. She crossed to her table – another of her new acquisitions – and poured water from the jug into a small basin.

Mikim sat cross-legged on her bed, watching her with a half-smile. His oiled body was like a sculpture. When he worked the pillow rooms, he wore wigs and headdresses, but now his bald head was utterly unadorned. Runt liked him best that way. Unpainted and pure.

Runt placed the basin on the bed, then set the votive afloat inside it. It was a decorative tangle of flowers and techwork. Once, not so long ago, she would have thought it the height of recklessness to touch techwork. But Ba Casten's entire business was built on the buying and selling of tools crafted from Scathed artefacts, creations that could light a room without flame or create fire with the turn of a handle. Or this: ostensibly a contraption to make water run clean, but the Chedus' newest version was something more besides.

'Locals place these in their water buckets,' Runt said. 'Helps the water run sweet and keeps off the sickness.'

'I know this,' Mikim said. 'As children, back home, we make her for the snows.'

'Ah, but not like this, you don't. Harvell makes these; and yeah, they do clean water, but they also do something extra. Watch. *Akatavaat.*'

This was the second time Runt had bought one of Harvell's votives. It was the older woman's main source of income now. Usually, she was reluctant to give them to anyone, saying the Seng Family were unfor-giving of those who breached the terms of their exclusive agreement; but since Harvell had shown everyone what they could do at Casten's birthday party, Runt had been desperate to buy one for Mikim, and Harvell had finally relented.

At first nothing happened, and Mikim raised a sceptical eyebrow. Runt licked her lips: it still felt deliciously perverse, to be speaking the Forbidden Tongue. *Akatavaat* was one of the few words Old Feyin had taught her, but it was an important one. He said it was the word that could breathe life into any Forbidden relic, if there was life still to be found within.

The water began to shimmer, and Mikim smiled and leaned forward.

'Wait!' Runt said, lifting a hand. 'This is just the beginning.'

The water shifted again, then swelled upwards, and Mikim laughed and leaned back. Then a viscous stream of shifting colour spilled up out of the basin, undulating as it stretched towards the ceiling.

Mikim cried out in surprise and extended one hand. 'Warm!' he said as the shifting colour swirled over his fingers. Higher and higher the stream of colour crept, until it arched over them and spilled across the ceiling. As they stared, the images began.

'Watch!' Runt said. 'Beautiful, eh?'

Waves and fish and boats and sky overlapped each other in a heady rush. Runt saw the city, as she might from the gunwales of a barge. Mikim's dark eyes shone as he stared, transfixed, and Runt allowed herself a small smile of pleasure.

'She is much soft!' Mikim said, pressing his cheek to the stream of blue-green, like a cat. 'She feels—'

Something lashed out from within the water, scraping across Mikim's cheek. He cried out in pain and fell backwards, but the thing crawled after him. Runt backed away; this had not happened at Ba Casten's party. Had she made a mistake; spoken the Forbidden word wrongly?

A man crawled out of the light, a man shrouded in cloak and hood. Chains clinked at his wrists. Runt recoiled, her hand plunging into empty air as she reached the edge of the bed. As she fell backwards, the man knifed through the air and fell upon Mikim like a rabid dog. Runt saw nothing of his face and form; only his chained hands as his claws slashed at Mikim's chest and arms. Blood sprayed as Mikim batted at the creature. His eyes locked with Runt's, and the terror she saw there roused her from her stupor.

'Stop!' she shouted, pushing to her feet. '*D'akatavaat!*' It was the only other Forbidden word she knew. But more of the creatures climbed out. Two set upon Mikim, pinning him, raking his chest, his arms, stifling his cries. Runt knew she should move. Mikim needed help. But something terrible – something wondrous – was happening. The voices of the pendant tittered within her as Runt watched.

'Please!' Mikim cried.

'What are you?' Runt said to the creature. It turned sharply, and she caught a glimpse of its skeletal face.

Only then did she realise that once it finished with Mikim, she would be next. The votive. Runt dove for the basin, still on the bed, and seized the votive. The metal felt blisteringly hot against her skin, but she willed herself not to let it drop. She leapt for the window as the creature pounced on her head and shoulder, slicing deep into her skin. A line of hot pain knifed up along her cheek.

Runt shoved open the shutters and tossed the votive out into the street, from where cries of fear and alarm rose. The creatures followed it out, dragged in the votive's wake as though tethered to it, and Runt drew in a great breath.

'Run?' came Zee's voice from the next room.

Runt turned back to see Mikim lying motionless on his back, surrounded by an expanding pool of blood. How beautiful he looked, even now, his face and torso a ruin. If he lived, he would be scarred. Bad for his trade, certainly. But perhaps not for her.

Zee was on his feet when Runt crossed into the lounge that connected their rooms. The book he'd been reading lay on the ornate Vushemi chaise. Zee was learning his words and numbers. Casten said he was quick enough that one day he might keep the Cascade's books.

'What's happening?' Zee said.

'Just stay there,' Runt said. 'Mikim's had an . . . accident. Wait there for me, you hear?'

She closed the door on him, then strode back to the window and peered down into the street. Three elders stood over the remains of the votive, lengths of wood still gripped in their hands. The thing lay in shattered pieces in the dirt of the road. A man sat outside the teahouse opposite, bleeding from one leg, and one of the old women had a gash across her stomach. But nobody was dead. And the chained monsters were gone.

'The ancestors turn from those who touch techwork!' one of the old women shouted up at the Cascade, before making the sign for ancestral protection and then hobbling off to tend to the wounded man.

The door banged open, and there stood Harvell, Lakoz at her side. Harvell smiled softly, but Runt caught the alarm in her eyes.

'What happened?' the older woman said. Her eyes flicked to Mikim and she took a step back. 'Ancestors!'

434

'Some kind of . . . monsters came out of the water votive,' Runt said. 'They tried to kill me. Mikim fought them off.'

Harvell stood in the doorway, her mouth a grim line as she watched Runt kneel at Mikim's side. It looked fruitless to Runt, but she knew everyone would expect her to try. Mikim was breathing, she was surprised to discover, but his heartbeat was swift and shallow. She stroked his cheek. How strong people could be, even when their bodies lay in ruin.

Runt pulled the pendant out from beneath her shirt and called softly for the healing voices to come. The Cloistered – that was what they called themselves now – swirled out of her in a laughing blue cloud. Some sped over to Harvell and Lakoz, smiling mockingly at their inability to see, while others formed a vortex above Mikim.

'You said *monsters* came out?' Harvell said.

'Yes,' Runt said, as the unseen blue vortex spun above her. 'Cloaked figures – three of them. They would've torn me apart if I didn't throw the votive into the street.' She kept her hands extended towards Mikim, though in truth she knew now that this was not needed. Once the Cloistered came out, they could act entirely alone.

'Did you say the wrong words? Or use something other than water?'

'No,' Runt said, with more certainty than she felt. 'I did everything right.'

'Perhaps it is just one,' Lakoz said, but Harvell was shaking her head. She had grown pale, Runt realised, and was staring through the window, deep in thought.

'We need to tell Casten,' Harvell said quietly.

'Why?' Lakoz said. 'This is only one mistake. If we—'

'It's not one mistake!' Harvell cried, rounding on him. 'If one is like this, then so are the rest. They have already gone on to the Sengs, and then who knows where!'

'Surely you wouldn't make the same mistake more than once?'

'You idiot. This isn't me. This is *her.*'

'Her who?' Lakoz said, touching Harvell's arm, but Harvell shook him off and strode from the room.

435

Runt turned back to Mikim to find the Cloistered still swirling above him. He had stopped breathing, she noticed, and his eyes stared sightlessly ahead.

'What's wrong?' Runt muttered. 'Fix him! He was still breathing!'

[We cannot!]

[Oh, we cannot!]

[Not this one.]

[He has been touched by something powerful.]

[Something familiar.]

[Something we did not think to find here.]

Then they streaked away, fading in a ripple of laughter, leaving Runt alone with the mangled corpse of her lover.

FORTY

Jinao

'Here,' the Bairneater said, tossing him a coconut. 'Eat.'
Jinao knocked the shell open on the nearby rock and then
sucked hungrily at the flesh. His cracked lips stung as the sweet liquid
ran over them. He knew the Bairneater was watching him, but he lifted
his eyes, scanning the wetwoods. Dense trees loomed above him, and
through the dripping canopy, the sun was a harsh white smudge. The
air hummed with insects and the distant whoop of monkeys. There
was no path out here save the one the Bairneater carved for them with
its jagged machete, and the last village they'd passed near had been
ten days ago.

Jinao did not take his eyes from the Bairneater as he chewed. When
the opportunity to flee came along, he needed to be ready. It no longer
mattered which way he ran, so long as he kept going. The creature
only let them stop once a day for food and water. Jinao wasn't sure if
it was trying to keep him weak, or if it simply forgot humans needed
sustenance. But within those few moments lay his greatest chance of
escape.

'Mizito,' Jinao muttered, 'spirit of my mothers, hear me.'

'Why keep trying?' the Bairneater said, lowering its great bulk onto
a nearby rock. 'You are cursed. He will no longer answer your call.'

The silence Jinao felt now, the aching absence, was a thousand times worse than it had been before he had made the Bond. His missed the heat beneath his skin. He missed the smoothness of Mizito's voice. The emptiness he felt now gnawed at his insides night and day.

'Did she command you to curse me?' Jinao said.

'You mother?' the Bairneater snorted and turned to watch a colourful bird swoop between branches. 'She does not *command* me. And very soon, I shall be free of her.'

'Delightful, isn't she?' Jinao tossed away the coconut shell. 'The two of you are well suited.'

What a great irony it was. Perhaps the Bairneater would be free of the spirit of Sulin, but Jinao never would. Sulin Mizito had lived unchallenged in his head for decades. Wherever he went, her criticisms and judgements followed. Her chastisement haunted him with every step he ever took, and it was the worst sort of damage to a person's soul. The sort that rewrote their sense of self. She lived on in his mind, and that was a version of his mother from which he would never, ever be free.

'So that day on the beach,' Jinao said. 'She knew she was going to die.'

'She had prepared a copy of her consciousness for me,' the Bairneater said. It grinned and leaned forward. 'I agreed to take it. I expect the rest came as quite a surprise.'

So the creature had betrayed her. Jinao supposed he should feel grief, or anger, but he felt only a grim lack of surprise. 'What about me? Did you know I would be there?'

The Bairneater snorted. 'Of course not. I was supposed to find you in the palace. But you had to be punished for what you did to my arm.'

The bush to Jinao's left stirred: the second greyblood – the one that had pinned Jinao down while the Bairneater healed itself. It had followed them at a distance for all the long leagues of their journey, never speaking as its narrow head tracked ceaselessly left and right, keeping watch.

438

'Why won't you tell me her plan?' Jinao said, and not for the first time. *Rebellion.* That was the word the Bairneater had used. The idea of Sulin Mizito, bastion of discipline and loyalty, rebelling against anything had sounded absurd. But as the days had passed and they had headed west out of the mountains, Jinao began to realise that perhaps it was not so laughable. His mother's loyalty was to her family, to her people, to her vow to protect. No soul living or dead, not even a king, could stand in the way of that.

Usually when Jinao asked the question, the Bairneater growled and stalked away, or else gagged him for the remainder of that day. But this time, the beast turned to face him. Glyphs glinted in the sunlight as it pulled *Valour* from its back.

'She promised me this,' the Bairneater said, eyeing its length. 'Its core is made from kemamium. I do not think you even know what that is, do you? To your people, it is indistinguishable from steel. But to us . . .' The Bairneater closed its glowing yellow eyes. 'It is getting increasingly hard to find.'

'Take it, then. And let me go.' With one hand, Jinao scrabbled in the dirt, never lowering his eyes from the Bairneater. 'I've done what you wanted. What *she* wanted. I've killed you. Even if you did come back.' If he just could find a sharp enough rock. A shard of something hard enough.

'Killing me was never the true objective,' the Bairneater said. It tipped its head to one side, assessing him in a gesture so like Sulin that Jinao had to look away. But her spirit hadn't appeared again, in that ethereal, miniature light form.

'Do you know why she chose you?' the Bairneater said.

'She didn't choose me for anything.'

'I've told you: she did. She has groomed you since childhood for this. Everything she did. Everything she said. All of it was to mould you into what you are now.'

'What, her hidden shame?'

The Bairneater straightened. 'No. Never that. She loved you. That is why it was such a sacrifice. She loved you deeply, and yet still she did what needed to be done.'

'What needed to be done,' Jinao muttered, and snorted.

'Yes. And—' The Bairneater groaned and pressed a colossal hand to its head. 'Ah, but she does not want me to see that. Yet still, I know what she feels. I know what you meant to her.'

'Greybloods do not have feelings,' Jinao said.

The Bairneater sighed and looked away.

'So was she in control when you killed Julon? Or was that all you? And what about Aranduq?'

'She torments me,' the Bairneater said, standing. 'Every day, she torments me. So I torment her.'

'Take the staff,' Jinao said. 'Set me free. I don't care about my mother, or any rebellion she had planned, and neither should you. You've got what you want. This is the end.'

'Unless I fulfil my vow, her thoughts will remain welded to mine for ever.' The Bairneater lifted its head to the gently dripping trees. 'Mizito lived in the shadow of his five older siblings – did you know that? He was the smallest among them. The slowest. The least skilled. But do you know what he had that they did not?'

'I've no idea,' Jinao said. He had found something, there beneath the mud. The hard edge of it felt sharp against his fingers. 'A techwork staff? Black warpaint? A really big cock?'

'He had tenacity. He was a cautious man, a careful man. But he was dogged. Determined. When his siblings died through their hubris, he remained. And he grew stronger. Your mother alone understood this about him. He would not be drawn to the brilliance of Jethar, or the fury of Jemusi, or the bravado of Julon. He would be drawn to some-thing more stoic.'

'By which you mean me?'

'Yes, I mean you. Why do you think you never Bonded his spirit, in all those years? Why do you think suddenly, miraculously, when your mother fell, that you were able to Bond Mizito at last?'

440

The rock was free now, a solid weight in his hand. 'Luck?' Jinao said. 'The ancestors love a grim coincidence.'

'There's no such thing as luck,' the Bairneater said. 'She arranged it all. She, and Warlord Daloya, with the help of their techdoctor Lakari Tob.'

And unbidden, Jinao recalled the last time he had seen Lakari: on the Day of Choosing. He recalled the way Lakari had taken his hands, how he had spoken words sacred to his people. The Forbidden Tongue, Jinao realised with a twisted smile. That was what he had spoken. Words to unlock whatever foul barriers Sulin had erected in Jinao's mind.

'You're lying,' Jinao said, tightening his grip around the rock. He kept his gaze on a lizard climbing a distant tree, while every muscle in his body prepared to spring.

'Don't you see? Your mother told Lakari that once I arrived, he was to remove the curse she had placed in your tataus as a child. This would mean you were ready to fulfil your destiny as the greatest invoker that has ever lived, and the figurehead of her rebellion.'

Jinao flew. He had no strategy, no plan. He screamed wordlessly and leapt across the undergrowth, bringing the shard of rock high above his head. The Bairneater turned, and Jinao slammed the rock down.

Too slow; the Bairneater twisted sharply to one side, and though Jinao missed the beast's head, the rock came down in its colossal shoulder.

The Bairneater howled in pain as Jinao staggered backwards. It was a shallow wound; scarcely a scratch to a greyblood so strong. But it was enough to give Jinao a chance, and so without hesitation, he turned and ran.

The forest was a dripping, shadowy maze as he pelted blindly through it. The floor was thick with mud and vines and insects, but Jinao pushed them from his mind. He ran with all the strength he could gather, sucking in the humid air, batting away the branches that flew at him.

441

An inarticulate roar sounded from somewhere behind Jinao. He scarcely had time to register the heavy pounding of the Bairneater's feet before the creature was on him. Something struck Jinao hard between the shoulders, and then he was down, tumbling to the mud, his legs a tangle.

'Stop!' the Bairneater thundered as Jinao crawled away on hands and knees. The creature's hand struck to his left, but Jinao rolled, and then he was up, staggering forwards, tearing at the vines in his path . . .

'Enough!' Something whistled through the air, striking the top of his head, and sending him crashing to the damp ground.

Jinao woke to a gentle swaying motion and a pounding between his ears. He opened his eyes to an upside-down world: the ground lurching above him, the darkness of the canopy far below. The Bairneater's left arm was clamped around Jinao's upper thighs as it carried him over one shoulder like a wayward child.

Valour lay tantalisingly close, swinging just beside Jinao on the Bairneater's back. But as his muscles tensed, he realised his hands were bound. The Bairneater, sensing his movements, chuckled deep within its techwork throat.

'It won't work,' the Bairneater said.

Jinao remained silent as his thoughts cycled back to what the creature had told him. His mother had nurtured him. She had kept Mizito from him as she trained him in determination and tenacity. When the time had suited her, she had released him from whatever spiritual chains she had placed upon him as a child and sent him out on the longest training session of his life. Had she involved Nirere, or was it simply good fortune that the Clan Kzani techdoctor had found him and opened him fully to the ancestral realm? The Bairneater mentioned his mother had been working with Warlord Daloya. So this was their great plan for ending the greyblood war. Rebellion. And him.

Jinao wondered if he was supposed to feel honoured. His mother's great lifework had been . . . him. His entire existence had been shaped by her scheming. He was the clay she had moulded since his birth. But he felt no sense of triumph . . . only a mounting disgust.

The truth was, Sulin Mizito had sacrificed one of her own children to her ambitions. All the times she had chastised and humiliated him; all of it had been to serve her plans, whatever those plans might be. She had hardened him like diamond, and even when Jinao achieved the impossible, invoking an ancestor to which he was not Bonded, the achievement was hers, not his. No matter where he went, there was no escaping her reach. Even if he fled, he would never be free.

Something snapped in the undergrowth over to the left, and the Bairneater dropped to the ground as an arrow sailed past. Jinao was thrown loose, and let himself roll away, then craned his neck, scanning the bush for his saviour.

A pair of yellow eyes glinted amid the dark foliage, and then a heavyset, man-like greyblood stepped forward, next arrow already nocked. Jinao covered his head as best he could with his bound hands, but the arrow was not for him. The Bairneater went rolling again as the new arrival tracked it.

It was the opportunity Jinao needed. He crawled away on elbows and knees, keeping his head low. Whatever madness was occurring between the greybloods, he wanted no part in it. He had just rounded a tree when a shape soared over him and landed before him in a spray of mud.

The Bairneater's lookout. But it was not coming for him. It sprinted away, through the trees towards the bow-wielder. Jinao lifted his head to see the two greybloods tearing at each other like lowblood drunks, while the Bairneater stood watching with folded arms. Jinao knew he should crawl into the foliage, but he was transfixed. The greybloods fought like humans – punching, kicking, blocking. The new arrival tossed away its bow and snatched a knife from its belt. Their lookout danced and dodged, then lashed out with one fist. Its reach was longer; it caught the attacker in the chin, sending it sprawling. As the bow-wielder fell, the Bairneater's lookout snatched the knife from its grip and slammed the blade through its adversary's eye.

'That's enough,' the Bairneater said, as its would-be assailant twitched and jerked. In three long strides, the Bairneater had reached its attacker's side. Jinao thought it meant to smash the thing to pieces, but instead, the Bairneater placed a colossal finger in the damaged eye socket and closed its eyes.

Jinao roused himself. The bush was dense to the left, but if he could crawl between the wide ferns and into the darkness, he might stand a chance. He had just begun to turn when a hard hand seized him by his hair.

'No you don't,' the Bairneater said, but when Jinao looked up, he saw that it was the bow-wielder that held him, though it had spoken with the Bairneater's voice. The greyblood's smashed eye was dim, but the second eye blazed bright yellow.

'Bring him,' the Bairneater said from beyond the trees, and the one-eyed greyblood hefted Jinao over its metal shoulder. And so they resumed their journey, now a silent company of four.

Jinao was too shocked to muster the energy to fight. The Bairneater had done something to the one-eyed greyblood. Somehow, it had brought the creature under its control with the touch of a hand. Why one greyblood might attack another Jinao could not imagine, but if it had happened once, it could happen again.

Jinao began to sing a folk song Jemusi had taught him, a bawdy rhyme in their father's tongue. He was not much of a singer, but he could make his voice carry if he chose to.

'Keep quiet,' the greyblood that held him said. Its voice was indistinguishable from the Bairneater's, and Jinao wondered if they now shared one mind.

'Why?' Jinao said. 'You don't want us to be noticed?'

'Keep quiet or I will knock you unconscious again. Your choice.'

They were attacked three times more that day, and on each occasion, the Bairneater let its cohorts do the fighting before it touched the captive and somehow turned its will.

'Why do they hate you?' Jinao said that night as he sat bound to a

444

tree, eating a dinner of kola nuts. 'Is it because they know you have the spirit of my mother?'

Twelve greyblood heads shot up in unison; their entire party now. 'I do not have her *spirit*,' the Bairneater rumbled from the shadows. 'And they have no idea that something resides within me.'

'They,' Jinao said, spitting out shell. 'You mean the other greybloods?'

'*Greyblood*,' the Bairneater muttered, shaking its head. 'The names you people give to things in order to delude yourselves.'

'What should I call you then?'

The Bairneater stared at him out of the darkness, visible only as twin points of glowing yellow. Jinao chewed and spat and held the beast's gaze. Finally, the Bairneater said, 'Not all of us are in agreement about how best to solve our . . . predicament. Many of us have yet to achieve free will. And some of us have forgotten who we are entirely.'

'I can remind you. You're monsters. Killers without souls.'

The Bairneater snorted and turned away.

By the time the land began to climb upwards, the Bairneater had an army of over thirty under its command. Most were of the more human-looking variety of greyblood, but there were also three canine creatures, and a lumbering, six-legged monstrosity with a slab of crystal for a head.

It was late into that morning when their convoy stopped in unison and the Bairneater said, 'This is the place.'

Hot metal hands lifted Jinao down. His legs gave way immediately, numb from so long spent hanging over the greyblood's shoulder. Then another greyblood tore the sleeve off its tunic and stuffed the stinking material into Jinao's mouth. So he lay in the dirt and stared through the trees at the clearing up ahead.

The Bairneater held itself still, apparently listening. After a time, it said, 'He is ready.'

The Bairneater closed its eyes and lifted a hand to its head. It spoke no words, but Jinao was certain some exchange was taking place. The army of greybloods the Bairneater had gathered marched forwards, drawing weapons. The Bairneater opened its eyes and then strode across to Jinao, before hefting him back over one shoulder.

A clearing lay up ahead, at the edge of a sheer drop. A scattering of people sat there at a cook-fire. Behind them stood a makeshift wooden hut. At the centre of the group knelt an elderly monk and a warrior with a familiar face. As the humans turned, realising an attack was upon them, the Bairneater strode out into the open.

'Here,' it said, addressing the monk, a man Jinao realised he also knew. The Bairneater dumped Jinao at the centre of the group of Adataliland warriors. 'He is ready for you.'

Father Boleo frowned as all around him, warriors stood unsheathing weapons and nocking arrows. 'Lord Jinao Mizito? He is the final piece?'

'Yes,' the Bairneater smiled. 'And he is ready for the Bond.'

FORTY-ONE

Boleo

'Lower your weapons!' Boleo cried, standing quickly, raising both hands. 'Please, all of you! Lower your weapons!'

'That is the Bairneater!' Nchali cried, arrow pulled back to his ear. 'It destroyed Aranduq! Stand aside and let me show it what justice looks like! *Batide! It is time!*'

The Bairneater. The creature loomed over Boleo, radiating heat, a faint smile playing across its ghastly face. The Bairneater was here, accompanied by a man who looked remarkably like First General Sulin's soulbarren son. The boy was scarcely recognisable. Gone was the lost, awkward look Boleo remembered from Sulin's funeral. Instead, the gaze that bore into him was full of angry determination. The Bairneater had bound the young man by ankle and wrist and had even stuffed a gag into his mouth. As Boleo watched, the creature dumped Jinao on the grass at his side and lowered itself to the ground.

'I suggest you do not attack me,' it rumbled, sitting cross-legged at the cook-fire. Behind it, two dozen greybloods melted out of the trees. 'My friends here will not permit you to harm me.' It lifted its eyes to the wooden structure Boleo had spent so many days erecting. 'She says you have done well, puzzling it all out.'

'Who does?'

'Sulin Mizito. It was she who sent me.'

At the Bairneater's side, Jinao squirmed.

'I don't understand,' Boleo said.

'Let me finish him!' Morayo said from behind, lifting his hands. 'In my father's name, let me take the monster who killed his oldest friend.'

'I am Nchali!' Nchali cried. 'Named—'

'Please, everyone; just wait!' Boleo said. 'Speak, creature, and quickly. What do you mean, Sulin sent you?'

'It was the two of them who sent me to finish their work. Sulin and Daloya.'

'Explain,' Boleo said, watching warily. He had his staff now – had stooped to lift it. With his free hand, he groped for his pouch.

'I was required to prepare Jinao Mizito here and deliver him to a Jebbanese monk I would find in the Busharn wastes. I was told you would know what to do once I had.'

'He does not seem a willing party in all this,' Boleo said.

'He was completely unaware of what was planned,' the Bairneater said. 'It wouldn't have worked any other way.'

Boleo squatted down and pulled the gag from Jinao's mouth.

'Don't listen to him!' the young man cried at once. 'He's insane, completely insane! He and my mother both. She – she possessed him somehow and made him train me. It was she who cursed my ancestral Bond for all those years! They keep talking about a rebellion, and that I am part of it. They're insane, both of them!'

Boleo turned. 'Captain Nchali, help me bring Jinao into the shrine.'

'Father?' Morayo said, lowering his hands. 'What are you doing?'

'This is the one!' Boleo said, pointing at Jinao. 'Him! Jinao! I told you, only a particular mind. *This* is the particular mind.'

'I won't do it!' Jinao cried. 'Whatever you have planned, I won't do it!'

Boleo leaned forward. 'Our king is invading the Feverlands. Tens of thousands will die. Meanwhile, your home city lies in ruin, leaving the Nine Lands unprotected. It's possible that there, in that shrine behind me, lies the means to reclaim Aranduq: an ancestor that your mother and Warlord Daloya – two of the most skilled, most respected, most learned invokers to walk these Nine Lands – dedicated their lives to finding. Perhaps they're wrong! Perhaps your mother was consumed by hubris! Perhaps Daloya was led astray in all his research! Perhaps I . . . Perhaps I have only seen what I wanted to see. But we have to try. *You* are our only chance to try. The things I have learned these past few moons . . . well, they have made me see that anything is possible.'

Jinao wet his cracked lips. 'You have learned things?' His gaze grew distant; with memory or with inner conflict, Boleo could not tell. 'So have I.'

'Think what you could do, if this ancestor is all they believe it to be,' Boleo said. 'You could return to Aranduq and drive out the greybloods that infest the city now. Surely you owe it to your people to try?'

Jinao looked away. 'Do I truly have a choice?'

'No,' Boleo said softly. 'No, you do not. If you won't cooperate, then I suspect the Bairneater will use force. But I believe it will go better for us all if you are willing. Please, Lord Jinao. As a last way to honour your people.'

Jinao shifted his gaze to Morayo. He swallowed, then said, 'Take me to the shrine.'

Nchali, radiating disapproval, helped Jinao to stand and remove his bindings, and together they crossed to the shrine. Boleo smiled to himself; despite all the scenarios that had played through his mind over the last three days, he would never have considered this. A named greyblood, and one out of legend at that, bringing him Sulin's Mizito's very own son. The gangly, awkward youngster he had seen so briefly at Thousand Domes had been replaced by a man of wiry muscle and watchful eye. When he entered the shrine, Jinao stopped and laughed.

'What is it?' Boleo said.

'I made something like this,' Jinao said. 'Not so long ago. The ancestors work in mysterious ways.'

Boleo sat Jinao down at the edge of the shrine, then connected the boy's tatau to the spirit wood using his staff. As Boleo straightened, he heard a stir behind him, followed by shouts of warning, and then the Bairneater appeared, almost doubling over to squeeze through the shrine's entrance.

Its eyes glittered with amusement as it took in the carvings and flowers, before finally settling on Boleo. 'I'll need a moment alone with him,' it said, 'in order to remove the curse on his link to the ancestral realm.'

Now that was interesting. So there were ways to prevent an invoker from reaching their ancestor; ways that this greyblood, at the least, knew. That was information the Nine Lands could certainly do with knowing, and with keeping from their enemy.

'We will wait outside,' Boleo said, signalling to Nchali and the others who had entered with him.

'And I warn you, holy man,' the Bairneater said over its shoulder, 'if you stand close enough to listen, I will know. I can hear your heartbeat. I can smell your deceit.'

When Boleo stepped out into the sunshine, Morayo joined him at once. 'Can we really trust a greyblood?'

Boleo's jaw tightened. 'It seems we have no choice.'

'Do you think it was human once too?'

'The Bairneater? No. No, there isn't a shred of humanity in that beast, I'm certain.'

'It is time!' came the Bairneater's shout.

Boleo slipped back into the shrine. His heart was pounding, he realised. This was it. They were going to invoke someone momentous. Someone Daloya believed powerful enough to end a war.

'Everyone spread out!' Boleo commanded. 'This ancestor killed Chinnaro Itahua and her entire company. We need to be able to contain them if they try to attack.'

'I'm sorry, what did you say?' Jinao said, looking up.

But Boleo lifted his arms. 'Spirit of Vunaji, attend me! We humbly offer ourselves to you!'

450

The moment he spoke, the network of spirit wood began to hum. Boleo hadn't even uttered a syllable in the Forbidden Tongue yet, but the connection had been made. Here indeed was a soul who had been created for this moment.

'Spirit of Vunaji, attend me! We humbly offer ourselves to you!'

A rattling started up as every length of spirit wood in the shrine began to tremble. This was good: it was a sign of how powerful the ancestor was. Beside him, Jinao's fists were clenched, his eyes squeezed tight.

Boleo knelt beside him and switched to the Forbidden Tongue. '*Spirit of Vunaji, attend me! We humbly offer ourselves to you!*'

Blue fire sprang from the shrine, along Boleo's staff, and into Jinao's arms. Jinao cried out, his body convulsing, his eyes rolling back.

'Somebody hold him!' Boleo cried, and at once Nchali was there, stopping Jinao from sliding to the floor, holding his arms to his side as he jerked.

'*Spirit of Vunaji, attend me! We humbly offer ourselves to you!*'

The air before Jinao fissured open. Ancestors, but they were going to see Vunaji come through! Beyond, Boleo glimpsed a cloying darkness – nothing like he imagined the ancestral realm to be. But it didn't matter. This was a different ancestor. A powerful ancestor. They would not reside where the others could be found.

'Spirit of Vunaji, attend me! We humbly offer ourselves to you!'

'Father, he's biting his tongue!' Nchali cried. Boleo looked round and saw that Jinao had begun to foam at the mouth. Boleo's stomach twisted. Something was wrong.

'We're nearly there!' he cried. 'Spirit of Vunaji, attend me! We humbly offer ourselves to you!'

451

FORTY-TWO

Temi

The rainy season came, the River Ae swelled to its fullest, and the bakers of Arrant Hill clung to existence. Two moons after they'd been forced to close the bakery, Old Mama Elleth grew ill. A simple fever, it seemed, but for days she could not leave her sleeping mat. Not long after that, Temi's pale-skinned cousins came down the river from Yenlund. Strange to think it had been half a year since Uncle Leke had returned to the ancestors. Jonneth, orange haired and ruddy faced, came with two youngsters Temi didn't know. Their boat contained only a fraction of their usual techwork scraps.

'Everyone's gone,' Jonneth said as he sat by Mama Elleth's sleeping mat and stroked her hand. 'Your Aunt Gilli, two of her daughters, and everyone on Uncle Tommo's farm except Tommo himself, and him with a bad leg and all. Half the town had fled by the time the monks came, so they took double and triple from some houses.' He rubbed a cloth over his sweaty face. 'It's a bad time, and no mistake.'

The monks hadn't come for them yet, and Temi supposed that was a mercy. But that surely meant it would be only days now.

Each Starsday, Harvell arrived to collect the votives, and the knot of rage in Temi's stomach tightened. Twice, she'd planned to venture

452

north to the Cascade herself, just to watch awhile, but the Chained Man soon persuaded her of the folly of that.

[Patience,] he said. [Patience. We will hear when the time comes.]

'What if it doesn't work?'

[It will work. The votives will fail. And the Seng family will blame Harvell.]

Temi had always loved the river. Since childhood, it had been her window onto the wider world. There was not a province, not a region in all the Nine Lands, whose people she had not glimpsed upon its waters. So she noticed at once when things began to change.

It wasn't just the people, arriving in their hundreds from the west, or else passing through on packed galleys to safer lands. It wasn't even the greybloods that increasingly crawled from the waters, first in ones and twos, then in larger groups. There was a tension on the river, a fearfulness she'd never experienced before. The sailors that came to the Adashola's Drum spoke of sacked villages all along the Ae. A gloom hung over them all, an impenetrable dread, and with each passing day it grew more pervasive.

'Is your plan gonna be over before the monks come?' Temi said as she trudged up the hill from market. 'Because if I'm the one what gets sent to war, I need to know my family's safe first.'

[We are close now. A few more days at most.]

Each night, she sat at the shrine and crumpled some of her rice for Uncle Leke and Tunji. She dropped some for the ancestors she'd been named after, too, and for Adatali and Tarsin.

Then one morning, as she was heading to the borehole for water, all eyes were turned west, towards a plume of smoke rising into the rich blue sky. Temi had no interest in fires in the highblood districts: the wealthy had entire contingents of bluehawks ready to extinguish blazes with water and sand. But by the time she was climbing Arrant Hill again, sweating under the heavy weight of the bucket balanced on her head, she could hear a lone convent bell – greyblood sighting, somewhere distant, and the people she passed were gathered in excitable clusters that meant big news.

'What's going on?' Temi said, stopping by a group of elders seated outside the ogogoro inn, smoking pipes and chattering excitedly.

'Didn't you hear?' toothless Old Javesh said, squinting up at her. 'Cursed water votives!'

Temi felt a thrill go through her. 'Cursed?'

'They're saying a greyblood climbed out of a votive north of the river and murdered a whole street full of people.'

'That's not it!' Yaya snapped, waving their cane at Javesh. They leaned forward. 'The greybloods was drawn to all that techwork the Chedus took, and attacked one of their inns.'

'A greyblood?' Temi said, taking a step back, a creeping chill stealing over her. He'd promised. Promised nothing would be done that could endanger her family. Promised only Harvell would be harmed.

'It's the fire what done it!' Javesh said. 'They said this cloaked greyblood ran across the city, starting fires, attacking people—'

'*Nine* greybloods!' Yaya snapped. 'It was nine different greybloods, you dense fuck. How's one greyblood gonna get across the whole city in a single morning?'

'It moved through walls,' Javesh snapped. 'It don't need to get on a bloody river boat, does it?'

'My grandchild said there was a fire,' Yaya continued, 'out in Lordsheart, exact same time a whole household of highbloods over in Lordsfury was stabbed in their sleep. And all this was right after the son of that general was quartered and his innards strewn over his garden.'

And so they argued on, but Temi had already begun to turn away, muttering her thanks and offering bows, and then heading back up the hill. She was trembling, she realised, so much that she had to lift one hand to steady the bucket.

'What do they mean, stabbed, quartered,' Temi said, her voice high and thin. 'What are they talking about?'

[I am not certain.]

'Don't lie to me!' Temi closed her eyes as several people looked her way. She set the bucket down outside the door to her family's yard and leaned on the wall. 'Tell me. Now. What did they mean?'

And then without warning, pain seized her. It was as though a hand had reached into her head and was twisting, twisting. Temi knew she had fallen to the ground, was aware of the morning sky spinning around her. But all she could focus on was the pain; the searing, world-devouring pain.

'What's . . . happening . . .?' Temi grunted, her vision clouding.

[Someone else is attempting to Bond with me.]

'You mean . . . split your soul?'

[Someone is seeking to take me from you.]

'No,' Temi muttered. Dimly, she heard the gate opening and Aunt Yeshe shouting. But even those sounds faded as another voice filled her mind. A chanting, rapturous voice, low and deep and rhythmic.

Spirit of Vunaji, attend me. We humbly offer ourselves to you.

Darkness. A darkness so absolute that for a long time she did not even know her own name.

'Temi.'

She had no form in this place, no body. Her mind was untethered; a nebulous thing. Thoughts came and went with no pattern, no logic. It was neither pleasant nor unpleasant. It was nothing.

'Temi, listen to my voice. I need you to hear me.'

A heat pressed upon her. Ah, that heat; familiar as the beating of her own heart. She reached for it, and as she did so, something flitted past her, a presence of light and warmth and churning thought, gone as soon as she had registered it was there. She turned towards it, if there was turning in this place, but the darkness had already swallowed it. She found she mourned its loss.

What had that creature been? It was no ancestor, nothing that had once been mortal. Yet she had felt its intelligence keenly. It was like a memory, she realised, or perhaps a dream: familiar and yet utterly intangible.

'Do not let them claim you, Temi. They will try to claim you, but you are mine. Do you hear me? You are mine.'

For a moment, confusion consumed her. Just who was trying to claim whom, to take whom?

Spirit of Vunaji, attend me. We humbly offer ourselves to you.

Another swell of something passed her, this slowing as it neared. She felt a glow like the sun upon her. When she looked, if there was looking in this place, she sensed an unknowable beauty, countless faces and strange, distant lands. It was as though history itself unspooled before her. It lay just beyond reach, but if she stretched—

'No!' The voice filled her mind, terrible and wondrous. 'Temi, open your eyes. Look at me.'

She opened them.

The Chained Man floated before her, though she scarcely recognised him now. His body shone with health and vigour. His hair was long and black and hung to his waist in tiny braids, and his face was strong, dark eyes aflame. But the chains that bound him had grown, too; they encased his legs like cruel armour, and encircled the bare brown skin of his arms. A collar shone at his neck; another at his brow. They bit into his flesh, and Temi reached out, meaning to comfort him . . .

The Chained Man drew back.

'Someone is trying to Bond with me,' he said, speaking aloud now. 'To take me from you. We can stop them, but it will not be easy.'

Temi looked down, then gasped as a vertiginous panic seized her.

She floated above a forest of curious, colourful plants. The ground beneath them was pale as sand, and within their gently waving fronds flitted fish.

An ocean floor.

'How can I breathe?' Temi cried.

'What surrounds you is not truly water.'

'This is the ancestral realm,' Temi said softly. 'But we're not on your island.'

'We are beneath it,' he said.

456

And Temi found that if she looked straight up, she could see circles of darkness above her – dozens of them, and from their bases hung the ragged brown roots of grasses and trees.

'We're in that ocean?' Temi said.

'In a manner of speaking. We are beneath my island. But we must sink lower still.'

'And Vunaji . . . that's you.'

A curious emotion clouded his proud features. '. . . Yes.'

'Why are they trying to take you?'

'I do not know,' Vunaji said, but his eyes shone as he spoke. 'They will not succeed. But if we simply repel them, they will try again, and again, until we are both spent.'

'What do we do?'

'We give them what they want.' Vunaji turned in a swirl of cloak and light, and then they were plunging downwards, faster and faster towards the ocean floor, until it seemed they would crash into it. Temi cried out and covered her face, but when she looked again, she found that they had passed beneath the sand, and that the fish and plants now hung above them.

Shapes flitted past her, each as beautiful and unfathomable as the golden being she had sensed before. Like glowing doorways onto eternity, each seemed filled with endless promises.

'Do not look upon them for long,' Vunaji said. 'They are as drawn to you as you are to them. You could lose yourself for ever here.'

'Maybe I want to.'

Vunaji smiled. 'Of course you want to. Now listen. This person has come seeking to Bond a being of great power, and we must give them that.'

'One of these things?'

'These? No! These are but . . . but a fraction of what is sought. Of what I am. I must take you further in. To the deepest place. It will not be pleasant. When we are there, hold on to one thought. That you must open yourself to whatever comes.'

Distantly, she heard the chanting again: *Spirit of Vunaji, attend me. We humbly offer ourselves to you.*

'Yes,' Vunaji said. 'They have opened a doorway to us. But we will send something else through it. Something to sate their desire. Something that, to their eye at least, will be indistinguishable from that which they seek.'

'There's more of you?'

Vunaji laughed but made no reply. Then he took the chain from about his waist and pulled on it. As he did so, his face contorted, whether in pain or effort, Temi couldn't tell. She watched, horrified, as the chain passed through his body and out the other side.

'Quickly,' he said. 'You must be held here or you will come untethered and they will consume you.'

Temi drifted to him. She found she could pass through the chain easily. Then Vunaji's body cradled hers, warm as a lover. The chain snapped back, clasping her to him, binding every part of her. Its weight throbbed through her, dulling her senses, pulling on her thoughts.

Spirit of Vunaji, attend me. We humbly offer ourselves to you.

'Are you ready to descend? Remember, you must open yourself to whatever you see.'

And they descended.

A rushing seized her, a great sense of falling. High above, creatures gathered to watch. Vunaji was a glorious heat at her back, an anchoring of her soul, and she found herself leaning deeper into him. The chains weakened him, she realised. Weakened him terribly.

She had expected more darkness as they went to this deepest level, but instead, a brilliant light greeted her, fading from white to blue. A city, she realised. A city rushed up to meet them, and soon it spread from horizon to horizon, an unending forest of crystal towers. When she looked up, a bright morning sky shone down upon her, filled with curious flying objects, like small settlements taken flight.

The city itself was beautiful; a pastel-coloured marvel of vast parks

458

and winding boulevards. Flowers and shrubs clung to the sides of the towers. And within the windows—

'Stay with me,' Vunaji said.

'What is this place?'

'A memory. A dream. It comforts them, in their solitude. In their exile.'

'A memory? They look like Scathed towers—'

'Be ready.'

As he spoke, a rush of energy seized her, and she looked up to see a tangle of light streaking their way in a furious tumult. A rage, a roaring despair, radiated from it, and as it drew closer, its presence was an icy chill upon her skin. It pulled on her with a touch like knives, and Temi found herself cringing.

'Do not look away! Their misery is difficult for you to bear like this but bear it you must.'

It drew closer still, filling the sky now, its voices crying and railing. Some of those voices had passed beyond intelligence into madness. As the cloud churned and roiled, its occupants pulled upon her again and again, each trying to seize her. And when they did, just for an instant, she knew them. Knew their sadness – a desperate, aching sadness, aeons old. Knew their hunger – such a pure and all-consuming hunger, a hunger they knew could not be fulfilled, not any longer. And they knew her. They always had.

'Are they ancestors?' Temi found herself saying. 'Lords, can't we help them?'

'Be strong,' Vunaji said. 'It does not matter what they are.'

The cloud filled her vision now, the city receding as it did. Hands of flame and frost groped for her. Temi cringed from them, even though another part of her wanted to reach out to comfort them, to know them, but Vunaji held her fast.

Then came a hand of deepest violet. Forbidden glyphs played upon its length. She glimpsed a leer within the cloud; a swell of pride.

'Yes! That one!' Vunaji cried.

459

Temi reached out, and the leering creature lurched towards her. No sooner had they touched than they were rushing backwards, further and further back, and the creature Temi held – it had assumed the form of a man now, his face knowing and arch – clung to her. Reached for her, almost tenderly. Cradled her face. Back and back they streaked, up through the darkness.

Spirit of Vunaji, attend me. We humbly offer ourselves to you.

'Now!' Vunaji cried. 'Now! Throw him to the voice!'

For a moment, she hesitated. The creature's eyes were like pools of midnight. She wanted to dive into them, immerse herself in them . . .

'Temi!'

Temi turned and flung her arms wide. The leering creature plummeted away, tumbling upwards and backwards, drawn towards the chanting and the mortal realm. For a moment, she thought she glimpsed a room beyond, and a highblood kneeling while a monk stood over him. As she watched the creature streak towards them, it smiled, and she felt a wave of gratitude, of elation, and then—

'Oh, ancestors!'

It was as though the being were a fruit she had plucked from a tree, only to find one half rotten and swarming with maggots. Its smile turned to a snarl. She saw teeth. She felt the press of it, the vile and corrupt.

'No!' Temi cried. 'We can't let him out. He's dangerous, he—'

'Stop,' Vunaji said, pressing his will upon her, and the familiar calmness washed over her. 'It is too late now.'

They watched until the creature they had found became a point of light in the darkness, and then became nothing. Temi realised then that the chanting had ceased. The press upon her mind, the tugging that had been with her since the moment she collapsed outside the bakery, had fled also.

'Well done.' Vunaji loosened his bonds, pulling them free enough that she could slip from his grasp.

'Did it work?'

'Yes.'

Temi turned to face him. He looked sad, and so very human. 'Those chains,' she said. 'Can't you take them off?'

Vunaji chuckled softly. 'Alas, no. I cannot. I might . . . weaken them for a time. But I cannot free myself from them yet.'

'Why'd you have them?'

'Because those who did not understand me sought to contain me.'

'Who?'

'Enough. We must go. It is not wise for you to linger here.'

Vunaji drew her up and up through the darkness, faster and faster until her vision blurred, and then she was blinking, and three faces swam before her. Yeshe, Selek and Old Mama Elleth. The three-headed beast that kept their family together.

'Thank the ancestors!' Yeshe cried, as Temi fell back into a blessed, dreamless sleep.

FORTY-THREE

Jinao

Jinao's entire body was aflame, as though the heat of invocation had spread to every pore of his skin. His vision swam in and out, but he was aware of a fissure opening before him. The chanting of that old monk, Father Boleo, seemed distant as the stars. He tasted blood as his teeth rattled in his head.

A chorus of cries rose around him as something appeared in the fissure. A clawed hand reached out, followed by another. Jinao felt the pull of it like a current, like a strong wind. He felt himself lift his own arm in response. A face leered at Jinao – little more than an outline with two white orbs at its heart. The weight of it pressed upon him. Assessing. Judging.

This was it. The moment his mother had prepared him for, ancestors curse her. Jinao extended his hand. He supposed he couldn't really fight his fate.

Then came an abrupt easing of the pressure. The ancestor's gaze shifted from him to someone else.

Father Boleo.

For one brief moment, ancestor and monk faced each other.

'Not me!' Boleo cried, his voice strained. 'Not me! You are meant for him!'

But in one swift motion, the ancestor twisted towards the old monk before plunging deep into his chest.

Boleo's back arched. His arms stretched wide. The force of the Bonding hit them all like a raging storm. It threw Jinao to the ground and blasted apart the far wall of the shrine. Boleo slumped forward and was still.

'No,' Jinao heard himself say. 'It didn't work. Why didn't it work?'

The tall Batide warrior who had been supporting Jinao released his grip. 'Father?' he said. 'Father Boleo, are you well?'

'I did everything they said,' Jinao muttered.

[The Bairneater is leaving,] Mizito said, cutting across his thoughts. [We cannot let it escape again.]

Jinao staggered to his feet. Belatedly, he stooped and grabbed a jagged piece of blackglass. The tall warrior had crossed to where Father Boleo lay sprawled across the spirit wood of the shrine. Was he dead? Jinao couldn't tell as others rushed to tend to him.

'Bairneater!' Jinao cried, stumbling towards the door.

He blundered out into the sunlight to find the Batide warriors kneeling with their backs to the shrine. Some were shouting names at the wind, as though that might help them fend off the enemy. The Bairneater rose from the cook-fire as Jinao approached, its greyblood army at its back.

'I am free,' the creature rumbled, looking down at its own hands. 'I am free of her!'

'We have to stop it leaving!' Jinao cried. He scanned the warriors for Lord Morayo and found him towards the end of the line. 'It has knowledge about us! We can't let it escape!'

Morayo lifted his hands to the skies. 'I call upon you Adatali!'

'Batide! Return!' someone yelled.

'Goodbye, Jinao,' the Bairneater said from the far side of the clearing. 'My work is complete. And everything is mine now. Her plans. Her *words*. All of it, mine.'

'Mizito!' Jinao cried, breaking into a loping run. 'Sumalong!'

His ancestors charged out of him, sprinting to either side as the Bairneater's greyblood recruits surged towards Morayo and his warriors. Jinao was aware of the sky splitting somewhere off to his left, and a rushing energy that could only be Adatali entering the mortal realm. Then a roar of new voices rose up behind him, and he looked round to see a line of people materialising out of the air. Ancestors . . . more ancestors, in battle skirts and crane helms, invoked much as Sumalong had been, but coming in their dozens. Coming, it seemed, from the Batide.

Jinao turned back to the Bairneater. His hand tightened on the shard of blackglass, the only weapon he possessed. The Bairneater swept around as Mizito closed in from one side and Sumalong from the other. In one fluid motion, it pulled *Valour* from its back.

'You never know when to give up,' the Bairneater rumbled. It brought *Valour* round in a sweeping arc, aiming for Mizito's head. Mizito dodged backwards out of range, then swung his own staff. Sumalong leapt in, one kali stick slicing towards the Bairneater's head, but the creature blocked, then struck out with its foot, sending Sumalong flying.

Jinao lifted the blackglass above his head. 'You killed my mother. My brother. You destroyed my home!'

'Your royal overlords destroyed your home.'

Jinao closed the space between them. Ten paces. Five. Behind him, he could hear the Batide and their ancestors engaging the Bairneater's horde. Jinao was nearly upon the creature itself when the Bairneater lifted a hand.

'Your ancestors turn from you,' it said. 'All of them. You are an insult to their memory.' Then it spoke a string of words in the Forbidden Tongue, and a searing pain sliced up Jinao's arm and into his head.

Sumalong and Mizito snapped from existence mid-attack. Jinao crashed to the ground, the blackglass tumbling from his grip. The Bairneater straightened, a triumphant smile upon its face.

'No,' Jinao said, dread crawling over him. 'No! You cannot keep them from me. Mizito, can you hear me? *Sumalong!*'

Nothing. Only the familiar stillness. Only the aching absence.

'Your mother's plan has failed,' the Bairneater said. 'Vunaji has gone to the wrong person – oh the irony.'

'Remove the curse!' Jinao cried. But the Bairneater was already backing away, a cruel smile on its hideous lips.

'No,' it said. 'No, I don't think I shall. I think this is better for everyone. I think this is a sign of things to come.'

'Bring them back!'

'Of course, now she has sealed her people's doom,' the Bairneater said. It gave Jinao a terrible grin as it reached the edge of the precipice. 'Best get going, Jinao. We are coming. All of us. And this time we will not retreat.'

Despair uncoiled within Jinao as the Bairneater gave the battlefield one final glance. Then it leapt out over the edge, *Valour* still strapped to its muscular back. At once, its remaining greybloods broke off their attacks and leapt past Jinao. Heading west. Heading towards the Feverlands.

Jinao was still standing at the edge, looking down, when someone's hand closed on his arm.

Morayo Adatali. Gently, he pulled Jinao away. 'That's a jump you can't make,' he said softly.

'You have to send scouts!' Jinao cried. 'Send warriors in pursuit—'

But when he looked up, he saw how poor their numbers were. Morayo had fewer than twenty Batide in his party. Two had been injured in the fighting. All looked weary and defeated as their ancestors faded from the mortal realm.

Jinao flopped down in the long grass.

'Nchali tells me the spirit of Vunaji chose Father Boleo,' Morayo said, sitting beside him. 'After all our days of trying, it chose him.'

Jinao heard himself laugh. He had come full circle. He had returned to that day on the beach, rising among a circle of the dead, no ancestor to call his own.

'Mizito, spirit of my mothers, hear me.'

After everything, one simple sentence had been all it took to sever his Bond with his ancestors, and it seemed he would forever be at the mercy of those words.

'I suppose we should be pleased,' Morayo said sourly. 'Father Boleo has fulfilled our parents' aims. We were just . . . unfortunate pawns.' He flicked silvery blood off his hand. 'I saw what you did. You Bonded a second ancestor. How did you do it? I thought it must be something only Batide can do.'

'I am not fully certain,' Jinao said. He looked away. 'Not that it matters. They're gone now. The Bairneater has seen to that.'

'What do you mean?'

'It cursed me. There are . . . *words* in the Forbidden Tongue that can curse our Bond with our ancestors.'

Morayo shifted. 'I have learned recently that we are closer to our ancestors than we are led to believe. I cannot believe a curse can truly keep us from them.'

'The curse was lifted once before,' Jinao said, 'by my mother's aide. So I suppose the Bairneater isn't the only one who knows how.'

Morayo shuffled forward. 'Then come back to Three Towers with me! My father knows many people. I'm sure one of them could find the right words, then teach them to you so that you can never be cursed again.'

'Teach me the Forbidden Tongue?'

Morayo waved a dismissive hand. 'Do you know *why* it's forbidden? To keep us all in our place. That's what I've learned, watching Father Boleo. There is nothing dangerous about it. It won't melt your mind, nor will it bring ill luck upon your bloodline. It's just a language.' Morayo gripped Jinao's shoulder. 'Come back to Ewo with me. We can learn together. And you can meet my father. Lords know, he owes you an explanation.'

An unfamiliar warmth spread within Jinao. An ally to Invoker Morayo Adatali. A guest of the legendary Warlord Daloya. An opportunity to share what he had seen of the ancestral realm. To see Sumalong again. And perhaps to find warriors to help reclaim Aranduq . . .

But then he looked over at Morayo. Clan Adatali had been part of his mother's schemes, too. And perhaps those schemes hadn't failed. Perhaps the monk could continue Sulin's work for them. In which case, what use was Jinao to any of them – the soulbarren son of a dead general from a dead city.

'I can't,' Jinao said. He looked west, over the edge, out across the wetwoods. There, on the horizon, shimmered the hazy glow of the Feverlands. He could almost feel its arcane energy.

'Why not?'

'I have to carry on. You don't need me any more, and I made a promise to my brother that I would kill the Bairneater. I don't think my mother's spirit will pass into the ancestral realm until the creature is truly dead. If it knows our parents' plans, then it has to be destroyed. Did you hear what it said: that they are all coming?'

'At least gather supplies—'

'No. Things don't go well for me when I allow others to lead me. And I don't think the ancestors ever meant for me to be an invoker.'

Morayo offered him a conciliatory smile. 'Would you like me to convey a message? I could ask them to send you soldiers, horses?'

Jinao realised then that he hadn't given Liet a thought. He'd last seen her at the clearing in the Riani mountains, when the Bairneater had first captured him. He hoped she had the good sense to find her way home.

'No,' Jinao said. 'They have enough to worry about with the river undefended. Besides, I work better alone.' Then he pushed to his feet before he could change his mind and began the slow climb down into the heat.

FORTY-FOUR

Runt

Over the days that followed, a grim picture began to emerge of a new blight that had descended on the city. All across Nine Lords, a vengeful greyblood was crawling out of uncleansed techwork; something bent on destruction, cloaked and chained, with the aspect of a man. Some whispered that it came from the ancestral realm, but that couldn't be so, because only the spirits of the slain dwelt there, and only the nine founding warlords could return.

The first reports Ba Casten's messengers brought told of a merchant household in southern Lordsheart. The throats of all who dwelt there had been opened from ear to ear. One of the servants had survived long enough to tell neighbours that a man in chains had done the deed.

Then came word from deeper in the highblood districts – clan captains, silk traders, ship owners. Runt was amazed at how far the tendrils of information extended.

One story reached them that a group of nuns had been near the creature when it emerged, and when they had tried to banish it, it had done something: turned to them and spoken some Forbidden word. At the sound of that word, the jewels in each of the nuns' heads had begun to burn, striking them down dead where they stood, leaving smoking holes in their skulls.

Then the whispers started: a pattern was emerging, of something each of the victims had in common. As some claimed that it was the will of the ancestors – punishment for using techwork known as water votives – others noted that each of the votives had been purchased from the same source. The Seng Family was large and as well respected as a Fallen Family could be: they even had members in the lower ranks of some invoker households.

The day that news reached them, Ba Casten called the entire household together in his circleroom. 'The Sengs have gone to the Council of Elders,' he told them all. 'Now when someone petitions the elders, it's a closed council. We don't get to hear what's said, and we don't get to hear the outcome. I only know it happened because I got friends in the Mbolu Family, and they got eyes and ears in everything. They might ask for money to compensate. They might ask us to confess.'

'Or they might ask permission for our execution,' Harvell said. 'Mightn't they?'

Ba Casten held her gaze until she looked away. Over the days, Runt had seen Harvell slowly start to unravel. She'd lost weight, and her normally radiant face had grown pale and drawn.

'Now, we can pre-empt whatever they might do,' Casten said, 'by explaining how this happened. So I'm gonna ask you one last time, Harvell, in front of everyone here – because this affects us all. How did this happen?'

'I simply made a mistake,' Harvell said in a rush. 'The links in the veins, sometimes it's—'

'Feyin, come here,' Casten said, gesturing to his scrawny old techdoctor – for that was what he was, Runt knew now. 'Get her to show you what she means. This is one of yours, yes? Show us what you mean about the veins.'

Feyin slid a votive across the smooth floor to her, his grin wide. Harvell lifted it in shaking fingers. 'Well, you see, this knot here, in the techwork vein—'

'Ho ho!' Feyin cried, rocking back and forth. 'Nice try, Vell! Nice try!' He glanced at Casten. 'You remember when I tried to teach her techwork, son? You remember how it went?'

'You said she got no skill.'

'No skill!' Feyin cried, as Harvell's cheeks began to colour. 'Don't matter how you tie them knots, that ain't gonna pull a vengeful ancestor out of the ancestral realm. As it happens, I don't know anything what can.'

Harvell straightened. 'I found a new technique that—'

'No!' Casten shouted. 'No!' To Harvell's right, Lakoz stood, pulling Harvell to her feet by one arm. Runt had thought him little more than Harvell's bed-warmer, but now she saw he was far more dangerous. Runt would have to watch him closely, she decided.

'What are you doing?' Harvell hissed.

But Lakoz shrugged and replied, 'The will of the ancestors.'

Only when Lakoz began to bundle Harvell towards the open balcony did she seem to register his intention. 'Stop! Stop, please! I admit it. *I admit it!*'

'Admit what?' Casten said, in a way that told Runt immediately that the man already knew.

'I don't make the votives! It's just a girl! Some girl south of the river! She makes them, and I—'

'And does this girl have reason to hate you? Hate us?'

Harvell drew in a shaking breath.

'Well, now we know our culprit,' Casten said.

'I'll punish her!' Harvell said. 'Kill her, her entire household. They have a bakery; I'll – I'll burn it to the ground!'

'Not yet you won't,' Casten said. 'It ever occur to you that someone capable of this might not be someone we want as an enemy?'

'She's nobody,' Harvell said. 'She and her family are *nothing.*'

'So you say, but Feyin here ain't never seen the like of this techwork. I even got a message from Gamani – he's back in Nine Lords, and he promised me he'd sort this mess out. But he gave strict instructions that we do nothing until he's here. So we sit tight, and we wait for him.'

'He's definitely coming this time?' Krayl said.

'Yeah, he is. So until then, we sit tight.'

After that day, Runt considered leaving. She'd noticed several of the card dealers and pillow workers slipping away, like rats fleeing a sinking ship. Even Tarn, the man who had stolen from her, went out to collect a local payment and never returned. Zee wandered their rooms like a ghost, muttering that the Quiet One, his imaginary friend, wanted them to leave too, wanted them to run, until Runt yelled at him so loudly he began to cry. Then, one morning, Krayl came to tell them all that Harvell's room was empty. Runt had expected him to send out scouts, but Casten seemed unconcerned. 'We'll deal with her later,' he said.

Runt even went as far as to pack after that, but when she emerged from her room with a bulging sack of essentials, it was to find Lakoz sitting reading to Zee. He had one muscular arm around Runt's little brother, and when he looked up, he smiled in a way that chilled Runt to her core. He didn't comment on her sack. He didn't utter a word. But his hand closed on Zee's shoulder, and that told Runt everything she needed to know about what would happen if she tried to leave the Chedus.

Every day, she heard mention of Gamani's name: she discovered he was some kind of superior to Casten himself, someone high up in the inner Chedu Family. But the man did not appear. Then, one afternoon, as Runt stood wiping down the tables in the taproom, there came a shout from outside.

'High Hill Chedus! Judgement has been given by the Council of Elders. Open your doors to receive it!'

Runt crept to the window to see a long-haired man standing in the near-deserted street. He had a pleasant, smiling face, but Runt had seen enough smiling monsters in her time to know what lay beneath their polished exteriors. He pointed left and right, sending youths in dark clothing streaking off to nearby rooftops and alleyways. Lookouts, Runt realised. Surrounding the building. At last, the Sengs had come.

Their high-collared shirts spoke of Zumae, but their faces suggested a dozen ancestral lands. If Runt had learned one thing about the Families, it was that loyalty meant far more to them than shared blood.

'High Hill Chedus!' the Seng man called. 'Open your doors!'

Runt sprinted up the stairs and into her lounge, where Zee sat reading aloud to his imaginary Quiet One.

'You remember what I told you,' Runt said. 'About how one day soon, you'd have to hide? It's now.'

'But Run—'

'Now, Zee!' Runt said, bundling him towards the wardrobe that stood against the far wall. 'You get in there, and you don't move. No matter what you hear, you don't move.'

'I want to come with you!'

'I'll be all right. There's no one that can touch me.'

'The Quiet One says we can help!'

'No! You got to hide, you hear?'

'Where's my healer?' came Ba Casten's shout from downstairs.

Runt shut the door on Zee's protests and hurried back out into the corridor.

Down in the taproom, Ba Casten and the entire remaining household had gathered. Casten had a heavy axe strapped to his back, and his fists were bound with cloth.

'I'm here!' Runt cried, running down the stairs from the mezzanine.

Casten met her at the foot of the stairs and took hold of her shoulder. It was the first time he'd ever touched her, and Runt felt her cheeks colour. It was a friendly touch. A touch between equals. A touch that said her place in the Family was now secured.

'You get in the back room there, and you stay hidden, understand me?' he said. 'You are our last defence.'

'Your time is up!' came the voice from outside.

'Get back there now!' Casten said, and Runt hurried across the floor and slipped behind the bar.

The room beyond was cramped and windowless and filled with

Casten's ledgers and records. A small, rickety desk stood against one wall. Runt crossed to it and squeezed into the tiny space under its bulk.

In the distance, she heard the sound of the main door unbolting. Of booted feet entering the Cascade.

'Casten Chedu,' came the long-haired man's voice, 'there was a problem with our last purchase from you. Where is Harvell?'

'Gone,' Casten said. 'Good luck finding her. But she claims it weren't her and that the votives was sabotaged.'

'Sabotaged?'

'Turns out she weren't the one making them. So believe me, I'm angry with her too. She's betrayed me too, betrayed all of us. And—'

'Fifty of our highblood clients are dead, as well as three of my own cousins, out in Lordsbasin. Our reputation is ruined. And now we have monks and bluehawks on our tail. Do you really expect me to believe all this was Harvell?'

'I expect you to believe whatever the fuck you want,' Casten replied. 'I'm just telling you the facts.'

Runt heard the man crossing the room; she imagined him taking Casten by the throat or perhaps pointing a blade at his neck. 'No one will buy techwork from us again. My cousins have crossed the pyre. Those things can't be undone. And can you imagine the bribes that will be required in order to appease the authorities?'

'We can compensate you.'

'I know. But, you see, the Council of Elders has decided you've crossed the line.'

She didn't hear weapons being drawn, nor any command to attack. But the room beyond erupted in cries and the crash of breaking furniture. The heavy thuds of bodies hitting the floor punctuated the tumult, and something else: a curious crackling surge that Runt couldn't name.

Runt squeezed her eyes tight as the Cloistered swirled and tittered within her. The violence excited them. The shouts of pain, the heavy ring of weapons, fuelled their joy. After a time, Runt realised her pulse

473

had slowed and she was smiling, actually smiling. The cries of the dying were sweet as a symphony as the Cloistered spun within her.

All too quickly, she heard a final thud, followed by silence. The booted feet were on the move then. Searching the house, she realised. Checking for survivors. Runt closed her eyes again and begged the ancestors to grant Zee the good sense to stay still.

When the door to the small room clicked open, Runt covered her mouth with both hands. The booted feet came right up to the desk, separated from her only by thin wood. There they paused, and for one moment of swirling terror, she thought perhaps they had heard her. But no: the clink of coins being emptied from boxes told her they had come only to take whatever of value they could find.

It was well into the night by the time Runt dared to uncurl herself and creep out of her hiding place. She pushed back the desk and wandered out into the taproom to find a landscape of slaughter awaiting her.

The Sengs had smashed the bar and all the glasses, and several of the tables too. In places, the furniture was singed, as though by fire. The bodies of Casten and Krayl and Feyin and the others were already drawing flies. They lay sprawled within the dark circles of their blood, eyes staring, mouths agape. It only occurred to Runt then that she might be too late. Perhaps their spirits had been untethered from their bodies for too long for the Cloistered to call them back.

Runt hurried across the blood-soaked floor and headed up the stairs and back into her rooms.

'Zee!' she called. 'Zee! Zee, come out!'

A moment later, the door to the wardrobe cracked open and Zee's brown face appeared.

Runt pulled him into her arms, the solidity of his body a balm. She swallowed against the tightness in her throat and buried her face in the soft scent of his neck. 'You're all right. You're all right,' she said. 'Thank the ancestors you're all right.'

'Is it over?' Zee asked.

'It's over,' Runt told him. 'But I got work to do. You – you stay here and don't come down, you hear?'

'Is everyone dead? Did they kill them all? The Quiet One heard weird noises, Run. Chanting, and—'

'Don't worry. Nobody's dead.' Runt lifted the pendant out from beneath her tunic. 'They got the best healer in the land.'

Back in the taproom, Runt surveyed the carnage again. Twenty in all lay dead. The floor was black with their blood. Casten had called her their last defence, and he was right. Runt closed her eyes and savoured that thought. If she stood there long enough, the High Hill Chedus would be no more. Their building would rot and decay. The name Casten would be forgotten.

Runt drew in a deep breath, inhaling the metallic tang of death. She had never felt more powerful. More alive.

[We can heal them.]

[Fix them.]

[Make them better.]

'Yes,' Runt said. She strode over to Casten. His sightless eyes stared at the ceiling. His twisted body didn't seem quite so imposing now.

The Cloistered chuckled excitedly and swirled out into the world.

FORTY-FIVE

Temi

[Temi. Temi, wake up.]

Temi blinked. Brilliant light angled through the shutters of the family sleeping room. She lay still, relishing the simple joy of being back in command of her own body.

'She's awake!' Mama Elleth cried.

Temi's head throbbed and her throat ached, but she felt rested. And strong. Aunt Yeshe appeared, clucking over her, pressing water to her lips. Temi's cousins crowded the doorway.

[Temi, listen to me. We need to leave.]

'How long've I been asleep?' Temi asked, glancing through the window.

'All night,' Yeshe said. 'It's nearly highsun.'

A clanging reached her ears, distant and crisp.

'Is that the convent bell?' Temi asked.

'Yup. Been going for a while,' Yeshe said.

'That sound's for greybloods.'

'Probably just more of 'em coming out the river. You know how many we get now. The bluehawks'll take care of it.'

'Temi!' came a cry from the street. 'Temi of the Arrant Hill bakers!'

Cold terror twisted Temi's stomach as she recognised the voice.

476

Harvell.

Temi crawled to the window, pulse quickening as she remembered Javesh's words. Her votives had killed dozens, even highbloods. A greyblood had crawled from them to tear people apart.

A woman stood out in the street. Even without seeing her face, Temi knew Harvell was not herself. Her shoulders hunched defensively, and stains marred the delicate blue of her torn dress. She looked thin and haggard, a far cry from her usual self. And she stood completely alone.

'Temi!'

'It's that bloody Chedu woman,' Yeshe muttered. 'She's early.'

Temi pushed to her feet. 'Auntie, please – please stay inside. I need to talk to her.'

She slipped out into the family room, her head spinning from the sudden movement.

'You said we'd be safe,' Temi muttered as she padded across the stone floor. 'You promised we'd be safe!'

'You're awake!' Selek said, looking up from where she knelt at the shrine. 'Don't you think—'

'Auntie, lock the door behind me and stay inside, please.'

'Why?'

Temi strode through the silent bakery and out into the heat.

'I'm here,' Temi said, looking south down Arrant Hill. If she could just lead Harvell away . . .

Harvell turned. Her face was manic, her eyes wild and bright. A single tuft of hair had become dislodged from her sleek, dark tail. It was this tangle of hair, more than anything, that unsettled Temi. She had never seen this woman look anything less than immaculate.

'You think you're so clever, don't you?' Harvell said. The men playing cards outside the ogogoro inn turned to watch. Others stopped, or leaned out of windows, even as some hurried to clear the street.

'You said she wouldn't come for us,' Temi whispered.

[Remain calm. We will discuss this later.]

'What is it you want?' Temi said to Harvell.

'Don't play the fool with me,' Harvell replied. 'You sabotaged the votives. Now they are dead. My cousin. Three Sengs. Their highblood customers!'

Temi steadied herself on the wall. 'S-so many?' The world seemed to be closing in again. 'I had no idea that—'

'You've started a war, you know! The Sengs blame us for the loss of their kin, of course, but they'll think somebody put us up to it. They and the Mbolus are arguing about who's responsible. We were their *allies*. Now the bluehawks and the monks will be tracking us! They'll say we've broken the Invoker Pact, and—'

'I didn't know!'

'What I don't understand is what you were hoping to achieve!'

Temi swallowed. 'He said the votives would fail. I didn't think anyone would get hurt.'

'He who?'

[And fail they did. We did not stipulate *how* they would fail. In time, you will thank me. I did what you did not yet have the strength to do yourself.]

'I didn't know!' Temi shouted.

Harvell continued to advance. She stood scarcely two strides away now.

'Listen to me,' Temi said, holding up her hands. 'I didn't know this would happen. It was someone else. An – an ancestor. If I could just explain—'

Harvell lunged, fast as a cat, closing the space between them in a heartbeat. Temi only had time to register movement before the other woman's fist caught her chin, the force snapping Temi's head back, sending her reeling. Temi staggered, her head ringing, her neck blazing. Then Harvell was on her. She swept her legs out, then slammed Temi down into the dirt of the road.

The breath burst from Temi as she hit the ground. She heard distant shouts – Yeshe? Selek? She tried to call to them, to warn them off, but she could not draw breath. Harvell's hands closed around Temi's neck, squeezing, squeezing, her face a mask of rage.

[Fight back. Throw her off. This woman has sought to control you, to control your family. Do what needs to be done.]

But instead, Temi closed her eyes. She thought of Tunji, waiting for her in the ancestral realm. She thought of her father, of Leke, and of all the people she didn't even know, whose lives were now gone because of her blindness.

Temi went slack. She looked up at Harvell and tried to convey her sorrow, her shame. She let her hands flop to the dirt and begged the ancestors that it would be quick.

There came a roar of rage, and then Harvell tumbled sideways. Instinct took control, and Temi drew in a rasping, painful breath. Kierin stood over her, shirtless, his milk-pale face screwed up in anger.

'Wait—' Temi tried to call, her voice hoarse.

She pushed herself up on her elbows. Harvell lay groaning in the dirt. Yeshe stood before the bakery, kitchen knife in one hand. Behind her stood Selek and Old Mama Elleth and Old Baba and Uncle Amaan.

'Get out of here,' Kierin growled, limping towards Harvell, his broken arm cradled against his torso, 'or so help me, I'll smash your brains out right here on the road.'

In response, Harvell threw her hands into the air. 'Ancestors, hear me!' she cried, and Kierin paused, confusion knotting his heavy brow.

'Blood of the deep, hear me!' Harvell said, rising shakily. 'Chedu, hear me! Rise from your swamp to defend those who remain!'

A murmur stole across the watching crowd as Harvell's tataus glowed like sunlight.

'Kierin, get away from her!' Temi hissed as she pushed to her feet.

'Is she an invoker?' Kierin said.

'Just get away!'

Out of Harvell's body spilled a cloud of light that resolved into a towering man. His tightly curled hair hung in long hairlocs down his muscular back. He wore a beaded war-skirt of red and blue, and where he stepped, the ground turned to viscous black liquid, an oily pool that spread and spread. Before him he swung a mace that shimmered with ever-changing glyphs.

'Temi, run!' sounded a scream from off to the left, and Yeshe came charging forwards like a vengeful ancestor, her kitchen knife held high. She sped towards Harvell, and Harvell turned almost lazily, the ancestor she had invoked turning with her.

'*No!*' Temi screamed. She reached out, knowing she was too far away to stop what would come next. As she did, all her fear and anger pooled into the tips of her fingers, burning, bursting forth.

Vunaji leapt out of her outstretched hand so fast Temi was dragged after him and onto her knees. He coalesced in a swirl of cloak and chains, materialising between Yeshe and Harvell, both arms outstretched.

Yeshe staggered to a halt, naked fear on her dark face, the knife still held high over her head.

'Of course!' Harvell said with a bitter smile. 'Of course! Now everything makes *sense*! No simple slum rat could make techwork such as that. Now I understand. But your ancestor has no weapons. He looks scarcely able to hold himself upright!'

It was true. Though Vunaji had placed himself between Harvell's ancestor and Yeshe, he looked a small and desperate thing before the mighty warrior Harvell had invoked. He held out one skeletal hand, as though his will alone might fend off the one who advanced. Temi had always dreamed of seeing an invoker. But she had never imagined it would be like this.

'Go *inside*!' Temi screamed at Yeshe, but her aunt didn't move.

'I'm going to tear your pitiful ancestor apart,' Harvell said, trembling where she knelt with outstretched arms. 'Then I'm going to flay the skin from your back. And your family here are going to watch me.'

FORTY-SIX

Runt

The Seng Family took possession of the Cascade two days after
executing the High Hill Chedus. Runt had watched them from
the alleyway opposite, arriving in a dozen rickshaws, the long-haired
man from that night at their head. He stood surveying the building
while his lieutenants swarmed up the steps carrying crates.

Bringing Ba Casten and his household back from the edge of the
ancestral realm had made for slow healing. In was near midnight before
they regained consciousness, and mid-morning the following day
before Ba Casten was strong enough to stand. When he'd seen Runt
squatting beside him, holding a mug of water, he'd gripped her shoulder
and grinned.

'You done good, girl,' he had said, his voice low and slurred. 'You
done good.' He'd turned to the others, still splayed out in their own
dried blood. 'The Sengs'll be back for this place! If the Council of
Elders gave 'em leave to settle things with us, then that includes our
assets.'

'Where will we go?' Krayl growled, holding his head between his
hands. 'I— What was that?'

'What?' Casten snapped.

'I thought I heard . . .' Krayl lowered red-rimmed eyes. 'Never mind.'

Perhaps it was due to coming so close to rejoining the ancestors, but as the rest of the household began to stir and work movement back into muscles, a distracted fearfulness seemed to hang over them like a cloud. The furtive glances, the sudden starts and questions to voices no one else heard . . . It was the Sengs, Runt decided: the fear that the Sengs would return too soon and find them alive. All the same, she thought of Zee and his imaginary friend, the Quiet One, and she wondered.

At highsun, with the streets quiet, they made their escape. South of the Cascade lay an old warehouse owned by a local brewer. It took half the afternoon for Runt to help each of the Chedus limp out of the building and across the yard. The warehouse was large enough to house them all and filled with barrels of drink from across the Nine Lands.

That night, the warehouse owner had arrived with two of her daughters, burly women all. Ba Casten had risen from his hiding place, knife in one hand.

'This can go two ways,' he said, smiling in that predatory way he had. 'You keep quiet and take the payment we give you when my superior comes to collect us – fifty suns, if you bring us food and water, not to mention the friendship of the Chedu Family. Or, you and your strong girls die here. What's it to be?'

Krayl had risen then, and Lakoz and the others, and though Runt had wanted to rise too, she stayed hidden. Her face was unknown, meaning she was free to come and go, and that was invaluable to them now.

The brewer had lifted shaking hands and said, 'Didn't see nothing. We didn't see nothing.'

Then they had backed out of the warehouse, and by sunset, two dozen rice balls and some Yennish ale found their way to the warehouse doors.

Days passed. Harvell did not return. Gamani, Ba Casten's superior, did not arrive. Runt knew they could not risk crossing the city, not with the Sengs now controlling most of the region and their scouts and allies swarming everywhere.

'He'll come,' Casten told them all each night. 'Gamani'll come. So you sit fucking tight and you keep quiet.'

Then one morning, when there came a tap at the door that usually indicated their food had arrived, Zee muttered, 'The Quiet One says to run, Run.'

'We need to talk,' came a well-spoken, unfamiliar voice.

Casten waved them all to silence, then stood slowly, knife in one hand. 'Who's there?'

The door creaked open and a man slipped into the warehouse: a beggar, by his look, despite his clipped accent. A torn travelling cloak hung from his malnourished frame. But his eyes, sunken deep within his skull-like face, shone with alertness as he scanned the warehouse.

'We got no food,' Krayl said. 'Get going.'

But the beggarman lifted his head and his curtain of black hair fell away from his face. He had the look of Cagai about him and bore terrible scarring to both arms. 'My name is Lord Jethar Mizito,' the man said quietly, 'and I am tracking a thief.'

'Don't care who you are,' Casten said, stepping round from behind the barrels. 'Get out of here.'

The stranger didn't move. 'I'll say it again. My name is Lord Jethar Mizito, son of First General Sulin of Cagai. And there is a thief in your midst. Bring them to me now.'

Casten strode forward, his hands loose in the way they always were when he was preparing himself for a fight.

'I heard of Lord Jethar,' Casten said. 'Died rains ago, somewhere out at sea.'

'I heard he come back!' Feyin called out, grinning. 'Heard he lost his mind and slit his own throat.'

'Let's see your throat,' Casten said, pointing. 'Come on, son. Lift your chin.'

The beggarman was trembling, Runt realised, as though with a terrible fever. Or with rage.

'We have to go!' Zee hissed, pulling on Runt's hand.

Runt snatched her hand away as the beggarman took a shuddering step forward, then another, as though his travelling boots were filled with glass. 'Please!' he said, his voice a hoarse whisper now. 'Please, just do as I say, or—'

'Let me slit his fucking neck!' Krayl cried, leaping to his feet.

'I'm warning you!' the beggarman shouted, staggering back against the door. 'Please, just—'

Before he could finish, his body gave a great jolt and a blinding light streamed out of his eyes and mouth. Casten took a step back. The man claiming to be Jethar spoke no words, nor did he lift his arms. And the silvery form that coalesced before him wasn't one of the nine warlords of old.

The creature that bled into the mortal realm was winged and luminescent, with the subtle suggestion of a feminine body. Though she seemed naked, every contour was smooth: no nipples, no genitals. She tossed back hair that undulated like river plants, her doll-like face split in a knowing smile.

'All of you,' the creature said, in a musical, highblood accent, 'sheathe your weapons, or I shall tear the hearts from your bleeding bodies!'

Jethar stood hunched and shaking. 'Do as she says!' he said. 'Please! She is incredibly dangerous!'

'What is this?' Feyin said, hobbling forwards. 'That ain't Mizito.'

'No, I am not,' the winged shadow said, smiling her broad, feral smile. She lifted higher above them, her iridescent wings a shimmering blur, her arms spreading like a dancer. 'You may call me Aan.' She pointed one clawed finger at Jethar. 'And this is my human. He does my bidding. Threaten him, and you threaten me. Now listen closely. Something has been stolen from me. Something I was charged with protecting. I have traced its *essence* to this building. So I ask again. Which of you is the thief?'

'No one calls the Chedus thieves!' Krayl said, and he threw himself forward.

'Wait!' Feyin shouted, but it was too late. The winged creature's head

484

snapped around. She raised an arm, and a streak of light surged from her hand. The others leaned away, shielding their eyes, but Krayl was too slow. The light caught him by the throat, and he stopped dead. His eyes bulged as he clawed at his neck and the band of light closed tighter and tighter. Casten remained unmoving, his face a mask as his son's skin turned blue and the whites of his eyes red. Then, finally, the creature tossed Krayl away. He crumpled where he stood, his neck blackened and flopping.

The Cloistered crowded Runt's mind, pushing against her pores with gleeful urgency.

[We will heal him.]

[Fix him.]

[Make him better.]

'Not yet!' Runt hissed, but they sped out of her, swirling into the air, and though no other soul reacted, Aan rounded on Runt at once.

'You!' she cried, her face coming alive.

The Cloistered streaked past, giggling and rolling, encircling Krayl's limp body. They formed their vortex around him, spinning faster and faster, but it was Runt Aan focused on.

'So the warrior-woman was right,' Aan said. 'You have already drawn them. And I have found my thief.'

'I didn't steal from nobody,' Runt said, standing.

'That storage device. Around your neck.'

Runt's hand went to her pendant. 'My baba gave it to me.'

'How many have you already recruited? Ten? Twenty?'

'Recruited?'

'Answer me!' Aan screamed, lurching forwards, her skin changing from silver to red to purple. 'How many?'

And as though in response, Krayl came to his feet, a terrible grin crossing his smooth face. The band of light that had strangled him fell away.

'We healed them,' Krayl said, in a voice that was his own and yet not. A second, ageless voice crossed over his. 'Made them better.'

For a moment, a laughing blue face seemed to flit across Krayl's features.

'Healed them,' Old Feyin said in his own dual voice.

'Made them better,' said Lakoz.

'Made them much better,' Zee said, rising beside Runt, his eyes now glowing yellow.

'Zee!' Runt cried, cold fear closing around her heart. 'Zee, what are you doing?'

But she knew at once that the thing stepping out from behind the barrels was not her brother. It wore his skin, yes, but the smile was not his; those yellow eyes were not his. And she knew to whom they belonged.

'What have you done?' Runt said, gripping the pendant. 'What have you done to them all?'

[We healed them.]

[Made them better.]

[Much better than they were.]

'You've changed them!' Runt cried. 'You changed my *brother*!'

[They lost their lives.]

[So they join ours.]

[And we continue the Great Hunt.]

And as one, the High Hill Chedus stood and out of their bodies melted swirling blue figures.

'No, Zee!' Runt said as her brother's eyes rolled back, as the Cloistered swept towards Aan and Lord Jethar. Aan extended both arms, her hands turning to blades, and as the first Cloistered struck, she sliced through its torso. The creature melted from the world in a burst of smoke and laughter.

'Cut one of us, and we become two,' a Cloistered said. 'Cut two, and we become four. How to defeat us all?'

Runt seized her brother by the shoulders, then snatched her hands back; beneath his thin tunic, his skin blazed like fire. Aan, meanwhile, swept upwards, her body expanding until it covered the entire ware-house ceiling. Runt glanced across at Jethar, hunched and trembling by the door. He was the lynchpin. Whatever it was he'd invoked, this Aan creature, she was tethered to him.

Runt was half his size, but Jethar could scarcely hold himself upright. So she dived forward, slamming into him, knocking him through the door and out into the narrow dirt road beyond. Together, the two of them rolled across the ground in a tangle of limbs.

In a heartbeat, Runt found herself pinned. However distracted Jethar was, he was a warrior and an invoker, and she was only a runt. From somewhere, he produced a tiny blade. Runt felt the bite of it in the skin of her neck. It was nearing highsun, and the alleyway was crowded with people. Runt felt dozens of pairs of eyes on them. Jethar loomed over her, trembling, sweat standing out on his brown brow, his face creased in concentration.

'Die!' Jethar growled, between clenched teeth.

But as he spoke, the Cloistered surged out of the warehouse, not in their usual merry circle, but in a storm, one after the next. They slammed into Jethar, each one knocking into him and driving him back. Soon, Jethar was sent sprawling, and Runt scrambled backwards, her breath grating in her throat.

This time, Runt wasn't the only one who saw the Cloistered. All around her, people murmured and pointed, and many slipped away into their huts or into the shadows between buildings.

Then Aan appeared, encircling Jethar protectively with her wings. When the Cloistered threw themselves against her, they fizzed from existence. But always with a laugh. Always with a cackle of pleasure. Always with the sense that this was a game.

'Enough!' Aan cried with a burst of energy that drove everyone back and gusted down the narrow road like wild wind. She hovered above Runt as Jethar struggled to his feet.

'They're protecting me, ain't they?' Runt said, as the Cloistered giggled within her.

'Surrender,' Aan said. 'Or I will destroy this region.'

487

Runt stood. The entire street watched her now: the dockworkers and marketgoers and elders . . .

They watched her in fear and wonder. And it was glorious.

'No,' Runt said, straightening. 'Go. Before I let them kill you.' Runt had no idea whether the Cloistered were capable, but it was clear that Aan feared them and what they could do. Runt had watched Aan dispatch them with ease, yet they had kept coming. As though they were impossible to truly destroy.

'Very well,' Aan said. 'You have been warned.'

Aan plunged into the ground, momentarily brightening the dirt with a silver-white glow. For an instant, Runt saw a flash of Forbidden glyphs play along the road. Jethar turned and began shuffling away. Runt realised then that Krayl was at her side, hefting his knife in both hands.

'Want me to get him in the back of the head?' Krayl said.

[Unwise.]

[Foolhardy.]

[We cannot defeat her.]

[Cannot fix her.]

'No,' Runt said. 'No, that thing will only attack again.' She looked up at her audience and realised how many of them she knew. Kalan, the Yennish fruit-trader, flashed a nervous grin. Ayoda, who worked in the teahouse, jerked his head in a nod of approval. Many were already turning away, some with nervous laughter, others in bursts of conversation. To them, she had dispatched an attacker, and they were thankful.

'He's just some lunatic,' Runt called to them. 'He won't be back. We'll see to it.' She glanced over at the warehouse then. Their cover was blown now, surely. The Sengs would know where they were hiding. They would have to leave, and quickly. If—

A scatter of shouts sounded at her back, followed by the ring of breaking glass. She turned as the ground trembled beneath her feet.

'You hear that?' Krayl said. 'It's the convent bell.'

Runt heard it; the steady, rhythmic clang that meant one thing: greybloods.

The crowds came to a stop again, murmuring worriedly, while shoppers scooped their fallen wares back into baskets.

Then a young girl carrying water screamed as the ground before her split apart. A silver hand thrust out through the fissure. Then a second. Figures dragged themselves free of the widening gap, sloughing off dirt as they rose. Their rusted eyes flickered, coming to life in the sunlight. Their techwork heads turned Runt's way.

'Greybloods!' someone screamed in the distance. 'Greybloods!'

Everywhere Runt looked, more fissures yawned open in the road. The greybloods that crawled out were battered and rusted and stiff. But as the sun touched their skin, their strength seemed to grow. Though they looked ancient, vigour returned with every passing moment.

Runt cried out as a face appeared in the ground beneath her toes. She staggered backwards, grabbing Krayl's arm. 'Aan sends her regards,' it said, then reached up and seized her foot.

FORTY-SEVEN

Temi

A single thought pulsed through Temi's mind as she stood watching Harvell's ancestor advance: he was not one of the nine warlords of the invoker clans. *Chedu*; that's what Harvell had called him. Temi had thought that was just a Family name, some word in one of the province tongues. But no, this was the name of Harvell's ancestor, the towering man with long hairlocs who stood beside her now. As the street cleared and Temi's neighbours fled back into their homes, only Yeshe remained, eyes narrowed determinedly, knife still gripped in her hand.

'Auntie, please go!' Temi cried, her voice tremulous and high.

Then Harvell grunted, and Chedu launched himself forwards, bringing his mace down in an overhead strike. Vunaji lifted his arms, and where the mace struck, sparks of light flew. Then another blow came, and another, each driving Vunaji down until he was kneeling.

Temi felt each blow like a burst of fire in her gut. Vunaji pulled on her mind, a force draining the energy from her. Harvell advanced, a terrible leer on her face as Vunaji fell. Chedu raised his mace high, glyphs trailing in its wake as he prepared the killing blow. Yeshe pressed herself to the bakery wall, her eyes wide.

'All those people you hurt,' Harvell said. 'All the lives you took

490

with your clever little plan. All for nothing. Because you die here. As does your family.'

A dizzying panic overcame Temi. It was true. In her folly, she'd caused the deaths of people she'd never even met. She should have known there could be no peaceful end to Harvell's control. She should have known the woman would not go quietly. Temi closed her eyes, pushing down the looming horror. She had caused all this. And it was right that she should pay the price.

Then, from Vunaji, came a strange sound, low and raw.

Laughter.

He was laughing, deep in his chest. Harvell paused, head tilted in confusion.

'Do you not recognise what I am?' Vunaji said, lifting his head to Chedu. 'Have your minds truly been that warped?'

And to Temi's astonishment, Chedu took a step back.

Temi had never imagined that invoked ancestors could show emotion, least of all horror, but that is what she saw on Chedu's face. He lowered his glimmering mace. Behind him, Harvell trembled, her brow furrowed with effort as she thrust her hands forward in frustration.

'What are you *doing*?' she shouted at her forebear.

In one smooth motion, Vunaji leapt. He sprang at Chedu with the grace of a cat. He seized the larger ancestor, both his chained hands pressed to Chedu's face. Beneath Vunaji's touch, Chedu twitched. Vunaji's hood fell back to reveal the ruin of his head. He looked nothing like his regal form in the ancestral realm. Thin, white braids flew from his ravaged scalp, and the cords of his neck stood out as he squeezed and squeezed.

Harvell screamed, and Chedu screamed with her, collapsing as he did. The swampy blackness he'd spread faded from the world. Temi stared in terrible fascination as Chedu's body flickered, changing form beneath Vunaji's touch. It lost cohesion, collapsing into a curious mass of light and then a knot of shifting glyphs.

Then Vunaji plunged forwards, enveloping Chedu entirely. Consuming him whole.

491

It was as it had been that day, seemingly an age ago, when Vunaji had first consumed someone in the ancestral realm. Then, as now, he seemed remade by what he had done. He arched his back as his body grew and flickered. With a cry of triumph and rage, he swung his arms apart and his blue chains snapped, then fell loose at his side. His cloak, no longer rags, shimmered a liquid black and gold. His hair remained white, but was thicker now, and new skin stretched across those knotted muscles. Even his face seemed more human as he turned to Temi, his smile ghastly and triumphant.

On the dirt road, Harvell moaned and cradled her head. 'What have you done?' she cried. 'Where is Baba Chedu?'

Vunaji drifted towards Temi, hands outstretched. His chains hung loose at his side, clinking as he moved. The flesh that covered those fingers looked almost as hale as it had in the ancestral realm. He glanced at Harvell, mouth curled in distaste. 'What a pitiful creature,' he said. Even his voice sounded richer. 'What shall I do with it?'

Temi drew in a trembling breath and let Vunaji take her hand. His fingers felt hot beneath her grip. The energy that pulsed from his chains ran up her arms into her head.

Harvell cowered, looking from Temi to Vunaji, her cheeks streaked with tears.

'Go,' Temi told her. 'Run. I told you; I didn't sabotage the votives. *He* did.'

Harvell nodded vigorously as Temi spoke. Outside the bakery, Yeshe lifted her knife, thin arms trembling. Temi could not remember ever seeing such fear on her aunt's face. But she realised with shock it was not directed at Harvell. It was directed at her.

'You took my brother from me,' Temi said. 'So I've taken your ancestor from you. Let's call it even.'

'We didn't kill your fucking brother!' Harvell screamed.

'*Liar!*' Temi took a step towards her, pushing down the urge to seize Harvell's head and smash it to the ground. 'Go. Now!'

Harvell scrambled to her feet, stumbling once and then turning east

492

up Arrant Hill. But she had not taken ten steps before Vunaji said, 'You are too merciful. Allow me to assist.'

And though Temi cried out, she was too late. Vunaji twisted his free palm upwards and light bled from it. Chedu stepped from that light – or what had once been Chedu. A wild-eyed ruin charged into the world, half-formed and screaming. His skin shifted with jumbled glyphs. When Harvell turned, he lifted his mace.

'Baba?' Harvell said, stumbling, eyes wide with horror.

In one sweeping motion, the thing that had once been Chedu brought his mace down and cleaved Harvell in two from shoulder to groin.

Temi fell to her knees, her gorge rising as the two halves of Harvell peeled away from each other. A cascade of entrails slopped on the dirt road in an inhuman heap. The only sound was the distant tolling of the convent bell, and Temi's own pulse, hammering in her ears. Harvell's delicate blue dress was red now. One eye stared down Arrant Hill, as though still seeking escape. The other seemed fixed glassily on Temi.

Temi swallowed down bile, but Vunaji, still holding tight to her fingers, jerked her back to her feet.

'Control yourself. Do not let them think you weak. Show them only strength.'

As he spoke, his heat pressed upon her, and her terror and disgust receded. Instead, a curious detachment took their place. Some deeper part of Temi pushed back against the bubble of feelings that were not her own, but the part that controlled her gaze took in Harvell dispassionately. Perhaps this was justice. Perhaps this was inevitable. That dispassionate part of her found something almost beautiful in the splay of blood and innards; something almost intimate in the way what was once inside was now smeared across the road for all to see.

'So much blood,' Temi muttered.

Then she looked up and saw Yeshe and Kierin, standing hand in hand, and the world came crashing down upon her again. She had killed someone. Perhaps not with her own hand, but she was responsible. Elleth and Old Baba watched her from the doorway, faces tight with dismay. Temi wanted to run to them and be enfolded in the comfort of their arms. But their silence, their revulsion, hit her like another blow.

'Don't ever do that again,' Temi said. 'Enter my head like that . . . Ancestors, what have I done?' She thought of the way Harvell had turned to her ancestor, so trusting. In that moment, she had seemed like a child. What power could turn a person's ancestors against them? Nothing natural. Nothing good.

Temi rounded on Vunaji. 'I didn't want to kill her.'

'Yes, you did,' Vunaji said. 'We both know what was in your heart. And it was right that she should die.'

Temi jerked her hand back, but Vunaji's grip tightened, hot as the heart of Elleth's oven. His heat bore into her skin, sending lines of energy coursing up her arm.

'Look at me,' he said. 'Look! It was necessary.'

She looked. 'You planned all this,' she said, understanding rising within her like a great wave. 'Didn't you? *Didn't you!* You knew Harvell would come here. Just as you knew all them people would die. You planned everything from the beginning, just so she'd invoke and you could take her ancestor.'

Temi tore herself free and backed towards the bakery while Vunaji said, 'I did what needed to be done for us both.'

'You're a monster,' she hissed. 'You disgust me. I wish I'd never—'

Her words were cut short by distant screams, and a crash from within the bakery. Beneath her bare feet, the ground shifted. Those few people who remained out in the street stared not at Harvell's mangled corpse, but down the hill. Off to the west, near the border with Lordsheart, a line of smoke rose above the rooftops, like a sandstorm lifting towards the sky. The ground rumbled again, knocking the fruit from a stall, tipping over the buckets of water by the ogogoro inn.

'What's happening?' Temi said.

'Must be a fire,' Kierin said, joining her.

'That ain't no fire,' Yeshe replied, her expression fierce.

The rumbling continued, and as the sandy cloud lifted, Temi saw it left something strange in its wake. A slate-grey line, running across the whole district.

'Someone is raising the wall,' Vunaji said. He stepped towards her, now a cloud of light and smoke, and slipped back into her body. Temi shivered as she felt Vunaji crawl back into her mind, a weight behind her eyes. Despite the betrayal she felt, the disgust, the anger, something else swelled within her now. Relief. A sense of rightness, that they were one again.

'There is no wall in Lordsgrave,' Yeshe said, marching over, knife now hanging at her side.

'That is a wall,' Elleth said. 'Look! It's lifting out of the ground.'

[We need to leave. Now.]

'I told you, I ain't going nowhere,' Temi said.

Then she heard Kierin's distant shout and spotted him up on Bakery Mount, overlooking the house and the street. Temi darted after him, climbing the thin grass hand over hand until she too stood above her yard, beside the ruined Scathed wall and the sheer drop down to the Ae.

A perfect ring had formed around the district of Lordsgrave, a circle of rising dust enclosing the district whole. It cut through the city like one of Elleth's pastry circles.

'Who's doing this?' Kierin said. 'The bluehawks?'

[No. Temi, we must leave. Hide.]

A cry split the air, mournful and inhuman, followed by the echoing blast of a horn. Shouts of alarm rang up and down the street below as, for the second time that morning, her neighbours retreated to their homes.

[There. Look.]

Temi looked north. A new column of dust had appeared, moving steadily down Iron Street: the dust of dozens – perhaps hundreds – of feet, marching in formation.

'Greybloods,' Kierin grunted. 'We've been sealed in to die!'

'Get down here, you two!' Yeshe called up from the street below. 'We'll be safest in Old Baba's workshop. That's why these old buildings have cellars. We wait there, and ride this out. There's no need for panic. The invokers'll come and they'll drive the greybloods back.'

Temi followed her cousin back down the hill. The street was deserted, save for Harvell's steaming corpse, laid out like some macabre offering to the ancestors. Silently, they stepped into the shop.

'We ain't safe here,' Kierin said. 'Didn't you see? Someone's put a fucking wall around Lordsgrave, and the greybloods are on this side.'

'There's probably only a few of them,' Yeshe said.

'That weren't a few. You see the size of that cloud they sent up?'

'When do greyblood armies ever attack Nine Lords?'

They passed through the main room and out into the yard, where Amaan stood helping Elleth down into Old Baba's workshop. They would be safe there, and at least they were all together.

Temi turned to Kierin. 'When did you last see my ma?'

He shrugged. 'I dunno. Two days ago, maybe? Down by the docks.'

'Don't you worry about your ma,' Yeshe called over. 'She can take care of herself.'

'How many greybloods are there?' Temi said, coming to a stop.

[Are you asking me?]

'Yes, I'm asking you. You knew it was a wall. You knew they was coming. So how many are there?'

[That is . . . unclear.]

'Don't lie to me!' Temi shouted, and Yeshe turned towards her as Kierin climbed down into the cellar. It was just the two of them now, standing out in the yard. In the distance, there came another greyblood cry. 'Tell me now: how many greybloods are coming? Twenty? Forty? Tell me!'

'You're talking to him,' Yeshe said, stomping over. 'Ain't you? That ancestor you invoked.'

[Five hundred.]

'Five *hundred*?'

[The exact number is unclear without me getting closer. There may be eight hundred the size of you. Or fifty the size of this house.]

'Temi,' Yeshe said. She closed the space between them and lay a gentle hand on her arm. 'If five hundred greybloods are marching across Lordsgrave, we need to hide. You know what Old Baba always says. They come for the metal and the techwork. They don't care about us none, not unless we get in their way. Come on. Your ma'll be fine.'

But Temi found she couldn't move. Five hundred greybloods. An army. Surely so many couldn't have crawled out of the river, not here in the heart of all things.

'You saw what he can do,' Temi told her aunt. 'The one I invoked.' She swallowed. 'I'm gonna find Ma.'

[It is not safe for you.]

'Then tell me where she is! You owe me that much! You lied to me, over and over. You put my whole family in danger.'

[I can detect living people, but only given time.]

Yeshe stood watching, her expression sorrowful. 'Temi, your ma'll be fine. If there's one thing that woman knows how to do, it's survive.'

'How far away are the invokers?' Temi said softly. 'You said it takes time to detect living people. But you can detect ancestors. How many are coming? When will they get here?'

[They won't.]

'What do you mean?'

[The nearest *invoker* is four leagues away. They are not moving in this direction. None of them are.]

'The bluehawks, then. Where are they?'

[I've told you; I cannot detect—]

'Come on!'

[I cannot detect living souls. But I can detect how many souls have crossed the newly raised wall into your district. None have crossed it.]

'Then nobody's coming in? Nobody's coming to help us?'

[No one is coming to help.]

'Temi, it's time to go,' Yeshe said.

'I can't,' Temi said, backing away.

'I'm not leaving you!' Yeshe whispered, her voice hoarse.

'It's OK,' Temi said. 'I won't be hurt. Didn't you see Vunaji fight? I'll get Ma and bring her straight back.' She slipped out of her aunt's grip and backed away. 'I've hurt a lot of people,' she said, her throat tightening. 'People I didn't even know. The ancestors turn from those who don't make amends.'

Temi turned away from Yeshe, still clad in her apron, dark eyes sparkling. She ducked through the family room and into the shop. But as her hand closed on the handle of the door, a searing pain knifed through her head.

'Not again,' Temi muttered, as her vision began to mist. 'Are they trying to take you again?'

[I cannot let you put us in unnecessary danger.]

'What do you . . .?' Temi's voice trailed off as understanding seized her.

[I could take all the energy from your body. Here. Now. Force you to sleep.]

'Do that, and you'll lose my trust for ever.'

[It is for your own good.]

'No,' Temi muttered, grinding her teeth, pressing her forehead into the door to keep from passing out. 'No.'

[I am sor—]

'I said no!' Temi shouted. She closed her eyes, thinking again of the creatures she had seen in the ancestral realm. The pitiful, needful creatures. She had felt their power, yes, but also their yearning. Also their desire to join to her; their need for mortal connection. 'You do this,' she said, 'and I will never help you again. Ancestors turn from me, but I'll throw myself into the Ae if I have to. Then you'll be alone.'

[Temi—]

Temi clenched her jaw, focusing on Vunaji's heat, there in the tips of her fingers and the base of her skull. They said nuns could detach

498

their minds from their bodies and suppress their own pain. If nuns could do it, why not she? 'You are not my master,' Temi said. 'We work together.'

She pressed her will upon him, filling her mind with only one thought: open the door. All that existed in the universe now was her desire to open the door. If she could do that—

[Very well.]

The pressure between her ears eased and fell away. Her vision misted, then swung back into focus. Temi inhaled, straightening. Had it been the weight of her resolve, or something more? Had she actually managed to deny him?

Temi pulled open the door and stepped out into the street. Already, the heat of highsun was upon them. The greybloods would be at their strongest.

'If we're going to be a partnership,' Temi said, 'if I'm going to help you get your freedom, then things have to flow both ways. I've done terrible things so you can further your power. All I ever wanted was to sell bread and keep my family safe. You brought me into . . . whatever this is. You made it about more.'

[I cannot fight five hundred of those abominations.]

'Who's asking you to?' Temi said, then set off down the hill.

FORTY-EIGHT

Runt

As metal fingers closed around Runt's ankle, the street descended into chaos. Everywhere she looked, people were fleeing, while others climbed onto roofs or barricaded themselves into huts. Runt growled and stamped down with her free leg, but it was like trying to fight rock. The greyblood's grip on her tightened and tightened until she screamed.

Dozens of greybloods now crawled free, and more poured in from between the buildings. The Techwork Graveyard, she guessed, out there beyond the collapsed wall: thousands of techwork parts lay among the ruins. Shells, she had thought, but it seemed even shells could be dangerous. Had these greybloods been lying in wait all this time, dormant through the millennia?

The holy ones taught that the greybloods came only for metal, but that was not what Runt saw. Everywhere she looked, greybloods were setting upon the terrified people of Lordsgrave: a girl, desperately swinging her basket; two elders wielding lengths of wood; a young man, being dragged through the window of his hut.

[We can heal them.]

[Fix them.]

[Make them better.]

500

Krayl drove his knife down into the hand that gripped Runt's leg, and she was free. As she turned to thank him, a second creature leapt at them from the next building.

'Get inside!' Krayl cried, swinging his blade at the greyblood. He pulled at Runt with his free hand. 'Come on, we need to get inside!'

Runt stared, unable to move. All around her, people scattered or fought, but Runt's gaze was caught by something more alarming, rising over the vista of bamboo rooftops. A dark line, lifting between the buildings, lifting inexorably higher and higher.

'It's the wall,' Old Feyin said, hobbling out of the warehouse. 'My Old Baba told me the myth of the Lordsgrave Wall when I was a nipper.'

Runt closed her eyes. She had never called upon the Cloistered before. But she'd never thought they could do anything more than heal wounds. 'How many of you are there?' she said. 'Dozens? Hundreds?'

The Cloistered tittered coyly as they swirled within her.

[Many.]

[Many upon many!]

A greyblood grabbed at Runt, but Feyin swung his stick, batting it away. Bodies already littered the street. The boy who delivered vegetables. Two elders. The beggar with the lame foot. She could do something. Whatever the Cloistered did to those they healed, it made them stronger. And yes, it seemed they also became the creature's hosts, somehow allowing them a gateway into the mortal realm. But surely that was better for people than death? All the Cloistered had ever done was heal and defend. And yet she could not banish the sight of Zee, her baby brother, his eyes glowing yellow . . .

'Do it again,' Runt told the Cloistered. 'What you did when Aan attacked me. But spread out this time. All of you.'

[What do you mean?]

'Make a protective area!' Runt snapped. 'But larger. Not just round me, but round this whole street. Push the greybloods back. Do it now!'

[She will know.]

[She will come.]

501

'I don't give a shit. Just do it, or so help me I'll find her myself and let her take my life.'

Krayl's eyes rolled up, as did Feyin's. A Cloistered streamed from them both, and from the open door of the warehouse behind. They joined hands, like children at play, and became formless streaks of blue swirling all around her. Runt, standing at the heart of the tumult, turned towards the road.

'Did you see how they looked at me?' Runt said, unable to stop the grin. 'All them people, when we faced Jethar? Did you see how they loved me?'

Runt went to the beggar first; Lichuen, that was his name. When she reached the man's side, she knelt down and lifted his chin.

'I can heal you,' Runt murmured. 'Make you better.'

She closed her eyes, and a single Cloistered sped out of her. It streaked forward gleefully, then plunged into Lichuen's chest. When Lichuen lifted his head, his eyes gleamed yellow, but his smile was full.

Yes. This was better than death.

Runt walked on in her bubble of protection, stepping from body to broken body. The youth who lit lamps at sunset. The fruit-seller's son. The song-teller who sometimes came to the Cascade. She worked her way south, darting from person to person, offering her hand and a quiet word. After a time, she no longer heard the fighting or the screams or the ceaseless ring of the convent bell. All that existed were the Cloistered and whoever she knelt beside at that moment. She was almost surprised when she realised she had reached the Riverside Bridge. This was Ida Square, the great statue of Warlord Adatali looming over the abandoned marketplace below.

[She is here!]

[She is back!]

Runt looked round to see a figure striding across the square towards her. Lord Jethar Mizito. The Cloistered protecting Runt cringed away as he advanced. He looked stronger now and more upright. Runt closed the space between them and offered him her most contemptuous smile.

'Get out of Lordsgrave,' Runt said.

'Your face is familiar,' Jethar said. 'Where do I know you from?'

'You don't know me,' Runt said, then grinned and added, 'But you will.'

'Surrender,' Jethar said. 'She has given you just a taste of her capabilities. Surrender now, or she will kill everything that lives in this district. Make no mistake; she can do it.'

'I have an army with me,' Runt said, and lifted her hand. She had no idea if the Cloistered would know her intent, but they did, and it was glorious. She had left a sea of groaning, slowly healing people in her wake, but blue forms rose from them now. Up and down the street, in the alleyways and between buildings, the Cloistered melted into the world, their smiles mocking, their yellow eyes agleam.

'You can't touch us,' Runt said, the thrill of it coursing through her body. This was what the Cloistered had meant when they said she was chosen. This was what her baba had meant. She had been born for this moment. She had been preparing for it her whole life. Perhaps Baba had left the pedant to protect her – that had to be it. Perhaps he had known only she possessed the will to use it properly.

The trill of a horn cut across her thoughts, sounding from the river at her back. And drums, advancing, already very close. Instantly, Runt's sphere of protection fell away. Cloistered streaked back to their human hosts in their dozens, popping from existence with peels of excited laughter. To Runt's left and right, wounded people sat up in confusion. They blinked as though waking from a deep slumber. For one chilling moment, Runt thought it was Aan's work. But no: a look of terror had seized Jethar. And neither he nor Aan, hovering above him, made any move to attack.

FORTY-NINE

Temi

Temi sprinted down Arrant Hill, the heat of the sun like a whip on her shoulders. The stillness terrified her more than the distant cries of the greybloods. Every rickety door stood closed, every window boarded. A child's thin cry rang out in the distance, but that was the only human sound she heard. When she looked out over the sea of bamboo rooftops, the city looked almost peaceful. It was only when she lifted her gaze to take in the dark line of the newly risen wall that it became clear everything had changed.

'Where'd that wall come from?' Temi said.

[It was always here. Though most had forgotten it.]

She turned west onto Iron Street, sweat trickling down her back. The teahouse loomed above her, but her mother did not sit in its shadows, nor did Temi find her outside the carpenter's hut or in the alleyway beside the pillowhouse. The only people she saw at all were the beggars – Enji, who saluted her with a bottle; scarred Chaakin. They showed no fear, but then these were souls for whom fear was as familiar as the hard ground at night.

'You seen Kerlyn?' Temi asked Old Loteth, a toothless beggar swathed in rags.

'Temi,' he muttered, 'you got any coin?'

'No coin, Teth. Sorry. You seen my ma?'

'No, girl. You should go home. Ain't safe out.'

'And you should go to the convent. They'll hide you in the catacombs, if you don't let on you're drunk.' She left the beggars standing in a muttering huddle and continued on down the hill.

A desperate hope kindled within her as she ran on through streets emptied of all life. Perhaps Vunaji had been mistaken. Perhaps the greybloods had turned back. Or perhaps, miraculously, they had already been defeated.

Then, at the junction with Cur Road, she saw one. At first, she thought it was a human, stuck outside their own door. But the creature that tore at the boarded window was too tall, and its movements too fluid. Its left arm had no skin at all, formed instead from a tangle of techwork veins. Its bright eyes glowed yellow from within the shadows of its face when it turned towards her.

Temi froze, her heart hammering as another appeared, crawling down over the roof of the Yennish alehouse. With a creeping terror, she realised they surrounded her – emerging from the shadows, descending from the rooftops . . .

[The vermin you see are barely sentient,] Vunaji said. [Walk on calmly, and do not hold their gaze.]

And so she moved, walking slowly, though every instinct within her screamed that she should run. From the corners of her eyes, she saw them prising open doorways and hacking at windows. Every alleyway she passed seemed to contain more of them, climbing walls or chittering to each other. It was as though she had stepped through an invisible border, was no longer in Lordsgrave but some hideous parody of it.

When she heard the first sounds of fighting – a woman's scream of rage, followed by the ring of something shattering – Temi turned instinctively towards it.

[We came here only to find your mother. Didn't we?]

As Temi hurried on, she passed more fighting. A man barring the doorway to his home; elders leaning out of their windows, hacking at the greyblood that scaled their walls; a band of youths armed with kitchen knives, standing over a twitching, sparking body. The enemy might have come in numbers, but the people of Lordsgrave fought back, and they numbered many too.

'Where are the invokers?' Temi said, her throat tightening.

[You expect them to save you?]

Outside the convent, nuns swung fighting sticks, side by side with their raggedy orphans. Temi scanned their ranks for Sister Poju, but the old nun was not to be found.

'Has anyone seen Kerlyn of the Arrant Hill bakers?' Temi shouted above the racket. 'Yennish Kerlyn, with yellow hair?'

'Get into the catacombs!' one of the older nuns called. 'They're everywhere!'

Only the river remained now. Temi headed east, past the shanty built by people who had fled Cagai and Vushem. They stood shoulder to shoulder along the street, armed with household objects. The grey-bloods had already driven them from one home, and their hard eyes said they would not permit it to happen again.

The newly risen wall loomed over the rooftops to her right, a mass of pure blackglass. Shifting Forbidden glyphs played along its length. High on its battlements, she glimpsed movement. Bluehawks, marked by their bright blue tunics, their gold-tipped spears glinting in the sun. Perhaps, at last, help had come.

Before her, the road opened out onto a riverfront swarming with people. The bridge beyond, the only crossing in the district, lay half collapsed. She ran towards the new wall, where an opening crowded with people led out into the city beyond.

'Ma!' Temi called at the crowd, scanning streaming faces lined with rising panic. '*Ma!*'

A woman with a baby strapped to her back grabbed her arm. 'We need to get out! They're coming down the riverfront!'

'You seen a beggar-woman with yellow hair?' Temi asked.

The woman dropped her hand. 'We need to get out!'

Temi watched the woman join the throng massing at the wall, an all-consuming desperation uncoiling within her. Because ancestors, her mother wasn't among any of the faces that streamed by. Her mother was nowhere. If she lay bleeding in a darkened alley, if the greybloods had carried her off, Temi would never know.

Shouting punctuated the low rumble of the crowd. The press of people at the wall had stopped entirely now. Temi craned her neck, trying to see what caused the screams. Then she spotted it. Something was descending across the opening, sealing the only way out of the district. The clamour at the wall rose in a crescendo of terror and disbelief.

'Let us through!' someone cried. 'Please let us through!' And then a dozen voices took up the call. Some leapt at the sheer side of the wall in attempt to scale it. Others pounded on the blackglass with their fists.

[We must seek safety,] Vunaji said, as still more people poured in from the riverfront.

'Where?' Temi cried, gesturing at the wall. 'There's no way out!'

Up on the wall, a dozen bluehawks looked down at the crowd, gold spears still strapped to their backs.

'Where are the invokers?' a voice called to them. 'We're trapped down here!'

One man had gained the top now and was hauling himself over with his right leg. But a bluehawk set upon him immediately, jabbing him with their spear until he went plummeting back into the crowd.

An inhuman cry rose behind Temi and she turned to look back the way she had come.

Greybloods swarmed the road she had run down, spilling out between buildings and alleyways and over rooftops. They flowed like a living river, a chittering, bristling mass. A distinctive greyblood marched before them all, armoured entirely in blackglass. Its angular, featureless head topped a body of long, jagged limbs. Glyphs streamed across its torso. The surrounding greybloods appeared to crowd towards it, as though drawn to its fearsomeness.

507

Cries of alarm rippled across the crowd as realisation leapt from person to person like fire. They were trapped here: trapped between a greyblood army, a river and a solid wall, while still more people poured in from the riverfront.

'There's greybloods here!' a man screamed up at the bluehawks. 'Let us through!'

'That's an army,' Temi said. 'A fucking army.'

[I can see.]

'The children!' one woman called, holding her squalling baby up to the wall. 'Leave us to die, but take the children!'

A dozen others took up this cry, and more children were lifted into the air, while others shouted threats or brandished bribes of tawdry jewellery.

[These people are doomed. Help is not coming. They mean nothing to your king, nothing to your highbloods and your so-called invokers.]

Temi glanced at the alleyway to her left. It was as good a place as any. If she was lucky, she could ride out the massacre that was to come. But the cries of the people of Lordsgrave cut through her thoughts. Many had already begun to turn away from the wall, away from the ruined bridge and the growing crowd. Some pushed children behind them, while others tugged at the rubble of ruined buildings, seizing lengths of woods, twists of metal . . .

Where are the invokers? That was what the man had said. And the ancestors turned from those who did not use the gifts they had been given.

'Can you do it again?' Temi said. 'With Chedu. Bring him out. Can you fight again?'

[Yes,] Vunaji said, his voice almost a purr. [But I cannot fight them alone.]

'What about all them others? The other creatures you took from the ancestral realm. They're still in there, like Chedu.'

[Yes. However, bringing them all out will be . . . taxing for you. It will leave you unprotected.]

But she didn't miss the hunger in his words. And she found that she

508

shared it. Something had been kindled within her now. She would die here today, she knew that. Standing where she was, she would be among the first to fall.

But she would not go without a fight.

Something moved near Temi's feet and she jumped back before recognising the misshapen, mangled form of No-Cat, padding through the panicked crowd as though heading for a nap.

Vunaji swelled with amusement. [Perhaps you will not be unprotected. Look.]

'That's the bloody cat!'

[That is no cat, as you well know. Do you recall the words of your grandfather upon the hillside? He said this device is a doorway. It can be no coincidence that the contraption has been following you around.]

'I don't understand!'

[It is a doorway, Temi! Open the doorway!]

As the greybloods charged forward and the people around her roared their fury in response, Temi squatted down. No-Cat padded forward and lifted its chin. On instinct, Temi reached out and scratched the hot, clumpy fur. 'Ancestors, this is stupid,' she muttered. 'I don't see how a doorway can—'

Something clicked beneath her fingers, a tiny bone-like protrusion. At once, light spilled out of the gaps in No-Cat's matted fur, where the techwork beneath blinked and hummed. A glowing line bisected the creature's back and No-Cat splayed apart, its body unfolding like a book. A cloud of darkness bled out of its torso. Temi's throat closed as she glimpsed grainy figures beyond.

[Call to them, Temi!]

'Call to who?' Temi cried, but she knew at once. Ancestors smile upon her, because she knew. 'I don't know how to do it!'

[You do not need to know how. They are part of you! Call to them, and they will come!]

Temi swallowed against the tightness in her throat. 'Please,' she said, keeping her eyes upon the grainy figures. 'Help me.'

As she spoke, the figures solidified, as though made tangible by her words, her need: a man in a travelling agbada, looking up in confusion; a young woman, braids piled high on her head. Hawk-faced Raluwa and tiny, fierce Sede. Temi could see little of the shadowy place in which they dwelt, but ancestors be praised, it was them.

'Temi,' Uncle Leke said, stepping out into the world. 'Where . . .? What . . .?'

Temi pointed at the advancing greybloods. 'Can you help me, Uncle? I need—'

A greyblood leapt towards them, and Leke swung his arm in a hook, knocking it out of the air.

'Where are we?' he said.

'The river. I need your help. Can you stop them reaching me?'

Leke nodded, and the four of them spread out around her, asking no more questions, knowing only that she was family in need. Temi lifted her arms high and Vunaji's heat flooded her scar. With a surge of fury and exhilaration, he leapt out into the world.

Behind her came cries of *invoker* and *ancestor* as Vunaji lifted his hands, unchained now. Chedu charged out of the air beside him, hair-locs flying, mace raised above his head. Next came the winged creature with green-blue hair, the very first to be consumed, in a streak of laughter and wings. As Vunaji stood amid the chaos, his cloak billowing, the ones he had taken peeled out of his body and charged to meet the horde. With each life he brought into the mortal realm, Temi felt part of herself diminish. Her vision misted. Her pulse thrummed in her ears. She was aware of Leke shouting, of Abeni stooping to lift a metal bar. Temi dropped to one knee as the city, the world, receded.

'*Protect your cousin!*' Leke cried as the slaughter began.

FIFTY

Temi

While battle swirled around her; while people fought in loose, wild-eyed groups; while Vunaji stood untouched amid the tumult, his circle of invoked spirits cutting down greybloods left and right, Temi squinted up at her uncle's face, her heart soaring.

It was him. Leke. His tidy beard. His close-shorn hair. His eyes, wide and kind, as Tunji's had been. Every time a greyblood leapt in, Leke's fist jabbed out. He and her cousins had one metal bar between them, which they tossed from hand to hand.

Then a greyblood sprang from behind Temi and brought its club down in an overhead arc. Leke, just turning, took the blow full in the face. Temi cried out as Leke's body faded to mist. But No-Cat, still splayed apart on the ground, jerked, and a moment later Leke came charging back through the doorway, a grin spread across his face.

Temi worked her mouth. She wanted to thank him. She wanted to ask him a thousand questions. Was he truly dead? Had he reached the ancestral realm? Did it hurt when they struck him, when they killed him and he came back?

Greybloods swarmed everywhere: descending from rooftops, leaping up from the river. There could be no question that these had come to kill. Whatever Aunt Yeshe claimed, this group wanted human blood.

But around Temi, the people of Lordsgrave fought. Youths and elders and parents with infants strapped to their backs. They fought with all that they were.

Bodies already dotted the riverside, the dead and the dying. Temi knelt on the ground, sweating with the effort of remaining conscious. The need to keep breathing in and out had so consumed her that she did not spot the trio of greybloods until they set upon No-Cat as a group. One swung out with a club, and though Abeni shouldered into it, the second caught No-Cat square in its splayed innards.

Instantly, Leke, Abeni and the others winked from existence.

'No!' Temi croaked. She knelt alone on the roadside now, without even the strength to call for help.

'Who are you?' one of the greybloods said as it advanced. A man, it seemed, its ragged cape unable to fully hide the gaping techwork of its arms. But as it lifted the club it had used to strike No-Cat, Temi felt another presence at her side.

Sutesh the apothecary, leaning on their stick as they hobbled forward. They wore an orange lungi, and yellow cloth bound their scrawny chest. She had not realised how many tataus they had, far more than most in Lordsgrave. Their necklace of metal charms shone in the highsun light.

When they lifted their hand and uttered a word in the Forbidden Tongue, the ground beneath Temi began to shake. As they danced, slowly spinning and chanting in a tight circle, glinting things crawled out of the earth: angular, slicing creatures like lizards, which thrust up through the dirt, tiny jaws tasting the air; silvery arachnids; flecks of blackglass that were little more than jagged shards. Out they poured, streaming forward. Some set upon the greybloods who came for Temi, crawling, burrowing, sending their victims staggering back with screams in their techwork throats. Others spread out to join the battle. Most looked no larger than Temi's hand, but their claws gleamed dangerously. They scuttled forwards, marching to meet the encroaching enemy as Sutesh chanted and spun.

Temi swallowed. Sutesh was a techdoctor, as she supposed she had always known. Sutesh's voice lifted in song, the smooth, rolling syllables of the Forbidden Tongue tumbling over each other like waves lapping the shore. As the scuttling creatures swarmed over the nearest greybloods, slicing and ripping, Sutesh squatted down to examine No-Cat.

'Fixable,' they said, as though looking at a broken bowl and not a living doorway to the ancestral realm. 'But I'll need my tools.'

Another greyblood leapt in from the left, and Sutesh swung their stick. The attack caught the creature in the shoulder, exposing blinking innards within. Then one of Sutesh's crawling things burrowed into the greyblood's eye, releasing a gout of silver fluid, and the creature fell to its—

Temi felt the wind of movement behind her and knew it was too late for Sutesh to protect her from the blow to come. All Sutesh could do was cry out in alarm as the length of wood swung downwards. It caught the side of Temi's head, sending her crashing back, and for several long seconds the world was a hazy muddle and a ringing in her ears.

When she sat up, she realised the tightness in her chest and muscles had gone. The blow had severed her link with Vunaji. Temi pushed to her feet, only now noticing the soreness in her hands and knees. Her head throbbed, but the rest of her body coursed with energy now that she could move. As she looked around, she realised how few humans remained. A diminishing circle of people had taken on the black-helmed greyblood. A dozen corpses lay at its feet as it fought and roared. Some of those who remained looked barely out of childhood, and one was an elder with a missing arm.

'We cannot win here,' Sutesh said, swinging their stick.

The black-helmed greyblood had fallen to one knee as great gouts of fluid steamed from its leg. Sutesh's creatures burrowed into this opening and set to peeling back the plates of its skin. Whatever they were doing seemed to have disrupted the greyblood's mind. Its limbs thrashed wildly and after a moment, the creature fell still altogether, before gracefully crashing sideways.

As Temi lifted her head, preparing to bring back Vunaji, she noticed a gilded barge sliding through the river towards the far bank. Warriors in gold stood upon its deck, alongside what looked to be a highblood litter. A strange, shifting light played over the rooftops on the far bank in a spreading haze.

'Is that a royal barge?' Temi said. She turned, looking for more witnesses, but all she saw were the wounded and those who aided them. Many greybloods had fallen too, but she saw far too many human bodies. Those few who fought on stumbled with exhaustion, their attacks laboured and slow.

Temi heard a cry off to her right and turned to see a circle of grey-bloods clustered around someone – still alive, from the way their bare legs twitched. Temi grabbed a nearby length of wood and staggered forward, her heart throbbing in her ears. If she could subdue one greyblood, distract the others, their victim might be able to escape . . .

The greybloods turned, and Temi came to a stop. That was no human lying there, but another greyblood. Her brown legs seemed as much flesh and bone as Temi's own, but her torso, torn open, was a nest of shimmering silver veins. The eyes that rolled in that small head glowed with the yellow light of the enemy. The greybloods were helping a friend, Temi realised: two strove to fold the creature's innards back in, while a third had connected to her by the veins in its own wrist. And one . . . one wept as she looked on, silver tears sliding down her grey cheek.

Temi let the length of wood fall, then backed away as two of them drew to their feet.

'I don't want to hurt you,' Temi said, lifting her hands. 'I didn't realise . . .' She trailed off, not certain what she had meant to say next. Didn't realise that greybloods were capable of compassion? Didn't realise that they might care for one another? The one who wept brushed her cheek and then stood. She was impossibly lithe, silver from her bald head to her slender feet, and dressed in the tight black armour of the desert. One of her companions babbled something in their language, but the weeping greyblood ignored them, advancing slowly. Her hands twitched, and then just like that, she was armed, a jagged blade in each of her black-nailed hands. Her eyes blinked ceaselessly, never leaving Temi's face, radiating emotion. Hatred, Temi realised. Radiating hatred aimed at her.

'I'm going!' Temi said, stumbling over the body of an old man, keeping her hands lifted. 'I'm going!'

In a heartbeat, the weeping greyblood stood before her, knife pressed to Temi's side. She hissed, catlike, and looked Temi up and down before muttering something unintelligible.

'Please don't hurt me,' Temi whispered, her breath catching. She let heat pool into her hands. She could call Vunaji back. Let him bleed out of her and destroy them all. And yet she hesitated. 'I only want . . . only want to help my people,' Temi said.

'As do I,' the greyblood replied, tilting her head like a bird of prey. She jerked, then laughed as Temi flinched in fear. 'You people. You disgust me. You are pathetic. Worms, grubbing in the dirt.'

'You kill our elders,' Temi said, her eyes flicking to the man she had tripped over. 'You destroy our homes.'

The greyblood looked over her shoulder and rattled off a series of words, and her companions laughed. Their language sounded strangely like the Forbidden Tongue. Their fallen comrade had been healed, Temi saw. She sat up now, twisting life into her hands, while another greyblood bound her leaking torso with a length of cloth.

'You kill *our* elders,' the weeping greyblood said, pressing the knife until Temi felt the sting of blood. 'You destroy *our* homes. You will not be content until you have annihilated us all.'

'You attack *us*!' Temi said, a single tear leaking from her eye.

The woman laughed, hard and sharp. 'Because most of us do not have a choice,' she said. 'Because it is what we were made to do.' Then she paused, her eyes flickering in a new pattern. Her gaze sharpened as she studied Temi's face. 'What – what is that?' She tossed her knife away. Long fingers brushed Temi's cheek: searingly hot, but so like the touch of real skin. Temi willed herself not to flinch, willed herself not to look away as the woman studied her longingly. 'The Intelligence that resides within you.' The greyblood's hand jerked and she seized Temi by the neck. 'Give him to me.'

'Give you what?' Temi croaked.

The greyblood's grip tightened, cutting off Temi's words, forcing water from her eyes. 'The Intelligence you have drawn from the underplane. I have never seen his like. Give him to me.'

'I—'

'Give him to me, or I will crush every bone in your body and extract him from your corpse. You do not deserve such magnificence.'

'Vunaji,' Temi rasped, heat pooling in her hands, 'is mine.'

'Give me the Intelligence,' the greyblood said, 'and perhaps I shall let you live.'

And then she froze.

Temi swallowed. She waited for the greyblood's hand to seal off her breath. But the creature remained frozen.

It was a trick. Some ploy to terrify Temi further. Yet the greyblood stood motionless, her head still cocked to one side. Temi slid her gaze round. Yes – the creature's companions had frozen too, one caught mid stride, another poised with his sword raised. Sutesh stood amid a circle of unmoving attackers that were as still as the standing stones of the Yenlund moors. And there on the rooftops and in the alleyways, every greyblood stood lifeless as the dead.

FIFTY-ONE

Runt

'No . . .' Jethar muttered. He winced, his hand going to his head as Aan faded to nothing.

For a moment, Runt felt a swell of triumph. But as the drums grew louder, she realised Aan had not fled because of her. Something was happening. The greybloods had fallen still. Every greyblood within sight had become motionless as rock. Just as suddenly as Aan had brought them to life, it seemed they'd fallen dormant once more. As the drums drew closer, Jethar looked left and right in panic.

Then Runt spotted a golden barge, mooring just before the broken bridge. People leaned out of windows and down from rooftops to watch. A swathe of warriors in brilliant gold warpaint leapt onto the bank, some bringing with them a wide platform. On the deck, Runt spotted a litter, its golden curtains drawn. A score of strong warriors lifted it and began to march it down into the square.

Runt looked left. Jethar, beside her, had collapsed to his knees as though in pain. As the litter advanced, the drummers on the deck sounded out a crescendo, and more nuns and monks than Runt had ever seen in her life spilled over the gunwales onto the bank.

Jethar had begun to crawl away on hands and knees, moaning as he dragged himself across the ground.

'Stop that person, in the name of your king!' came a voice from the litter.

Why Jethar didn't simply call upon Aan, Runt could not guess. But when the golden warriors intercepted him, he fought with his fists. It did not take them long to beat him to the ground. Meanwhile, a man had descended from the litter, a soul unlike anybody Runt had seen in her life. He was tall, and as graceful as a reed, and wore a narrow skirt of embroidered gold. The brown skin of his bare chest and arms was covered with luminous gold tataus. The patterns within them shifted under Runt's gaze. Sometimes she saw waves, and sometimes the sun. She saw an old man, stooped in contemplation, and then a powerful young woman, her head held aloft. Finally, Runt lifted her gaze to the newcomer's face. His eyes were of a gold so penetrating she could not bear to look upon them. There could be no question: this was a member of Clan Ahiki.

'Invoker Jethar Mizito,' the Ahiki said, and the crowd murmured as they took in the battered Jethar anew. 'We are Princen Hetemam Ahiki, Arbiter of the King's Justice, and his great-nephew. You are to accompany us back to the Garden to answer for your crimes.'

'What crimes?' Jethar growled, from where the warriors held him pinned to the ground.

'The murder of Invoker Cantec Itahua. And the abandonment of your sacred duty to carry the spirit of Mizito in your veins.'

'I didn't abandon anything,' Jethar said. 'It was her. All of it her.'

'Her who?' Princen Hetemam said.

In answer, Jethar smiled grimly, and Aan's terrible light bled out.

She lifted into the air and spread her wings, her body radiating power. She looked magnificent in those moments: Runt could not deny it. Dozens upon dozens lined Ida Square now, with more arriving every moment. No matter the danger, no matter the attack that had just taken place, an Ahiki princen had come to Lordsgrave. It was an event that would be talked about for decades.

But when Aan's light fell upon them, many cringed away. Even the royal warriors could not tolerate her for long. Only Princen Hetemam Ahiki, his golden eyes blazing, seemed unimpressed. He lifted his head, his long black braids spilling down his back, his jagged golden crown catching the sun. He was the most majestic, most arresting soul Runt had ever beheld. There was no hint of surprise or fear on his youthful face as he stared.

'Who are you?' Hetemam said.

Aan lifted higher in the air. 'I am fire and water,' she said, her body expanding as she spoke. Within the smooth, pearlescent skin of her body, shifting visions started to appear. Stars and the greatest depths of the ocean. Lush forests and the vastness of the desert. 'I am life and death,' she continued, filling the square. 'I am mercy and vengeance. Do as I say, and you shall live. Defy me, and you die.'

Hetemam stepped forward. He was close enough now that Runt could see the thick kohl that rimmed his glowing eyes. 'You are to submit to—'

'I submit to no one!' Aan thundered, surging downwards, her face streaking through the air to stop a handspan from the princen's. 'That human has stolen from me.' She extended a hand in Runt's direction. 'I come here seeking what is mine. I have no quarrel with anyone else. And you have no idea of the danger you are in.'

Princen Hetemam's gaze flicked to Runt, taking her in, dismissing her at once. Runt painted on her most gormless expression and glanced behind her in a display of apparent bemusement.

'Where is the spirit of Mizito?' Hetemam said.

'You need to kill her,' Aan said, still staring across at Runt. 'If you don't, they will multiply and overrun your entire continent.'

'We said, where is Mizito?'

'Please,' Jethar mumbled, his face still pressed to the dirt. 'Please, don't anger her. Just let us go.'

Hetemam straightened. 'You are to submit to—'

'No!' Jethar said. 'If you let us go, no harm will come to you!'

'No harm will come to us?' Hetemam said, amusement dripping in his voice. He tipped his flawless head to one side. 'Bring our servant Mizito into the light,' he said softly. 'We command you, Lord Jethar. In the name of your king.'

A look of stricken anguish crossed Jethar's face. 'I can't,' he said.

Hetemam stepped forward. 'Can't? We said, bring Mizito into the mortal realm. Now.'

As he spoke, he gestured, and one of his gold-robed monks strode forward bearing a metal box. Though featureless and unadorned, when the monk twisted it in their hands, its top fell open, and a great keening rent the air.

Runt winced and grabbed her head in both hands. The note it struck made her teeth ache. She was not alone in this. All around the square, people cried out or backed away.

The effect on Jethar was greatest of all. He groaned and strained beneath the warriors who held him. High above, Aan spun around and knifed towards him, like a child fleeing to their mother's arms. But she could not escape: Jethar jerked, and Aan was dragged back out through his eyes and mouth. Princen Hetemam advanced, balancing the box on one hand and gesturing with the other.

'Hold him,' Hetemam said, and as the warriors hauled Jethar to his feet, Jethar's skin brightened, and Aan slid gracefully towards the box. Though she clung to Jethar with elongating hands, the call of the box proved too strong. It snatched her free of her human and sent her spinning towards Hetemam, though she groped desperately at the air as she fell.

'What have you done with Mizito?' Hetemam said as Aan hovered before him.

'The abomination?' Aan said, her voice strained, her full lips curved up in a dangerous smile. 'Gone.'

'How were you able to take his place?'

'Power down the code limiter and I shall tell you.'

'Pardon?'

'I said shut the techwork box!' Aan snarled. 'Then we can talk.'

'No,' Princen Hetemam said. By now, Aan had been dragged so close to the box that her legs and the tips of her wings had disappeared within. Lord Jethar sagged in the arms of the warriors who supported him.

Princen Hetemam turned, and Aan turned with him, held fast by the techwork box. Her skin flashed with Forbidden glyphs, faster and faster, ever changing, as though, if they found the right combination, she might be set free.

'I am not alone, you know,' she screamed as she collapsed in upon herself. 'There are more of my kind within your kingdom! Eight! Eight lie in wait, each bound to a soul of power and influence! Should you stand in my way, my brethren will awaken and we will take these lands! Do you understand me? We will take these lands!'

'Of course you will,' Princen Hetemam said mildly, watching as Aan's body diminished.

'Maybe one is your sibling,' Aan said, her voice hoarse now. 'Maybe one is your lover. Maybe one is your child. They will see what you have done, and they will awaken! You will quail before—'

Then she was gone, and the box snapped shut, and Jethar went limp, his eyes rolling back in his head.

'Put the prisoner in the cage,' Hetemam said to his soldiers.

Jethar's head rolled forward as they dragged him towards the waiting ship.

'You're making a mistake,' Jethar told them, his voice slurred. He seemed scarcely able to lift his head as he peered at them through ribbons of sweat-soaked hair. 'That box will not hold her. Nothing will. When she frees herself, her wrath will be terrible!'

'That is our concern,' Hetemam said. 'You are an enemy of the king and the Royal Protectorate of the Nine Lands, and you are to face justice.'

'You fool!' Jethar cried, his voice rising as they dragged him away. 'Don't you understand the danger we're in? During the voyage, there was a man with me. A spy! From the Fallen Families! He planned it all! Arranged it all! Everything that's happening, it's all to destroy you!'

'Put him in,' Hetemam said.

'Listen to me!' Jethar cried, craning his head round as they bundled him onto the deck. 'He planned it all! He gave them to *her*.' And he locked eyes with Runt. 'He wants to force your hand, don't you see?'

Jethar braced his legs against the gunwales, but two more soldiers joined the group, and soon the eldest child of First General Sulin Mizito was being dragged away, ranting and screaming all the while, a soul unhinged, a man whose mind was gone.

Tension melted from the crowd in Ida Square. Several of the onlookers laughed softly behind their hands. Others looked pensive. Princen Hetemam climbed back into his litter, and his gold-clad party turned towards the river. Then they marched back aboard their golden barge while the people of northern Lordsgrave looked solemnly on.

All around Runt, people stirred. Some carried away the wounded, while others prodded the immobile greybloods, sending them crashing to the ground. Runt strode towards the edge of the river, where a lone greyblood stood staring, its sword raised. She tapped its face: lifeless. In a single stroke, something had snatched the life from an entire army. The Ahiki princen had done it, somehow – she was certain of it. But if so, couldn't he end the greyblood war with a snap of his bejewelled fingers?

As she turned towards the river, watching the royal barge and wondering, her gaze passed over a woman standing on the far bank; a solitary figure, not much older than Runt herself, her tightly curled hair a midnight halo about her brown face. Perhaps she too had fought to defend her home. Runt lifted a hand in salute and then turned away.

FIFTY-TWO

Temi

Temi reached up with both hands and tried to prise the greyblood's fingers apart. Frozen. The greyblood army had frozen, the flame of each life snuffed out in a single instant. The heat of the fingers that still gripped her neck had cooled, but the hand remained solid as stone.

'Sutesh!' Temi croaked. 'I'm stuck!'

Sutesh ducked under the unmoving arm of an axe-wielding greyblood and hobbled over to Temi's side. 'We must thank the ancestors,' they said. 'Someone has called them off.'

'Called them off how?'

'They are creatures of obedience,' Sutesh said, removing a metal disc from around their neck. 'If one above them tells them to stop, they must do so instantly.'

'They just gonna stand here?' Temi said, as Sutesh worked at the fingers. 'Why don't they retreat?'

'They have not been commanded to retreat,' Sutesh said. 'They have been commanded only to stop. We are fortunate: there are few greybloods left in the world upon whom such commands still work. I am more interested in where this group came from in the first place.'

'So . . . who commanded them?'

523

'Likely a more powerful greyblood.' Sutesh cursed under their breath. 'I am going to have to cut her hand off.'

Temi studied the creature's face, so human despite the silvery hide. Her small nose had a slight upturn, like a northerner. Her full lips were still parted, mid-sentence. She had a graze to one cheekbone, and beneath the silver skin, Temi glimpsed fresh grey blood. 'Will she ever wake up?'

'Perhaps. Perhaps not. Stand back.' Sutesh pulled a machete from the wide belt at their waist and marked the greyblood's skin with a gentle touch of the blade. The blood welled in a line, but still the greyblood woman did not move. Was she awake, behind her faded gaze, screaming for release as Temi had been when she had fallen into the ancestral realm? Could she feel pain?

'Stop,' Temi said, and swallowed against the greyblood's grip. 'Stop, I – I don't want you to cut off her hand.'

'Would you have said the same if she were still trying to kill you?'

'No, but . . . don't seem a fair fight, is all.'

Sutesh touched her shoulder. 'Temi Baker, no fight is ever fair.' Then with a cry, they swung their machete round and sliced the greyblood's hand from its body.

Temi fell sprawling. The greyblood too toppled sideways, her body stiff as old wood, her smile still fixed in its mocking rictus. All around them, survivors tossed aside weapons or crept out of hiding spots. Some warily circled the greybloods or poked at them with lengths of wood.

'Her hand's still stuck on my bloody neck!' Temi croaked.

Sutesh squatted beside her and took another metal shard from their necklace. This was larger than the others, and made of blackglass, Temi saw. When they passed their hand across it, it sparked to life with blinking glyphs. Sutesh hummed to themself and pulled one of the veins from the greyblood's severed wrist, heedless of the silver ichor that oozed onto their fingers.

[This is a person of skill,] Vunaji said. [You would be wise to keep them close.]

'Why did you disappear?' Temi muttered as Sutesh began to chant softly to the shard of blackglass.

[I did not wish to be seen.]

'That ancestor you invoked,' Sutesh said, not meeting her gaze. 'Best to keep him locked away. Best not to bring him out again.'

'Chedu?'

'No. The shadow in chains.'

'Do you know what he is?' Temi said.

'No. I do not. But they will come for you, Temi. The monks. You are not of the clans or the Families, so they will come for you.'

'The Families Bond ancestors too, don't they?' Temi said. 'The Chedus and the Sengs. All of them. That's what they are. Lowblood invokers.'

'Many can,' Sutesh said. 'But they are sworn to never invoke. If they break the Pact, they are eliminated. I have seen it happen myself, back home in Riani. Ahh, there we are.'

Blessed air rushed into Temi's lungs as the greyblood's hand fell away. Temi massaged her neck and tried not to look at the severed hand that had fallen at her feet.

Sutesh scooped up No-Cat's body. Light still flickered beneath its matted fur.

'This creature is quite remarkable,' they said.

Temi looked across at them. 'Did you see my cousins?'

'I saw,' Sutesh said. 'I saw them come through this doorway. A person of great skill created this, specifically to find your kin.'

Temi stood. The survivors had set to piling the greyblood bodies together, and two elders were already trying to light a fire beneath. Some clustered around the wounded and the dying, lifting their heads, offering water.

'Who are you?' one woman called over to Temi, as a child clung to her side.

Temi opened her mouth to say she was no one – just a lowblood, like them – but Sutesh turned and said, 'She is the Invoker of Lordsgrave!

And none must know she was here!' Their gaze flicked to Temi. 'I must return to the apothecary. I will be needed now.'

'You mean you wasn't before?' she said, and let out a strained laugh.

Temi turned towards the river. The golden barge was sliding gracefully away: heading west, back towards the Garden. On the far bank stood a lone figure: a waif-like girl, with skin much the same mid brown as Temi's, but pale hair. On impulse, Temi lifted her hand: part greeting, part salute. After a moment, the stranger raised her hand in response.

'Time to go,' Sutesh said, placing their hand on Temi's shoulder. 'Before the monks drag us both to the White Isle.'

FIFTY-THREE

Runt

Jimiki, a tailor who lived off Ida Square, had the privilege of taking them in. She'd been one of the many people Runt had healed during the massacre, after Jethar and the princen had left. Runt had moved from person to wounded person, offering aid, and once she had finished, she'd been deluged by invitations to rest and eat.

As Ba Casten spoke to them, explaining Runt was his personal healer, with a rare and powerful techwork that had been Cleansed by a kindly monk, Runt spotted a group of people in the shadows of an alleyway: three youths, and with them, the long-haired Seng man. Runt lifted her chin in challenge. She had no fear of them now . . . no fear of anyone. The long-haired man had smiled in a way she couldn't interpret, and then he and his lieutenants had disappeared back into the shadows.

'Run!' Zee said, throwing himself on her. 'They said there was a princen here!'

'There was,' Runt said, kissing her brother's head, inhaling his salty-sweet scent. 'He came to take Jethar and that thing away. They won't trouble us again. Nothing can trouble us again.'

'Ain't we got to hide?' he hissed, scanning the crowds that were only now beginning to disperse.

'Not no more,' Runt said.

'My house is yours!' Jimiki declared as they all followed her across Ida Square. 'You will want for nothing.'

'Just one night,' Ba Casten said. 'Then we're heading to the Family compound.'

As Jimiki prattled on, gleefully aware of the envious eyes she drew, Krayl fell in step with his father. 'We're not waiting for Gamani?'

'The Sengs won't dare touch us now; not since they seen what we can do.'

'And what about the monks?' Krayl hissed.

'That's why we're only staying here one night,' Casten said. 'Back in the compound, they got ways of keeping the monks away. We'll be safe from everyone there.'

As they climbed the steps into Jimiki's brick townhouse, Casten stalled. Runt watched him opening and closing his hands, turning them over and running his palm along his tataus. 'Something ain't right,' he muttered. He looked over at Lakoz. 'Can you feel him?'

Lakoz, ever smiling, gave a nonchalant shrug. 'No. But I'm sure he'll be back.'

Behind them, Feyin chuckled. 'Interesting!'

'We talk about Chedu later,' Casten said. 'Come on.'

Jimiki plied them with food out in her yard, and told them the names of all her children and which were eligible for marriage. Runt sank into a plush chair, Zee at her side drinking spiced coconut water, while the Cloistered swirled excitedly within her veins. Jimiki kept dozens of cats, and Zee dropped onto the polished wood to play with them. He seemed a child as she watched him, just the brother she knew, who liked fried bean cakes and jumping over roofs. But when he laughed at a kitten chasing its own tail, her skin chilled and she felt herself tense.

'Are you still my brother?' Runt said. She'd meant it to sound firm, but her voice shook as she spoke.

'What do you mean, Run? Course I am!'

But every time he caught her eye, she found herself watching for flashes of yellow.

It was evening when one of Jimiki's grandchildren came in saying there was a man at the door asking for Ba Casten.

'At fucking last,' Casten said, lumbering to his feet. 'Gamani! What took you so fucking long?'

Runt sat with her back to the door, Zee asleep now across her lap, so she heard Gamani before she saw him. 'I'm sorry,' came a familiar, soft voice. 'I was busy out east.'

A thrill rippled over Runt's skin. Gently, she lifted Zee's head onto the chair and stood. She knew the owner of that voice. But she couldn't quite believe it.

When she turned, she didn't see him immediately – Lakoz and Krayl and all the others were enfolding him in embraces, slapping his back or rubbing his long, braided hair. Then, finally, he stood alone: a slight, plain man with mid brown skin and the look of a dozen lands about him. Just like Runt.

'Baba?' Runt said, folding her arms across her body.

'There's my girl!' Gamani said, walking towards her. 'You been good?'

'You know the Chedus?' she said, a dozen emotions crowding her mind. Her cheeks grew hot. 'You're . . . Gamani.'

'Yes, sweet,' Baba said, grabbing her head and pulling her into a hug. Runt closed her eyes and inhaled. Her father smelt sweet and smoky, like incense and clean sweat. He was as beautiful as she remembered him, his features even, his eyes wide and caring. Just standing beside him suffused her with a calm she hadn't known she craved. He was here. All was right. Her baba was at her side.

'Runt's your girl?' Casten said, frowning. 'Why'd you never say? We've had her scrubbing pots!'

'This one's meant for big things,' Gamani said, pulling her close again. 'Don't make for a strong mind to grow up too soft. Besides, her ma and me . . . we had our disagreements.' He looked down at her. 'But she's gone now, ain't she, Runt?'

'That's right,' Runt murmured, remembering the smell of the blood, the way her mother's hands had batted feebly.

'The Family's waiting for you all at River House,' Gamani said. 'You ready to go home?'

They said their goodbyes and thank-yous to Jimiki and her family. Gamani gave the woman fifty suns, and Runt stifled a smile at the way Jimiki tried to mask her awe. Jimiki giggled like a smitten adolescent when Gamani bowed to her as he would an honoured elder, and when he kissed both her cheeks, her dark skin flushed darker still.

In the twilit street outside stood two wooden wagons pulled by oxen. A gang of admiring children had gathered around them, and one of the drivers had set to tossing coins for them to chase. 'You lot get in the back there,' Gamani called, gesturing to the larger of the wagons. 'I need a moment alone with my two bairns here.'

Runt's heart swelled as she climbed up into the wagon. She'd never ridden in one before. Inside, it was as though someone had lifted up Jimiki's sumptuous family room and placed it on wheels. Zee climbed in beside her, his face long and serious.

'What's wrong?' Runt hissed at him as Gamani pulled shut the door.

'I just want to go home,' he muttered. 'To our real home.'

It took Runt a moment to work out what he meant. 'What, our hut?' she laughed. 'What for? There's nothing there for us. Don't you want to go to a Family compound? We're Chedus now!'

Zee shrugged and turned towards the window.

Despite the darkness as they pulled out into the street, the full extent of the devastation caused by the greyblood attack could not be hidden: broken buildings, collapsed walls, injured people being tended to out in the street. The Cloistered swirled eagerly at that. Yes: there were more people for them to help. So many more.

She felt a certain energy in the air, too. A potent awakening. When they reached the new wall at the edge of Lordsgrave, a mass of people had gathered. A gate stood open in it now, but the crowd was arguing

530

with the bluehawks who stood atop it. *Where were the invokers?* she heard voices shouting. *Why'd you leave us here to die?*

Gamani sat opposite her, studying her with his soft, dark eyes. As they passed into Lordsheart and the panorama of highblood estates and affluent avenues spread out before them, above which rose the jagged ruins of Scathed towers, Runt's father leaned forwards.

'Tide's beginning to turn out there,' he said. 'People are starting to see. Starting to understand.'

Runt was quiet for a long while, her mind turning over and over. 'You knew what was in the pendant,' she said. 'When you gave it to me. You knew, didn't you? That's why you brought those two men to me. You wanted me to give them the Cloistered. Which means there's even more out there.'

Gamani laughed softly. 'Cloistered? Is that what they're calling themselves now?'

'They lied to me,' Runt said. 'They said they heal, but they don't. They use people as – as a gateway.'

[We make them better.]

[Much better.]

'They do both,' Gamani said. 'That was a close call, you know. With Jethar. Came very close to ruining everything.'

'You know Lord Jethar?' Runt said.

Gamani waved a dismissive hand. 'We'll talk about that later. I need you to understand that we've been summoned before the Council of Elders – that's the alliance of all the Families. And since our little blue friends were seen by so many monks and nuns, well . . . We'll have that to deal with, too. Which means we'll have to speed our plans up a bit.'

Outside, the sun had nearly set. Down one of the streets they passed, Runt spotted a slow-moving column of people. The war draft. Royal monks led the way, their floor-length golden robes shimmering like mirages, the jewels of their holy staffs gleaming red or silver or green. Bluehawks in sapphire tunics marched ahead of them, rapping on doors with their spears, calling for people to open up, open up in the name of their king. She couldn't see the faces of the bedraggled people who came behind, but she felt the resignation, the despair, in their hunched shoulders. How strange to think that, not so long ago, she'd considered her life over. How strange to think she'd no longer be joining the masses heading west.

'I've got another present for you,' Gamani said. He tossed something through the air and Runt caught it: a velvet pouch. Inside lay a tiny, nine-sided dice covered in markings. It looked like blackglass, and though Runt didn't know her words and numbers, she knew enough about techwork to recognise Forbidden glyphs.

'This is something else I brought back with me.'

'From the place where spirits gather?' Runt said, looking up sharply. 'That's where you were, ain't it? All them years. You was with Jethar trying to find that spirit land. That's why he knew my face. It was you he was ranting about when they took him away.'

Gamani smiled.

'Can't you tell me what it is you're planning?' Runt said, sitting forward. 'I mean, if I'm guardian of the Cloistered. Shouldn't I know?'

'When the time comes.' His gaze was on the sky, where the golden clouds that hung above the Garden shimmered. 'For generations, our Family has been building towards bringing down our true enemy. And now we're in the final stages. Just know that you're doing a great service to your kin and to everyone in the Nine Lands.'

'What are the Cloistered? They're ancestors, right? But not normal ancestors.'

Gamani pulled a face. 'What they are is . . . complicated.' He sighed and tapped her knee. 'Now. We got work ahead of us. You ready to meet the rest of the Family?'

'Yes, Baba,' Runt said. She'd forgotten how good it felt to say those words. How right. She wanted to ask him more. About the Cloistered; about his plans. Above all, she wanted to ask him if, finally, she had earned herself a name. But instead, she took Zee's

532

hand and watched her father's face, while somewhere deep within, the Cloistered giggled.

Brother Danadu, acolyte to Arch Curator Ngbali the Just, a man who until recently had never left the distant town of Ninshasi, melted back among the shadows as the two wagons rolled past. He touched his holy staff and closed his eyes and the techwork afforded him a vision.

'What is it?' Ngbali said, sitting at his desk before a plateful of plantain. 'If you've come to tell me you've lost him again, I am not interested.'

'No, Your Holiness!' Danadu said. 'I found him! And I know his name now: Gamani Chedu. He is a man of high standing within the Chedu Family, one of the lowblood crime syndicates who—'

'Yes, yes, I know what the Families are. If you are sure it is him, then bring him in for questioning. And whatever it was he took from Jethar's ship, I want it recovered. Grand High Curator Boleo was expecting an update from us two moons ago.'

'Um. Your Holiness, about that. As I said, I have been watching him for some time now and, well, I believe you need to hear what he's been doing.'

FIFTY-FOUR

Temi

Temi stood looking at her reflection in the chipped mirror that leaned against the sleeping-room wall. When word came over the river that the monks had finally arrived in the district of Lordsgrave, she'd put on her best wrapper dress – red, with gold patterns; the one Aunt Yeshe liked so much. She'd piled her freshly braided hair high on her head, and even applied some kohl Meliti had given her.

'Don't matter what they say,' Temi said, inhaling, 'they have to let me do it. What's the point in being an invoker if you don't fight grey-bloods, right?'

[I am still at a fraction of my capabilities,] Vunaji said. [If you die, I too will be cut adrift.]

'Then you'd best protect me, hadn't you?'

[I still advise against this.]

'But you want it, don't you?' Temi said. Her heart had been racing all morning, and she knew he could feel it. But what did it matter if he felt her fear? Only a fool would walk willingly to war without knowing a crushing dread. All it showed is that she was human. 'You want to fight. I can feel it, just like you can feel my fear. You'd enjoy it. Wouldn't you?'

Vunaji didn't respond, but she felt the swell of his heat and the stir of his pleasure like warm air on the tips of her fingers.

'Why didn't you tell me No-Cat was a doorway to the ancestral realm?'

[Doorways can be dangerous.]

They were all sitting around the table when Temi strode into the family room. All except the children: Temi could hear their squeals out in the yard, where Old Baba had ushered them with the promise of dried mangos and coconut. Uncle Amaan leaned back in his chair, his hairlocs freshly twisted. Kierin sat opposite, his arm healed now, his yellow hair shorn almost to the scalp. Yeshe and her painted wife, Selek, held hands at the head of the table. Temi's cousin Mtobi wore a simple blue tunic rather than their usual elaborate Jebbanese robes. Two dozen sombre faces looked up at her as she strode across the uneven floor.

'What took you so long?' Yeshe said from the head of the table. 'And where you going dressed like that? You got some new fancy man?'

Temi smoothed down her skirt. 'I'm an invoker,' she said. 'You know that. We all know that.'

'I don't know what that thing was,' Yeshe said, pointing, 'but I do know I don't want to never see it again. So you sit down here and—'

'I'm going to join the draft,' Temi said. 'When the bluehawks come, I'm stepping outside. And none of you can stop me. You saw what *he* can do—'

'Temi, no.'

'He tore that Harvell woman in two!' Temi shouted, raising her voice above their cries of incredulity.

'Hush!' Yeshe said.

'No, Tem,' Uncle Amaan said. 'Fair's fair. Sit down and let's draw the lots.'

'You can't stop me,' Temi said. 'When they come, you can't stop me signing up.'

Uncle Amaan shook his head and then turned to usher his youngest child back out into the yard. Many of them couldn't meet Temi's eyes, all except Mtobi, who grinned knowingly at her. Yeshe stared across the table, her jaw tensing. When her wife Selek placed a hand on her shoulder and tried to whisper something, Yeshe shook her off.

'The best chance for one of us to come back is me,' Temi said quietly. 'So it's got to be me.' She gestured at Yeshe, hoping they hadn't heard the tremor in her voice. 'So go on, Auntie. You pull the second name out. We only need one now.'

Yeshe straightened. 'Temi-girl, you're the only one that can build them water votives proper now Tunji's gone. If your name comes out, then it's the will of the ancestors and that's that. But you ain't volunteering yourself. And that is also that.'

Temi inhaled slowly. She could run outside. She could volunteer before any of them knew what was happening.

'Who's gonna clean the water round here, with you gone?' Yeshe said, her eyes beseeching now.

Temi found she couldn't speak. Wordlessly, Yeshe reached into the bowl that stood in the centre of the table. She rummaged through the two dozen scraps of papyrus.

They all watched Yeshe silently as she unrolled the papyrus and read.

'Who is it?' Kierin said.

Yeshe held up the scrap, showing them all the symbol for her own name. 'Me,' she said. Her lips grew tight, but Temi saw the resolve in her eyes; a hardness that would brook no argument. 'It's me.'

'No,' Kierin said, his light skin flushing red. 'No, not again!' He made a grab for the bowl, but Yeshe jerked it out of his reach.

'Fair's fair,' she said. 'Let's see who the second one is.' She shot Temi a warning look, then reached into the bowl.

They watched again in silence as Yeshe unrolled the second scrap. 'Amaan,' Yeshe said, her voice cracking. 'It's you, Amaan. Ancestors preserve us.'

'No,' Kierin said. 'No, he can't go! The kids! No.'

'It's OK,' Amaan said, standing. 'Honestly, it's OK.'

They all crowded round him, hugging him, offering to go in his stead. His eyes were bright, but Temi saw no fear in them. Only resignation. Temi felt no grief as she watched him, not even sadness. Something else swelled up within her, powerful, insistent. A simmering anger – contained, for now, but an anger that would not be swift to leave.

[By what right does your king do this?] Vunaji whispered, his words soft as silk. [With every rain, every decade, he takes more from your family, your city, your people. On and on, without end. He is like the Chedus. But infinitely worse.]

'Let me go speak to the lil'uns,' Amaan said, extracting himself from his family. 'Explain it. I told them there was a chance it might be me, but . . .'

He trailed off and they watched him step out into the yard, where Old Baba looked up from his chair with sadness heavy in his rheumy eyes. As the others sat back around the table, pouring out the last of the Jebbanese red, Temi sought out Yeshe.

'How many times d'you put your name in that thing?' Temi said quietly, taking her aunt's shoulder. 'There's more than thirty pieces in there.'

A faint smile tugged at the corner of Yeshe's lips. 'Don't know what you're talking about, Temi-girl.'

'You can't go back,' Temi whispered. 'You said . . . you said it was as close to a waking nightmare as anything could ever come.'

'It was,' Yeshe said tightly. 'That's why I don't want none of you lot to go through it.'

'You ain't nineteen no more.'

'Fuck you,' Yeshe muttered, shoving at Temi, and Temi laughed softly.

'I could protect you out there,' Temi said, taking her aunt's warm, dry hand. 'Amaan's kids need him, his women need him. Let him stay. Let me go with you. We stick together and we can just let Vunaji do the rest. Family protect each other, that's what you always used to say.'

But Yeshe was already shaking her head. 'We can't do that. There's no telling where they'll send us. Could be different jobs, different companies, even.' She turned until she faced Temi, then took both her hands. 'You can't go. You hear me? You *need* to make the votives. Besides, the minute them invoker lords see you call that . . . whatever the fuck that monster was, they'll take you away. You hear? Execute you, or send you to the White Isle, or haul you up in front of the king, I don't know. It'll be something bad. It ain't *allowed*, Temi. It ain't allowed for the likes of us.'

'Fuck that,' Temi muttered.

They didn't need Maiwo running in from the street to tell them when the monks arrived. Temi heard the shouts from outside, the crying. Amaan had come back into the family room, his children clinging to him. Larmi, his muscular eldest daughter, wept bitterly. His youngest daughter was too small to understand as Mtobi prised her away and lifted her onto their hip.

Yeshe squeezed Temi's hand one last time before standing to join Amaan, the rest of the Arrant Hill bakers falling in behind. Kierin tried to shove past, his travelling sack over one shoulder, but Yeshe seized his arm.

'No!' she snapped, jerking him round. 'You hear me? No!'

'Auntie,' Kierin said, his green eyes filling with tears. He gestured helplessly at Yeshe and Amaan.

'Drop some rice for us on the shrine,' Yeshe said stiffly, then drew her hand back and punched him square on the temple.

Kierin toppled backwards, his fall broken by his heavy bag. Yeshe winced and flicked her hand as she stepped over his unconscious form. 'Out of practice,' she muttered, rubbing at the soreness.

The bakery stood empty as they all passed through it. Outside in the street, their customers hung about in an uneasy cluster, all of them looking south.

They came up the street like a funeral procession – more bluehawks than Temi had ever seen in her life, marching either side of a mass of locals with travelling sacks. Old and young. Hale and frail. Many with downcast eyes. Some boasted the fresh cuts and bruises that said they had not come quietly. Locals heckled the bluehawks from left and right, asking where they were during the greyblood attack, cursing them in the ancestors' names. Beggar children threw fruit peelings from the rooftops, then scampered away before they could be caught.

Dozens of monks flanked the procession, their golden cloaks blinding in the afternoon light. At the next building – the ogogoro inn – they stopped, and the lead monk lifted his staff. The crystal at its tip spun, displaying a stream of glyphs.

'Arrant Hill brewers!' the monk called. 'Submit your volunteers for conscription!'

There was a scuffle further up the street: a youth had bolted out of a hut. A couple lived there alone, Temi recalled, and as bluehawks dragged out the woman, two more set off in pursuit of the man.

'Don't wait for me!' the woman screamed, pulling at the soldiers. 'You run and don't wait for me!'

She laughed through her tears as her lover made it to the top of the hill and disappeared around the corner. But not long after Remmy and Lade, the two eldest sons of the Arrant Hill brewers, came silently out of their house, packs on their shoulders, the bluehawks returned, carrying the youth between them.

'Arrant Hill bakers!' the monk called, turning away from the ogogoro inn and towards Temi and Amaan. 'Submit your volunteer for conscription!'

Yeshe took Amaan's hand, and together they stepped out of the shade of the building and into the sun's glare.

'We need only one of you,' the monk said. 'This individual has already volunteered for your household.'

There was movement further down the line, and a ragged woman with pale skin stepped out of the line of conscripts. Behind the matted yellow hair that obscured much of her face, she grinned. It was the first genuine smile Temi had seen on her mother's face in years.

'Ma, no!' Temi cried, closing the space between them.

'I'm gonna find him, Tem,' Kerlyn said as Temi pushed through the crowd to reach her mother, eyes swimming. 'I'm gonna find your baba and I'm gonna bring him home.'

The bluehawks did not try to stop the two women when they clasped forearms, nor when Kerlyn pulled her daughter into a sweaty embrace.

'You stay here,' Kerlyn whispered in her ear. 'You look after them. They need you. Lordsgrave needs you.'

'Ma—'

'Go on,' Kerlyn said, pushing her away. She shifted her gaze to Amaan. 'You go back. Them kids need you. I'll look after Yeshe.'

Amaan looked stricken, his eyes moistening, his lips quivering behind his beard.

'It's OK,' Yeshe said, pulling her youngest brother into her skinny arms. 'It's the will of the ancestors. And my will too. You do this for me, Ammy; I'm your elder and you're doing this for me.'

She released him, then turned to Temi, pulling her into a final embrace. 'Take care of them,' she whispered into Temi's ear. 'Them Chedus'll come back for us. Make sure that monster of yours is ready.'

Without another word, Yeshe kissed Temi on both cheeks, then strode to join Kerlyn. Temi's aunt looked so small beneath her travelling pack. So old. Temi crossed to where Amaan stood weeping and put her arms around him. Together they watched as the procession started moving again, and Temi's chest tightened as Yeshe offered them a small wave before turning away.

'It ain't right,' Temi said. 'None of this is right. They shouldn't get to do this.'

'I know,' Amaan muttered, his voice thin. 'But it's the will of our king.'

'Fuck the king.'

She was still watching her aunt and mother when one of the monks stepped out of the column to stand before her.

'Do you speak for the bakers of Arrant Hill?' the monk said. He was of middling years, mild-faced and slight, but something about his glittering dark eyes unsettled Temi. His composure spoke not of good humour, but of control. Of a suppressed power straining for release.

Temi glanced at Amaan, still weeping beside her.

'Yes,' Temi said. 'It's me what speaks for the bakers. I help you?'

'There have been reports of the use of Uncleansed Forbidden relics in this region,' the monk said. He lifted his eyes to take in the locals at her back and the faces that watched from surrounding windows. 'I ask you all, as subjects of the king, to report anything unholy to us, as your sacred duty to the realm and the ancestors!'

'Goodness!' Temi made the sign for ancestral protection. 'Well, we most certainly will report anything suspicious of that nature, Father. You can count on us.'

The monk flicked his gaze back to her. Yeshe and Kerlyn walked arm in arm, near the top of the hill now, the sun touching their bare shoulders.

'Additionally, two halves of a woman's corpse were found in the river near here,' the monk said. 'Sliced in two by a blunt object. Do you know how much force it would take to slice a body in two like that, from shoulder to crotch?' He lifted his staff and traced a slow line down from Temi's shoulder, not quite touching her body but so close that if she shifted, the sharpened tip would nick her skin. Temi knew when someone was trying to intimidate her, so she grinned broadly and held the man's gaze. 'I can think of battle-hardened warriors in their prime who could not do such a thing even armed with the heaviest axe.' He lifted his voice again, addressing them all. 'Perhaps one of you saw something?'

'Yeah!' Old Javesh said immediately, hobbling out of the huddle of spectators to lean on his stick. 'Yeah, I saw it all! Nasty business. Greyblood got the poor woman during the massacre. Just jumped down from the roof and carved her up with its massive hand. Then carried her parts off to the river. Saw it with me own two eyes.'

'Yeah, I saw that greyblood!' piped up Kiko, one of the Ekari children from the dockside shanty. 'Fucking massive fucker!'

More voices chimed in then, piling over each other in their eagerness.

'Biggest I ever seen!'

'Bloody ugly, too!'

'Just carried her right off!'

A dozen heads nodded in agreement as the air filled with more descriptions of the hideous killing that had left the entire neighbourhood traumatised.

Temi swallowed against the tightness in her throat and met the monk's gaze. 'Everyone here knew someone who got killed in the massacre,' she said. 'I hope this woman, whoever she was, fares better with the ancestors.'

The monk offered her a thin smile. 'Indeed. In the meantime, do let us know immediately if you suspect Forbidden relics are being used or traded here. As I'm sure you know, there are untold dangers to handling it.'

'Oh, I do most certainly know that, Father. And I'll be sure to shout if I see any.'

'Good. Because know that anyone who withholds information about cursed relics betrays their ancestors and their king.'

The monk turned away slowly, sweeping his eyes over the bakery and the crowd one final time before rejoining the procession heading up Arrant Hill. Temi could no longer see her mother and Yeshe. They were lost to the mass of figures heading to their doom.

FIFTY-FIVE

Jinao

Lord Jinao Mizito, soulbarren son of the late First General Sulin of Cagai, trudged west through the abandoned lands of Clan Kzani. He didn't need the constant shifting colours in the sky to tell him the Feverlands lay ahead. He felt it in the growing heat. He saw it in the increasing numbers of greybloods he had to evade. It was a throbbing in the pit of his stomach and a pressure behind his eyes. The Feverlands weren't just hot; they were inhuman. Nothing mortal that ventured inside came out again. And now, the king planned to invade.

He glimpsed only fleeting signs of the Bairneater on his journey. A pile of greyblood corpses, neatly stacked. A flattened area of bush. The remnants of that strange green fire the creature sometimes lit.

He found himself thinking often of Mizito's words to him in that Kzani cave. *There were no Scathed. These lands were always ours. And Ahiki was not our saviour.* For centuries, millennia, the Nine Lands had looked outward for its enemy. Yet as his ancestors had shown him, all the time, their enemy had lain within.

'We are the Scathed,' Jinao muttered to himself as he hacked at the bush with his makeshift machete. 'Humans are the Scathed. That lost, mythical, all-powerful species: that is us. The Ahikis did something to us. Damaged us. Took our powers. Smashed our cities. Stole our techwork and twisted our histories.'

The woods around him seemed to mock him with their indifference. Had his mother known? Had Daloya? Was this why they deemed their work, deemed their moulding of *him*, so important? He'd thought they meant to send him to battle greybloods, but now he suspected his mother's great rebellion was for something quite different. Well, he supposed all their hopes now rested on the shoulders of that old Jebbanese monk, Boleo. He wished the holy man well. Him, and whatever that Vunaji spirit was. He supposed the monk knew the truth of things. And the Bhuten Wives, too. That was surely what Neena had meant when she'd told him to think about who the true enemy was.

When the Greyblood Kings rise again, so too will the ancient Warlords ninety-nine. That was how Neena's version of the Song of Legends Lost had begun, yet he had been told there were only ever nine warlords, nine lands, nine peoples. They were in there, then. The other warlords. They were in the ancestral plane. The Ahikis had kept the people from their ancestors, but soon that would change. He had brought back Sumalong. He had seen the Batide bring back their own namesakes. Perhaps others could return. And if it was not about blood, as Mizito had told him, then anyone could make the Bond.

After a day of trekking steadily westward, Jinao came to a place a great fire had once swept through, turning trees and undergrowth alike to char. No, not a fire, he realised, as he trudged through that dead and desolate place. Something else. The plants were rotten rather than burned, rotten from the inside out, as though everything that lived had been poisoned. He realised then that he saw no insects, no lizards, no birds. Nothing.

By the next morning, the land began to descend and the trees fell away, and he saw it up ahead: the Feverlands. The trees there stood unnaturally tall, looming like living Scathed towers, a confluence of colour and movement. Purples and pinks and scarlets and blues; vines thick as his waist, trunks large as greathouses, all of it in constant motion, as though the Feverlands breathed, as though they were a single living organism that sought to swallow the Nine Lands whole.

Already, he could feel a headache building. That was the sickness of the Feverlands; the terrible twisting of human minds. Already, the air felt thinner.

And down in the valley before him, as far as he could see to north and south, lay an army. The king's army. Thousands upon thousands of human souls, massing to march to their doom. He saw banners from across the Nine Lands: every clan, every province. Command pavilions rose above smaller tents for warriors, and a thousand cook-fires dotted the twilight. It was folly, all of it. The clans were only meant to hold back the greybloods, not venture into their lands. Every soul before him now would not live out the next rainy season.

Jinao closed his eyes against the world as something within him crumbled. The Bairneater had made it. It had returned to its home with his mother's staff and with her secrets. And Jinao could follow it no further. He'd failed. Ancestors forgive them, they'd all failed! They hadn't stopped the war that was to come, and Jinao hadn't fulfilled his vow to his brother. Now, he stood at the very edge of civilisation with no way to continue the pursuit.

He knew what he should do. Turn home. Help Jemusi reclaim Aranduq. Find Lakari Tob and try to remove the curse on his Bond. Tell the clan what he'd learned about their history. There was nothing left for him here. Nothing but the promise of death.

Rain pounded down on the canvas of the processing tent. Water pooled beneath Captain Iju's boots. But as he packed away the last list of names, he heard a new sound. Footsteps, squelching through the mud.

'I'm not processing any more conscripts tonight,' Iju snapped, without looking round. 'And tell General Rei that if they're as useless as the last lot, she may as well slit their throats now. All we get is soft city fops and blubbering babes. This is no way to run a war.'

'I'm the last conscript,' said a voice in the rolling accent of the Isles. 'I got a bit lost.'

Captain Iju turned to squint at the newcomer. He was a tall man with the look of Cagai about him, but wearing a Riani kameez. He carried no weapon, but he wore good sandals, which was more than could be said about most of the lowbloods they were sent.

'Name?'

'J-Janzen, sir. Janzen of the . . . Aranduq farmers.'

'Janzen.' Iju looked back the scrolls he had just rolled up. 'Are you going to make me go through all of those again to find your name?'

'No, sir. Just – send me anywhere. It doesn't matter.'

Iju regarded the man. Most conscripts weren't nearly this keen. And there was something curious about him. His accent was of the Islands, yes, but it carried a highblood lilt. And his arms, beneath their heavy cloak, were crusted with mud, as though he were ashamed to show his family tataus.

'Well . . . Janzen. Do you have any combat training?'

'No, sir. None. I'm just a farmer.'

'Come with me.' Iju stepped out into the drumming rain, not bothering with his triangular rain hat. There was no point – in rains like this, everything got wet. There would be no cook-fires tonight, and yet the vastness of the war camp was still palpable through the gloom.

'You see over there,' Iju said, pointing to a faint line of tents. 'Those are the conscripts from Cagai. I'm trusting you to go to the third tent and join the group there. Don't be running off now. The holy ones have a way of knowing, and you don't want to end up swinging from a gibbet come sunrise.'

'Yes, sir. And thank you.'

Iju blinked against the rain. Nobody had ever thanked him before. Mostly, they came in screaming, or beseeching the ancestors, or lashing out until they had to be chained. Or else they walked like they were dead already, all the hope gone from them.

546

'There's something familiar about you,' Iju said, scratching his chin. 'Have we met before?'

'No, sir. Definitely not.'

Iju shrugged and watched the man until he disappeared into the rain.

EPILOGUES

Lucy, Sister Poju, Lyela

Lucy

'This is for you,' Father said, opening his travelling sack.
Lucy's breath caught: a kitten, with four white paws, a black body and a little white chin. Its ears looked too big for its head, and its fur was ruffled from the journey. It stood on Lucy's bedding, looking about, no fear on its face; only curiosity. It took in the towering canopy of colourful trees, ears twitching. Lucy reached out with her good arm and the kitten cringed away, but then she remembered what Father had taught her about being patient and gentle, so she let it smell her fingers first.

'I rescued her,' Father said, watching. She felt the intensity of his gaze like a physical weight. Once, it had frightened her, the strength of his love – but she understood it now. As their numbers had declined, as Mother had faded and died, Lucy had come to understand that fear of loss. 'The Silent Ones I found her with were mistreating her. But I saved her from them and punished those who sought to harm her. Their kind have no regard for life; they do not know how to nurture and cherish it. Life and living come so easily to them that they have forgotten what a precious gift it is.'

Lucy saw then that the kitten had lost a chunk of its tail. Like her, it was broken. Not quite complete. 'I hate them,' she said.

'So do I,' Father replied, sitting back. 'Now: I have something very important for you to consider. Listen closely. What are you going to call her?'

'I don't know,' Lucy said, as the kitten sniffed her fingers. She looked over at Father's tired face. She had been so overjoyed at his return, so relieved to see him alive, that she had not truly taken him in. His clothes were rotten. His eyes bore that haunted look she'd come to know as exhaustion. And his arm; one of his glorious arms had been injured, and badly. It was healing, she saw, but there was a scar. And when he sighed and leaned back against the tree, she saw an even greater scar at his throat.

'What happened?' she said, swallowing.

'Nothing that couldn't be mended,' Father said, closing his eyes. 'Nothing for you to concern yourself with.'

'I'm not a baby any more,' Lucy said. 'I'm older now. Someone hurt you.'

Father sighed, his eyes still closed. 'Yes, Lucy. Someone did hurt me, but I'm not hurt any more. And what matters is that I got the medicine.'

Lucy looked up, to where Seema sat near the fire, burning a long staff, a Silent Ones' weapon, over her smelting pot. The green greatfire beneath had reduced much of the outer material to ash, and the metal within was molten now. Almost ready for her to take.

'While I was in the lands of the Silent Ones, I . . . learned something,' Father said. 'About a plan they have, to wipe us out.'

'No,' Lucy said.

Father touched her cheek. 'They will not succeed. I have all the details now. And I know the words to stop them.'

'You mean you're going away again,' Lucy said, drawing back.

But Father ignored her. 'Seema will be coming soon for your first dose.'

Lucy's muscles tightened at that. 'Can't I rest first? And play with the kitten? I—'

'Lucy,' Father said. 'Listen to me. When I left to get the medicine,

Seema told me . . . she told me that there was a good chance you would not be here when I returned.'

'I know,' Lucy said, not meeting his gaze. The kitten had climbed onto her bedding and was sniffing at it. Lucy thought if she stayed very still, she might be able to coax it onto her lap.

'When I came back,' he said, 'when I saw you . . . There is so little of you left, daughter. You are so very weak.'

Lucy opened her mouth to reply, to tell him he was wrong, that she was strong, when she saw Seema coming up from the fire, carrying her medicine crate. Her bright yellow eyes flicked over at Father, then back to Lucy.

'Have you thought of a name yet?' Seema asked as she took out her vials and needles. 'My mother always told me that the name you give a pet determines its nature. So choose carefully.'

Lucy tried not to focus on Seema's deft, silver hands as she poured the medicine into the mould.

'Give me your arm,' Seema said.

Lucy looked down. It had been six days since her arm had died, and she'd managed to hide it from them. But now . . .

Seema threw back the covers and saw Lucy's light grey arm, resting in her lap. There was no warmth in it now. No life glowed beneath the skin. Seema sighed, then took hold of Lucy's arm, lifting it. Lucy felt nothing at all. And she felt nothing as Seema found the place where her arm opened and folded back the skin to reveal the life within, the bristling nest of silver and black.

'I should leave you to your work,' Father said.

'Don't you move,' Seema replied. 'Your neck needs looking at, and your arm.'

'They're fine.'

'No they're not. Sit still.'

Father chuckled – that warm, comforting sound – and settled back against the tree.

Seema worked quickly, pulling out the dead wires, threading in the

553

new. Replacing the cracked thinking plate with the new one she had moulded. Then she placed five pins in the end of each of Lucy's fingers.

'I'm going to breathe life into them now,' Seema said. 'This will sting.'

'I'm ready,' Lucy said.

Seema pressed Lucy's hand to her black healing box, and life leapt from it to the ends of the pins, and for a moment all was fire and blinding brightness, and Lucy gasped, and Father, his voice strangely distant, was saying, 'You're hurting her! Stop!'

But Seema ignored him, sliding her palm up the black box, and the life leapt through Lucy's body. For a moment, her whole arm tingled with blessed awareness. Then it was too much. Lucy felt herself falling back. The last thing she heard was Seema snapping at Father, telling him to sit down and let Lucy rest.

Lucy woke some time later to wetness on her face. She opened her eyes to find a pair of tawny orbs looking back at her. Lucy laughed, and without thinking, lifted her left hand to stroke the kitten. It moved as smoothly as it had done sixty years ago, when she'd been a baby, and Mother had still been alive. All of Lucy felt fluid, and supple. She sat up.

It was night-time now, and all around her, people slept under blankets, or up in the branches of the trees. The greatfire still burned, as it always did, and a number of people sat around it, talking. She recognised the low rumble of Father; saw his towering bulk silhouetted against the flames. But for the moment, all she cared about was the kitten. When Lucy uncurled her legs, the creature leapt at her feet. Lucy found a twig and swished it back and forth, and the kitten capered after it, pouncing and leaping.

After a time, the voices at the fire grew louder, Father's strongest among them.

'Why do you think I risked so much?' he said. 'Sulin Mizito's memories are mine now. It is as Regent said: they have a plan to wipe us out. A plan that has nothing to do with the armies massing at the border.'

'It changes nothing,' said an aged, cracked voice. That was Adebayo. He had sat at that fire for ten years now. No soul had found the medicine to heal his body. The flowers and grasses had grown up around him, but his eyes, bright yellow, remained keen, as did his mind. Until his light went dim, he would continue to lead them. 'Any day now, Ahiki's forces will invade our lands. Let them hurl themselves against the Horde. They will be annihilated.'

'And what happens if this invasion does not destroy them?' Father said. 'We will have to enter Ahiki lands again, and when we do, they will execute this plan Sulin had.'

'They cannot win against the Horde,' Tanaka said. 'They never have, and they never will. They are sending tens of thousands this time. What was it? Two from every household in the Nine Lands. The Horde will wash over them, and their civilisation will fall.'

Father stood, looming over the greatfire, his arms spread, black against green flames.

'Sulin's son took my head,' Father said. 'He is closer than anyone I have ever met to awakening fully. He managed to separate the two Intelligences that bonded with the coded spirit of his ancestor and attract a banished spirit. What if he learns how to mend the corrupted code? Or . . . or draw something more dangerous out of the under-plane? We have the knowledge now to stop the link. I used it on Jinao himself. We must unite the factions and lead an assault on the Ahiki king while his people are distracted by this invasion.'

'You say this man has two freed Intelligences and a coded spirit?' Adebayo said quietly. 'How?'

'I am not certain.'

'Do you not think it a curious coincidence? That the very man you chased for that staff was the single person in the realm to encounter an active Intelligence? What happens if it metamorphosises? If—'

The horn cut across the night like lightning, sharp as Father's sword. The conversation died at once, and several of those at the fire rose. Lucy did not think; when she had been tiny, she had been one of their best lookouts. And now; now, renewed life coursed through her. She leapt for the trunk of the nearest tree, her strong fingers and toes digging holds into the wood. She climbed, faster and faster, until she swayed within the multicoloured canopy. She spotted Carlos, their scout, a dozen trees away. And beyond him, beyond the end of the forest . . .

'It's them!' Lucy called down, her voice quavering, the life quickening within her. 'They've found us!'

Beyond the treeline, in the Wastelands, crawled a dark mass. An army. She could have sharpened her vision, changed it to see more clearly, but what was the point? The Horde had come to face Ahiki's army. Towering above the mass were larger shapes; so, they had brought their generals and kings. Perhaps they truly would wipe out the Silent Ones this time.

'Lucy, come down!' Father called. 'We have to go.'

'I'm coming!' Lucy said. She cast a final glare at the army, then scrambled back down the tree.

The camp around her had descended into chaos, people waking abruptly, their eyes lighting up with alertness, the clicks of their movements filling the air. Father bundled their bedding into his travelling bag. Lucy thought of Adebayo, too heavy to move, stuck there by the fire. Several of the children were covering him with vines and sticks. If they were lucky, he would be missed again, taken for a tree.

Lucy scooped up her kitten.

'Hope,' she said, touching Father's scarred grey arm. 'That's what I'm going to call her – Hope.'

Father smiled his wide, metal smile. 'It is a fine name.'

556

Sister Poju

Grand High Mother Takali summoned Sister Poju just before highsun.

'Mother!' the noviciate called, stumbling round the corner and into Sister Poju's chambers. 'Grand High Mother Takali commands your presence immediately.' She flattened herself to the earthen floor, keeping her forehead pressed low. The girl was perhaps ten rains of age, and a light stubble covered her dark-skinned scalp. Sister Poju sighed. She had known this moment was coming, but that did not make it any easier now that it had.

'Does she indeed?' Poju muttered.

'Yes, Mother. She said I should return with you.'

'I see. Well. Go and get yourself a drink from the fountain. I shall meet you outside.'

Poju waited until she heard the child's footsteps receding, then pushed to her feet, knees creaking.

Poju's accommodations were mean, even by convent standards. A stone slab to sleep on. A bucket for washing. The bookcase in the corner heaved with useless tomes she never read. Every convent heaved with useless tomes that were never read. A thousand thousand volumes of Nine Lands history. All worthless. All as meaningless as the games of pass-the-whisper that street children played. But it was important to show people what they expected to see. That had been her first lesson as a green girl, when Takali had plucked her from the pillow-house. Being a nun meant showing people what they expected to see. Then they did not look for anything else.

Poju pulled open her wardrobe and fetched her cape – the only item within. As she did so, the jewel in her head trilled.

'Yes?' Poju said.

[I commanded you here immediately,] Grand High Mother Takali's voice said in her ear.

'I'm just getting my cape. There's a breeze outside.' She tapped her skull, cancelling the connection, then pulled open the bottle of vintage Vushemi raki that she had been saving. If Grand High Mother Takali meant to punish her, then Poju planned to go to the next life having sampled the legendary drink. She allowed herself three deep swallows; the tales did not lie. It was the smoothest, subtlest raki that had ever passed her lips, and it filled her with resolve.

Outside, the sun was harsh already, and climbing towards its zenith. The noviciate stood obediently by the drinking fountain, hands behind her back, while the orphan children leapt naked in the convent fountains.

'Come,' Poju said, and the girl fell into step. Outside the gardens, Poju joined the throng in the street. She hated the period before highsun; always the busiest, as people hastened about whatever urgent business they had before the heat drove the sane indoors. As Poju passed down Iron Street, shutters were already closing and children being called home. Vendors covered their carts, and beggars withdrew to the shadows. Still, signs of the recent destruction lay everywhere. Abandoned buildings. Broken walls and doors. The Lordsgrave Massacre – that's what they were calling it. Thousands of souls had lost their lives. Then, thousands more had left for the king's accursed war.

Poju passed through it all serenely, and by the time she reached the avenue that ran along the River Ae, she and her companion were alone with the streets.

'Lower body temperature,' Poju commanded.

[Request complete,] the ancestors replied. A blissful chill spread over her, as though a cool summer breeze had come down from unseen mountains. She had been out in highsun many times without the protections of her implant, but it was never a pleasant affair.

Beside her, the noviciate sweated and sighed.

'How many rains in training are you, child?' Poju asked.

'Three,' the girl said, blinking sweat out of her eyes. 'Three this rainy season.'

'Then you must have an implant already,' Poju said. 'Command it to cool you.'

'But . . .' the girl said. 'Mother Briani says that a nun must have complete control over herself, body and mind, and that pain is an illusion that we must master.'

'If pain is an illusion, then what is there to master?' Poju said. The girl blinked up at her, and Poju sighed. 'Never mind. If you faint, I'm not carrying you to Highrose Convent. I'm too old. And if you pass out around here, you'll be lucky to still have the clothes on your back when you awaken.'

'Yes, Mother.'

'So command your implant to cool you.'

'The improper use of Forbidden relics is—'

'Yes, yes, I know, and one of the first things you'll learn when you come to the Trials is which rules to break and which to adhere to.' Poju leaned towards her. 'It's all a trick, you see. They tell you to follow the rules, but noviciates who slavishly do so spend their entire lives in training, and never obtain a circle of enlightenment. Why, in my old convent as a girl, there was a noviciate who was a hundred and ten rains old.'

Truth be told, Poju had no idea how old Sasenna had been, but to a wild girl of twelve, she had seemed ancient beyond measure.

'Lower body temperature,' the girl said at last.

After that, they made better headway. How peaceful Lordsgrave was when empty of its people. Poju wouldn't go so far as to call it beautiful, but there was a certain serenity, a certain calmness to it now. The buildings were not ramshackle, but lived in. The streets were uneven, yes, but they were like the wrinkles in an elder's face – evidence of life well lived, of tales to tell. As she began the climb towards the edge of the district, she realised there was nowhere else in the Nine Lands she would rather be.

Soon they had crossed the newly risen Lordsgrave Wall into Lordsheart, and padded down empty, paved streets lined with white-washed buildings.

Highrose Convent was a narrow, white building set back from the deserted road. They came upon Grand High Mother Takali clipping the flower bushes that flourished in defiance of the city heat. Takali was a tall, upright woman even older than Poju, with a perpetual sour look on her pinched face. The noviciate bowed and then scampered away. Poju could not blame her. Stepping before Mother Takali was among the most terrifying tasks any nun might face.

Poju tapped her skull as she walked. '*Encrypt conversation.*'

[Commencing encryption,] the ancestors said.

'So,' Takali said as Sister Poju drew near, 'I gather progress is being made with the Spirit Eater.'

'Yes, Mother,' Poju said, bowing. 'Things are progressing swiftly, but well.'

'And how is the incumbent?'

Sister Poju shrugged. 'Fine, so far as I can tell. I'm sure you heard she was involved in some heroics during the massacre. But all is proceeding as it should. With luck, we will be able to send her out against the Ahikis before the next rains. Too late to avert the start of the war, granted, but hopefully not too late to prevent our complete annihilation.'

'Mm, and tell me.' Takali clipped the head off a yellow rose. 'When you told Sister Relina where to find a suitable candidate, did you know this young woman's background? Choose someone simple, I said. A normal lowblood of no consequence. Selected at random, preferably. Someone pliable, who will evade notice.'

'And so I did,' Sister Poju replied, painting on her most innocent face. 'You cannot get any more common than Temi Baker.'

'Then explain why her grandfather is a master programmer who barely escaped execution in the Bronze Lands, and her entire family earns its keep selling techwork that they smuggle from coast to coast?' Takali fixed her with that hard stare that had turned Poju's stomach to water when she'd been a green girl. 'I suppose that wretched cat contraption was your doing, too. Don't think I don't know about it. That was not a good start.'

Sister Poju swallowed. 'I thought it prudent to add another layer of protection. As for the family, I found out later that her kin have some rudimentary skill with Forbidden relics. And the grandfather you mention left the Bronze Lands as a youth.'

'There is another complication. Our shadedaughters informed us that the criminal Gamani Chedu intended only to *threaten* the Clan Ahiki with the release of the Spirits of the Hunt. But it seems his own daughter has already brought them into the world.'

'Surely not!'

'They were there, during the massacre. It is likely she has already mutated dozens. And we've received word that they are also present in large numbers out in the Itahualand province of Intiqq. Believe me, this is a disaster. When I said we should cover up what we knew of Gamani's plans and what happened during Jethar's quest; when I said we should make contingencies of our own to overthrow the king; it was not so the Fallen Families could run rampant across the Nine Lands with the deadliest weapon in the history of humanity.'

'Can't we just . . . kill this Chedu girl?'

'Oh, believe me, you are welcome to try.' She clipped another rose head, which fell neatly into one liver-spotted hand. 'In the meantime, you must keep a close eye on the Spirit Eater's host. Temi has become even more important to us now, with these twin threats.'

'I have her family completely under control.'

'Under control? Then please explain this.'

Takali uttered a low incantation and then opened her palm. An image appeared there: a piece of torn papyrus, words in the Jebbanese language Urobi scrawled hastily across it.

'Oh, my,' Poju said, forcing herself to look shocked. 'Wh-where did that come from? Goodness! Tunji is the girl's dead brother!'

'Don't play games with me. I know you tried to hide the note from us. Have you shown it to the girl?'

Sister Poju slumped. 'Not yet. But she deserves to know.'

'No. Do you hear me? No. It's a mercy, not telling her. Your instincts were correct in that. Let her believe him dead and let her grieve and move on. We both know it is better this way.'

'It could complicate matters.'

'Yes,' Takali said, throwing her a stern look. Then she shook her head. '*Rudimentary* skill with Forbidden relics, you said?'

Poju shrugged. 'Um . . . perhaps *moderate* skill would have been more apt?'

'If you try to hide something from me again,' Takali said, rounding on her with the shears, 'I will have your implant wipe your mind. Understood?'

'Yes, Mother.'

'Good. Then proceed to the next phase.'

Lyela

'Rejoice, for you are about to enter the inner household of the Royal Clan Ahiki,' the steward said as he regarded the line of robed servants that stood before him. 'You have been selected for your perfection. For your skill and your demeanour. Many wish to stand where you do now, but few achieve it.'

He strode along the line, inspecting each of them in turn. They wore identical white silk robes, clasped at the throat with the golden sun of Clan Ahiki. Before them stood the Great Golden Road, that sacred avenue that led to the Central Palace itself. Each side was lined with looming statues of Ahiki kings, some as tall as the palace itself, and all wrought from gold. They matched the brilliance of the golden sky above, but Lyela couldn't look at that. She had spent a lifetime trying to forget the ever-present golden clouds that hung above the Garden, and feeling them there now, bearing down upon her, was enough to turn her stomach.

'You are silk-bearers,' the steward said as he continued his inspection. 'You have only one task. Carry silken sheets to the bedrooms of the mighty. Do not speak, unless spoken to. Do not smile, unless smiled at. Do not—'

The steward paused before Lyela, a curl of distaste tugging at the corner of his mouth. He slid his gaze up and down Lyela's body, taking in the roundness of her arms and thighs, the thickness of her waist. The Blessed Family tolerated only perfection in their midst. There were strict measurements for this perfection, to which every soul who appeared before them must conform. She knew what he was thinking. That it was too late to send her back now. That sending her back would draw more attention to the error than sending her on. That he would find her later, spirit her out of the Garden if he could, slit her throat if not. Lyela smiled sweetly. She could have found a techdoctor to adjust her physique to more acceptable proportions, but where was the fun in that? Her body had never felt more her own than it did in its present form, and she was so very tired of contorting herself to fit the ideals of others.

'Do not look into their eyes,' the steward continued, pacing on up the line. 'For the eyes of the Blessed Family are sacred and powerful, and you will find yourself weak-kneed before them.'

And on it went, as the sun beat down through the palms, and swarms of silent servants swept up and down the avenue. Sometimes, Lyela saw bluehawk commanders, and occasionally a monk or a nun. But none of the Royal Clan were abroad. It was too early in the day for that.

The steward led them down the Great Golden Road, and up the Thousand Steps of the Central Palace. By the time they reached the top, Lyela was sweating, but she was not breathless. Larger she might be now, but she was stronger, and fitter, and faster than she had ever been. The waif-like, precious things behind her did not let their discomfort show. They had been trained too well for that. But she could see it in the tenseness of their jaws as they trudged up behind her.

After a tour of the servants' basements, they were sent to begin their morning's duties. Nobody asked why the palace got through so many servants. It was one of the many secrets of the Garden that few who had not lived there were aware of. But the requirements and the appetites of the Royal Clan of Ahiki were many, and required a large turnover of staff.

Lyela padded through ornamental courtyards and tiered gardens.

She slipped past ornate fountains and up grand, sweeping stairways. More than once, she saw souls she knew, but no one recognised her. How could they? It had been nearly twenty rains, and she looked very different now.

It was not hard to reach the king's chambers. They were in the highest levels of the Central Palace. She came to the gold bridge that led to the doors of his sleeping chamber and counted the guards that stood there. Six bluehawks, in the gold and blue of the palace guard. Three with spears, three with swords. They would be expecting a silk-bearer, albeit not one with her girth, so she need not worry about them until she was near.

She padded across the marble and gold bridge, the sun scorching on her bare shoulders. She'd planned for this moment so carefully, over so many rains, and yet now that it was here, she felt the stirrings of fear in her gut. It was the old fear, she knew; that which had been instilled in her when she was a child. That she was powerless. That she was insignificant. That her fate was not her own.

'Good morning,' Lyela said as she approached the guards. She was almost level with them when she tripped, stumbling into the largest. She let the silks drop to the floor, and her hand closed around the guard's sword in its scabbard.

'Forgive me,' she said, and leapt back with his blade.

The spear-wielders were her biggest concern, but she had the element of surprise. While the man she had bowled into was trying to right himself, she slipped low, passing under the tall woman to her left, thrusting up with her sword, taking the first spear-wielder under their chin. As they staggered backwards, gurgling, Lyela spun and caught the blow of a great boar of a woman with a sword. The space was narrow, and that worked to her advantage. She leapt back, landing on the wall of the walkway, not looking down to the dizzyingly distant ground, praying no one below could see.

'Fetch help!' the woman shouted, and the spear-wielder on her right sprinted back along the walkway.

Lyela threw her sword as she leapt down. It spun end over end and buried itself between the running guard's shoulder blades. He staggered on a few paces before collapsing onto his face, but Lyela did not stop to watch. Four guards remained, and she was unarmed again.

Lyela pressed her hand to the wall and issued a command, then leapt into the air as her fingers flashed yellow.

The golden markings on the ground sparkled blue with cracking energy. Lyela landed carefully, placing her bare feet on the marble and not the gold, but two of the guards were not so lucky. The sparks caught them, dancing up their body, making them jolt and jerk. One fell where she stood, but the second toppled over the edge and down to the ground below.

'Shit,' Lyela muttered. No chance a falling corpse would go unnoticed. Now she would have to be quick.

'Who are you?' said the boar-like woman – their captain, from her tataus. She advanced carefully and held Lyela's gaze.

'Why, I am a silk-bearer!' Lyela replied, then dropped into a sliding kick.

The captain was fast, but as she struck down, Lyela rolled to one side and shoved her weight into the final guard, knocking him over the edge too. The captain cursed and swung again, but Lyela seized the sword of one of the fallen guards and caught the captain's blow, and the next, and the third. By the fourth, Lyela was on the attack. The captain had her in height, but Lyela was stronger. She drove forwards, slicing mercilessly, left, right, left again. She caught the captain in her shoulder, then in her arm, then kicked out, cracking her knee and sending her sprawling.

'I'm sorry,' Lyela said, and then sliced the sword down into the woman's neck.

It was over. Lyela smoothed down her white robe. It was splattered with blood, but there was nothing to be done about that now. She stepped up to the towering gold doorway of the king's bedchamber and placed her hand to the marble for it to open.

She had expected to find him awake and armed, but he was not – she'd been lucky. He lay asleep within the vast silk-and-cushion landscape of his bed. The room opened out at the far end onto a vast balcony of flowers and palms. A tiny fountain tinkled away in one corner. Lyela padded across the marble floor until she stood before the king.

Jakhenaten II Ahiki, High Warlord of the Invoker Clans, Holy Unifier of the People and King of the Nine Lands, was a young man in his prime. His long black hair hung in a smooth curtain over one brown shoulder. He was bare chested, save for the beaded decoration at his neck. He wore no crown, not when he was abed, but the gold tataus of his clan ran from his temples down to his waist, where the silken sheets covered him. He looked peaceful, amid the splendour of his bed. Lyela turned away, crossing to where the king's two cheetahs sat, their jewelled collars winking in the sunlight.

'Good morning, Your Blessed Majesty,' Lyela said brightly, keeping her back to him, offering a hand to the first cheetah. Amethyst: that was her name. The beast lifted its chin, letting Lyela scratch the fine, tawny hairs. The great cat's brother, Opal, was not to be outdone, however, and nudged at Lyela's hip until she scratched him, too.

'Be careful,' the king said. 'They bite.'

She glanced over her shoulder to see his eyes were open now, and he was watching her. Those eyes – a gold so bright they dazzled like the sun. Even now, she had difficulty looking into them. 'Not me, Your Majesty,' she replied. 'They like me.'

'They are trained to kill any who touch them.'

'Then perhaps you need to speak to their trainer,' Lyela said, as Opal licked her hand.

'You are not one of my usual silk-bearers. You do not . . . look like them.'

'No?' said Lyela, glancing down at her body in mock confusion.

'I like it. Why don't you come over here?' As she looked round, he patted the cushions to his left and offered her a wolfish grin. 'Let me examine you.'

'Oh no, Your Most Golden Majesty,' Lyela replied, rubbing between Amethyst's eyes. 'I'm afraid my father would never approve.'

'Your father?'

'He is a stern and unforgiving man and rules every aspect of my life.'

'Not any longer,' the king said. 'Now, you are a Child of the Garden, a servant of the Blessed Royal Court of Ahiki. You are free of your father's bonds. You belong only to me.'

'I'm afraid I can never be free of my father,' Lyela said. 'Why, he slew the last boy I loved, and took our child from me. I would not like the same fate to befall you.'

'You are safe from him here, I assure you.'

'All the same, I—'

'Take off your robe and come here, you insolent wretch. I am your king and I command you.'

Lyela unpinned the golden clasp at her throat, letting her thin white robe fall to the floor before finally turning. The king had a thousand concubines; he was unused to any refusing him. Most servants would throw themselves at him, if not for the glory of having lain with the man who ruled the Nine Lands, then for the sheer beauty of his form, for there was no denying that he was beautiful. She reached under her heavy breasts, unknotting the thin length of twine she had used to pin Elari's jewel in place, then crossed slowly to his bedside.

'What is that?' the king said, taking her wrist.

'A gift,' she said. 'For you.'

'Let me see.'

Lyela crawled to the king's side and let the twine dangle from her hand. The jewel wasn't much to look at: a small black orb, opaque and scratched. The king took it and turned it over in his long brown fingers.

Lyela uttered a command.

The king flinched. 'It's hot,' he said. 'Here – take it back.'

'Oh no, Your Most Golden Majesty. It is for you.'

The king flicked his hand, trying to remove the jewel, but it held fast, adhering to his skin.

'What is this?' he said. He glanced towards the door. 'Guar—'

Lyela clamped a meaty hand over his mouth, pressing hard. 'Your guards are dead, Your Majesty, but I'd like you to remain silent all the same. You see, you only have a few minutes now, and I have much to say.'

Beneath her hand, the king squirmed. His tataus brightened, setting his skin aflame, but there was no keening in the air, no inrush of energy.

'He can't hear you,' Lyela said. 'Terrifying, isn't it? That voice that has been with you all your life . . . that presence, guiding you, encouraging you: terrifying when it's torn away.'

The king clawed at her hands, but Lyela was strong, and as heavy as the king himself now. What were a few scratches compared to the joy of this moment? 'Imagine, having all that power, all that pleasure, ripped away. Such a cruelty. But I can sympathise. You see, it happened to me.'

The king's eyes widened, and his attention turned back to his hand. The jewel was sinking into his skin, and though he clawed at it with his free hand, it was soon buried within him.

'Can you feel it burning into you? Into your mind? First, it will take your ancestor. Then, it will take you. Piece by piece, it will take all that you are, until all that remains is your mindless body.' Lyela smiled. 'You took everything from me, you know. Everything. The one I loved. My child. *My ancestor.* Now, I am going to take everything from you, and you are going to watch. I've spent the last two decades planning for this moment. And this is only the beginning.'

Beneath her hand, the king had gone slack. His eyes remained wild and roving, but his body was inert. It was happening, then. Lyela stood, and the king's head flopped to one side, drool spilling from his open mouth.

'I'd imagine it's nearly done now,' she said. 'Of course, they'll keep your body here. In the hope that you'll return to it. But you won't. No, you'll be with me.' Lyela reached beneath the king's sleeping mat and removed the tiny, jewelled knife she knew he kept there. The king's eyes went wide, but he was powerless now.

Princen Lyelatuana Ahiki, the Breeze on Water, leaned close. 'Goodbye, Father.' Then she brought the knife down onto his wrist, sawing through flesh, tendon and bone. Three quick jerks were all it took to sever the hand with a satisfying crack. Then she padded away from the dribbling, mindless, one-handed thing that was her father the king, and found her robe. In the distance, a bell rang out. The alarm had been raised. But Princen Lyelatuana knew the palace, knew the Garden, like she knew her own soul. She had spent over a century imprisoned within it, and those memories did not fade.

'Come, Father,' Lyelatuana said to the severed hand she held. 'It is time for you to watch my ascension.'

Acknowledgements

It takes a village to raise a book, and there are many, many people who held my hand as I brought this one into the world. I set out to write the sort of epic fantasy I wanted to read, with all the richness and complexity I craved, and inspired by the multiple cultures I grew up around. Yet I sometimes wondered if the result was too heartfelt, too personal, too ambitious. The wonderful people below helped me see that there was a place for this world and these characters, and I honestly would not be here without their encouragement, love and support.

First and foremost, thanks to YOU, the reader, for joining me on this journey. I spent countless self-doubting years never showing my work to a soul, so it is such an honour and a joy to be able to share this story with you now. Thank you to my amazing agent and fellow city lover Jennie Goloboy. Thank you for being my rock, for championing this novel, for seeing from the very start what I was trying to do with it, and above all, thank you for giving me the confidence to believe in it and myself. To my wonderful and talented editor, Emily Byron – thank you for *getting* this novel, for your attention to detail and for your boundless enthusiasm. And thank you for enabling me to tell this story the way I always sought to tell it. Heartfelt thanks to Anna Jackson and the entire Orbit UK team for making my debut experience such a dream, including Nazia Khatun and Nadia Saward (thank you both for making me feel so welcome at my first in-person con), Blanche Craig, Joanna Kramer and Alison Tulett. Thank you also to Nivia Evans and the rest of the team at Saga Press, my US publisher, and thank you to Richard Anderson for really capturing the spirit of the book in this glorious cover.

Eternal thanks to Ben Aaronovitch, Adjoa Andoh, Sarah Shaffi, Andy Ryan and to everyone involved in the Future Worlds Prize, for picking the opening of this novel as the winning entry back in 2021, and for continuing to uplift voices of colour in the UK SFF field. Future Worlds Fam forever! Thank you also to Kasim Ali for reading the whole of this beast of a book and providing such enthusiastic insight. Thank you to Lane Robins of Odyssey Workshop for your feedback on an early version of the opening – I still laugh when I think about that clown-car reference. I am also thankful for all the kind authors I have met over the last couple of years, both online and in person, who provided such reassurance, warmth, encouragement and community. And deepest thanks to DaVaun Sanders and the team at *FIYAH* literary magazine for publishing my first ever short story, a piece set in this world, and for showing me that there was a place for me in this industry when I most needed to hear it.

To my amazing sister Adesola Akinleye, thank you for sending me that story as a kid (the one with the cockroaches!), with blank pages at the end for me to continue writing in . . . I guess I never stopped! Thank you for being an inspiration to me all my life. Love and thanks to my two sisters from other misters, Sabitri and Maleene, who have been listening to my madcap ideas since we were teenagers – never mocking, always believing, forever lifting me up. Thank you, Sabitri, for always having my back and for entertaining my kids on all those afternoons while I wrote. And also for that time when I spent our entire walk from Crouch End to Wood Green telling you the history of the very first incarnation of this world. (It involved talking chickens. You probably don't remember, but it meant a lot to me!) Thank you,

Maleene, for feeding me a steady diet of videogames and books over three decades of geeky sisterhood, for introducing me to *Final Fantasy* back in the day (it's been a huge influence on my writing ever since, never more so than in this series), and for being the unstoppable trailblazer that you are. Thank you to those who gave me encouragement in the very early days, especially Nicks, Ilona and Lavie. Love and thanks to family members who have always uplifted me – Kyi, Mint, Will, Keith, Wale, Jeanne, Gavin, Reynaldo, Ronnie, Zara, Tamsin, Riyah, J, M, C, and Hasu. Thanks also to the friends I have had at my side, especially Anne P, Beena, Fatima T, Iselema, Jenny DD, Jo B, Karla, Mariam, Neeta, Phil, Reshma, and Sam S.

Finally, thank you to my husband, my soulmate, Marc, for your unwavering patience, faith, support and, above all, love. Thank you to my three kids for putting up with all the evenings and weekends when I had to do my 'nerd stuff'. And thank you to my parents, Pat and Alarape Ayinde, for never questioning my chosen path, for always believing in me, and for supporting me in every way imaginable. Daddy – look! I wish you were here to enjoy this moment with me. But I know you are cheering me on somewhere in the ancestral realm.

About the author

M. H. Ayinde was born in London's East End. Her short fiction has been published in *FIYAH Literary Magazine*, *Omenana Magazine*, *Beneath Ceaseless Skies* and elsewere, and she was the 2021 winner of the Future Worlds Prize. She is a runner, a lapsed martial artist and a screen time enthusiast. Modupe lives in London with three generations of her family and their Studio Ghibli obsession.

Find out more about M. H. Ayinde and other Orbit authors by registering for the free monthly newsletter at orbit-books.co.uk.